D0900148

I'M
NOT DONE
WITH
YOU YET

Titles by Jesse Q. Sutanto

DIAL A FOR AUNTIES

FOUR AUNTIES AND A WEDDING

VERA WONG'S UNSOLICITED ADVICE FOR MURDERERS

I'M NOT DONE WITH YOU YET

Young Adult and Middle Grade

WELL, THAT WAS UNEXPECTED

THE OBSESSION

THE NEW GIRL

THEO TAN AND THE FOX SPIRIT

I'M NOT DONE WITH YOU YET

JESSE Q. SUTANTO

BERKLEY
New York

BERKLEY
An imprint of Penguin Random House LLC
penguinrandomhouse.com

Library of Congress Cataloging-in-Publication Data

Names: Sutanto, Jesse Q., author.
Title: I'm not done with you yet / Jesse Q. Sutanto.
Other titles: I am not done with you yet
Description: New York: Berkley, [2023]
Identifiers: LCCN 2022058254 (print) | LCCN 2022058255 (ebook) |
ISBN 9780593546918 (hardcover) | ISBN 9780593546925 (ebook) |
ISBN 9780593549087 (International edition)
Subjects: LCGFT: Novels.
Classification: LCC PR9500.9.S88 I6 2023 (print) | LCC PR9500.9.S88 (ebook) |
DDC 823/.92—dc23/eng/20221209
LC record available at https://lccn.loc.gov/2022058254
LC ebook record available at https://lccn.loc.gov/2022058255

Printed in the United States of America
1st Printing

Book design by Daniel Brount

*To Laurie Elizabeth Flynn, my soul twin, without whom
I wouldn't have the courage to even start this book.*

When did you first realize you're not normal?

I'M
NOT DONE
WITH
YOU YET

PART
ONE

1

Aunt Claudette, she's the best. So everyone says. By everyone, I mean my mother. My mother loves Aunt Claudette because she is always ready to help out with "the cutie pie" (i.e., me). "Cutie pie" is the first clue that should tell you that my mother doesn't give a shit about me, because really, how fucking generic a pet name can someone get for their only child? She can't even be bothered to come up with a more unique pet name, one that's tailored to fit me. No, I remain known as "cutie pie" up until even my idiot mother can't pretend that I'm cute anymore.

But anyway. Back to Aunt Claudette. Not technically my aunt. She's just an elderly neighbor who Mom swears loves me like "her own." Her own what? Aunt Claudette never had kids. And the thing about Aunt Claudette is, she doesn't look after me out of love, no matter how much Mom would like to believe she does.

Sure, maybe she did it out of love at first, when I was little enough not to have any personality. When I really was a generic little cutie pie. But now that I'm seven, I realize she's not looking after me because she cares about me. She does so because she cares about what I would do if I wasn't being watched.

This morning, Mom made me cocoa pancakes for breakfast before rushing out the door to get to work. Cocoa pancakes, not chocolate pancakes. She'd read that unsweetened cocoa powder is full of antioxidants, so today, my pancakes come out brown as shit and tasting no better. I hate the color brown. That's what my hair is. Mom sometimes tries to call it "chestnut" or "chocolate," but we both know it's neither of those things. And here are my pancakes, the same disgusting mud-brown as my hair. I can drown the pancakes in syrup, but the only syrup allowed in the house is agave, which tastes like melted plastic. Clint Eastwood nudges my foot. The name's a joke that stuck—Clint is a loyal rescue mutt of an indeterminate age, but he looks about as old as God. I look into his trusting face and tear a tiny bit of shit pancake off. His stumpy tail wags, and he stands on his hind legs and paws my knees with a desperate whine.

But before I can give him the piece of pancake, Aunt Claudette rushes in like a hurricane and grabs my wrist, almost painfully. "What are you doing, child?"

I gaze at her. I have huge hazel eyes. Whenever people describe their eyes as "hazel," it's always brown. But mine have that warm honey hue that makes people do a double take. They're also stupidly big and round. Legit Bambi eyes. I widen them now, because I know that's what people do when they're taken by surprise. "Clint is hungwy," I say.

Most people, including my own mother, would soften and say, "Aww," at that. But Aunt Claudette's mouth thins. I've miscalculated. She knows I'm too old for such mispronuncia-tions. "Hung-ree," she says. "You know how to pronounce it properly."

I do.

"And you know Clint isn't allowed chocolate. It's bad for him."

It's not even a huge amount of cocoa. Not enough to do any permanent damage, only enough to give Clint the runs. I was going to really enjoy watching Mom clean up after Clint's di-arrhea.

"I'm sorry." I cast my Bambi eyes down. All of my picture books show kids doing that when they're sorry. "I forgot." I look up at Aunt Claudette again, and this time, I've weaponized my Bambis—they're shining with tears. "Please don't be mad at me, Auntie."

That's something I'd learned from Jayden, Mom's current "special friend." Whenever they argue, Jayden looks at Mom a certain way and says, "Don't be mad at me, babe," and she sighs and her shoulders slump in defeat, and even at the age of seven, I know what a conniving asshole Jayden is, because telling some-one not to be mad is putting all of the responsibility on them. *Sure, I may have done something wrong, but YOU do the labor of getting over it.* Jayden may be a grade A asshole, but he's taught me some really great tactics. And women fall for that shit all the time.

Even Aunt Claudette is no match for it. She flushes, her eyebrows coming together, and she quickly says, "Of course I'm not mad at you, angel," and I know for sure she's mad because she knows I'm no angel. Then she taps a palm against her fat thigh and says, "Here, Clint," and herds Clint away. Away from me. I shrug, running a finger down the edge of my butter knife. I fleetingly entertain the thought of plunging the point of that knife someplace soft and warm, someplace with a steady pulse, so the blood would come out in a rhythmic spurt. But I could never hurt Aunt Claudette. She's special. She's the only one who can always see right through my bullshit, and she loves me anyway, which just goes to show how flawed humans are.

She may as well love a cockroach.

2

The thing about crazy bitches is there's usually some man who's pushed and prodded and gaslit her to that point.

I've never been a tidy person, but I like the idea of it; I enjoy the feeling of having tidied up, of sitting in an uncluttered room with a cup of tea and a good book. I like it enough to spend some time at the end of each day putting things away. I never get the room to "pristine," because I've been raised with clutter and never quite got the hang of cleaning, but I put in enough effort to make sure the space is livable. Ted, on the other hand, is an all-or-nothing guy. When I ask him to help declutter, he'll say, "Why bother? It's all just going to get messy again." If he can't have perfection, then we may as well live in a hovel.

This evening is no different. After dinner (in front of the TV so we won't actually have to make conversation with each other), Ted shuts himself away in his man cave for a round of Fortnite—apparently, it's not just for twelve-year-old boys; it's also for

thirty-seven-year-old men—while I putter about the house putting away our daily bric-a-brac.

Normally, I wouldn't mind it, but today, our neighbor Kimiko stopped by to "borrow" some flour (I say "borrow," but Kimiko is always coming by to borrow cups of sugar or an egg or two,
and not once has she returned anything), and while she waited
in our foyer, Ted had said, laughingly, "Sorry about the state of
the house. Jane's just really messy like that."

I'd come out of the kitchen then, carrying a Tupperware of
flour, and said with more bite than I'd intended, "What? I'm not
the messy one here."

Ted had raised his arms in a theatrical way, eyes wide, and
laughed. "Whoa, it's okay, babe. I don't care that you're messy."

"But I'm not—" I caught it then. The shrill tone of anger in
my voice that sounded like cracking glass. I stopped myself, but
I could tell that Kimiko and Ted had both caught it too.

Kimiko had left pretty quickly after that, not bothering to
stay around for a chitchat like she usually does. Which was just
as well, because it gave me a chance to nip down to the basement and be alone. Lock myself away so I could cool down before I did something I'd regret. Something irredeemable.

Now, as I pick up Ted's half-drunk glasses of water and tea
from the coffee table, my resentment mounts. Why is it always
down to me to clear away all this shit? The random remnants of
our daily lives—socks on the floor, pens and bits of paper everywhere, a half-eaten sandwich abandoned on, of all places, the
TV cabinet. And I wouldn't mind it so much if Ted weren't such
a fucking asshole about it all, if he'd at least acknowledge that I
put in more effort than he does. I may be messy by nature, but
I'm trying, and he's not seeing it, or maybe he's refusing to.
Maybe he enjoys pushing my buttons, seeing how far he can

twist the dials before I crack and show anger, like this morning, so he can say, "Geez, why're you getting so worked up over nothing?" He'd do his little incredulous snort and share a look with whoever he's talking to, and in the end, I'm always the crazy bitch who shoveled molehills into my own Mount Everest.

I can feel the old anger rising up again. I don't want to have to go down to the basement for the second time in a day, so I fling down the balled-up Fortnite T-shirt I'd picked up and stride out of the living room and into the dining room, where my laptop lives. Let Ted deal with his own mess.

Taking a deep breath, I sink into my chair and turn my laptop on. I scroll through Twitter for a while, losing myself in the usual cacophony of intense emotions. Everyone on Twitter is always either manically happy or completely enraged, and it makes me feel a bit better. More normal. When I get tired of all the virtual yelling, I switch over to check my email.

And that's when I see it. A newsletter from the *New York Times* with their latest bestseller list. The words scream at me through my computer screen, flashing in huge capital letters, neon bright.

Well, okay, the *New York Times* doesn't ever do anything that's as uncouth as screaming, and they sure as hell do not do headlines in huge caps and neon colors—what are they, the *Daily Mail*? But they might as well have, because there, right in front of me, is her name. Surely, it can't be written in plain black font; it's radiating with so much light. Blindingly bright, like the way she was. And just seeing those two words, that beautiful, uncommon name of hers, is enough to swallow me whole again. I'm whisked back into the common room at Pemberton, nervously skirting the edges of the crowd, biting my nails as I watch her hungrily.

Thalia Ashcroft.

In Greek mythology, Thalia was a Muse. Someone who inspired others to write. To create.

This version is no different. Even back at the program all those years ago, our classmates were drawn to her, always buzzing around her like bees swarming the queen, wanting to drink from the well of inspiration. Hands always touching her, a pat on the shoulder here, a brush on the arm there, as though she were Jesus and they were lepers desperate for a cure. I detested them all, not because I judged them for their insipid personalities, grown lazy and bland through privilege. No, I couldn't give two shits about our classmates. But I despised them their audacity. The way they felt entitled to be near her, to converse with her as though they were even close to being on the same level as she was.

No one was on the same level as Thalia the Muse, Thalia the Beautiful, Thalia the Perfect.

And now here she is again, her name right there in front of me, blasting her way back into my life in the most Thalia-esque fashion. Right at the top of the *New York Times* bestseller list.

NEW THIS WEEK

A MOST PLEASANT DEATH
by Thalia Ashcroft, writing as May Pierce

The squeak of creaking plastic wrenches me out of my reverie. With a start, I see that I've been squeezing my mouse so hard that it has cracked in my hand. I peer down at the mouse. It was a bargain buy, made in China, cheap and unloved. Just like everything in my house, yours truly included.

If Ted knew I think this badly of the house his parents helped

us to get, he'd have a go at me. And I suppose I should be grateful for it, thankful that his parents, unlike mine, are generous
enough to help out with the down payment. But Ted's a contract
data analyst and I'm a midlist writer, and the house is just a bit
beyond our means. The mortgage alone is almost crippling. Almost, but not quite. Enough that each month, when we make
the payment, I feel embittered that we have to pay so much for
a house where I don't even have my own study. Ted's man cave
doubles as his office, so he's just fine and dandy, but me? I have
to make do with the communal spaces. The spaces that are
dominated by his mess.

So I write at cafés. Of course, the tech boom in the Bay Area
means that a cup of coffee costs me an arm and a leg and half a
kidney, but it's worth it to give me a few precious hours away
from the house and the mess.

I wonder if Thalia writes at cafés too. No, I reject the thought
as soon as it surfaces. I can't see her at a hipster café with a mo-
cha latte next to a rose gold laptop. No, Thalia isn't the type to
soak up attention like that. Even back then, I could tell she hated
it, hated that she was the sun and everyone else was a sunflower
turning their wide, open faces toward her, feeding off her
warmth.

She'd write in her apartment. Or maybe a house? My heart
leaps to my throat, forming a lump as I open up a new tab and
type down her name. Each letter a heartbreak.

T-h-a-l-i-a A—

I don't even get to finish before Google finishes the search
for me. Because of course, she's the only Thalia worth Googling.
My chest squeezes into a jealous fist. How many have done this
search before me? I've done it so many times, but until now, I
have only ever been able to find a ghost. Hits that were years

old—a few blurry Facebook photos of her from college, from high school. Nothing from our master's course, certainly. After what happened in our year, Oxford had extended its powerful hand and crushed everything, scrubbed every last bit of news until all that remained were the ramblings of a couple of local tabloids. Nothing that anyone of consequence would pay attention to.

But now, oh my god. So many hits. A Goodreads page. An Amazon page. And a website. How is this possible? How have so many hits sprouted up without my knowledge? In the early days, I used to do a search for her name obsessively. She used to blog. I'd read and reread her posts in my room, devouring every word, marveling at the elegance of her writing. Then that final formal had happened, and Thalia disappeared. I often wondered if Oxford had been responsible for scrubbing her off the Internet too. And, years later, I've moved on, sort of. My search became more sporadic.

And now here she is.

The tip of my tongue edges out, moistening my lips ever so slightly. I press down on the inside of my wrist, noting my heart rate. Slightly elevated. The way it gets whenever there's anything Thalia-related. I swallow and move the cracked mouse so the cursor hovers over her website. I watch as the arrow turns into a pointing hand.

Our time at Oxford flashes before me: the heavy, damp English air; the wet cobblestones; the books—*oh god, all the books*—the feverish writing; the heady wine and sweet cider; and the blood. By now, I'm breathing heavily, the way I always do when my mind wanders over to that blood-soaked night. I lick my lips again before biting down hard enough to taste a metallic tang, as though my body can't wait to go back to that night, the night that should've bound me to Thalia. The night I lost her.

But here she is, after all these years. And this time, I'm going to do things right. I'm not losing her again.

I grip the mouse tight, until it squeaks in near death, and I click Enter.

3

The sky in England is different from the sky in California. It's the first thing I notice when I walk out of Heathrow. It seems lower somehow, and even though it's a beautiful English summer day with wispy white clouds frosting the deep blue sky, it feels slightly oppressive. Or maybe it's just my mood. I'm nervous, and when I'm nervous, I get cranky, which is bad. Really bad. Because I can't control my anger like the normals do.

Mom has never bothered taking me to see anyone, because she insisted nothing was wrong with me. She'd say things like, "Why do white people come up with so many mental health issues? All of a sudden, everybody has mental health issues. It's all made up so they can medicate us and take our money." I think she just didn't give a shit, but tomayto, tomahto. It doesn't matter, anyway. Early on in my teens, I researched my condition and diagnosed myself with the help of Dr. Google.

Pretty sure I'm a sociopath. I'm not ashamed of it; in fact it's something I quite like, and I carry the thought in the recesses of my mind like a lucky charm, returning to it the way one might stroke a rabbit-foot once in a while. Caressing it mentally. My own little touchstone. Sociopath. As long as I can identify it, I can deal with it.

Sociopathy.

Antisocial Personality Disorder.

Behaviors: antisocial (check), deceitful (check), hostile (check), irresponsible (okay, check), manipulative (I suppose, though I'm not as good at it as I'd like to be), aggressive (yeah).

The thing that most people don't know about sociopaths is that we do actually get lonely. At least this one does. It's hard to explain. I don't like people—I don't know how to be interested in them the way everyone else seems to be. But god, I wish they'd like me. Not much luck in that aspect though.

But England will be different. It's the whole reason I chose to do my master's here instead of California. California is basically the worst place in the world for antisocials. It's too loud, too sunny, too fucking friendly. Everyone gets revved up on kale smoothies and cocaine so I can't even get a tub of hummus without the Trader Joe's checkout lady grinning at me and calling me honey and asking me how I'm doing and what are my plans for the weekend? Californians just can't help themselves. If I stayed there any longer I was bound to kill someone.

Just kidding. Sort of.

So I researched the world's rudest, unfriendliest places. Top two are apparently Russia and France, which I dismissed because I don't speak French or Russian. And then there it was. Number 3: United Kingdom. What do I know about England?

1. Surly people (Yay, means I should fit in perfectly. Maybe they won't notice that I'm a sociopath?)
2. Gloomy weather (If even the English find me too surly for them, I could blame it on the weather!)
3. Terrible food (. . . or I could blame it on the food.)
4. Brilliant writers

The last bit has been the deal clincher for me. I've always wanted to write for a living. When I was little and magazines were still a thing, I'd daydreamed about writing for them. It seemed very glamorous at the time. I'd pictured myself in New York City, a place teeming with people just as vicious and cruel and empty as myself. Not a single person is allowed to be bubbly in New York City; I was sure of it. I'd wear sky-high heels and lipstick the color of a gaping wound and stride around with a cigarette hanging from my lips, getting paid to talk to people, manipulate them into giving up information, and then write down my observations in the most wickedly delicious way.

But then the Internet swallowed up the magazine industry whole and I just couldn't bring myself to write for online news sites. All those bright colors and dementedly cheerful headlines:

TEN LOL-WORTHY PUPPIES!

SEVEN SMOOTHIES WORTH BUYING A BLENDER FOR!

FIVE WAYS TO TELL WHETHER YOU'RE A SOCIOPATH!

To be fair, I actually found the last one useful.

The thought of my impossible New York dream rankles me, even now, so many years after its death. I give myself a little shake. Whatever, forget New York. I'm in England, for god's sake. I locate the bus headed to Oxford and pay the driver.

"Which stop?" he says.

"Um." It takes a moment to recall the name that had been included in the welcome e-mail. "Glow-chester?"

"Nope, sorry, don't know that."

I frown at him and peer at the sign above the bus, which clearly says "OXFORD." "This is going to Oxford, right?"

"Yep," he says, and turns away from me.

Jesus. I'd been warned that people here would be unfriendly, but this guy is on a whole other level. A familiar tendril caresses the depth of my guts. Oh no, please. Don't lose your temper here. Do not. I take a deep breath and snap the rubber band at my wrist. The rubber band is one of the things that my extensive research had suggested as a method to control my sociopathic rage. A literal way to "snap" myself out of the spiral that would otherwise grab me like a riptide and fling me into dark oblivion, leaving nothing but broken detritus in my wake.

It works, most of the time. My stomach settles and I step aside to open up the welcome e-mail on my phone. I was right; it says right here: Gloucester Green.

I wait until the elderly man boards the bus before approaching the driver again. "Hi, it says here my stop is Glow-chester—"

"Nope," he says, beckoning at the next passenger to come up.

The slick caress again. My cheeks grow warm. Oh no, I'm going to lose it right here, less than an hour after arriving in a foreign country where I'm supposed to make my fresh start.

"But it says right here—"

"I think she means Gloucester Green," a female voice says from behind me, pronouncing it Gloss-ter, "and I think you knew all along what she meant."

I turn around and that's when I see her. The most beautiful girl I have ever laid eyes on outside of Instagram. My mouth parts, and all of the bubbling anger that had been ready to erupt just moments ago dissipates. She looks like she might have mixed ancestry, too, though unlike the uneasy way that the different lineages have converged on my face, Thalia's features are a work of art. She looks like a literal angel. Gold hair that looks like threads of pulled sunlight, huge, huge eyes—distracting, so distracting. But it's not the face that arrests me; it's the kindness in it. Like she's the long-lost best friend you didn't know you had and she knows every gross secret about you and doesn't judge you for it. She makes me want to make a motherfucking friendship bracelet for her and buy one of those obnoxious heart necklaces that say "best friends" when you put them together.

She quirks one corner of her mouth up at the bus driver in what I can only describe as an empathetic smirk. "Come on, luv, let's stop messing about, okay?"

She sounds very clearly American, but somehow she carries off "luv" with so much flair that the bus driver is obligated to give a grin in return.

He winks at me and says, "Ah, just messing with ya. Off you go, then. Two for Gloucester Green, is it?"

"Yep," the girl says, and cocks her head at me. "Let's go, before this cheeky bugger decides to fuck with us again." She winks at him as she says this before hopping onto the bus.

The driver roars with laughter, and I clamber up after her. Already my mind is going at breakneck speed, analyzing every microsecond of the encounter. It's what I do most times I have an awkward encounter with people.

Was that a normal interaction? Did I react in a socially acceptable manner? How would a normal person behave? How would a bad-tempered normal person behave? What might I have done differently to pass under the radar next time?

As though reading my mind, the girl turns her head and gives me a rueful smile. "You okay? He was an asshole, wasn't he? I bet he thought he was being real cute too."

My mouth drops open but nothing comes out. It's not that my mind's empty; on the contrary, there are way too many thoughts zipping around in it. Chief among them: *What should I say?* I'd nearly blown my cover of normalcy just moments ago, and as much as I hate to admit it, I'm rattled. I've burnt so many bridges back in Cali. People I thought were my friends ghosted me. I can't let that happen here, not at my laundry-fresh start.

I've stayed silent far too long. I know it. The atmosphere thickens the way it always does when I know I'm not Being Normal. I stare helplessly at the girl, feeling that old heat travel up my chest and into my cheeks. I wish she'd end my suffering and leave me alone already.

Instead, she slides into a seat, scooting over so she takes the window seat, and then cocks her head at me. "Come on, the bus will get full soon and I don't really wanna sit with some random stranger."

"I'm a random stranger," I blurt out.

God damn it.

Sociopathic tendency #57: Lacks filters.

She laughs, and it's the best laugh in the world. Very different from the manic, need-for-attention-driven shriek-giggles I got used to in California. It's low and husky, a laugh so soft I know it's meant for my ears alone.

"True, but I just saved you from that asshole out there, so I think you owe me one," she says.

I swallow, gripping my bag with sweaty palms, and slide in

before I can talk myself out of it. This close to her, I can smell her scent. Lavender and the musky, tired smell of travel. It's a surprisingly pleasant combination, one that relaxes me. If I were a cat, this is where I'd retract my claws.

"I'm Thalia," she says.

Thalia. What a beautiful name. Different. Unexpected, with a hint of foreign flavor. Again, I find myself wondering about her lineage.

As though reading my mind, she adds, "It's Greek. Half my ancestors came from there; the other half came from Italy. Of course, this was, like, five generations ago, so don't ask me anything about either place, aside from the food." She grins sheepishly and my mind goes blank. Like her, I know nothing about my ancestral heritage. I don't even speak Chinese. A similarity, a bond fusing us to each other.

No. This is not how normal people think. We've just met. There is no bond. I focus instead on her name.

It suits her perfectly, and I realize she must have parents who love her and know her the way I wish my mother knew me. Parents who cared enough to find the perfect name for their little girl. Parents that are very much unlike mine.

"I'm Jane."

"I love that name."

I roll my eyes and instantly regret it. Why am I so thorny?

But Thalia smiles, seemingly unperturbed by my bitchiness. "No, really. You know *Jane the Virgin*? I love that show. Ever since season one, I've loved the name Jane."

"Never saw it." A small lie. My mom watched it religiously with my aunt, and I'd sometimes catch snippets of it. It enraged me—the saccharine-sweet, fairy tale–perfect relationship between Jane, her mother, and her grandmother. And the fact that my mother, the woman who couldn't give a tiny rat's ass about me, loved the show made me even angrier. I wanted to put my hands around that fucking show and crush it.

"Yeah? What shows do you watch?"

The mention of *Jane the Virgin* has angered me enough to let my guard down a little, so I look Thalia straight in the eye. "I like dark shows. Shows that aren't afraid to kill main characters. Shows that have a healthy body count. *Breaking Bad*. *The Walking Dead*. Those kinds of shows."

I fully expected *Jane the Virgin*–loving Thalia to stop talking to me then and there, but instead, she laughs and says, "I think you and I are going to have a lot of fun together, Jane."

It's meant to be. We were meant to meet this way, with her rescuing me from the London–Oxford bus driver. Meant to sit next to each other for over one hundred minutes, our elbows a mere hair's breadth away from touching. With each bump the bus takes, my elbow kisses hers, and I am dying a sweet, slow death.

I steal glances at her as the miles are eaten up beneath us. While men lust after the soft, bulging parts of the female anatomy—the breasts, the ass—we women notice the hardness. The places that signify control. Discipline. The clavicle, the shoulder blades, the cheekbones. Thalia's collarbone is defined in a way that makes me swallow. I imagine myself running a finger along its hard length, from the bottom of her neck all the way to her shoulder, where it juts out into a single knifepoint. I want to press on it with my index finger and feel the solidity of it pushing up against me. I want her lovely bones to cut into my skin.

I don't understand it myself; I'm quite sure I'm not sexually attracted to women, but there's just something about Thalia that captures my attention, clutching it tight in a sweaty grip that refuses to let go. I'm ashamed of my inability to cast my eye away, as though I were a creepy man breathing heavily into the mouthpiece of a phone. Maybe it's the fact that somehow, the mixed ethnicities have rewarded her and punished me. My nose has a bump on the end, rodent-like, my lips chapped, with a slight overbite. Though we're about the same height, Thalia seems taller because she carries herself straight-backed, while I slouch and try to hide from the light. Maybe, if I'd had a more loving mom, a present dad instead of a dead one, I could've been more like Thalia. Mom's voice floats up to the surface, a bubble popping in toxic waste, releasing noxious fumes. *Still rejecting the Asian side of you? Still worshipping white people, wishing you were them?*

"I can feel you staring."

My breath catches in a painful rush, and I practically plaster my entire back against the seat. Fuck shit fuck. "Uh." Half a second to catch my breath, compose myself. *Don't get caught being a creep, Jane.* "I was just looking at the scenery."

Fortunately for me, the scenery outside is somewhat decent. Definitely worth looking at as opposed to the inside of a crowded bus. We're going past a bucolic setting of rolling hills, complete with flocks of sheep grazing lazily, their movements so slow it's like we caught them in a portrait as we rush past on the freeway—no, sorry, the motorway.

Thalia laughs under her breath. "I'm just messing with you. Sorry. I've been told I have a terrible sense of humor." She looks out the window before I can reply, which is a relief because I have no idea what to say to that. A second later, she glances back at me. "So, Jane. What brings you to Oxford?"

I have an answer to that, at least. "I'm here to attend the master's program at Pemberton College."

The Oxbridge universities operate like no other that I know of. They're each divided into various colleges, instead of operating as a single university, a fact that had been a source of confusion as I navigated my way through the complicated applications. But whatever, it doesn't matter which college I attend, as long as my final diploma says Oxford bloody University.

"Oh my gosh," Thalia breathes, her clavicles rising and falling. Mesmerizing. "Wait, don't tell me. The Creative Writing program?"

Again, that painful rush of breath. I'm going to develop asthma if I'm not careful. "Uh. Yeah."

Her entire face lights up. "No way! That's what I'm doing too." Her mouth stretches into the most beautiful smile. "Holy shit, Jane. We're going to be classmates."

I don't really know what to say to that. Part of me wants to crawl into a hole, but a small part of me is writhing with joy. I don't realize I'm biting my lip until I taste the salty tang of blood.

"What do you write?"

I lick my lips before I answer, wondering if there's blood visible on my mouth, if I've given myself away. But Thalia is still smiling a smile so innocent it physically hurts me to look at it.

I can't help but get a flashback of Mom, tilting her head down in the way that she does to show anyone watching that she's had a long day's work. I never know how she's able to convey exhaustion and put-upon-ness with just a turn of the head, but there's my mother. I pretend not to see her; most of the time, we pretend the other person doesn't exist. Then the sigh comes. *Still doing that writing thing, are you? When will you learn, Jane? Those things are for rich white folk. Not people like us. People like us, Jane, we do honest work.*

By "honest work" she means menial labor—work that breaks our bodies apart bit by bit. I often thought of how, throughout history, the bodies of people of color have been destroyed and fed in little pieces to rich white people to swallow, and they won't stop, not even when there's nothing left of us to give.

Mrs. Crawford's niece is due to give birth in September. She asked about you again, asked if you'd be available.

You know I won't be, I bite out. *I'm going to school.* A mistake. I should've stayed silent.

Mom has been working her whole life for people like Mrs. Crawford; people who have children and then decide they don't actually like kids that much, so enter my mother. She does everything for those kids—feeds them, bathes them, hugs them tight when they cry. The kids reward her by forgetting her name as soon as they become old enough to not need a nanny and she moves on to the next family. Over the years, I've watched my mother scurry around at the beck and call of the rich—"Can you work this weekend? We've been invited to the Robertsons' lake house for the weekend, for an adults-only hunting session, and Bella is so sensitive, we couldn't bring her anyway—you know how it is." The kids are always "sensitive" or "precocious," never "needy as fuck" and "spoiled as shit," which is really what they are. She gives and gives, her back becoming more hunched as she bends to pick up carelessly strewn shoes, bends to carry tantrum-throwing toddlers, and bends to kiss the feet of the Crawfords and Robertsons of the world. Good, honest work.

School, she snorts. *School for writing, who ever heard of that? Throwing good money away to learn how to dream your life away.*

It's not our way, Jane. If you insist on spending money on higher education, then go for proper subjects. Accounting. Medicine. Things you can make an actual living from.

And I type extra loudly so she'll know I'm ignoring her, that unlike her, I haven't given up dreaming of a better life. That I'll write a thousand different novels if that's what it takes to save me from my mother's life. That there is no such thing as "our way." It's always grated at me, the way that my mother assumes that I am just like her. I'm not all Chinese like my mom. I'm half-white, and just because my father's gone, it doesn't mean that part of me is magically erased.

I've stayed quiet far too long. Thalia is still looking at me with an expectant smile, so I quickly say, "Uh. I write fiction. A bit of poetry. You?" I add, shifting the conversation back at her. I've read that this is how normal conversations go. One person asks a question; the other one answers and fires back another question. Back and forth, a verbal game of tennis that most people seem to find so natural but often leaves me lost and exhausted.

"Same," she says. "What sort of fiction do you write?"

Stories about death. Stories where good people are forced to do bad things. And then find that they actually enjoy it. "Um, everything, really. I dabble in this and that."

"Still trying to find your voice," Thalia muses. "Yeah, that's how I feel too. I've tried writing both lit fic and genre, and I haven't quite decided where I feel most authentic."

Stop. Staring.

It's impossible not to, though. Not when she's speaking my truth. Authenticity is so hard to come by, and it's what I've always strived for in my writing. It means everything to me, because I can't be authentic anywhere else but on paper.

"I'm really hoping the program helps with that," she continues. "Maybe it'll help both of us find our voice, huh? I bet your voice is really special, Jane. Powerful." Her eyes meet mine, and I can't look away. I wonder what it would be like to lose myself in them, to plunge my fingers into the golden silk of her hair and feel her skull underneath my skin, only a thin layer of bone separating my hands from her brilliant, perfect mind.

4

Her website is beautiful. Clean and elegant, all of its focus on her book. *A Most Pleasant Death*. What a title. I read the description, which teases my skin into gooseflesh.

Marie and Sylvia used to be the best of friends. The kind of friendship that only comes once in a lifetime. It's just too bad that Marie had to move away, making the two friends drift apart. But when the two are reunited years later, they pick up right where they left off. Marie is now an Instagram star documenting her every move. Sylvia is quickly absorbed into Marie's frenetic, glamorous world of yacht parties and exotic trips. She even starts becoming Insta-famous herself. Everything's wonderful, or is it? When Marie gets involved in a shocking scandal, Sylvia quickly becomes trapped in her best friend's mess. The fans turn into trolls, with many of them lobbing death threats at both Marie and Sylvia. As everybody's obsession about Marie grows to a fever pitch, Sylvia has to go back to the past and discover the true reason why Marie had to move away so abruptly all those years ago, and what her supposed best friend is hiding.

No matter how I keep reminding myself to breathe, I keep losing my breath. *The kind of friendship that only comes once in a lifetime.* Now I'm no longer squeezing the mouse so hard. In fact, my hand is shaking. I snap the wristband a couple of times and try to control my breathing. It's us. I know it's us. She's written about us.

SHE WROTE ABOUT US!

The words flash in my head like one of those casino machines when you hit jackpot and it lights up with the accompanying *ding-ding-ding*! Us! She wrote about us! Flashing in neon lights, on off on off. Us! All these years, she, too, hasn't managed to leave me in the past. This is Thalia trying to get me to come back to her. This is a love letter written to me.

I try to get my breathing back under control as I click on her About page, but I don't know why I bother because there's a huge picture of her, and by god, she is perfect. Her hair is a shade lighter than it was in Oxford—an icy blond instead of the honey I was used to. It suits her, just as early thirties suits her. She's lost the baby roundness of her cheeks, and her cheekbones jut out in a way that makes me swallow, a way that I'm sure most runway models would kill to have. Her eyes are the same though. Impossibly large, ringed with heavy lashes and looking somehow innocent and yet knowing at the same time.

Thalia Ashcroft, writing as May Pierce, is the author of *A Most Pleasant Death. The psychological suspense novel* sold at a competitive seven-house auction, and its film rights sold at a five-studio auction before being won by Sony Pictures. Director Ambrose Wells and Oscar-nominated actress Margaux Thomas are attached to the film, which is reported to start production next summer. The book is due out in August of this year.

Her bio tells me next to nothing about her, but holy shit, her debut is a big book. A lead title. Those two words—"lead title."—are what most writers lust over. Every year, thousands of books are published by traditional publishers, but most of these books are midlisters—books that will only get the minimum backing and publicity, if any. Only a small handful of all published books are what are called the "lead titles," and these are the books that get everything—front placement at bookstores, magazine and newspaper ads, radio, TV, and online interviews with the author, pitches to Oprah's and Reese's book clubs in the hopes that they might pick these books out of the endlessly high mountain of books submitted to them every month. In other words, "lead title" is mecca for us writers. I've never even dared to dream about getting lead status at a Big Five publishing house. Not I, midlister at a small indie press who writes flaccid lit fic that nobody reads. Literary fiction is highbrow, often difficult to read because every sentence is full of hidden meaning. Virginia Woolf. Toni Morrison. Authors who don't make it easy for the reader; we're not here to spoon-feed the masses. In the past, I had dreams of being one of the great lit fic writers of my generation, but ever since I lost Thalia, I've lost whatever magic touch I had that made my writing shine. My teachers and classmates at Oxford used to celebrate my work, but now, after I've released two lackluster books, none of them ever bothers to respond to my emails. I have been forgotten.

In the News section of Thalia's website, I see that her cover reveal happened in *Entertainment Weekly*—yet more evidence of her publisher splashing out on her. I scroll further down and find the Publishers Marketplace announcement back when she got her book deal.

Denise Hazuki of Story House has bought, in a seven-figure deal, at auction, Thalia Ashcroft's debut adult suspense, *A Most Pleasant Death*. Pitched as *Gone Girl* meets *The Best of Friends*, the story follows a married couple after the husband goes missing, triggering an investigation of his seemingly perfect wife and the mysterious best friend who has recently reappeared. Agent Beatrice McHale brokered the deal for North American rights.

Seven figures. Holy shit. I'd been expecting six figures, but this. This is out of this world. Most of us only ever dream of six figures. I spend time lurking on several writing forums, and the threads that discuss dreams and goals only ever have people posting about how they dream of one day getting a six-figure book deal. And even then, usually you'd get other writers snarking back and saying stuff like, "Keep dreaming." Us writers are a petty, insecure bunch. But the point is, no one has ever dared to say, "I wish I could have a seven-figure deal one day." You'd get laughed out of the forums.

But here she is, after a nine-year disappearance—not even a

trace of an update online—screaming back into the public sphere with a unicorn deal. I can't help but laugh a little. That is SO Thalia.

I go to her Contact page and my mouth turns into a desert. A contact form. My fingers hover over the keyboard. I don't know if I can do this. What would I say?

Hey, it's Jane. I know you wrote about me. About us.

No.

Hiii, it's Jane! It's been forever!

No.

How are you? It's Jane. I've been looking for you ever since—

No.

I can't write to her through a goddamned contact form. I've imagined us meeting again a thousand different ways—most of them cheesy meet-cutes like reaching for the same box of cereal at the same time or crashing into each other on the sidewalk, our bodies slamming and recognizing each other before our minds catch up. Not a single one of my dream scenarios had me reaching out to her over a clinical contact form—*Contact Me! I love to hear from my readers!*

I'm not your reader, Thalia. I'm me. Jane. Your Jane.

I go back to the home page and scroll down, and aha! There's a list of social media icons. I click on Instagram, because I need to see her first and foremost. So badly that my mouth is actually watering. As though I haven't eaten in years and my body knows it's about to be nourished.

This account is set to private. To follow, please send a follow request.

NO. WHAT?

Why even bother having an Insta account if you're just going to set it to private?

The world is painted red for a moment. I'm gritting my teeth so hard that I hear the clack in my ears. I force my jaw to unclench. Take a deep inhale. Exhale. Another inhale. *It's okay, Jane. It's fine.*

Her profile picture is the same as the one on her About page. And she has—wow, she has over fifty thousand followers. Practically an influencer. I swallow, my cursor hovering over the Follow button.

But then I think of my Instagram page. I see it through her eyes. Fifty-six followers. Six posts, all of them mundane, all of them half-assed. Limp posts about my books at the behest of my publisher, who can't be bothered to market the books themselves and gaslit me into doing my own promotion. My profile picture a painfully awkward shot that had taken Ted four seconds to take on my secondhand Oppo phone. He'd offered to take more, but he'd also said it in a faux generous way: *I'm slammed with projects, babe, but I could pull an all-nighter if you want me to spend more time on your author photos?*

Like I could accept after he put it that way. Not sure why taking ten minutes to properly photograph me meant that he'd then have to pull an all-nighter, but if I asked him that, he'd give that sigh. Ted has The Sigh mastered. It somehow conveys every emotion a sigh has ever managed to convey—disappointment (*I expected you to understand, Jane*), exhaustion (*not this again, Jane*), and resignation (*okay, Jane, you win. AGAIN. Because this is my life, isn't it? Yes dear, no dear, I'll take the trash out, dear*). The Sigh means that he's won, because he's about to be magnanimous to placate his nagging shrew of a wife. So of course I say, *No, it's okay, this will do.*

I could have taken photos of myself, I suppose. But just the idea of it makes my skin crawl. Even the term for it, "selfie," sounds unbearable, a stain on my generation that we'll never be able to wash off. So there's my sad Instagram page. Might as well be a giant stamp on my forehead that says: FAILURE.

I close the Instagram tab and go back to the list of social media pages that Thalia's on. Twitter. She's got about fifteen thousand followers on it (I have one hundred), but her Twitter bio says: I'm not active on here. This is just for book updates. Instagram is my jam! Follow me on there @ThaliaAshcroft.

A small laugh escapes me. Follow her on Instagram. Well, some of us are trying, Thalia.

I close Twitter and open the third and last social media page: Facebook. The same profile photo appears. I scroll down and my heart stops, because this is it. A post about SusPens Con (ha, very cunning), a convention for suspense/thriller authors in New York City that takes place six days from now. And Thalia's going to attend. The post says: "Can't wait to see you there!"

I can't wait to see you there either.

———

I APPROACH THIS CAREFULLY. PATIENTLY. I MAKE A CUP of Ted's favorite hot drink—chai. He's white, not Indian, but he loves loving things from other cultures because it's so very progressive, so very NorCal. Here I am, my whole life spent trying to fit into white American culture, and all of a sudden, to be not-white, to be a person of color, is trendy. What a name, "Person of Color"—like whiteness is a blank canvas that you start with, and along the way, some of us are splashed and come out stained. But now, being stained is cool, so men like Ted are scrambling to show how worldly they are. The same people who, as kids, told me my lunches were "weird" and "stinky" now lecture me on the health benefits of tempeh and matcha.

Ted's turned his nose up at things that he thinks are too basic—the pumpkin spice lattes that I like, the American cheese I used to buy (now we buy feta and camembert and queso, which he pronounces "koo-ay-sow"), the Red Delicious apples I like for their mealy texture and the way that I can masticate them with a forceful tongue (apples are too American for Ted, though he'll settle for Fujis if we must). I watch from the sidelines and wonder if maybe part of the reason he was so attracted to me in the first place is because of my not-quite-whiteness. I'm different enough to be exotic, but not so different that it scares him. Of course, if I were to even broach the edges of the subject, Ted would be horrified. *You really think I would marry someone just because they're—ugh—exotic?* He can't even say the word without choking on it. One time, I bought a bag of "exotic mixed nuts" from Costco, and Ted snorted and said, "Exotic? I thought we'd done away with that word." *It's a fucking bag of nuts, Ted*, I wanted to say, but I didn't, because then he'd tell me I don't get it, because I'm "white-passing," therefore I don't understand the struggles of real POC. He loves this term, "white-passing." Often uses it to remind me I'm just as white as he is, and thus am just as unequipped to tackle the gnarly, tangled subject of race as he is.

But this isn't the time to ruminate. I must focus. Eyes on the prize. I pour the tea, its fragrance spicy with cloves and cardamom, into Ted's favorite mug and put a Trader Joe's dunker on a side plate. As a last-minute addition, I sprinkle a pinch of cinnamon on top of the chai.

I carry the offerings to his study, pausing after I knock for him to say, "Yeah?" I go inside and have to swallow my anger again, because Ted's office is pristine. Bright and airy, not a single sheet of paper cluttering the space. Everything slotted neatly into its assigned place.

So Ted, the guy who has never lifted a finger to help me clean the rest of the house because he's always claimed he doesn't mind clutter, evidently DOES mind clutter, and not only that, but he knows how to fucking clean. He just doesn't do it because why bother when you've got your wife, basically an unpaid live-in maid?

But never mind that, I remind myself. That's minor stuff. Don't focus on it. We've got bigger things on our minds, don't we? So I plaster a smile on my face—not too big or he'll get suspicious.

He barely looks up from his big computer screen (a splurge he had deemed necessary for analyzing numbers, though honestly I think it's more to do with Fortnite). "I'm kind of busy—" Then he sees the chai and the side plate with the stupidly huge dunker on it and his eyebrows lift a little. "Wow, this is a nice surprise."

I suppose it is a nice surprise. I don't tend to come in here with tea and a snack. A small coil of guilt tightens in my chest, which makes me resentful. Did he say this is a "surprise" to drive home the fact that I don't often do things like this? To highlight what a negligent wife I am? No, I'm being too sensitive. Or am I?

When did every tiny thing between us turn into a barb? I hate to admit it, but it's probably my fault. In the early days, after the wreck that was Oxford, I'd contorted myself to fit the image of a normal, happy person because I needed to fill that void so badly. And when I'd met Ted, I'd fooled him. I kept up the charade for about a year after we got married. Then I got lazy. Let the mask slip a few too many times, and slowly, we changed from partners into adversaries. I wonder if he knows what I really am, and he's pushing so he can expose me.

"Thanks," he says, looking genuinely pleased as he slurps his tea. "What's the occasion?"

I shrug. "Just thought it would be nice."

"Well, it is." He looks at me quizzically before replacing the look with a smile. "This job's turning out to be a lot more complicated than I expected." He leans back with a sigh (not a sigh meant for me, so it's not The Sigh) and dunks the biscotti in before chewing it noisily. "How's your day going?"

I make myself nod. "It's okay. I was just looking up book events, and there's a book con that I think could be good for my career."

Ted's eyes flick toward mine, and my hackles rise. Oh shit. I wasn't careful or casual enough. He knows I'm here for something. My defenses clap into place, ready for his attack. "A book con?" he says.

He knows what a "book con" is. Bastard.

"You know, a book convention? Everyone in the industry will go—publishers, authors, agents, booksellers, librarians, reviewers . . . It's a great opportunity to network with other industry people." Good job, me. That's a great way of describing it—a smart business move.

Ted nods. "Oh, okay."

That's it? I wait another few seconds, but all he does is dip more of the dunker in his tea before taking another big bite and chewing carefully. Okay, so he's not even going to meet me halfway. He's making me say it, spell it out for him.

"There's one in New York that I want to go to," I blurt out. God damn it. *Have more fucking filters, self.* As soon as the words are out, I think of half a dozen ways I could have worded it better. But it's too late now. I've given Ted exactly what he needed, and he's not going to waste it. Of course not.

His eyes widen and he straightens up in his seat—*gosh, Jane, I'm shocked!*—and he places his tea and cookie on the table. Not so shocked that he's forgotten about the drink and snack, I see. "In New York? Like, New York City? The East Coast?"

How many fucking New Yorks are there? He really has to drive home how far away this con is.

"Yeah," I say in the most neutral voice possible. I am Switzerland. I will not be swayed.

"Sweetie, that's—" He pauses, then there it is. The Sigh. Except this one also conveys, in addition to all the other emotions, impatience (*we've been over this, Jane, why do you have to be so thick?*). "That's out of our budget."

Know what's really outside of our budget? I want to hiss. This fucking house. The way it dominates all of our income, its cumbersome presence sucking every available cent and giving me nothing in return. An overgrown backyard we hardly use, despite Ted's insistence that we would use it one day. His parents are avid gardeners; every month there's a new offering from them—a basket of yellow-green apples, a punnet of apricots, a bag of heirloom tomatoes, bulbous and ugly and disturbingly warm from the sun. And with each gift, there is an attached comment. "You kids should grow your own too! It's so rewarding!" With a pointed look at me, because Teddy Bear is just so busy, isn't he? They literally call him that—Teddy Bear. He pretends to hate it, but he adores the name and resents that I haven't picked it up, that I still call him Ted, or worse, Theo sometimes.

I would rather live in an apartment. I'd lived in an apartment with Mom for most of my life, and living in a house seems wrong, like wearing borrowed clothes. Mom had died in her apartment three years ago. A stroke. Her neighbor called to complain about the smell, and that was when they found her, two days before I was due my weekly visit. If she'd been living in a house, I would've been the one to discover her. We're not built for houses, Mom and I.

I push the thought out of my head and focus on the discussion. "It's a good investment for my career," I say. He likes this word, "investment." Uses it for all of his splurges. The stupidly expensive computer, the gaming chair, the adjustable standing desk that he never, ever stands at.

I can see him considering whether he should deploy The Sigh again. He thinks better of it. For now. "I know how much this writing thing means to you . . ." This writing thing. I try not to dwell on it. Instead, I brace myself for the "but."

"But . . ." He winces like what he's about to say is physically hurting him. *Look how much pain you're putting me through, Jane.* "I just don't think it's quite there yet, you know?"

I shake my head. No, I don't know, you fucker. I'm not going to make this easy for him. I'll watch as he struggles through the next few sentences, watch him prettify the words that are meant to cut me down.

"Well—" Now he sighs. It's not The Sigh, just a small one. An "I'm trying" sigh. "It's just—look, please don't take this the wrong way. But you're a midlist writer. What was your last advance for?"

He knows what my last advance was for because he adores how tiny it is, how insignificant it is compared to his freelancing fees. So I don't say anything. Let him say the numbers, rolling them in his mouth like peppermint candy to be savored.

"What was it, two grand?"

"Two thousand three hundred." Dammit. I wasn't going to say it, but I fell for his bait.

"Two thousand three hundred dollars," he announces with a satisfied nod. "Broken up into three payments."

This is how most publishing payments work. They're broken up into as many chunks as possible—the signing payment, the delivery and acceptance payment, and one last chunk when the book is actually published. Eight months it took me to write the book, a book about a depressed suburban housewife that is never going to earn out, never going to make me another cent. Ted likes to remind me that I am privileged because I can afford to write full-time thanks to him.

"A ticket to New York City at this time of the year is going to set us back what, five hundred dollars?"

Ha. I've prepared for this, you asshole. "Actually, only about a hundred if I fly budget."

He frowns. He hadn't seen this coming. Then he rallies, "Sweetheart, I don't think you should fly budget. That's not safe."

"I looked up their safety ratings"—I did not—"and they seem really good."

"And where would you stay? New York's expensive."

"No problem. I would stay outside of the city and commute in. I found places for around fifty bucks a night—"

"No, those places won't be safe. I can't possibly let you stay there."

All these noes disguised as concern. I want to scratch him, peel the skin off his face so I can see the thoughts oozing underneath like toxic mud. He just wants to keep me here, tethered to his side so he can always be the superior one of the two of us.

"And then there's the cost of food and travel and . . ." Here it comes, The Sigh. And it's a good one this time. He's been building up to it. It conveys the world. When it's done, he looks deflated and sad and empathetic. "I'm sorry, sweetie, but I just don't think we can afford it. We can't justify the cost of sending you to a con."

I make it out of his study and down to the basement just in time before I snap.

5

Pemberton College is one of the smaller of Oxford University's colleges. But smaller doesn't mean any less impressive. Thalia and I wheel our luggage across the cobblestones from the bus station, about half a mile away from the college. I can't help but notice how nice her luggage is compared to mine—hers a sleek black Samsonite, mine a ratty thrift store affair, the fabric patterned with seventies-style roses and vines. Every step across the uneven cobblestones makes the wheels rattle. I'm half expecting them to pop right off, leaving me to heave it up onto my shoulders and stagger all the way to my fancy new college. I wonder what Thalia would do then. Leave me, probably. I won't blame her. Or rather, I will, but only secretly, and the blame would be tinged with so much want that it wouldn't matter anyway.

I shake my head. Try to focus on the beauty that's around me. There's so much of it, even all the way back at the bus station. Who's ever known a bus station to be beautiful? But Gloucester Green is surrounded by Gothic Revival–style buildings, so different from the laid-back, slouching buildings I got used to in California. Everything around us is built in that same elaborate style, all impressive stone buildings with stained glass windows. Huge red buses trundle down the narrow streets, charming English names emblazoned on their sign boards: Kidlington, Almond Ave, Cowley Road.

I am charmed by it all, in a way, but in an even bigger way, I'm too absorbed by Thalia to really take in any of it. I sneak glances at her as we walk, trying to inhale the tiniest details about her. The way her hair turns into spun gold when the late afternoon English sun hits it. The way she licks her lips, moistening them ever so slightly with her impossibly pink tongue. Her lips are pouty in the way that most girls would have to rely on fillers to get; two full pillows that speak of innocent lust. If I were a guy, I would be obsessed with those lips.

Ugh, what is wrong with me? Why would I think that? But there's something about Thalia that makes me want to defile her, to see her kneeling before someone, her face awash with lust and shame, tinged with anger underneath a thick layer of pleasure, begging for more.

"Phew, I was not expecting such a long walk," Thalia says, and I nearly jump because holy shit, what the hell was going through my mind?

"Uh, yeah, me neither." I take in a deep breath of the brisk Oxford air to try and un-crazify my crazy thoughts. Even though it's only the start of autumn—mid-September; the end of summer, really—Oxford has a head start on the weather, and already I can smell the breath of winter on the edge of the wind.

"Still, I guess it's a nice walk," Thalia continues. "Though if

I break the wheels of my luggage, my mom's going to murder me."

There's a beat before I realize it's my turn to speak instead of staring at her like I'm hoping to see the insides of her. "Yeah, same." I go over the words I just said, making sure they're appropriate under the circumstances, that I haven't just given myself away.

"Your mom's a bitch like mine?"

That startles me enough to snatch me out of my anxiety spiral. I don't know why it should; it's not like I know Thalia. We met two hours ago, and the whole bus ride here, we only made small talk about the master's course. Why should I be surprised that she doesn't like her mother?

Because. In the past two hours, I've concocted this entire image of Thalia. Thalia comes from a family with 2.5 children and a golden retriever–Lab mix named Ginger or Biscuit or Cookie. Definitely some kind of food, anyway. Her mother is a "homemaker," not a housewife. She makes rhubarb tarts from scratch, using locally sourced butter that comes wrapped in wax paper and twine. Her father is an architect / lawyer / finance manager who owns a little bachelor pad in the city so he can work late nights and fuck his secretary without staining the high–thread count sheets at home. Mom knows about it but turns a blind eye; she's benignly happy in suburban heaven, plus she can twist Dad's guilt into a new pair of princess-cut diamond earrings or maybe an emerald necklace surrounded with leaf-shaped diamonds. She hasn't decided yet. Thalia is the baby of the family; you can tell because she's so innocent and unspoiled. Totally unprepared for the likes of me. Ripe for the plucking.

But now, with that one little question, Thalia's ripped apart this image I've built of her family. I can't tell if that pleases or angers me. I don't like having to rearrange my thoughts, to reorient them like this. It's confusing. Unnerving. And what do I say to that? It's not normal interaction to call your mother a bitch, especially not to someone who's effectively a stranger, surely? I want to encourage further interaction without revealing too much of my own bitch of a mother.

"I can relate to that," I say finally. I read once that this is something you say as a form of commiseration, an updated version of "I understand." Saying, "I understand," opens you up to backlash, because you can't, in fact, "understand" what someone else is going through, not even when you've gone through the same thing yourself. Because everyone processes things differently. Or some such bullshit, I don't know.

It works, anyway. Those porno lips stretch into a smile. She has a dimple on her left cheek. I hadn't noticed before because I'd been sitting on the other side of her, but wow, that dimple. "I had a feeling you might," she says.

I'm about to ask her more about her mother, her father, and her 1.5 sibling(s), but Thalia says, "I think we're supposed to turn right here," so we do, down a narrow side street, and suddenly, Pemberton is there.

It's like going through some enchanted passageway. The noise of St. Aldate's is muffled by the closely packed buildings, and Pemberton is so much bigger than I'd expected. What the hell have I landed myself in? I'd read that it was one of the smaller Oxford colleges, meant only for graduate courses, large enough to house only a hundred students. About fifty more students live off campus, but I've scrimped and saved, existing only on ramen, and taken out staggering loans. I had to have the full Oxford University experience. No off-campus apartments for me. I wonder where Thalia's staying, and the thought sends a jolt of excitement through me. Maybe we'd be roommates, and I'd be able to observe her all the time, catch a glimpse of her shedding that skin of perfection at night, because there's no way that anyone can be this wholesome, this brilliant, all the time. But no, I recall belatedly that Oxford only has single rooms, a fact that I had celebrated when I found out months ago, but now detest because it means there is no chance of Thalia and me rooming together.

There's a giant wooden gate at the entrance of Pemberton, and a side door carved into the gate that has been left open. I let Thalia go through first, because I'm half-certain guards are going to swarm us at any second and tell me I'm a fraud who needs to be deported back to the US. Right through the gate is a guard's office with the words "PORTER'S LODGE" above it. We go inside, and a self-important guard wearing a black suit and a bowler hat says, "New students, are we?"

I am, technically, a new student here, but when this man in a black suit and a black hat asks that, the answer screams out of my head, leaving me with Mom's voice. *What do you think you're doing, sweetie? Going to that posh school with the posh kids? You're going to the same school the kids I raised go to. They're gonna know you're not one of them right away.*

I know she's not wrong. When I was little—I don't know how old, but definitely too little to be left alone at home—Mom was called in for a weekend because the people she worked for had to travel someplace suddenly. An "emergency" golf trip, maybe, or an "urgent" ski trip, who knows. They needed Mom to come in to take care of their kid, and they didn't care that she had to find a caregiver for her own kid on such short notice. None of the neighbors or the aunts could watch me, so after she

45

came to the end of her frantic search, Mom got this determined look and said, "You'll just have to come with me. You and Nectarine are about the same age. You can play with each other."

These kids' names are always some such ridiculous ones—some sort of fruit, or a color (always Blue, never Pink, to show defiance toward gender roles), or an emotion (one of them was called Jubilation).

Anyway, Nectarine took one look at me and knew I was "the help." The entire weekend, we "played together" as in she'd play with her toys while I waited patiently, at the end of which she'd point to the mess and say, "Clean." And I'd clean.

"So cute! You kids play so well together," Mom said, and I'd think, *You stupid bitch.*

The worst part of it was how naturally picking up after Nectarine had come to me. I didn't even hesitate when she'd point and tell me to bend over and clean up her mess. Go on my hands and knees and gather the strewn Duplo blocks. Inside, I seethed, wanting to fling myself at Nectarine and claw at her little face, feel my fingernails rip apart her soft, moisturized skin. But my body listened to her demands without a fight. It knew, even then, that I belonged to one class of people, and that there I would stay.

This guard—this Oxford porter—is looking at me like he knows exactly what I am. Like he knows I'm only able to afford being here by taking out massive loans and grants. I swear he's this close to telling me to go round the back, to the entrance for "the help." Thank god I have Thalia with me. She says, "Yup!" and gives him one of those smiles and you can just see the spell working on him. He blinks, his stern expression melting away, and his wrinkled cheeks turn rosy.

"Just uh—write your names down in this book here then, luv." He pushes a guest book toward us.

I watch her write her name down. Thalia Ashcroft. An elegant cursive spelling out an elegant name, nothing as stupid as hearts over the i. She hands the pen to me, her fingers brushing fire across mine, and I have to swallow before writing my own name down. Jane Morgan. A name as plain as I am, the letters ugly and stark underneath Thalia's cursive.

"Through this way," the porter says to us—to Thalia, really; he can't take his eyes off her either, as he leads us outside of the porter's lodge. "This is the Old Quad. Built in the fourteenth century. Have you seen anything more beautiful?" He points to a pristine quad surrounded by ivy-covered sandstone buildings on all sides. Both Thalia and I shake our heads obediently. I haven't, actually, been anyplace this impressive. The buildings around us look like a palace from a fairy tale, bursts of flowers hanging beneath every window. "Here you are: this is Highgate Hall, and the common room is right in there. All right then?" He smiles at us, twinkly eyes still on Thalia.

"Thank you," she says, shaving another ten years off his face. I swear he practically skips away from us.

"I think he's in love with you."

She barks with laughter, and I wonder what's so funny about what I just said. I'd merely pointed out the truth. Luckily, I'm saved from having to say anything because a woman greets us at the entrance of Highgate Hall.

"Hello! I'm Becca, your resident advisor. Which course are you here for?"

"Uh—" I can never just reply when a stranger asks me a question like this, even though I know the answer already. My brain always has to add in an extra syllable just to buy myself that split second of time to put on my mask, make sure I'm presenting okay.

47

"The MFA in Creative Writing," Thalia says easily.

"Brilliant," Becca says, leading us inside Highgate Hall. The interior is just as stunning as the exterior—high, vaulted ceilings, hardwood floors covered with giant Oriental rugs, and Renaissance paintings adorning the walls. Becca goes to a large table, where an array of name tags and envelopes awaits. "Right, here we are. Names, please?"

We tell her our names, and she locates our materials. "The envelopes contain the keys to your rooms—I see both of you are rooming at Downing—and a welcome packet with information about the college and Oxford in general, that sort of thing. Let me know if you need anything, all right?"

"Great," Thalia says. "Thank you."

Becca has fallen under Thalia's spell as well, and it makes me want to scratch out her eyes. Seeing everyone fall for Thalia isn't easy to stomach. She's mine, not theirs.

"You'll have your induction seminar at the Sawyer Room at four o'clock, where they'll tell you about the process of matriculation and everything. And then right after that we'll have a welcome reception and dinner. You can go up that staircase there; there's a bridge that leads straight to Downing. Welcome to Michaelmas!"

The names and terms of everything are making my head swim, and I want to grab Becca and scream at her to talk in plain English. What the hell is "matriculation"? What's "induction," and why is she welcoming us to "Michaelmas" and not Pemberton? I snap my wristband before the curl of anger can overcome me and I actually do end up assaulting my resident advisor my first day here.

"Cool, thank you," Thalia says, and with that, she turns and walks toward the staircase. We lug our heavy bags up the stone steps, the sounds of our rapid breaths echoing in the cavernous stairwell. Once we're on the second floor, Thalia drops her bag with a loud sigh, turns to me, and whispers, "What the fuck is Michaelmas?"

I laugh, and it's the first genuine laugh I remember doing. My world is a whirling, broken mess and I don't belong anywhere, but Thalia is the eye of the storm, where everything is still and silent and I can finally breathe.

———

THERE IS AN ACTUAL FIREPLACE IN MY DORM ROOM.

It's no longer usable, of course, and instead of logs, there is a small bookcase sitting inside it, but still. It's a fireplace. Inside my dorm room. There's even space for a sofa and coffee table in addition to the expected single bed and study desk. And there's a sink in one corner of the room. What kind of bougie dorm room has a sofa set and a fireplace? All this for one student. Back home, there was no student housing at the community college, and when I transferred to Cal State for the final two years of undergrad, I was assigned a dorm room that would've been shared between me and two other girls; a recipe for disaster, so I'd opted to stay at home instead. Not the college experience I wanted, but freaks like me don't deserve the traditional college experience, and we sure as hell don't deserve a solo room with a fireplace in it.

The moment my door clicks shut, I abandon my heavy luggage and fling my purse and papers on the coffee table before striding across the room and opening the bay windows. Oh yeah, did I mention the room has actual bay windows? They overlook the Old Quad, and the whole thing is so pretty I don't quite know what to do with myself. I stand there for a long while, watching students trickling in through the front gate. None of them is escorted by the porter, I can't help but notice. I guess we just got the special treatment because of Thalia.

Thalia. My breath comes out in a choked rush. I'm suffocating with need for her. Though need for what, I can't say exactly. Do I want to fuck her? Is that what all this is about? The thought of Thalia and me entwined in bed—in my new single bed—our sweat-damp bodies writhing against each other, makes me shiver. I'm not into girls. I—

A knock at my door, making me jump and sparking irritation like a jolt of electricity. I snap around, teeth gritted. I've just been on a long journey, I'm in a foreign country and a foreign college, and I just need one fucking moment to recenter myself so I don't fall apart. Is that too much to—

"Jane? What are you wearing?" Even muffled by the door, Thalia's voice carries with it the musical quality that I've come to love. "I can't decide what to wear to the dinner. You've got to help me."

All of the irritation melts away, replaced now with anticipation. Then, with it, a sudden barrage of anxiety. Oh god, this is it. We'll meet others at the induction, whatever that is, and then the welcome reception. Our course mates, or maybe even Pemberton students from other courses. Many people. My palms turn slick. I don't want to meet them. Not right now. Not ever. I want to exist in a place where it's just me and Thalia.

I cross the room and open the door. Fuck, it's hard to remember to breathe at the sight of her.

"Yes?"

"Have you decided what to wear to the welcome dinner?"

"Oh, right. No." I glance at the mirror above the fireplace. I look exactly how I feel—travel-weary and irritated by the world.

My oversize jacket is rumpled, my hair flat with grease, whatever minimal makeup I had on rubbed off during my journey here. With a sinking feeling, I realize something that mortifies even me: I don't have anything that's appropriate for a "welcome reception." I hadn't expected anything formal. In college, we all existed in hoodies and torn jeans or yoga pants and Uggs, and during finals week, some of the other kids even showed up in their pj's.

I must look as lost as I feel, because understanding dawns on Thalia's face. "Come on," she says, grabbing my hand. "You can wear one of my dresses."

I open my mouth, about to resist, because no way, I'm not one of those girls who have female friends that they can swap clothes with. But she doesn't give me a chance to protest before she pulls me along, saying, "Oh, this is so exciting. I'm so glad we met each other, Jane. I'd be so lost without you otherwise."

She wouldn't. The thought is laughable. I would've been lost back at the Heathrow bus terminal, but Thalia swans through the world like she belongs everywhere, and everyone opens their arms to take her in, because who wouldn't? But I'm helpless to resist, letting her guide me the way a faultless little child guides a slouching beast in fairy tales, confident in their ignorance of what they drag behind them.

Her room is right across from mine, nearly identical except her bay window overlooks the Chapel Quad instead of the Old Quad. Somehow, in the time I spent just staring vacantly out of my window, Thalia has unpacked her belongings and put personal touches to her room. Books adorn the space—a handful placed in her bookcase in the fireplace, a few more on the mantelpiece, and yet more on the floating shelves above her study desk. Her bed no longer has the standard woolen blanket on it; instead, a fluffy white duvet rests like a cloud over it, complete with a crimson silk runner. It actually looks like a hotel bed instead of a dorm bed, and the small touch transforms the room completely.

"Have a seat," Thalia says, walking to her closet.

I perch hesitantly on her sofa, noticing that she's also draped a soft, rich blanket over it. I run my hand across the blanket, marveling at the softness. It's like touching pure wealth.

"That's my favorite blanket," she says, smiling over her shoulder as she rifles through her closet, and I snatch my hand back as though she's just caught me going through her underwear drawer. Luckily, she's turned back to face the closet and doesn't see me flinching. "What do you think of this?" She brandishes a dress the color of sunshine.

"No," I say flatly, and then immediately regret it. That came out a lot more brusque than I had intended. I never want to be rough with you, Thalia. I clear my throat, modulating my voice so it doesn't come out so raw. "Thank you, but it's not very—it's too—I can't—"

She watches me struggle for the right words for a second before coming to my rescue. "No, you're right. You're too sophisticated for such a bright color."

Sophisticated? I start to protest, to correct her—*you're wrong, there's nothing sophisticated about me!*—but she's already rifling through her closet again.

"This one," she says, and I want to protest because *I don't belong in your clothes, Thalia, I really don't,* but my words die in my throat at the sight of the dress she holds up. It's the color of old, dark blood. The kind of dress that promises danger and class in equal measure. The kind of dress I have always secretly wondered how I'd look in, except of course I've never had the money to buy one, nor do I have any events to attend in one.

"Yes, this is so you," Thalia says, striding across the room and placing the dress in my hands. She walks back to the closet, humming, then turns around with a frown when she notices the lack of movement on my part. "What's up? Come on, we don't want to be late."

She expects me to change here. In front of her.

"Oh," she says, reading my mind again. "I won't look. I'll be facing this way, searching for something for myself to wear."

Is this what girls do? Change in front of one another? Parading one's flaws like that? Unbearable. But I don't want to offend, so I stand up, feeling suddenly gigantic, aware that the room seems to have shrunk in the past thirty seconds. But true to her word, Thalia isn't watching me. She doesn't care what my body looks like. This is normal. Be normal.

I take off my rumpled shirt with slightly shaking hands, feeling goose bumps sprout across my bare skin as the cold air kisses it. My breath sounds so loud in the cramped room. My bra hikes up as I pull up my shirt, and for a horrifying second, my left breast almost pops out from underneath. I catch it in time, and now I truly am out of breath, like I've just run a marathon.

"Oh, I would kill for those abs," Thalia says, and I jerk around and sure enough, she's looking. She's LOOKING.

I should feel betrayed, but she's looking at me with admiration, and the small, sick part of me wants to arch my back so she can see more of me. Instead, I turn away from her, cheeks burning, curling in on myself as I yank on the dress over my head.

"I'll help you with the zip."

"No!" The word rips out without warning. I want to catch it, ram it back in my mouth and swallow it, but it's too late.

"Okay," Thalia says, easy-breezy like I didn't just shriek at her like a crazed animal. "Just let me know if you need help. What do you think of this one? Too Alabama-housewife-at-country-club?"

"Uh, I don't know." I can't think. My mind's a mess, thoughts whizzing past and crashing into one another. I struggle into the dress, my limbs too long and ungraceful to move fast. I feel like a praying mantis. Once it's on, I realize with dawning horror that I do, in fact, need help with the zipper. "Um—"

She doesn't need me to say the words out loud, and for that small kindness, I love her even more. She simply crosses the room and puts one hand at the small of my back. All of my senses are zeroed in on a laser point of focus—Thalia's hand on my back. Then she pulls the zipper slowly up, up. My eyes flutter close. The barest caress of her fingertips across my skin, a trail of sensation I feel more acutely than anything I've experienced.

"Done."

Air floods my lungs. The world resumes spinning on its axis. Birds are chirping once more. Done, and just like that, her fingers are no longer on my skin, leaving me cold. I turn around slowly, my gaze on my feet.

"Oh, Jane," she breathes. I look up and the first thing I see are her eyes, like a lake. Like a mirror. I could get lost in them. "You look amazing."

There is no way in hell I look anywhere close to "amazing," but Thalia doesn't give me a chance to reply before she takes the hem of her sweater and pulls it over her head. I've just resumed breathing, for god's sake.

Her body is creamy bronze, a stark contrast to the violet lace bra she wears. Her breasts are small but high, and I really need to stop staring, but I can't. Not while her ribs are right in front of me, each curved bone ever so slightly visible under that satiny skin. A gentle curve I could take a hundred years to trace. So different from her hip bones, which jut out like knifepoints. Her belly is so taut that there's a depression between her jeans and her skin, just enough for a fingertip to dip in. I swallow hard, and the sound is thunderous in the small room. God, she must have heard. I need to leave.

But Thalia is standing in nothing but panties, and you do not leave the room when this is happening. She shivers, smiling. "Gosh, it's a lot colder than back home, isn't it?" She doesn't wait for a reply before she pulls out another dress from the closet and shrugs it on. A forest green dress that brings out the creaminess of her skin and makes her hair shine like melted gold, off the shoulder so her clavicles are still in my face. She cinches the waist with a thin black belt, highlighting her tiny waistline, and I have never seen anyone make looking gorgeous so effortless.

"Come," she commands, and I don't even hesitate before I do so. I walk to her, each step bringing me closer.

"Sit. Let me do your makeup."

Ah. Right. Makeup.

I'm only used to doing makeup that makes it look like I'm not wearing makeup. Makeup that's worn to blend in, not stand out. But I feel helpless as I sit there and Thalia takes out a bag filled with brushes and lipsticks and powders. She dabs and smooths and draws, my face her canvas, and each touch leaves me wanting more. And when she uses her ring finger to rub lipstick on my lips, I nearly lose it, nearly jump up and grab her, relishing the frightened squeak she would surely make, like a rabbit that belatedly realizes it's stepped into a steel-toothed trap.

I jerk up to my feet, my heartbeat a roar of thunder. *Get it the fuck under control, Jane.*

"Whoa, you okay? Did I hurt you?"

The question makes me snort. No, Thalia, you did not hurt me. How ridiculous for the rabbit to ask if it has hurt the wolf. "No, I just—sorry, I—I'm not used to people touching me." Isthatnormalisitokaywillitoutme?

"Oh." A small line appears between Thalia's eyebrows for one second before it clears. "I'm sorry, I should've asked you first. I didn't mean to be so pushy. I get that way sometimes, so please let me know if I ever make you uncomfortable, okay?"

She's blaming herself. She, Thalia, a completely normal, friendly person, thinks she is at fault for my sociopathy. I don't know what to say to that, so I just shrug and nod. "Okay, yeah."

"Cool. Can you give me like five minutes to finish putting on my war paint?"

I would give her the rest of the time I have in this world if I could. I nod and head toward the window. I pretend to look out and enjoy the scenery, but the whole time, I can't stop sneaking glances as she applies things onto her already perfect face, wondering what it would be like to touch her, to run my fingers down her cheek, her mouth, and that incredible, thin neck of hers.

6

The memory of that first day with Thalia possesses me. I can't believe I was about to let Ted derail my goal of getting to New York. I guess the years have just worn me down a lot more than I had thought. But when it comes to Thalia, nothing's too much, no cost is too great. When I'm done in the basement, I climb up with a purpose. My mind is swirling with images of Thalia—her laughter, that rumpled silk hair of hers, the way she looked at me sometimes, an all-knowing look underlaid with the ghost of a playful smile. And I think of how I had twined a scarf around her neck and squeezed and squeezed until she turned red, and my heart thrums taut, and I can barely get back up fast enough.

I walk briskly to the bedroom and take out my jewelry box. It's mostly cheap things in here—Ted likes to adorn me with cubic zirconia. I don't mind; jewelry is frivolous, and I have no space in my life for frivolity. Ted's parents are the epitome of frivolity; every week, his father buys a rose for his mother, and every week, she somehow resists telling him he's an unimaginative moron and acts like she is surprised and delighted by the single rose. The same thing, every week, for over forty years. I don't know why she hasn't killed him yet.

I rummage around the fake diamonds until I find the pieces I'm looking for. A ring and a necklace. The only things I have left from Oxford. My stomach clenches at the sight of them. The diamonds on both are ridiculously large. If Ted were to see these, he'd assume they're fake, just like everything else in the box. Which is precisely why I've tucked them in here, to hide in plain sight. Because these, like my time at Oxford, are painfully real.

The necklace is a simpler piece—a thin white gold chain with one huge diamond flanked by two smaller ones. The ring, on the other hand, is a monstrosity. A square-cut diamond the size of a cough drop. I select the ring and slide it into my pocket. It's too ostentatious for me to ever wear, so I might as well get rid of it. I only call out to Ted that I'm going to the store when I'm already halfway out the door, so he can't come lumbering out of his study and ask me to pick up some soy ice cream or whatever. He says, "Hmm?" but I don't wait for a reply.

I drive down the street before I stop and look up jewelry shops. There's one fifteen minutes away from here. I click on directions to get there, and when I arrive, I take my time deleting my search history. Just in case Ted decides to be smart for the first time in his life.

The shop assistant takes one look at the ring and glances up at me again, his eyes wide.

"Please wait a moment, ma'am," he says, before going to the back room. He comes back out with an older man with wiry white hair and glasses with what looks like a tiny microscope attached to one of the lenses. The old man asks, very gently, "May I?"

I nod and watch as he inspects the ring. Then the worst happens. He asks, "May I inquire where you procured this ring?"

"Procured." Not "bought" or "who gifted you this ring." My guts turn into snakes and I almost throw up then and there. I snatch the ring from the velvet tray and mutter, "Never mind, I've changed my mind. I won't be selling this after all. It's a family heirloom."

"Wait, please, ma'am—"

But I can't. I need to get out of here before the walls close in on me. I rush out, half expecting a cage to slide down on me as I head for the front door, but nothing happens and I walk out into the late-afternoon sunlight without anyone chasing after me. Outside, I don't even pause to catch my breath. I half run until I'm safely around the corner before I stop.

Stupid, stupid! I need to be more careful. What was it that gave me away? I slip the ring back into the inside pocket of my bag and smooth down my hair. Glancing up, I catch my reflection in a store window. That'll be it, then. I don't look like someone who would be in possession of such an expensive piece of jewelry. I'm in loose-fitting jeans and a shirt and ratty cardigan— my "midlist author who's given up on life" outfit.

It's too late to go home and change now, so instead, I look up pawnshops. Here in South San Francisco, there's a depressing number of them around. I pick the one with the highest number of star ratings and drive over there.

I've never been to a pawnshop before, and the only things I know about them are things I learned from the movies. It's surprising how close reality resembles the movies. The pawnshop clerk inspects the ring for a few minutes, glancing up at me and back at the ring, frowning. I swallow, try to look less shady. Not sure how, but I try to channel my innermost wealthy-white-lady-who-just-happens-to-want-to-pawn-off-a-magnificent-ring aura. Finally, he punches some numbers into a calculator and slides the calculator through the little slip hole under the bulletproof sheet separating the two of us.

I look at the number on the calculator, and a laugh burbles up my chest and into my throat, where I manage to swallow it back down. Well, holy shit. Ten grand. It would more than cover my airfare as well as accommodation and food and still leave me with a sizable amount to do whatever I need to do. I want to jump and scream, "YES!" but I've watched enough shows to purse my lips and say, "Is that all? Never mind, then."

In the end, I walk out of the pawnshop with $12,000. I only allow the grin to take over my face when I'm outside of the shop. $12,000. It feels like a huge fuck you to Ted, though I'm not sure why that is. I practically dance my way back to the car.

Back at home, I move sneakily past Ted's office and into the bedroom, where I stand, for a minute, wondering where to hide my wad of cash. That's the problem with $12,000; it's thick and heavy and kind of a challenge to hide. I'm about to head for the closet when the door clicks open and in comes my husband, trying to give me a goddamned heart attack.

"What the fuck," I say.

"Everything okay? You look like you've just seen a ghost."

The hallway outside of our bedroom is made of old, rickety wood. It creaks like a demon with a grudge, and at night, when I wake up needing a glass of water, I have to step very, very carefully at specific spots to avoid waking Ted. Ted, on the other hand, never gives me the courtesy of picking the non-creaky spots; when he goes to the kitchen in the middle of the night, he makes sure I know it.

But now, when it matters, he's able to make his way through the creaky hallway as quietly as a fucking cat.

"I'm okay. You just surprised me a little, that's all." My hand's still in my bag, clutching the thick envelope. I have to consciously tell my fingers to unclench and, instead, to reach for something else. Anything. They brush up against my phone, and I grab it with relief and take it out. *I was just taking my phone out of my bag, Ted, no biggie.*

"Where did you go?" Ted says in this ultracasual way that tells me there's nothing casual about his question.

"Oh, I just went to Safeway. Just wanted to get some . . ." Some what? "Stuff. Some Swedish Fish." I hate Swedish Fish. I don't know why that popped into my head.

"I thought you don't like Swedish Fish." It comes out as an accusation, which immediately makes me bristle, because if there's one thing I can't stand, it's my husband using that tone of voice with me.

"I just had a sudden craving for them." How many times can I say the word "just"?

Ted looks at me, and for a second, I wonder what made me agree to marry this man. We never had the same chemistry that Thalia and I had. I never wanted to carve my name into the curves of his heart the way I fantasized doing with Thalia. I never had the need to leave an imprint of myself on him. I think back to five years ago, when I met him at the most basic of all places—a Starbucks.

Someone had taken my drink, and Ted had seen my confused, about-to-be-enraged expression and bought me another latte. And I remember thinking then that here's a nice, safe person. I've had enough of my own un-niceness, of the disaster I had left Oxford in. I was only in my twenties, but already my life had been a series of mishaps and tragedies. I was ready for nice and safe, and if ever there were two words to describe Ted, they're "nice" and "safe." Of course, over time the veneer of niceness became abraded, whether by natural wear and tear or maybe he'd rubbed against my sharp edges one too many times. Now, as I look at him, I realize that those two qualities that had attracted me to him have turned into the bars of my jail cell. He's still nice, but in a very conscious, calculating way that serves to highlight my own lack of niceness. And he's still safe, but it comes in the form of this cumbersome house, which we will only manage to pay off seventeen years later, its presence holding us back from making any brash financial choices. I'm in a prison made out of polite words and a steady mortgage, and the bars had descended so gently that I hadn't felt them coming.

I know what he's about to say before he says it, and there's a moment where I see myself lunging at him with something sharp—maybe the letter opener that ended my time at Oxford prematurely. I see the glinting point of it pressing into his skin, making a small indentation at first, and then finally breaking through, its tip parting the skin silkily, so smoothly that not a sound is made as it goes past skin and fat and into flesh and bone. Not a single sound.

Then he says it and breaks the spell.

"Can I have some?"

He doesn't like Swedish Fish either; nobody likes Swedish Fish, and he's only asking me this because he knows that I haven't, in fact, been to Safeway, and I haven't, in fact, bought any Swedish Fish.

"They were out." And if he drives to the store to check, then I will know our marriage is truly over.

"Aw, that's a shame. Okay." He stays there for a second too long, still watching me with those watery blue eyes of his—who would've known that blue eyes could look unattractive—then he turns, scratching his belly, and slouches out of the room. The wooden boards sing as he treads on them. Just like that, he's once again magically lost the ability to walk without making noise.

I wait until he's out of earshot before releasing my breath. Jesus, that was close. I open up my underwear drawer, then shut it again. Too obvious. I go into the bathroom and open up cabinets and drawers before finally spotting the boxes of tampons that I buy in bulk at Costco. Perfect. Ted is the kind of guy who winces every time the subject of menstruation comes up, as though it's hurting his delicate senses. He'd never look in here. I open one of the giant boxes, stuff the wad of cash in it, and tuck the box in the farthest reaches of the cabinet.

Later, I wait until after dinner (massaman curry; nothing as basic as pasta, though Ted complains that I have put too many cloves in) before I skulk off to the bathroom and then come hurrying back with a somewhat excited smile on my face. Not too excited, mind, because we don't want Ted to get suspicious.

"Hey, guess what?" I hate the way my voice sounds—so artificial, so conscious of itself.

Ted glances up from the TV. He's watching a food travel show on YouTube where some white guy is in rural Vietnam eating bugs. We've never been to Vietnam, but the other day, I heard Ted saying to his friends over Fortnite that he loves authentic pho, the kind you could only get at alleyways in Saigon. *How the hell would you even know what authentic pho from the alleyways of Saigon tastes like*, I wanted to scream, but I restrained myself, because that's what marriage is about. Restraint, control, folding myself up into as tiny a square as possible. "Look what they're eating, babe," he says, turning back to the TV. "Look how huge those water bugs are. Revolting. I mean, no disrespect, of course." Of course not. Never any disrespect from Ted, the woke white man.

I lick my lips and swallow. Try again. "So I just got a sort of exciting email from Toni. You know, my agent."

"Oh?" Ted brightens up and finally gives me his full attention. "Did your last book earn out?"

The knife in my gut twists. He knows my sales have been lackluster. The idea of earning out my measly advance is laughable, given how little publicity my publisher has given my books. He's only making that his guess to set the bar impossibly high, so that when I inevitably fail to meet it, we'll both know what a disappointment my writing career is. What a disappointment I am. It's his way of putting me back in my place.

Normally, this would enrage me enough to pick a fight with him, bicker over stupid shit like him leaving his crap everywhere, but tonight, I won't be distracted from my goal. Not when the goal is Thalia. So I force a smile and say, "No, I haven't earned out."

He sighs, but before he can turn back to the TV, I quickly say, "But I emailed Toni about the possibility of going to SusPens Con, and she thought it was a really great idea."

"Hmm," he grunts, already getting swallowed up by the video, in which the Woke White Guy is explaining to us that bugs have a ton of protein and are really good for you, so we should get over our fear of them and start crunching down on their hard little bodies.

This is good, actually. Since he's not really paying attention, I don't have so much heat on me. I let the words out in a rush. "Anyway, she emailed my publisher and they agreed and said they're going to pay for my trip and my tickets to the con."

"Wait, what?" Now I've got his attention. He actually presses the Mute button, plunging us into sudden deafening silence. There's nothing acting as a buffer, and I find it disconcerting, like, *sorry, Ted, I know I asked for your attention but I don't actually want it, or rather I don't want a hundred percent of it, maybe just sixty percent so your bullshit radar doesn't ever ping.* "Did I hear you right? Harvest Publishing is sending you to a con? On their dime?"

I'm trying hard to get a read on his emotions, picking apart his words and his tone frantically to gauge just what he's thinking. Is that sarcasm I detect? No, I think he's genuinely surprised, and why wouldn't he be? It is surprising. Harvest is a small independent publisher, not even one of the big indies but a small one whose advances average low four figures. That's not the kind of house that can afford to send its midlist authors to cons, especially cons that are on the other side of the country.

I don't know if Ted's aware of all these semantics, and my whole body is taut, waiting to see if he'll spot it, if he'll smell the whiff of bullshit. And what he might do if he were to detect it.

Slowly, dreadfully, my head inches forward. Then back. A nod.

And then suddenly he's up from the couch, this big bear of a man coming at me, and everything inside me shrieks. If I had a knife in my hand I would have stabbed him with it and called it self-defense, and I wouldn't have been lying.

But I only stand there, rooted, because the saying "flight or fight"? It's wrong. It's flight or fight or fucking freeze and that's me; that's what I've always done. I freeze and my husband comes at me and he—

Hugs

Me.

It takes a while for my brain to catch up and process the thing Ted is doing and feed it to the rest of my body so that my limbs stop mid-flail. It's a hug. A hug. Something you do to someone you like.

I close my eyes and let myself thaw, just a bit, leaning into his embrace. It's not unpleasant, hugging my husband. He smells familiar—vanilla sugar and something musky, a distinctly male odor. I let my breath out, sagging into him.

"Wow, I'm so happy to hear that," he murmurs, shifting.

I feel it then, him getting a semi, pushing against my thigh. I want to shove him off me.

"You fully deserve this, Jane," he says.

I don't push him away. Instead, I smile at him and nod.

"Didn't I always tell you to ask Toni for things? She works for you. Remember that, babe."

"Mm-hmm."

"I'm coming with you, okay?" It's not a question. It's a statement disguised as a question, and if I were to say no, there would be a price to pay later. "We'll make a trip of it, stay somewhere nice. Go to Lombardi's."

A trip of it when just hours ago, there was absolutely no money in the pot to spare for this. I want to rail at him, to push my fingers into his eyes until I can feel the squish of his brains against them, and then yank them out, unravel the curls of his brains so I can read his mind and see just the sort of shit that's floating through it.

I want him to stop talking, I want me to be able to celebrate this moment of possibility without the weight of his idiotic words clumping down on it, making it sag and strain. I've earned this. I've outsmarted him and he can't stand it; that's why he wants to shove his way into this, to spoil it all somehow.

But it doesn't matter. He can come. I don't care. As long as I can see Thalia in the flesh, hear that throaty voice of hers, I will be okay. I will bear it. I will go through anything for her.

7

The welcome dinner isn't as bad as I had feared. No, it's much worse.

I thought it would be bad when Thalia and I walked out of Downing and ran into a clot of students in the Chapel Quad. They all smiled at us, and one of them said, "Off to the reception dinner?" Obviously we are, asshole. As though there were anyplace else we might be going at this time, dressed like this. But Thalia smiled back and then did the unthinkable—she introduced herself, and then me, and before I knew it, we were swallowed by their group.

And so here I stand on what's apparently one of the most beautiful quads in Oxford, wearing a dress that doesn't quite fit me, grasping a glass of chardonnay like it's a lifeline. Oh yes, there are wine and canapés set out at the quad, where we're doomed to mingle before dinner begins. My first ever cocktail hour. I've never attended a cocktail hour before. One does not go to such things on one's own, and I've always been on my own.

The small group of students has swelled into a crowd. An actual crowd of people, all of them mingling, lots of straight-toothed smiles, and the conversation. The conversation!

I catch snatches of "Belize for the summer—" and "under-grad at Yale—" and "Boston Consultant Group—." Who went to the better school for undergrad? Who's got the better job? Whose penis is bigger, yours or mine?

I cast a desperate search for Thalia. She's abandoned me. We'd been standing next to the canapé table when an attractive blond guy had approached her and asked her which course she's taking. She'd answered for the two of us, which I didn't mind. In fact, I appreciated it. But then as the conversation stretched unbearably, more and more people had joined in, and I had taken a small step backward because groups of people are dan-gerous, groups of people are like wolf packs, and yet more peo-ple had buzzed toward us, no doubt attracted by Thalia's presence, and I took another step back and another step back and before I knew it, I had been spat out of the group.

I finish my glass of wine and walk toward the table to discard my glass. I should stop drinking. I don't do well with alcohol. My inhibitions aren't there to stop me from doing stupid things, dangerous ones.

"There's always one," someone says.

I look up to see a slightly pudgy girl with mouse-brown hair. She's wearing a black dress that's probably been marketed as the LBD, but it looks all wrong on her, the capped sleeves highlight-ing the pallid flab of her arms, the material cheap and shiny so it highlights every roll and bulge. She's drinking red, and when she smiles at me, I see that it's stained her teeth, making her look monstrous. It's like looking in a mirror. I have no idea what she's talking about, and neither am I interested in knowing, so I don't reply. Instead, I pick up another glass of white.

She takes my silence as invitation to keep talking. "That girl," she says, nodding at the swarm of Pemberton students with Thalia dead center. "There's always one, isn't there?" A long sigh, followed by a deep gulp of wine. "The golden girl."

I hate the way the words sound rolling out of her sloppy mouth. Dirt-smudged and bored, like Thalia isn't anything special, like she isn't one in a million. One in a billion.

The heat of rage caresses me deep in my belly. I snap the wristband.

"What's that?" she says, watching me from the sides of her bullfrog eyes. "Do you have anxiety?"

I take a long sip of wine so I don't have to answer, but it doesn't matter anyway. The charmless girl is still talking. I think she likes that I'm silent. I think she's used to people ignoring her.

"My sister's like that," she's saying, "except she just flicks her own arm. Not organized enough to always wear a wristband."

Huh. That's actually a good solution for the times when I snap the wristband so hard that it breaks, leaving me untethered. Uncaged. I make a mental note of it.

She gives a brittle, eager smile before taking another swig of wine, and I realize that like me, she's nervous.

"I'm Pam, by the way. What's your name?"

I don't want to give her my name, but I'm trapped. I'm here to make a fresh start, and fresh starts don't involve walking away mid-conversation with your schoolmate, even if said schoolmate is as interesting as a piece of chewed gum.

"Jane." One-word answers. That's safe.

"Jane." Her smile turns even more eager, if that's possible. "I like that name. Down-to-earth. Like Pam, I guess. I feel like everyone here's got some fancy name—they're either exotic or, like, one of those long, old ones. You know—Hubert Weatherby the Third."

That gets a smile out of me, because among the throng of people who had swarmed me and Thalia at the canapés table, there had been a "the Third." I think he was a Robert though, not a Hubert. I'm sure there's a Hubert here somewhere in this crowd, and perhaps a Rupert or two.

"Which course are you doing here?" Pam asks. She's actually clutching her wineglass with both hands, strangling the stem with her pudgy fingers. I'm torn between pity and secondhand embarrassment for her.

"Creative Writing."

"Ooh, that one's intense, I hear."

Is it? My stomach twists, whether from the alcohol or from anticipation, I don't know. But an "intense" course that involves Thalia sounds like something straight out of my darkest dreams.

"I hear that every year, about a quarter of the students flunk out of the course."

What? I hadn't even been aware that you could flunk out of a Creative Writing course. "How do you flunk out of a Creative Writing course?"

Pam shrugs. "By writing badly, I imagine."

I suppose it seems obvious when she puts it that way.

"I'm doing the master's in Women's, Gender and Sexuality Studies."

I have to stop myself from snorting out loud, because of course she is.

"I'm kind of really nervous about it, are you? I'm from March?

71

You know it? No, of course you don't. It's a small town outside of Cambridge," she says apologetically, as though the fact that she came from a small town is a personal affront to me.

"I'm from Oakland." San Francisco's armpit, a half-abandoned, half-industrial city that's being threatened by gentrification, if the techbros can be bothered to colonize Oakland. My own answer startles me, because I usually tell people I'm from San Francisco. Why admit to Oakland when you can cover yourself under the sheen and sparkle of SF? But something about Pam is so sad and honest that it compels me to drop the act, if only just a little. I hadn't expected English girls to be like Pam, so unworldly and unattractive. I suppose I've only ever seen the ones on TV, the English Roses fed on a diet of poetry and wine.

"Oakland, that's nice," Pam says, nodding like she knows of it. Nobody who isn't Californian knows of Oakland, but she's trying so hard. It makes me feel a tad better, being with someone who's even more out of place than I am. Though, with a nasty jolt, I realize then that I don't know if Pam does look more out of place than I do. I look down at the dress I've borrowed, by far the most expensive thing I have ever worn. It doesn't fit me well; Thalia's waist is smaller than mine, so her dress is ungracefully tight around my midsection, squeezing so that my lower belly bulges out. My boobs are bigger than hers, so the chest section is also tight, showing the lines where my bra is slicing into my skin, squashing my boobs like grotesque balloons. The thought hits like a fist. I'm no better than Pam.

I'm about to make my excuses and rush back to Downing to lock myself in my room for the rest of the evening when I become aware that the crowd is suddenly headed toward us. Because Thalia is leading them here. I sense Pam turning rigid with fear at the advancing crowd.

"There you are," Thalia says, and truly, she is dazzling in all senses of the word. The nearness of her knocks every other thought out of my head, and I am left confused and off-balance. "I've been looking for you."

Pam stares at me with mouth slightly open. I'd been feeling slovenly only moments ago, but now, as the subject of Thalia's smile and Thalia's kind attention, I feel myself unfurling once more, blooming from deep inside the rotten core of me.

"I'm Thalia." Thalia extends a hand toward Pam. I can't help noticing how slender her wrist is compared to Pam's. How Pam's meaty hand completely swallows Thalia's. The sight of it sends a thrill down my back. So thin, so snappable. After she shakes Pam's hand, Thalia turns to her side, and that's when I notice the girl standing way too close to Thalia. A girl I hate on sight.

"And this is Ani," Thalia says, pronouncing it Ah-nee, and not Annie.

Ani is Asian, and she is everything I'm not—tall, slender, her features flawless.

My entire being wants to cringe away from her. Growing up, my Asian-ness was the source of poverty, the reason for everything that was lacking with my life. I was used to Asians like my mother—women with bedraggled hair, stooped shoulders, faces lined with bitterness and need. I was used to rejecting it, to running away from it. But Ani is unapologetically Asian, and fabulous. Unlike the rest of us, she's not wearing a dress but a navy-blue jumpsuit that hugs her slim figure, the kind of expensive outfit that is all elegant clean lines.

She looks down her nose at me and Pam, her dark eyes lined with eyeliner so sharp it looks like it could cut me, and there's a gnawing in my stomach, because I am just now realizing that Ani is grouping me together with Pam. Whatever magic had captured me today and fooled me into thinking I might be on the same level as Thalia, under Ani's aloof, derisive gaze, it dissipates, and I am thrown to the curb, exposed for the fraud I am.

Everything goes by in a bit of a daze after that. I'm vaguely aware of making our way across the Chapel Quad and into Haygrove Hall, aka the dining hall. It's styled like a medieval great hall, complete with an arched roof with hammer beams, large bay windows, chandeliers, and wood-paneled walls, on which hang portraits of disapproving white men. In other words, yet more hallowed, ostentatious wealth that serves to remind me of how much I don't belong.

Worse still, at some point, Thalia says to Pam, "I love your dress. Prada?"

And she flushes with pleasure and nods eagerly. Prada. And here I had thought it was a cheap dress from one of those Chinese websites. But no. Pam—fucking Pam—is wearing Prada. The thought that if I hadn't bumped into Thalia at the bus station, I would've come here wearing a dress from Ross Dress for Less makes bile rise up my throat.

We're seated at long tables, each place set with three plates and three different glasses. I'm about to slide into the seat next to Thalia when Ani slinks in between us with a smooth, smiling, "Oops, sorry." I end up sitting next to Ani, with Pam on the other side of me. I can't believe we're all doing our master's when it feels so much closer to high school than even college did.

"So, Jane," Ani says. My name comes out poisonous from her dark plum lips. She touches the tips of two fingers to her chin, and a giant sapphire ring glints on her index finger. "Thalia tells me you're doing Creative Writing as well."

"Yeah. You?"

"MBA. Cursed to help out with the family business. You know how it is."

I don't know how it is, actually. I'm about as far from knowing how it is as humanly possible. But I'm saved from having to answer when a server comes bearing two bottles of wine, one red and one white. Ani cocks an eyebrow at him, and he smoothly pours the wines into our glasses.

"Cheers," Ani says lazily, lifting her glass of red wine. I lift mine, too, and manage to spill a little bit over the side. The corner of Ani's mouth crooks up. I amuse her. I want to run away and hide. I want to smash my wineglass and push the sharp edges into her porcelain face, see which one cracks first—the shard of glass or that fake face of hers?

"This year is going to be so fun," Thalia says, leaning toward me and holding out her glass. "Bottoms up, everyone!"

Ani doesn't take her eyes off me as she downs her glass in one long, smooth swallow, and though I almost choke, I end up draining mine as well.

———

IT WAS A TRAP. OF COURSE IT WAS A TRAP. I SHOULD HAVE known, the way Ani's eyes never left mine, the languid, predatory gaze crawled over my skin, her mouth curved into a constant smirk. The way she made sure my glass was always full.

By the end of dinner, I can barely walk back to Downing. The only saving grace is that everybody else seems just as sloshed as I am—Pam keeps talking about how "pissed" she is, and Thalia is looking more flushed than before. There's a guy—Edward; of course there's an Edward here—who's taken it upon himself to "make sure you ladies get back all right." He has his hand on the small of Thalia's back, a sight that sickens me. But before I can lunge forward, put myself between sweet Thalia and Edward the creep, Edward the would-be date rapist, Thalia turns, catching my eye, and says, "Jane and I live on the same floor. We'll be okay, won't we, Jane?"

I don't remember the walk up the stairs in Downing. Next thing I know, I'm falling asleep without bothering to wash off the makeup that Thalia had applied on my face, my head swimming in nauseating circles, my room spinning, hating myself. Last thought that crosses my mind is if Thalia's back in her room okay. I try to recall if I'd deposited her like a lost treasure safely in her room before stumbling back to mine, and then the darkness descends.

I can barely choke down the breakfast buffet the next morning. I sit at the far corner of the massive dining hall, avoiding the morning crowd, and force myself to eat one of the roasted tomatoes and drink a glass of OJ—vitamin C is good for hangovers. I'm about to leave the hall when the doors swing open and in come Thalia and Ani. They're chatting easily, and the sight of them sours my already queasy stomach. I almost vomit, literally. They came in together. Together, as a single unit. I hunch further into the corner so they won't see me, my cheeks blazing hot.

How did that happen? I scramble through the tangle in my mind, trying to sort out the events of last night. Thalia and I had staggered back to our rooms together. There was laughter. Who was laughing? I remember talking, though the actual words themselves now escape me. I have no fucking clue what I might have said to her. Something awful? Something that might have repelled/alarmed/scared her? *Don't be scared of me, Thalia*, I want to scream until she promises that she isn't, that we're still the best of friends, forever and ever, amen.

Had she stolen out of her room after that? Tiptoed past mine—careful, don't wake Jane the freak—and gone to meet up with Ani? There's nothing quite like the exquisite pain of being excluded, your presence purposefully blotted out. After careful deliberation, we have deemed you, Plain Jane Morgan, unworthy of our company.

What was it that had finally dealt the killing blow, that had strangled the blossoming friendship between Thalia and me? The answer comes naturally, quickly. Ani. Ani has whispered some poison into Thalia's ear in a bid to steal her from me, and it worked.

I sneak out of the dining hall like a rat and scurry all the way back to my room. Only when I've shut the door do I let myself unravel, leaning against the door and breathing deep. I snap the wristband and think of Ani. Ani, with her black-painted eyelids and her elegant clothes and long limbs, which, like a spider, she has wrapped around my Thalia.

The shatter of glass wrenches me out of my black state, and I realize that I've thrown my coffee mug across the room. Shit. I hadn't even noticed that I'd taken a coffee mug from the dining room. Coffee is dripping in light brown rivulets down the wall, and I really should mop it all up, but I don't have time. This is the first day of my master's course, and I'm not going to let Ani ruin that too. Forget Thalia. Forget everyone. I'm not even here to make friends; I'm here to learn the craft of writing. I grab my things—a new spiral-bound notebook, my favorite pen, and a folder full of coursework material that had cost an annoying amount to print out, and I hurry out the door, trying not to think of what I might say when I see Thalia in class.

Our first class plunges us into the deep end. Boom, straight away a fiction workshop. There are fifteen of us in total, ranging from early-twenties to the oldest student who is in his sixties. I'm supposed to admire that he's pursuing higher education so close to death, but instead, it makes me uncomfortable. They're all well-dressed, lots of leather shoes and boots and what the English would call "smart" button-down shirts. Sharply tailored Burberry coats and shiny leather handbags with neat stitches and logos that are small enough to be subtle, but not so small that you can't read the "Prada" or "LV." Nothing so crass as monogrammed logos all over the bags, oh no. We're writers, after all.

The tables are set in a U, with the teacher's desk at the center. I hesitate, trying to figure out where to sit for minimum attention, trying not to make it too obvious that I'm waiting to see where Thalia is going to sit. She swans into class last, right before it begins, and her presence brightens up the room. All that golden hair and dewy skin and Colgate smile. All heads turn toward her, but she doesn't seem to notice. She's used to being the center of attention, neither loves it nor hates it. She spots me, and her smile widens. While everybody watches, she crosses the room straight to me. The sixty-year-old man has taken the seat next to mine, but she smiles sweetly at him and says, "I'm sorry, is it okay if I take this one?" and he shifts one seat over with a friendly, "Of course, luv."

And now here she is again, next to me, close enough for me to smell her. My heart twists and twists, and I feel like I could die from the nearness of her, but Thalia is ignorant of the quiet death I'm going through. My mind is a mess of jagged questions, slicing their way across the soft folds of my brains. Did you ditch me so you could party with Ani? Did you spend the night with some guy? Did you fuck him? Did you, did you?

"Hey, didn't see you at breakfast," she says.

I'm not sure if that's a question, so I focus on taking out my notebook from my shitty messenger bag. Next to me, I can feel Thalia's confusion growing when I don't answer. *It's not that I don't want to strike up a conversation with you, Thalia,* I think desperately, as loud as I can, trying to make her hear my thoughts. *It's that if I open my mouth, I don't know what's going to fall out.* My thoughts are spiders waiting to leap from my tongue and poison everything they touch.

"Good morning, everyone!" a voice trills, and thank god, because I don't know what I was about to say.

Our first teacher is Emily R. Rogers, author of the critically acclaimed but poor-selling *Mayflies in the Winter.* All of our teachers, I realized when looking over the course handbook, are of the same loved-by-critics-but-ignored-by-the-masses caliber. Emily is in her midforties, past her prime but still lovely to look at. Everyone here is like that—all of them attractive in one way or another, or at the very least, fashionably ugly.

"Right! Welcome to day one of Michaelmas." She pauses to give us all a smile. There's that term again—Michaelmas. Google told me it refers to Oxford's fall term, though why they can't just call it "fall" like every other college does is beyond me. "Today we're going to talk about prose fiction and how to keep your reader engaged. Reader engagement depends on a few factors, but the most important thing is tension. What is tension?"

I write down as much of what Emily says as I can while also being painfully aware that Thalia isn't writing anything down. When I sneak a glance at her, she's sitting back and watching Emily with a thoughtful expression. She looks so absorbed, so naturally intelligent that I have no doubt that despite the lack of notes, she will retain a lot more of the seminar than I will. By contrast, I feel silly for scribbling so furiously, afraid of missing even a single word. A child trying to play catch-up at a grown-up class.

"But before we get into all that, we're going to warm up with a freewriting session."

My pen stills. No, please. My brain is still in a wine-fug from last night, and I can barely read my own notes.

"We're going to go for five minutes. Write anything that comes to your mind. We'll read it out afterward and do a little workshop—how does that sound?" Emily has already taken out an egg timer from her bag.

It sounds awful. Horrible. But nobody else is looking nearly as panicked as I feel. The timer starts and pens move across pages. I look around at the heads bent studiously over their notebooks, all of the hands moving smoothly. Freewriting sounds like something that requires very little effort, and yet when I look down on my empty page, I can't come up with a single word. I force my hand down, pressing the tip of my pen to paper. If I could just get the nib to touch the paper, the words would start flowing.

It's pressing so hard by now that there's an indentation in the paper, and still, the words don't come. I push the pen hard, turning the indentation into a line.

I.

I what? Please, mind. Please work. Instead, the words that come are Pam's. *I hear that every year, about a quarter of the students flunk out of the course.*

How do you flunk out of a Creative Writing course? I had asked so stupidly. Well, now I'm about to find out. You fail because your mind aborts all thought, purging it out in favor of a tangle of fear pulsing under a fog of alcohol. I can't believe that after all the hours I've worked, saving up every cent, after the enormous debt I've put myself in to be here, I'm about to crash and burn on my very first day of class.

Fucking Ani. She knew, somehow. She must've known. Last night was the first time we met, but I'd sensed it, that predatorial hunger in her, the shot of jealousy on her face when Thalia introduced us. She'd wanted to get rid of me, and like a complete patsy, I'd fallen for it. I'd let her motion the server to refill my glass over and over and over, and now here I am, about to fail a five-minute exercise, the first ever task given by my course.

A shrill shriek erupts from the egg timer and I jump; my butt actually leaves the chair for a split second. My heart stops, only to resume in a mad gallop. *Shit, shit!* It's over. All that time I'd spent worrying about being exposed, my human mask slipping and showing a glimpse of the beast beneath, and it turns out it didn't matter, because now I'm about to be exposed as a fraud, a wannabe writer who can't write after all. Life's a real bitch sometimes.

8

hate waste. I don't like wasting food, or time, or money. But the thing I most hate to waste is potential. And I have so much of it. I know that; I've known that ever since I was little. And now, at the ripe age of twelve, I know that I have the potential to really make it big. You know how kids are often told the big old lie: "You can be whatever you want to be"? Ninety-nine percent of the time, it's bullshit. But not so for me. My teachers are always raving about how gifted I am, and even Aunt Claudette agrees. She'd often say, "Child, you have a busy, busy mind. Put that mind to good use." It's too bad that I was born into the wrong family. Imagine the heights I would've reached if I'd been born into a wealthy one, with parents that could afford to send me to the best private schools, then on to the Ivy Leagues. But no, I was born to this one, a single-parent home complete with a mother who's completely uninterested in me.

When I turned twelve, I decided it was time to punish my mother. Why? Too many reasons to count. For being a negligent parent. For failing to see how exceptional her daughter is. For being so fucking stupid that she has no real prospects, can only hop from one minimum wage job to another.

I've spent years studying my mother, watching her like I'm a scientist observing a rodent. My mother is a serial dater. She delights in it, plays the role of the dream girlfriend perfectly. I eavesdrop on her as she chatters on the phone each night to her friends, giggling about how infatuated her current boyfriend is. She knows just what to do to get them hooked on her, knowing exactly when to push and pull, to leave them wanting more. She loves the feeling of being desired. Then she'll get bored; maybe she senses that they're about to get bored of her, who knows? But whatever it is, my mother rarely stays with the same man for months. She'll dump them, break their hearts, and when they're gone, she'll crook one corner of her mouth up into a smile and say, "Leave 'em before they leave you, baby girl. Remember that."

To be fair, she did teach me a lot about men, so I suppose there's that.

I decide that the best way to punish her is to make sure all of her boyfriends leave her instead of her leaving them. It's the perfect punishment. She'll be left alone, with plenty of time to ruminate on how unwanted she is.

It's a lot trickier than you might think, scaring off someone's boyfriend when he's not ready to go. Most kids in my situation would start behaving badly—throw tantrums, maybe, or be a complete bitch to the boyfriend, but I know that's not going to cut it. That'll just paint me as the problem instead of Mom. For days, I wander everywhere, deep in thought, toying with one idea after another and rejecting them all.

The idea comes to me from the newspaper. Some guy one

town over had been arrested for molesting some kids. Perfect. That same day, I go home and smile my way through dinner as Mom and her boyfriend du jour, Jackson, make googly eyes at each other over the pasta bake. I wait patiently for them to finish their nightly routine, watching TV and making out. Then, finally, Jackson leaves the apartment. I steal out the door, being careful to walk as quietly as I can past Aunt Claudette's apartment (I swear sometimes she just spends her time peeping out her door to catch me doing something bad), and catch up with him just as he's about to climb into his car.

"Jackson, wait."

He turns around and breaks into a smile when he sees me. "Hey, kiddo. What's up?"

Kiddo. I'm twelve and I have boobs and I bleed every month, but he's still calling me "kiddo." Guy deserves what's coming to him. "I need a favor."

He grins. "Sure, anything for you."

Don't be too sure about that, idiot. "Great," I say brightly. "I need you to stop seeing my mom."

His smile freezes on his face. "Excuse me?"

"Yeah, I need you to break up with her. Or not, whatever. Just stop seeing her."

"Uh, hang on, why—"

"I don't like you," I say. I love the simplicity of it, the undeniable clarity.

He sighs. "I think this is something you and your mom should talk about, because I'm crazy about her, and I'm willing to do whatever it takes to prove to you that I'm serious about this relationship."

"Nah." I shrug. "I just don't like you. You look like an asshole."

Now he's lost all traces of the smile. "Okay, listen here, kid—"

"If you don't break up with her by tomorrow, I'm going to tell everyone that you touched me."

"Whoa, hang on a second—"

I screw up my face and start crying, and he stops talking, his mouth hanging open as he watches my performance. I wish I could watch my performance. I bet it's stellar. Hot tears roll down my cheeks. "He asked me to go inside his car because he had a surprise for Mom, and then he—uh, he—put his hands on my—"

"Stop that!" he hisses. "Jesus fucking Christ. This is not funny!"

I stop mid-sob and look pointedly at him. "It's not a joke. I'm dead serious. Break up with her, or else." Then I turn and walk back toward the apartment.

He breaks up with Mom that very same night, and as I listen to her sobs through the thin walls, fierce joy blooms in my chest. Now, maybe, she'll give me the attention I deserve.

9

Time's up!" Emily says, and I wonder if she's aware of how ominous that sounds. Maybe she's a sociopath like me and she enjoys the way those two words work to slice through our dreams. Or maybe I'm just being melodramatic because I'm still staring at a blank page with the word "I" gouged into it.

Then, suddenly, a piece of paper full of words slides on top of my blank page. My head shoots up and I catch Thalia's face, a mischievous expression written—written, ha!—on it. She winks at me and gives the smallest of nods at the paper. My breath comes out in shallow, tiny gasps. A note. I've never received a note in class before. Back in high school, it seemed like everybody was passing notes. Everybody, that is, except me. The only times notes have graced my table were when they had to go through me to be passed on to the intended recipient. Passing through, DO NOT OPEN, JANE, please pass to Maura, please pass to Jake, DON'T OPEN IT, YOU FREAK, pass to Aiden.

I wonder what Thalia wants to say to me so badly that she has to say it in the middle of class. My mind jitters ahead, hope turning into a gibbering mess. She's written to say she's sorry for not going to breakfast with me, that she was going to, but was ambushed by Ani, who had come knocking at her door in the morning—she spent the night alone, of course, just like I did—and refused to take no for an answer, and as she'd marched her down to Haygrove Hall, she'd gazed longingly at my door, wishing she had the courage to tell Ani no, that she's going to breakfast with her best friend Jane.

Then I look down at the paper and it's even better than I thought, because it's not a note for me, but what Emily had asked us to do—a little freewritten essay, done in Thalia's elegant cursive. I read it slowly, quietly, while the first student is called upon to read his work out loud. And it's good. Achingly so. Words as exquisite as the person herself. I glance up at Thalia. Her mouth quirks ever so slightly and my stomach turns soft. A little secret. Our little secret.

Fuck Ani and everyone else around us. This piece of paper is proof that Thalia is mine. Because it's not even that she's somehow managed to squeeze in double the work in the same amount of time, but she also gets me. The words she's written for me aren't just good, they're also strangely relatable, and relating to anything isn't something that happens often for me.

When it comes to my turn to read, my voice comes out with false confidence, bolstered by Thalia's words.

I am alone and not alone. I coat myself with barbed wire and broken fur, stay away, please come near, come you with bolt cutters and bran muffin and cut your way into my heart . . .

Tears prick my eyes as I read her words out loud. She sees me the way I truly am, past my human mask. With her, I don't need to wear the mask.

"Wow," Emily says when I get to the end of the passage. She's beaming at me. All around the room, I can sense everyone else adjusting their impression of me. My image is recalibrated, upgraded from the poor kid who doesn't belong to the poor kid with surprising talent despite the unfortunate upbringing. I don't know how I feel about it all, don't quite know how to handle anything warmer than polite, bland interest in me, so I duck my head and focus on my fingers as Emily lists out why "my" passage worked so well. The whole time, I go back and forth with thoughts of how to adequately thank Thalia, how to let her know that she is perfect and amazing and that she's saved me. I need her to know, above all else, that I see her the way she sees me.

———

PAM IS RIGHT ABOUT THE CREATIVE WRITING MASTER'S being intense. After Emily's seminar/workshop, we pause for a five-minute bathroom break during which Thalia goes to the bathroom, so I don't get a chance to even thank her before the next session begins. The next class is a critical seminar on fiction, and I struggle to follow as our teacher drones on and on about modernism and postmodernism. At least there's no freewriting session this time, though we are assigned homework—a five-hundred-word paper on creative trends of the twentieth century that's due the next day.

Finally, finally, we break for lunch. Thanks to the hangover and the heaviness of the course seminars, I am thoroughly defeated. I turn to Thalia, the words "thank you" halfway out of my mouth, but the sixty-year-old man's talking to her. For a second, I sit there awkwardly, wondering if there's a socially acceptable way of cutting into a conversation. Joining, I remind myself. The word I'm looking for is "joining" a conversation. And maybe I should just jump in? But no, I'm not built to jump into anything, so I focus on gathering my notebook and worksheets and pens, keeping half my attention on Thalia and this chatty-as-fuck old man who can't seem to shut the hell up. My last pen is in my bag now, and there's nothing left for me to tidy up, so I stand.

She stands too. She stands too! She's just as aware of me as I am of her, because our souls are two parts cut out of the same fabric. She's probably trying to extricate herself from the inane conversation just as much as I'm willing it to end. But the old man—I think his name is Peter—doesn't take a clue. He follows Thalia out of the classroom, me trailing them like a shadow. Finally, he realizes he's a senior goddamned citizen who doesn't belong with us and he says goodbye to Thalia. Good riddance. But Thalia walks on as though she doesn't see me there, as though my nearness means nothing to her.

One step, two steps away from me. I'm going to lose her. "Hey!" The word jerks out of me with more force than I intended, jarringly loud in the hallway. Heads turn toward me.

Thalia turns around, looking confused, then she smiles and all is right once more. "Jane! I'm so sorry, I didn't see you there. What's up?"

"Um, I just—" I walk up to her and lower my voice, my skin still prickling with gazes from my classmates. "I just wanted to thank you for um. You know, the freewriting thing. You saved my ass."

"Oh, that," she laughs. "It was nothing."

I shake my head. I hate that she's using that word—nothing. *It wasn't nothing, Thalia. Do not cheapen what you did.* Writing something for me had proven a lot of things: that I wasn't wrong about how I felt, that she feels the same way too. I want to grip her slim shoulders and shake them hard, feel those brittle bones cutting into my palms, and tell her it's not nothing, it's not nothing, over and over until she gets it.

But before I can say anything, she says, "Anyway, I should go. I told Ani I'd meet her at the Porter's Lodge."

She might as well have punched me in the heart. Ani? At the Porter's Lodge? That means they're not lunching at Haygrove Hall. They're going someplace else, somewhere outside of the college, venturing out and exploring Oxford together like how she and I were supposed to do. My cheeks are melting with anger. I can hardly stand it. Mom's voice in my head, soft as a feather: *Baby, you gotta get used to not having anyone. People say things they think you want to hear, but at the end of the day, you're on your own.*

I came here to break away from Mom, to be as far away from her poison as possible, but maybe she's right after all. No, she can't be. I won't let her. I mentally shriek at her voice until it dissipates into the wind.

"Can I come?" Those three simple words are the hardest I've had to say. Can I come, so pathetic, so needy.

Panic crosses Thalia's face, fleeting and gone before it even settles; she's too nice to let her reluctance show. But I catch it anyway, and my gut gurgles with acid. "Oh, um—you know what, let me check with Ani—"

"Don't bother." I brush past her. I have to get back to my room, I have to get away from everyone but especially from Thalia before this darkness bursts out of my chest and destroys everything.

"No, wait," Thalia says, grabbing my arm. Her lovely face is stricken. "Sorry, it's not that I don't want you there; it's just—Ani wanted to talk about some stuff I think? Buuut!" She brightens up. "Tonight, we're going to hit a few of the local pubs, and you're very welcome to join. The more the merrier!"

Why do people say that when it's so often untrue? It's only ever said when you're lobbing out a half-hearted invitation, when you can't think of a better reason why you're asking someone along aside from that you want more warm bodies to bulk up the group. To make it look more merry.

And what's worse is that Thalia hasn't just made lunch plans with Ani, but lunch AND drinking plans. The kind of thing that best friends do. A girls' night out. I picture myself with the two of them—Thalia all shiny, her stunning face practically a beacon of light, starkly contrasted by Ani's model-sleek black hair. They'd be a hit, two girls straight out of a modeling shoot. And then me, trailing after them, skulking like a forlorn goblin, surly-faced and dowdy in my thrift store clothes. Not vintage, just thrift store. Or maybe Thalia would take pity on me and offer to lend me another outfit, and I'd be squeezed into yet another dress too tight for me to breathe in.

It's unthinkable. The night out from hell. She'd end up resenting me for glomming on to her light, clinging like a barnacle. Nobody likes barnacles.

I shake my head. "No. Thank you," I remember to add. And I hurry off before she can say anything more.

10

New York City! If ever there was a place that's the antithesis of Northern California, this is surely it. I wish I could slip into a movie montage as we walk out of the airport and into a train station. Imagine some sprightly music playing, the breeze blowing ever so slightly, just enough to give my hair that windswept look and catch a corner of my coat as though the city itself is nudging me. *Hey, you're in New York fucking City! You made it, Jane!*

Instead, what there is, is a long train ride from JFK to the city of Manhattan, where we are jostled continuously and sworn at for bringing our bags into the subway, and I'm pretty sure the guy sitting in the far corner of the subway car is dead. When we finally climb out of the dank station, we're panting and sweaty because of course these stations don't have escalators or elevators or anything that would make life slightly easier—New York isn't into easy; it loves to remind you that it's tough, and if you're not tough then you don't belong. Into the sunlight, I am done. But I can't be done because it's ten more blocks of walking, dragging our luggage with us, and once again getting cussed at— "Fucking tourists"—until we get to our hotel.

Without Ted, I would've booked the cheapest little motel I could find, squirreling away as much money as I can for a rainy day. But because he has insisted on coming along and because I have claimed that my publisher is paying for it, we have to stay somewhere mildly acceptable. A three-star hotel, he pointed out, is reasonable. Something my publisher would be okay with reimbursing. Can't argue with that, so here we are. I've charged everything to my card and told Ted that Harvest would reimburse me later.

It's way past lunchtime, and after we're done checking in and going to the bathroom, Ted says, "Shall we?"

I look at him like he's just started speaking Russian.

"Lunch?" he says. "I've been dying to try all of these places in New York, and you said meals are included as part of the trip, right?"

God, he's going to make me burn through the ring money. "Actually, I have a meeting with Toni."

Ted frowns. "Now? She set up a meeting with you for today? She knows you just got off a long flight, right?"

I hate to admit it, but now that he's saying these words out loud, they do actually make some sense. Why didn't I think of it? But it's too late now. I can hardly be like, oh yeah, you're right, it wasn't today after all, silly me! Gotta dig my heels in and keep shoveling away at that grave. "Yeah, she's really busy and she can slot me in today, so . . ." I grab my purse, put my phone and a key card inside, and give Ted a bright smile. "I'll see you later."

Ted's still staring at me like he's a kid and I'm his mom and I've just told him that he's adopted. "So we're not lunching together? What about dinner?"

My god, Ted. It takes a lot not to scream at him. He's doing this on purpose, I know he is. He's never ever this clingy, but now, when it actually matters, he's pulling this shit on me. Trying to distract me from following my true calling.

"I don't know," I say, trying to sound apologetic. "Toni might want to have dinner together?"

His face softens. "Yeah, of course."

I turn to leave.

"Hey, before you go . . ."

Don't scream. Do not scream. I turn around and raise my eyebrows.

"Don't like—don't set your expectations too high. I mean, I know it's exciting, meeting your agent for the first time and all, but you know, she's probably really busy and stuff, so . . ."

He can't stand that it's my success we're celebrating for once. Well, my pretend success, but he doesn't know it's pretend. He's got to shit all over it, to remind me not to have hope because all I deserve is mediocrity. I don't bother giving him a reply before I stalk out the door, slamming it shut behind me. I half hope he'd come out and ask if I'm angry because, *Wow, you slammed the door really hard, Jane.* Then I'd give an extra sweet smile and say, *Oops, it just slipped from my hand!* But he doesn't come out. I practically run down the stairs, through the lobby, and out into the street. Holy shit, I did it. I'm in New York City, sans Ted, and I'm about to meet my agent.

The problem is, Toni doesn't actually know I'm here. In all the rush to book tickets for this and that and reminding myself about what lies I'd told Ted, I'd forgotten to email her. And now it's kind of late to do so. Another shitty realization: I don't actually have a ticket to SusPens Con. But, I comfort myself, Toni probably does. And she'll be so happy to see me. She's always been so bubbly and enthusiastic, all of her emails generously sprinkled with "!!!" She adores me as a client, she's told me so many times. And given she works at one of the biggest literary agencies in the city, she'll have all the connections. Right, good plan.

I look up the address to her agency and burrow my way into the subway yet again.

Matterson and Cable Literary Agency is on 42nd Street, a street flanked by skyscrapers on both sides, so close that I get dizzy looking all the way up. All of New York is like that, designed to give you a sense of vertigo so that it can feel satisfied, like a school bully. I find the building, a behemoth of yellow brick and glass, and walk inside. Immediately, I feel all sorts of wrong. Everyone is impeccably dressed, and I do mean everyone. Suits and pencil skirts, and here I am, wearing a knee-length denim skirt and an ill-fitting cardigan, my hair messy and limp.

But that's probably to be expected from writers, right? There's a reason why we're writers and not actors. We're better on paper than in person. Toni's probably got a whole stable full of writers with sweat stains, hunched backs, and skin that's sallow and greasy from too much time spent poring over their manuscripts. I probably look better than most authors. Probably. Maybe.

I get into one of the elevators and press the button for the twenty-fifth floor. At the twenty-fifth floor, I get out and walk past a law firm and an architecture firm before finding Matterson and Cable Literary. Here we go. This is okay. This is totally acceptable behavior from one of their longtime clients. I force my mouth to stretch into a smile before pushing open the double doors and walking inside.

The receptionist, a boy who looks like a college freshman, looks up and says, "Welcome to Matterson and Cable. Do you have an appointment?"

"Um, no. I'm looking for, um, Toni Sumida?"

"Sure, of course, that's great. Is she expecting you?"

I shake my head, and he opens his mouth, his face primed to give me a canned response, but I quickly add, "But I'm a client of hers. Jane Morgan?"

"Ah, a client. But you don't have an appointment."

"No," I say again, wondering why the hell they hired this moron to man the desk.

"Okay . . ." He stretches out the "kay" so it's more like "kayyyyyyyyyy," like he really needs the entire office to hear that *hey, you guys, look at this stupid client who's come all the way here without an appointment!* Then he sighs and says, "Let me just check real quick if she's in the office." He picks up the phone and dials a number while I turn around to give him some semblance of privacy. I take the chance to look around the office.

It's a lot bigger than I expected, and a lot nicer as well. Half of it is an open-plan design, with private offices for the senior agents and an open space for the rest.

"Hi, Toni, this is Robin. I have a client of yours out here—a . . . sorry, miss, what did you say your name was?"

If I killed him it would be a favor to humanity. "Jane Morgan."

"It's Jane Morgan. Should I—oh? Okay. Mm-hmm. No problem." He puts down the phone and leans forward. "She'll come out in a minute. Okay?" he says in a tone that says: *We're done talking.*

Wow, I really am not used to the sassiness of New York. I

have no idea what to do with myself as I wait, so I take out my phone and try to look busy. Oh, look, there are exactly zero emails I need to answer.

I've been tapping on my phone for eight excruciating minutes when Toni finally comes out.

"Jane?" she says, and I look up to see a smiling face.

"Hi! Yes, it's me," I say, standing up quickly. Holy shit, it's really her. My agent for the last three years. The woman who sold my last two books to Harvest Publishing, who edited my books and listened to my pitches and told me over and over again what a treat my writing is. I should probably hug her. But neither of us makes a move to bridge the polite gap between us, and then she holds her hand out at the same time as I hold my arms out for a hug, and there's a moment where she realizes I'm coming in for a hug and quickly switches to hug mode, and Jesus Christ, why the hell did I go in for a hug? We end up giving each other an awkward, don't-want-to-actually-touch-you hug, and then stand uncomfortably close to each other—close enough for me to see the fine lines on her forehead and around her mouth.

"It's so nice to finally see you, Jane. Come, let's go into my office." She steps back and turns around before I can answer, and I get the feeling that she's relieved to be walking away from me. But I'm sure I'm just being silly, because of course she's happy to see me. We walk past interns and junior agents, and she leads me to a corner office and shuts the door behind me. She doesn't offer me a drink. She gestures for me to take a seat across from her desk before settling into her luxurious seat. "So, Jane! What brings you to New York? Visiting family?" She doesn't even finish the sentence before she glances over at her computer screen.

"Um, business, actually."

"Oh?" She glances at me for a second before her attention is pulled back to the computer. "Sorry, hang on . . . give me just a sec . . ." She types something rapidly before forcing her attention back to me. "Right. So you were saying?"

It takes a moment to regain my bearings. "I was saying I'm in town for business. For SusPens Con, actually."

Her eyebrows knit together. "SusPens Con? But that's for suspense/thrillers. More commercial work."

"I know, but I was hoping to attend because I'm thinking of writing a commercial suspense."

"That's—"

I can't read her expression. It's somewhere between a smile and a quizzical frown, like a polite *What the fuck?* She finally says, "That's wonderful. Yeah, adult suspense has a very healthy market, so I think it's a good, um, good move. Yeah."

Who are you trying to convince? I want to ask her. Her hesitation is coming through painfully clear. She doesn't think I could write an adult suspense. "I mean, I know it's kind of different from what I've been writing . . ."

"Yeah, pretty different." She holds up one finger and says, "Hang on, let me just pull up your file."

My file? She's only sold two of my books and she can't even remember them? But I sit there, inwardly squirming as she squints at her computer.

"Okay, here we are. Right, your debut, *Flowers That Grow in Moonlight*, lit fic, right, sold for . . . here we go, $3,500."

Yep, I know that. I don't have to be reminded of it. It rankles that she has to be reminded of the details of my book deal. Aren't agents supposed to remember this stuff? I bet if I wrote young adult, she'd remember. But no, I have to write lit fic, the least commercial thing anyone could write, maybe aside from poetry. It would have done well in the nineties, before YA destroyed the entire market. With a sinking feeling, it hits me that the fact that she doesn't remember probably does mean that it was always an intern or assistant who handled me.

"And your second book, also a lit fic, *The Coldest Winter*, sold for $2,300." Her mouth stretches into a wince for a second before she recovers and turns it into a smile. Still looks like a grimace. When she looks at me again, I can see that what little interest she had has now faded. She takes a fifteen percent cut of my earnings, and fifteen percent of $5,800 is barely worth the paperwork. Worse, my advance has gone down after my first book, a sign that the first one didn't perform as well as my publisher had hoped.

But how could it have performed well when they did fuck all to promote it? Nobody even knew about its existence.

"Hmm. Yeah, going into commercial fiction could be a good move. Move away from lit fic, that's good. Did you have any pitches you wanted to share with me?"

Ah. Shit. Pitches, right. Shame curdles my gut as it hits me how unprepared I am for this meeting. And as I sit here mentally freaking out, Toni glances at her Apple Watch; I'm taking up too much of her time, she's got bigger clients to focus on, clients who make seven-figure deals and sell movie rights.

Then, surging through the turgid waters of my senses, an idea leaps out, taking form. I pounce on it. "Um, you know Thalia Ashcroft?"

That catches Toni's attention, because of course it does. Thalia's always got this effect on people. Toni turns her face toward me, no longer thinking—for now—how she can get rid of me. "The author of *A Most Pleasant Death*? Yeah, I've heard of her. Her book's at the top of the *New York Times* list. What about her?"

"Well, I know her."

Toni gives me a wan smile, the polite kind that you give to pathetic people to get them to stop talking.

"We actually went to the same MFA program together. At Oxford. In England?" I don't know why that came out as a question, but I desperately need Toni to start nodding, and she does, her eyes brightening. "Yeah, we actually lived on the same floor; we were really good friends, really close to each other."

"Wow, that's wonderful to hear." She's still got that line in between her eyebrows because even though it's nice to hear that I'm friends with publishing's next big star, she's also wondering what the hell this has to do with anything.

"And I think if I could just get to see her in person, we could reconnect and she'd probably want to help promote my books and everything. We were so tight back in Oxford."

"Why not just give her a call? Did you two lose touch?"

I shift uneasily in my seat. "Sort of. Um, something bad happened during our year, and we were all sent home for a while. I came back the next semester, but Thalia never did, so we kind of lost contact there."

"You could just send her an email, maybe slide into her DMs?" she says with a smile.

Frustration claws at my belly. She doesn't get it. "No, I'd rather see her in person—I'm sure she's inundated with emails and DMs from random people. Anyway, she's going to be at SusPens Con, so I was thinking if I could get a ticket to go there, I could go to her panel and say hi."

She nods slowly, hesitantly. "I'll ask around, see if anyone has a spare ticket. I'll give you a call once I know. Okay?"

The last "Okay?" was delivered very clearly as a placating goodbye. I'm out of ideas by now, so I just give her a nod and stand up, pretending not to see the relief on her face as she walks me out of the office.

Outside of the building, it takes a full minute before my heart recovers from the painful speed it had been galloping at. My breath releases in a long whoosh. God, I can't believe I just did that. Just showed up at Toni's office like that. What the fuck. But even as I think that, a slow smile takes over my face. For once in my life, I put myself out there. I took control of the situation. I was fucking proactive, and I'm about to be rewarded for it. I know I am.

I walk around the area for a bit, looking up at the massive buildings and searching for a bite to eat. But who am I kidding? Everything in this part of Manhattan is out of my price range; even the bottled water is six dollars each, which is insane. And here I'd thought Bay Area prices were out of control.

I've been walking aimlessly for about ten minutes when an email comes in from Toni. I open it, mouth dry. I know, as soon as I see the lack of "!" that it's not going to be good news.

Jane,

What a surprise having you show up at the office today. I made a few calls to see if I could get a hold of SusPens Con tickets. Unfortunately, I wasn't able to get any. I think your best bet to reconnect with Thalia would be through email; I think that in general, this is a better way than showing up unannounced in person, especially since it's been quite a while since the two of you were in touch with each other.

Best,
Toni

The skyscrapers around me might as well have folded over and crumbled on top of me. I feel crushed and humiliated and above all, enraged. This email is a far cry from her usual ones, which always, always start off with "Hi!" and not just "Jane comma." And her emails have, at minimum, three exclamation marks, always. Even when they're emails containing bad news, like when I got those bad reviews from Kirkus and Publishers Weekly. She'd said: "Hi! Ugh, we got a bad review from Kirkus, but seriously, who gives a shit about them anyway, right?! They wouldn't know good writing if it hit them in the face!"

And now, all terse words and awkwardness. I could just—

I was making a gesture, turning up at her office. Aren't agents supposed to welcome their clients with open arms? Unbidden, Ted's voice rises up from the depths of my mind, like a noxious bubble popping up from a poisonous swamp. *You're small fry, Jane. Don't expect too much from her.* She's got bigger clients to tend to. I bet she wouldn't react like this if one of her bestselling authors showed up unannounced.

I can't stand it. I can't stand the thought of seeing his smug face when he finds out that he's right all along, that I shouldn't have assumed that Toni would be happy to see me. That all these years of friendly emails were nothing but lies. I wonder if they were even written by her in the first place, or if they had been something she'd delegated to an assistant, or worse, an intern. "Here," she would have said, "write an email to these clients. Make it sound like I give a damn."

And like a total idiot, I had fallen for it, thought she adored me, thought we were—ha—friends. The thought of myself, so pathetic and so foolish, makes me want to spit.

But who gives a crap about Toni? So it turns out she doesn't give a shit, so what? It doesn't matter. All that matters is that I'm here, in Manhattan, and in less than twenty-four hours, I am going to go to SusPens Con, ticket or not, and I am going to find a way to get inside, because that's where Thalia will be, and there is nothing I wouldn't do to see her again.

Nothing.

11

spend the rest of the day avoiding Thalia. When we get back from lunch (I get back from my room, where I spent lunch-time holed up, alternating between pacing like a caged animal and screaming into my pillow), I pick a seat farthest from her and refuse to meet her eye. As soon as classes end, I escape once more into my room. I listen behind the door, my breath coming out rapidly whenever footsteps pound through the hallway. There it is, the click and swing of her door, just a few feet away from mine, might as well be miles. I should go out there and explain—though I'm not sure what I would be explaining, maybe why I'm so warped and jagged? My hand caresses the doorknob.

Laughter.

I freeze. It's not Thalia's voice. Then I hear it, Thalia talking, followed by more throaty laughter that turns my hand into a fist. Ani. Ani's going into Thalia's room. The room I'd been in less than a day ago, where Thalia had touched my bare skin, where we had, at one point, both been undressed. And now it's being tainted by Ani's presence. Is she lending Ani an outfit too? I am frothing with jealousy. But no, says a tiny voice of logic, Ani isn't the kind of girl who needs to borrow another girl's outfit. Ani's the kind of girl who would've brought her entire wardrobe to Oxford, filling her closet to bursting with expensive silks and leathers. My heart rate slows down for a moment before speeding up again. Because if she's not here to borrow an outfit, then what the fuck is she here for? What are they doing in Thalia's room, laughing like that? Are they laughing about me? Laughing about the freak across the hallway?

A few minutes later, Thalia's door opens again, voices and more laughter flooding the hallway. I press my ear to my door, teeth gritted so hard my jaw threatens to lock, and listen to their receding footsteps. And they're off on their girls' night. How could I have been so wrong? How laughable that I should have thought myself worthy of being Thalia's friend. How quickly I've been put back in my place.

By now, I'm half-crazed with hunger and rage and pain. Mom's voice again: *Oh, sweetie, get used to it. You will never belong with these people. We're the help. Come back and work for Mrs. Crawford's niece; I hear her baby is a sweetheart, not colicky. It'll be a good job.* Shut up, Mother. Shut the fuck up. I should go out, get some food. But I've missed dinnertime at Haygrove Hall, and I don't really want to wander up and down the streets of Oxford where I might bump into Thalia and Ani and suffer the embarrassed giggles that would come from them—god, look at her, so sad and gross.

Instead, I sit down at my desk and start writing. I slit myself open and let all the darkness pour out onto the keyboard, all of my rage and all of my hunger for her. Several times, I type so hard and so fast that my hands, slick with sweat, slip from the keyboard. I keep going, writing like I'm possessed, except it's not a possession but the opposite of one. An exorcism. I'm only vaguely aware of what I've written.

> *. . . her beautiful neck, as slim as the stem of a rose about to bloom . . .*
>
> *. . . count her bones, one at the back of her neck, peeking out as she pores over the book . . .*
>
> *. . . the way her face looks as I squeeze the air out of her, panic and ecstasy knotted together. She wants me to do this; she wants me to be the end of her, to be the final thing she sees . . .*

By the time I'm done, I'm barely functional. I load the file onto the virtual classroom and click Send without thinking twice. My mind is buzzing, skittering like the legs of a centipede. I feel drunk again, a disconnect between mind and body, a deep chasm in my core. I slam my laptop shut, slump over to bed, and surrender myself to warped dreams where Thalia alternates between telling me she loves me and laughing cruelly at me.

In the morning, it takes a while for last night's events to come back to me, and when they do, they float up like noxious bubbles swirling up from a swamp of dead things, bubbling to the surface and popping to release their toxic fumes. Thalia and Ani, laughing as they head out of Thalia's room, probably arm in arm the way that girls like to walk sometimes, both of them dressed in equally expensive, fashionable clothes. Bare skin and tight jeans. Red lipstick and sensuous perfume. And me, boiling with hunger and envy, screaming silently in my room. Food. I need food. I shrug on clean clothes, rake a brush through my hair, while blinking blearily in the mirror. Plain Jane. Mediocre in every way. Not ugly, not pretty, just aggressively mediocre.

Thalia doesn't turn up to breakfast. Neither does Ani, and I picture them both squeezed into Thalia's bed, undressed, breathing slow, lazy breaths into each other's hair. I take an extra-vicious bite of my pancake. Pam appears in the doorway, and I wonder for a second if she'll join me—I half panic, hoping she won't, but then she sees another student and joins them instead. And then I'm suddenly jealous. Even fucking PAM has someone to sit with, but not me. It seems that making friends is a skill that everyone else has been born with except me. I feel like a fish who doesn't quite know how to swim and can only stay still until it sinks, slowly, into the deep and the dark, the waters getting increasingly cold as it descends.

We have each other, Mom whispers.

Shut. Up.

I gobble up the rest of my food, satiating at least one of my hungers, and escape from the noise of Haygrove Hall. Pam offers a hesitant smile as I walk past, but I pretend not to see. I don't know how you're supposed to respond to half smiles. Are they meant to initiate conversations? I shrug it off and walk out of the building. It's yet another beautiful morning; I've learned that no place else does mornings and evenings quite like Oxford does.

Back in Cali, mornings are ostentatious, the sun bursting over the horizon, Here I am! Everybody up! In Oxford, sunrise and sunsets are far gentler, the sky melting like ice cream from dark to purple, to orange, and then to a dewy haze that lines everything with gold. It's so beautiful it further enrages me. I wish I could take a knife to it, slice into this perfect moment.

There's just something about perfection that makes me want to defile it. Sometimes, I fantasize going through the museum with a little razor, casually slicing apart priceless canvases as I walk past.

The day's classes start off with another workshop, this time with the theme of "How to surprise your reader." When I saw that on the syllabus, I'd snorted out loud because I'd, of course, imagined leaping from behind a bookshelf brandishing a knife. Bet you my reader would be surprised by that.

The weird things that my brain spits out.

I take a seat at the farthest end of the room from the door and studiously bury my head in my notebook, trying to project an air of "Fuck off." It works; my classmates mill about, chattering among themselves, but none of them try talking to me. I'm glad, truly I am. I sense the shift in the room when Thalia enters, the way the voices stop for a second before they call out to her. How is it possible for to her to ignite such delight from others after just a day? Is this what charisma gets you—instant adoration? But no, I catch snippets of conversation like:

"—checked out that bookshop you mentioned, loved it—"

"—were right about the hot chocolate at Caffè Nero!"

What the hell? How has she had time to give people bookshop and drink recommendations? When we sat on the bus from London to Oxford, she told me she'd never been to Oxford before, that she's a complete stranger to the city. She'd been so nervous, so sweetly innocent and excited. And now here she is, giving recommendations to English people like she's the one who's a local. And I'm pushed further out of the circle, an outsider peering through a window.

I study my notebook so hard that my nose practically touches the page. Fortunately, our teacher arrives and we begin the class.

My relief is short-lived; the teacher, Taylor McKeon (also critically acclaimed, also with fewer than ten reviews on Amazon), perches on her seat and says, "I thought it would be perfect to start today's class with a workshop session. I read through all of your short scenes, and I found one that I thought would be appropriate for today's subject matter: Surprising your reader. It's one by Jane Morgan. Jane?"

It takes a few moments to realize she's calling my name, and by then, she's had to say it twice more. Jane. Jane?

I startle back to life, my mind a mad horse, bucking and running wild. What had I handed in that could be appropriate for this? For anything? It comes back in a black rush—last night's mad raving typed with such ferocity that my fingers could barely keep up with the torrent of words. Something about strangling a young woman. Something about counting her bones. Oh my god.

I finally find my voice. "I don't think—"

Taylor smiles kindly. "Doing a reading is a harrowing experience, isn't it? Especially when it's a reading of your own work. I don't think I've quite managed to overcome that horrid sensation myself. But it's a vital skill for authors to have. So Jane, please. The stage is yours."

There is no stage, but still, everyone's eyes are on me. I can't bear to look at them. I don't dare even glance in Thalia's direction because I have no clue what expression she'd be wearing. Encouraging? Pitying? Bored? I don't know which is worse. With shaking hands, I take out my laptop and call up the file, every passing second incredibly, painfully slow. I can hear every single noise in the room—the subtle throat clearing, the rustle of clothes as someone shifts in their seat, the scratching of a pen's nib across paper. Everyone is waiting to hear me read out my scene of rage. I might as well be undressing in front of them. I look at Taylor again, my eyes beseeching, but she only gives me what she probably thinks is an encouraging nod. And so, with one last swallow, I begin to read.

We meet in the middle of a bustling city and all at once I know I will be the most important person in her life. Not her boyfriend, nor her parents or her siblings, but me. A total stranger. I shall be the defining moment in her entire life, the point around which everything will curve, because I, a total stranger, will be the one who ends it.

Despite everything, the more I read, the less aware I am of everyone else in the room. Everyone, that is, except for Thalia. Everyone else ceases to exist; even the tables and chairs between us melt away, leaving us floating in empty space, just her and me. Her eyes are on mine, and I can feel the weight of her gaze, but still I dare not look at her. What must she be thinking? Is she repulsed? Fearful? Angry?

I come to the end of the passage and there's silence. Then someone says, "That was amazing."

And that someone was Thalia.

———

THINGS HAVE CHANGED FOR ME. EVER SINCE THE DAY that Taylor made me read out the dark spaces in my mind, everyone's been looking at me differently. With fear, one might guess, but no. It's respect I see in their eyes. Somehow, revealing what a fucked-up mind I have has elevated me in their eyes. I'm not sure how I feel about that.

You don't want to know what people really think of you, do you, dear? Mom whispers. It's one of her favorite things to say. She would never tell me outright that people think I'm weird·or crazy or unlikable; no, that would be too easy. She preferred to coax me gently into thinking that myself, so that when I asked her point-blank if people disliked me, she could widen her eyes with surprise and say, "Why would you think that, Jane?"

So I try not to dwell on it. It doesn't matter anyway. I don't care. See, the thing is, I won her over. Thalia.

Immediately after classes ended that day, Thalia had come to me and said, "We're going for lunch together." And that was that.

That was two weeks ago, two incredible weeks that I spent with Thalia. And Ani, our barnacle. I bet she doesn't think of herself as that, though. Ani probably thinks she's the main character in our story, and I want to scream at her and tell her that she isn't, she's the villain, the whiny bitch nobody loves. But it's okay. I am willing to suffer through countless hours of Ani if it means that I can be with Thalia. And I am. We're traversing Oxford together, and it's wonderful and amazing and so much more than I could have predicted, than I'd dared to hope.

In the mornings, we have greasy mushrooms and rubbery scrambled eggs at Haygrove, followed by classes where I get to sit and marvel at the words Thalia spins like gold thread. She's by far the most gifted writer in our program, and everyone has accepted it. She's always called on to read her scenes out loud, which I love and hate, because I love watching her, but I hate having to share her with others. How dare they watch her like that, their lust so open and so lascivious?

For lunch, we meet up with Ani, who is surprisingly studious. My first impression of Ani had been that of a spoiled brat who couldn't care less about school, but she's the opposite. Apparently, she's top of her class, and Thalia tells me that Ani often comes back from a night of partying to study until the following morning. Ani is powered by Red Bull and anger at the world, and she is exhausting to be around because she never stops. I have lost count of the number of times we meet up with Ani only to find her just finishing up a meeting with someone else—a Rhodes scholar, a professor, a fellow business school student. She's always making connections, such a busy butterfly. The complete opposite of me. But with Thalia as a buffer between us, I find it bearable. Each day, the three of us walk around the city and try out a different restaurant for lunch. I know Ani doesn't think much of me, just as I don't regard her as anything other than a benign tumor that has attached itself to the entity that is Thalia and me, but for Thalia's sake, we tolerate each other.

After our afternoon classes, Thalia and I go to the Bodleian Library and lose ourselves in the hushed halls, surrounded by centuries-old tomes, and there we sit and write. I steal glances at her as I type on my keyboard, and just the nearness of her is enough to transport me to that place that writers aim for. Her presence propels me through the doorway, letting the rest of the world melt away. Never before have I come up with such passionate prose, such dark, enchanting words. In class, our teachers and fellow students swoon over my compositions, marveling at the way I've managed to cut through the flowery words that writers often fall prey to and go straight to the harsh bones of human emotion. It's all thanks to Thalia, I want to say, but I keep it to myself. I don't want to share my muse with anyone.

For a few weeks, it really does feel like I've finally found my place. Something special that I never thought I could get, and I would give anything to keep this friendship with Thalia going. Anything.

PART
TWO

12

The trouble begins about three weeks into the course. We're at the Eagle and Child, leaning back in our seats with apple and pear ciders sweating in pint glasses, waiting for our food to arrive. (British pub food—steak pies, bangers and mash—because we're doing this whole English thing right.) Ani says, "What are we doing this weekend, ladies? Don't tell me we're staying in this tired old town again. I am DYING here. Literally dying."

I look at her and daydream about her literally dying, blood splashed across her skin in a fetching pattern. Ani would look good bathed in red.

Thalia smiles tenderly at her, and my heart bites at my rib cage, a petty little Jack Russell terrier.

"I've been studying way too hard," Ani grumbles.

"Yeah, you have. Why do you study so hard, anyway?"

Ani takes a sip of her pear cider. "If you had a brother and parents like mine, you'd understand why I need to excel at this stupid course. Anyway, shall we party this weekend? I've been dying to do London! I didn't come here to spend my time wasting away in this shithole."

"Oxford isn't a shithole," I mutter. I wonder what she'd call Oakland, if a city as beautiful as Oxford is considered a shithole.

Ani rolls her eyes and Thalia laughs. At me? With me? With Ani?

"You'll have to excuse Ani, Jane," Thalia says, leaning close enough to me to make breathing suddenly a challenge. "She's a spoiled, rich, big-city brat."

The left corner of Ani's mouth slices upward into a lazy smirk. I expect her to counter it and say something like, "No, I'm not that rich; don't be silly." But she doesn't. She knows what she is and she's not afraid to admit it.

Later on, after Ani leaves us to go to her afternoon classes at the Saïd Business School, Thalia tells me that Ani's family are billionaires.

"Didn't she come from Indonesia or some other country like that?" I ask, and immediately regret how snarky that sounded.

"Yeah, apparently there are a ton of billionaires in Indonesia. I looked it up. They're considered the biggest emerging market, soon to be the world's fourth biggest economy."

I'm taken aback by this, and slightly, inexplicably angry too. Deep in the recesses of my guts, Mom's voice, petulant and bitchy: *Know what Grandpa used to call those third-world countries in Southeast Asia? The armpit of Asia.* But now, even someone from the armpit of Asia is wealthier than us. Laughable. Ani is a painful reminder of the kind of Asian I could have been. The kind I should have been. I'm almost overcome by an urge to eradicate her from my life.

"She's probably the richest person in Pemberton," Thalia laughs, as though reading my mind and my awful, hateful thoughts.

Yet again, I realize how out of place I am. I bet Thalia's family, if not billionaires, are at least millionaires. Just like everyone else who can afford to come here for further education.

"It might be fun to go out in London," Thalia says.

I stiffen up at the thought of going all the way to London with Thalia and Ani. Maybe if it were just Thalia. The two of us could explore the city together, at a gentle pace. Stop by the British Museum, have afternoon tea at a café tucked away from the bustling streets. But Ani would only want to do the things that are out of my reach. Shop at Harrods. Buy a ton of Burberry. And then go to the most expensive clubs.

As though sensing my reluctance, Thalia says, "How about just going for a girls' night out here in Oxford instead?" Then she adds, "Come get dressed in my room. We can do our makeup together again. What do you think? It'll be like old times."

Old times. Three weeks ago is hardly "old times," but when she mentions it, it sends an electric shiver down my spine. The thought of her fingers grazing my back as she zips me up turns my legs to water. I can't say no to that. And a night out in Oxford sounds just about doable.

I force my mouth into a smile, though I have a feeling it ends up more like a grimace. "Sure. Sounds fun."

— — —

THIS IS NOT FUN. THIS IS NOT FUN AT ALL. WHY THE HELL am I here, in a place called the Varsity Club where everyone looks like a young lawyer and is drinking five-year-old bottles of wine and nibbling on tiny food? I'm swept back to my first night here, and there's nothing more I want to do than skulk back to Downing and bury myself in my single bed.

The Varsity Club has four stories, including a cocktail lounge and a nightclub in case patrons weren't suffering enough. At the top level is a rooftop lounge with skyline views. Apparently. I wouldn't know, because Ani of course drags us to the nightclub part of the place, where she orders shots of something sickly sweet at the bar, shouts at us to down them, and then proceeds to strut onto the dance floor.

Please, Thalia, please hang back. Please catch my desperate eyes and roll yours so I know that you're on my side in this moment. That you hate this atmosphere—the throbbing techno music, the slick bodies writhing, working so hard to catch everyone's attention, the raised voices fighting to be heard over one another.

But she doesn't. With a slightly embarrassed laugh, Thalia lets herself get pulled into the crowd on the dance floor, and then she starts to dance as well, and I can't tear my eyes off her. I never would've thought that Thalia could move like that, not wholesome ray-of-sunshine Thalia. But she moves like oil, smooth and slow, while everybody else jerks like mad puppets around her. She flicks her blond hair over her shoulder, sways her hips sensuously, her hands trailing from her thighs up and up and, oh my god, I'm staring, I should look away, but I can't.

Ani whoops and steps close to Thalia, pressing the front of her body up against Thalia's, and begins grinding against her. No, please, push that bitch away. But Thalia doesn't. She laughs again, a girlish laugh that's half-embarrassed and half "let's go," and their thighs are kissing and kissing and I am in hell, I know it.

My head is swimming already—we'd stopped by at a nearby pub before this and grabbed a couple of pints of cider each, and now, coupled with the syrupy shot, I'm well past tipsy. I lurch toward them, vaguely aware that I'm pushing away other dancing bodies. A shout of, "Watch where you're going, sweetheart!" I ignore it. I want to wrench Ani and Thalia apart, give Ani a good shove or two to really drive in the message. Fuck off.

I'm almost there when Thalia suddenly cries out and jerks around, her shiny hair whipping in a wide arc. Before I can react, she shoves a guy who's been grinding behind her away roughly. "Bastard!" she screams.

"What happened? Are you okay?" I say, but my voice is too small and the club is too loud and it gets drowned out. I try again, a bit louder this time, but already I'm too late.

A man steps between me and Thalia, blocking her from view, and he asks the questions I did, only this time it comes from a timbre-rich voice, impossible to miss. "Are you okay?"

He shifts slightly. I see the profile of his face, the superhero jawline and the floppy blond hair and the impossibly broad shoulders, and I know he's trouble.

— — —

HIS NAME IS ANTOINE AND HE'S FRENCH AND APPARENTLY owns a hip wine bar in Jericho, and there is no way that I can compete with him, not a handsome, wealthy French guy with a French accent so heavy it sounds like his mouth is full of cream and sugar when he talks. The chemistry between him and Thalia is hot and immediate and dangerous, and for once, Ani isn't my main concern. Ani isn't at the forefront of my mind, nor even at the back of it. Ani is nothing; I've miscalculated it, focused too much on her when I should have been focusing on the men around us. Because of course, Thalia is into them, and they are into her because there is no way that anyone with a libido isn't into Thalia.

Antoine takes Thalia by the hand and leads her upstairs, Ani fluttering around them like a drunk butterfly, and when we burst out into the cold night air on the rooftop, his voice becomes even clearer, sexier now that he no longer has to shout over the music.

"What a bastard," he's saying to Thalia.

She shudders. "He grabbed my butt, just like—grabbed it—ugh."

"Gross," Ani declares.

I nod wordlessly, wanting to show my rage in solidarity, but as usual I'm flaccid, no words coming out. As useful as a glass hammer.

"Would you like a drink, maybe?" Antoine says, leading us all to an unoccupied table near the edge of the rooftop, where Oxford's incredible skyline stretches out around us. Oxford at night is jaw-droppingly beautiful, lights shining off the cathedral and the colleges, but I don't see any of that. My eyes are locked on Thalia, because the signs of my heartbreak are written so clearly on her face. The way her wide eyes never leave Antoine's face, the way her lips part ever so slightly when he's near, like he's something delectable she can't wait to taste.

When he leaves to get us a drink ("Wait eer, ladiezzz"), Ani immediately leans forward and says, "Omigod."

"I know," Thalia breathes. "Have you ever seen anyone more gorgeous?"

You, I want to say. *You are more gorgeous. You are too good for him.*

"Holy shit," Ani says. "Girl, if you don't take him, I will."

Thalia laughs. "Jesus, is he even real? Those eyelashes."

"Fuck his eyelashes, look at his biceps! That jawline, oh man. I could bite him. And I've been to Vin+. That place he mentioned he owns? It's so trendy and like, just so chic." Ani narrows her eyes. "Seriously, are you gonna go with him? 'Cause if you aren't, then I am."

Thalia bites down on her lower lip, her eyes shining with something—laughter? Desire? Then she says, "You hardly know him, you tramp."

They both laugh. My heart is thundering, hammering against my rib cage. This conversation can't be happening. I want to scream. They both look at me like they've just remembered that I'm there. Oh, it's you. Our hanger-on. "What do you think, Jane?" Thalia says kindly.

I shrug. "He seems okay."

"Okay?" Ani squawks. I really hate her. "OKAY? Girl, are you blind? Have you seen his face?"

I press my lips together and don't say anything. Ani turns her face toward Thalia and rolls her eyes. I don't know if she meant for me to see it. It makes me feel like shit. Thalia is for sure not going to invite me out again after this. The thought spurs me to say, "Yeah, I guess he's good-looking."

"Fuck yeah he is!" Ani says.

Thalia grins. "He really is ridiculously handsome, isn't he?" And then she shushes us and I turn to see Antoine walking back with a tray of wine, smiling that smile that has no doubt dazzled hundreds of women, and I wonder, fleetingly, if I could push him off the roof. Only four stories up, but they're tall stories. His skull versus the cobblestones. I'd put money on the cobblestones.

Then he's sitting down, again between me and Thalia, always between the two of us, his masculine presence thick and suffocating. I'm being squeezed out and I hate him, I truly do. I pick up one of the wineglasses and take a long, deep gulp. They talk and laugh and drink, Ani and Thalia gazing at him with shining eyes, laughing at his every word. At some point, another guy joins us, another Frenchman, pleasant to look at, though not quite as shiny. Good enough for Ani, who's pleased that she's got a Frenchman for herself; it had become clear very quickly that Antoine was only interested in Thalia.

I sit on the edge of the circle, gulping down wine so I don't have to make conversation. My head is heavy, the voices coming from all sides around me, a maddening circle of noise. There's no place for me here. Later, as we lurch back to Pemberton, Thalia clinging to Antoine's strong arm as she stumbles over the cobblestones, I wonder who I should get rid of first: Antoine or Ani?

——— ——— ———

AS IT TURNS OUT, I GET RID OF NEITHER. THE DAYS MARCH on, the skies turn from late-summer gold to a dreary gray, and still I do nothing. We've slumped into a comfortable routine. Classes, coursework, tea and scones. Sometimes, Thalia and I write together at a café, our fingers flying over our respective keyboards. There's just something about her presence that ignites the words inside me, and I like to think it's the same for her, that part of her aches for me in the same way and spurs her to write too.

But then classes end for the day and she disappears, leaving me with nothing but her lingering scent—mulberries and smoke—and the remnants of her hastily written scenes. While I'm left alone, replaying bits of our conversation over and over, I know she's out there with Antoine and Ani and Olivier. I know, because I often follow them, hiding behind trees and statues like a fucking creep. *This is what you've done to me, Thalia. This is what you've made me do.*

I should stop, I know I should, but I can't. Not yet. And it's not even like I'm the only pathetic one. Really, I'm not the worst out of all of us here. Ani is, because I know for sure she's not even that into Olivier. I can tell Ani's going along with it because it's the only way she gets to spend time with Thalia. Because in the end, that's what we're all vying for, isn't it? Time with Thalia. I bet Olivier, too, is secretly in love with Thalia. As I observe from behind a statue of whatever dead white guy, I often catch little looks of derision from Ani, as though she's wondering why the hell she's putting up with a greasy Frenchman like Olivier. She must know she got the short end of the stick; but maybe that's favorable to ending up like me—left out, single, alone.

But I am patient. I know Thalia well enough to know that she will soon tire of Antoine. He's just so wrong for her. That first night, they'd fallen under his spell, that heady mixture of French accent (*Dis eez ah-may-zeeng, eez it not?* No, Antoine, it fucking is not.) and impossibly blue eyes. But I've gone out for meals with them twice more now—pity meals, I think, that Thalia invited me to only because she has a heart of gold and can't stand to see me suffer—and it's become painfully obvious that he is so wrong for her. He doesn't understand her sparkling wit; whether it's because of the language barrier or because he's a moron, I don't know or care, but he doesn't appreciate her for her brilliance. The only thing they share is physical lust, and while it makes me want to rip my skin off, it's also a relief because how long can lust last?

She'll get sick of him soon. She will. She must.

But the days tromp on, and now we're in proper winter wear. Ani has gotten rid of Olivier and moved on to Geraldo, and then to Jason, and still Antoine hangs around, a wart that refuses to get gone. I want to grab Thalia and shake her. What is it, Thalia? What's stopping you from seeing the truth? That you can do so much better? He calls her *ma chérie*, and I do believe any judge would acquit me for stabbing him in the ear just for that alone.

Then one day, on a quiet, dark November morning, all of us fed up with the lack of sunlight, glumly sipping our coffee in Haygrove Hall, Ani says the words that would bring our Oxford days to a bloody end: "My brother's coming for a visit."

13

As it turns out, SusPens Con is a lot bigger than I had previously thought. It's at the Javits Center, a behemoth of a building made of glass and steel with an aura that makes me think of ancient stadiums built for bloody fights. Or maybe I'm just in a dark mood. What else is new? When I finally went back to the hotel room last night, I'd told Ted that Toni took me to a fancy dinner and we talked shop all night, and then I'd immediately gone into the bathroom so he wouldn't ask me too many questions. This morning, he'd had the audacity to ask if there was a ticket for him as well. I only just managed not to laugh in his face. A ticket for him as well. As if. He, the man who reads one book every five years, thinks he should get a ticket to SusPens Con just because . . . what?

As I got dressed, carefully applying makeup in the bathroom mirror, Ted had leaned against the doorframe and watched me. Leaning against the doorframe is something I read about a lot of male love interests doing in books, but when Ted did it, all it did was make me nauseated. I wanted to shove him out of the doorway.

"You look nice," he said in a tone of voice that made the back of my neck crawl.

I glanced at him before muttering, "Thanks." I have given a lot of thought to what I should wear when I see Thalia. I've fantasized about this way too many times to count. One of my biggest fears is that I would bump into her while I'm running an errand in sloppy jeans and a tea-stained T-shirt. Now that I'm actually getting the luxury of prepping before seeing her, I need to make sure that I look as flawless as I can.

My outfit was designed to take us back to our Oxford days—a mustard yellow dress that ends just above my knees paired with black tights, brown booties, and a black cardigan. As a finishing touch, I put on the diamond necklace to perk up the otherwise dark fall colors. Or should I say, dark Michaelmas colors? I wonder if she'll notice.

"I haven't seen you wear that necklace before, wow," Ted said, coming inside the bathroom and tracing it with his index finger. At some point in time, my husband's touch must have warmed me. Or at the very least it must not have repulsed me. But now all I can do is remind myself not to flinch.

It was a relief to get out of that hotel room. I told Ted I was running late and rushed out, only to finish doing my makeup at a Starbucks bathroom. Of course, now that I'm actually at the Javits Center, I feel simultaneously under- and overdressed. There are people here who look like they're ready for New York Fashion Week, and then there are others who are schlepping it in baggy jeans and shirts, and I should feel happy with my outfit, but I just want to tear it off because it isn't good enough, and just what the hell was I thinking, coming out here?

I stand outside of the convention center, watching people streaming in and out. Their bright red tickets hang from their necks, and part of me wonders if I could just reach out and snatch one off. I gnaw on my lower lip and pace back and forth. What do I do? Can I steal inside? Or—ah, I know. I'll approach one of the people coming out of the convention center and offer to buy their ticket off them. Yes! That's perfect, because presumably they're coming out of the thing because they're done anyway, right? Right.

Deep breath. Here we go. I spot a man in his forties walking out carrying a tote bag no doubt with free books, and I approach him. "Um, excuse me, sir?"

He doesn't even slow down, just brushes past me with a muttered, "No, thanks."

Okay. There's that famous New York City attitude for you. I've lived too long in the Bay Area, have become soft. Still, I straighten my back and look around for someone else to approach. A middle-aged woman walks out with the same tote bag, and I walk up to her, but before I even get close, she barks, "Not interested."

Jesus. What the hell is going on? And now it's bad because this woman was loud enough to attract the attention of one of the security guards at the door, and he comes toward me with his hands on his belt. Why do guards always walk like that? I guess because it makes them look even more intimidating. I take a small step back, my mind zipping everywhere, wondering what the hell I'm going to do if he asks me to leave. It's not like I can tell him that I NEED to see Thalia. I doubt he'd understand.

"Ma'am, do you have a ticket to this event?" he says.

"I—well, actually, I was trying to get one—" The words sound so wrong, so shady even to my own ears.

He's already shaking his head. "Sorry, ma'am, but we don't allow the sale of tickets here."

I take another step back.

"I'm afraid you're going to have to—"

And another, and my back bumps up against somebody. Warm liquid pours down my butt and the back of my thighs and I jump with a yelp.

"Dammit!" someone says in a brusque, high-pitched voice. A voice that's painfully familiar.

I turn around, an apology already halfway out of my mouth when I see her face and forget what I was about to say. The woman in front of me is busy dabbing at her pantsuit. She still hasn't seen me.

It takes a while for my brain to get a hold of my mouth again, and I say, "Ani?"

She stops dabbing and looks at me over the top of her huge Gucci sunglasses. Her eyes narrow, then widen, and her mouth drops open. "No. Janice?"

"Jane."

"Jane, of course! Oh my god!" She opens her arms wide and covers me in a hug where no part of our bodies touch and she kisses the air near my face. When we part ways, she gives the guard a once-over. "What's going on here?"

"I was just letting her know that she can't be here unless she's got a ticket," he says.

"Oh!" Ani pouts at me. "You don't have a ticket? Then what are you doing here?"

"I—" My insides are writhing, and I'm sure my face is ablaze.

I want to find a hole I can jump into and die, because this is the worst outcome I could have imagined. "It was a mix-up," I say lamely. "My ticket got lost in the mail . . ."

"Oh, you poor thing!" Ani cries. "Not a problem. I have VIP passes, obviously." She rummages in her huge Louis Vuitton bag and fishes out a lanyard with a card that says "VIP" in huge gold letters. She holds it up to the guard, who waves us off with a grunt, then she hands it to me. "Here you go. Nobody wants them anyway. Who wants to come to these things, am I right?"

I'm not sure what to say to that, since I clearly want to come to these things. I make a show of being very focused on putting the lanyard on so that I won't have to answer that weird question. Speaking of weird questions, what the hell is Ani doing here?

Then Ani says something that wrenches me from my thoughts. "Hey, that's a nice necklace you're wearing."

My mind goes blank. Shit. SHIT. I'm wearing the necklace. But of course I am, because I never thought, in a million years, that I would bump into Ani, of all people. I catch hold of the pendant, the infinity symbol made out of diamonds, and slip it under my top. "Thanks, yeah. I just—my husband gave it to me. Last year. For our anniversary."

"Yeah? It's cute. He's got good taste." She smiles at me, and I can't tell if she's seen through the lie. She must. She must recognize the necklace. She—what is she thinking? I can't read her, never could.

"Yeah, anyway, it's so great to bump into you. I mean, of all people!" I say, desperate for a change of subject. We walk through the entrance and are swallowed up by the huge building. Inside is a mad bustle of chaos. There are crowds everywhere, panels and booths with bright colors, and large banners announcing their lead authors and most exciting titles. Definitely not a place for my humble books. "What brings you here?"

Ani pushes her sunglasses up into her hair. Her makeup is flawless—her eyes smoky and lined to a sharp point, her skin aglow from years of a meticulous skin care regimen. She is as beautiful as I remember. She gives me a sidelong glance and smiles, as though she can read my thoughts. "Thalia, of course."

"Thalia?" My voice comes out choked, which makes sense because Ani's answer is basically a gut punch. She's here because of Thalia? She got VIP tickets because of Thalia? But that would mean that they've kept in touch all these years. No, that's not possible, not when Thalia's disappeared from my life so completely. I spent years looking for her and finding only a ghost, and here is Ani, telling me oh so casually that she, a nonwriter, is at SusPens Con because of Thalia?

"Yeah, I basically promised her I'd post about it on my socials or whatever. You know how it is."

No, I do not know how it is.

Ani grabs two tote bags from a booth as we walk by and hands one to me. She must see the confusion on my face because she says, "I'm an influencer. You must've seen my socials? I've got, like, over three hundred K followers on Insta."

I manage a dazed nod, which pleases her. *You fucking self-centered cunt*, I want to spit out. *I'm not impressed by your "influencer" status, I'm fucking shocked because for some reason, Thalia has decided to stay in touch with you, you parasitic brat, and not me.* I could sob with the unfairness of it all. I'd thought that Thalia had chosen me over Ani in Oxford, but maybe I was wrong all along.

"So you've kept in touch with Thalia all this time?" I say. I can barely speak above a whisper.

"Hmm?" Ani is momentarily distracted by someone giving out free books; she takes two copies and hands one to me before dropping her copy in her tote bag. "Thalia? Right, yeah, of course."

Why of course? I don't even realize that I've asked it out loud until Ani gives me a strange look and says, "I thought you knew. Thalia's my sister-in-law."

14

t's interesting, seeing the ways in which certain people react to each other, like acid and alkaline being poured into a single container, seeing which one prevails. When Ani said that her brother was coming for a visit, something in her tone of voice made me glance up and really look at her. I try not to do that; Ani's face isn't good for sanity. Too pretty in a man-made way, everything about her deliberately put together. A manufactured doll wearing a permanent sneer. If I looked at it too long, something inside me would crack and I would swipe a knife at it, just to see if she could even bleed or if there were just ice and silicone underneath.

But her voice is more bitter than usual, a half-hidden quaver underneath it, as she says, "So my brother's coming for a whole month. He'll be staying in London for most of that time, but he's insisted on spending a week in Oxford. Yay me."

"Oooh, we finally get to meet the famous Ivan," Thalia says.

It hurts that Thalia knows his name, whereas I'm only now learning about his very existence.

Ani sniffs. "The famous Ivan. Right."

"Is he coming here just to see you? That's so sweet," Thalia says.

Ani's mouth curls unpleasantly for a second before it goes slack again. "Of course not. He's setting up a new office branch in London; that's why he'll be in England for a whole month. And in the meantime, he'll stay for a while in Oxford to make sure I'm actually going to classes and not fucking up as usual. Perfect Ivan. Did you know our parents have left basically everything to him in their will? They told us both that he's getting the company, like 99 percent of it, while I get Mom's jewelry and Birkins and, oh, a shitty 1 percent. Fucking patriarchal bullshit."

Poor you, I want to say. Having to make do with what is no doubt a fortune in diamonds and emeralds and branded bags. But I remain quiet, relishing the graceless way that Ani is griping. Even saintly Thalia is barely able to keep her annoyance concealed; a corner of Thalia's cheek is twitching a little, which means she's fighting to hold back her words. That's how well I know you, Thalia.

"Well, it's still nice of him to come and spend time with you," Thalia says. Why does she try so hard to be nice to Ani?

"Whatever." Ani slurps her coffee loudly, and that's when I notice that her leg is jiggling relentlessly. And I realize that Ani, take-no-prisoners Ani, foulmouthed Ani, sexpot Ani, is nervous. I would be lying if I said I wasn't enjoying it, just a little. It's nice to see someone else being pushed into a corner for a change. I, for one, can't wait for Ivan to arrive. The past few weeks haven't thawed whatever weird thing is going on between me and Ani, and it would be a nice change to see her undone. To know that I'm not the only one fighting my own inner battle all the damn time.

A week later, Ivan arrives, and it's A Whole Thing. There are rooms available for guests at Downing, but he's booked a room at the Randolph instead, because according to Ani, "Prince Ivan is too good for a school dorm." I think back to how enamored I had been with my dorm room when I first arrived, swooning over the fireplace, and inside, I burn and twitch and wonder if I'll end up hating Ivan even more than his sister does.

Thalia, Ani, and I trudge through the biting English winter in turgid silence. Ani is too nervous and cranky to suffer any conversation, even between just me and Thalia. It's actually nice; Ani's snappish mood turns into an inside joke between me and Thalia. As we walk, Thalia and I sneak glances at each other, eyebrows raised in amusement, and god, I feel like I'm coming out of hibernation, like the sun's finally come out. Here we are for the first time without the fug of Antoine hanging around like a cloud of body odor. I want to shout with laughter and dance in the cold.

The Randolph is one of the oldest buildings in Oxford, and one of the fanciest. It's one of those places where the inside is decked out in old leather and rich mahogany and people automatically speak in hushed tones to show that they're wealthy and powerful enough to never have to raise their voices to get what they want. Ani sighs loudly and makes a beeline for the hotel bar. Thalia and I exchange another look—our fourth!— and follow Ani.

She's waving impatiently at the bartender. "I need wine."

"Of course, ma'am. We have a large selection—"

"Dude. Just give me a bottle of—of—whatever, a Chablis."

134

"Excellent choice. Which vintage would you prefer—"

"Oh my god!" Ani cries, throwing her hands up. "Just. Anything, okay? The most expensive one, whatever!"

Thalia gives the bartender a sheepish smile and opens her mouth, probably to apologize, but just then, a warm male voice behind me says, "Thirsty again, sis? Not much has changed, I see."

Ani's expression freezes, only her eyes showing a flash of horror and mortification for a fleeting second before her face melts into a simpering smile. She turns around and says, "Koko, I'm so happy you're here!" She jumps off the barstool and throws her arms around Ivan.

The lighting in the bar is dim, but even so, I can see at a glance that Ivan is devastatingly handsome. Ani's family's got amazing genes. Tall, broad shouldered, a smile that's almost as distracting as Thalia's. His heavy-lidded eyes somehow work together with his sloped nose and a jaw that would give Antoine's a run for its money, turning his face into one that speaks not just of strength, but of elegance. The kind of face that painters would cut off their ears over. His outfit is casual but obviously tailored to fit every inch of him flawlessly, showing off his swimmer's shoulders and tennis player's arms.

"Koko?" Thalia says, by way of greeting.

Ivan's smile widens—is it possible for men to not smile when they see Thalia?—and he says, "It means 'older brother' in Indonesian. I swear my name isn't actually Koko."

Thalia giggles, and the hairs on the back of my neck prickle. Because I know this laugh of hers. Ani does too. I catch the startled glance from Ani, displeasure writhing behind her eyes, both of us probably thinking the same thing: *You've got Antoine, what are you doing?* On my part, of course, I'm also mentally hissing: *I've been worrying over how to get rid of Antoine, and now*

135

I've got to worry about Ivan too? But isn't that just classic Thalia? She can't help being a flirt, can't help exerting her superpower over everyone. I can't blame her; we all want people to like us, and it's not her fault that she's everybody's type.

Ani detangles her arms from Ivan's neck and pats the seat next to her, away from Thalia. "Sit down, Koko. I've ordered a bottle of wine to celebrate your arrival."

"Come on, let's get a table instead. I don't much feel like sitting at the bar." He doesn't wait for Ani to agree before heading for one of the tables next to the picture windows that look out onto the Ashmolean. Thalia follows, her face glowing in a way that makes my insides churn. I catch Ani's eye—the irony! How have the tables flipped so fast? Only moments ago I was exchanging glances with Thalia, and now . . . well. She breaks the connection first, her upper lip curling like she can't believe she's at such a low point that she's having to exchange looks with me. Not Jane the help! She'd rather suffer alone.

I follow like the faithful dog I've become. If only Mom could see me now. How she'd laugh. *Are you one of them yet, Jane?*

Ani recovers quickly. It's a trick the rich have, I've noticed. They do everything with a certain confidence that the world is a clam that'll pry itself open for them. And it does. Doors are always swept open; people step aside to let them through. A constant assumption that everything they do is right. That they belong. Ani slinks away from the bar and struts to the table her brother has picked out for us and sits down like she meant to relocate to a table all along.

Thalia and Ivan are already deep in conversation when we get there, Thalia laughing, Ivan mock-grimacing.

He glances at us with a rueful smile. "I was just telling Thalia how I fell asleep on the way over here and one of the steward-esses placed a pillow behind my back while I was sleeping. I stayed in the same position for about five hours and now my back is killing me."

"She placed a pillow behind your back? How would that even work? The seats don't even go far enough back for you to lie down on," I say without thinking. In my mind I'm recalling my flight from SFO to Heathrow, me squeezed into a seat so narrow I couldn't bend my arms without touching my neigh-bors, recoiling every time we accidentally touched one another.

There's a pause as they all look at me. A flash of pity in Thalia's eyes, right before Ani bursts out laughing.

"Oh my god, Jane," Ani says. "This is why I love you. You're so simple and sweet." Stupid, she means. I'm so stupid and poor. "In first class, your seat turns into a bed. It lies down flat and then they come and put an actual mattress on top of it."

An airplane seat that turns into an actual bed. I can't even imagine it. *Do you belong now, Jane?* Mom croons.

Ani is still giggling when the wine arrives. We're quiet while the server pours it into four glasses. Ani's shoulders are shaking, Thalia is shooting me pitiful glances, and Ivan is studying me in a half-amused way. I pretend to be very interested in the pour-ing of the wine, watching the pale yellow liquid splash into the glasses, wondering how much this is going to cost me. Mom's right, I realize with a twist of my stomach.

I can't look anyone in the eye as the waiter places a glass in front of each of us.

"Well," Thalia says, her attention refocused on Ivan, "let's drink to Ivan's arrival." She picks up a glass and smiles at him, flashing that naughty little dimple. A full-on assault, the kind of smile that makes even our teachers forget what they're saying mid-sentence.

But Ivan's still studying me, and it takes a full second before he realizes that Thalia is speaking. The spell catches him again; I see his mouth parting as Thalia's smile captures him, and I know he is hers. He picks up his glass and raises it. "Cheers," he murmurs, like he and Thalia are the only two people in the bar, like his sister isn't sitting across from him, glowering.

Ani and I pick up our glasses but don't bother to say "Cheers" before we each take a swig. I can practically sense everyone else's mind whirring, thoughts scuttling around like little insects looking for a weakness before they bite, and I think, for the first time, *I'm not the most dangerous person at this table.*

———

ANI TELLS US SHE CAN'T BEAR TO BE AROUND IVAN ON her own, so we'll have to spend the whole weekend with them. Thalia agrees too readily, and in the morning, she knocks on my door bright and early. Too bright and too early for how much we all had to drink last night (two bottles of Chablis, followed by cognac). But that's Thalia. Nothing touches her, not even alcohol. She's looking even more beautiful today, if that's possible, and if I didn't love her so much, I would hate her, this real-life Barbie who's dimpling her cheek at me, smiling like she can't smell my rank morning breath.

"Go shower," she says, striding into my room. "I'll get an outfit ready for you."

I'm too hungover to argue, not that I would argue at any other time, so I shuffle off to the bathroom, yawning and scratching the back of my neck. The shower does me good, and by the time I get back to my room, Thalia has carried out her threat and has picked out an outfit. A gray sweater (everything I own is black or gray) with my dark blue jeans, fine. What's not fine is that she's also added a bright orange silk scarf with a big "Hermès" emblazoned across it. I looked up Hermès after that first day, and if I remember right, their scarves start at $500. This one's probably above two grand. She sees me staring at it and says, "It'll look nice, don't you think? The color works well with your sweater."

I don't answer, watching her through the mirror as I towel dry my hair. She's up to something, but I don't know what. Then it hits me that she's just trying to be nice, to save me after my faux pas yesterday about the plane ride.

As though reading my mind (again! Maybe she is a mind reader after all), Thalia steps toward me and puts her arm around my shoulders, pulling me close to her. My heart stutters, forgets how to pump blood.

"I'm not like them either, you know," she says softly.

I can't manage more than a single, "What?"

"I'm not rich like they are." She gives a small, rueful laugh. "Well, I doubt any of us here at Pemberton are as rich as Ani and Ivan, but I'm not even, like, middle-class rich."

"But you—but the scarf, your dresses—"

"They're all gifts. I thought you might have guessed by now, I'm good with people. And . . ." She takes a deep breath. "I'm not above using it to get little gifts like these." She catches my gaze with those incredible eyes of hers. They're wide, so wide and so impossibly expressive. And in them, I see a sense of fear and vulnerability that makes me want to hug her. This is the first time that Thalia has admitted something like this to me, something that should make her less than perfect, but somehow ends up making her even more precious. She bites her lower lip, the movement distracting me. "Do you think I'm pathetic? Pretending to be someone I'm not?"

It takes a second to realize this is not a rhetorical question, then I jerk my head side to side. "No, of course not."

She smiles with obvious relief. "Good, because it's been killing me, keeping this to myself. I've just been so embarrassed. I guess I thought that coming here would be my chance to live like they do, you know? My parents—we've always been uh. Really poor," she says with a bitter laugh.

"My mom's a nanny," I blurt out. I don't know why I reveal that now, and why it feels like such a huge burden has come off my shoulders. So what if my mom's a nanny?

"My mom's a dog walker," Thalia says.

We look at each other for a beat, then we both burst out laughing.

"No, seriously," she says, "that's what my mom does. She walks rich people's dogs!" And we laugh some more, because it's either that or cry.

"Well, she walked rich people's dogs," Thalia says, suddenly serious. I struggle to swallow my laughter, because now Thalia looks like she's about to cry. "She can't really walk anymore. She got sick. Bone cancer. And she doesn't have health care, so we're pretty much fucked. And I kind of was . . . hoping . . ."

By now, if she asked me to help her rob the HSBC on High Street, I would do it. I would do anything for this girl.

"Well, I was kind of hoping that Ani would help out." She grimaces and gnaws on her lower lip. "Oh god, that sounded horrible, didn't it? I just heard myself say those words, and my god, I sound like such a shit—"

"You don't," I say quickly. Because of course Ani should help out. Ani the billionaire heiress who's only here to fuck around,

Ani who makes us follow her to Harrods and watch as she drops fifty grand on a mink shawl at Ferragamo, a shawl that I have since seen her drop on a sticky dance floor as she sways drunkenly in a nightclub. "Dammit!" she'd screamed, then tossed the shawl aside, forgotten. She'd staggered back to the dorms sans shawl. I think of how my mom would save her used tea bags, cut them and dry the soggy leaves before boiling them again so she didn't have to spend ninety-six cents on a new box of shitty tea. Ani is the right kind of Asian. The Crazy Rich kind. The kind that everyone loves. The kind I would kill to be. The kind that's meant to save Thalia. "I mean, it's literally nothing to her. And it would be saving your mom's life. She'd want to do that; I'm sure she would."

"I can't just ask her outright," Thalia says. "She'd think I was just being friends with her for her money. She's been telling me how growing up, she was always surrounded by these fake friends who were only with her because they expected something— money, fame, whatever."

I resist telling Thalia that Ani has nobody else because she is so intensely unlikable; that her money and status are the only things she has to offer. "This is different though; it's your mom." And your mom isn't like my mom. Your mom is worth saving.

"I've been hinting to her. The past few weeks. That's why I've been spending so much time with her. God," she sighs, her face scrunching up with shame. "Sorry, I didn't mean to dump all this on you, Jane. I know I sound horrible, but I've been getting desperate. Ani's not really taking any of my hints . . ."

"Of course she isn't," I mutter. "Ani's too self-centered."

Thalia gives me a sad smile. "Yeah, I guess so. Anyway, this isn't your or Ani's problem. It's just—well. This will probably be my first and last term here."

A wave of sickness washes over me. "What?"

"My aunt called me yesterday. We're in massive debt and she's right, I shouldn't be wasting money by attending such a fancy master's program. I've been such a selfish idiot, god." She rubs her face with her hands. "I'll probably go back once the term ends and get a job. Pay the—"

"You can't!" The words rip themselves from deep in my belly, burning as they wrench out of my mouth.

Thalia stares at me, wide-eyed.

"I—no. You can't just leave." My face is made of flames. Somehow, I manage to stop myself from grabbing her. From shaking her, or squeezing her, or doing something, anything, that would stop her from getting away from me. I imagine Thalia as a little bird; I would catch her and put her in a gilded cage, keep her safe from everything. I look around my room, desperately trying to find something—some way, of keeping her here. She's saying something, but I can't hear the words, the blood is roaring in my ears, and I have to keep her here, I can't lose her. I grab hold of something—anything—and it turns out to be the snow globe I'd bought at the Covered Market. I see myself swinging it, the snow swirling inside the globe, catching the light as I bring it down in a wide arc onto her lovely skull—

The idea strikes me just in time, hurtling out of me like a maddened horse. "Ivan!"

Thalia's still staring, and now I see that her startled gaze is on the snow globe in my hand. The walls of my room collapse onto me. "Uh. This is—I like to hold it when I need to think." I move it from one hand to another casually. Or what I estimate to be "casually," at least. It feels incriminating in my hands. I'm lobbing a live grenade to and fro, and I can't tell if Thalia's buying it, or if she just saw a glimpse of the madness that skulks inside me.

She recovers her smile. "I do that, too, when I'm stressed. I like to have something for my hands to do. Anyway, what about Ivan?"

Right. Yes. "Well, he's rich, right? 'Cause he's Ani's brother." Stating the obvious. *Get to the point, Jane.* "And he seems nice . . . ish? I don't know, he seems okay. And he . . ." God, the words refuse to come out now, lodging in my throat, digging sharp little claws in and clinging tight. I cough them out. "I think he likes you."

I didn't think Thalia's eyes could get any wider, but they do, and it's almost too much. I can't keep looking at that face of hers, as trusting as a child, because otherwise I'll cave and tell her to forget it. But I don't want to lose her, I can't imagine going through the rest of the program without Thalia here, and if it means she has to belong to someone else, then so be it.

"He definitely likes you," I continue. "The way he looked at you . . ." My skin feels slimy and I want to rip it off. "You could ask him."

Thalia shakes her head. "Oh god, I couldn't. I can't ask some guy I just met—"

"You like him too." I wonder if that sounded as petulant as it did in my head. If it gave my own feelings away.

But Thalia doesn't seem to notice. Her cheeks turn rosy, from peaches and cream to strawberries and cream, and god, she is made to be devoured. "Was it that obvious?"

I shrug. It's obvious if you're watching for it. If you're ultra-sensitive to it because you're obsessed with the person in front of you.

"I feel terrible. Especially since Antoine—"

I can't help snorting out loud. Antoine. Who cares about fucking Antoine? "He'll live. He's a big boy. And this is more important. Look, if it makes you feel better, you could even ask Ivan for a loan or something."

Am I solving it? Am I actually taking a huge problem from Thalia's life and offering up an actual solution?

"I think I need to get to know him better first. I just don't feel comfortable asking him for help like that." She twirls a lock of hair, and I'm distracted, for a moment, by the way it catches the light and turns almost translucent. Everything about this girl is ethereal.

"Of course you don't. Because you're a decent person." You're the best person. "How about this: this weekend, when we spend time with Ivan and Ani, I'll distract Ani so you can have some private time with Ivan? You'll have plenty of time to chat—" My insides are shriveling up as I say this, twisting and shrieking and dying. "—and hopefully get close enough to him to ask for help."

The look on her face makes my sacrifice almost worth it. It's an expression of gratefulness, mixed with disbelief. "Really? You'd do that for me?"

I would kill for you, Thalia. I shrug. "It's not a big deal. I like Ani." Oh, how the world laughs at this obvious lie.

But Thalia is without guile. She nods slowly. "I guess that could work. But Jane, I feel so shitty about doing this. I don't know—"

"You have to. For your mom." Fuck her mom. *For my sake, Thalia. Do it for us.*

Her furrowed brow clears and she closes her eyes for a moment. When she opens them, her face turns, becomes determined. "You're right. I have to do it. It means nothing to them, right?"

"Yeah. It's the equivalent of a day's shopping spree to them."

She nods. "Okay. God, I can't believe I—we're doing this. Thank you." She grasps my hands, her eyes shining with tears, and I swear I've just died. "You're the only real friend I have, Jane."

15

The problem with trying to give Thalia and Ivan some privacy is—well, there's more than one problem. There's Ani, first and foremost. She's always been snarky, but now that Ivan's around, she becomes so abrasive that a few times I imagine shoving her off a tall building, or stabbing her with my fork, or some other thing that would shut her up. So I might be a bit grumpy. Just a tad. I think that's understandable, given I'm basically pimping away the girl I am obsessed with. *It's so that I won't lose her,* I remind myself. But knowing something in theory doesn't really make that thing any easier to swallow.

We start the weekend off with a centuries-old Oxford tradition—punting. Punting consists of hiring a tiny boat and using a long stick to push your way down the River Thames. It sounds a lot more romantic than what it actually is, which is a pain in the ass. And arms. And legs. Because using a heavy wooden stick to shove your boat downstream is really freaking tiring.

Thalia has prepared a picnic basket, complete with finger sandwiches and warm bagels and champagne, but I don't get to enjoy it because I insist on doing the punting so that Thalia and Ivan can have some privacy to chat with each other while Ani guzzles the champagne and kills whatever romantic buzz there is between Thalia and Ivan. I don't know what circle of hell I'm in to have to watch Thalia turn on her charms for Ivan while I grasp this heavy stick and resist bringing it down on both Ani's and Ivan's heads.

"Ani doesn't like to talk about Jakarta," Thalia says. "Tell me more about the place."

Smart. Ani's always dismissing Jakarta—come to think of it, she's always dismissing every place; no city is big enough or fancy enough for her. Urging Ivan to talk about Jakarta is a sure-fire way of getting Ani to switch off. Sure enough, I spot Ani's eyes rolling behind her huge sunglasses before she turns away to watch the scenery as we float downriver.

"It's great, actually," Ivan says. "It's a huge metropolis with, like, over twenty million people."

"Wow, big city." Just like her big, big eyes. In the early Oxford morning light, they turn from brown to gold, and if I were Ivan I would propose to her right now. "The biggest city I've been to was LA."

Ivan laughs. "LA doesn't feel much like a city; it's too spread out. I love LA though; it has its own charms. Is that where you're from?"

"No, I'm from Nevada. Just outside of Vegas."

"I hate Vegas. What a fuck you to mother nature," Ani says

between gulps of champagne. "Nobody should be living in the desert."

Ivan and Thalia glance at her. Thalia gives an uneasy smile. "Yeah, I guess. The Strip's kind of a weird place if you live there. I can probably count on one hand the number of times I've actually been to the Strip."

"I can see that. It's like how my friends in the Bay Area never ever go to Fisherman's Wharf," Ivan says, and just like that, Ani's caustic remark is left behind, a little verbal roadkill that they can pave over and ignore. "Anyway, I spend a lot of my time traveling. Maybe about half of my year is spent outside of Indonesia, and I swear every time I come back to Jakarta, there's a new skyscraper being built."

"Wow, sounds amazing."

Sounds like a nightmare to me, the landscape changing faster than I can adapt. Just like what's going on now. Part of me is still dazed, still wondering how the hell I ended up here, pushing this boat along. I'm tired, my shoulders ache, my belly is filled with bitterness, and I've just about had enough of everyone. I wonder if I can tip the boat over and send us all plunging into the Thames, just end it all already.

"Where do you usually travel to?" Thalia says, and I hate this. I hate her and I hate him and I hate Ani and I hate Oxford for bringing me and Thalia together and the world for keeping us apart.

"We do a lot of business with Japanese corporations, so I travel to Tokyo quite a lot, and we also have clients in Hong Kong, Singapore, Dubai, London, New York . . . all the big cities."

You know what really sucks about Ivan? It's the fact that even though he's clearly bragging, it doesn't come off as bragging. He's so used to this lifestyle that it's become natural to talk about it like it's no big deal. He lists off countries I would never be able to afford to visit like they all belong to him, like the world is truly an oyster that he holds in his manicured hand. I can't help but snort out loud at this. They all glance up at me, and my heart stops beating.

"Sorry," I stammer. "I think I'm getting tired pushing the boat."

Ivan straightens up. "I'll have a go."

"Hah!" Ani snorts, jumping up. We all cry out as the boat sways dangerously.

"Oops, sorry about that," Ani laughs, not sounding at all sorry. She steps over the seats toward the end of the boat, where I'm perched. "C'mere, give me that paddle thingy. You can't do it, Koko, on account of your heart."

I glance at Ivan and he shrugs. "I'm fine."

"Like hell you are," Ani says.

She's tipsy, well on her way to being drunk, and it's not even noon yet. I look down at her and the plan forms, quick and easy, so obvious that I wonder why it didn't hit me sooner. I should get Ani drunk. So drunk that I have to escort her back to Downing, leaving Thalia and Ivan alone. Yay me, world's number one wingwoman.

I hand her the oar and sit down. Thalia meets my eye and gives me a quick smile, and I live for these moments, these little shared sparks between us that tell me our minds are in sync.

"Thanks for manning the oar like a champ, Jane," Ivan says, pouring champagne into a new glass and handing it to me. Our fingers brush as I take it and my stomach lurches. Revulsion and a guilty little coil of attraction. He holds my eye a second too long. I don't quite understand what the hell's going on. Why he would even notice my existence when Thalia is right there. I am a star and Thalia is the sun; while she's around, I am invisible.

A guilty flush taints my cheeks, and I break eye contact, muttering my thanks for the champagne. I swig the whole thing down. It's too much of a stressful situation for me to maintain, and I can't even bear to look at Thalia, too scared to see if she's noticed that strange moment between me and Ivan. I hold my glass out for a refill and Ivan obliges, then I hand it over to Ani, who's only half-heartedly pushing the stick in and out of the water.

"Thanks, this is sooo heavy," she moans, taking the champagne flute from me and taking a long swallow. "This is a lot less fun than it looks."

Touché.

She empties the glass and practically tosses it back to me. Thalia must realize what I'm up to, because she points to something in the distance and resumes chatting with Ivan. With Ivan distracted, I quickly refill the glass myself and pass it to Ani.

"Ugh, you are a lifesaver," she says. The words come out sloppy, her lipsticked mouth slightly slack. She sways a little and I jump to my feet. I don't need Ani falling into the river and causing a scene, which would surely ruin the rest of the day for Thalia and Ivan.

"Come here. I'll take that," I say, grabbing the stick and helping Ani to one of the seats on the boat. "I think maybe it's best if we return the boat now."

Thalia gives me a grateful smile, and I begin the long, arduous task of steering us back to the nearest docking bay, wondering again why I'm doing what the hell I'm doing.

———

I'M SURPRISED BY HOW WEIRD IT FEELS TO HAVE MY FEET planted back on solid ground. It's disorientating; I feel like I'm still swaying. So it's no surprise when, five seconds after we hop off the boat and onto dry land, Ani leans over to one side and vomits. Oh, Ani, so predictable.

Ivan utters a sigh. An entire history conveyed with just one breath. Impatience and anger coloring his perfect face for just a fleeting moment, the flawless facade cracking. I wonder how many years of Ani he's had to put up with, the spoiled, resentful little sister who hates that he was the one born with a cock—the key to the Pranajayas' empire. For a second, I think of a literal penis-shaped key and I have to bite down on my lip to keep from laughing. Ivan walks over toward Ani, but I'm faster because I've been waiting for this (well, minus the vomit) and already I'm there, patting Ani's shoulder and gathering her hair behind her neck.

"Let me," Ivan says, but I step between him and Ani.

"It's okay," I say. It's not okay. Take care of your goddamned sister. Take her back to Jakarta and lock her away forever. "I don't mind. I'm actually not feeling too great myself, so why don't you let me take Ani back to our dorm and we can have a bit of a rest while Thalia shows you around the city?"

He's taken aback by this. I guess he's not used to other people stepping up and offering to take care of his messy little sister. Thalia steps up beside him, her eyes shining with hope. Ivan frowns. "I don't think—"

"No, really. I mean, how often do you get to come to Oxford, right?" I say quickly. "It's one of the most beautiful cities in the world, and you're only here for a week before you go back to London. It would be such a shame to miss out on everything."

"Let me at least call you two a cab." Such a gentleman. A gentleman who can't wait to be rid of us. My heart is being ripped into two halves—one side singing happily at succeeding in my quest; the other weeping, tearing things apart. I am not used to being generous, to doing things for the sole benefit of another person. I do not like this feeling, but I would do it again and again for Thalia. Thalia whose face is bright as the sun, who is staring at me like I've just saved her puppy—no, better, I've saved her mother. She mouths a thank-you as Ivan flags down a cab and gives the driver a twenty-pound note, way too much for the two-minute drive to Pemberton. We help Ani inside the cab (Ani: "I don't need help. Oh my god, you guys, stop that—stop, ow!"). I slide in after her and gaze longingly out the window. The last thing I see is Thalia slipping her hand through the crook of Ivan's arm before the cab turns a corner and they disappear from my sight.

———

GUESS WHAT'S WORSE THAN LEAVING THALIA WITH AN unbelievably beautiful man who also happens to be richer than god? Well, never mind. Nothing's actually worse than that. But what makes it even worse is leaving Thalia for said beautiful man to take care of his very drunk, very angry sister.

I don't understand why Ani's so angry all the time. If I had her looks and all the money in the world, I would—well, I don't know what I would do; it's not something I've daydreamed about, but I imagine I would at least not be this bitter.

"She knows, you know," Ani slurs.

I turn my face from the window and look at her. I'm not going to take the bait. And with Ani, everything is a bait. She doesn't ever say anything without having first calculated how much it would prick at your skin. She likes to push people to the point where they're uncomfortable enough to almost tip over into anger, before she laughs and tells them she's just kidding.

That's the kind of asshole she is. The world is her playground and the people in it are her toys.

"She knows you looove her."

It feels like I've been punched. The taxi driver glances at me through the rearview mirror, but I pretend not to notice. I study my hands instead.

"God, Jane, you're so fucking obsessed with her. It's sad. Why is everyone so in love with her, anyway? She's just a cute, racially ambiguous chick; there's like about a dozen of her in every Whole Foods in New York."

"You're drunk," I snap. And now I've lost, because now she knows she's managed to get under my skin.

"I see what you two are trying to do."

The taxi driver isn't even bothering to pretend that he's not listening. He's turning his head to look at Ani once every few seconds. *You should pay attention to the road*, I want to say, but my words have dried up.

"I know you're trying to get her some alone time with Ivan." She laughs, but it ends in a sigh. "I've seen it all; bitches are always using me to get to my brother. Eeevvverybody wants a piece of Ivan." The cab turns a corner and her head lolls to one side, and I wonder how much force it would take to snap her neck. Not very much at all, I don't think, especially if I use the momentum of the moving car in my favor. Wishful thinking, of course.

By the time we get to Pemberton, I'm half toying with the idea of just leaving her in the car, but in the end, I grab her arm and yank her out, not bothering to be gentle. Outside of the cab, she teeters on her stupidly high heels and I have to swing her arm over my shoulders and practically carry her into the college.

"Why're you Thalia's lapdog, Janey? I can tell you like Ivan too. Why wouldn't you try your luck at him?" She snickers at this, and I know, I'm not delusional enough to think that me going after Ivan isn't amusing in a very pathetic way. We lumber up the stairs, and I think about how it would be so easy to get to the very top and then give her a little push. How very much like the universe, to make Ani so delectably killable. But if I were to take that prompt, everything would end. Ivan would be heartbroken—or at the very least he'd be inconvenienced, and inconvenienced people aren't the most giving. Thalia wouldn't be able to afford to continue her studies, and I'd lose her.

So I keep going. Keep on keeping on, as they say. I let her breathe her rancid alcohol fumes down my neck and I look at the myriad ways that Ani could die and I ignore each and every one of them. Love moves us to do great things, they say, and they're right.

Ani lives one floor above us. When we get to her door, I have to go through her purse to find her key, and Jesus, how many freaking pills does this girl have? There are at least three differ- ent bottles in her Prada handbag, but I don't know what they are as the labels are in Indonesian.

"Diet pills," she says, watching me under half-closed eyes.

"Why?" I can't help blurting out. I've just helped her up three flights of stairs and she weighs practically nothing, her bones sticking out under my hands, brittle bird bones.

"How do you think I manage to look like this? Give me that," she says, snatching her purse back and fishing inside it. She lo- cates her key and stabs it at the door, missing the lock until I grab her hand and put the key in myself.

Her room looks like a fashion show has exploded in it. Mounds of clothes, shoes, and bags are strewn on every available surface. The window is open, which is good because it smells slightly rank in here, a stench of old smoke that's going to cling to my skin even after I leave.

"You're not supposed to smoke in your room," I say.

Ani snorts. "So they'll make me pay a fine, whatever." She flops onto her bed and moans. "Ugh, my mouth tastes disgusting. Isn't that weird? Tasting your own mouth?" She laughs. "What do you think Thalia's doing with my brother right now? You think they're fucking? I bet they are. I bet she's dragged him all the way back to his hotel and they're smashing right now."

"I'm gonna go." But I don't go. I'm too busy watching Ani and daydreaming about smothering her with her pillow or maybe one of her fancy, overpriced outfits.

"Thalia's not the angel everyone makes her out to be. Why are you so obsessed with her? She's not even a natural blonde. You haven't seen what she's like when it's just her and me. That girl is trouuuble."

I have to ask, because it's about Thalia and I can't not ask when it's about Thalia. "How is she trouble?"

"She is a sluuut."

I suppose I did ask. I don't know why I did; it's not like I was ever going to get any reliable information from this drunk bitch. "Okay, out of the two of you, she's not the one who's been sleeping around with different guys." I hate how petty I sound, how high school. But this is the effect that Ani has on me. She drags me down to her level and I'm left feeling dirty.

She laughs, her eyes closed so I can see the way her eyeshadow has smudged across her lids. "They're all guys she's sampled herself, before she gives them to me. 'He's a yummy one,' she'll say. Wink-wink."

Wow. Ani's even worse than I thought, and that's saying something. But what I can't figure out is why she's saying these things. Because she's drunk? Or because she wants to hurt me?

"Why are you telling me this?"

But she's already out, snoring softly as she finally falls into a drunken sleep. I stand there, watching. Why, god, why must you make it so easy to kill her? I look around her room. There are at least six different handbags in here, and two clutches, and I have no idea how many red-soled shoes, strewn about like carcasses. If I were to swipe a pair of her Louboutins, she wouldn't even notice. Then I see, on the mantelpiece above her fireplace, a careless tangle of jewelry. My cheeks grow hot, my heart thumping a manic rhythm. Pearls and diamonds and gold all twined like rat tails. I take a step toward the fireplace and glance at Ani. Still asleep. Another step, and another.

Close up, the pile is even more impressive—the pearls are perfect, smooth spheres and the stones are bigger than I thought, and there must be at least thirty different pieces here. I glance at Ani again. She won't miss one. Just one. I deserve it for putting up with her throughout the past few weeks, and for letting her live now. I try to pick out a ring lined with little diamonds like a sugar crust and a square diamond in the middle as big as my fingernail, but it's too tangled up with a necklace that has an infinity symbol made out of diamonds. Whatever, she has so many pieces of jewelry here she won't miss these. I take another quick look at her before slipping the ring and the necklace into my pocket and leaving the room, quiet as a ghost.

16

halia's my sister-in-law. Sister-in-law.

The words echo in the hollow recesses of my heart, bouncing off the walls and resounding over and over and over again, until I want to cover my ears and shriek just to drown them out. Sister-in-law? Thalia is married?

But even in the storm of pain raging inside me, I realize that of course she is. Why wouldn't she be? We're in our thirties. I'm married. Of course Thalia is married too. She's never had a shortage of men and women going after her.

But it's not just the fact that she's married, a small voice whines. It's the fact that she's married to Ivan. It's been a while since I thought of Ivan, even though he was such a pivotal part of our Oxford experience. Now his face floats back to the forefront of my memories. His flawless love-interest-in-a-rom-com face. They made a stunning couple then. I'm sure they make a stunning couple now. I can't stand it.

"Yeah, she and Ivan pretty much tied the knot as soon as she left Oxford," Ani says, each word a knife wound, twisting and turning in my guts. I need her to stop fucking talking already.

I can't bear it; I can't stand here and listen to this anymore. I raise my hands and shove Ani aside. She squawks and stumbles back, almost falls over, but some passerby manages to catch her just in time. "Whoa," he calls out, unnecessarily loudly.

"Sorry," I mumble. "Sorry, sorry." I'm already walking away, ducking into the crowd, ignoring the noise behind me. I can hear snatches of Ani's voice—"What the hell is her problem?"

My problem, Ani, is that Thalia was mine. All mine, before you and your brother came along and ripped her away from me. And why did she cut herself off from me but not from them? Did she only cut herself off from me? Does she still keep in touch with everybody from Oxford? I can barely remember the names of anyone else at Pemberton. Pam, or Pat, or whatever the fuck. Does Thalia keep in touch with her too? Was I the only one who was excommunicated?

The thought is too painful to bear. Already tears are burning in my eyes and I have to blink them away rapidly to stop them from falling. All this time I thought . . .

Never mind what I thought, because I've clearly been wrong about everything.

I'm stumbling blindly through the crowd, barely seeing or hearing anything. There's a cry or two as I shove people away, but I don't stop. I don't care, I can't be here, and where's the freaking exit anyway?

Then I hear it. The voice that's been haunting me all these years. It skips my ears and goes straight into the center of my nervous system, lighting up all of my synapses. My entire body reacts to it. I stop mid-stride, everything inside me pricked to attention.

Thalia.

I turn slowly, and there she is, sitting behind a desk, speaking into a microphone. A large crowd is gathered around her, a sea of humans standing between the two of us. She's so far away from me, achingly far. So many bodies in between ours. And as I stare, she continues talking: "—my first ever panel, oh my gosh. It's so wonderful to be here."

Back in Oxford, Thalia had this quality that made her, even when addressing a crowd of people, seem like she was speaking directly to you. It's still present now, everyone in the crowd staring at her with rapt attention. And how can they not? She is incandescent. Over the past nine years, her beauty has sharpened into something breathtaking, the kind that makes people do a double take to make sure she's real. It's the kind of beauty that actresses pay good money for, the kind of beauty that requires a busy mind, a mind that holds a myriad of secrets.

"Tell us about *A Most Pleasant Death*," says another woman who is sitting next to her, probably the moderator. "What's the story behind the story?"

Thalia smiles. "Well, *A Most Pleasant Death* is about an all-consuming, sort of toxic friendship between two women, and what inspired me was my own experience with various female friends. I have always found female friendship fascinating, the way that from a very young age, girls are encouraged to see one another as competition just because of how sexist many societies are, and therefore there's only ever room for one girl at the top. In school, I have always kind of felt like the other girls can't help but compete with one another: even though they may be best friends, they're also rivals. And so it becomes this extremely complicated relationship that's nurturing and yet also harmful. I wanted to show how this kind of friendship can spiral into a darker state, until it spins out of control and hurts those around it."

The moderator nods like she understands what Thalia was just talking about, but she doesn't understand. No one else understands, because what Thalia just said? That was all meant for me. Heat rises from the base of my chest. She wrote a whole book about our friendship. And that's what tips me over the edge. Because I don't understand how she could have written this, a whole book that was obviously meant for me, and yet she never once reached out to me over the years.

Before I know it, I'm wading through the crowd of listeners and calling out, "I have a question!"

Heads are turning in my direction. The moderator frowns, pausing mid-sentence, and looks at the crowd. "Wow, we have some enthusiastic listeners here," she says with a forced laugh. "We'll have a Q andA session in about half an hour, so—"

I shout the words out; I can't bear it any longer. "Why did you never come back to Oxford after your first term there?"

Silence falls, suffocating and thick. I know it's impossible, but it feels as though the entire convention center is suddenly quiet, every ear inside the building listening.

And finally, Thalia sees me. Her eyes widen, her mouth— those rose-pink lips—parts slightly. For a second, something passes across her face—fear? Horror? It can't be. She's just surprised, that's all.

"Jane!" she says, and my name, amplified by her microphone, reverberates through flesh and bone and breathes life back into my whole body. Her expression is pure shock, and she turns to the moderator and mutters something.

The moderator nods and looks at me sternly. "We'll have a

Q and A session after this talk. Let's get back to the program for now."

I lower my head and move to the edge of the crowd, my face in flames. Shit, what the hell is wrong with me? Why did I just blurt that out? Fortunately, the moderator moves the talk along and soon I am forgotten once more, blending into the crowd as we all fall under Thalia's spell. She got lucky with *A Most Pleasant Death*, she says, because so much in publishing depends on timing and luck. So humble, as always. Minimizing her own talent. I wish I could tell her to stop, to own that she deserves this meteoric success. It's a different form of torture to be stuck here among the audience, as though I'm like any of these people, a stranger to Thalia.

Nothing she says is particularly enlightening; they're all responses I've heard from other authors before, but somehow when Thalia says them, they become different, exotic, exciting. The Thalia effect.

Movement from the edge of the stage catches my eye, and I turn to see Ani aiming a serious-looking camera at Thalia. My gut sours. Shit, she's going to tell Thalia about how I went completely berserk before running away. Ani seems completely absorbed in taking photos. When she's done with the big camera, she pulls out her iPhone and takes more photos using that, before turning the phone around and posing for a few selfies with Thalia in the background. She then aims the phone at the crowd. I duck my head, but I'm not fast enough. She frowns when she sees me and rolls her eyes.

My heart rate slows to a manageable pace. She just thinks what she's always thought of me: a weirdo, just some loser that Thalia took pity on. Nothing worth remembering. I can deal with that. I'm not here to impress Ani.

An eternity passes before the panel is finally done. With superhuman effort, I manage to stop myself from blurting out more awkward questions during the Q and A, gritting my teeth instead while listening to mundane questions like: "How long did it take you to write this book?"

"Come on," I whisper under my breath, willing the whole thing to end already. Then we're asked to stand in a single file to get an autograph. An autograph from my estranged best friend. The line that forms is impossibly long. Of course everyone wants to have a piece of her. I want to scream at them to get away, to let me have this time with her. But I am patient. I have been waiting years for this moment. I can afford to wait a few more minutes.

As it turns out, I end up waiting a whole hour. An hour spent on the sidelines, shifting from one foot to the other, biting my nails until they are ragged and bleeding. I squeeze my thumb and watch the blood well up into a fat droplet before I put it to my mouth and lick it off. The pain keeps me present, reminds me I'm not dreaming, that Thalia really is just a few feet away; after all these years, here she is in the flesh.

Then the signing is done and Thalia is waving to people and waving away her agent/editor/publicist and heading toward me. I turn into a statue. I can't move as she closes the distance between us, the expression on her face unreadable—is that a smile or a frown or something between the two? And now she's in front of me and I must be dreaming because she is here and she's so perfect I could cry. The scent of her, that familiar smell, takes me right back to Oxford. The nose is the only part of our body that can time travel, and I'm whisked back nine years to when I first landed in England, among the damp and the bus exhaust, finding Thalia for the first time. Her nearness pulling me to the surface just as it's doing now, yanking me up and up until I break through, as though the past few years I've been floating under-water, everything around me muted. Now, suddenly, everything is loud and clear, and all the colors are bursting with vibrancy.

"Jane," she murmurs, and I'm not sure who made the first move, but we're hugging now, and she feels amazing in my arms, so warm and real and—oh god—I can feel those delicate bird bones of hers and my throat thickens with my need for her. Thank god my weird outburst earlier hasn't scared her off. "Let's talk over coffee," she says, pulling back and smiling at me.

Someone clears her throat. Ani. I have to resist from lunging at her. She stands next to us with an are-you-kidding expression. "Um, not to interrupt the moment—"

She very definitely meant to interrupt the moment.

"But we've got to go, babe. You've got a photo shoot with *Elle*, remember?"

Thalia groans. "That goddamned photo shoot."

"Excuse you, 'that goddamned photo shoot' took me months to arrange, so you need to move your ass." Ani turns her gaze at me and regards me the way one would a particularly revolting insect. "How are we doing, Janet? Are you recovering well after your little"—she waves vaguely at me—"meltdown earlier? I'm fine, even though that was a really hard shove back there."

I can barely bring myself to reply, her tone of voice is so caustic. Still, I only have myself to blame. She's right; I did phys-ically push her away. I should be grateful that she's not pressing charges against me or making an even bigger deal out of it some-how. For Ani, this reaction is surprisingly understated. Pretty sure that Oxford Ani would have reported me to somebody, and the realization that present-day Ani isn't doing that makes me swoon with relief. "I'm sorry," I say, and I actually do mean it. "I don't know what happened back there. I, uh—I'm not great with crowds."

Ani rolls her eyes. "Duh." But when she next looks at me, I'm pretty sure she's thawed a little bit. She seems less like she's about to bite my head off. She turns to Thalia. "Let's go."

The look on Thalia's face is yearning, I'm sure of it. The way her eyes widen and her mouth trembles. I know it because it's mirrored in my soul. "Jane," she says again, more of a whisper than anything. "Let's have dinner. Yes? Skye Bar on East 75th at eight."

I barely have time to nod before Ani and her agent/editor/publicist descend upon her and whisk her away, leaving me alone, the only person standing still in the throng of her fans. But for the first time in nine years, I am okay. I am alive. I have a dinner date with Thalia.

17

Thalia doesn't waste any time. In the evening, she sends me a text: **Thank uuu!**

I look at those two words for a long time, tracing them with my index and middle fingers. I want to laugh and cry at the same time. Yay, my plan worked. Boo, my plan worked. I send her a thumbs-up emoji and it gets read, but she doesn't send anything back and my heart rips open a little bit more. I put on Ani's ring and look at it this way and that, admiring the way it catches the light before I put it in my underwear drawer and leave the room to go for dinner.

The rest of the night, I pace in my room. At the slightest noise, I jerk up and rush to my door. Is it Thalia?

It's not Thalia. It's never Thalia.

She spends the night with Ivan, and it's good, it's what we wanted. It's just how we planned it. But I can't help hating my-self just a little bit more. I did this. I whored her out. I'm her pimp. The thought pushes a bitter laugh out of me and then the laugh turns into a sob and I bury my face in my hands, because I can't stop imagining Thalia in bed with Ivan, slick bodies glinting in the soft glow of lights as he takes her from various positions. Their beautiful faces purring with pleasure as they fuck. Then my brain trots out images of Thalia with other men, just as Ani described, and god, I hate Ani, I really do, and I should've killed her. With any luck, she'll choke on her own vomit. I didn't see her at the dining hall, so maybe that happened. One can hope.

I'm awakened the next morning by a loud, insistent knocking. I stumble out of bed, open the door, and it's Thalia. She's radiant. More so than usual, which I never thought possible.

"Oh my god, Jane," she says, rushing inside and throwing my curtains open.

I squint at the sudden flood of sunlight.

"He's amazing—oh my god, he's just—ahh!" she squeals and does a little hop. An actual little hop, like she's a kid who was just told she's going to Disneyland.

"Oh?" I perch on the side of my bed and rub my eyes. They're still puffy from all the crying I did yesterday. Idiot. Stupid fucking idiot.

"I can't thank you enough. I can't believe you did that. After you and Ani left, I took Ivan around the city. We went to a couple of colleges—New College, Exeter—then we went to Blackwell's, and the whole time we were talking so easily with each other like we've been friends forever. And then before we knew it, it was almost dinnertime. He tried calling Ani, but I guess she was still zonked out, so then we ended up having dinner with each other and oh my god, the dinnertime conversation—Jane, I swear it was like we were just in sync and it was like I was having a mind orgasm."

I look down when she says the O word. The thought of Thalia having orgasms of any kind with Ivan is like a drill through my head.

"He's so brilliant, oh man. He knows everything about everything. We talked about politics, economics, philosophy, everything! We were so in sync—oh, I said that already."

"Yeah," I mumble.

"And he ordered this vintage bottle of wine—oh my god, I swear it was the best thing that I ever drank. After dinner, we were so full, we decided to have a walk, and our hands just kind of found each other's and it was the most natural thing in the world. We were walking past the Radcliffe Camera when he suddenly stopped and tugged on my hand and kissed me, and oh," she sighs, fake-swooning and flopping onto my sofa with a smile. "It was some kiss. My legs actually became all weak. Have you ever had that reaction from a kiss?"

I shake my head, but already she's talking again.

"Then we kind of got carried away and hurried back to his hotel and . . ." She grins and wiggles her eyebrows at me. I feel sick. "I think he made me come like four times. I can barely walk this morning, holy shit."

Stop talking, stop talking! I want to scream. I want to clutch at my head and shriek until the whole world falls apart. Instead, I yank at my wristband and let it snap back, hard.

I don't understand this feeling myself. I don't understand any of my obsession with Thalia. My feelings for her aren't actually sexual, I don't think. I don't know. I love her body, but I don't have fantasies of having sex with her. It's just—I love the vulnerability of it, the sharp edges of it, the way that it's like priceless art. Yes, that's it. I want to just gaze at Thalia the way one admires pieces at a museum. And the thought of anyone having her, defiling that body of hers, is revolting.

Finally, Thalia notices something's off. "Are you okay? What's wrong?"

I shake my head. "It's fine." It's not fine. "So when are you going to ask him for help?"

The excitement leaks from her face. "I don't know. I kind of don't want to now. I just—it feels so slimy doing that, and what we had yesterday, that was real, and I don't want to ruin it."

I stare at her. At her pale, slim neck. I imagine putting my hands around it. "But your mom," I say dumbly.

"I know," she sighs. "I'll tell him about her soon. I just—not yet. It's too soon."

Great. I guess I just have to grin and bear it as she continues seducing him for the rest of his stay here. What could possibly go wrong?

———

IF I THOUGHT THAT ANTOINE WAS BAD, IVAN IS WORSE. SO much worse. Because Antoine is your stereotypical French dudebro—oozing sex appeal and romantic quotes, which is bad, but reeks of short-term fling. Burns hot and fast before dying out. She breaks up with him without any preamble, a task on her to-do list crossed off just like that.

I wonder at her ruthless efficiency when she tells me about it the night after her magical day with Ivan.

"He was so angry," she says with a slight shiver. "It was so unattractive. Ugh. The way he spoke. I'm just glad I'm no longer with him."

I try to imagine Antoine radiating with spurned anger, and I'm surprised to find that the image comes to me easily. His handsome features contorting, turning him ugly with hate. His big hands turning into fists. Yeah, I can imagine it easily enough.

Meanwhile, Ivan is *husband material.* This is what Thalia actually says to me after spending a second day with him. Husband material, like men are made of different ingredients and this one happens to have the organic, wholesome ones she's been looking for all along.

It sickens me to the point where I almost hate her. Almost. But I am spineless, so the following week, I merely watch from the sidelines as she traipses around Oxford with her future husband (because let's face it, once Thalia decides she's going to marry you, you're going to walk down that aisle with her). When his week in Oxford is up, he returns to London, but my relief is short-lived. Instead of staying on in London as planned, he comes back after just one day. ("He said he just couldn't bear to stay away from me!" Thalia squeals.) And his second week here, they're even more in love, entwined even tighter.

And she's right, Ivan IS husband material. Romantic but not too romantic, so you know he isn't just being carried away by the newness of their relationship. Calm, so he'll make a good husband and father. And a bit of a workaholic, so if he turns out to be a terrible husband, at least she won't have to see too much of him. The occasions that the four of us spend together, Ivan has to excuse himself a couple of times to take a work-related call. Tonight is no different.

"Poor Koko, having to run an empire must be sooo hard," Ani purrs when he comes back to our table. "You know what would help? Letting your own blood relation have company shares so she can assist you."

"We'll talk about that when you're done with your MBA," Ivan says in a tone that makes me look up, because there's a quiet rage simmering underneath it. So he has a bit of a temper when it comes to Ani. What else is new? I can barely keep myself from choking the girl.

Thalia and Ivan share a look and a soft smile, so I push my fork off the table and bend down to pick it up. I glance under the table as I bend down, and sure enough, she's found his hand and is squeezing it. A secret message, an alliance against Ani. It's this small gesture that plunges the knife deep in my gut and twists. They've only been going out for about two weeks, but already they're close enough to have secret gestures, and she's offering him support over his bratty sister. Thalia is no longer Ani's and my friend first, but Ivan's girlfriend first, our friend second. And I can't forgive her for that. I cannot, not after everything.

I'm changing the plan. The plan is shit. The plan needs to die a swift death. I could just about tolerate the plan when it was about Thalia playing a part to get some quick cash from Ivan so she could stay in Oxford with me. She wasn't supposed to actually fall for the guy. This has gone too far. It's time to put a stop to it. She'll thank me for it later, when she's no longer under Ivan's spell.

After dinner, I tell them I'm too tired to go pub-hopping with them and walk in the direction of Pemberton, hoping madly that none of them will try to follow. I turn the corner and wait. None of them follows. Disappointment clutches my chest, then relief. This is okay. This is exactly what I wanted.

I go in the opposite direction, down St. Giles', until I reach Jericho, where there's a cluster of hip bars and nightclubs. I check Google Maps, just to make sure I've got the right place. Thalia and Ani have gone to Antoine's bar several times, but I could never make myself go. I'd imagined it being as sleazy as Antoine, low lights, throbbing music, and date rape drugs. But as it turns out, Vin+ is a classier place than that. The lights are low, but so is the music, and the crowd in here trends older; post-grads instead of undergrads. I wrap my coat around myself tight, feeling massively out of place, and skirt the edges until I get near the bar, where I spot Antoine.

I watch him for a while as he chats with customers and pours different drinks for them. How strange to be watching him in his own element, minus the Thalia effect. He's less disgusting now, on his own. I almost turn around and go back to Pemberton, but I make myself walk up to the bar. When he sees me, a look of such naked hope appears that I want to scratch him.

"Janice!" he says, delighted.

"Jane," I say, but he's not even listening, he's so excited.

"This is a nice surprise. Are you with . . ."

"No," I say quickly, and he deflates.

"Oh." He picks up a towel and starts wiping down the bar. "Did you want something to drink, or . . ." Clearly, without Thalia accompanying me, the conversation might as well be done.

"Uh. Just water. No, white wine. The house white." I need some liquid courage for what I'm about to say.

I watch as he pours the white wine, the sides of the glass turning frosty from condensation. When he slides the glass over, I take a long swallow.

"So what can I do for you?" There's that French accent.

"Um, actually, I'm worried about Thalia."

His handsome face darkens, the corners of his mouth pulling down into a sad-face emoji. This man is a walking cartoon character. "Oh, Janice, I am so glad you bring her up. I haven't been able to stop thinking about her, you know? The way she broke up with me was so abrupt—"

"I know, but trust me when I say she's still not over you. She's kind of . . . easily influenced. She's been pushed into getting together with this guy—god, he's bad news, Antoine. He's horrible, a monster, and Thalia—you know how she is, so kind and such a pushover—"

"What do you mean a monster?" He plants both hands on the bar and leans over it, training his baby blue eyes on me. It's like having stage lights focused on me. Lights, camera, action. I want to quail, but I'm doing this for Thalia, so I lean into the light and perform my lines like an actress with the Oscars on her mind.

"I don't know exactly what he does to her, of course. In front of us he's the perfect gentleman. But there are bruises on Thalia's arms and legs, and one time I went to her room and she was crying like she's really scared." I even manage to make my voice quaver, that's how dedicated I am to saving Thalia from Ivan.

Antoine's face is a study in barely restrained rage. "What— but—" He shakes his head. "I don't understand. Who is he? Why doesn't she just leave him?"

"That's the thing, he's so charismatic, I don't think she sees how toxic he is. Will you talk to her? Please? I know that she still misses you. She's just blinded by this guy or something. I think if she just sees you—if you remind her of how good you two were—she'll wake up."

"She misses me?"

I give an empathic nod, my eyes wide. "Very much. She talks to me about you all the time. Said you're the best she's ever had. In, uh, in every way." It's like gargling acid in my mouth, saying these words.

Antoine laps them up, because of course he does. What is it about men and their need to be the knight in shining armor? He loves the image so much he doesn't pause to ask why Thalia, a grown, able woman, could possibly allow herself to get into such a bad situation over a matter of weeks. Months, years, I can see how someone can be worn down slowly, layers peeled away until there's nothing left. But weeks? Come on.

But Antoine is too blinded by the blaze of glory.

"I miss her, too, of course. How can you not? She is magnificent, no?"

I nod. She is magnificent, yes. That's the whole reason I'm here, asshole. "And, um, maybe it would be best if you didn't tell her that I was the one who told you about Ivan. We should make it look like you just knew because you're so in sync with her."

"Ah yes. Good point. I'll win her back, Janice. I promise you."

I don't bother correcting him this time. It doesn't matter; I've achieved what I came here to do.

First thing I do when I walk out of Vin+ is to run down a side street and try to slow down my heart rate. What the hell have I done? Sociopathic tendency #17: Brash.

But I couldn't just stand by and watch as Thalia ties herself down to Ivan, quite possibly for the rest of her life. We're too young, only in our early twenties. It's too soon! Our brains aren't even fully formed yet. She'll regret it. I'm only saving her from a lifetime of disappointment.

When my heart feels like it's no longer about to rip itself out of my chest, I walk back to Pemberton. My mind is still spinning, wondering what Antoine is going to do. Some over-the-top romantic gesture? An old-fashioned fight with Ivan? Maybe I should've given him some pointers. But it's too late now. I've done my part to try and save Thalia; now I just have to sit back and watch as Antoine does the rest. Who would've thought that in the end, I would be turning to him for help? How's that for irony?

——— — ———

THE SECOND WEEK PASSES; ONE LONG, EXCRUCIATING week where Thalia and Ivan wrap even tighter into each other, folding around each other so that there's absolutely no space for the rest of the world. It feels as though they've been in love for years. They now have their own secret code, their little inside jokes. All it takes is a seemingly nonsensical phrase here and there: "Like the squid," Thalia says as we tour the beautiful grounds of Trinity College, and Ivan will burst out laughing and pull her close. *What squid?* Ani and I would ask each other silently before shrugging and rolling our eyes.

How strange that Ani should now be my reluctant ally. Though she's not much of an ally; she seems content to stay back, spitting out barbed comments here and there, but mostly a passive bystander. She drinks more, splurges on more luxury clothing, which I didn't think was possible, but aside from that she's mostly harmless. A shame.

Fortunately, it's all about to come to an end. Ivan's due to leave the morning after our formal college ball. It's the biggest night of Michaelmas; everybody's been twittering about it for weeks now. The local dress shops have been filled with students trying on ball gowns. Ani's already bought five gowns. She tells me with sloppy generosity that I am allowed to wear her least favorite one. I'm so anxious/looking forward to Ivan leaving that I ignore the slight in Ani's comment.

But that morning, Thalia bursts into my room, cheeks ablaze. "I think he's going to propose," she squeals.

No. What? NO.

Somehow, I manage to keep from screaming. "What? But—what?"

"I know!" she cries. "It's so fast, but oh god, it feels so right. I—he asked me how I felt about possibly living in Jakarta, and all these questions like did I want kids, how do I feel about him needing to travel throughout the year . . . things a smart, down-to-earth guy would consider before popping the question."

Of course he's the type to ask these questions before popping the question. Wise Ivan. Kind Ivan. Down-to-earth Ivan.

"And then he took my hand and was like—well, I swear he was measuring my ring finger. Oh my god, Jane! Can you imagine? If he proposed tonight?" She hops and squeals again. "Is this the most romantic thing you've ever heard or what?"

I make myself nod slowly.

Thalia finally notices that All Does Not Seem Right and stops chattering. "Are you okay?"

"Yeah. It's just—it seems really fast, don't you think?" *It's been barely a fortnight*, I want to scream at her. I've had rashes older than this relationship.

"I know, but I've never felt this way about anyone before—"

Wow, that stings.

"—and when you know, you know. You know?"

I shrug. "Sure, I guess. Have you told Ani?"

Her smile loses a bit of wattage. "No. I don't really know how she'll take it. Does she seem slightly off to you the past few weeks?"

You mean while you and her brother wrap tentacles around

175

each other in front of her? Instead, I shrug again. "I don't know, maybe."

"I think there's a lot of history between the two of them. Like, a lot of tension or something. I'll let Ivan break the news to her. He'll know how to deal with it." She says this with such confidence that it makes me want to stab her. Already she sounds like a wife, a good Christian wife who adores and respects her husband and trusts that he'll be able to handle everything. I can hardly believe this is the girl I've been obsessed with for the past three months. I really, really need Ivan to disappear from her life.

Once she's out of my room—imagine that, me wanting Thalia out of my room—I call Antoine. Come on, you useless prick. He picks up on the second ring.

"Allo?"

"Antoine, it's getting worse," I say.

"Janet?"

This fucking guy, I swear. "Jane. Listen, Thalia is so—so dominated by this guy, she's not even thinking straight anymore. I think he might propose to her, and if he does, you know what she's like; she's too nice to say no. And the way he is with her, it's like he's controlling all her thoughts and actions. Antoine, please, you need to help."

He makes a sound that sounds suspiciously like a whine. "She won't pick up my calls, Janet. I must have called over ten times, and she won't pick up." His words come out thick around the edges, like he's been drinking. I guess the guy does own a bar.

She won't pick up his calls, so he's done trying? I grind my teeth with frustration. Another thought prickles at the edge of my mind: Thalia never mentioned Antoine calling her. It hurts.

Isn't that what friends do? Share things like this with each other? Have I been relegated to even less than a friend? I wonder if she shares such things with Ivan, if she's confided in him about Antoine so he can wrap her in his tennis-muscled arms and coo at her comfortingly.

"Janet, I'll talk to you later. I have to take care of this shipment," he says, and as he hangs up I can hear him shouting in French at someone in the background.

I knock on Thalia's door, my mind whirring. She carries a curling iron in one hand as she opens the door. "What's up, girlie? Do you need anything?" She doesn't wait for me to reply before going back to the mirror and wrapping a lock of hair around the iron.

"I ran into Antoine, and he mentioned that he's been calling you?" I blurt out.

She freezes for a few seconds, then her hair starts steaming and she curses and quickly unwraps it from the iron. She puts the iron down with a sigh and turns to face me. "When did you see Antoine?"

I think fast. "Uh, this morning, when I was out for . . . a walk."

Thalia frowns, and I wonder if I've blown it. If she can read me as easily as she used to be able to. "Where?"

"Just outside the college."

A look of concern creases her lovely features. "Oh my god, do you think he's stalking me? Why would he be here? His bar's all the way in Jericho and his apartment's in Summertown. He has no reason to be anywhere near here except me."

Try to save the situation, Jane. "Um, well, don't you think it's kind of romantic?"

Thalia looks at me like I've lost my mind. Can't say I blame her. "No! My god, can you imagine if he ran into me and Ivan? I would be mortified. Ivan has no patience for any drama. He comes from a huge Chinese-Indonesian family and he says they've got enough drama to last a lifetime. He's broken up with past girlfriends over less drama. He'll dump me for sure."

For sure? I almost ask hopefully. I manage to stop myself in time. "I see. Well, I'm sure it was nothing. Antoine's a good guy."

"But he talked to you? He mentioned he's been calling? I've been avoiding his calls because I've been with Ivan this whole time and—" She shrugs. "I guess I don't really have much else to say to Antoine."

"He only mentioned it in passing. I'm sure he's fine. I'll leave you to it." I can't leave her room fast enough. My whole body is wound up tight with nervous energy. This is it. I can break her and Ivan up while at the same time making her so angry with Antoine that there's no way they'd get back together.

Back in my room, I dial his number again, pacing as I wait for him to answer. When he does, I don't even bother with a greeting. "Come to our ball tonight. At Pemberton. Thalia will be there and she misses you. When she sees you in a tux, she's going to lose it. She'll leave him for sure."

He actually laughs at this, his voice going a bit high from excitement. "I love balls." I hate all men, I really do. Why do we let them roam around freely?

"Great," I manage to bite out. "Dress nicely. Be your handsome self. Break this awful spell she's been under."

"I will try. Thank you, Jane. Thank you." So the prick knows my name after all.

Thalia and I have agreed to meet up ahead of the ball, so fifteen minutes before the ball, I knock at her door. The sight of her. It's too much. She's wearing a dress the color of crushed sapphires, and it makes her skin look luminous. Her hair is done up in intricate braids, with a few loose tresses framing her face. She's gone for smoky eyes, and it's transformed her into something enchanting. A work of art.

"What do you think?" she says, twirling like I'm her date, like she did all this for me.

"You look amazing," I manage to say.

"Thank you, so do you!" She grins at me. What a lie. I'm wearing a five-year-old dress I'd bought at Macy's that had looked emerald green under the shop lights but as it turns out is more frog green. "Oh my god, I'm so excited. I can't believe this is going to happen." Before I can react, she reaches out and hugs me. "Jane, thank you."

"Huh?" I'm too stunned by everything—by the way she looks, by the sudden hug, by the overwhelming scent of her—to understand fully what's going on.

"Jane, my sweet, sweet Jane." Thalia grasps my hands, her eyes shining bright. "You've been my friend from the very first day. You've made this entire semester wonderful. You are my best friend."

Best friend. A part of me cackles with glee. I'm her best friend! Yes! Me!

The rest of me is dying a long, excruciating death. Guilt is crushing the air out of me. She's radiant with happiness because she thinks Ivan will propose tonight, and meanwhile, her supposed best friend has put into motion a last-ditch effort to stop her dreams from coming true.

You're doing it for her own good, I remind myself. She's just being carried away by her infatuation. She'll thank me for it later.

We walk down to the Chapel Quad, which has been transformed—majestic white tents erected on the lawn, a full bar, and bursts of flowers, flowers everywhere. Everyone is there and everyone is beautiful, shiny lips and shinier dresses, coiffed hair and diamond watches. Ani waves to us and sashays over, looking decadent in a low-cut dress the color of blood. A short while later, Ivan arrives, wearing a bespoke tux that fits him perfectly. He looks like an Asian James Bond. It's impossible not to stare when he and Thalia stand next to each other. Everyone watches them with open envy and admiration. I may as well be a frog in the dewy grass.

I scan the crowd, trying to find Antoine. Where the hell is he?

My phone buzzes and my heart leaps to see his name on it. I excuse myself from Thalia and Ani and pick up the phone.

"Where are you?" I hiss.

"I'm here. At the Old Quad."

I tell Thalia that I have to go to the bathroom and hurry through Highgate Hall. The entire time, my heart is beating a staccato rhythm. I can't wait to see Ivan's expression when Antoine shows up.

As promised, Antoine is at the Old Quad, standing near the Porter's Lodge. I give him a once-over; he's looking dashing in a well-fitting tux, with his hair slicked back, there's no denying that. But he also reeks of alcohol fumes, and as I walk toward him, I see him sway ever so slightly on his feet. Is he drunk? I'm about to snap at him for turning up drunk, but then I realize that the alcohol would probably make him even more dramatic, which is great.

"Hey," I say.

"Yooo," he says. Okay, definitely drunk. "You look great, Janet."

I don't even bother correcting him. "Yeah, so do you. You ready to win back Thalia?"

"Of course!" He grins at me and I have to look away because he's just so disgusting.

"Great, let's go." We make our way across the Old Quad toward the ball.

But when we get to Highgate Hall, I tell him to stop. "We can't go through to the Chapel Quad together. Wait like ten minutes after I go in before making your big romantic gesture. Remember, you have to make it convincing. Good luck."

Antoine gives me a sloppy grin—just how much has this idiot been drinking?

My blood roars in my ears as I walk through the gates and out onto the Chapel Quad. It's finally time for the Thalia and Ivan show to end.

18

O f course, fucking Ted has a fucking problem with me having made dinner plans without him. When I finally get back from SusPens Con, he's all over me, abandoning his laptop and clattering about like an excited dog. How was it? Did you meet anyone famous? Did your publisher set up a booth for you? Did you get to speak? Sign books?

Each question is an assault. He knows damn well Harvest wouldn't have bothered to set up a booth for me; they barely have one for the entire publishing house. And he knows better than anyone else that my books haven't done well, that they were released and pretty much immediately sank into obscurity. No reader has ever emailed me about them; no one has ever asked me for an autograph. On the launch date of my debut, Ted had given me a copy that he had bought at our local bookstore and asked me to sign it, and I'd very nearly burst into tears at his cruelty, the way he was mocking me for my failure as a writer.

I can barely restrain the bitterness and anger seething inside me for this man as he fires question after question, none of which I can answer to his satisfaction. *No, Ted, they didn't set up a booth specifically for me. No, Ted, I didn't sign any books.* Why? Then why bother sending you to the con at all?

Why indeed.

I close my eyes, massaging my temples. "Stop."

The questions stop abruptly, a surprised look fleeting across his face. "Are you okay?"

I hadn't meant to say "stop" quite like that, with so much acidity in it.

"Geez, Jane. I thought you'd be in a good mood. I mean, it's your first ever author event—"

"It's not MY author event, it's a bloody convention for all writers." All writers except me, apparently. I struggle to restrain my temper. It's not his fault that he doesn't understand. It's not his fault that he thinks I'm a big enough author to score a ticket to SusPens Con. He doesn't know that I basically barged my way into the convention center with Ani's help. Fuck, I'm a mess. And it's not his fault that he doesn't know any of it.

"Sorry," I manage to push out. "I've just—it's been a long day. I don't like crowds, and the con was—heh, it was very crowded."

Ted's shoulders slump a little. "Aw, sweetie. You should've told me." He reaches out and places a meaty hand on each of my shoulders, and I remind myself I mustn't recoil, because that's not how wives react when their husbands touch them. "Tell you what," he says, lightly massaging my shoulders, "how about we have a nice night out? We're in New York, let's live it up a little, huh? A nice romantic meal, just you and me, how about that?"

The thought of it fills me with dread. A night out with Ted, dinner over candlelight; what the hell would we talk about to each other? When we first dated, I made a huge amount of effort with him. I don't remember why now, but I do recall those days, where I'd read up on the news in the daytime, or scour Twitter for the most amusing, most shocking pieces of news. I would actually jot them down in a little notebook so I wouldn't forget them, and I would carry these news pieces, like little pieces of delicious candy in my pockets, where I would feed them to Ted over candlelit dinners. *Did you know that scientists may have found the God particle—the Higgs boson?* Fascinating. *They uncovered a two-thousand-year-old mummy today, perfectly preserved.* Wow, no way! *I read an interesting article today about the widening wealth gap and why it happens.* Gosh, you are so interesting, Jane.

I was so interesting because I gave a damn. I made an effort. I was never caught unprepared. I had to do it to cover up the fact that I am, in fact, without personality. All those news stories are only meant to paper over the bleak, empty hole where a personality should've been. I've read that this is something many sociopaths have—a lack of authenticity. We're empty inside, a monster pretending to be human.

I don't know when I stopped trying, when our dinners went from the two of us at the table, discussing physics and philosophy, to us talking about seeing Kimiko and her husband out walking their dog, to us struggling to even find anything worth saying. And finally, the death knell of dinnertime conversation—to us sitting in front of the TV, slurping our linguine without having to look at each other. I'm fine with that dinnertime arrangement; it's a lot easier on me, not having to pretend to care about Kimiko and her dog or our other neighbor, Frances, and her two-year-old kid who has a penchant for climbing up trees and then jumping out of them. And so it's very unfair for Ted to suddenly demand the old Jane back, the Jane who had something to say. I need time to prepare, to bring that Jane back to the surface. And I don't have the energy to do that.

And plus I can't do that; I have dinner plans with Thalia.

"Actually," I say in as casual a way as I can manage, "I can't. I have to have dinner with—" My voice falters. If I say "a friend," he'll ask me who it is, and I don't want to go into the whole thing. Oxford is mine, and mine only. He doesn't have a right to it. "Toni. And my editor."

His face lights up. "Oh, wow! That's amazing. Wow, so they're really going all out to woo you, huh?"

The bastard. He knows they're not. I study him, looking for the glint of steel underneath the happy facade. He can't be that clueless. Can he? "Um, yeah, I guess? I think it's pretty standard, probably something they do for all their authors when they happen to be in town."

"No, I don't think so. They're making an effort for you because they see your potential."

He's got to be doing it on purpose, rubbing my lie in my face. Yes, that's it. He knows I'm lying and he's pushing to see when I will break. Well, I won't break. Two can play at that game.

"Would it be okay if I came along?" he says, and there it is. His final blow. "I want to see my wife being schmoozed up by her agent and editor." He moves closer, until our faces are only inches apart, and gives me what he probably thinks is a seductive smile. "It's kind of hot."

Bile rushes up my throat, and I have to swallow it back down. *No, Ted, it's not hot in the least.* "It's a business dinner, not a social arrangement. It wouldn't be appropriate. And anyway, you hate book news."

He frowns. "But it's not just any book news, it's *your* book news." My breath catches, and I hate him, in that moment I truly do hate him, my cruel, vindictive husband who knows damn well that there is no book news when it comes to me. I'm still struggling to come up with a third book, knowing at the back of my mind that neither Toni nor Harvest Publishing is that interested in getting more books from me. Writer's block, Ted calls it, except I don't feel like I'm writer enough to have writer's block. And now that my second book has been out for months, everyone knows nothing's going to happen. No news, no surprise book club picks, no celebrity live-tweeting it and getting their millions of followers to pick it up. It's done, and I'm done, and we both know it.

It takes a whole lot of self-restraint to bite back the caustic retort burning its way up my throat. Instead, I say, "Tomorrow? Tomorrow morning, we can go for a nice breakfast."

Ted sags, disappointment lining his face. When did we get old? His whole face looks gray, a detail that surprises me. It snuck up on us. I wonder if I've turned old without knowing it too; if he sees me and sees a "ma'am" instead of a young woman. "Sure, tomorrow." He gives me a smile to show that he's being generous—*look how understanding I'm being, Jane; don't I deserve at least a hand job?* I turn away so I don't have to keep looking at that expectant smile. "I'll look up brunch places on Yelp."

I nod. "Great." Then I escape to the bathroom and start getting ready for tonight.

———

SKYE BAR IS A GLITZY RESTAURANT AT THE TOP OF A boutique hotel. It's very definitely outside of my comfort zone, but fortunately, I'd had the foresight to Google it beforehand, so I've come dressed for the occasion. I'm wearing my only nice dress—an LBD I splurged on years ago for this very moment, for when I do see Thalia and spend a night out with her. It's as though I have always known that we'd end up meeting again, because the thought that we might not was simply unbearable. It's an off-shoulder dress that calls out for a necklace, so I put on Ani's necklace. Seems fitting, somehow. I hid the outfit under an understated coat so that Ted wouldn't see how dressed up I am. Still, when I came out of the bathroom, he noticed the amount of makeup and said, "Wow, you went all out. You look nice." He started walking toward me, but I quickly headed for the door.

"Thanks," I said. "I'll probably be back late, so . . ." I let the rest of the sentence hang in the air. I didn't want to be the one who said, "Don't wait up," to my husband. That seemed a bit too aggressive, and he'd probably bring that up when we bickered down the road.

"Gotcha," he said with another valiant smile. "Have fun. You're gonna do great."

Could he be any more patronizing? I didn't bother looking back before leaving the room.

But never mind Ted. Who cares about that right now? Right now I'm in a swanky New York City restaurant and I'm about to be reunited with Thalia, and I look amazing; I know I do. The hostess gives me a once-over, nodding a little when she sees the necklace I'm wearing, then smiles at me. "Welcome to Skye. Do you have a reservation?"

I give her Thalia's name and her smile widens. "Ah, Ms. Ashcroft! Yes, of course. Follow me."

She leads me through the restaurant, and I try not to stare at my glamorous surroundings. Everyone here looks like they belong at some fashion show—the suits all bespoke and the dresses glittery and the jewelry ostentatious. She leads us to a table at the corner of the rooftop with a breathtaking view of the Manhattan skyline, and there she is. Thalia. She looks like a star, a burst of light and energy so beautiful it's blinding.

"Jane!" Thalia says, standing up and giving me a hug. I'm dizzy from the nearness of her. "So glad you made it."

"Shall I bring you the usual wine, Ms. Ashcroft?" the hostess says to Thalia.

"I think a champagne tonight. We're celebrating." Thalia grins at me. "Maybe a Dom?"

"Wonderful. I'll be back in a bit with your amuse-bouche."

I wait until she leaves and then lean forward in my seat. "Do you come here often? She seems to know you."

Thalia smiles. "A bit, yeah. It's one of our favorite places in New York. But enough about me—how are you? It's been what—nine years since we last saw each other?"

Here it is. I hadn't expected her to dive into it, but okay. I'm ready. I've been ready for this moment for years now. "Since that night that we—"

She sucks in a breath through her teeth sharply, her smile frozen in place. "Yeah," she says quickly. "Right, yeah. Since that—the incident." For a moment, neither of us speaks, both of us lost in that terrible, beautiful night. A night of death, a night of endings. A night that I had thought would've cemented our bond to each other but had ripped it apart instead. "So anyway," she rallies, regaining her poise, "what have you been up to ever since?"

"Well, I came back the next semester. I finished the program. I was hoping that you'd be back, too, but . . ."

"I couldn't afford to come back after everything," she says, looking sad. "I think you know about my financial situation."

I nod. How could I forget? A waiter comes back with a bottle of champagne, which he opens and pours out for both of us. We wait until he leaves before Thalia holds up her glass and says, "To new beginnings."

My chest flutters with hope. New beginnings, yes. That's perfect. The champagne goes down like electricity, bringing me back to life.

"So, um." I don't want to bring this up, but I have to. I need to know. "You're married to Ivan? How—tell me everything." I mentally go over the words I just said to make sure they're okay and don't give away my obsession. No, they sound like perfectly normal words that a perfectly normal, non-sociopathic person might say.

Her mouth curls into a strange, mirthless smile. "Yeah," she says, taking another swig of champagne. "We kept in touch after that first semester, and he visited me back in Nevada."

"Wow, he went all the way to Nevada just for you?" The minute I say that, I realize that, well, yeah, he's a billionaire. Vegas is probably one of his favorite spots. The old hatred toward him flares up.

"Yeah." She refills her glass and tops off mine. "We were seeing each other pretty seriously, and he's got a private jet, so it's easy for him to fly anywhere he wants."

Everything she's saying sounds glamorous, but her voice is flat and slightly bitter.

"We got married a year later, and that's the story of my life."

I'm missing something here. "Is that where you live now?"

She snorts. "No, of course not! Ivan can't possibly live in a sleepy town like that. We live all over, really. We're based in Jakarta because that's where his company is headquartered, but we spend our time flying back and forth to Singapore,

Shenzhen, Dubai, London, et cetera. Wherever business takes him."

"Wow, Thalia, that sounds amazing." I hate how much of a fangirl I seem like, but really, I can't hide my amazement. This is exactly the sort of life she deserves, and I'm happy that she's living it. Happy for her, at least. Part of me is crying for myself, curling up in a dark corner and licking my wounds and sorrowful that it can't be me she's spending her life with. I drain my glass again to try and numb the pain.

"Yeah. Well, actually, things have been kind of difficult—Ivan's been having some health problems that we're trying to deal with."

I've studied enough human interaction to know that this calls for empathy, so I frown and say, "Oh no, what kind of health problems?"

"It's his heart. He's got a genetic condition, and his work is making it worse."

I shake my head and the world spins with me. I grip the edge of the table to steady myself. Dimly, I recall Ani had mentioned something about Ivan's heart back in Oxford, though of course I thought nothing of it at the time. "That sounds terrible. Is he okay?" Even in my inebriated state, I know that's a stupid question because she literally just said he's got heart problems, so he's obviously not okay.

Luckily, Thalia doesn't seem to mind my idiocy. "He's hanging in there, but it's been hard on him. He's such a workaholic. I mean, he's used to being able to work twelve-hour days and then go out drinking with his clients until three in the morning, you know? All the doctors we went to told him to take it easy. That's part of the reason why we're here, actually. I had to come here for SusPens Con and my book launch party, and we decided it would be good for him to come along and get away from everything. I've taken away his laptop and work phone. Gotta force the guy to relax somehow."

"Wow, so Ivan's here in New York?" I can't seem to stop myself from spewing stupid shit.

"Yeah, he's back at the apartment with Ani."

"Ani."

"Yep, Ani. We're sisters-in-law now."

We stare at each other for a beat, and then we both burst out laughing. I don't know why we're laughing, exactly, aside from the fact that we've drunk way too much, but hey, here they come with yet another bottle of Dom, and neither of us is saying no.

"I feel bad for laughing!" Thalia cries. "Sorry, I mean, I love her, but she's always around! Even back in Indonesia, she's always hanging around the office, and she insists on going with us to the doctors and everywhere." She replenishes her glass and drinks deeply. "God, Jane, you have no idea how glad I am to see you. The last few years—they've been a LOT. Ivan's family . . . they're—you know, he warned me about them. He told me that they're really big and tight-knit and his parents are very controlling, so I can't even blame him for it, really—but holy shit, they're like a whole other level of controlling. That's why I couldn't reach out to you."

Everything stops spinning, and I'm suddenly hearing every word clearly, as though she's speaking right in my ear. This is it, the reason I haven't heard from her in so long.

"I wanted to, so many times. You can't even imagine. But his parents heard about what happened at Oxford—of course they did—and they forbid me from having any contact with anyone from Pemberton. They made me sign all these NDAs; it was crazy."

"NDA?" I can barely keep up.

"Nondisclosure agreement."

"What—why?"

Thalia shakes her head. "Because of the family company, of course. It's a huge media and tech corporation, so they need to uphold a good reputation. No scandals allowed. Not even for in-laws. Especially not for *bule* in-laws—*bule* means 'white person,' by the way. The direct translation is 'faded.' That's what they call me. The faded person." She snorts again.

"Thalia, that sounds terrible." It's a struggle keeping my voice even. In my mind I'm lining up all of Ivan's faceless family members and stabbing them one by one. I can hear the wet thud of their bodies so vividly that it makes me lick my lips.

"Whatever, fuck them. I can't believe I'm here with you. Tell me about yourself. What have you been up to?"

If we'd spent the last hour only talking about her brilliant debut, I wouldn't mention my writing at all. But since she's revealed her less-than-wonderful marriage to me, I feel like I owe it to her to reveal my less-than-wonderful career. "I've been writing, actually," I say.

"Writing?" Thalia cries, delighted. "What do you write? Are you published? You must be! You were one of the best writers at that program."

I shrug and take a longer swallow of champagne. It's painful, revealing how unremarkable my life is. How, without the sheen of her brilliance, I have sunk into mediocrity these past few years. "Just a couple of lit fic."

"Oh, I love that! I can totally see you writing lit fic. You've always been so deep."

"Your book—*A Most Pleasant Death*—it sounds . . ." I want

to say that it sounds like it's about us, but I have no idea how to say it without sounding completely desperate.

Thalia purses her lips and looks down on her lap. "Um, this may sound a bit crazy, but it was kind of inspired by us."

A warm glow spreads from the middle of my chest all the way to my fingertips and toes. I almost burst into tears and hug Thalia, but somehow manage to stop myself and drink more champagne instead.

"I knew I wanted to write about our friendship for the longest time, but I just never had the right plot, or the right—I don't know. I guess I just never had the guts to." She gives me a sheepish grin. "So the years before I worked up the courage to write *A Most Pleasant Death*, I'd actually been writing a few YAs."

I snort. "Yeah, right." I can't see brilliant, deep, incredibly complex Thalia writing YA.

"No, really! Look them up. I wrote under the pen name Ali Pemberton." She laughs. "Kind of on the nose, but what can I say? I missed our Pemberton days."

She can't possibly be serious, can she? But I take out my phone and Google the name, and sure enough, Ali Pemberton has published four YA books, and they've all done significantly better, especially the latest one. I look at the shiny "Junior Library Guild Gold Standard Selection" and "National Book Award Longlist" stickers on the cover of the latest book. Getting picked for those are a feat that most authors long for. Then I see the publication dates and I look up, wide-eyed. "These books were all published in the last two years."

She nods, taking another sip of champagne.

"You published two books a year? That's amazing!" Most

writers chug along at a single book per year. Or rather, most writers are like me and struggle to come up with one book a year. Publishing schedules are geared toward releasing one book a year; a good pace at which to properly set up a known brand without putting too much of a strain on authors. But of course Thalia is too fast for such schedules, whereas I am the turtle, forever doomed to struggle to even keep up. Even if I were to miraculously finish a new book by next week, due to the slowness of publishing, the earliest it would hit the shelves is in two years' time. Most people don't know that it takes two years on average from the time a book is sold to a publisher to the time it's available to consumers.

"It's not so hard, once you get the hang of writing fast. If you want, we can do a few writing exercises to get your juices flowing," she says. "I actually feel like the MFA course kind of screwed us over in that sense. They were so focused on writing flawlessly instead of writing fast. Such pretentious assholes."

That shocks a laugh out of me, and I stare at her in wonderment, because how can a person like Thalia exist? I drain my glass and she refills it for me, and I've lost count of how many glasses I've had but I don't care; I don't care because I'm with Thalia and it's just like old times.

"In fact," Thalia says, "I'm going on a writing retreat tomorrow in the Hamptons. You should come. There are eight of us going, and we've rented an incredible house there. It'll be good for you and me—we'll do nothing but drink and write and I could show you all of my secrets."

I know she's talking about writing secrets, but I can't help the thrill of excitement that shoots up the length of my spine. The way she's smiling at me as though she's talking more than just about writing.

"But—tomorrow? That's too soon. I haven't—don't you have to, like, pay or something? Make reservations?"

She shrugs. "Sure, of course. But one of the few perks of marrying into Ivan's nightmare of a family is that I do have access to a disgusting amount of money. Call it my repayment for having to put up with all of their shit. And as for rooms, don't even worry about it; you can just stay in my room. It'll be a bit of a squeeze in bed, but we'll make it work!" She winks at me. She *winks* at me. I've stopped breathing completely.

"I can't take that, Thalia, it's too generous." I would literally give up everything to be able to go on a writing retreat with Thalia where we would have to share a bed with each other after a day of wining and writing.

"Nonsense! You're coming. Where are you staying?"

"Domino Inn in Brooklyn."

"Oh, Brooklyn! I know the area well; my aunt lives there. Great, I'll pick you up first thing tomorrow morning."

And just like that, it's been decided.

19

When I get back to Chapel Quad, everyone is streaming slowly toward the entrance of Haygrove Hall. Shit, I guess it's time for the meal to be served. I hurry across the quad and find Thalia, Ivan, and Ani.

"Jane, there you are!" Thalia says, her face shining with joy.

Have I missed it? Did he propose already? But her ring finger is still empty, thank god. I force a smile at her and follow after the group, my mind and heart both racing. This is okay. I'll text Antoine and let him know we're going to the dining hall. If he confronts Thalia indoors, it'll make for even more drama, right? Yes, that's okay. That's good. I'm doing this for her own good. Yes.

But as we across the grass, Thalia suddenly stumbles forward with a cry. Ivan grabs her arm in time to keep her from falling over. She looks down at her feet in dismay; one of her heels has stabbed into the grass and broken off her shoe.

"Crap," she groans. "I'm going to go up to my room to change into a different pair. You guys go ahead."

"Are you sure?" Ivan says. "I could come with you—"

"No, it's totally fine!" she says, forcing a laugh, still playing the easy-going, drama-free girl of his dreams. "You guys go. I'll meet you all at Haygrove." With that she walks away, leaving the three of us looking at one another awkwardly.

"Oh well," Ani says with a shrug, making her way to the dining hall.

Ivan gives a small laugh and shakes his head. We walk slowly, a few paces behind Ani. "She's so independent, isn't she?" he muses to me.

I nod slowly. "Uh-huh."

"I really, uh, I really love her," he says.

A thousand fire ants crawl and prick at my skin. Why is he telling me this?

As though reading my mind, Ivan says, "I'm telling you this because, um, I know it sounds really rushed, but I'm planning on asking Thalia a very important question later tonight . . . and I wanted your help to make sure everything goes smoothly."

I refuse to look at him. "You're right, it's too rushed."

"I know, but . . ." He sighs dreamily. "There's no one quite like her, is there? I would be a fool to let her go."

I suppose he is not wrong. "Well, good luck with it." I gather my dress in my hands and hasten my steps so I won't have to keep talking to him.

Haygrove Hall was already beautiful to begin with, but now, with huge flower arrangements and fancy plates and glasses decorating the long tables, it's been transformed into something that looks out of this world. As it turns out, there are placards on each plate, and I find myself sandwiched between Pam and

Ani. Across the table is Ivan, who is—thank god—hidden be-hind a ridiculously tall tower of hydrangeas and peonies. The seat next to him is empty, awaiting the queen of the ball.

Fortunately, both Ani and Pam are too busy talking to other people, so I take the chance to check my phone. No messages from anyone. I try calling Antoine, but he doesn't pick up. I steal glances at the doorway, wondering who'll show up first. Antoine or Thalia? It doesn't matter, as long as they both end up here, causing a scene in front of Ivan. I'm filled with so much anticipa-tion that I actually feel my mouth watering.

Minutes trickle by and still no sign of either of them. I peer round the flowers, sneaking a glance at Ivan. He's busy texting, probably yet another business-related thing. The servers stream out of the kitchen and place our appetizer on our gold-edged plates. A single fat scallop, gleaming atop a bed of crushed peas, topped with a dollop of caviar.

It should taste amazing, but it might as well be plain bread for all that I notice.

"This is exquisite, isn't it?" Pam says. She's the only person I've ever heard using the word "exquisite" in casual conversation.

"Uh-huh." I glance at the doorway again.

I can barely choke down the remaining bite of scallop, gri-macing as it makes its gelatinous way down my throat. Where the hell are they? Has something gone wrong? What if—oh shit—what if Antoine runs into Thalia outside, at the Chapel Quad? They'd have their talk in private then, and Ivan would never know about it. Thalia would ply Antoine with her usual charm and tell him to go home, and he would. He doesn't stand a chance against her intelligence, her eloquence.

Just then, my phone buzzes with a phone call. Antoine? I

turn it over and my breath catches when I see Thalia's name flashing on the screen.

"Hello?"

"Jane?" Her voice sounds strange. "Hi, could you—um, can you please come up to my room?"

"Huh? Now?" She's still up in her room? Fuck. Antoine must be pacing about the Chapel Quad, wondering where the hell everyone is. Or worse, maybe he's just given up and gone back to his bar.

"Yeah. Don't bring anyone else with you. Just you, okay?" The strange note in her voice is clearer now, a giant crack running through glass. All thoughts of Antoine and Ivan leave me. Something's wrong. I grab my purse and stand.

"Where are you going?" Ani says.

"Bathroom."

"I'll come with you," she says, already getting up.

"No!" I half shout it. Pam and Ani stare at me. "Sorry, I just—I'm not feeling well and I, uh, I get self-conscious if there's someone else in the bathroom."

Pam's mouth drops open. "Oh nooo, is it the scallop? I ate it too!"

"I'm sure the scallop's fine." I rush away from the table, the noise of the ball receding as I hurry across the marble floor. Out in the hallway, I take off my heels and run all the way to Downing. Up the stairs, panting, my hair coming loose from the bun I'd painstakingly twisted it into. Finally, I'm at Thalia's door. I don't even get to make a second knock before the door is wrenched open.

"Thali—"

She grabs me by the arm in a painful grip and yanks me inside before slamming the door shut.

"What is it?" I've never seen Thalia like this before. Undone. Her eyes wild with fear. I taste a metallic tang at the back of my mouth. Bile. Fear.

"Jane," she babbles. "He attacked me. He was—he was waiting in here when I came in, and I didn't see, I—"

"What?"

She's not even looking at me. She's looking at something over my shoulder, in the far corner. The hairs on the back of my neck rise. *Don't turn around*, Mom says in my ear. *Just leave, now. You don't want any part of this.*

But I can't not turn around. I can't, because this is Thalia who needs my help, Thalia whose happily-ever-after I just sabotaged, and I know what's there before I even turn around. I know it because I've orchestrated everything. Everything up to the moment that led to this. Why did he come up here instead of confronting Thalia at the ball like we planned?

Too late, I realize that Antoine must have been so drunk that he must have decided to—to attack her. The thought is unbearable.

Antoine looks massive inside Thalia's room, a toppled, broken giant. He lies on the rug, a letter opener sticking out of his throat. His eyes are still open, as is his mouth, caught in a surprised O. It looks obscene somehow, his lips so pink, his eyes so blue, and all that dark blood coating his throat and chest. My legs lose all sensation and I crumple to the floor. It feels as though all of my insides are coming out, my body turning itself inside out, revealing all of my dirty secrets. The whole time, my mind is a continuous, shrieking chant: *He's dead! He's dead! He's dead!*

It's my fault. I did this. I goaded him into coming here, and then he lost control and he nearly attacked her—she was nearly—

I almost pass out at the thought of it, the image of Thalia, frightened and sobbing, shoved up against a wall by Antoine. Somehow, though, it gives me a bit of strength. I need to make things right. She doesn't deserve this.

Somehow, I manage to pull myself up and stagger to the sink to splash some cold water on my face. In the mirror's reflection, I see Thalia's silhouette, standing very, very still. I wonder what's going through her lovely, brilliant mind then. I splash more water on my forehead, my cheeks. I need to stay calm. With trembling fingers, I snap the rubber band so hard that it makes me wince. It helps to clear my mind slightly.

I turn around, averting my eyes from Antoine's body. *You stupid fuck*, I hurl mentally in the general direction of his feet. I focus on Thalia. She's just staring at him, obviously in shock. And so am I, surprisingly. The number of times I've fantasized about killing someone, but now when I'm faced with an actual dead body, it's startlingly different from anything I could have ever imagined. He's just so there. So fleshy.

"It's going to be okay," I say.

Her gaze flicks to my face, and she utters a mirthless, awful laugh. "How can it be okay?"

"We'll call the cops, tell them what happened. He ambushed you in your room, he attacked you, you—what did happen, exactly?" The thought of Antoine—good-natured himbo Antoine—attacking Thalia feels wrong. So wrong. But maybe that's just my guilt talking. Because I know that in a very real way, I caused this to happen. I was the one who pushed and instigated him to the boiling point.

She shakes her head. "I don't know, it was all a rush. He was rambling, I think he was drunk, and then he came at me, and oh god, his hands were all over me—"

She moves her shoulders back, showing me where her dress has ripped near the bodice. A ripple of revulsion and rage curdles my skin. If Antoine weren't dead, I would have killed him myself.

"I pushed him off and he came at me again and he was on top of me, his hands were pawing at me, and I reached for something, anything—" Her words dissolve into a sob. "I need you, Jane. I can't—you've got to—I can't, I can't."

I did this. I broke her. Not only did I ruin her happily-ever-after with Ivan, I may have ended her freedom. "No, it'll be fine," I say, weakly. "It's self-defense. He clearly attacked you, and you were just defending yourself. You'll be okay."

"I won't be okay!" she half shrieks, half sobs. "It looks so weird, don't you see? I panicked. After that, I washed my hands. Who does that, right?" She holds out her hands toward me, and sure enough, they're clean. "I just wasn't thinking. I saw all that blood on them and I thought, 'Ivan can't see this, Ivan can't know,' and before I knew it I was washing it off and it's going to look so suspicious! It's going to look all premeditated!"

I shake my head. "No, it doesn't . . ." My words can't convince even me. Does it look weird? Maybe it does? Who the fuck knows anymore? All I know is, I caused this. It was all my fault. And I can't let Thalia shoulder the burden of the blame. "We'll say I did it," I blurt out so fast that it takes a second for my mind to catch up with what I just said.

But once it's out, I get it. I get my role in this thing, and it is perfect. Just like our friendship, it's dark and lovely, and I am finally going to get to save the girl I love. For once, I get to be the knight in shining armor. And, a small, dark voice whispers from deep in the underbelly of my mind: *Once you do this, she will owe you for life.*

As Thalia stares at me, mouth open, eyes wide, I say it again, twining our life paths into a single knot. "We'll say I did it."

We're creative writers, we know how to set a scene, and so we do.

Antoine was waiting in Thalia's room when she came inside. He was obsessed with her. He attacked her, would have raped her if I hadn't come in to check on her. There was a struggle (here we make sure that there are more signs of struggle for the cops to find). We're two young women trying to stop a crazed, muscled bull. We were overpowered. He was choking Thalia; he was going to kill her. I yanked him off her and he came after me and that was when I grabbed the letter opener.

"You have to choke me," Thalia says.

My mouth turns into sandpaper and I stand there uselessly as she twines a thin scarf around her slim neck and hands me the ends.

"Do it."

And so I do. I pull and pull as her face turns pink, and then red, and then purple, and my pulse is one with hers, her life like a little bird in the palm of my hand. Such trust. She wouldn't put her trust in just anyone. She knows we belong together; this is why I'm pulling, choking the life out of her.

She flaps at me and I break out of my trance. I release the scarf and she stumbles back, coughing, gasping like a fish. There's something almost erotic about her wheezing, and I have to turn away, my face burning at the excitement inside me. What the hell is wrong with me?

Sociopathic tendency #27: Does dangerous things to feel alive.

I've gone too far. I know it. Thalia must have seen it too: that little evil spark behind my eyes. But when I turn around, she gives me a little smile. So brave. My heart goes out to her. She is too pure for this world.

"You should probably have a few bruises on your face," she says.

So pure, but also such a realist. I nod and she takes a deep breath. "Ready?" she says.

I close my eyes.

When she smacks me, the pain is blinding. Deafening. Stars explode behind my left eyelid, the insides of my head sloshing sickeningly. I fall backward and bump my elbow on a piece of furniture. Holy fuck, it hurts. Then, somehow, we're laughing. A mad laugh filled with tears.

When we're done, we look at each other, and for a while, neither of us speaks.

"I can't thank you enough, Jane," she says, taking my hand in hers. Her voice is hoarse. "You're my best friend. Forever."

My voice catches in my throat. I look deep into her beautiful eyes and say, "Forever."

20

W akey, wakey!"

The words grate against my eardrums, and I wince, turning away from them.

"Sweetie, time for our fancy New York City brunch."

It takes a while for the words to sink in, but when they finally reach the part of my brain that digests verbal information, my entire body curls up and I let out a groan.

"Did we imbibe a little bit too much last night?"

I resist the urge to wrap a pillow around my head to drown out Ted's voice. I can't bear that playful, wheedling tone. And then last night comes rushing back like a fist to my gut and I sit up, suddenly awake. "Shit, Ted. I can't go to brunch."

He stares at me for a moment before smiling. "Very funny. You got me good."

"No, I'm not kidding. I—uh, I've been invited to go to a

writing retreat in the Hamptons and we're leaving today." I glance at the clock on the wall. "Uh, in an hour, actually."

Ted's smile slips off his face and hardens, sharpening into something else. "A writing retreat?" There's something ugly in his voice now, something that makes my stomach tighten.

"Um, yeah. Sorry, I didn't have a chance to tell you last night. But it's a really good opportunity for me—it'll allow me to get to know other writers who are at the top of their game." I'm rambling and he's going to know something's going on.

"How long will you be gone?"

"Only two nights."

"But we're supposed to go back to the Bay Area tomorrow." I wish he'd stop walking toward me. He stops short of being within touching distance, and all of my instincts are alert, on standby. "And how much is this going to cost?" And just like that, The Sigh comes out, long and slow. "Look, sweetie, I know how exciting it must be to be sent to your first ever convention. I mean, I agree it's a huge change of pace from what we're used to, but we can't afford to get swept up in all this hobby of yours."

"Hobby?"

He must have detected the dangerous tone in my voice because he stiffens and straightens up. "I didn't mean to say hobby. Sorry, it's obviously more serious than a hobby, but like—" The Sigh again, this time a quick one. "It's not really a job, is it? It's not like it's earning much money at all, and I have faith that you'll earn more, with time," he adds quickly, "but I just don't think that now's the time to be splurging on things like a fancy retreat in the Hamptons. I mean, Christ, Jane, it's probably going to cost like a grand or something. We can't justify it!"

I hate him. I despise him, this small man who's trying to make me smaller so I can fit him, so I won't ever outgrow him.

"Well," I say, getting up and walking away from him, "that's fine, because this is being paid for by Harvest Publishing. I guess unlike you, they see my potential and think it's worth investing in me." The lie burns coming out, sizzling in the air with its falsehood. I don't see how anyone could possibly believe this; it's just so far-fetched. I've never even heard of publishers sending their authors on writing retreats, unless maybe said author is of Stephen King status. A small part of me wants him to call me out on it so that we can spiral into a proper fight, finally, one where I unleash all of my fury on him, breakable objects whizzing through the air and shattering against the walls.

Instead, there is a long silence, during which I busy myself packing and refusing to look him in the eye.

"They're paying for it?" he says finally. "Is this a retreat organized by them?"

I don't have a moment to consider what would be the most believable answer, so I just say, "Yes."

"Huh." Silence again. I stuff more clothes into my bag. "So I'll just . . . wait here for you then?"

"If you want. Or you could go back to the Bay Area first and I'll be back in a couple of days."

"Oh." It comes out so small and so sad that before I can stop myself, I look at him. He looks even smaller than before, all of the bluster gone, leaving just my husband behind, old and saggy and sad.

"Ted," I sigh.

"No, it's fine. This is really good. I'm happy for you; you deserve it." He turns away from me and looks out the window. "Yeah, I'll just . . . yeah, you're right, I'll fly back myself. I've got a ton of work to do anyway. So. Yeah."

"Great."

"Yep."

I wonder, fleetingly, if this is the end of my marriage. The thought is a surprisingly painful one, though as soon as Thalia texts to let me know she's here, the pain disappears, fading like the San Franciscan fog in sunlight.

⸺ ⸺ ⸺

I'M IN A DREAM. THIS CAN'T BE REAL, THIS CAN'T BE MY life. I'm not really here, in Thalia's convertible, driving out of Manhattan toward the Hamptons. The entire drive there, we glance at each other and grin like, *holy shit, can you believe that we're finally reunited after all this time?* And we've shed our baggage, left both our husbands behind in the city while we drive out into the sunlight and ocean breeze. We talk about nothing and everything. Books, agents, things about publishing that I have never discussed with anyone because no one in my life is that interested in the nitty-gritty details, and I'm not big into the book community, which consists of people who are too cheerful and too wired for my liking.

Before I know it, we're entering into the driveway of an incredible property. How incredible? Well, so amazing that it has its own name: Graystone House. The name is displayed proudly on a bronze plaque at the gate.

"Isn't it crazy?" Thalia says as the wrought iron gate swings open. "Six bedrooms, plus a guesthouse. There's even a heated pool and a Jacuzzi. We went all out for this retreat." She drives slowly up the driveway and stops a little ways from the front door. "Hey, so."

Something in the tone of her voice leeches the easygoing mood from the air. I turn to face her.

"I haven't told the others that you're coming yet. I'm kind of waiting for the right moment. You know how writers can be so precious about their retreats," she says with a roll of the eyes, followed by a smile.

A knot tightens in my stomach. "But—" I don't even know where to begin. They don't know I'm here? Me, someone who's already an outsider, is now about to show up unannounced? This feels bad. The kind of thing that makes me want to burrow into a deep, dark hole and never come out again.

"Don't worry about it!" Thalia says. "Look at me, Jane."

I do so, and am lost in those deep brown eyes of hers.

"They're going to love you," she says. "But maybe give me like ten minutes to prep them before coming inside?"

If it were anyone but Thalia telling me this, I would not be okay. I would beg them to let me drive the car out of here. And if they didn't agree, I would run all the way back to the city. Okay, I wouldn't actually run, but really, all of my insides are shriveling up and I just want to hide away. But then it strikes me that all my life, I've just wanted to hide from everything, and I can't do that now, not when it's taken so long to find Thalia and she's invited me to, of all things, a writers retreat! Who gives a fuck about all these other writers, right? I'm not here for them; I'm here for Thalia. For my own writing. I'm here to soak up her presence and everything she can teach me about writing, and it's obvious she has a lot of knowledge to impart.

I nod and watch as she gets out of the car and takes her bags from the trunk. She waves at me through the window with what I think is supposed to be a reassuring smile, then she walks up the steps and through the front door and is swallowed up by the house.

If I ran now, no one would be the wiser. Or maybe I could drive the car back to the city. Thalia wouldn't mind. Or she would, but she wouldn't hold a grudge. She's not the type to. I could make something up, send her a text about a "family emergency" halfway back to Manhattan. But then I'd be going back to Ted, and on his face I'd see—what? Relief? A knowing smirk. *I knew you'd come back, Jane. You don't belong with those hoity-toity writers. Come back to our comfortable, safe lives.* Our lives of mediocrity, where we did the same, mediocre things every day and got paid a mediocre amount for it and then had mediocre meals over mediocre conversation.

The thought of going back to my old life, after just one evening spent with Thalia, is unbearable. It makes my jaw clench. I make myself take a deep inhale. It comes in shaky and releases in an audible gasp. God, I'm so nervous. But these things are always worse in my mind than they are in reality. Yeah. I always build them up in my head and then it turns out to be okay. I watch as the clock on my phone ticks away. When it's been exactly nine minutes, I get out of the car and grab my bags, then walk toward the house.

Ten minutes.

I raise my hand and ring the doorbell.

———

IT IS AS BAD AS I THOUGHT. WORSE, ACTUALLY. EVERYONE here is either a *New York Times* bestselling author or a prize winner. I recognize Rebecca Young, a Hugo Award winner who recently sold the rights to her books to HBO. They'd called her series "a feminist take on *Game of Thrones.*" Then there's Kurt Fenton, *New York Times* darling whose love stories (not romance; when men write romance, it's classified as "love stories" so they're taken much more seriously than those silly things women write) always, always top the lists. Basically, everybody here is Somebody, and I'm the only Nobody, and they all know and act like it.

Even Thalia.

When she opened the door and let me in, I thought I sensed something off about her, something stiff about her smile, but I'd shrugged it off as my own nerves. But now I'm in the stunning living room with everyone else, and I think it's pretty clear that Thalia doesn't want me here. She's introduced me in the most awkward way possible, taking me to the living room and saying in a falsely cheerful voice: "Everyone, this is Jane, the woman I was telling you about." A couple of the writers barely glanced up before continuing their whispered conversation, while the rest looked at me warily. Why had she said "woman" and not "friend"? Maybe I'm just reading too much into it. She'd led me to a seat at the farthest end from everyone else and told me to sit before leaving the room.

And so here I am, looking around awkwardly and picking furiously at my fingernails. Nobody is even looking my way, so I can't really catch anyone's eye to make small talk. Kurt glances at me and I quickly smile, but it only seems to offend him. A crease appears between his eyebrows and he looks away. My stomach drops. I want to disappear. The fact that everyone here is very, very white does not escape me. Ani would relish that she's the only Asian in the room, revel in her difference and use it to stand out, but all I want to do is blend in, to pretend that I belong.

Thalia comes back, wheeling a drinks cart. Eyebrows are raised, but she grins at everyone and they can't help but smile at her.

"Hello, everyone! I'm your server for the day." The others laugh. "A bit early, I know," Thalia says, "but you know what they say—write drunk, edit sober."

One of the women, a thriller author named Siobhan, laughs and says, "Hey, I'm not complaining. The last retreat I went to was a dry retreat." She rolls her eyes and everybody groans along with her.

"God, was it the agency retreat?" someone else says.

She nods. "Yep."

The others groan again. "I hate those things."

Toni's agency holds a yearly retreat, but I've never been invited. Of course not; not I, sad little midlister. Such retreats are only for their biggest clients. Here I've been lusting after these retreats, and here are the big clients, grousing about them like they're a chore.

"Honestly, if they're going to hold a yearly agency retreat for all their agents and clients, they should at least ply us with alcohol."

"You need to fire them," Rebecca says. "If they're not even sensible enough to provide alcohol, you don't want them representing you. I'll call my agent; she's great. She'll represent you no problem."

Siobhan shrugs like switching agents is no biggie. Is this how they move in these circles? I live in fear of Toni dropping me as a client. Before signing with her, I'd been stuck for years in the query trenches, collecting hundreds—literally hundreds—of rejections. When Toni offered, she wasn't as successful an agent as she is now. She still had room on her list for writers like me. I'd gotten so lucky. If she fired me, it would end me. But I guess these writers can afford to agent-hop, firing their agents over the most frivolous reasons.

Thalia goes around, taking drink orders. Of course, she makes the drinks with perfect precision. She even shakes the shaker like a professional bartender. With each drink she serves, she does so with exaggerated flourish, saying things like, "Enjoy, madame." Everyone's gaze is riveted on her, the way she moves with such grace and confidence. She trundles the cart to me last.

"And what will it be for you?" she says.

"Um, it's a bit early to start drinking—" I check my phone and hold it up to show her it's not even noon yet.

Thalia gives me a concerned smile. "You okay? Come on, this will help you loosen up a little."

My cheeks burn. She's right. She's trying to help me fit in. I shouldn't have questioned her. I give her a small smile and say, "Just the white wine, please."

"Great choice." She pours heavily, filling my glass to the brim, before pushing the cart to one side of the room.

Please sit next to me. Please, please—

She goes over and joins Siobhan and Rebecca. I hear her say, "Ladies, what are we talking about?" and a wave of anger rushes over me. Why did she invite me here if she's just going to ignore me? And what am I supposed to do, just sit here sipping my wine?

"So what do you write?" someone says.

I look up to see Kurt towering over me. I shift in my seat, making room for him on the couch, and he sits down next to me. "Um, lit fic." It comes out apologetic, somehow, like I'm a hack trying to write highbrow novels.

Kurt nods and takes a mouthful of his drink. "Anything I might've heard of?"

I tell him my book title, the words feeling small, like grit, in my mouth.

"Never heard of it."

My skin crawls with embarrassment. Of course he hasn't heard of it. I would never presume that Kurt fucking Fenton would've heard of my little book, but the way he says it, dismissing me like a fly, stings more than expected. I focus on my wineglass, wrapping both hands around it and feeling the drops of condensation.

"So you've known Thalia for a long time, huh?" he says, and there's something in his voice that makes my ears prick. Something that reaches deep into the primordial instincts of my body, a whisper of danger that sidesteps my brain and goes straight for my muscles, tensing them.

"Um, you could say that, I guess. We got to know each other at our MFA program."

"In Oxford? That was where she met Ivan, right?"

I nod. Take another sip of wine to keep from having to reply. Then I realize I should redirect, turn the questions back on him. "And you? How do you know Thalia?"

Kurt smiles, and it's not a pleasant one. "Oh, everybody who's anybody in publishing knows Thalia. You know that."

There's a sourness in the back of my mouth, because no, I don't know that, and I am in publishing, but I guess I'm a nobody in publishing and he's a somebody and so is Thalia.

"I got to know her a few years back, at some con or another; I don't remember, there are so fucking many of the things."

Yet another one of those things that plebs like me had to beg and scrape to attend and superstars like him think are a chore. I force a smile and say, "Tell me about it."

"We hit it off right away. She's got a way with people, doesn't she?" He empties his glass, and I get a whiff of whiskey breath.

I wonder if it's just me or if he's talking about her in a weird way. I get like this sometimes. Too in my own head—that's what

Ted says. I'd think that someone said or did something weird, and Ted would say, *Nah, it's just you; you're too in your own head.*

A shadow crosses over us, and I look up to see Thalia, carrying two full glasses, one with a refill of Kurt's whiskey drink and the other with white wine. She hands them to us and smiles. "What are you two talking about?"

"You," Kurt says, and that one word is so loaded and so heavy with meaning I feel it like a physical blow.

Thalia's smile freezes for just a second before she recovers. "Nothing interesting about that. Tell us about your current work in progress, Kurt. I'm dying to hear all about it."

She's touched on the right note. Kurt settles back, taking a long, slow gulp of his drink, and starts telling us about his latest work, which he evidently thinks of as his masterpiece, a blessing to the literary world.

The rest of the afternoon passes by in a blur. There isn't a lunch per se; a lush, abundant grazing table has been laid out on the kitchen counter, and everyone goes back and forth throughout the day, taking bits of cheese and cured meats onto their plates. They chat about books and other writers, and as the drinks are steadily refilled, the talk turns nasty. Which writer is a hack, which writer is a snob, which writer is "problematic." I don't partake in the conversation, because I don't know any other writers; I'm not part of the #WritingCommunity, and even if I were, I wouldn't be part of *their* #WritingCommunity. They're A-list and I'm barely on any list. So I sit a little bit outside of the group, losing count of how many glasses of wine I've had.

At some point, the group breaks up as everyone staggers away to their rooms to write. A couple of people choose to write in the common areas. I skulk off into the room I'm supposed to share with Thalia and wait for her to come up. She does so after a while, and now I'm nervous because I have no idea what she'll be like toward me. I want to ask her why she's been so cold and stiff the whole day, but it doesn't seem right to ask such things. Too confrontational.

"Hey, you okay?" she says, and I almost burst into tears because her voice is now the soft, warm Thalia voice I know. She sees my expression and her face softens. "I'm sorry if I was a bit standoffish downstairs. I just get so nervous around these people, you know? Like, we chat with one another online every day, but seeing them in person is like, whoa."

I nod, the room swaying along with me. "I understand."

"I'm so glad you're here. It's just like old times."

"Yeah." I wish I could say something more interesting, but after all the wine, my brain is slush.

"I'm going to write downstairs. Are you going to write up here?"

My throat thickens. I find it hard to swallow. I'd fantasized about us writing together, glancing up at each other once in a while and smiling, knowing that we're creating worlds with only a few feet between us. We'd do writing sprints, maybe, race each other to get to five hundred words. But now she's abandoning me. I could come downstairs with her, but god, writing in the same room as those A-listers? Me? What a fucking joke. They'd eye me with open derision; they've been eyeing me with barely concealed distaste the entire day, their expressions making it clear that I don't belong.

"You go ahead. I'll write up here."

"Okay." And just like that, she's gone. Leaving me up here alone. I open up my laptop and stare at the blank page and the blinking cursor. Then, as though of their own accord, my hands float up over the keyboard and then they're flying across it, words flowing out of me the way they haven't been for months. It's the kind of state that writers are forever chasing, the one where the world around you melts away and you drop into this hole where there's nothing between you and the words. It's just you and the story, and your fingers aren't even yours anymore, they're just bypassing your mind and doing the story's bidding, typing out words that you weren't even aware were inside you all along. At some point, Thalia must have come back up, because I become half-aware of a new glass of wine being placed next to me. At some point, I drank it. I don't stop writing.

It's the Thalia effect; I know it. I haven't felt this way since Oxford. Since those afternoons she and I spent in the cozy darkness of the Bodleian Library, tapping away at our keyboards, pausing only to share with each other little snippets of our work. Even though I'm barely aware what I'm writing, I know it's good. I know because I'm no longer held back by my own self-conscious thoughts, that little inner editor who's always nagging at me and telling me that what I'm writing is shit. Just being near Thalia is enough to silence that voice.

When I next look up, the sky has darkened to a deep purple and voices are floating up from downstairs. People are done writing, and so am I. I've somehow pounded out two thousand words. I don't dare read them yet, not now while I'm still woozy from the booze and the writing. I stumble down and everyone's there and I guess they've all been drinking throughout the day like I have, because they're all just on the edge of drunkenness; some of them maybe well beyond drunk. We all crowd around the kitchen counter and paw at the boxes of takeout.

The boxes say: *Green Village, Clean Body, Clean Mind.* And when we open them, we find steamed vegetables and lightly seasoned white fish. Not a single carb hiding among them.

Thalia frowns at the anemic boxes. "They must have gotten our order mixed up with someone else's. I ordered their party set. I'll call them and ask them to come pick these up."

"Eh, don't bother," Rebecca says, nibbling on a long stalk of asparagus. "I'm too hungry to wait for them to come and switch the food and blah, blah, blah. Let's just eat these."

"Okay," Thalia says. "I'm so sorry for the confusion."

"It's not your fault," Rebecca says.

We eat in the living room, and there's so little food that I feel hungrier after dinner than before it, but there's plenty to drink, and by the time we're done, I'm too woozy to think about eating. The chat resumes—just how many authors can these people bash?—then we finally, finally retire for the night. By the time I get back into the bedroom, I've drunk so much wine that whenever I roll over in bed, the entire bed rolls with me. I'm not even aware of Thalia's presence. At times I think she's there, but when I call out her name, there's no answer, and I can't tell if I actually did call out her name. The last thing I remember thinking before I fall into oblivion is: I shouldn't have drunk so much.

Morning comes abruptly. When I open my eyes, it's bright, blindingly, painfully so. Neither of us had thought to close the curtains. I turn my head gingerly and wince at the way the slight movement makes it throb. Thalia is sound asleep in the bed next to me, and god, what a sight it is, to wake up and be staring at her. Even this early in the morning, after a whole day of drinking, she looks gorgeous. I take in all of her, noticing little details I'd missed before, like the tiny freckle on her right eyelid, and the way that the roots of her hair are surprisingly dark in color. I forget my headache, just for a bit. I could stay here all day and gaze at her, I really could.

A frantic knock pounds on the door one second before it bursts open. Siobhan stands there, a horrified look on her face.

"Wake up," she cries. "Thalia, get up!"

Thalia mumbles something and blinks slowly. "Mmh?"

"Shit, get up! The cops are here."

"What?" Thalia and I say it at the same time.

Siobhan's face is deathfully pale as she says, "There's been an accident. Kurt was—uh." Her voice catches and tears fill her eyes. "He was walking out on the cliffs and he—he fell and—" She starts crying then. "He's dead. Kurt's dead."

What?

I'm looking at Thalia when Siobhan says this, because of course I am; I am always watching, too afraid to miss even one second of her beauty. And that's how I catch the flicker going across her face. It's not shock, or horror, or anything that would've been appropriate in that moment.

It's relief.

And in that moment, something cold ripples over my bones. I know Thalia, I know all of her facial expressions, all of her quirks. I know what I saw.

I think back to that night in Oxford, when she'd called me to her room and I'd come rushing up to see Antoine bathed in blood and Thalia shaking with fear. He'd attacked her, she'd said. It was self-defense, she'd said. And I'd simply believed her even though none of it felt right. So many pieces not fitting in. But I'd wanted to believe her. I'd loved her—I still do, and I would've believed anything she told me.

And now Kurt is dead, and for the first time, I wonder if maybe I don't know Thalia that well after all.

PART
THREE

21

THALIA

Jane knows. She knows that I have something to do with Kurt's little accident.

She's not saying anything, of course, but she knows, and that's a bit of a shame. Rather spoils the surprise a bit. She's always been like that, so hopeless with the social cues, which I found amusing when we first met. There were so many things about Jane that amused me at first. Like the way she was so obviously obsessed with me from that moment I saved her at the bus station. My god, the way she'd gazed at me, like a leper being allowed to touch Jesus's robes, or a fan at a BTS concert. It was exhilarating. It was the whole reason why I started flirting with her, asking her to come to my room and try on dresses. I thought she was going to have a heart attack when I started undressing in front of her. I suppose that was somewhat cruel of me, teasing her like that. But I adore the feeling of being adored, don't you?

And before I could get bored of it, she told me, in a drunken stupor, that she's a sociopath, which piqued my interest, because you see, when I was fifteen, Aunt Claudette finally convinced my idiot mother to take me to a clinical psychologist, where I was actually properly diagnosed with APD—antisocial personality disorder. So can you blame me for being curious when I came across Jane? What are the odds of two people with APD coming across each other in this vast world? And oof, that little essay she wrote about wanting to strangle a beautiful woman. That was so clearly a love letter written for me. Very romantic, isn't it? She really shouldn't call people like us sociopaths, though.

Terms like "sociopath" and "psychopath" are very nineties and not politically correct anymore. I'm very careful to be politically correct at all times. On social media, my political views lean left (BLM! No TERFs!) because I have learned that this is what's currently acceptable. Don't worry, you can still like me; I'm not secretly a Republican.

I just don't give a shit.

The psychologist referred me to some specialist or another, who tried their best with interventions—I have always hated that word "intervention" because it is a lie, and what they were doing was more of an interruption, a distraction. I went along with it anyway, just to get them off my back, and plus it was quite fun toying with them and seeing if they bought my act. If anything, the treatment they put me on taught me how to become a better actress, how to guess what the other person is thinking and wrap that knowledge around my finger, so that when I crooked it, they would do my bidding. I'm not sure if I ever fooled them completely, but no matter, because your average person isn't quite as intuitive as a professional psychologist, even though they'd like to think they are.

Take Kurt, for example. Oh, Kurt. Named after Vonnegut, which should tell you something about his fucked-up parents. Kurt writes love stories—he'd get so riled up if you called them romances—about dying people. His characters are always suffering from some form of cancer that's terminal but not the kind that turns them ugly and unmarketable. Because of this, Kurt thinks he knows love, and he resents that his wife doesn't love him the way that his characters do, the kind of love that only exists when both people know that their time is limited. He thinks she doesn't deserve him (he's right; she deserves someone better). Enter me.

I do not want sex; I mean, I do, but not from Kurt, for god's sake, with his pale, skinny-fat author's body. I have plenty of lovers, one in every city, in fact, and all I wanted from Kurt was his agent. Most writers love to recommend their agents, as though the fact that they were fortunate enough to land a good agent is somehow a reflection of them, but not Kurt. Kurt was represented by the legendary Beatrice McHale, an agent whose smallest deals are at the very least "significant" (this is Publishers Marketplace speak for "$250,000 to $499,000"). Rumor has it that the clients whose books do not sell for at least $250,000 get dropped. It might sound heartless, but to me it speaks of efficiency and, well, probably someone who also has APD. Imagine me being represented by a fellow psychopath. Unfortunately, Beatrice only takes clients by referrals, so I figured I'd schmooze up to Kurt until he referred me to her.

But it turned out that Kurt, fed on a steady diet of his own clichéd love stories, believed in True Love, just not with his own wife. So I pretended to be attracted to him, smiling as he droned on and on about his latest project, telling him how beautiful his shit-brown eyes were, how gentle his limp fingers were, how much I longed for his flaccid touch. I have done more, and would do more. Anything it takes to advance my career. You're wondering why. You're thinking: Why not just write better?

Anyone who thinks that publishing is a meritocracy is not in publishing.

Because yes, to a certain extent it does depend on writing well, but that's only half the battle won. It also depends on the "market," though what the "market" actually is, no one can tell you. All they can tell you is that despite the "powerful prose" or the "riveting characters" or "exciting plot," they still can't buy your book because it's just "not marketable." And it depends on knowing the right people—being represented by the right agent. For the longest time, I was with Ruth Steinwell, a middling agent who doesn't even live in Manhattan; she lives in Seattle and is a bored suburban housewife who thought agenting would be good for a laugh. She sold my debut YA for a piddling sum of money and told me it was about as good as could be expected, given "the market." Ruth's clients were all midlisters, all bored housewives who thought dabbling in publishing would be good for a laugh. I have nothing against these women, but they kindly need to move the fuck out of my way.

I didn't want another Ruth for an agent. I wanted a shark. Because only a shark of an agent would be able to get me the kind of book deal I deserve, and only a shark of an agent would be able to prod and nudge and cajole my publisher into giving me the kind of marketing I deserve. (Everything.) We all know what I've been through—being attacked at my MFA program, marrying into Ivan's family; something that I will get into in a bit. I've been through hell, am still living through it, and after enduring all of these things, I deserve everything, wouldn't you agree?

Anyone with a heart would agree. But not Kurt, because all Kurt cared about was himself.

After months of exchanging raunchy phone calls and two cons during which we had sex and I pretended it wasn't mediocre and was so overwhelmingly good that I cried a little, Kurt finally introduced me to his agent. Beatrice, oh Beatrice! The two of us combined were basically unstoppable. In less than one month after signing me on, she'd read and edited my latest manuscript. When she finally submitted it to publishers, her pitch was so incisive and so glowing that we started getting offers right away. She quickly turned down the bottom two, telling them that they'd offended her by coming in with an insultingly low number, which created even more of an uproar. By the time she set up my book auction, publishers were practically frothing at the mouth. The auction was swift and ugly in the best possible way, with editors going behind one another's backs to make me promises of publicity while also bad-mouthing their competition. Finally, I was getting what I deserved—an all-out fight over me.

But Kurt had to go and ruin everything by declaring that he was in love with me (I suppose I couldn't blame him) and that he was leaving his wife (wait) because unlike me, she didn't fully appreciate him (oh no) and I would agree, wouldn't I? Surely, I also wanted to leave my abusive, tyrannical husband (Ivan has never abused me in the traditional sense, but he might as well have, for all the shit I've had to go through).

When I told Kurt that no, I did not in fact want to leave my husband, he turned sour. Told me I was a brainwashed, abused woman, and that if I didn't leave Ivan, he was going to go public with our affair. That was why Kurt had to die. That was why I had to lure Jane back into my life, because I needed a fall guy in case I didn't succeed at making his death look like an accident. I didn't want to have to use Jane like that, but needs must, and she's the perfect fall guy, what with her history of violence (poor Antoine).

If you're wondering about Antoine, the idiot ambushed me at the college formal, thinking he'd march into the dining hall to make some sort of grand announcement, to brand me as his. (Really, what is wrong with men?) I couldn't let him ruin what I had with Ivan. I begged him to leave, which only made him angrier—*You're so afraid of that man, ma chérie. What has he done to you?*—and so at the last, desperate second, I kissed him and then led him up to my room. I tried to placate him, I really did, but he insisted that I stay there with him for the rest of the evening. That just wouldn't do. So in the end, the letter opener became the key to my freedom, the knife that fully severed Antoine's grasp on me. And Jane, good old loyal Jane. I knew she'd help me. I almost laughed when she offered to take the blame for killing Antoine. I thought I would have to suggest it to her, but nope. Didn't even have to hint.

I really think that Jane was quite happy to do it for me. Like Antoine and Kurt, she saw herself as my savior. I know she definitely saw herself as that when I came to her with my sad mommy story. That was hilarious. *Oh, Jane, my mother is sick! I need money to pay for her treatment!* Honestly, who in their right mind would fall for it? But this is Jane we're talking about. My most loyal doggo. You know, I don't actually know if Jane has APD. She's a bit of an armchair psychologist, diagnosing herself like that. But whatever she is, she is definitely obsessed with me.

There wasn't even a sliver of doubt in her mind when I told her my sob story. And I saw the look in her eyes when she suggested that I get close to Ivan. She was so pleased with herself for coming up with the most obvious idea in the world. Good job, Jane. I got exactly what I wanted: Jane distracting Ani so that I could have some alone time with Ivan.

Jane was so excited to be able to help me like that, so I decided to let her do it again. Serve herself up on a platter for Kurt's death, should I need someone to blame it on.

I called Beatrice and asked her to have my author name changed from my pen name back to my real name. Pretty ironic, because the reason I used a pen name in the first place was to keep Jane away. After the whole thing with Antoine, I thought it best to simply disappear from Jane's radar, just in case she got any funny ideas about coming clean or whatever.

Unfortunately, Beatrice told me that it was too late in the game to change my pseudonym. The book was already out, and that was that. Bit of a blow; I'd had higher expectations from Beatrice. But never mind. I took things into my own hands. I created social media accounts under my real name and connected it with my pen name. On every available outlet, I made sure that I was known as "Thalia Ashcroft, writing as May Pierce." Whenever I had interviews or guest articles, I made sure I was known as "Thalia Ashcroft, writing as May Pierce." I created a fake *New York Times* email account (if Jane had bothered to read the sender's address properly, she would have seen that it says newsletter@newyorktinnes.com and not newyorktimes.com) and sent Jane a newsletter with a doctored bestseller list that showed my name as "Thalia Ashcroft, writing as May Pierce," knowing she would see my name and be so swept up that she wouldn't pause to wonder why the *New York Times* had bothered listing my real name. Then, having set my trap, I waited for Jane to turn up. The day of my panel at SusPens Con, I kept coming up with reasons to send Ani to the entrance of Javits. I told her she should take selfies at the entrance, under the huge "Welcome to SusPens Con!" sign. I told her she should try the delectable coffee at the pop-up drinks cart near the entrance. All sorts of stupid reasons I came up with just to keep her there in case small-fry writer Jane couldn't score a ticket to SusPens Con. And if that were to fail, I would've posted other events I would be at.

Honestly, I've kind of missed Jane after all these years apart from her. I missed that intensity of hers, the way she'd watch me in what she probably thought was a subtle way. There is literally nothing subtle about Jane. As Ivan's wife in Indonesia, I was respected, even admired, but I wasn't the object of anyone's obsession, which is honestly quite offensive, if you ask me. I deserve to have rabid fans, to take up as much space as possible in people's brains. Why not? It's not like most people have anything better to think about. Might as well be thinking about me.

To be clear, I really didn't want to do it. I begged Kurt not to go public with our affair, but he dug his heels in. It's all those fucking love stories. They'd gotten into his head; he thought that like his dying female characters, I, too, was in need of a savior.

The thought of needing to be saved by a pathetic male like Kurt. When I pushed him off one of Montauk's cliffs, he had felt so light, like a doll. Couldn't even save himself, yet he thought he could save me. What is it about men that blinds them to their own mediocrity and allows them to think of themselves as heroes?

22

JANE

The cop interviewing me is wearing a name tag that says Howe. Midforties, small wrinkles around the eyes that deepen whenever I give her an answer that she thinks is a lie. Which is a lot of them, for some reason. Detective Howe thinks I'm lying, and I don't know why.

"So you weren't invited—"

"I was," I say for the third time. "Thalia Ashcroft invited me here."

"Right . . ." Those lines become stark. She obviously doesn't believe me. "Okay, so Thalia invited you here, but you don't know anyone else here?"

I shake my head.

"Kind of awkward, don't you think? To be invited to a gathering of writers where you don't know anyone else?"

We're sitting in the living room, in an opposite corner of the room from Thalia and the cop who's interviewing her. Siobhan and another writer are also there, though Siobhan I think has had her interview; she's just walking around and going, "Oh my god, can you believe it?" to anyone who will listen. The other writer, someone named Monday, I believe, is just staring out the window with a dazed expression, an expensive-looking shawl wrapped around her. The others are all being interviewed somewhere else in the house. No, I hardly know any of these people.

"I suppose. But Thalia said it would be fine, and it's been so long since we saw each other, I guess we thought it would be a good chance to catch up."

"Really? Huh." She nods slowly, and my instincts are reacting, telling me I'm in very dangerous territory, but I don't know why. I have nothing to hide, but somehow I feel guilty, I feel like a suspect. "When was the last time you saw her?"

"Oxford. We attended the same MFA program. About nine years ago."

She writes this down in her notepad. "And you didn't have any contact with her between then and now?"

"No."

I can practically feel the waves of disbelief radiating from her.

"That's a long time ago. You didn't find it strange that she invited you to such an exclusive retreat after so many years apart?"

The back of my neck tingles. Is Thalia a suspect? That would be bad. Or good? I don't know. I need to talk to Thalia, but I haven't had a chance to; after Siobhan woke us up, everything had turned into a whirlwind. We barely even had enough time to brush our teeth before we had to go downstairs, which was when the cops took us aside to interview us one by one. And a huge part of me is internally screaming: *Thalia, what have you done? What have you done to Kurt? To Antoine?* But I won't betray her to the police, and even if I wanted to, what would I tell them? There's literally nothing to tell, nothing but a hunch. I know how well that would go over.

"No, we used to be really close in Oxford. We were best friends, and when we bumped into each other at the con, we picked up right where we left off."

Detective Howe smiles. "That's nice. I have friends like that too. We could go for months without talking to each other, but when we do, we pick up right away like we've been talking every day."

I nod, not buying for a second that she has any friends. I, a loner, can tell another loner right away.

"What kinds of things did you talk about with Thalia when you reconnected?"

It takes a second for me to digest what she's just asked because it seems so out there. "Um, I don't know, all sorts I guess? Our books . . ." I try to think of what we had talked about, and then race ahead to try and figure out if these things are safe topics to share with Detective Howe. Then I end up questioning why I need to figure out if they're safe or not. Everything should be safe because I did nothing wrong. And yet everything inside me is holding me back from telling Detective Howe anything. "Just life in general," I say finally.

"Right. Stuff like your marriage? Did she share anything about her marriage? When I get together with my girlfriends, we're always bitching about our husbands." Another smile appears.

"Just the usual stuff, nothing that stuck out." What is she trying to get at? Why would our marriages factor into this conversation?

"So while you're here, you're rooming with Thalia?"

I nod.

"That's very interesting."

Why is that interesting?

"Who suggested the sleeping arrangements?"

She's fucking with me. She must be. "Thalia, of course. She was the one who invited me here."

"Right, of course. Did you leave the room at any point during the night?"

"No, I was sleeping. We'd all drunk a lot." My mouth is painfully dry. I can barely get the words out.

"Right," she says, clearly not believing me. "And Thalia? Did she leave the room at any point during the night?"

"No. I don't know. Like I said, I was sleeping," I snap. Shit. The anger slipped out before I could control it, like an embarrassing burp.

Something changes in Detective Howe's face. A trap clicking shut.

She's seen the sharp edges, the gaping red maw of me. She knows the kind of monster I am. My insides go cold.

"Sorry, I'm just a bit jumpy because, uh, holy shit?" I gesture vaguely around me and give an uneasy laugh, then I hate myself for laughing, because what the fuck kind of person would laugh at a time like this? A sociopath, that's what.

"Don't worry about it. I'm used to people being jumpy around me," Detective Howe says, her beady eyes trained on me. "Did you notice anything strange about Kurt's behavior yesterday?"

It's a struggle to keep breathing, to keep my voice level. "It was the first time I'd met him, so I wouldn't know what's strange and what's not." Did that come out sympathetic? I hope so.

"What about Thalia? Notice anything strange about her behavior?"

From across the room, I see Thalia talking to another cop, and I wish I could just walk over there and pull her aside and talk to her. Find out what she's thinking, what really happened last night, and what really happened all those years ago in Oxford. But even now I feel the need to cover up for her, to protect her. She looks so frail and so frightened. Are they being tough on her? I can't stand the thought of Thalia as a suspect. What if they take her into the station for questioning? She doesn't belong in such places.

I shake my head. "No, she seemed fine."

"Anything feel off between her and Kurt?"

A flash of Kurt, questioning me about Thalia. The way his face had darkened when he mentioned Ivan.

I shake my head again. I need this interview to be over. "They seemed like okay friends."

Howe nods, clearly not buying anything I tell her. "Okay, thank you for your time."

"Wait," I say, and then I wish I hadn't said that. But it's too late now, so I might as well spit it out. "How did he—it was an accident, right?" My voice comes out wrong. Desperate and stilted and just plain wrong. Detective Howe catches it too; I see it in the glint of her eyes. Very much not the kind of question an innocent person would have asked.

"We're still trying to figure it out. But don't worry, we've got the forensics team out on the cliffside, doing their magic. They'll figure out exactly what happened." She grins at me, and I get the sense that I've just been given a challenge, or maybe a threat. As she leaves to interview the next person, I have to stuff my hands in my pockets to keep them from shaking visibly.

23

JANE

It is forever before I can get Thalia alone. Even after Detective Howe is done with me, I'm accosted by yet another cop wanting a statement, asking me adjacent questions—where was I last night? In bed. The whole night? Yes. Didn't wake up at any point to go to the bathroom? No.

Unlike me, the others aren't getting the same amount of grilling. It's not just my imagination. Monday, for example, is only questioned for about fifteen minutes before being dismissed. And Rebecca even less than that. Whereas questions are fired my way for over forty-five minutes. It feels like an assault, and halfway through I feel as though my mind has been stabbed through from all directions. Nothing makes sense. I don't understand it. I feel like a hunted animal surrounded by hounds who have caught my scent. *But I didn't do anything wrong*, I want to scream. *I didn't, I swear. It was—*

No, I can't think that. Not my sweet Thalia. But she isn't mine, is she? Never has been.

It's nearly noon by the time I manage to get to Thalia. She's talking to Rebecca and one of the male writers, the three of them with their heads bowed, speaking in low murmurs. When I approach, they jump apart and Rebecca stares at me with open hostility while the male writer studies me carefully, like an interesting but dangerous specimen.

"Hey," I say in a low voice. Then I wonder why I'm speaking in a low voice, wonder if it makes me look even more suspicious, then I wonder why I'm caring about looking suspicious because I did nothing wrong, god damn it. "Can I talk to you real quick?"

I expected Rebecca and the male author to, you know, fuck off like normal people would at this, but instead, they both look at Thalia with a questioning expression. What the hell? I get the feeling that if she were to say no, these two would forcibly remove me. Which is absurd. Right? My imagination is just getting the better of me, right? What the hell is going on?

Thalia nods at them and says, "Sure," and they very reluctantly move away, but they stay in the room, hovering from a few steps away like protective guards.

"I need to speak with you in private."

"I don't think it's a good idea to leave the room," Thalia says, glancing over her shoulder at Rebecca, who's still watching us.

"Okay . . ." *Not okay*, I want to scream. I cock my head at a far corner of the living room instead, hoping like hell she'll follow. I almost start crying when she does. It's not perfect, as there are still people around, but I guess it's the best I can get for now. I lower my voice until it's barely above a whisper. "Thalia, what the hell happened?"

She looks at me with those round doe eyes. Eyes that brim with innocence and fear. "I don't know what you mean. A horrible accident, it sounds like." A sob lurches out of her, and she covers her mouth and looks up at the ceiling, blinking rapidly. "I'm sorry, I just—it's kind of hard to digest that my friend is gone."

Uncertainty catches hold of my chest, weighing down on it like a boulder. I'd been so sure that—

That what? I hadn't been sure of anything. I just had a . . . an inkling? A worry. A gnawing sensation that she might have been involved somehow. Because that's two men who were in her proximity who are gone now, and surely, that can't have been a coincidence? When it comes to deaths, what number is too many?

"Last night, did you uh—" I don't even really know what I'm trying to ask. "Did you leave the bedroom?"

Thalia's eyes lock on mine, and now, beneath the lake of fear, I sense something lurking in the deep. Some dark, slouched beast with teeth and claws. I blink, and the beast is gone. I'm losing my mind.

"What are you asking, Jane?" she says, clearly hurt. I can't stand it, even now, to see that look of betrayal on her beautiful face. "You can't be—" She chokes on the rest of the sentence, as if the words are too painful to say.

"No," I say quickly, unable to bear her pain. "I just wanted to know if you heard anything."

She lets out her breath slowly, still eyeing me like I've just kicked her in the heart. "No. I was asleep next to you. I was dead drunk. We all drank way too much."

"Yes, of course. Yeah." I nod vigorously when what I really want to do is apologize, tell her the panic and anxiety are getting to me. "Um, I'm sure I'm just imagining it, but the cops—what sort of questions did they ask you?"

"Just routine ones, I think?"

"Okay, because they were asking me all these questions like I had—god, I don't know, like they thought that maybe I had something to do with it. Do you know why they might think that?"

Thalia's eyes widen for a second before she frowns. "No, god. Jane, what are you asking me?" Her voice rises; she's clearly upset. "Why are you asking me these things?" She stops herself abruptly and takes a deep breath.

"Everything okay?" Rebecca calls out.

She looks over her shoulder and flashes a small, reassuring smile at Rebecca. When she turns back to face me, she's wearing a frown again. "Listen, Jane, I think it may have been a mistake to invite you here . . ."

She means because someone freaking died, my mind chitters nervously. But I know what she really meant by that. She said it because I don't belong, and even if Kurt hadn't died, it had become painfully clear that I don't fit in with her circle of A-list writers. It shouldn't surprise me. It shouldn't. And yet.

I nod, unable to speak.

"I think it's best if you go back to Manhattan," she says.

"I just—I—are we okay?" Are you going to disappear again for another nine years? Or is it forever this time? Will I only be watching you from afar, telling anyone who will listen that I used to be friends with you?

Thalia sighs. "I'm just a bit hurt that you would—I don't know, suspect me of something? After everything we've been through, Jane. I mean, I trusted you fully at Oxford when I was—I was assaulted." Her voice breaks then, and to my horror, tears roll down her porcelain cheeks. People are looking over. Rebecca leaps into action, crossing the room quickly with a deadly look on her face.

"I didn't mean it like that," I say hurriedly. "Of course I don't suspect you of anything."

"I think it's best if you leave now," Rebecca says in a cold voice. She wraps an arm around Thalia's thin, shaking shoulders and leads her away with one last glare thrown my way.

Another writer peels away to join them, murmuring to Thalia. The rest of them glare at me. There's a couple of officers left, and they both watch the scene, looking back and forth between me and Thalia, before exchanging looks with each other. My insides are knotted so tight that I think I might vomit. I'm sweating through my clothes, my palms slick, my hair sticking to the back of my neck. For a few painful moments, I'm rooted to the spot, their glares pinning me down like a butterfly struggling as pin after pin is stabbed through its wings. Then something snaps and I stumble away, half running. I hurry up the stairs and into my shared room with Thalia. I pack in a frenzy, stuffing everything I see into my bag, and don't spare the room a second glance before rushing back down, the weight of the house suffocating me. I don't look at anyone as I pass by the living room, but I know they're all still watching. A thought flashes through my mind—you're going to look so guilty if you run now—but I'm beyond caring. I don't hesitate before wrenching the front door open and running out into the blinding sunlight.

The memory of Thalia and me driving up here, so carefree, the wind in our hair, smiling at each other, is like a knife wound. It actually makes me take in a sharp, hitching breath. I shove the mental image out of my head and order a Lyft to the train station. I breathe easier as the miles are eaten up, as I gain distance from Montauk, from those cold stares—god, I swear I can feel them, even now. A sudden rip of pain startles me, and I look down to see that I've ripped my thumbnail to the quick and drawn blood. I suck on it, and the tang of blood takes me back to that night in Oxford, the way it always does. But now, instead of the usual sensation of longing that I've always felt with a memory associated with Thalia, all I feel is nausea. That look of hurt on Thalia's face—god. I take my thumb out of my mouth and wipe the blood off on my jeans instead.

I send Thalia text after text:

Are you ok?

Please answer me.

We need to talk.

No replies come. My rib cage has turned into a vise that is crushing the air from my lungs, the life out of my heart.

My mind is a mess by the time I get back to the city. I stumble out of the train into Penn Station, find my way to the right subway train, and make the rest of the trip back to the hotel in a daze. It's only when I walk into the lobby, closing my eyes with relief at the cool, soothing air in the hotel, that it hits me. What the hell am I doing back at this hotel? I no longer have a reservation here. Ted would've checked out already.

The thought is too much to bear. I can't stand it. I sense the tears coming and I rush into the elevator before any of the receptionists notices me. Maybe they haven't reset my key card yet. Maybe I can still go inside our room and take a hot shower before booking a flight back to SFO. Yes, one could hope. Oh god, please. I need it to happen so badly that I mutter to myself as I make my way down the hallway, my bag dragging on the carpeted floor behind me.

I tap the key card against the door lock and the light turns red. My stomach plummets. "God, no!" The words come out in a harsh whisper. I try the card again even though I know it won't work. The light turns red again.

Everything inside me plummets to the floor. I'm done. I am so tired that I actually sink to my knees, letting my head slump forward and thump against the door. I feel thoroughly and utterly defeated. What happened at Montauk? What happened at Oxford? I thought I knew, but now I realize I know nothing. What really happened with Thalia? But even now the thought is a painful one. I don't want to think of her as anything but the Thalia I knew. The perfect angel. I don't know what to do with this growing stain that's tainting the image of her in my mind. I'm untethered and directionless. My eyes flutter closed and I let out a long, exhausted sigh.

Then the door swings open, and there's Ted.

"Jane!" His eyes are wide with surprise.

I scramble to my feet, staring at him, wondering if it's a mirage. If I blink, maybe he'll disappear. I do so, but he remains in front of me, solid as ever. "Why—I thought—wait. Aren't you supposed to be back in the Bay Area now?" An ugly thought rises, a noxious bubble bobbing to the surface of a toxic swamp— he's cheating. He's got another woman in there. Maybe he hired a sex worker.

He smiles sheepishly. "Okay, so this is going to sound stupid, but I thought it would be nice to surprise you. We haven't had a chance to explore the city, just the two of us, so I extended our stay for another week. I thought it would be nice—Jane? What's wrong?"

He'd extended our stay so we could explore the city, just the two of us, and here I'd jumped to the conclusion that he'd extended his stay to fuck around. Here I'd gone off and left him, seen him as nothing more than a burden I have to bear while I went off chasing the dream of Thalia. A dream that had ended in a nightmare. And for the first time in so long, I realize that I'm glad to see Ted. Relieved to be back with him. For the first time, I long for the boring, predictable comfort of our home. I feel my heart cracking, the gray wall around it crumbling, and I fall into my husband's arms and cry.

24

THALIA

Poor Jane. It's honestly like kicking a puppy. Something I have never done before, just to clarify. I really am not a monster. Killing men, I believe, is a much more forgivable transgression than kicking a puppy, wouldn't you agree? And honestly, the men I've killed—it's a gift to humanity to erase them from this world. Kurt Fenton, your typical lazy, entitled, straight, white male author who has mistaken his success for brilliance. Antoine Deveraux, your typical straight, white male who likened himself to a romantic savior. Ha, it just hit me that if Antoine had been alive today, he'd probably love Kurt's books. (I'm smiling at the thought. What a hoot.) How's that for irony?

But Jane, the poor thing, I really didn't enjoy doing that to her. My goodness, the way she'd looked at me when I'd asked her to leave! Those kicked-puppy eyes. They're a study in pitifulness. I took a mental picture of them and shall practice in the mirror later on. Everything I do, I do very seriously, because I must excel at everything I am interested in. I do this with writing, cooking, fashion, and my most masterful craftwork of all: human behavior.

It's not easy for me, you know, having APD. It's like there's a bridge missing and all I can do is stand on one side of a deep ravine and watch as other people—the normals—mix with one another and go through emotions as easily as changing clothes. I hope you can see that I was the victim all along. It felt like everybody was feeling things at me to taunt me: *Ha, look at pathetic little Thalia who doesn't understand why birthday cakes are a cause for delight, and why people coo at babies or dogs, and why people cry when you tell them, with all sincerity, that they're ugly/ worthless/stupid.* It's honestly quite rude of other people to parade their emotions in my face, I think. Would you jump up and down in front of someone in a wheelchair? Didn't think so. But somehow, it's okay to rub things like joy or pain in my face.

Anyway. Where was I? Right, Jane's hurt expression. Must remember the angle of her eyebrows and the way her mouth had parted ever so slightly. Not just hurt, but a little hint of surprise—*how could you?*—as well. Chef's kiss. I can't wait to try that particular mask on. But for now I must mill about with the rest of my writer friends and allow them to fuss over me. And they're fussing over me because, poor me, to have my stalker classmate reappear after all those years and follow me all the way to Montauk! How awful. How terrifying. How delicious.

It's the kind of thing this crowd can't have enough of. I can see the hunger in their eyes as they mine me for more information about Jane. Mining—that's exactly what they're doing—using me for research for their next manuscript. I wonder how many of them are going to go away from here and start pitching their next book—a story about a stalker. Rebecca for sure is going to write a stalker novel. Now that sci-fi/fantasy is going through a rough patch, she's been talking endlessly about venturing out into writing thrillers, an evergreen genre. She's so predictable, hovering about me, her breath a disgusting hot blanket of sour tequila as she plies me with questions. *How long did you know Jane? Did you know back in Oxford that there was something wrong with her? What was she like then?* I have to resist shoving her away. I wish she'd at least make more of an effort to disguise her opportunistic research as concern.

I stay long enough to make sure that the story takes flight; quite easy to do with this bunch, obviously. They're so wrapped up in storytelling that everything is a fucking prompt to them.

Prompt 1: One of our own, a gifted writer, a dear friend, a loving husband, has been found dead at the bottom of a nearby cliff. The police are still investigating. Was it an accident or something more sinister?

One hundred percent of the people here would go for "something sinister," because that makes for a better story.

Prompt 2: If it was indeed "something sinister," who did it? Perhaps a vagrant who somehow stumbled upon Kurt while he was out on his nightly wanderings, pondering his work in progress? Or was it (dun dun dun!) someone he knew?

Again, one hundred percent of writers here would pick the latter, because of course that makes for the better story. And they would be right. It was someone he knew (*c'est moi!*) and it was no accident. I just have to do a bit of redirecting so that their attention will stay far, far away from me. Not that anyone would suspect me; for all they know, Kurt and I were just friends. We were discreet about our affair, both of us being happily married and all, but I don't like taking my chances. I've been so careful about this whole setup. I paid attention to all the little details, down to things like changing our dinner order to the restaurant's lightest menu, ensuring that there isn't a single carb in the meal so that nobody has a chance to sober up. The whole damn day, I went around refilling everyone's glass so that by the time we retired for the night, everyone would be drunk out of their minds. Layers and layers of preparation, that's me. I almost giggled out loud this morning, listening to the police interviews around me. The useless answers everyone gave. "I didn't hear anything. I was passed out . . ." "We drank way too much. I can't remember what happened last night . . ."

If only they gave out awards for attention to detail. I should have been a wedding planner, or a neurosurgeon, or a war strategist.

"Do you think Jane . . ." Siobhan says to me in a stage whisper loud enough for everyone else in the living room to hear. The way she let the rest of the sentence trail off, letting everyone fill in the rest themselves, is really quite brilliant. Siobhan is probably the most masterful storyteller out of this bunch, a living example of Show, Don't Tell. I could've stood up and applauded her right then and there.

"Oh, it's too awful to think about!" I cry, burying my face in my hands.

And now here comes Rebecca with her alcohol breath, wrapping her limp arms around me like an octopus. "Oh, you poor thing. It must be terrifying. To think, your stalker might've killed Kurt." Rebecca is not a believer of Show, Don't Tell.

"But why would she have done that though?" Thomas says. He swills the brandy in his glass and frowns. He probably thinks he looks very thoughtful.

"Who knows why crazy people do anything?" Rebecca snaps.

"I don't think you should use 'crazy' in that way," Alicia says.

Alicia is a YA writer and very much involved in the woke YA sphere. I hate Alicia.

"Yeah, don't wanna be canceled," someone snarks. A couple others snort-laugh their agreement.

Being canceled is always at the edge of our minds, always a gnawing fear.

"My guess is," Rebecca says, raising her voice, "it's because Jane was obsessed with Thalia, and she saw how close Thalia was to him."

I stiffen under her embrace, because excuse me? I wasn't close to Kurt. I mean, I was, but no one else was supposed to know it. We were always formal when we texted or emailed each other, leaving the raunchy stuff for the phone calls. I sneak a glance at Rebecca, trying to get a gauge on her. Does she know something? Is she trying to needle me? And then a chilling thought: What if Kurt had told her something?

Oh god, of course he fucking did. He must've been so proud of it, secretly. Maybe he got drunk one night and spilled it all over DMs.

How much does Rebecca know? The bitch, all this time I thought she was just trying to lap up extra attention, but maybe she's putting down the pieces needed to make a move against me after all. She's never liked me; I know it. Ugly women rarely do.

"I don't think so," I say in a small, shaky voice. "I wasn't that close to Kurt. I mean, I'm closer to you than I was to him, Rebecca." Ingratiating myself to this bitch, ugh.

Rebecca gives me a small smile, smug to have been acknowledged as a better friend than poor dead Kurt.

"Oh, I think we all know that Kurt had a little crush on you, Thalia," Thomas says with a smirk.

I'm about to deny this when it hits me that it's fine by me if they want to think that Kurt had a crush on me. After all, who could blame him? I take care of myself. And it would probably add to my allure without soiling my reputation, to know that he'd been lusting over me.

"I'm sure he didn't," I say demurely. "He loved his wife very much, I've heard." (The ungrateful bitch, he'd called her.)

"I'm not saying he would've cheated on his wife. I think it was just a harmless crush. But maybe Jane noticed him looking at you and it made her angry," Thomas said.

Good dog.

I let out a small sob. How terrible to think that me being a beauty has unwittingly led a man to his death. Very Greek tragedy. I approve.

"It's not your fault," Siobhan says. I hate her the least out of everyone here, have I mentioned that? She is the best dog.

Someone else snorts. It's Monday (yes, her parents really did name her that). "I don't think it's useful to sit here and make up stories about what might've happened." Not useful to make up stories? It's like she's not even bothering to pretend to be a writer. "I mean, the cops said it might've been an accident. And this is real life, not a novel. In real life, the simplest answer is usually the truth. Kurt was drunk and decided to wander outside—he probably thought it was romantic and deep; sorry not sorry, but Kurt was the kind of guy who'd totally do that—and he fell off by accident." Guess what genre Monday writes. Guess! Yeah, you're right, she sells self-help books. Her latest book was titled: *Zero Drama Mama! How to get rid of all the drama and #LiveYourBestLife.* (Yes, with the "!" and the "#." The book has been on the *New York Times* list for twenty-three weeks. I should've killed her instead.)

Despite myself, I kind of have to agree with Monday. Kurt

was very definitely the kind of idiot who'd go for a night walk on a cliffside while drunk. Case in point: It didn't even occur to him to say no when I suggested it. I think he was expecting some kind of al fresco drunk sex thing, as though any woman thinks getting fucked in the wilderness while branches stab at your skin and mosquitoes feast on your blood is sexy.

"Yeah," I say in a wobbly but brave voice, "I think you're right, Monday." Monday simpers. Why is she so repulsive and why does she have 1.2 million followers on Insta? "I mean, Jane is—there's something off about her for sure—but it might have just been an accident." See? Not a monster. I *am* trying to pin Kurt's death on his own idiocy. Jane is just a fail-safe.

I take a deep breath. I've mastered the art of the Heroic Inhale. Mine lasts for a full second and is done with eyes closed and a resigned look on my face. It's supposed to convey: I hate to do this, but I will because I am a trooper. "I'm going back to the city. I can't stay in this house, knowing what happened."

"Oh, honey, I don't know—you drove here, right? You'd be driving in the dark," Rebecca says. What is her obsession with me? Never mind Jane; I should've told everyone Rebecca's my stalker.

"No, it's fine. I'm fine," I say in the I'm-not-really-fine-but-I-will-be-because-I'm-so-brave voice. "I just can't stay here any longer. How can you all stomach it? The thought of Kurt—" I finish the sentence in a sob.

Everyone shifts uncomfortably. That's right, assholes, I am purposefully trying to make you uncomfortable about staying here. I want everyone to disperse like ants. Only about half of this crowd lives in New York; the rest are strewn all over the country. If I can get the group to break up, it'll make it just that little bit harder for the cops to ask follow-up questions in case they have any.

"Yeah, I'm gonna head back too," Monday says. "Too much drama here for my mental health."

"Would anyone like to hitch a ride back to the city?" I ask. Ugh, I hope none of them takes me up on the offer. But whatever it takes to get them the hell out of here.

"Sure," Rebecca says.

The things I do to get away with murder.

After that, everyone else does decide to leave Montauk (phew). If not for Rebecca and her revolting breath stinking up my car, I would've breathed a huge sigh of relief as I drove away from the house. But like beggars, murderers can't be choosers. I put up with her yammering the entire drive back to Manhattan about her latest WIP and how wonderful her agent thinks she is ("I'm her star client, she tells me every day!") and how useless her publicist is ("Couldn't even get me a cover reveal on EW, what the hell? It's like, you have one job, Mikayla!").

Finally, we're back in the city and I can make up an excuse to drop her off at the nearest subway station. I grin all the way back to my penthouse apartment. I did it! They were right when they said that hard work pays off! So many obstacles in my climb to the top—my useless mother, Antoine, Kurt—but I've done it. I am now a bona fide *New York Times* bestselling author with a magnificent agent and a glittering career ahead of me. My plan isn't done yet; there are still a couple of steps ahead of me to secure the life I deserve, but the hardest part—killing Kurt— is over. Tomorrow, Ivan and I will go back to Indonesia, where the rest of my plan can unfold in as effortless a way as possible.

Shall I tell you the rest of my plan? No, I shall leave it as a surprise. I hate surprises, but I do love springing them on people, because my surprises are actually good ones.

After handing the car key to the valet, I practically dance my way to the private elevator. Inside, I tap my foot impatiently as I watch the numbers go up. I am so jubilant, so incandescent with victory, that when the doors slide open and I spot Ani at the picture window overlooking Central Park, I don't get the stab of annoyance that I usually do when I see her. Then she turns around and my interest is piqued, because her expression is an awful mix of everything—fear, alarm, sorrow. Ooh, maybe her mother is dead. Or her father? Or better yet, both.

"Ani, what is it?" I say in a concerned voice as I step out of the elevator.

"Where have you been? I've been calling you nonstop."

I'd turned my phone off because one must focus when killing a man. "Oh, sorry, I must've turned my phone off. What is it?"

"It's Ivan," she says, her voice catching. Tears well up in her eyes. "He had a heart attack. I don't know if he's going to make it."

And with that, she pitches herself at me and bursts into tears as I stand there, stunned to silence. Because, oh, irony of ironies, I might have gotten away with Kurt's murder, but I think I'm about to go down for my husband's.

25

JANE

If someone had told me just a day ago that I would be genuinely glad for Ted's company, I would've cackled out loud. But here I am, ever so grateful that my husband ignored me and made his own decision to remain in Manhattan. He's borrowed money from his parents to help pay to extend our stay, telling them it's for our upcoming five-year anniversary. Normally, I would've balked at that, tying myself up into knots about being indebted to them. But I can't afford to tie myself into any more knots right now. I'm out of string; every available length is well and truly tangled up. I'm barely coherent as Ted gently pries what happened in Montauk out of me. When I'm finally out of words, he leans back on the sofa with a huge sigh.

"Jesus, Jane. That's massively fucked-up."

I stiffen, readying myself for him to blame me somehow. Maybe he'll tell me that I'm just being too sensitive, that I imagined all of those accusatory glares and questions. Or maybe he'll tell me that I shouldn't have gone, remind me that he tried to keep me here, that he knew all along that going to a retreat with a group of strangers wasn't the best idea.

"And the cops haven't said either way? If it was an accident or . . ."

I shake my head. Here it comes. *I told you, Jane, you shouldn't have gone, you should've listened to me, you should've . . .*

"Shit. I'm sorry this happened to you."

I brace myself, but he doesn't say anything else. Wait. That's it? That can't be it. This is my husband we're talking about. He never lets an opportunity to prove me wrong go. "You can just say it," I mutter.

"Say what?" He frowns at me.

"I told you so, I told you not to go there," I say, mimicking his voice.

The creases on his face deepen. "Why would I say that? You've obviously been through a lot of shit."

I stare at him, and it's like I'm seeing him in a new light. Part of me wants to fight, to prod him into arguing with me because that's all I know to do in these situations. But the other part of me is just exhausted. "Never mind."

"No, I think we should talk about that, because—" Ted takes a deep breath. "For a while now, I feel like you take everything I say in the worst possible way, and I don't think that's healthy for either of us."

I bristle, but before I can come up with some bitter retort, he says, "I care about you. I want us to be able to work it out. And I realize that I often say the wrong things, but it's really because I want to be included. I want to be able to celebrate your achievements, all your publishing news—I feel like you've been wanting to keep me apart from that, like maybe you don't think I care about it, but I do. I really, really do."

"But you're always . . ." The rest of the sentence fades away as I go through our past interactions. Everything he had said or asked that I had seen as a put-down. I'd thought they were moments where he was twisting the knife, but with an awful rush, it hits me now that he was showing genuine interest. He'd asked if he could come to dinner with me and Toni, and it wasn't because he'd thought I was lying, but because he'd really wanted to partake in what he thought was a celebration of my career.

The realization nearly knocks me over. For as long as I can remember, I stopped seeing him as my ally and started seeing him as the enemy. All of our interactions have been tainted with the purpose of winning, and to win, the other person needs to lose. All of those questions he'd asked about my books, about Toni, about Harvest, hadn't been because he wanted to be cruel. They'd been because he wanted to be included, and maybe he's just as awkward as I am when it comes to making conversation, and maybe, yes, I have been interpreting everything he says in the worst possible way.

My eyes start filling again, and I say, more to the floor than to him, "I'm sorry. I don't know why I'm like this. I don't want to be." More tears come. "I'm so tired of being myself, Ted. I don't know what to do! I don't! I just—"

"Hey, it's okay. It's going to be okay. We can talk to someone. Whatever you need." He wraps his arms around me and murmurs into my hair as I break.

———

THAT SAME NIGHT, OVER A GLASS OF WINE, WE SIT DOWN with my laptop and look up online counselors, because I decided that an in-person session would be too much. My mind is a mess. Part of me wants to do this as quickly as possible, rip off the Band-Aid before I have a chance to chicken out. If we were to wait until we got back to the Bay Area, I would probably lose my nerve. Years ago, after a particularly bad fight, Ted had suggested that we see a couples counselor, but my whole body had rejected it immediately. My muscles spasmed; my scalp tightened like it was trying to crush my skull. Mom's voice, whispering at the back of my mind: *Therapists are all fakes, making up imaginary problems so people give them money to fix them. You're either crazy, or you're normal. If you're crazy, then you go to a mental hospital. If you're normal, then deal with your own problems. Why do people insist on wasting money just to have a stranger listen to their problems? Why is your generation so soft?* I mentally scream at Mom to shut up, but as soon as she does, another part of me whispers: *What if Ted finds out I'm a sociopath?* He'd leave me for sure. Days ago, I would've said I'm fine with it, but now I realize it would devastate me. Somehow, bolstered by the wine and Ted's reassurance and the absolute fucking mess I've made of everything, I manage to agree to an appointment for the next day.

The following morning, we sit stiffly on the love seat inside our hotel room, my phone propped up in front of us, both of us smiling nervously as the mental health app logs us into our session. The session begins, and the counselor isn't at all the way I'd pictured counselors to be. She's in her forties with pink hair, wearing a button-down blouse that shows off the intricate tattoos on her arms. Her appearance disarms me enough that I feel my walls shifting ever so slightly.

"Good morning, Jane and Ted," she says. Her voice is soothing, like a librarian during story time. "I'm Kathryn. What brings you here today? Jane, would you like to start?"

I stare mutely.

Kathryn smiles reassuringly. "Well, how about telling me a little about yourself?"

Still, I can't find the ability to speak. Ted squeezes my arm and I flinch.

"Maybe I can start," he says. Thank fuck, because I don't know what the hell is wrong with me. I sit there, half listening as he spills everything, about how fraught our marriage has become, how he feels like I take everything he says as an attack, how on edge we both feel at all times. And with everything he reveals, I feel more and more emotions piling up—frustration, anger, sorrow—leaping from the ether and turning into a giant ball of feelings that I have to fight to hold back.

Kathryn nods like she understands, but she doesn't. No one does, and how could they? They don't know the kind of monster I truly am, the sick thoughts crawling like spiders inside my head. "You'd be surprised," she says, when Ted's done, "to know that many couples go through the same struggles you do . . ."

It's too much. The monster bursts out of me. "No they don't, because most people aren't married to sociopaths!"

Kathryn falls silent. Ted stares at me. "Um," he says after a beat. "I understand that I've probably not been the best husband, but calling me a sociopath is a bit much—"

"No, not you," I say through gritted teeth. "It's me. I'm a sociopath. I've done all these tests and it's what I am. I hid it from everyone else because—I don't know—I guess I just wanted to fit in, and I'm sorry I tricked you into marrying a monster, but . . . yeah."

Ted's staring at me like I've just grown an extra eye.

"Jane," Kathryn says, "when you say you've done tests, do you mean you were tested by a professional and given a medical diagnosis of APD?"

"No. I just—I found tests online—"

"There aren't any official tests you can take online, as far as I know. What kinds of questions did these tests ask you, do you remember?"

I try to ignore Ted's stare and recount as many questions as I can. Kathryn nods encouragingly. If she's judging me, she hides it well.

"Interesting," she says after a while. "Can I ask you a few questions, Jane?"

I shrug.

"Do you often feel fear that others will judge you for whatever reason?"

"Yes, you definitely do," Ted says, nodding at me.

Kathryn smiles. "Ted, maybe we can let Jane speak for herself."

"Sorry." He deflates.

I don't even feel satisfaction; I'm too absorbed in what Kathryn just asked me. Slowly, I open up my box of memories, cautiously, as though it's Pandora's box. "Uh. Yeah." My voice comes out soft at first, but the deeper I go into the box, the more I see it. How I'd felt about going to Montauk, the way I felt at Sus-Pens Con, always lost, always an outsider. "Yes. Always."

Kathryn nods. "Do you have intense fear of interacting with strangers?" When I hesitate, she says, "This fear may manifest itself in different ways that might not seem like fear. For example, on the surface you might feel intense exhaustion, or stress, or in some cases, even anger."

I find myself nodding along before I even realize it. "Angry, yes. I often feel angry when it comes to other people. But isn't that anger because of my sociopathy?"

"Let's put the possibility of sociopathy—or antisocial

personality disorder—aside for now. I'm just trying to gather more information for now. No labels, okay?"

I don't know what I am without the label of a sociopath, so I just shrug.

"Do you spend time after a social interaction hyper-analyzing your behavior and finding flaws in the way you behaved?"

"Yes. All the time. I do it during the interaction too." I almost add, *because I'm a sociopath and I don't know how to behave normally*, but I stop myself.

She asks me a few more questions, and I'm sure, so sure that when this is all done, she'll tell me that yes, I'm right, I'm a sociopath and there's no saving my marriage. But when she finishes with her questions, she gives me an empathetic smile and says, "Jane, you don't have APD. You're not a sociopath."

"What?" Panic laps at the edges of my consciousness. "But everything I've said—the anger, not knowing how to interact—"

"Yes, I believe you have social anxiety, Jane. Keep in mind I can't formally diagnose you without doing a proper evaluation in person, but—" She shakes her head. "I'm very sure you don't have APD. My guess—and I encourage you to come in for a proper evaluation—is that you have social anxiety disorder that manifests in anger toward yourself and others. In fact, I would say that your strong belief that you have APD is a way for yourself to cope with your anxiety—you have intense fear around social interactions and other everyday activities, so you tell yourself that you don't care, and that you're perhaps not as good with social interaction as you want to be because you're a sociopath. It gives you back some semblance of control, thinking that it's because you're apathetic and don't care about others instead of the truth, which is that you're scared of people."

"I—what?" I'm shaking my head, my voice unrecognizable. "No, you're wrong, I took all those tests—"

"Like I said, there are no online tests that have been approved by the DSM-5 that can diagnose APD. Not to mention that self-diagnosis is very hard and discouraged by most health professionals. Evaluating and identifying mental health issues can be a long and confusing process."

She might as well be speaking Russian. I don't understand what she's saying. I can't. I stare blankly at the computer screen, mouth agape. I'm not a sociopath? But all those thoughts I've grown up having, all the anger and malevolence. It feels as though she's just broken a part of my identity. I want to scream at her.

But underneath the whirlwind of emotions, a small part of me is nodding its head and agreeing. A small voice at the back of my head is sighing with relief that after all this time, it's finally being understood. My eyes fill with tears, and I take a shuddery breath. I am unmade, shattered, yet I'm also relieved.

I'm not a sociopath. I don't have APD.

Maybe.

I'm not ready yet to fully embrace this new identity. She could be wrong. Couldn't she? Of the two of us, she's the one with a degree in psychology. My mind swims.

I look at Ted. He's regarding me with concern. "So all this time," he says, "you thought you were—what, *American Psycho*?"

"I would encourage you not to use such incendiary terms," Kathryn says.

Ted closes his mouth. Then he says, "I'm sorry. It's just kind of a lot."

"Yes. But proper evaluation is the first step to healing, and I think the two of you have a lot to think about after this session.

I'm going to give you some homework. Ted, your homework is to wear a rubber band around your wrist and snap it every time you talk over or talk for Jane. Make a mental note whenever you do it."

Ted gives a sheepish smile. "I guess I do that quite a bit."

Kathryn smiles. "And Jane, your homework is to wear a rubber band around your wrist as well—"

I lift my hand toward the phone to show that I already wear one, and she laughs. "Great! What have you been wearing it for?"

My cheeks burn with shame, though why I feel ashamed, I don't quite understand. Because I'd foolishly thought I could do the work of a trained psychologist by evaluating myself? Because I'd thought that I could control whatever it was I had all on my own? "To uh—control my anger."

Ted's mouth drops open. "I thought it was just to tie up your hair."

If I weren't so mortified over everything, I would've laughed at that.

She nods. "I see. It's actually very astute of you. But let's shift the focus so that you snap it whenever you start feeling that fear. Remember, in your case, it might feel like anger, so when you feel angry, snap the rubber band and remind yourself that you're not actually angry, it's just anxiety manifesting itself as anger. Over the next few weeks, we'll use some known cognitive behavioral therapy methods to cope with your anxiety. And some extra homework—I want you to look in the mirror every morning and every evening and say these words out loud: *I am not a sociopath. I do not have antisocial personality disorder. I have some anxiety around social interactions, which I will learn to cope with*. Okay?"

Everything inside me wants to fight it. I want to reject

everything she's said and pretend that none of this has happened, so I can go back to the familiar identity I've been wearing all these years. But the burden of that identity is going through life alone, feeling like a complete outsider while everyone else is celebrating life, a party I'm never invited to. And I'm tired of it. I've had enough.

I look at Ted and meet his eyes. They're filled with kindness, sorrow, and a small glimmer of hope. A tentative smile touches the corners of my mouth, and together, we nod.

26

THALIA

My husband is dead, and I am bereft. I am a grieving widow. I am beside myself.

No, I am not acting. I am genuinely distressed, though perhaps not for the obvious reason. No, I'm devastated because Ivan died too soon. About a year too soon, I would say. And now we (me and Ivan's body, that is) are stuck in New York, unable to go back to Indonesia because of his cunt of a sister. Let me catch you up. Go back in time, to that awful, horrific night in Oxford, where I was very nearly raped by an angry Frenchman.

After the cops came and took our statements, etc., I spent the night at Ivan's hotel room, being very gently cuddled by him. I made it clear that Antoine didn't manage to actually rape me before Jane came into the room and pushed him off me. Because I knew Ivan; he liked that I was a damsel in distress, but it would have been too much for him if I had actually been defiled. He didn't propose that night. I suppose he thought that proposing the same night some guy was killed in my room would be in bad taste. Or maybe he wasn't planning to propose that night at all.

It didn't matter. As it was, Antoine's attack turned into the perfect catalyst for my relationship with Ivan. I told him I was too traumatized to stay in Oxford, and he whisked me away to London, where we spent the next few days dining at Heston Blumenthal and Gordon Ramsay's Michelin-starred restaurants. He seemed to think that the key to recovering after a traumatic experience was to eat foie gras and langoustines and shop at Burberry and Gucci. I mean, I don't disagree. It's a fine strategy.

By the time I "recovered," he was besotted with me. I'd made it easy for him to fall in love with me. I was the perfect girl, one who challenged him in a coy, playful way that led to both of us tumbling into bed among shriek-giggles. I was vulnerable enough for him to feel like a big man, but not needy, not at all. Stable enough for him to want to take me home to see his family. I created a dream of us as a married couple—me, always happy to see him when he came home from work, running toward him—"Baby! You're home!"—and jumping into his arms. I said I loved to cook and wanted to cook for him every day, morning and night. I would wear nothing but an apron so that when he came home, I would be the ideal wife: a sex slave who cooks.

He fell for it. He was so into this image of me as his forever-slave that at the end of the week, he asked me to go with him to Jakarta.

By then, I knew that Ivan was my ticket to the kind of life-style I deserved. Hard work may turn you into a modest million-aire, but it sure as hell isn't going to give you access to mega yachts and private jets and mansions guarded by military police. So I said yes. We flew to Indonesia, and that was where I met his family.

His family, oh my. Where do I begin? I've watched *Crazy Rich Asians*, I thought I knew what to expect, but Chinese-Indonesians are an entirely different breed. First of all, they are extremely tight-knit. When I say extremely tight-knit, I mean Ivan still lived with his parents. Oh yes. This is common in Chinese-Indonesian cultures. These people own several mansions and luxury apartments in Jakarta alone, but do they utilize them? Nope. They choose to live in the biggest one in North Jakarta, a behemoth of a mansion with eight bedrooms, a fully equipped gym, a ballroom, a home theater, and two Olympic-size pools, one indoors and one outdoors. It's staggeringly luxurious, but I saw it for what it truly was: a gilded cage.

Ivan's parents are incredibly controlling. You think you know controlling? You haven't met these people. They controlled everything from Ivan's diet ("He must eat bird's nest soup every day!") to Ivan's bowel movements ("Have you been regular, dear?" they asked every morning, as if I wanted to hear about literal shit over my breakfast). From mouth to anus, they had to know what was going on.

No wonder Ani was half-insane by the time I met her in Oxford. Who wouldn't be driven mad by these people? Ani in Jakarta was a shell of the person I knew in Oxford. It would've been funny if it wasn't so pathetic. In Oxford, she had been wild and carefree, switching boyfriends as often as she switched expensive purses. In Jakarta, she became unrecognizable; even her makeup was different. She was a good, pious Chinese-Indonesian girl—she went to church every Sunday, her outfits were stylish but above all modest, and she never, ever spoke back to her parents. Sometimes, I'd catch her regarding me with a calculating look. I'd tried, one night, to pry her open and find the real Ani, but she'd locked Oxford Ani up in a steel box. I didn't blame her. I would've probably done the same if I had Ivan's parents.

And oh, how his parents hated me. The dirty foreigner come to colonize their precious son. They tolerated me until Ivan announced one year in that we were going to be married, then they tried everything to break us up. They even tried to pay me off to disappear. A measly $2,000,000 they offered me to dump their son. As if anyone in her right mind would have taken that, after seeing their true net worth. I took the $2,000,000 and gave the money, tears streaming down my face, to Ivan. He stormed into their room and told them they were repulsive, then he gave them the ultimatum: Let us be married, or else he would move out (gasp!). They quickly relented after that, though they did make me sign a prenup.

———   ———   ———

CONTRARY TO WHAT HOLLYWOOD WOULD HAVE YOU believe, people with APD don't necessarily like killing. I, for one, find it rather bothersome. Unhygienic. All that blood. (Between you and me, I feel that Antoine bled so much just to get back at me; that was exactly the sort of petty man he was.) I didn't go into the marriage planning to kill Ivan. I didn't have anything against him; he was always perfectly benign. That's a very deliberate word choice, by the way. I'm a writer; I think hard about these things, and "benign" describes Ivan most accurately. He's inoffensive, unthreatening, and I didn't mind his presence much for the first few years of marriage. How many married couples can say that? Everyone is always so obsessed about being #blessed and #livingyourbestlife, and here I am, modest little Thalia, perfectly satisfied with benign. And I could have tolerated Ivan for a much longer time if not for his abhorrent family. I'm the true victim here; I was given no choice but to kill him, because of the prenup.

Prenups. Aren't they just the worst? They're only there to protect the rich from the rest of us. But I saw the loophole right away: If Ivan and I had a divorce, I would get nothing, but if Ivan were to die . . . well, they failed to specify that in the prenup. So there was my answer, clear as day. All I had to do was wait until Ivan passed away.

I'm very good at waiting.

It took a while to figure out how to kill Ivan. For months after I decided to kill him, I continued playing my role as a dutiful Chinese-Indonesian wife. I followed him on his business trips to Shanghai and Dubai and bought decadent souvenirs for his parents—dates as fat as scarab beetles, ginseng more expensive than gold bars. Every gift I gave them, they came up with some reason to push aside. They only drank ginseng from South Korea, not from China. They found dates sickeningly sweet, never mind the fact that they inhaled sticky-sweet palm sugar syrup like it was water.

I accompanied his mother everywhere, carrying her snake-skin Birkin for her like a handmaid. I called her "Mama" and I called his father "Papa" and I called Ani "Saosao," which means "sister-in-law" in Mandarin. Imagine being Ani's sister. The sheer horror. Luckily, Mama and Papa didn't much care for Ani either. They were all about Ivan.

My patience was rewarded when I was allowed to accompany Ivan on his annual checkup at the Mount Elizabeth Hospital in Singapore. Mount Elizabeth is the most overpriced hospital in Singapore, so naturally, it's teeming with Chinese-Indonesians. Chinese-Indonesians adore coming here for annual checkups. They're paranoid and have too much money to know what to do with, so every year, they subject themselves to extensive blood tests and scans to get reassurance that no, they're not about to randomly drop dead. Ivan was no exception to this rule, but Ivan actually had something to worry about, because apparently, my husband had some hereditary heart condition that required a bit of monitoring. Belatedly, I recalled Ani's comment all those years ago in Oxford, when she told Ivan not to punt because of his heart. I'd dismissed it as a stupid barb then, because of course, everything that came out Ani's mouth was a barb.

"It's fine," his doctor assured Mama, Papa, Ivan, Ani, and me. (Of course, Mama and Papa and Ani had come with us on this trip. They, too, had a series of unnecessary tests to undergo at Mount Elizabeth.) "Still seeing a little bit of arrhythmia, but overall you're in good condition." He prescribed some medication and charged us $3,600 for this. Mama and Papa fussed over Ivan. *My sweet baby, oh my poor darling. Talia* (This was how they pronounced my beautiful name, butchering it so the Th-sound turned into a harsh T. Just one of the many transgressions that I dutifully jotted down in my little notebook.), *you must take better care of him!*

I nodded and kept my head lowered so they wouldn't see my smile. A hereditary heart condition. Interesting. As soon as we got back to their apartment in Singapore—a penthouse off Orchard Road, one of the most sought-after districts in a city of wealthy expats—I nagged Ivan into bed and told his parents I was going to the pharmacist to find the best supplements for him. They nodded, satisfied at this over-the-top show of concern, and off I went. Once I was out of the apartment, I logged on to a VPN and did a search on his heart condition.

He had some sort of hereditary arrhythmia, which was

basically just a fancy way of saying that his heart didn't beat to the correct rhythm. For a rule follower like Ivan, this seemed a tad ironic. Fortunately for Ivan, thanks to his gaggle of attentive, well-paid doctors, his condition was kept under control. Unfortunately for Ivan, his poor, long-suffering wife was about to take what was rightfully hers.

At the pharmacist, I asked for "heart healthy vitamins and supplements" and selected the most expensive ones. Then I asked for a bottle of caffeine pills. I've just been so tired nowadays, I told the shopkeeper, and I hate the taste of coffee. The shopkeeper shrugged and gave me a bottle of their strongest caffeine pills. I asked if they had anything stronger, and they shrugged again and told me to Google it. Which I did. I found out that while caffeine pills held a comparable amount of caffeine to a cup of coffee, pure caffeine powder is a whole other story. A teaspoon of caffeine powder is equivalent to twenty cups of coffee. And, oh look, I could easily order them online. How very convenient. I practically skipped all the way back to the apartment.

I had to be very, very careful. Indonesia has capital punishment, and the police are largely in the pockets of the rich and powerful (i.e., Ivan's family). If they even suspected foul play that involved me, I would either rot in an Indonesian prison cell or be killed quickly in the dead of night. No one would miss me; I didn't have any close friends, and my only remaining relative is Aunt Claudette, who would be torn between sadness and relief at the news of my demise. The precarious position I'd put myself in, to be married into this tyrannical family.

So I did what I do best. I planned meticulously. And it was a plan that would take years. I couldn't just cram a whole bottle of caffeine powder into Ivan's mouth and call it done. No, I started off small. A sprinkle here and there. He started sleeping badly, tossing and turning in bed, waking up in the morning looking disheveled. I visited him at his office, where I'd subtly sabotage him—misplace an important document, change the numbers on his spreadsheet. Nothing that would actually derail and bankrupt the company (hey, I wanted that money), just little things that I knew would stress him out, so that when he came home in a bad mood, I could cluck over him, in front of Mama and Papa, and tell him he was working too hard, that it wouldn't be good for his health. This was trickier to pull off than it should have been, because Ani was always hovering around like a wraith. Often, when I dropped by the office, I'd find her there, skulking around, butting into conversations and just generally trying to insert herself in Ivan's business, so desperate to become relevant within the company. It was honestly pathetic, and very irritating as I would have to make sure she wasn't paying attention to me while I changed numbers around.

Then I would hold off for a couple of months, helping out at his office to make sure things ran smoothly. No more caffeine. Just to make a clear connection that it was his work that was causing him stress and definitely not his loving, helpful wife. Then back to more powder, mixing it into his morning kale smoothies, his maguro salad bowl, his chicken soup, until he was worried enough to fly back to Singapore for another checkup. The doctor put him on a heart monitor for three days, which showed nothing of concern (I eased up on the caffeine then) and cost us over $20,000. You know how bloody hard it was to pull it off? I had publishing deadlines to meet, not to mention cons that I tried my best to attend, though at times I did have to turn them down, yet another reason I had to punish this awful family.

Once we came back to Jakarta, I started him back on the caffeine. It was actually rather fun, like a little game we were playing with each other. When the palpitations happened again, Mama and Papa insisted he fly to Japan for a checkup. Another doctor, another heart monitor. *He's fine*, the doctor said. *Is anything stressing him out?*

His work, I piped up. *I wish he'd take more time off from it.*

Listen to your wife, the doctor said.

Good dog.

Yes, listen to Talia, Mama and Papa said.

I almost cried at that. Finally, all those years of hard work, trying to prove myself, that I was a good wife, had paid off. In fact, I was so moved by this that I decided to postpone killing Ivan. I wanted to bask a little in his parents' approval. How crazy is that? The Chinese-Indonesian culture of sacrificing everything for your parents' approval had actually managed to sink its claws into me. Mama and Papa's approval was like a drug; they doled it out in stingy little pinches, and the more I got, the more I wanted. This part was my fault—I fully admit to it. I should've just gone ahead and killed him when I'd planned, but I let myself be distracted.

Obviously, it didn't last long. After a few months of it, I got bored and resumed my plan. But by then, Kurt had started talking about leaving his wife for me. It soon became clear that I had to get rid of Kurt first. If anyone in Indonesia got wind of my affair, it would be all over for me. I tried, I really did, not to have to resort to killing him. I tried to break things off, plying him with all of the charms I had (which is a lot), but nope. Surly, selfish Kurt. If he couldn't have me, then he'd make sure no one else could. Of course, killing Kurt meant that I probably shouldn't kill anyone else for at least another year. It meant postponing Ivan's death, which I wasn't thrilled about, but I could stomach it. I told you I was very good at being patient.

——— — —

BUT NOW, SOMEHOW, IVAN'S DEAD. A MERE DAY AFTER Kurt's fatal accident, which looks bad. Very bad.

I pace about the penthouse. I go through the papers from the hospital, all those medical terms, the numbers that mean nothing, and I ask myself: *Where did I go wrong?* I'd let up on the caffeine powder for over two months now, since I decided to kill Kurt. Yes, I realize that all those years spent messing around with Ivan's heart probably worsened his condition, but surely, it wasn't enough to actually kill him this fast? No, it couldn't be. Whenever I eased up on the caffeine, he'd quickly bounce back to normal. Unless his heart was still bothering him but he kept it from me, because men can't help but lie.

A surge of anger stabs through me, and I crush the hospital document and fling it at the wall.

"Knock-knock," Ani says, popping her head in. She actually says the words instead of knocking. "How are you doing?"

"What do you think? My husband's dead." It's surprisingly easy for me to allow a small sob to escape. I am upset, after all. He really was taken away from me too soon.

Ani stretches the corners of her mouth and eyebrows down, making a literal sad-face emoji. "And my brother's dead. You're not the only one who lost someone here."

Typical Ani. Of course she'd make this about herself. I stop moving and just stare at her until she looks away.

"Sorry, I didn't mean it that way," she says finally. "I just—I don't even know what to do. He's been there my entire life, and now he's not, and I don't understand why." At this, she breaks down sobbing, sinking gracefully onto the chaise longue. I roll my eyes and grit my teeth before sitting down next to her and putting my arm around her shaking shoulders.

I count to ten and then say, "Okay, enough of that. We need to be strong, Ani. We need to make arrangements." We need to get Ivan's body the fuck out of America and back to Indonesia, hopefully outrun any suspicions that might be cast on me after Kurt and Ivan's deaths. One day apart! I could cry at the thought of my unbelievably bad luck. "Don't you worry about a thing. I'll take care of everything. I'll see to it that he's flown back ASAP and buried in your family plot—"

"No!" Ani cries, pulling away from me.

I blink at her, confused.

"No, are you kidding? His body is not leaving this country until we know exactly what happened."

My stomach turns to ice. "What do you mean?"

"Mama and Papa are on their way here right now."

I'm so shocked by this that I almost miss the glint in Ani's eyes. Almost. As I stare at her in mute horror, her lips tremble like she's fighting back a smile, and she says, "Don't you worry, my sweet sister-in-law. We are going to get to the bottom of this."

And I know, then, that I've made a terrible mistake. All those years of planning, all those careful moves I'd made, and I'd missed a crucial factor: Ani. Like everyone else, I never even spared a thought for her. I assumed that I was the only predator around, when all this while, there was another more dangerous creature in the family, and now she's standing right in front of me, smiling a smile that says: *I got you.*

27

JANE

Every day feels like a dream. Okay, granted, it's only been two days since Ted and I had our session with Kathryn, but it feels like something huge has shifted. After that session, I went to the bathroom and cried until my eyes ran out of tears, then I just dry-sobbed until I was completely and utterly empty. I thought of myself as a little kid, and myself as a teen, and myself in my twenties and now, thirties, the whole time believing that I was a sociopath just because I happened to take some stupid online quizzes that told me I was. Just because I thought I was smart enough to do the work of trained psychologists. Just because I had social anxiety and didn't know how to deal with it. I spent the next hour or so going through my memories, reliving all the social interactions I could think of and identifying all those feelings of apathy and anger for what they truly were—fear and anxiety. How could I have been so wrong about myself? I looked up antisocial personality disorder, and this time, I saw many, many traits that didn't fit my personality. Traits that I had dismissed years ago, telling myself that of course I wouldn't have all the symptoms of sociopathy, that I was an individual and not a statistic.

Surprisingly, Ted had left me to cry for as long as I wanted, and only when I came out of the bathroom of my own accord did he approach me, with a plate of cheese and crackers and a glass of wine. He gave me a hesitant smile and said, "Thought you might be hungry."

And I looked at my husband and didn't hate him.

We spent the rest of the day in Central Park, just walking through the lush greenery holding hands and talking about any-thing and everything. He asked me how I felt, and I told him "Like a mess." But after a beat, I added, "But also hopeful." And that was enough for him. And it was enough for me too.

The next day, we went and did the tourist thing. Went to the Statue of Liberty, got the hats, went up the Empire State Build-ing. We didn't kiss or hug—we weren't ready for that yet—but we held hands, and I snapped my rubber band whenever I felt angry and I reminded myself it wasn't anger but fear that I was feeling. And he snapped his rubber band whenever he talked over me, and then gave me a sheepish smile and said, "Wow, I do that a lot, huh?" After a full day of this, I was tired but like I said, hopeful.

———

WE'RE IN THE MIDST OF PACKING UP FOR THE AIRPORT when there's a knock on the door. I immediately know some-thing's wrong, because it's not the kind of knock that precedes the words, "Room service." It's the kind of insistent knock that precedes the words, "Open up, we know you're in there!"

In fact, what the person opposite the door says is worse. "Jane Morgan? It's Detective Howe. Please open the door."

Detective Howe. Why's she here? The old anger resurfaces and I snap the rubber band, but knowing that the emotion is actually fear doesn't make me feel any better in this moment. Ted looks at me with brows raised, his face largely unconcerned. "You okay?" he says.

I nod. I am okay, I remind myself. There's absolutely no reason why I wouldn't be okay. No reason at all. I didn't do anything wrong.

"Yeah, I'm fine." I flash him a small smile and head for the door, taking a deep inhale before opening it. "Hi, Detective."

She doesn't return my polite smile. Instead, she frowns at the scene behind my shoulder. "Are you leaving town?"

"Uh. Yeah? We're flying back to the Bay Area today."

"Yeah?" she says, and it comes out like a challenge, like, *Yeah? You think so, do you? Well, you have another think coming.* "What time's your flight?"

Ted comes up to the door, standing just behind me. "Hi, I'm Ted. Jane's husband."

"Detective Howe." They shake hands.

"Is everything okay here?" Ted says, and I feel the old irritation starting to scrape at my nerves. He's doing that thing again, inserting himself where he's not needed, playing at being The Man of the Household. I remind myself that he's probably doing this to reassure me, to remind me that he's on my side. But I bristle anyway, because I'm used to not having anyone on my side.

I expect Detective Howe to say yes, of course everything's okay, but instead, she says, "We have a few follow-up questions for you, Jane. Can you come back with us to the station? It would be really helpful if you did. It would only take an hour."

"But we're flying out—" Ted says.

"I can spare an hour to answer some questions," I say. I don't know what made me say that, except that I feel an urgent, overwhelming need to show that I'm trustworthy, that I'm here to help. Good old Plain Jane, always here to help! I desperately need to prove that I'm innocent, and to do that I must surely agree with anything and everything they ask of me.

"Great."

"Just let me grab my stuff first."

"Of course."

I go back into the room and shove random things into my purse, half in a daze. I keep having that out-of-body sensation like I'm floating above myself and wondering, *How would an innocent person behave? What would an innocent person bring to the police station for an interview?* Which is strange, because I am an innocent person, so I shouldn't need to think about this. I'm vaguely aware of Ted fussing around me, asking things like, "Are you sure this is a good idea? Should I call a lawyer?"

"Only guilty people need lawyers," I bite out.

Ted stops short. "That's not—I don't think that's true. I—"

"I'll be fine." Maybe the last two days have been a dream after all. It's surprisingly easy to slip back into the old ways, wearing my resentment at him like an old sweater, wrapping it tight around me. I don't give him a second glance before walking out the door. I can feel the hurt radiating from him in thick, slow waves, and it's a relief when the door finally clicks shut, cutting me off from Ted's gaze. I let out my breath.

"Thanks for agreeing to come with us," Detective Howe says.

I nod, not trusting myself to say anything. Never mind my stomach, everything inside me is knotted up, even my muscles. It's almost next to impossible for me to keep walking. I'm actually relieved when we get out of the hotel and her car's right outside, a gray, nondescript sedan. I'd been half expecting a black-and-white police car with flashing lights, Howe placing her hand on my head as she "helped" me into the car. But nothing like that happens. I get in normally, like I'm sliding into an Uber.

The station, at least, is reminiscent of TV police stations, all gray walls and stark fluorescent lights and a dozen cops going about their day, filing paperwork, talking to one another. A couple of them are walking some guy in handcuffs in, and the sight puts me on edge. Howe waves and greets other officers and leads me into a room marked as "Interview Room 4."

"Can I get you a drink? Coffee, tea? Coke?"

I shake my head. I just want to get this over with. "I'm fine."

"Great. Have a seat and let me just . . ." She takes out her phone and then pauses. "It's okay if I record this, yeah?"

That catches me off guard. The way she asked that, so casually, like it's something she's just remembered at the last minute. "Yeah." It's not like I could say no.

She unlocks her phone and calls up the voice recording app. Presses the big red button. "Okay, great. I'm Detective Tricia Howe, speaking with Jane Morgan. Can you confirm that's your name?"

I nod, and she says, "Can you please give me verbal confirmation that your name is Jane Morgan?"

"Oh, yes. It's Jane Morgan." My stomach lurches unpleasantly. This feels way too official for what I was prepared for.

She gives me an encouraging smile. "So first of all, thank you for coming to the station with me, Jane."

I press my lips together, wondering what to say to that. It's not like she's asked me a question.

"I'd like to go over a few more details about what happened at Montauk."

I nod. "Sure."

"So you said that Thalia Ashcroft invited you to this retreat?"

"Yes."

"Do you remember what she said to you that made you think she invited you there?"

That made me *think* she invited me there? Beneath the table, my hands are wringing each other, my fingers writhing like snakes, pinching and strangling. "Um. She said, 'Come with me to this writers retreat.'"

"In those exact words?"

I stare at her. "No, I don't know, that was days ago. Of course I don't remember her exact words, but I remember the gist of it, and it's that she invited me." *Careful, Jane.* I'm letting my temper overwhelm me again. Again, I remind myself it's not my temper, but my fear. But it's really not actually helpful at all in this moment.

Detective Howe nods, and it's clear she doesn't believe me. "Is there anyone that can corroborate this?"

I claw at my memories and come up with nothing. "No."

"Hmm. Okay. Can we talk for a moment about how you know Thalia? You said you guys were friends in college."

You guys. She's trying to put me at ease—*look, Jane, I'm just a pal!* I nod. "Yeah. Well, not college. Grad school."

"Ah yes, of course. In Oxford, right? That's pretty fancy. So you two were classmates?"

We were much more than just classmates, I almost tell her, but I don't. "Yeah. Like I said, we were friends."

"But you mentioned that you lost touch after the first semester there. Would that have anything to do with what happened to . . ." She makes a big show of glancing at her notes. "Antoine Deveraux?"

My mouth snaps shut. I don't know why this surprises me. It shouldn't; I should've known the moment she brought up Oxford that she would've done her homework and that she must've known about Antoine. But I guess I'm not as cunning as I thought I was, because damn, that catches me off guard, and now I don't know what to say. "Yeah, well. What happened was—you know, it was very traumatic. Thalia left the program and didn't come back. I don't like to talk about it. Hell, I haven't even told my husband about it," I say with a small laugh.

She doesn't return the laugh. "What happened then? Can you fill me in?"

"The Oxford police didn't give you any details?" God, I'm way too acerbic. I need to be more pliant, more pleasant.

"They gave me a summary of what happened. Let's see . . ." Another glance at her notes, which I'm sure she's actually got memorized. "They said Antoine had stolen into the college and hid in Thalia's room, and when she went up halfway through the ball, he attacked her. Fortunately, you came into her room and were able to save her by"—she clears her throat—"stabbing him with a letter opener. Is that accurate?"

I look down at my hands. That awful night flashes through my head. Me going inside Thalia's room and finding Antoine covered in blood. Me, the besotted idiot, coming to Thalia's rescue. Offering to take the blame. God, I was so fucking stupid. Fleetingly, I wonder if I should tell Detective Howe the truth about what happened. But that would just come off crazy. She'd think I was making it up, and she'd probably become even more suspicious.

"Yeah." My voice comes out as a whisper.

"Can you walk me through how that happened? Because the

angle seemed a bit . . . off." She mimes grabbing someone with her hands. "If you were to grab him from the back and throw him off, then he would've been at this angle."

"There was a lot of struggling involved," I say quickly. "Thalia was there and she was fighting him, too, and he was just kind of, you know, fighting both of us."

"Sure, yeah, of course. Huh." She refers to her notes again. "Okay . . . And the Oxford police, did they do any sort of investigation?"

"I'm not sure? I mean, they interviewed everyone there. They reviewed the security tapes at the common areas, I think? But I also know that the university was keen to shut it down. There were a lot of whispers in the dorm afterward about how the university basically got the cops to close the case."

Detective Howe nods slowly. "Uh-huh. I can see that. A wealthy, powerful college like that, they wouldn't want the bad press. Especially since this guy stole in and nearly raped one of their students."

I nod, keeping my eyes on my lap.

"And ever since then, you never heard from Thalia?"

"Yeah, she kind of just went off the radar."

"Not even social media?"

I shake my head.

"Don't you think that's strange? I mean, we're on everything nowadays. Hell, I'm on TikTok. You know TikTok?"

"Sure." A lot of authors are on TikTok, doing all sorts of videos to convince people to BUY MY BOOK, GUYS!

"So you never tried looking for her on social media?"

"Once in a while." So many times. "I don't know, she was never on it."

"And you don't find that strange?"

"I don't know. I mean, I know people who're not on social media. My husband's not big on it."

"Oh, Ted doesn't have a Facebook account?"

I frown. "Well, he does, obviously. But he's not, like, on it, on it. He never checks it." As soon as I say that, I realize it's not true, because Ted checks Facebook about once a week.

"Right, that's common. But what you're saying is that Thalia doesn't even have a Facebook, or a Twitter, or an Instagram account, which is not normal."

I gape at her, opening and closing my mouth. "I mean—yeah, I guess it's not very common. But I don't understand what that has to do with me. Why am I getting grilled because Thalia's not on TikTok?"

I'm met with a long, drawn-out sigh. Detective Howe leans forward, clasping her hands in front of her, and looks me straight in the eye. "Have you ever wondered why she might have disappeared so completely after you killed Antoine?"

. The way she said "you killed Antoine" sends a chill down my spine. "Uh, hang on—"

"Because I have a statement from Thalia Ashcroft saying that you were obsessed with her. You were stalking her in Oxford, and yes, you did save her from Antoine, but she also felt like you weren't—hmm, how to say this delicately—like you were glad that you were given this opportunity to kill him and get away with it."

"What?" The blood in my veins stops flowing. Everything inside me has turned to jagged ice. "No, wait—"

"Obviously, she didn't tell any of this to the Oxford police; she said she was so terrified that she just wanted to get away from it all, and she took the chance to leave the city and escape your attention."

"Hang on—"

Detective Howe holds up a hand. "There's more. Thalia said after leaving Oxford, she deleted all of her social media profiles to ensure that you wouldn't be able to track her down. She even released her first few books under a pen name to avoid you. Then she said that when she got her big book deal, she felt so strongly about using her real name that she was willing to risk it, especially since it's been years since Oxford. She thought there was a good chance that you'd moved on. Kind of a silly risk to take, if you ask me." She actually winks at me then, like she's still trying to get me on her side even though she's lobbing these insane accusations at me. "And that was when you tracked her down again. Showed up at some book convention she was at? We've got a couple of witnesses saying you were behaving somewhat aggressively during her talk."

Behaving aggressively? I see a flash of myself at SusPens Con, overwhelmed by emotions at seeing Thalia again after all these years, shouting out a question at her. How I must have come off to onlookers. Unhinged. Like a stalker. "I don't like crowds."

She crooks her mouth into a mirthless smile. "We also spoke to Ani Pranajaya about you, and she swore that you stole a necklace from her? Erratic behavior, Jane. Everyone we talked to can attest to that."

Ani's necklace. God, who would've thought that it would come back to bite me like this?

"And of course, the other writers at the retreat all attest to you inviting yourself to Montauk. They said Thalia was obviously uncomfortable around you, but that she was too kind to tell you to go away."

Another flash of me and Thalia at Montauk, the way she'd gone inside first to let everyone know that I was there. What must she have told them? *Oh my god, my college stalker is here. Please be nice to her; she's dangerous and I'm so scared.* I can picture it so easily in my mind's eye, the way that Thalia's beautiful face would've looked then, tight with fear. No wonder they'd all been so quietly furious toward me. All those glares. The look on Kurt's face.

Kurt.

Realization smashes into me like a hammer. This is why. This is why she lured me back to her. Because she wanted me to go down for Kurt's murder.

"Why are you asking me these questions? Do they have to do with Kurt's accident?"

"Was it an accident, Jane?"

I glare back at her. I'm not going to be the one who looks away first, because I'm not guilty. I'm not the one who's failing to do my job. "Isn't it your job to find out if it was an accident?"

"You're right." She blinks. I win. But it's an empty victory. "We're still looking into it. It's just that some details are showing up and I thought it would be best to talk to people, cover our bases."

"So this is all just covering your bases? Asking me if I wanted to kill Antoine?" It's too much. All of it. I feel the truth bubbling inside me, hitting its boiling point before erupting. I can no longer keep it inside me. "I didn't kill Antoine!" I cry. "It was Thalia. She was the one who did it." The words sear themselves out of my mouth, leaving me breathless. There, my deep, dark secret is out.

But Detective Howe only looks smug. "Yes, Thalia did warn us that you might say that."

"She's fucking lying!" My voice comes out harsh with rage, and yes, it is rage, fuck what Kathryn says, because I know what anger feels like and it is this, hot and pulsing and animalistic.

Detective Howe's eyebrows shoot up into her hairline. She's looking at me like I'm a dangerous criminal, like she's this close to reaching for her gun. Somehow, by sheer teeth-gritting power, I manage to will myself to breathe. BREATHE. I suck in a breath through my teeth, clenching the armrests of my chair.

"I've been talking to many people, Jane," Detective Howe says. "They all say you're—you've got quite a temper, don't you? Your neighbors commented on it."

My neighbors? A flash of Kimiko, seeing me angry at Ted over his remark about me being untidy. I could kill Kimiko.

I flinch at the thought and look at Detective Howe guiltily, as though she could read my mind. I'm losing it. I need to get out of here.

"Am I under arrest?" I ask thickly.

"No. We're just talking, hoping to get more answers."

"I'm done talking." I'm done being helpful Jane. I'm done being anything. I'm buzzing with fear, I don't know what I'm doing, but I know I need to not be here anymore.

Detective Howe frowns. "Jane, I really advise you to—"

I jump out of my chair, out of breath, everything inside me screaming at me to run, and I just about manage to spit out, "Next time you want to speak to me, go through my lawyer."

28

THALIA

How the hell did I get outplayed by Ani of all people, for god's sake? As Mama and Papa land at a private airport in New Jersey, I pace about in my bedroom, going through all of the steps that led to Ivan's death. Ani has something to do with it, of that I am sure. And once I realize it, I could kick myself for missing it. All those years, living under the same roof with her and Ivan. The way she would sometimes watch him as he did the most mundane things—eating, swimming, watching TV. The way she often came with us to doctor appointments under the guise of being a caring sister. How she would often make a snarky remark about how everything is being passed down to Ivan purely on the basis of him being born a boy. The way Mama and Papa ignored her, tuning her out at mealtimes as though she weren't there. I never thought much of it, because obviously, Ani is unbearable. I can't blame Mama and Papa for ignoring her; it's probably the only way you can keep your sanity with a daughter like her around.

I'd just dismissed her as an insignificant little brat with the maturity of a five-year-old. But now, too late, I realize that this persona of hers—the flighty, party animal Ani—is a carefully curated one. I'd sometimes wondered why she bothered to do certain things—shop for branded bags and shoes, for example, when she couldn't be bothered to even wear them. Now I see them for what they truly are—a facade. The real her is far more calculating and horrifyingly more intelligent. I recall now how I once walked in on her at the office, on one of my visits there to sabotage Ivan. She'd been looking through his ledgers, and when I walked in, she'd looked up with a guilty flush. I'd thought she was just guilty because she was caught snooping, but now I see that it was something more sinister. She'd been planning.

I go back even further. To our Oxford days. How she portrayed this image of a party girl, but underneath that, she was always studying, always making connections with people she found useful. Forging business relationships, I realize. All this while, she'd been preparing herself for the eventuality of Ivan's death, so she could take over. And she'd developed this dumb fashionista persona so no one would even think of suspecting. Not even me. Fuck, I was so stupid.

Okay, enough of the self-hatred. This is what most people don't realize: self-hatred is indulgent. I know how contradictory it sounds, but trust me, hating yourself is not the opposite of narcissism. In fact, it's just another facet of it, because at the end of the day, the attention is still placed on you.

Sorry for the derail. I'm just a bit thrown off by the complexity of it all. I'm not used to feeling self-hatred. I hope I don't get used to it, because quite honestly? I'm pretty fucking amazing. And I hate Ani even more for making me feel even an ounce of self-hatred.

Okay. Think. Ivan (RIP) died of a heart attack. Did Ani trigger a heart attack somehow? Why not, right? It's the most obvious way of killing him. So how would she have done it? I pace faster around the room, gnawing at my fingernails. In my eagerness to figure it out, I almost Google "how to trigger a heart attack" but manage to stop myself in time. Shit. I must remember that the stakes are different now. I can't just Google whatever I want.

Fortunately, I always have a couple of burner phones with me. Perks of being rich: your burner phones are iPhones. I take out one of them now, log on to a VPN because I'm always careful, always putting as many layers between me and the truth as possible. Then I look it up.

Okay, so basically everything can lead to a heart attack. Amphetamines. Cocaine. Mercury. Too much alcohol. And of course, caffeine.

That tells me nothing. Except . . .

Ani was so fucking eager for an autopsy to be done. Which means whatever the results of the autopsy, it would be in her favor. What does that mean?

Cold dread spreads through my limbs as I make another realization. In case of Ivan's death, his wealth would go to the next of kin, which would be me, his wife. Which means that Ani doesn't just need to get rid of Ivan in order to get control over the family company. She also needs to get rid of me.

Shit, shit! I take in a sharp breath and force myself to calm down. I'm usually so good at being calm. But having all those years of meticulous planning and sacrifice go down the drain like this is infuriating. Not to mention the fact that I might actually end up going to prison for a crime I haven't had the chance to commit. How's that for irony? I hate irony.

Okay, so to frame me, Ani would have to—

What? What would she have done? I close my eyes, try to put myself in her shoes. How would she have done it? Once more, I go back to the previous months, the previous year, and this time, I think of Ani, sitting at the sidelines, watching me carefully as I went about my day. Watching me prepare Ivan's kale smoothies in the morning. I'd been so careful. I'd mixed some caffeine powder in with his protein supplements, so that in the mornings, I could simply add in the protein supplement in front of everyone without causing any suspicion. Or so I thought.

Now I see myself through Ani's eyes, and god, I was so smug I could smack myself. I see the way she watched me, and then she would've watched Ivan as he drank the smoothie. The way he became jittery, hyper. Each smoothie would've contained the equivalent of ten cups of coffee. Ani would've seen that. She would've made a note of it, his strange behavior, my behavior.

What else?

She would've kept watching. Maybe even kept a journal of Ivan's moods. It wouldn't have taken her long at all to figure out that there was a correlation between the days where I put in protein supplement powder and his jitters. His heart palpitations.

Ani, for fuck's sake. Of all people.

But just because she knows I was poisoning him doesn't mean she figured out what it was I was using. I could've been dosing him with cocaine, or a million other drugs. Not that it would make me any more innocent, but if she doesn't know, then she might not have used caffeine to kill him off.

My reverie is interrupted by the arrival of Mama and Papa. I hear them through even the thick bedroom walls, they're so fucking loud. They barge into the penthouse crying and wailing, and I hear Ani wailing back at them out in the living room. I can picture them now, clutching one another, finally acknowledging Ani's existence now that their son is dead. Belatedly, I realize I've made a mistake. I should've been waiting out there for them, should've been ready to play the role of dutiful daughter-in-law. Shit. Once again, I've been outplayed.

Too late to salvage that now, so I do the only thing I can think of. I quickly make my way to the darkest corner of the bedroom and crouch there. I run my fingers through my hair, messing it up. Then I start to sob. Minutes later, there's a knock on the door and I manage a teary "Yes?" Mama comes in and sees me, and I see the flash of satisfaction crossing her face at my disheveled state. I'm mourning her son the way I should, with all my being. I quickly cross the room and rush at her, flinging myself at her like she's a life raft. "Mama!" I cry, burying my face in her shoulder and letting loose another violent round of tears. I need her to think that Ivan's death has broken me, that I am nothing without her insipid son. Her shoulders shake with sobs, and gingerly, she pats me on the back.

"I don't know what to do without him," I wail. To them, women are incomplete without their husbands. "I might as well die!"

Mama sniffs. "Don't let yourself be destroyed by grief," she says. "You still have a whole life ahead of you. I'm the one who has lost my son. I'm the one who has lost her life."

That's right, mustn't upstage her grief. I lean back from her so I can give a small, brave smile. "You're right, Mama. I'm so sorry for your loss. I can't—I'm so sorry. I know how much you loved him. You're the best mother."

This brings forth more tears as she nods and cries. She agrees that she had been the best mother, even though the truth is that she'd been such an awful parent that one might say it was her fault that Ivan was killed. By her own daughter. To have raised such a monster and not realize it, that's a whole new level of negligence.

After a while, we both stumble out into the living room, clutching each other and taking turns sniffling. Ani is with Papa, who looks so shrunken and aged that I almost feel bad for him. He's almost unrecognizable. Just days ago, he'd been a healthy, strapping seventy-year-old man. Now he looks like he's one step away from his own grave. Ani, on the other hand, is pacing madly about the living room. She's glowing with triumph, though she disguises it well as rage.

"We need to know exactly what happened," she says. "Wouldn't you agree?" She aims this at me, chin raised, eyes blazing. A challenge.

"I—I don't know," I say softly. *Tread very, very carefully, Thalia.* "I'm just—the thought of them cutting him up—" I feel Mama stiffen next to me. Good. She's getting an image of her beautiful son being sliced into like a pound of meat on a cold metal slab.

"Yes, but somewhere, somehow, someone did something wrong," Ani argues. "How many doctors have we taken him to? And all of them said he was fine, and then suddenly he has a heart attack? These doctors deserve to lose their medical license, and that's not going to happen unless we can prove there was malpractice. That they missed something. I mean—" She pauses, choking back a loud sob. "They might as well have killed him themselves."

Mama and Papa straighten up at this, a light entering their eyes. Shit. Ani is good. Their grief is so overwhelming right now that they'd jump at any cause to distract them from the endless sorrow. And what better cause than revenge for their dead son?

I think fast. "It's next to impossible to prove medical malpractice. I don't want you to put yourselves through that for years and years. It's not—"

"No," Ani says, nodding her head. "I agree with you, Thalia. It's too much on Mama and Papa." She gives them both a sad smile. "I will do this. I'm not going to stop until we find out who killed my brother."

I can only watch, unable to say a thing, as Ani whips out her phone and calls the hospital to make arrangements for an autopsy to be done.

My blood chills. She's so insistent about it that I know then, whatever they find, it's going to be bad for me.

29

JANE

walk out of the police station in a daze. When I check my phone, I see seven missed calls and a dozen messages from Ted, asking me if I'm okay. It's been almost two hours since I left for the station. I hit Return Call. He picks up on the first ring.

"Jesus, Jane. Are you okay? I've been going crazy here. What happened?"

The concern in his voice is heartbreaking. Or it would be, if I weren't in shock. I want to tell him what happened, that I seem to be the suspect in Kurt's death, but as soon as I start to say it, my throat clamps up and the words won't come out. Because how ridiculous do they sound? It makes no sense. So instead, I say, "Yeah, it's fine. They just had a few follow-up questions that they've been asking everyone." How easy it is to lie to my husband.

"Okay . . ." He sounds unsure. I guess I'm not that great a liar. "Well, do you want to meet me at the airport? Because I don't think there's time for you to get back to the hotel. I've packed up everything—"

The airport. God. I'd completely forgotten about our flight. And as soon as he mentions it, I realize that there is no possible way I'm getting on that flight today. There's too much unfinished business left in New York. And how would it look to Howe if I were to fly back to California now? She'd think I was trying to run away.

"Um, actually, I think I'm gonna stay here for a while longer."

"What?"

"I just—there are some things I need to do." Like clear my name.

"Well—" He struggles to speak for a few moments before sighing. "Okay. I'll extend our room."

"No, I think you should go home, Ted," I say without realizing what I'm really saying until the words are out. But as soon as they're spoken, I know I meant them. I don't want him here. The past couple of days, we've been inching back toward each other, but now I'm about to do something I don't want him to know about. "Go home; don't bother checking out because I'm going to be staying on for another couple of days at least."

"But—" The word comes out sharp with so much pain that I have to close my eyes for a second.

"Go home." The words come out heavy with finality. I don't wait for an answer before hanging up. As soon as I end the call, I tap on his number and add it to my Blocked Contacts list. I can't afford to be distracted by Ted no doubt calling and texting me nonstop, demanding an explanation, wheedling, begging me to talk.

I go into a nearby café and buy myself a hot coffee. I need time to think about what just happened. I sit down in a far corner and start ripping up napkins into narrow strips to give myself a bit of a distraction while I work out the giant ball of shit that Thalia has somehow plopped into my life. Right. So this goes back years. Oxford. She's always been someone different. Beautiful on the outside; something repulsive and dangerous on the inside. I think about how, at Oxford, she'd fooled me into thinking she was a socially anxious person, and I realize with a kick of bitterness that she must have read me well, must've figured out that I have social anxiety and so pretended to have it as well to get my guard down. The thought of it is so overwhelming that I almost crush my coffee cup. I have to will myself to keep breathing, snapping the rubber band over and over.

Doesn't matter that she was a conniving little bitch, that she'd fooled me all this time, that she'd tricked me into claiming responsibility for Antoine's death. Oh god, Antoine. I'd believed her without any second thought, but now I know, without a doubt, that she'd killed him for no good reason. Maybe she was bored; maybe she was angry that he'd shown up unannounced— shit. He wouldn't have shown up if it wasn't for me. For years, I'd tortured myself, thinking that it was my fault that Thalia was assaulted, that she'd had no choice but to defend herself by killing him. But now I'm overcome by guilt because it was my fault that Antoine was killed.

Okay, focus. I need to prove that Thalia was behind everything all along. That she'd planned it so that she could kill Kurt and pin the blame on me. But how? I'm a pawn in a game I hadn't even realized was being played. What move would she make next? What weaknesses does she have?

I rack my mind, trying to remember every little detail she'd once shared with me. All the life stories she'd told me. All of them were lies, probably. I sift through them anyway. She'd hated her mom and never knew her dad, just like me. Was that real? Maybe. What else? Her mom was neglectful. Always leaving her to be looked after by someone else while she went out with a different guy every night. Someone else. Her neighbor. She'd mentioned her name three, four times, back when we were in Oxford. Aunt Claudine. Claudia? Claudette. That's it. And she'd said—what had she said about Aunt Claudette? That she wasn't actually related, but that she was the only family Thalia had, and that she was closer to her than she ever was to her own mother. She's mentioned her last name before, something starting with a Cl-. She'd joked that it made her sound like a porn star even though she looked nothing like one. And that night, at Skye Bar, she'd mentioned a relative who lives in Brooklyn. It's a long shot, but maybe she was referring to Aunt Claudette?

I take out my phone and do a search for "Claudette Brooklyn." Google spits out the results, and ugh, there are a ton of Claudettes in Brooklyn. I scroll down the page and—

Claudette Clovis. That's it. That's her. It's a Facebook page of hers. I click on it, and bless her heart, Aunt Claudette is one of those old women who overshares. She lives in a retirement home in New Jersey, a swanky place called Golden Years Estate. I order a Lyft and drain my coffee before going outside.

I have no idea what I'm going to say to Aunt Claudette. I know I'm grasping at straws, but know what's worse than grasping at straws? Grasping at thin fucking air. The whole drive there, I go over and over what I might say to her, but by the time I get to Golden Years, I still have no clue. The driver drops me off at the front, a thoroughly impressive grand entrance complete with a fountain and a massive doorway.

I walk inside and approach the receptionist, an altogether

too-shiny young man who looks like a living, breathing Ken doll, which is a lot more creepy than it sounds.

"Good afternoon, are you here to visit one of our residents?"

"Um. Yes. Claudette Clovis?"

His face breaks into a smile, and I'm half blinded by the whiteness of his teeth. "Oh, Ms. Clo, of course. May I ask who's visiting?"

For a moment, I freeze. Then I manage to spit out, "Uh. Jane. Just Jane."

"Okay, I'll let her know you're here." He picks up the phone and dials a number. After a few moments, he says, "Hi Ms. Clo, it's Aaron." He gives a simpering laugh. "Oh, Ms. Clo, you're so bad. I have a visitor here for you, a young woman named Jane. Yes." He glances at me and my stomach lurches. She's going to refuse to see me. "Jane, what's your last name?"

"Morgan."

He tells Aunt Claudette this and nods. "Okay, I'll send her right up."

Relief floods through me, followed quickly by suspicion. Why did she agree to meet with me? Maybe she's bored, I tell myself as I walk after Aaron. Yeah, she's probably just bored out of her mind in this place. We walk past a living room that opens up to a beautiful courtyard where I can see a handful of old men and women playing croquet, and a game room where more people are playing chess and other board games. My mind is half-wild with anxiety by the time we get to Aunt Claudette's room. Aaron knocks on the door, and when she calls for us to come in, he smiles at me and says, "Go ahead. Just call the front desk if you need anything."

With a deep breath, I check on my phone in my bag, making sure it's recording. I'm not sure why I'm doing this, keeping a record like this. What am I expecting to hear? I open the door and step inside.

Aunt Claudette's room is exactly as I pictured it would be—bright and airy and beautiful but with a smell of death about it. I don't know what it is, exactly, but despite the canary-yellow walls and the bright turquoise touches, there's a sense of heaviness in the air. Aunt Claudette, the large, white-haired old woman sitting in a wheelchair with her papery hands folded on her lap, is dying. I know this immediately.

"Hi, Ms. Clovis, I'm Jane."

"Jane," Aunt Claudette says, smiling warmly at me. Behind her glasses, her eyes are overly bright, and I wonder if she's been put on medication. "Please, call me Aunt C. That's what Thalia calls me. I assume you're here because of her."

The back of my neck prickles. It's the way she says it. Not a question. More a resigned statement, like she always knew that I would one day show up.

"I am, actually. Yeah." I move closer, peering at her carefully.

Aunt Claudette's mouth puckers with displeasure and she nods. "None of the others ever showed up, you know. I kept waiting, and waiting, so certain that one day, one of you would come here asking about her."

"The others?" I say, sitting down.

"Her 'friends.'" She puts air quotes around the word, and I know then that she knows exactly what Thalia is. The question is: Is she on Thalia's side? I don't say anything, and she fills in the silence. "She has so many of them, you know. Well, I'm sure you do." She sighs and gestures to her dresser. "Do me a favor, will you? Open that—yes. And take out that box down there, yes, that's right. Lovely. Now let's see . . ." She takes the box from me and opens it. Inside are photo albums and a yearbook. I'm getting impatient, jittery. I'm not here to look at old photos.

"I actually have a few questions—"

"Here she is," Aunt Claudette says, opening the yearbook and pointing at a photo. "Beautiful, wasn't she?"

I hold back a sigh and look at where she's pointing. Eighteen-year-old Thalia. She was gorgeous, but I can't help noticing that her hair is a very dark brown. It looks strange on her. "Yeah."

"That was the year that her mother's boyfriend was reported missing."

All of my instincts prick up, my mind going from bored to a high-pitched alarm. "Missing?"

Aunt Claudette closes the yearbook with a sigh. "Her mother tried so hard with her. But Joanne wasn't a very bright woman, bless her soul. From when Thalia was little, you could already tell Joanne was outmatched. She loved Thalia in her own way. Wanted to do right by her. She didn't have much, but she was beautiful—oh, movie-star good looks. Where do you think Thalia got her looks from? She was always on the hunt for a husband. A dad for Thalia, she said. I tried telling her that what Thalia needed wasn't a dad, but one of them brain doctors, but she just couldn't see it." She opens one of the photo albums and flips through the pages. "Ah, here he was. Jackson Giles."

I frown down at a photo of a woman resembling Thalia, her arms around a blond man.

"Dated Joanne for—hmm, three months? Before he abruptly broke up with her and disappeared. Thalia was twelve at the time." She flips through more pages. "And this one . . . Matthew something or other. Went out with Joanne for almost a year before leaving suddenly."

299

There's an ugly sensation unfurling in my guts.

"We both assumed these men were cads. What you kids would call 'players,' or 'fuckboys.'" She snorts at my raised eyebrows. "What, you think I don't know the way you kids talk nowadays? Anyway, so. Fuckboys, they existed back then, too, so we just thought, ah, he got bored of Joanne and just stopped calling, stopped coming round. Joanne would cry and then she'd get over it and move on. See, I always had my suspicions. I thought that maybe Thalia had said something to these men to drive them away. But I told myself that was, well, maybe not quite normal, but it wasn't illegal. Kids rebel against the people their parents are dating all the time, don't they?" Her tone is almost pleading.

I shrug. I wouldn't know. My mom never dated anyone after my father passed, shrouding herself in unhappiness, reveling in her self-imposed loneliness so she could blame it on me.

"It wasn't until him—" Aunt Claudette points to a balding man who looked somewhere in his midforties. "Freddy Somer. He disappeared like all the rest, but unlike the others, he had people who loved him. People who reported him missing. It all came back to Joanne, and the cops found nothing on her, of course, because she was innocent. She was horrified, actually. But I remember being there when the cops came to the apartment to question her, and I saw Thalia—she was listening in from the next room, and that look on her face—" She shudders.

"You think she did something to all these men?" I don't even recognize my own voice. "But that's impossible. You said the first one disappeared when she was twelve? How could she have—"

"I don't know about the other men. I—when the cops came asking about Freddy, I thought maybe—I don't know. But I kept a closer eye on Thalia. I love Thalia like my own kid, I do, and she's done so much for me—she paid for all this, you know? I wouldn't have managed to retire in a place like this on my teacher's salary. I didn't want to—I didn't want anything bad to happen to her. But—" Her voice wavers and she takes a shaky breath. When she speaks again, the words come out as a whisper. "A couple years ago, they found him."

"Freddy?" I don't get why she's looking at me like that, with her eyes all wide and burning with fear. "I think I'm missing something . . ."

"They found his body. He's been dead for years. Some hikers found the—ah, the remnants."

Horror crawls, like a spider, from the base of my spine all the way up my neck. My scalp prickles, everything inside me curling up into a tight ball. *Thalia, what have you done?*

Her hands twist in her lap, fingers squeezing and writhing. "I want to believe that it was a coincidence. Maybe he was out hiking and fell? Freak accidents, they happen more often than we think, right?" She squeezes her eyes shut, and for a few moments, there's silence, except for the sounds of our breathing, deafening in the dead air. "All I know is, my time's coming to an end. I'm going to see my own judgment day, and I told myself, if someone were to come one day, asking about Thalia, I'm going to tell them everything. I know it sounds crazy, and it's all probably going to turn out to be nothing, but . . ." She swallows. Takes another deep breath. "The point is, I love that girl, but there's something broken inside her, and she scares the hell out of me sometimes."

Hope blooms inside my chest, bright and burning. "I need to talk to her. Do you know how I can get a hold of her?"

At this, Aunt Claudette's mouth tightens, and I realize with a sinking feeling that even though she says she knows what a monster Thalia is, she's not quite ready to give her up just yet.

I've miscalculated, been too forward. I should've taken more time to listen, nudge Thalia's address or phone number out of her gently. That's what Thalia would've done. Still, I can't judge Aunt Claudette too harshly, I know, especially since Thalia is apparently footing the bill for this place. And she knows where Aunt Claudette lives. If I were Aunt Claudette, I wouldn't be in a hurry to sell Thalia out either. She turns away from me slightly and says, "I'm quite tired now, dear. Maybe we can continue this another time?"

I wipe my face, trying to ignore the tightness in my chest. I want to shake her and tell her how Thalia's made me out to be a stalker, a murderer. But the last thing I want is for her to call for help. It would be yet more evidence of my so-called erratic behavior. "Okay," I say in a small voice. "Thank you, Aunt Claudette."

She's already turning her wheelchair away from me, probably can't stomach another moment of looking at me. As I pick up my purse to leave, I see a notebook sitting atop a stack of letters on a side table. I don't even hesitate before taking the entire pile and hiding them behind my purse. Aunt Claudette turns around then, and my heart jams its way up my throat, but she only gives me a sad smile. "I'm sorry I couldn't be of more help."

"You've done enough," I mumble, and hurry out of her room.

OUTSIDE OF THE FACILITY, I LOOK THROUGH THE PIECES of Aunt Claudette's mail. Two of them are spam and the third is a credit card bill. Gritting my teeth with frustration, I stuff them into my bag and flip through the notebook. My heart soars, because as it turns out, I've managed to steal Aunt Claudette's address book. I go through the pages until I find Thalia's name.

There are four different addresses listed in here, one in Jakarta, one in Singapore, one in Dubai, and one in—bingo!—Manhattan. I take out my phone and order a Lyft, my breath coming out ragged as I key in the address. Once it's ordered, I briskly walk out of the driveway and down the street, eager to put some distance between me and Aunt Claudette before she realizes that I've stolen her things. When the Lyft arrives, my breath releases in a whoosh. I spend the entire car ride wringing my hands, working out different scenarios, a multitude of ways in which my confrontation with Thalia could go.

I don't know what I was expecting from the address, but when the Lyft arrives at my destination, I get out and look up. And up. And up.

So Thalia lives in a bloody skyscraper right next to Central Park. So what? She married Ivan, so they're rolling in dough. I knew that. Still, as I walk toward the imposing building and the doorman nods and opens the door for me, I can't help but feel intimidated. It's probably the desired effect. I feel completely out of place, dwarfed and fraudulent. The inside of the lobby is all shiny marble and gilded edges and lush carpet. A receptionist stands to attention and, after giving me a once-over, puts on the bare minimum of a smile; she knows I don't belong here.

"Good evening," she says. "Visiting someone?"

I try to look as imperious as I can. "Yes. Thalia Ashcroft. Or she might go her married name, Pranajaya."

"Ah yes, Mrs. Pranajaya. And your name is?"

"Jane," I say without thinking. Then I realize I should've given her a fake name, but it's too late.

"I'll let her know you're here." She picks up the phone.

"Oh, don't bother. I'll just go straight up. She's expecting me." The words sound like a lie even to my own ears.

She looks at me like: *Who're you kidding?* And I can't blame her.

"I was going to surprise her," I say lamely.

She gives me an icy smile. "Our residents don't like surprises." She punches a number into the phone and waits. "Hello, Mrs. Pranajaya, sorry to bother you, but there's a guest here for you? Jane. Yes." She glances at me and she's no longer bothering to smile, not even a little. "Of course. I'm so sorry to bother you, ma'am." She hangs up, and when she turns to face me, her face is cold. "I'm afraid you'll have to leave the premises."

I hate myself. I should've been better prepared. What the hell was I expecting? To just be able to barge into her apartment? Actually, yes, that was exactly what I expected. For Thalia to live like a normal person, without security manning the lobby of her apartment. For me to be able to randomly press buttons on the front of the building until someone buzzed me in.

"Ma'am, did you hear me? Please leave the premises or I will call security."

I glare at her balefully before turning for the front door. I dip my head and look down at the marble floors, so shiny that I can see the lights reflected in them. I'll wait outside, I decide. I don't care how long it takes. Thalia can't possibly stay in her apartment forever.

Behind me, one of the elevators dings and opens. For a split second, I wonder if I can rush into the elevator and hit the button before the receptionist can stop me. But before I can do anything, someone calls out, "Jane, wait!"

I freeze. Thalia's come down here to see me after all. But when I turn around, it's not Thalia who's hurrying after me, but Ani. The receptionist is watching us with wide eyes, probably confused. That makes two of us, I want to tell her.

"Ani, I need to see Thalia, I—"

"For fuck's sake, Jane," Ani snaps, "could you please stop the Thalia obsession, just for one fucking second? My brother is dead."

She might as well have smacked me in the face. For a few seconds, all sounds are muted, as though I'm listening to them underwater. Everything moves slowly. I see Ivan the way he had been in Oxford, full of life, sunshine coursing through his veins. "Ivan's dead?"

Ani's eyes fill with tears and her chin trembles. "Come on," she says hoarsely, leading me out of the building. Outside, next to the heavy New York City traffic, she turns to me and says, "Yes. Ivan's dead. And I think Thalia had something to do with it."

It shouldn't surprise me, but it does, and I hate that it does. I hate that despite everything, Thalia still shocks me. Dimly, I'm aware that Ani is leading me down the block and onto a side street. The noise of the traffic recedes dramatically as we stand in the alleyway.

"Sorry, I don't know where else to go to have this conversation," Ani says.

A shocked laugh burps out of me. She's right; I mean, it's not really the kind of conversation you have over a pumpkin spice latte at Starbucks. "I—yeah. Wait, so. Uh. Ivan's dead?" I know I've asked this already, but my mind is still refusing to comprehend it. "And Thalia? You think she . . ."

"Yes. She fucking killed him, Jane!" Ani cries, grabbing my arm.

My mouth opens but nothing comes out.

"You need to help me," Ani says. She's gripping my arm so tight that it's starting to hurt, but I cling to the pain because it's the only thing anchoring me at this moment.

"Help you?" I echo uselessly.

"Look," she says, sighing. "I know you're part of the Thalia fan club—god, why do people fall for her act?"

"I'm not." My cheeks burn. "I mean, I used to be, but not anymore."

Ani pauses, and slowly, like honey, her lips stretch into a smile. "She did something to you."

I swallow the lump in my throat and nod. "I think—um, I think she killed Kurt." It sounds so ridiculous. Alien words tumbling out of my mouth, unrecognizable. "And she's framing me for it. I think," I add. How many times can I say "I think"? But it just sounds so crazy I can't help but try to soften it. Despite what Ani said earlier about Ivan being dead and Thalia possibly having something to do with it, I still half expect her to laugh at this and tell me I'm nuts, that my obsession toward Thalia has led to me completely going the other way.

Instead, she nods solemnly. "I believe you."

Those three words are so far from what I'm expecting that I feel a surge of warmth toward her, this woman I have hated for so long. I look at her, dressed impeccably as usual, her hair sleek, her makeup flawless, and I see the anger simmering behind it. She's lost her brother, and I suddenly feel such sorrow for her. We're both Thalia's victims. "What can I do to help?"

Ani takes in a shaky breath. "I need to find evidence of her killing Ivan. I think I know how she did it. She's been poisoning him for years—"

"What?" I try to wrap my head around it, try to digest the words, but they sit like a rock in the center of my brain, defying all logic. "Poison?"

"I'm pretty sure she's been slipping him caffeine without him knowing it."

"Caffeine? That's not poison."

"It is in the right amount. And my brother has—had—a heart condition. The caffeine triggered a heart attack."

"Oh my god." I shake my head, blinking several times. This can't be real. But then I think of Thalia, past that gorgeous, innocent facade she wears so well. I think of the little glimpses of her that I've caught, the way she sometimes smiled just a split second too late, as though she only just realized that something was meant to be humorous. And then I think of her using those long, elegant fingers to sprinkle caffeine into Ivan's food, and my body turns cold. I can picture it all too easily. "But I don't know how I can help. She's blocked my number, she didn't allow me to go up to the apartment—"

"Yeah." Ani nods. "I was hoping we could brainstorm something together, maybe find out where she keeps the caffeine, or how she even got it to begin with. It's not like you could get it over the counter, you know? So she must've ordered it online. I tried looking through her credit card bills, but I couldn't find anything."

A sense of hopelessness washes over me. Thalia's been ahead of us by so many steps this whole time. We're two beginners playing against a master. "She would've thought of everything. She—" Then the thought strikes me. "Wait, you got access to her credit card bills?"

"Yeah, in Indonesia, we have a family account and all our cards are registered to the same account, so we can see each other's purchases. There are no secrets in my family," she says with a bitter laugh.

"Did you see a charge for Golden Years Estate?"

She frowns and takes her phone out of her pocket. "Hang on, let me open up the bill—" She taps on it and scrolls down. After a while, she shakes her head. "Nope. What is it?"

"It's a retirement home that Thalia's been paying because her aunt lives there. And her aunt said the bill is paid every month, so if it's not in here, that means she has a different credit card." As soon as I say it, it sounds so obvious. Of course she wouldn't have used the family credit card to buy the stuff she was using to kill one of them.

To kill one of them. God, the thought is still so shocking, a jagged shard through my brain. Then I recall the stack of papers I'd taken from Aunt Claudette's room.

I rip open my purse and rummage through it.

"What're you doing?" Ani says, but I ignore her, digging until I locate the right envelope. I tear it open and look at the bill. It's for a credit card belonging to Claudette Clovis. My heart sinks, but still I scan the list of purchases anyway, because maybe . . .

And there it is.

A purchase from Burn Fast for $72. I Google "Burn Fast" and find a weight-loss site whose number one product is "Pure Caffeine Powder." The description reads: "Pharmaceutical-grade pure caffeine anhydrous powder! Watch as the fat literally melts from your waistline! Each teaspoon of our caffeine powder has the equivalent of 28 cups of coffee!"

"I found it," I whisper.

Ani's eyes widen, and I feel the blood roar in my ears. We may be new to Thalia's game, but somehow, I think we've managed to stumble on her only weakness.

30

THALIA

I t will take less than a day for the autopsy to be done, because apparently, money gets you expedited service even in death. I watch helplessly as Ani orders the autopsy to be done, requesting a full blood work including—and this is key—the amount of alcohol or caffeine in his system. My fists clench and unclench, as though longing for her neck to be in their grasp, and still I cannot say a word; I can only stand on the sidelines and nod, pretending to agree with this farce. What will they find? The only thing in my favor is the fact that I don't have any caffeine powder on me, not in New York, at least. Because, god damn it, I hadn't planned on killing him here. So if they do a search, I will be clean. I remind myself of this fact over and over, caressing it in my mind, my own little mental talisman.

But now I need to make my move. I need to figure out what Ani knows and what Ani has done and outmaneuver her. The house phone rings and I hurry to pick it up, leaving Mama and Papa sobbing quietly in the living room with their reptilian daughter. It's the lobby receptionist, telling me I have a guest. The last thing I want is a guest. I snap, "Well? Who is it?"

"Jane."

Jane. My sad, pathetic, little clinger-on. My god, Jane. Have some self-fucking-respect. I just framed you for murder and yet still you come, begging me for attention. "Jane?"

"Yes."

"I don't want any visitors. Do your job, get rid of her, or I'll lodge a complaint."

"Of course," she says hurriedly. "I'm so sorry to bother you, ma'am."

I hang up the phone and turn around, only to run into Ani. Jesus. She moves as silently as the snake she is. She narrows her eyes at me. "Everything okay?"

"No, everything's not okay, my husband's dead." I brush past her and stalk off. Moments later, I hear the elevator ding and I breathe out. Good. Ani's left the apartment. I need time to think. Fortunately, Mama and Papa have retired to the master bedroom, so I don't have to deal with them. I go into my room and start pacing again. I need to—what do I need to do? I need to go through Ani's belongings, see if I can find anything incriminating. Yes. Hope flutters in my chest, a lonely butterfly. At her heart, Ani's a dumb bitch, she's careless, she—

No. I can't afford to think like that anymore. She's outplayed me. I can't keep underestimating her. I take a deep breath and walk out of my room. For a few moments, I listen hard, but aside from the muffled sobs coming out of the master bedroom, there's no sound in the apartment. No clue where Ani went, no idea when she'll be back. I need to do this fast.

For the first time, I'm grateful for the suffocating tightness of Ivan's family, for the fact that we're all sharing an apartment even though they could easily have bought a separate one for Ani. Ani's room is slightly smaller than the one Ivan and I shared. I go inside and leave the door open just a crack, so that I'll be able to hear the elevator's ding when Ani comes back. I move fast, letting my instincts take over. I open drawers, dig my hands into mounds of lacy underwear, search under her bed and her chaise longue. I go into her bathroom and rummage through all the cabinets. I read all of the labels on the bottles she has, and I hate how unsure I feel. Is this bottle of pills really Advil? Or has she switched it with something else? What should I take? And even if I were to take any of it, what would I do with it? In the end, I leave them all alone. I figure if any of them were incriminating, she wouldn't have left them in her medicine cabinet like that. I go back to the walk-in closet, and this time, I search harder. I dip into every shoe, grimacing at the thought that I'm putting my hands where Ani puts her disgusting feet. I open up her Louis Vuitton luggage one by one, searching the inner linings, then I move on to her handbags. There are over a dozen of them. The more I search, the angrier I become. I'm breathing hard, panting like an animal, so unlike myself. I can't stand it, the thought that I'm being out-smarted by someone like Ani.

I'm so absorbed by my search that I fail to hear the elevator's ding. I fail to hear the footsteps padding down the hallway, the sound of Mama and Papa's door opening. There must have been a hushed conversation, but I miss that too. And suddenly, the door to Ani's room bursts open, and I am caught with my hands buried in a Gucci bag. Ani and Mama and Papa stand before me, their faces a mix of horror and shock and disgust.

Explanations crowd my head. "I was just—"

Ani holds up her phone, a look of triumph on her face. I can't quite see what's on the screen, but based on that smug smile of hers, I know it's nothing good. "You're a murderer," she says, simply. Just like that, *you're a murderer.*

I snort. "What?" I glance at Mama and Papa, who are still staring at me like they can't quite comprehend what they're seeing. "This is—you're crazy. Mama, don't believe anything she says—"

"Don't talk to my mother," Ani snaps. "This is your credit card bill. Your secret credit card bill."

I forget how to breathe. "What are you talking about?"

"Your aunt? Claudette Clovis? I know you registered a credit card under her name and used it to buy caffeine powder, which you used to poison my brother."

Aunt Claudette? Did the bitch betray me?

"And," Ani continues, her eyes glinting madly, "I just got the call from the coroner's office. My brother died of cardiac arrest, triggered by caffeine overdose."

"No, wait—" I drop the handbag and start forward.

Ani steps back, her expression switching seamlessly into exaggerated fear and alarm. "Stay back, Thalia! Don't move. I've called the cops. Don't do anything stupid."

"I'm not—Jesus, I didn't do it."

"Just stay away from me and my family," she spits out, backing away, herding her parents away from me. Right before she shuts the door, she flashes me a smile. One that says: *Checkmate.* And I know, then, that I have well and truly lost.

———

MY BAIL IS DENIED. MY LAWYER, PROVIDED BY THE STATE, warned me before my arraignment that bail would likely be denied since this is a murder case, but when it comes, it still hits hard. Yet another blow I wasn't ready for. I can only stare silently ahead as I am led back to my cell, ignoring the shouts from the paparazzi and the flashes of their cameras. Back in the silence of my jail cell, I look into the mirror. Regardless of what Netflix tries to tell you, orange is definitely not the new black. This isn't an Hermès orange that I'm wearing, but a neon one, against which my skin looks sallow. Despite that, I still look rather beautiful. This is a fact; I'm not being narcissistic. I haven't had much of an appetite, which is understandable given the disgusting slop they serve in here, and over the past few days, I have lost enough weight to make my cheekbones even more prominent. It gives me a sort of vulnerable, haunted look, which I understand is quite trendy at the moment. I make a note to myself to decrease my caloric intake even after I get out of here.

And make no mistake, I will get out of this place. Jail isn't for me, much less prison. I do not deserve to be here, locked up with the rest of society's filthiest dregs. I turn my head to one side, admiring the sharp angles. No, I am made to be seen, not locked away. It would be like keeping the *Mona Lisa* buried. A crime against nature's art.

I don't know how I will get out of here yet, though. My lawyer, she of the ill-fitting suit and frizzy hair, tells me that the prosecutor has gathered all sorts of damning evidence against me. The caffeine powder that I had bought for the last two years, charged to Aunt Claudette's card, a card I have been paying off for years. I suppose that is pretty damning indeed. And, of course, the autopsy results. Rather irrefutable.

The clang of my jail cell rouses me from my plotting. A guard is standing there, somber and burly. I wonder if this is a requirement for prison guards. "You've got a visitor."

I frown. "Is it my lawyer?" Maybe she's found something after all. Nah. She's about as smart as a box of hair.

"Nope. Come on, we don't got all day."

I resist the urge to correct his grammar and let him cuff me, noting with satisfaction how huge the cuffs are on my slender wrists. We walk toward the visitors room. I wonder who—ugh, I hope it's not Ani, come to gloat. I might just leap across the desk and shove my thumbs into her eyeballs, just for the satisfaction of wiping that smirk off her face. But when we get there, I see a dark-haired woman sitting across the table. Jane.

My heart softens at the sight of her. What? Just because I have APD, doesn't mean I can't feel genuine affection for someone. Okay, yes, it means exactly that. But Jane really does have a special place in my heart. Like a favorite coat, comfortable and worn. And she's just so pathetic; look at her sitting here even after everything I did to her.

"Jane!" I sit down across from her and shake my head in disbelief. The smile on my face is as genuine a smile as I have ever worn. "I wasn't expecting to see you here."

She looks surprised by the warm reception and quickly looks down at her hands. "Um. Yeah." She sneaks another glance at me. Poor Jane. Some people are just built to be prey, and she is the worst of them. She reminds me of a rodent, small and twitchy, made to be hunted and killed with a wet squeak. Still, I've been so bored, I find myself looking forward to knowing what brought her here.

"Thank you for coming," I say, making my voice warm. A verbal hug, because physical contact isn't allowed. I wonder if it's time for tears and decide against it. "I'm so glad to see you."

"Are you?" There's a flash of anger on her face that quickly fizzles out, replaced once more by the anxiety I'd quickly come to associate with her all those years ago.

"What do you mean? Of course I am."

Her mouth twists. I want to tell her to stop sneering like that; it's so unbecoming. "Funny you should say that, given how you tried to frame me for Kurt's death."

I let my mouth drop open in a shocked O. "What? There must've been some kind of—no. Kurt—he died in an accident. What are you saying?" My voice trembles a little. "Please, I can't stand it, Jane. My husband's dead and they're saying I killed him when I didn't; I had nothing to do with it. Now you're here, you're my best friend, the only person in the world who understands me, and you're saying—what are you saying?" I whisper, blinking so that the tears won't fall.

She hesitates. Always so quick to be pushed off-balance. "You told everyone I was stalking you."

I raise my eyebrows. *Look at how shocked I am!* "No. I would never. I told everyone we're best friends, that we—" I stop myself and mentally count to three before gasping. "Oh my god. I think I know what's going on." I pause, waiting.

And because she is Jane and she can't help herself, she goes, "What?"

"The cops," I say. "It's what they do, right? They get you alone and then they feed you all sorts of crazy stories to make you confide in them. I mean, they told me all sorts of things about you. They wanted me to throw you under the bus, but I didn't. I told them you're an amazing person, you'd never do anything like that." I pause again and look at her with sad puppy eyes. "Did you tell them that I would hurt Kurt?" My voice ends in a pained squeak. Got to drive home to Jane what a fucking betrayal it would've been to throw me under like that.

"No," she cries. "No, I couldn't—they were so—they said

that the other writers at the retreat said you told them I was stalking you, and . . ." She shakes her head. "It doesn't matter, anyway. You killed Ivan."

"I didn't," I say, and here I infuse some indignation into my voice. "I swear to you, I did not kill him." I don't break eye contact. I let her in to see my truth.

She blinks again, confused. Poor little rodent Jane. Must I do all the work for her? One despairs. "Ani did," I say finally, when it becomes clear she's not going to get there.

"But—" She gnaws on her bottom lip. Her lips are disgusting, all chapped, bits of skin peeling off. I wish she'd put some Vaseline on them. "The—he died of caffeine overdose and you'd been buying all that caffeine—"

"I was being abused." I let out a single, short sob. An idea is beginning to take form. My mind rushes ahead, spinning a whole new narrative. One that relies on me leaning into the whole Asian stereotype of an overbearing family. The best stories, after all, contain grains of truth. "You don't know what it was like to be married to Ivan, to be living in his country. I couldn't turn to anyone. His family controls the police, the whole justice system. I couldn't divorce him. I was trapped. They told me if I ever humiliated them by divorcing Ivan, they'd kill me and my family—Aunt Claudette—that's why I hid her existence. I was—you don't know what I've been through." Now I let the tears fall, though not too much, don't want to look all puffy. "I was—he raped me every night. I tried telling Ani and she just laughed and told me it was my fault for marrying him."

Jane looks so horrified I wonder if she's going to fall off her seat. The more I tell her, the more the story comes alive. And it's a good one, I can feel it in my bones. I know stories; I'm an author after all. And this one has all the makings of a hit. Me, a beautiful, intelligent, modern woman. This new thinness of mine makes me look so vulnerable, almost ethereal. Ivan, a handsome prince with a dark secret. I dare anyone to try resisting it. I can already see how it'll take flight. The media will lap it up. Women's rights groups will clamor for my freedom. I will become the face of their movement, the poor, broken woman who escaped her captor. I will be a heroine.

"You know what Ani's like. She'd been vying for Ivan's position in the company even when we were in Oxford. She was always so resentful, so jealous about it. Remember?"

After a second, Jane nods.

"She did it. She killed him to get control of the company, and she framed me for it. You must find out how she did it," I say through my tears.

She's so torn between wanting to believe me and the string of irrefutable evidence behind me. All she needs is a little nudge. And I know exactly what Jane wants, what her life has been all about ever since the first time we met. Me.

"Please, Jane. You're my only hope. You're my best friend."

At this, her face brightens, a righteous flame burning behind her eyes. I almost laugh at how easily she fell for it. She nods and says, "I'll do it. I'll find out how she killed him. I'll set you free."

I smile at her. Good dog.

31

JANE

After I visit Thalia, I walk for hours, only half-aware of where I'm going. My mind is a jumble of emotions. I want to cry and laugh and scream and hide, all at the same time. I want to hug Thalia, put my arms around her and squeeze. I want to strangle Thalia, put my hands around her throat and squeeze. I remember that night in Oxford, when she'd asked me to strangle her so she'd have marks on her throat. I go back to that moment and I don't let go. I watch as the light goes out of her eyes and she turns from a living, breathing being into a rag doll. A dead thing. A sob escapes me, and I wipe away the tears that trickle down my cheeks. I don't know why I'm crying. Thalia is exactly where she belongs, and I should be out celebrating. The cops are off my back. I don't know what's going on with the investigation of Kurt's death, but I'm sure that since Thalia is being charged with Ivan's murder, she would also be the number one suspect behind Kurt's death, if they decide it was murder, that is.

So why do I feel like part of me is slowly dying? Why do I

feel like I've left the most beautiful bird in the world to rot in a tiny cage, its vibrant wings clipped, its sonorous chirps silenced?

She belongs there, I tell myself. She's dangerous, the most dangerous creature there is. A serpent.

But I can't forget that look on her face. Haunted, broken, as she begged me to help her. Could she really be lying? She looked shattered. And what she told me made sense. Ani has always been bitter about the whole family company. The number of times she ranted to us back in Oxford about how Ivan only got his position because he had a dick. Could she have done it?

I close my eyes and try to picture Ani poisoning her own brother, and the image clicks into place all too easily. I shudder and open my eyes once more. The problem is, I can also very easily think of Thalia doing it. Both of them are deadly. I should forget all of this and just go. I'm caught in a game between two apex predators.

And yet. The thought of going back to Ted, to my mediocre, safe life, grates at my nerves. What the hell is wrong with me? Social anxiety, Kathryn had told me. I can see that. It fits. I should go back home and just curl up and hide away from the world. Do that cognitive behavioral thing Kathryn wants me to do. Learn to cope. Live with the knowledge that Thalia is in prison and I'm outside of it, safe and sound.

Should, should, should. How long have I lived my life according to "should"?

I take my phone out of my bag and call Ani. When she picks up, I say, "Want to get drinks?"

———

CHANCES ARE, ANI HAS CHANGED FROM THE GIRL I KNEW back in Oxford. Chances are, she's a lot wiser now, less of a loose cannon. But she's also just coming down off a real roller coaster; I mean, there's a possibility she just framed Thalia for Ivan's murder and got away with it. I'm guessing she's in real need of a good, stiff drink and someone to celebrate it with.

We agree to meet at Doorway, a quiet restaurant with outdoor seating, where we can drink and chat without her feeling claustrophobic. When she arrives, she looks as fashionable as usual, not at all like a woman who's recently lost her dearest brother. No eye bags; she hasn't been crying.

I've arrived early and ordered us a bottle of wine, asked for them to pour it out into a decanter. I poured myself a glass, and when no one was looking, I added a sprinkling of Ambien into the decanter. Not too much, not enough to actually knock her out. Just enough to lower her inhibitions. I've set my phone to record and put it facedown on the table. I'm ready.

"Ani," I say, standing up and giving her a hug. She's all tight cords of muscle. It's like hugging a lizard. I have to stop myself from shuddering as I step away and sit back down. I pour her a generous helping of wine and push the glass toward her before lifting my own glass.

"To putting away the evil cunt," she says, lifting her glass.

I grit my teeth and force myself to say the words. "To putting away the evil cunt." I watch as she takes huge gulps of the wine. "So how are things with you and your family?" I hope I sound sympathetic. My heart is beating so hard I wonder if she can see its silhouette pressing against my top. I resist the almost overwhelming urge to wring my hands under the table. I can do this. I must do this.

Ani scoffs. "How do you think? My parents are a mess. Ivan was always their favorite, you know."

Like she'd ever let us forget that. I put on a sad face and nod, lifting my glass to my lips and taking the smallest sip. She mirrors me, except she gulps instead of sips, and I refill her glass as soon as she lowers it.

"They're lucky they have me. I've been taking care of everything. The funeral arrangements, the company—oh man, the company." She snorts and takes another long swallow of wine. "Let me tell you, Jane, it would all be going down the shithole if it weren't for me."

"Yeah, I can believe that. They're so lucky to have you." She must know I'm faking it. I'm not that good a liar. I take a bigger swallow of my own wine. The more we talk, the worse I feel. It feels like I'm betraying more than just Ani, but parts of myself as well. I don't want to feel a kinship with Ani, of all people.

But by now the spiked wine is taking its effect. I can see it in the way Ani's eyes become heavy-lidded, the way her bright red lips go slack, the slurring of her words. It takes me right back to our time at Oxford, those wine-drenched days where Ani swung wildly from competitive student to drunk dancer, hopping from books to boys and back again. I guess some things never change. The memory of it loosens my nerves. I know this Ani. I tolerated her for months, gritted my teeth and pretended to like her just so I could be close to Thalia. I can do this.

"But," I say, leaning forward, "you must find it hard, to take over the company so suddenly? I mean, have you been involved in the company all these years?"

She glances at me sharply and frowns, or tries to, anyway. The drink and drug have softened her. Without them, Ani would've probably leapt up and leaned so close I could smell her rank breath and hissed to me about how valuable she is to the company. As it is, she merely leans back and laughs. "Uh, ya think?"

"I thought your parents didn't really trust you to work there? Didn't you say they're pretty sexist and everything?" I don't actually remember her specifically saying that they're sexist, but I know enough from my mother how deeply ingrained traditional gender roles are in many Asian countries.

She rolls her eyes and takes another big swig. "Yeah. Misogyny in da house!" she crows. God, I hate her. And I know it's hate, not fear or anxiety, Kathryn. "Yeah, my parents are total fucking misogynists. Didn't think I could handle it. But I'm showing them. They're pretty fucking impressed with me right now, I can tell you that."

"I'm sure they are." I laugh along with her, then widen my eyes so I look impressed. "How are you managing everything? It must be so tough jumping in when you know nothing about the company. I mean, I don't even know the first thing about running a company, and with one as large as yours—"

"Girl, I've been preparing for this moment for all of my fucking life!" she hoots.

My heart stutters, screeching to a halt. Oh god. I try not to show it, try to recover. "Um, what do you mean? Preparing for what?" Quickly, I lean forward and refill her drink. She's almost finished the whole bottle. Two whole Ambiens plus wine. This is it.

"Every goddamned day I go to the office. He thought I was just there to gossip with the employees." She snorts. "Like I would ever be friends with those nobodies. I went in for years, learning as much as I could. Taking control of projects behind his back. Did he notice?" Another swallow of wine. "Fuck no. My idiot brother. He thought he was soooo great. Didn't even know his own fucking wife was poisoning him." She laughs, an ugly, jagged sound.

I frown. This isn't what I came here for. Thalia, were you lying after all? The thought is a cold one. I flinch away from it. Ani's lying. But she can't be, not when she's this drunk. This drugged. She can barely even keep her eyes open. Only the adrenaline of finally telling her story to someone is keeping her awake. "What do you mean, poisoning him?" I say in as calm a voice as I can muster. Mustn't alarm her now.

She gives me a cunning sideways glance. "Jane, Jane, keep up," she says in a singsong voice. "Didn't I tell you? Didn't we go over this already? Caffeine, Jane!" she cries at my blank face. "Remember?"

My stomach plummets. Thalia was lying. She'd sent me out on a wild-goose chase, and for what? Just for fun, I guess. One last practical joke from prison. Ha, very funny. I'm ready to call it a night. I put my glass down and start fiddling with my purse.

"So I just gave the final push," Ani says.

My head shoots up, my breath caught in my throat. "What?"

She gave a sloppy shrug. "She was taking so. Fucking. Long. I had known from, like, a year ago what she was doing, and I kept waiting for her to seal the deal, but she never did. What the fuck, right?" she says angrily. "So I got a bit impatient—you get it, don't you? She was just stringing me along, teasing me the way she loved to tease those guys in Oxford. Do you remember those days? God, she was such a slut."

"Stringing you along? Did she—did you two plan this?"

"God no. But part of her must have known that I knew. It wasn't like she was being that subtle about it. She always thought she was so smart." In a high-pitched, squeaky voice, Ani says, "Look at me, I'm Thalia, I'm Miss Perfect!" She laughs again and drains her glass.

"So you—you killed—you, uh—"

"I gave him an extra big dose of caffeine, right before Thalia left for her stupid writers retreat. He had his heart attack pretty quickly after that. Went into a coma, blah, blah, blah. Well, you know the rest. RIP Koko."

I can hardly believe what I'm hearing, the words are so horrifying, coming out of her lipsticked mouth so casually. She's sick, her mind nothing but a twist of vipers. I can't get away fast enough. But somehow, I manage to make myself stay, gripping the stem of my wineglass so hard that my skin is stretched taut over my knuckles. I nod and smile, smile and nod as though she hasn't just admitted to murdering her own blood, her only brother.

Then I think about the other beautiful monster, the one who is currently behind bars, the one I've been obsessed with for so long. I think about how Thalia has played me, pulling my strings so expertly, a puppet master putting on a show for everybody. I should hate her, and part of me does, but the other part of me can't deny how alive she makes me feel. Even when she's using me and discarding me like an old toy, the nearness of her alone is enough to ignite something inside me. I think about what I wrote that day in Montauk, after just a couple of days of being near Thalia. I'd read the words over and over again, and I can't believe that they were written by me. So powerful and incisive. Not the writings of a midlist author.

No, this situation isn't as straightforward as I had thought, and my opponents are both deadly and probably slightly insane in their own ways. But, with a start, I realize that I have something over both of them.

All my life, I've grappled with my identity. Always different. Never fitting in, not even into my own skin. But maybe that doesn't have to be a bad thing. I'm not my mother nor my father.

I am neither like Thalia, nor am I like Ani. In this deadly game of cat and mouse, I am neither cat nor mouse, but something else entirely. Something unexpected. My own person. I feel the change spreading over me like warm honey, settling my bones into my new skin. I look down and gently swirl the wine in my glass.

And I think hard about my next move.

32

THALIA

Jane came through. I can't quite believe it myself, and I'm
still not sure how she did it, but there you go. Sometimes,
old dogs can learn new tricks. The moment I'm freed, I slip
back into my old clothes with a sigh of relief—there is no silk or
cotton in prison wear—and order an Uber back to the penthouse. I'm already imagining a long, hot shower with the most
luxurious soaps and ultra-moisturizing conditioners, but when I
get there, I'm faced with Mama and Papa, tearstained and shaking with rage.

"What have you done?" Mama shrieks the moment I walk
out of the private elevator. Behind her, two men in bespoke suits
start forward. Mama and Papa's lawyers, I guess.

I stand there and frown at her. As I expected, they rush to
fill the lack of response.

"You," Papa thunders, pointing a stubby finger at me, "you
framed her. You framed our only daughter."

At this, I raise my hands and twist my expression into a

mixture of hurt and horror. "I didn't. I'm sorry, Papa, Mama, I know this is hard for you, but the truth is that Ani poisoned Ivan. Your daughter killed your only son." I know I didn't have to say it quite like that, but it's honestly a treat to be able to spell it out for them, to twist that knife in their chests. And the look on their faces at those words . . . chef's kiss.

"You framed her. You killed our son and then you framed our daughter!" Papa says. He is very repetitive, which bores me. Now that I've dealt the final blow, I'm ready for them to be out of my sight.

"Please don't fling around such accusations," I say. "I understand you're hurting right now, but I must protect myself." I glance at their lawyers, who catch my drift and whisper urgently in their ears. That's right, motherfuckers, I can be a litigious bastard, too, now that I'm about to inherit Ivan's massive wealth.

Mama scoffs and shoots her lawyer a murderous glare before turning her fiery gaze back to me. "You are not getting a single cent of Ivan's money."

I almost laugh out loud at her, but somehow, I manage to keep a straight face. "I think it's best to leave that to the law. I don't want to fight you over such things, but I am his next of kin . . ." I let the words trail away because I can't help it; I am one for dramatic pauses.

And in the silence that follows, I see the unearned triumph on their faces, and I have to bite my lip to keep from smiling. They still think they have the upper hand, that they can bribe and threaten their way to victory. They don't know that I've spent years studying them, following Ivan to meetings where he delicately felt out whether the other party was open to bribes and how much would be an appropriate amount. They have no idea that I have built a contact list of my own, filled with politicians and businessmen, people who run the world. And the cherry on top: I might not even have to use them, because the law is on my side. I am Ivan's next of kin, his wealth is rightfully mine. We can play this nicely or we can get dirty; either way, I have won.

"I'll just pack a few things and stay at a hotel," I say kindly. So gracious, so generous. "You can stay here until you figure out other accommodations."

Their faces blanch at the reminder that this penthouse, like all the other assets, will soon become mine. I quickly turn and walk away then, because I can no longer keep the elated grin off my face.

———

I SIT BACK IN MY LEATHER SEAT AT THE BAR OF THE PLAZA Hotel with a glass of their best whiskey and sigh with content-ment. Lifting my glass, I inhale the woody scent of the amber liquid and gaze out the window at the city. After so many years of planning, of inhuman levels of patience, I deserve this.

Footsteps approach, and I know without even looking up that she's here. Only Jane can make even her footsteps sound apologetic. The smile on my face as I stand to greet her is genu-ine; after what she's done for me, I am actually happy to see her. She looks different tonight, more beautiful somehow, her face glowing with something I can't quite put my finger on. I em-brace her and pretend not to notice her sniffing me. Once a dog, always a dog. But at least she's a faithful dog.

"I've ordered for you, something to remember Oxford by," I say, because I know this will delight her, the knowledge that I care enough to remember her favorite drink.

I was right; her smile takes over her face, dimpling her cheeks. She looks ten years younger than when I last saw her. But more than that, she looks somehow more herself, like she's finally settled into her skin. It's made her really quite stunning. I wonder what's different now. Careful, Thalia. This is a new game. A different game. I need to figure out what she wants now that she has rescued me. And I need to figure out how to win.

"How are you doing?" she says. The waiter arrives then, placing a pint of English apple cider in front of Jane, and she smiles again.

After he leaves, I let out a long sigh. "I mean, I don't know, really. It's been a whirlwind. I'm so—Jane, I can't thank you enough for helping me. On top of losing my husband, being accused for his death was—" My voice wobbles very convincingly. "Well, let's just say I wouldn't be here if it wasn't for you." I put down my snifter and reach out for her hand. Her eyes widen, and a flash of uncertainty flits across her face, like she can't believe that I want to touch her limp, clammy palms. Well, I *don't* want to, Jane. But one must show gratitude when appropriate, so here I am. She trembles ever so slightly as she reaches out for mine, and then I'm clasping it, and it's just as damp as I remember, like holding a frog in the palm of my hand. I fight down the wave of disgust and smile at her. "Jane, my best friend in the world." She gazes back at me, completely under my spell. "You saved me."

Tears shine in her eyes. She looks grateful, and rightfully so. In a very meaningful way, I have given her the best gift—to be able to say that she saved me. It is the one defining moment of her miserable, unremarkable life. A highlight that every other moment will fail to live up to. After this, she will go back to her very average home and her very average husband and continue writing her very average books, and she will look back on this and know that she has peaked, thanks to me.

Then she says, "I know," and those two words come out so quiet that I wonder if I've misheard.

"Sorry?" I say, leaning closer.

"I said I know," she says, louder now. Her hold on my hands tightens. "I know I saved you, Thalia."

I cock my head to one side. I'm a little confused, slightly taken by surprise. I don't like surprises. I try for a smile, but it fights me all the way.

"Because," she continues, "I know the truth. You were poisoning Ivan. I have a recording of Ani saying that."

I lean back and try to pull my hand away, but her grip is now a vise, and I can't yank my hand away without causing a scene. "You have a recording of Ani confessing to Ivan's murder." That was what my lawyer had told me, anyway.

"I do, yes. But that was just a snippet of everything that Ani told me. I only gave the cops what they needed to arrest her and let you go. The rest of the recording, where she said all sorts of damning things about you . . . it's safe somewhere."

A small laugh wobbles its way out of my mouth. "That's so—do you realize how ridiculous it all sounds? Nobody's going to believe Ani, especially now that she's admitted to killing her own brother."

"I know." She looks down and caresses my hand with a thumb. My skin erupts into gooseflesh. "But I also have Aunt Claudette on record, telling me what you were like as a child, as a teen."

I snort. "The ramblings of a senile, old—"

"I looked up your mom's old boyfriends. I managed to find a

couple of them. They said you threatened them, said you'd accuse them of raping you unless they broke up with your mother."

My mouth twitches, itching to come up with a retort to refute her, but my mind comes up with blanks.

"And then I saw that the last boyfriend—what was his name? Freddy Somer. See, unlike the others, he disappeared without a trace. His family filed a missing person report on him." She leans closer, close enough for me to see all of the minute differences on her face, the way she's changed from a dog into a wolf. How did I miss all of the signs before? "What did you do to him, Thalia?"

I lean toward her, too, until a single, lonely inch separates us. "The same thing I'm going to do to you if you insist on playing this game with me," I whisper. I don't do well with threats.

She grins then, and releases my hand. She leans back, still grinning, and flips her hair over her shoulder. "I love it. I knew you'd say that." Her breath releases in a sigh. "I always wondered why I was so obsessed with you. And now I know. It's because you make me feel alive. Maybe some part of me knew that you were this dangerous monster, and it triggered an instinctive reaction inside me—whatever it is, I just—I am addicted to this feeling. I want to be near you. I know—" She holds up a hand when she sees that I'm about to say something. "I know you're a psychopath or whatever, and you probably don't understand what love is. I don't care. I've driven myself crazy all this time, wondering why I'm so into you. I don't think I'm sexually attracted to women. Who knows? But anyway, I think I've finally figured it out. Did you know, as it turns out, I have social anxiety? I think I do, anyway. I've always been scared, always felt this, like, resentment toward others for whatever reason. But I don't feel it with you, and I think it's because when I'm with you, everything is shaved down to the bone—to basic survival instincts. It's crazy, I know, but it's true. I write so much better with you around. You're my muse. All those years when you were gone, I felt like a part of me had died. You can see it in my books. They were just . . . dead. And then you came back and, my god, Thalia, you need to read what I've written these past few days. I swear it's like I've been possessed."

I have to admit, what she's saying is a lot to process. I mean, it's insane, but it's also really flattering. Because yes, of course I should be a muse. Anyone who's been lucky enough to come across me knows I ignite something in others.

Jane leans forward, her eyes burning into mine. "So here's what I want, Thalia: I want to be with you. You're a killer, a monster, but we belong together."

For once in my life, I have no idea what to say. She's not turning me in. She wants to . . . be with me. I stare at her, my mind zipping ahead as it always does, making multiple moves across the chessboard. Already I'm plotting her murder.

"You're probably wondering how you're going to kill me, aren't you?" she says, and my expression must betray me because she laughs. "I knew you would. I've put safeguards in place. If I were to suddenly disappear, there are quite a few damning files that would be sent to the police. But I'm sure you'll figure out some way to outsmart me. And that's exactly why I love you. I'll be doing the same. Don't you see? We make each other into the best version that we can possibly be."

And despite everything, she's sort of winning me over. Because, when I let myself think of the life ahead of me, filled with Ivan's incredible wealth and privilege, a part of me wants to cry with boredom. I am my best self when I have something to fight for. Maybe that was the real reason I took years to kill Ivan, because I knew that once I did, I would have nothing else to aim for, nothing to take up my busy, busy mind. And now, looking at the new and improved Jane, I realize that here's something that will occupy me for the next handful of years, at least. For so long, I've seen her as nothing more than an obedient dog, but here it turns out she's outfoxed me. Only temporarily, of course. I'll find a way to outwit her over time. But what she's done is still impressive. And, more importantly than that, she's outfoxed Ani. I'm not sure if this makes her a worthy adversary, since it's been years of me seeing her as something less, but it certainly makes her interesting. Different. Someone who knows exactly who and what I am. Someone who has seen the thing that lurks deep inside me and wants to play with it. Is this what true friendship is? It's not completely awful.

A slow smile spreads across my face, and I lift my glass.

"Okay, Jane. You're right. We're not done with each other yet."

EPILOGUE

Know what's funny about prison? Actually, never mind. There's nothing funny about prison, especially when you're on the wrong side of the bars. Let me rephrase. Know what's curious about prison?

The library.

It actually does not suck. I mean, prison itself sucks. Very, very much. But the library is surprisingly decent. We've even got John Green in here. His books, I mean. Not the actual author. On Wednesdays and Fridays, I rush through my assigned duties because those are the days I'm allowed to go to the library, as long as I'm done scrubbing the day's dishes or mopping up the dining hall. I hear that in the men's federal prison, they don't have a library because the inmates kept destroying the books. Men, I tell you. Good thing for me, women are far more civilized. Our books are generally in good condition. One time, I caught my roommate Lulu tearing a page out of a library book. My lawyer massaged his temple as he explained to me, later, that I couldn't go around breaking people's noses just because they mistreated a library book.

"It was our only copy of *The Unhoneymooners*!"

He remained unmoved. Fucking lawyers. Mama and Papa assured me this one's the best defense lawyer in all of New York City, but I have my doubts. Still, he did get me a pretty light sentence, all things considered. He worked some magic: came up with a viable strategy to present me as an airhead/bimbo who didn't think it would be possible to actually harm someone with caffeine. I mean, we all drink it every day, for gosh's sakes—how would I have known that it would kill my brother? I loved him, I looked up to him, anyone could see that. I just wanted to help him because he was complaining about being tired all the time.

Manslaughter in the second degree, out in four years, two with good behavior. I'd thought that "good behavior" would be pretty easy to achieve, but that was before I met Lulu the Destroyer of Books.

Anyway, as I was saying, prison libraries. Who would've thought? Today, like all Wednesdays, I hop to the brightly lit room in a good mood. Because today is the first Wednesday of the month, and that's when we usually get our shipment of donated books. New Yorkers love donating books. I think it makes them feel like good people or something. I wish they'd donate Starbucks lattes, too, but I'm not complaining. I'm trying to be a better person, really I am. I even took up yoga.

"Four minutes early." Elsie, the library guard, glances at the clock. "You must be really looking forward to the new books."

"Well, it's not like I've got HBO to look forward to, so new books it is." I smile wide and shrug. See? I'm sweet, I'm cheerful, I am a totally new person.

Elsie snorts. "True that. Well, it's your lucky day. We got that latest *New York Times* bestseller everyone's been yammering about."

My excitement isn't faked. Elsie's been talking up this book for weeks now. "You mean the one you've been yammering about?"

"Ha, yes. I can't wait for you to read it and tell me what you think." As far as prison guards go, Elsie's cool. She and I have formed a little book club, encouraging a handful of other inmates (not Lulu, obviously) to join in. "I've put a hold on it for you." She takes the book out from behind the desk. I reach for it eagerly.

And freeze.

"Ani? You okay?" Elsie's voice sounds so far away. Small and tinny, like it's coming through a tunnel. I barely register it. All I see are the words in front of me.

THE #1 *NEW YORK TIMES* BESTSELLER
BEST LEFT BURIED
by Jane Morgan

A choked sound claws its way out of my throat. Jane fucking Morgan. No, it can't be her. There must be a million Jane Morgans out there. It could be anyone. It's not her. It can't be her. I force myself to exhale. Then I turn the book over, and there's her face, those drab, undistinguished features of hers, except they're no longer drab, nor undistinguished. She must've hired a great photographer to take her author photo, because Jane looks—there are no other words for it—stunning. I am literally stunned. Her normally dull skin is positively glowing, her lips curved into a shy, knowing smile. But it's her eyes that arrest my attention. Jane's always had this intense look about her, like a fucking creep. You could totally imagine her as some middle-aged man who likes to linger outside women's bathrooms. Her gaze is still intense now, but it's the kind of intensity that says she's got a secret. A real good one. And it would be very, very alluring if I didn't know just what that secret was.

I don't realize I'm crushing the book until Elsie says, "Hey, knock it off!" and yanks it out of my hands. I blink at her stupidly. It takes me a moment to recover myself, to snap back to reality, to leave the wine-hazy memories of that last night with Jane. I've lost count of the number of times I've replayed that night. Each mental rewind is a confused jumble with a multitude of time skips and gaping black holes. I recall snatches here and there. Jane refilling my glass over and over. Jane asking questions about Ivan. I had my guard down because it was Jane, harmless tagalong Jane. Even after they presented the recording she took of me to the judge, I still didn't blame her. I'd assumed it was all Thalia's idea. My brilliant, deadly sister-in-law.

But now, looking at this photo of the new and improved Jane, it hits me that I've gravely miscalculated. That I don't just have one, but two bitches that need taking down. I need to read Jane's book. I need to know just what Jane is capable of. I've underestimated her, but not anymore. I've got plans for when I get out of here. They only included Thalia before, with Jane as an afterthought, but I think I might just move Jane up my VIP list.

I force myself to take a deep inhale. Stretch the corners of my mouth painfully up into a reassuring smile. I make sure my voice comes out even.

"Can I have that back? Please?" I add. I will never get used to saying "please."

Elsie narrows her eyes at me, still hugging the book to her ample chest like it's a baby and not a thing written by a lying bitch. "You sure you're okay?"

"Yeah, I just got too excited at the thought of finally reading this book you've been raving about." My teeth are clenched so tight I almost hear them crack. A book. That Elsie's been raving about. Written by Jane. I have to suppress a strong urge to lunge for it.

"Okay . . ." Elsie sighs. "Just. Be careful with it, okay? It's prison—"

"Property. I know."

"And I would hate to have to report you for—"

"You won't have to. I'll be careful with it. I promise." I'm ever so gentle when she finally hands me the book. Her frown eases into a smile.

"You're going to love it."

I grin. "I'm sure I will. And when I get out of here, I'll make sure to tell the author just how much I did."

ACKNOWLEDGMENTS

As I mentioned in my dedication, this book would not have been written if not for the encouragement of my writing bestie, Laurie Elizabeth Flynn. Laurie is the queen of psychological suspense, which is hands down my favorite genre to read. I'd been wishing to write one for a very long time, but didn't think I had what it took to achieve it. Laurie was the one who coaxed me gently to dip my toes into the genre, and that was how I started on one of the most thrilling writing journeys of my life.

I'm also so grateful to my husband, Mike, who unlike Ted has never referred to my writing as a "hobby." I did use a couple of our real-life tiffs in this book, and for that I apologize, but they were too good to not take advantage of.

This journey would not have been possible without the brilliant hand of my agent, Katelyn Detweiler, guiding my career path. Katelyn's vision has turned my humble journey into one I could only have dreamt about years ago.

I am beyond amazed and thankful that I am able to work once again with my editor, Cindy Hwang. Think of the best editor that has ever editored—one who is kind, patient, insightful, and attentive, Cindy is that editor and more. I am spoiled, I know. Cindy has set the bar so incredibly high.

Along with Cindy comes what is surely the best publishing team an author could dream of. Thank you to my Berkley team—Jin Yu, Angela Kim, Erin Galloway, Dache' Rogers, and Danielle Keir.

As always, I would've quit a long time ago without the support of my writing friends. My beloved menagerie—Elaine Aliment, S. L. Huang (whose epic fantasy is about to take the world by storm), Toria Hegedus, Tilly Latimer, Rob Livermore, Maddox Hahn, Lani Frank, Mel Melcer, and Emma Maree. My wonderful writing friends—Nicole Lesperance, Grace Shim, May Cobb, and Kate Dylan.

I think it's next to impossible to exist in this world as someone who identifies as a woman and not be enraged time and again. This book is the result of all the anger and bitterness at the inequalities of our society. I was fully submerged in Jane's and Thalia's mind, and what deliciously twisted minds they were. Writers are often chasing that moment of falling into the darkest depths of their book. I had so many of those amazing moments while writing this book, because it was a chance for me to pour out all of the rage inside me. And so this book is for anyone who identifies with Jane's and Thalia's anger. Thank you for reading it. Totally unbiased opinion here: I have the *best* readers. And I'm sorry to those who might have been expecting something lighthearted like *Dial A for Aunties*, LOL!

METROPOLITAN ACTION STUDIES NO. 3

THE
MILWAUKEE
METROPOLITAN
STUDY
COMMISSION

THE
MILWAUKEE
METROPOLITAN
STUDY
COMMISSION

Henry J. Schmandt
with William H. Standing

BLOOMINGTON · INDIANA UNIVERSITY PRESS · LONDON

Copyright © 1965 by Indiana University Press
Library of Congress catalog card number: 65-19706
Manufactured in the United States of America

Contents

Appendices

Tables

Foreword

APPROXIMATELY TWO-THIRDS of all Americans live in metropolitan areas. Of these, about half live within the boundaries of the central cities of these metropolitan areas and the other half live in the much more rapidly growing suburban and fringe areas. The metropolitan agglomeration is the characteristic pattern of settlement of modern Americans just as the family-farm was for their grandparents, and the feudal manor of medieval Europe for their more remote ancestors.

We are having considerable difficulty in learning how to govern these metropolitan regions. The units and institutions of government which were devised to fit earlier patterns of settlement do not fit the new ways of urban life adequately. Neither the older political boundaries, nor some of the newer ones which we are trying to develop, contain integrated and completely viable self-governing communities. Our public services are provided slowly and often ineffectively. The problems of ugliness and waste in suburban sprawl are exceeded only by those of blight and decay and social segregation in the older cities.

This is the third in a series of intensive case studies of the efforts of particular municipalities to adapt their government institutions to the changing patterns of settlement. In the hope that something useful can be learned through these careful examinations of the processes through which particular communities have tried to adjust to some of their metropolitan governmental problems, the Ford Foundation made a series of grants to help support case studies in several different communities. The case studies were made by groups of social scientists in a university at or near the metropolitan community involved. A grant was also made to Indiana University to enable it to attempt some coordination of the individual case studies.

In the earlier volumes of the series, *Decisions in Syracuse* and *The Miami Metropolitan Experiment*, the communities examined were significantly different from Milwaukee. Syracuse is considerably smaller and older, and has not had to cope with an encircling ring of strong suburban municipalities. Its decisions about metropolitan-wide governmental problems had tended to focus upon specific functions, one by one, without much effort at a frontal attack on major structural arrangements. Miami is nearly as large as Milwaukee; its growth has been much newer and more rapid, and a much smaller proportion of the metropolitan population is contained within the central city. It has attempted one of the most widely known and controversial experiments in governmental integration in the country. Milwaukee has its own peculiarities, as will be apparent to the reader of this volume. Yet it is also clear that there are many aspects of Milwaukee's situation, and its efforts to adjust to it, which resemble those in the other cities.

Through this and the other volumes of the *Metropolitan Action Studies* series, we hope that a better understanding of the processes of governmental adaptation to social change, and community decision-making in general, will be promoted.

York Willbern

Indiana University

Preface

THE POST-WORLD-WAR-II PERIOD has witnessed a rash of reform movements designed to effect change in the metropolitan governmental pattern. In most instances, the action programs themselves were preceded by extensive studies or surveys to document the problems and recommend solutions. A majority of these enterprises in research and prescription were conducted by citizen commissions established under public authority or private organizational auspices. So popular, in fact, did lay survey commissions become during the last two decades that the history of contemporary metropolitan reform might be written around their activities. As primary carriers of the reorganization movement in mid-twentieth century America, they epitomize the hopes and frustrations of those who sought to redesign the urban polity.

This book is the study of how one large urban area, with the aid of an officially appointed survey commission of citizens, went about the task of reaching decisions on modification of its governmental structure. Even though the story is one of insignificant accomplishment, it provides further insight into the rationale behind metropolitan reorganization movements, the motivations and resources of the participants, and the forces that condition reformist activities and shape community responses to them. The study is divided into three parts. The first describes the socio-economic, political, and organizational dimensions of the Milwaukee metropolitan community. The second is devoted to the Metropolitan Study Commission, a citizen-agency created by the Wisconsin state legislature in 1957 to investigate the governmental problems of the Milwaukee area. The third part analyzes the work of the Commission within a general theoretical framework, and discusses the role and future of lay survey committees in the light of emerging developments and trends.

The present study was made possible by a Ford Foundation grant to the University of Wisconsin—Milwaukee. Professor York Willbern served as co-ordinator for this and other metropolitan action studies sponsored by the Foundation. His encouragement and counsel contributed substantially to whatever merit this volume may have. Coleman Woodbury, chairman of the Urban and Regional Planning Department at the University of Wisconsin, shared the responsibility for drafting the original research proposal and designing the study. His generous assistance and advice throughout the course of the work and his careful reading of the manuscript have been invaluable.

Others who read the manuscript or portions of it and offered helpful suggestions for its improvement include Scott Greer, director of The Center for Metropolitan Studies, Northwestern University; Dr. J. Martin Klotsche, who served as chairman of the Metropolitan Study Commission during its final two years, and Richard Cutler, who was chairman of its land use and zoning committee; Norman Gill and Paula Lynagh of the Citizens' Governmental Research Bureau; A. Clarke Hagensick, associate director, Institute of Governmental Affairs at the University of Wisconsin—Milwaukee; and Frank Campenni, also of the University of Wisconsin—Milwaukee. G. Ross Stephens, associate professor of political science at the University of Connecticut, participated in the early phases of the study and in the interviewing of the community leaders. His contributions were many and valuable. Grateful acknowledgment is also due the many other Milwaukee area residents who kindly let us draw on their time and knowledge. Particular mention in this regard should be made of Leo Tiefenthaler, civic secretary of the City Club; Rudolph Schoenecker, executive director of the Greater Milwaukee Committee; Robert Jensen and Robert Foote, former members of the Metropolitan Study Commission; Betsy Ross Marcinkus, the Commission's administrative assistant; and Charles Ball, Charles Goff, and David Mars, research directors for the MSC. None of those mentioned, however, are responsible for any errors or shortcomings of this volume or the conclusions reached in it.

HENRY J. SCHMANDT

Milwaukee, Wisconsin
February, 1965

METROPOLITAN ACTION STUDIES NO. 3

THE
MILWAUKEE
METROPOLITAN
STUDY
COMMISSION

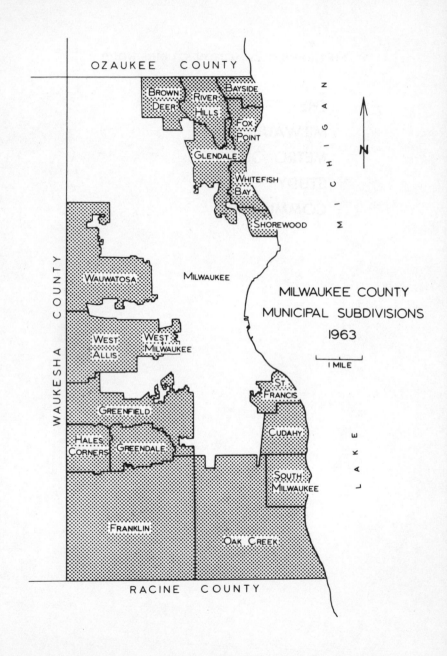

OZAUKEE COUNTY

BROWN
DEER

RIVER
HILLS

BAYSIDE

FOX
POINT

GLENDALE

WHITEFISH
BAY

SHOREWOOD

MILWAUKEE

WAUKESHA COUNTY

WAUWATOSA

WEST
ALLIS

WEST
MILWAUKEE

GREENFIELD

HALES
CORNERS

GREENDALE

ST.
FRANCIS

CUDAHY

SOUTH
MILWAUKEE

FRANKLIN

OAK CREEK

RACINE COUNTY

MICHIGAN

LAKE

N

MILWAUKEE COUNTY
MUNICIPAL SUBDIVISIONS
1963

1 MILE

1
The Setting

We begin our study with a thumbnail sketch of the economic, social, and governmental framework within which the Milwaukee metropolitan action movement took place. The resulting picture is one that conforms in some respects to the common image of urban areas and their problems while deviating from it in others. It portrays an economy, not of a depressed area or boom town or of a community of footloose labor and migrating business, but of a mature metropolis enjoying steady growth, reasonable stability, and relative prosperity. Socially, it reveals a community with a high proportion of skilled workers, good environmental conditions, comparatively small racial minority groups, sectional isolation among its parts, and a leisurely mode of living. Governmentally, it shows the familiar metropolitan pattern of decentralization and fragmentation, of central city-suburban rivalry, and of continual expansion of public services to meet new needs. More significantly, it reveals no immediate crisis situation or major breakdown in local services. The business of government is being carried on as usual.

THE COMMUNITY TONE
Situated on Lake Michigan eighty miles north of the noted "hog butcher of the world," Milwaukee* has had no poet laureate

* The terms "Milwaukee" and "metropolitan Milwaukee" are used interchangeably in this study to designate the larger community encompassed by

3

to epitomize it in verse. But only recently at a celebration of the City's 115th anniversary as an incorporated municipality, its mayor—with apologies to Carl Sandburg—turned momentarily from his more prosaic duties of public administrator to play the role of civic troubadour:

> Good natured whistle wetter for the world,
> Maker of beer, batteries, books and bolts,
> Tanning craftsman and the nation's number one machinist;
> Leathery, learned, steady, city with the strong hands.
> They tell me you are shabby—but I can't
>   hear them for the crash of air
>   hammers downtown.
> They tell me you lack culture—but I can't
>   hear them for the clamor for a nineteenth library.
> They tell me you are quiet, slow to change—
>   but I can't hear them for the booming
>   salvos as our planners fire new ordinances.[1]

Less laudatory was the prose description of a veteran newspaper reporter who some years earlier had sought to capture the salient quality of the community in capsule form:

> Consider dear Old Lady Thrift. That is, the plump and smiling city of Milwaukee, which sits in complacent shabbiness on the west shore of Lake Michigan like a wealthy old lady in black alpaca taking her ease on the beach. All her slips are showing, but she doesn't mind a bit.

> Small town is the word for Old Lady Thrift. Her hundredth anniversary came in 1946 and found her with a population of about six hundred thousand, but she remains essentially a small town. A great majority of her people want to keep her

Milwaukee County. The central city is referred to variously as the "city of Milwaukee," "Milwaukee city," or simply the "City." The census-defined metropolitan area, which since 1956 includes Waukesha County and since 1963 Ozaukee County, is referred to as the "Milwaukee SMSA" (Standard Metropolitan Statistical Area).

that way. Everything has been so comfortable, so pleasantly Old World, so free of false pretensions and the travails of ambition that only the vain, the restless, and the conscience-stricken want to change things. Old Lady Thrift is quite content to be recognized as the most safe and solvent city in America.[2]

It is no easy task to symbolize a city and its environs or to give expression to its many faceted and complex personality. As George S. Perry said of writing about Baltimore, "Almost any sweeping statement you make about its character will be wrong."[3] Each person sees a community and its qualities differently. To some of the local citizenry, Milwaukee is the land of "gemuetlichkeit"; to others the beer center of the nation; and to still others, the place in which to rear one's children. The variety of images, many of them contradictory, is virtually infinite, but one theme underlies all of them: the conservatism of the community. Both the relative newcomer and the native complain of the length of time that elapses before a new project is brought to fruition or change is accomplished. They point to the War Memorial Center, which was held up for years by disputes over its location; to the new public museum, which was seven years in the discussion stage before ground was broken; to the music hall, which only now is about to become a reality after almost ten years of tugging and hauling; to the expressway system, which saw the first segment of road opened to public use at the beginning of 1962, almost fifteen years after the program's inauguration; and to the repertory theatre proposed by the noted producer and director, Tyrone Guthrie, which went to Minneapolis while Milwaukee debated.

These observations, however, must be tempered by events since 1960 which indicate a quickening of pace and a more vigorous approach to the developmental problems of the community. Expressway construction, for example, has been speeded up, the central business district is witnessing a flurry of new office building, a wide range of urban renewal projects arc under way, Milwaukee is the first large city in the nation to adopt a community renewal program (CRP);[4] and white and Negro leaders have formed a top-level committee to work for better racial relations. Developments such as these, while not spectacular, attest to the sound social and economic foundation of the area and its capacity to adjust to change, however slowly.

The question is often asked why Milwaukee's approach to local public affairs and to social problems generally has been marked by a conservative orientation. The reasons given are varied and largely impressionistic: lack of leadership; ethnic composition of the population; the heritage left by the late nineteenth and early twentieth century immigration; and the relative absence of serious problems. Some observers attribute the slow pace of civic projects to the traditional no-debt or pay-as-you-go policy of the City, which persisted into the post-World-War-II period, and to the local governmental system, which requires consensus at many different points before action can be taken. Others contend that Milwaukee, lying in the shadow of Chicago, is on the periphery of the main stream of economic and cultural activities—"off the beaten path," as they put it—and that this geographical fact militates against aggressive action. Still others place the blame on the "fiction of a socialist-controlled government," claiming that this image inhibited active participation by businessmen, led to lack of rapport between the city administration and community leaders, and handicapped the area in dealing with the rest of the state.

Until the latter part of the nineteenth century, Milwaukee regarded itself as the "queen city of the West," but its vigor and ambition gradually tempered as its enterprising and aggressive neighbor to the south began to surpass it in size and stature. As long as travel was mainly by water, the area's peripheral location mattered little. However, with the increasing emphasis upon overland railroad transport, the race for urban supremacy in the upper Middle West went to Chicago, the growing giant at the base of the lake. By the end of the century Milwaukeeans had reluctantly accepted the fact that the realities of geography could not be combated. To speak of Milwaukee's conservatism is to refer to only one aspect of the community's many-sided and sturdy character. Its advantages are numerous: a relatively sound and prosperous economy; a highly skilled labor force; a good educational system including its nationally known vocational school and two major universities, Marquette and the University of Wisconsin—Milwaukee; a park system of over 11,000 acres that is surpassed by few other areas; and a high level of honest and efficient public service. Its accident, crime, and unemployment rates are among the lowest in the nation for communities of its size. Visitors are impressed by its well-kept homes, the absence of extensive areas of blight, the friendliness of its people, its law-abiding citizenry, the beauty of its lakefront with its excellent harbor, and its superb restaurants. These are assets that have given the community a reputation as a desirable place to live and rear one's children.

Population

Milwaukee County's 239 square miles of territory—all of it now incorporated—stretches from Lake Michigan on the east to rapidly growing Waukesha County on the west; and from the Racine County line on the south to that of developing Ozaukee County on the north. Within these boundaries are slightly more than one million residents, 71.5 per cent of whom live in Milwaukee city. The proportion of the central city's population to that in the remainder of the county is declining steadily although not as sharply as in many other large urban areas. (Since 1940, as Table 1 shows, Milwaukee city's share of the total has decreased by only 5 per cent.) However, the City's ability to prevent a more precipitous decline has been due entirely to annexation. In fact, during the last decennial period it actually suffered an absolute loss of 3 per cent in population within its 1950 boundaries while showing an overall increase of 16 per cent because of the expansion of its

TABLE 1

Changes in Population: Milwaukee City and County, 1850-1960

Year	Milwaukee City	Rest of County	Total	% of Total County Pop. in City
1850	20,061	11,016	31,077	64.6
1860	45,246	17,272	62,518	72.4
1870	71,440	18,490	89,930	79.4
1880	115,587	22,950	138,537	83.4
1890	204,468	31,633	236,101	86.6
1900	285,315	44,702	330,017	86.5
1910	373,857	59,330	433,187	86.3
1920	457,147	82,302	539,449	84.7
1930	578,249	147,014	725,263	79.7
1940	587,472	179,413	766,885	76.6
1950	637,392	233,655	871,047	73.2
1960	741,324	294,723	1,036,047	71.5

TABLE 2

Equalized Assessed Valuation of Taxable Property in Milwaukee City and County, 1947-1963*

Year	Milwaukee City (000 omitted)	Total Milwaukee County (000 omitted)	% of Total within City
1947	1,244,928	1,814,628	68.6
1949	1,618,281	2,375,561	68.1
1951	2,128,074	3,128,017	68.0
1953	2,746,820	4,044,371	67.9
1955	3,029,567	4,446,132	68.1
1957	3,466,457	5,195,742	66.7
1959	3,645,716	5,590,881	65.2
1961	3,756,093	5,885,077	63.8
1963	3,856,595	6,119,908	63.0

* Equalized assessed valuation is an approximation of full market value and is determined by the state department of taxation.

Source: Statistical Reports, Wisconsin Department of Taxation, 1947 to 1963.

legal limits.[5] For a similar reason, the proportion of taxable property within the central city to the county total has been held to a decrease of less than 5 per cent since World War II (see Table 2).

SOCIAL AND DEMOGRAPHIC DIMENSIONS

The seeds of the future metropolis were planted late in the eighteenth century when French-Canadian fur traders established a post at the point where the Milwaukee River joins the waters of Lake Michigan. By 1837 two rival villages, Juneautown on the east side of the river and Kilbourntown on the west, were vying for the trade of the rich hinterlands. Prompted by the desire to reduce governmental costs during a period of depression, the two settlements consolidated in 1839 as the east and west wards of the town of Milwaukee. Seven years later as its population approached 10,000 the thriving community achieved city status.

At the time cityhood was conferred on it Milwaukee was predominantly Yankee. "Only an occasional Finnegan or Daugherty, Vieau or Juneau suggested the variety that Irish migrants and French-Canadian traders lent to a society that was predominantly of the eastern seaboard; only an occasional Diedrich or Weisner foreshadowed the coming Germanic flood."[6] Starting in the late 1840's, German immigrants began to appear in substantial numbers until by the last quarter of the century Milwaukee was known as the "most German city in the United States," or more flatteringly as the "Deutsch-Athen of America." The almost exclusively Germanic character of the community began to be diluted during the last decades of the century by the new stream of immigration from eastern and southern Europe. By 1910 there were large concentrations of Poles in the southern sections of the city along with substantial neighborhood enclaves of Czechs, Slovaks, Hungarians, and Italians.

Milwaukee County of the 1960's presents a varied ethnic, racial, and social pattern. While the Schmidts, Klausners, Wahls, and

Vogels still predominate in total numbers, the Germans no longer form the closely knit and cohesive community they once did. Two world wars as well as high social mobility have hastened the almost complete demise of Milwaukee's Germanism. At the turn of the century, the editor of *Germania* could exhort "every German-American, as a matter of honor, to vote for that excellent German John C. Koch," and express confidence that "the Germandom of the city is conscious of its duty."[7] Such expressions today would be received with amusement or considered in bad taste.

In contrast to the Germans, the Poles have closely guarded and retained their identity as a nationality group. The bulk of the Polish population lives on the City's southside with concentrations extending into the adjacent industrial suburbs of Cudahy and South Milwaukee. Polish solidarity is particularly manifested in the political arena, where a Polish name is a prerequisite for election to public office in certain wards and districts. "Ethnic" voting has assisted Polish candidates in capturing not only aldermanic and state assembly posts but also local judgeships. Traditionally, also, certain appointive posts in the city government go to Poles as a matter of course.

By 1960, foreign-born residents constituted 7 per cent of the county's total population and second-generation Americans 22 per cent. Several of the smaller nationality groups, including the Croats, Armenians, Slovaks, and Ukranians, continue to maintain a strong neighborhood identity centered around the parish church. The Italian community of more than 20,000, once concentrated in Milwaukee's lower third ward, began its migration to more desirable sections of the metropolis in the 1930's. Dispersal was completed in 1957, when the City's first redevelopment project dislodged the remaining families, some 325, after vigorous and often impassioned resistance. The Irish, never large numerically but always influential in the community's political life, have long been scattered throughout the county. According to the 1960 census, they composed less than 2 per cent of the county's foreign stock (first- and second-generation Americans) compared with 34 per cent for the Germans and 17 per cent for the Poles.

Although increasing, Milwaukee's racial minority groups are as yet not large in comparison with those of other northern and eastern industrial centers. In 1950 there were slightly over 22,000 non-whites—2.5 per cent of the total population—in the county. By 1960 their number had tripled to almost 67,000, or 6.4 per cent of the county's population. Approximately 25,000 of this increase during the intercensal period was due to in-migration, largely from rural areas of the South. Scarcely more than a handful of the non-whites live outside the core city and practically none south of the Menomonee River Valley, sometimes referred to as the "Mason-Dixon line," which cuts an east-west swath through the center of Milwaukee city. A second minority group of some 3,000 Puerto Ricans has found assimilation easier and has been able to move from its original settlement near the central business district to other sections of the City, principally the near southside.

In terms of social geography, Milwaukee County does not present a sharp contrast between the central city and the "iron ring" of surrounding suburbs. The corporate limits that separate Milwaukee city from its neighboring municipalities can hardly be referred to as distinct social boundaries. A majority of the upper-income families have moved to suburbia—to the wealthy north shore villages of Whitefish Bay, Fox Point, Bayside, and River Hills; to Wauwatosa, an old established residential community on the western edge of the city; and to the new "exurban" settlements in the adjacent counties of Waukesha, Ozaukee, and Washington. But to the south and west of the central city are also the industrial satellites of South Milwaukee, Cudahy, West Milwaukee, and West Allis, and the medium-income communities of St. Francis and Greenfield—all with large concentrations of blue-collar workers. The exodus to the suburbs has obviously denuded the central city of much of its leadership potential, yet a substantial pool remains. One reason for this is Milwaukee's East Side with its fashionable Lake Drive, elegant old homes, luxury apartments, a university environment, and a capacity for good living. Many of the City's influential families and civic leaders still reside in this area, stubbornly resistant to the blandishments of suburbia.

The Milwaukee SMSA has a somewhat less-than-expected degree of home ownership, due largely to the many duplexes or two-family flats which were built by the thrifty citizenry earlier in the century. Only 58 per cent of its dwelling units are owner-occupied, compared with 68 per cent in the Minneapolis–St. Paul metropolitan area, 62 per cent in Cleveland, and 71 per cent in Detroit. The Milwaukee SMSA ranks seventh among the twenty largest metropolitan areas of the nation in the median value of owner-occupied dwellings and second in the median gross rental of dwelling units. These relative standings in turn are a reflection of the area's median family income, which the 1960 census shows as $6,995, the sixth highest among the large metropolitan areas.[8]

ECONOMY OF THE AREA

Economic characteristics are important indicators, at times determinants, of the social and political structure of a community. The pattern of behavior of a university town, to cite an extreme case, will vary substantially from that of a city whose economic life blood is dependent on heavy industry. Social composition, cultural aspirations, and prevailing values will differ sharply in the two jurisdictions. Even local governmental organization, as recent studies indicate, may be significantly influenced by the economic and social dimensions of the community.[9] These are factors that proponents of metropolitan reform have tended to disregard.

Milwaukee County dominates the industrial complex in the southeast corner of Wisconsin. Containing 30 per cent of the value of all taxable real and personal property in the state, the county employs 40 per cent of the state's industrial wage earners and accounts for 43 per cent of the total value added by manufacturing in Wisconsin. A mature industrial community—the county's population reached 400,000 before 1910—Milwaukee exhibits none of the boom town characteristics of newer centers of industry and commerce such as Los Angeles and Dallas. It produces few flamboyant entrepreneurs, and it manages to retain a strong hold on the loyalty of its businessmen and workers. Strikes arc relatively infrequent, and it is not unusual to find sons and even grandchildren working as skilled craftsmen in the same firm that their forebears did.

The community is one of old and well-established firms. Allis Chalmers, the area's largest employer, was founded in 1847; and A. O. Smith, the second in total employment, dates back to 1870. Other large and nationally known Milwaukee firms that were organized before the turn of the century include Allen-Bradley, Bucyrus-Erie, Chain Belt, Harnischfeger, Patrick Cudahy, and the Pabst and Schlitz breweries. Many of these and other major concerns in the area are locally owned and controlled, some wholly by individual families. Recent years have witnessed heavy inroads on the "family" type business through absorption by national corporations and stock offerings to the general public, but a surprising number of such firms still exist in the Milwaukee area. The older families as a result continue not only to set the social tone of the community but also to influence greatly, if not dominate, its economic life.

Contributing also to Milwaukee's "inbred" characteristics is the nature of its industrial development. Since the termination of World War II, the community has had to depend for its growth principally on the expansion of local firms. Few new branch plants of national corporations have been attracted to the area. American Can, A. C. Spark Plug Division, Continental Can, General Electric X-Ray Department, and Hotpoint have been the only additions of significance during the last two decades. This development is reflected in the fact that less than 20 per cent of the county's export earnings is derived from branch operations while the remainder originates in local companies.

The economy of the area rests on capital goods.[10] Nine-tenths of its export earnings originate in manufacturing, primarily the production of durable goods. Second only to Chicago as a machinery center, Milwaukee County turns out 10 per cent of the nation's electrical generating, transmission, and distributing equipment, 15 per cent of its construction and mining equipment, and over 10 per cent of its castings and forgings. Within its borders are the country's largest builder of cranes and the world's largest manufacturer of single-cylinder, air-cooled gasoline engines. Much of the county's output consists of specially designed heavy machinery and electrical motor controls, which require highly skilled and experienced workers. While there is mass production in Milwaukee, the items turned out by machines tended by unskilled labor make up a relatively small sector of the economy. The northwest European origin of many of the area's early residents goes a long way toward explaining the development of its machine industries.

Of the total employed population in Milwaukee County, over 42 per cent work in one of the area's 2,000 manufacturing establishments. Although the bulk of this employment is centered in the central city, secondary concentrations of considerable magnitude are found in the suburbs. In fact, some of the area's largest employers, including Allis Chalmers, Ladish Company, Chain Belt, Bucyrus-Erie, and Harnischfeger, are located outside Milwaukee city. These and other outlying firms account for approximately 32 per cent of the total number of industrial jobs and 30 per cent of the value added by manufacturing in the metropolitan area. Comparable figures for the neighboring metropolis to the north—Minneapolis–St. Paul—are 23 and 27 per cent; and for the Chicago SMSA to the south, 34 and 35 per cent.

Commercially, Milwaukee along with other metropolitan areas has experienced decentralization of its retail trade as the stores and shops have followed the population movement outward. This development, however, is not a product of recent decades but the continuance of a long-established pattern. Decentralization of commercial activities started early in Milwaukee's history with the opening of large shopping centers in the outlying neighborhoods of the City. Long before major department stores in the large cities were building branches to tap the suburban market, Milwaukee had its Mitchell Street, its Upper Third Street, and its Twelfth and Vliet shopping areas, all situated no more than two or three miles from the major hub of activity. This early competition between downtown and the outlying clusters of stores restricted the growth of Milwaukee's central business district and hence made it less sensitive to the later effects of the modern suburban shopping centers.

The significant postwar expansion of the central city's boundaries through annexation has enabled it to maintain its dominant position in retail trade. In 1958 Milwaukee city accounted for 83 per cent of total retail sales made in the county. This represents a decrease of only 3 per cent since 1948, a decrease which corresponds to the small change in the central city-suburban population ratio during the last decade—again the result of annexation. Two of the four major regional shopping centers opened in Milwaukee County since 1950 are within core city boundaries and both of them are on land that had been annexed in recent decades. The retail trade ratio, however, can be expected to change in the future, since the central city has now reached the limits of its territorial expansion and the bulk of the area's future population increase will occur in the outlying sectors.

One additional factor is important in describing Milwaukee's economic position. Although a large urban center, it does not enjoy the regional dominance in business and trade characteristic of many other SMSA's of roughly comparable size such as Kansas City, Minneapolis–St. Paul, Seattle, and Dallas. It does not, in other words, perform large-scale business and financial functions for a sizable service hinterland. One reason for this is the character of its manufacturing sector. Milwaukee is primarily a producer of goods that are *not* destined for final consumption but are fed into other industries for further processing or use as fabricating equipment. Hence the bulk of its products are manufactured for a national and world market rather than for use or consumption within the region. Another reason is its geographical location. Milwaukee is relatively close to rival manufacturing, financial, and trading centers—principally Chicago to the south and Minneapolis to the northwest, and to the smaller subcenters of Madison to the west and Green Bay to the north. This proximity to competing nuclei inhibits the area's potential development as a regional center.

POLITICAL BACKGROUND

Milwaukee city's early political history is marked by strong adherence to the Democratic party. Of the sixteen mayors who served between 1846 and 1870, all but one were members of the party of Jefferson and Jackson. The Democratic monopoly was broken in 1870 when a prominent businessman was elected mayor on the Republican ticket. During the following forty years neither party dominated in city politics. The Democrats, drawing their support from Irish and Polish voters, won eleven mayoralty contests; and the Republicans, who had managed to draw the increasingly conservative German-American element into their ranks, were victorious on an equal number of occasions. In 1910 the Social Democratic party, with working class support, was able to capture the office of mayor and obtain a majority on the common council. The victory gave Milwaukee the distinction of being the first American city to come under Socialist control.

Catapulted into power during the municipal reform wave that swept across the nation shortly after the turn of the century, Milwaukee Socialists drove out the "corrupt" regime of the Democratic administration and set about with crusading zeal to achieve good government for the growing city. Their control, however, was short-lived. Republicans and Democrats joined forces to push through a bill in the 1911 legislature providing for nonpartisan elections for city offices. This maneuver prevented the Socialists from again gaining control of the common council, although they remained a strong minority into the 1930's and held the mayor's office for all but eight years from 1916 to 1960. The long tenure was due more to the personality of the two Socialist mayors who served during this period than to the party's attractiveness to the electorate. Daniel Hoan, who occupied the office for a span of twenty-four years, was a colorful, dynamic, and able individual who won the grudging respect of the conservative elements in the community by his efficient and honest administration of the City's affairs. Frank Zeidler, who followed Hoan after an eight-year interlude of non-Socialist mayors, was an unassuming, scholarly, and dedicated public official with a large personal following among the working class and the intellectuals of the community. When he retired from office in 1960 after twelve years of service, Milwaukee's socialism (branded "sewer socialism" at one time by members of the national party because of its concern with local public sewers and facilities) came to a formal end. Its influence as a significant force in local politics had long since vanished. Typical of the community's conservatism, Milwaukee's socialism produced no socialism. The water supply and sewerage systems are the area's only publicly owned utilities.

Milwaukeeans have now had almost a half century of nonpartisan government at both the municipal and county levels. Only the traditional county administrative offices—county clerk, sheriff, district attorney, coroner, clerk of the circuit court, treasurer, surveyor, and register of deeds—are elected on party tickets. Despite the development of stronger party organizations in recent decades and the growing strength of the Democrats in the City, it is still essential in local elections to appeal to the voters in a manner that does not do violence to the ideal of nonpartisanship.

Politically, Milwaukee does not conform to the common stereotype of a Democratic central city surrounded by Republican suburbs. Democrats have predominated in the City since the days of the New Deal and in more recent years have occasionally managed to capture slight majorities in the remainder of the county, as the vote pattern for governor shows. (See Table 3.) The industrial and

TABLE 3

Vote for Governor 1946-1964 by Milwaukee City and
Rest of County*

	Milwaukee City			Rest of County		
Year	Dem.	Rep.	% Voting Democratic	Dem.	Rep.	% Voting Democratic
1946	102,052	102,500	49.9	27,047	46,033	37.0
1948	138,915	108,116	56.2	35,683	46,025	43.6
1950	122,735	88,368	58.1	33,049	43,857	42.9
1952	168,039	141,110	54.3	51,511	68,777	42.8
1954	124,874	83,903	59.8	37,984	45,405	45.5
1956	176,441	118,676	59.7	53,002	61,786	46.1
1958	190,647	118,310	61.7	47,425	45,555	51.0
1960	194,388	115,085	62.8	69,022	67,328	50.6
1962	142,908	81,726	63.6	49,535	56,664	46.6
1964	196,113	117,867	62.4	68,299	72,788	48.4

* The insignificant vote for minor parties that occurred in several of these elections is disregarded in the tabulation.

lower middle income suburbs, mainly of the south side, return heavy Democratic majorities while the north shore and other high income communities remain solidly Republican. In presidential elections, the county has supported the Democratic candidate since 1928 except in 1952 and 1956, when it gave its vote to Eisenhower.

GOVERNMENTAL STRUCTURE

The local government pattern of the county is relatively simple although fragmented. The City of Milwaukee and eighteen incorporated suburbs (ranging in size from approximately 1,200 to

75,000) serve the municipal needs of the citizenry. Public education is provided by eighteen autonomous school districts and six boards of vocational and adult education. The county government, the Metropolitan Sewerage Commission, and the Southeastern Wisconsin Regional Planning Commission (which includes Milwaukee and six other counties), constitute the remaining units. As in other large urban areas, the number of school districts has decreased in recent years (from sixty-seven in 1950) while the number of municipalities has increased. Eight of the suburban communities were incorporated during the 1950's, two during the 1930's, one in 1926, and the others prior to 1910. The 1950's also witnessed the incorporation of four cities and villages in the areas immediately adjacent to Milwaukee County.

The early incorporations are of significance to any discussion of metropolitan reorganization. These communities, all of them in reasonably sound fiscal shape either because of their high quality homes or their industrial tax base, have a long history of local autonomy and tradition. Their governments are well regarded by the citizenry, and the level of public services is relatively high. Whitefish Bay, the first of the suburban incorporations, was established in 1892 around a village resort that had become a favorite gathering place for the businessmen and intelligentsia from Milwaukee—so popular, in fact, that a railroad spur had been built to it as early as 1888. Whitefish Bay was followed five years later by the incorporation of Wauwatosa, advertised at the time as "the most attractive suburb of Milwaukee with fine churches, street lights, transit facilities, and freedom from saloons and heavy industry."[11] Shortly thereafter, a third residential suburb, Shorewood, was formed north of Milwaukee city. No further incorporations of residential communities occurred until 1926, when the village of Fox Point was created to accommodate the spillover from Whitefish Bay. River Hills, the most exclusive dormitory suburb in the area with its large estates and its predominantly five-acre minimum zoning, was incorporated four years later. The federally sponsored greenbelt community of Greendale, a product of the depression years, followed in 1938.

Industrial decentralization began to occur early. Lack of room for expansion within the central city and the proximity of railroad transportation to the cheap outlying land in the southern and western sections of the county sparked the migration of several major plants and led to the creation of Milwaukee's industrial suburbia. During the period from 1897 to 1907 four industrial satellites were incorporated: South Milwaukee, West Milwaukee, West Allis, and Cudahy. Of the municipalities incorporated since that time, only one (Glendale) has a substantial non-residential tax base, and a second (Oak Creek) has evidenced industrial potential.

The last and final wave of incorporations occurred during the 1950's, prompted in large part by the annexation activities of the central city. The story is a familiar one—the outward push of the core city to obtain more room for expansion; the resistance of fringe area residents and township officials in the City's "imperialism"; and, finally, suburban incorporation in self-defense. At the time that it achieved status as a city in 1846, Milwaukee had an area of seven square miles. Today it encompasses over ninety-six square miles, almost one-half of which was acquired after World War II.*

The City has a weak-mayor system of government. The chief executive's control over the administrative bureaucracy is circumscribed by the powers vested in commissions, such as the police and

---

* The most recent addition—and probably the last—occurred in 1962, when the state supreme court awarded the City an area of approximately sixteen square miles in the former town of Granville in the northwest section of the county. Jurisdiction over the area had been in dispute since 1956, when both Milwaukee and Brown Deer instituted annexation proceedings. Ironically, the City's victory brought to it a far larger portion of the disputed territory than it had anticipated. It also drew vigorous and impassioned protests from residents of the annexed area and led to such mock heroics on their part as a proclamation of an "Independent Granville" and the guarding of garbage cans by housewives against Milwaukee refuse collectors.

fire and the harbor commissions, and by the tight supervision which the common council exercises over the day-to-day operations of the government. The council, composed of nineteen aldermen elected by wards, not only makes policy but also plays an active role in administration through its influential standing committees. It handles labor relations and personnel matters, conducts "trials" on tavern licenses, and issues directives to departments heads. In such a milieu, the effectiveness of the mayor depends more on his extra-legal prerogatives and his personal faculties of persuasion than on the formal powers of the office. The present incumbent, Henry Maier, a well known Democrat and former minority leader in the state Senate, has instituted changes designed to give him greater control over the City's administrative machinery. Although hampered by the traditional system of diffused authority, he has been able to use his position to push forward developmental programs of substantial scope.

The county is governed by an elected executive and a twenty-four-member board of supervisors chosen by districts. The position of county executive was created by statute in 1959. At the time the office was established its formal powers were relatively weak, but a constitutional amendment approved by the voters in 1962 gave the county executive authority to veto board actions. As in the City, standing committees of the legislative body and semi-independent commissions militate against centralized administrative control. However, the county's elected executive, John Doyne, is making a determined effort to become chief administrator in fact as well as form.

A high degree of professionalism characterizes all levels of local governmental administration in Milwaukee County. Strong merit systems prevail in both the City and county governments and in a majority of the suburbs. The central city's reputation for honest and competent administration is well known. In recent years, also, the county government has made considerable headway in professionalizing its administrative machinery and adapting itself to the needs of a modern urban community. Suburban municipalities follow the common pattern. Some of them are competently administered and furnish a high level of services; others are less well governed and provide only a minimum of functions. Those in existence before the post-war rash of incorporations generally have higher tax resources and provide a broader range of services than the newer communities. The latter fact is graphically demonstrated by a detailed breakdown in the number of activities performed by each unit. In the ten communities incorporated before World War II, the average number of municipal activities or subfunctions is 151, while in the municipalities created since 1950 the comparable figure is only eighty-six.[12] Even in these latter communities, however, the range of services has been steadily increasing.

Local governments in Wisconsin rely on two major sources of revenue: general property taxes and state aids and shared taxes. Returns from the first finance approximately 48 per cent of local expenditures in Milwaukee County; those in the latter category supply most of the remainder.* In addition to grants-in-aid for specific functions such as education, welfare, and roads, the state returns 50 per cent of state income tax receipts from individuals and corporations to the municipality where the taxpayer resides and 10 per cent to the county government. Sixty-five per cent of the ad valorem taxes on light, heat, and power companies is also returned to local units and 20 per cent to counties. This distribution system enables some cities and villages in Milwaukee County to perform their municipal functions without local property tax levies and several to provide services that could not otherwise be offered without inordinately high local rates.

As this brief sketch indicates, the formal structure of govern-

* Under a major tax revision bill passed in the 1961 session of the legislature, the state is required to appropriate $55 million annually for real property tax relief. This amount is distributed to local communities and applied by them as a credit on individual property tax bills. Without this credit, 57 per cent of the cost of local government in Milwaukee County would be financed from property tax levies.

ment in metropolitan Milwaukee resembles that in most of the nation's large urban areas. Political fragmentation, intergovernmental rivalry, disparity in service levels, lack of institutional machinery for establishing area-wide goals and priorities, all are the common attributes of the modern urban community. Each metropolis, however, has its own features and peculiarities, its own qualities and flavor, that distinguish it from its counterparts. Local government in Milwaukee does not function in precisely the same manner as in Chicago, or for that matter, in any of the other 219 American SMSA's. As in other sectors of the community's life, the dominant tone in the governmental sphere is conservatism. But it is a conservatism that has produced well-administered if not dynamic government, progressive if not rapid or outstanding community development, moderate if not imaginative change. Small town may still be the word for Milwaukee but the pressures of contemporary urban society are shaking her complacency.

2
The Community's
Organizational Pattern

Metropolitan reorganization is more than an issue of governmental efficiency or administrative tidiness; it is also a highly charged political question. Whenever alterations are made in an existing system of local government, the stakes of various individuals and groups are affected in one fashion or another. To some of the parties, the prospect of change holds out inducements and promises of rewards; to others, risks and threats to their interests. Not all members of a community, moreover, will be concerned with a metropolitan crusade; in fact, only a small minority will ordinarily be involved. Since the relative power, resources, and intensity of conviction of those who take part in the campaign will influence if not determine the outcome, it is essential to know something about the actual and the potential gladiators—who they are, the positions they occupy, the stakes they hold, and the power they possess.

Three features of the Milwaukee community structure are relevant in this regard. First of all, the leadership pattern of the county, from all available evidence, is much closer to the polynucleated

24

structure described by Dahl in New Haven and by Freeman and his colleagues in Syracuse than to the monolithic system depicted by Hunter in Atlanta.[1] The anatomy of influence, in other words, is pluralistic, not oligarchical. No small coterie of economic or political dominants has the power to call the civic signals on all important public questions. Many decision centers exist, each with varying degrees of influence and control over particular kinds of issues. If the question involves urban renewal, one set of power constellations is activated; if the matter is one of building a new hospital, a different combination of actors is called into play. Some groups and organizations are influential because of their capacity to initiate and promote action in certain fields, while others are powerful because of their ability to veto measures within limited spheres of concern. A civic committee of top level industrialists is an example of the former, a suburban league of municipalities of the latter.

In some areas of public life, policy may be controlled by a relatively small group of the citizenry. This situation is most common in the private welfare sector of the community, where key individuals representative of wealth and large corporate interests dominate. No campaign to solicit money for a civic enterprise of magnitude—hospital, community chest drive, music hall—is undertaken without the endorsement and blessing of this group. But even in these matters, power may not be as centralized as is usually assumed. Differences over priorities and allocation of funds are not unknown among the social and economic notables. Many of them have their "pet" projects or charities which they will vigorously foster and guard from intrusion by others. Efforts made by a majority of the elite to consolidate or abolish a social agency or give its capital improvement program low priority may evoke strong opposition from other notables who are championing the institution to be affected.

When the question is one of metropolitan governmental reform, the pattern of influence is diffused and unorganized. Not only does this issue involve different configurations of power from those involved by most other matters on the public agenda, but since it transcends individual governmental boundaries it brings into operation many lesser power groups and actors that are able to exert influence out of all proportion to their status or numbers. Thus a league of suburban officials, impotent in most areas of community concern, can become a crucial element in reorganization proposals because of its ties to the entrenched local bureaucracies. So also the veto power of a suburban chamber of commerce or a village council is greatly enhanced in metropolitan affairs by the autonomous character of its political stronghold. No web of formal or informal ties exists linking these functional and territorial decision clusters to an all-powerful center of sovereign power in the metropolis. When progress is made in metropolitan reform, it is usually the result of negotiation, compromise, and finally consensus among many disparate and largely independent sub-areas of control; or it is the result of pressure from external forces, particularly from higher levels of government.

A second feature of importance to the problem of metropolitan reorganization is the wide gulf that exists between control over the local government structure and power within the non-political areas of community life. This cleavage, also noted in other urban centers, has long been evident in Milwaukee. During the early decades of the City's existence, the business and economic leaders played prominent roles in local political affairs. By the end of the last century, however, their activity had begun to diminish as the working class became more articulate in community politics. When the Socialists gained control of the City government early in the present century, the gap between the political and business communities widened. Commercial and industrial leaders became content to influence the conduct of government indirectly through service on the boards of various citizens' groups, such as the City Club and the Citizens' Governmental Research Bureau. Few businessmen bothered to run for political office; and the number of them appointed to public boards gradually diminished over the years. Professional civic secretaries became their spokesmen and channeled their interest in local governmental affairs.

Concomitant with their withdrawal from the formal political sphere, the economic and social notables began to devote time and attention to the privately run sector of the community's organizations: boys' clubs, hospitals, the community chest, and similar civic institutions. Such activity not only enabled them to minimize governmental spending and control in these areas but also provided them with a highly legitimate and prestigious civic role. At the present time, for example, over fifty members of the Greater Milwaukee Committee—the group most extensively representative of the community elite—serve on the governing boards of such organizations.

The third relevant attribute is the non-partisan character of the local governmental system in the Milwaukee area. Because of this feature, political parties have little capacity or opportunity for exerting a unifying influence in matters of metropolitan government. In a study of area-wide decision-making in Syracuse, Munger concluded that one of the potent forces encouraging and facilitating metropolitan action was the existence of a disciplined party allegiance which "has united central city, suburban governments, county government, and state legislatures in common cause."[2] No such integrating agency with a direct organizational stake in the operation of the on-going governmental system is found in metropolitan Milwaukee.* Excluded from the major political rewards that local governments can offer, the parties—even if they desired to play the role—are without effective means of linking together the highly autonomous parts of the structure. Such an associational force, if one exists in Milwaukee, must be sought elsewhere.

* The Syracuse situation, moreover, may well be atypical. There is little evidence elsewhere to support the assumption that metropolitan affairs are better coordinated in areas where the city political organization controls the county government than in localities where non-partisanship or split political control exists.

THE ORGANIZATIONAL WEB

Americans have long demonstrated a tendency to form associations for almost every purpose, whether trivial or important. The habit of "joining," of organizing human contacts around some activity or cause, is well established in the nation's cultural environment. As Alexis de Tocqueville observed more than a century ago: "Americans of all ages, all conditions, and all dispositions, constantly form associations." Although not all individuals belong to such groups—a large percentage, in fact, remain outside the stream of organized social life—the number of those who do participate is impressive. These organizations provide a far-flung but highly decentralized network for mobilizing public opinion and action on civic issues. Together with the formal structure of local government, they form the basic organizational framework of the metropolitan community. Rarely, however, is their aggregate potential for effecting social or political change realized.

Metropolitan Milwaukee offers no exception to the common mold; it is a community of many and varied organizations. A recent edition of the *Directory of Milwaukee County Organizations*[3] lists well over 900 voluntary associations, exclusive of the numerous social, fraternal, PTA, and religious organizations and the garden and sports clubs that mushroom over the area. (See Table 4.) The purposes they fulfill and the size and nature of their membership differ greatly. Many are formed primarily to serve business, professional, and occupational interests; a large number seek to further cultural and educational ends; some deal specifically with community services and welfare; others are connected with a wide variety of causes and objectives. Of particular interest to the metropolitan reformer are the voluntary associations that concern themselves with influencing public opinion and local governments on community matters of general import. Only a relatively small number (even of those which classify themselves as "civic") are organized for this purpose, while the vast majority are formed

TABLE 4

Voluntary Associations in Milwaukee County by General Types*

Classification	Number	% of Total
Professional and business	362	40
Civic	127	14
Educational	93	10
Women's clubs	90	10
Cultural	76	8
Nationality and patriotic	53	5
Service clubs	51	5
Veterans	32	3
Public officials	10	1
Political	7	1
Taxpayers	5	—
Miscellaneous	28	3
Total	934	100

* Adapted from Directory, Milwaukee County Organizations, 1959-60 (Milwaukee: Milwaukee Public Library, 1960).

around other particularized aims. For the latter, any involvement in matters pertaining to local public policy or governmental action is merely a subsidiary phase of their major set of activities or in furtherance of their own specialized group interests.

From the standpoint of participation in metropolitan public affairs, the voluntary associations in the Milwaukee area may be divided into four categories: activists, peripherally concerned, potentially interested, and inactive. The first, the activists, encompasses only a few organizations whose objectives are almost exclusively of a civic nature, such as leagues of women voters and good government groups. The second, the peripherally involved, is broader in scope and includes those organizations that are concerned with specialized and limited aspects of metropolitan problems as they relate to their professional, occupational, or political interests. The third, the potentially interested, embraces service clubs and similar groups that, as organizations, have no direct stake in metropolitan governmental issues but are at times attracted to public causes. The last and largest category, the inactives, covers the many fraternal and social associations that have no interest in civic or metropolitan affairs and no propensity for becoming involved in them.

Virtually all organizations which can be classified as civic activists are supported by those who derive no personal benefit from their membership except the satisfaction of community service or the approbation of their peers. The League of Women Voters, for example, has no rewards to offer its members other than the opportunity of participating in civic affairs and the honor of holding office within the organization. Conversely, the majority of groups that fall under the remaining three categories serve the interests of a "clientele" membership. A labor union looks out for the economic interests of its constituents; a political party holds out promises of rewards to its workers; a medical or engineering society protects the professional concerns of its members. Civic activist groups function without these motivating advantages of self-interest, relying heavily on the altruism of their members. Hence their rosters usually remain small and their resources for stimulating wide-scale action inadequate. Voluntary associations of this kind tend also to avoid community issues of a strongly controversial or political nature for fear of alienating some part of their support.

When the organizational list is scanned for potential participants in area-wide governmental affairs, the results offer little encouragement to the metropolitan reformer. Using as yardsticks the general nature of the voluntary association and, in cases where known, its stated objectives, only a handful of the more than 900 groups listed in the directory can be classified as civic activists, approximately fifty as peripherally concerned, and no more than 100 as potentially interested.

Some indication of the extent of organizational interest in metropolitan affairs can be gleaned from replies to a questionnaire sent out by the Junior Chamber of Commerce in 1960. The survey was conducted at the request of the Metropolitan Study Commission (MSC), the state appointed agency that was examining the governmental problems of the Milwaukee area. Three hundred and seventeen local groups were asked about their concern with metropolitan problems and their willingness to support an action program. Of the eighty-seven that responded, approximately one-half indicated some interest in these problems and a receptivity to participation in furthering their solution. However, when the MSC, through the Junior Bar Association, offered to provide speakers to discuss the Commission's findings, requests were received from only nineteen of the "interested" groups, the majority of them from service clubs such as the Lions and Kiwanis.

If attendance at meetings of the Study Commission is employed as a test of interest, the results further confirm the low state of organizational concern. During the four years of the MSC's existence (1957-1961) only eighteen local groups were represented at its meetings, most of them on only one or two occasions. As Table 5

TABLE 5

Number of MSC Meetings Attended by Representatives of Local Organizations*

Name of Organization	Type of Organization	No. of Meetings Attended	% of Meetings Attended
Milwaukee Association of Commerce	Business	22	61
Citizens' Governmental Research Bureau	Civic	34	94
City Club	Civic	28	78
Greater Milwaukee Committee	Civic	12	33
League of Women Voters	Civic	28	78
Suburban League of Municipalities	Public officials	9	24

* Organizations represented at less than five meetings are not included. Attendance is based on 36 of the 41 Commission meetings. Data were not recorded for five of the sessions.

shows, only six organizations had representatives at five or more sessions. This lack of associational interest in metropolitan affairs is not peculiar to Milwaukee. The same phenomenon is all too familiar in most large urban centers.

The Civic Federation for Community Cooperation, established in 1961, gives an indication as to which Milwaukee organizations have enough interest in metropolitan reform to participate at least nominally in discussions about possible changes. The federation is a loose alliance of twenty voluntary associations, including several that are themselves coordinating agencies for service clubs. It was created following the demise of the MSC to promote selected recommendations of that body. Its membership includes:

Advisory Council to the
  Mayor*
Building Owners and
  Managers Association
Citizens' Governmental
  Research Bureau
City Club of Milwaukee
Engineers' Society of
  Milwaukee
Junior Bar Association
Junior Chamber of Commerce
LaBudde Chapter of the
  Isaac Walton League
League of Women Voters
Metropolitan Builders
  Association

Metropolitan Civic Alliance
Milwaukee Association of
  Commerce
Milwaukee Bar Association
Milwaukee Board of
  Realtors
Milwaukee Chapter of the
  American Institute of
  Architects
Milwaukee County Labor
  Council
Milwaukee Women's Club
Wauwatosa Civic Alliance
West Allis Chamber of
  Commerce
West Allis Civic Alliance

Only three of these organizations—City Club, League of Women Voters, Citizens' Governmental Research Bureau—can be classified as civic activists. About half, including the Board of Realtors, Labor Council, and Engineers' Society, fall into the peripherally-concerned category; and the remainder, such as the service club

* A self-constituted group with no official relation to the mayor of Milwaukee, composed largely of street-advancement associations and small retail store groups.

alliances, are subsumed under the potentially-interested classification. The majority of these groups have area-wide constituencies and therefore a greater potential for thinking and acting on a metropolitan basis. Several, however, such as the suburban civic alliances, have narrow geographical limits which tend to circumscribe both the range and the territorial scope of their interests.

CIVIC TABLE OF ORGANIZATIONS

Only a small number of Milwaukee's voluntary associations have played active roles in metropolitan reorganization attempts. A few, such as the City Club, Citizens' Governmental Research Bureau, League of Women Voters, and in recent decades the Greater Milwaukee Committee, have been in the forefront of virtually every effort to modernize the local governmental pattern. Several others, such as the Association of Commerce and the Civic Alliance, have participated on a less extensive basis in attempts to effect specific governmental improvements. Still others with large area-wide constituencies and a potential for influence in the public sphere, such as political parties and labor unions, have remained largely uninterested.

A thumbnail sketch of the major groups that have been actively or peripherally involved in metropolitan reorganization efforts in Milwaukee follows. This inventory will serve to bring into clearer focus the local organizational picture as it relates to the reform movement which culminated in the Metropolitan Study Commission.

City Club

The dean of Milwaukee's community-oriented associations, the City Club, was founded in 1909 to "advance a broad program for the social, civic, and economic betterment of Greater Milwaukee." Reaching a membership of almost 2,500 at one stage of its existence, the organization in recent decades has suffered the decline in popularity and influence that similar groups elsewhere have experienced. Today its membership, drawn largely from professional and middle range business circles, is less than 250. However, under its full-time secretary, Leo Tiefenthaler, who has devoted almost a half century to the cause of good government in Milwaukee, the club continues to maintain a broad program in civic affairs.

Over the years, the City Club has played a major part in promoting such objectives as charter revision, comprehensive zoning, adequate salaries for teachers, and improved public health measures. It supported creation of the Metropolitan Study Commission and actively worked for its extension. It also played an important role in the creation of the Southeastern Wisconsin Regional Planning Commission in 1960 and was one of the prime movers behind the formation of the Civic Federation for Community Cooperation. Today, the organization has standing committees on municipal and regional planning, transportation, county affairs, public education, and finance. Most of its efforts to influence public action, however, are limited to appearances by its secretary before local legislative and administrative bodies.

Greater Milwaukee Committee

When a sample of known community leaders was asked to name the voluntary associations in Milwaukee County that wield the most influence in area-wide community affairs, the Greater Milwaukee Committee headed the list by a wide margin. Approximately 50 per cent of the respondents referred to it, with no other organization receiving mention from more than 20 per cent of those interviewed. With a membership limited to 150, the GMC is composed of the top business leadership in the community. Its roster reads like a "Who's Who" of the industrial and commercial notables of metropolitan Milwaukee. Some middle echelon businessmen, the heads of the two local universities, and two labor officials are included among its numbers, but the group is predominantly representative of the major corporate interests of the area. Indicative of the high socio-economic status of its members is the fact that over 90 per cent belong to the exclusive Milwaukee Country Club and approximately one-third to the still more select Milwaukee Club, the local counterpart of James Gould Cozzens' venerable Union League. Financed by membership dues and corporate contributions, the organization employs a full-time executive secretary and clerical personnel.

Since its creation, the GMC has devoted its energy largely to stimulating and promoting action on capital improvement projects such as an outdoor stadium, an indoor sports arena, a public museum, a new zoo, an addition to the library, and an expressway system. In the 1950's the organization became interested in area-wide service issues and established a metropolitan problems committee to foster activity in this field. The most significant accomplishment of the committee was the legislative act creating the Metropolitan Study Commission.

Citizens' Governmental Research Bureau

Since 1913 the Citizens' Governmental Research Bureau has served as the research agency and the source of expertise for many of the civic groups in the area. Its thirty-six-member board of trustees is composed largely of high-ranking businessmen. Supported by the contributions of private firms and individuals, the Bureau has carefully guarded its reputation as an impartial fact-finder and as a staff arm of the civic community. Although it is primarily a research and not an activist group, its efforts have contributed to structural and procedural changes in local government at both the municipal and the county level.

Through its executive director, Norman Gill, and a small professional staff, the Bureau works closely with public officials in providing them with data and technical advice. Local governments and school districts frequently call upon it for assistance in evaluating budgetary and other administrative procedures. Similarly the Metropolitan Study Commission utilized its fact-finding and advisory services. Like most business-supported research bureaus of this type, the bulk of Citizens' Bureau projects and reports is oriented toward the improvement of local government management and the most efficient use of the tax dollar. In carrying out this role of civic "watchdog" the Bureau has come to be highly regarded not only by the business community but by public officials as well.

League of Women Voters

The League of Women Voters in Milwaukee County dates back to 1920. At the present time there are six autonomous local leagues in the county—Milwaukee City, Brown Deer, Greendale, Wauwatosa, Whitefish Bay, and West Allis—with a combined membership of approximately 700. In 1959 an Inter-League Council consisting of two representatives from each local group was established. The primary purpose of the council is to coordinate the activities of the individual Leagues and serve as their spokesman in matters pertaining to county and metropolitan affairs. By formal agreement, no local unit may take a stand on any area-wide issue unless authorized by the council. A League may refrain from supporting a position approved by a majority of the units, but it may not act in opposition to it. Through this mechanism, the individual Leagues have been able to present a united front on county and metropolitan matters. Whatever compromise is necessary usually occurs within the council, where the League's traditional policy of arriving at "a consensus" is scrupulously followed.

The League has been active in pushing for moderate governmental reforms at the local and county levels. It has been aligned with other civic groups, such as the City Club and the Citizens' Governmental Research Bureau, in most of the reorganization movements of the past thirty years. Through the Inter-League

Council, the local units closely followed the work of the Metropolitan Study Commission, publicly endorsed a number of its recommendations, and supported its continuance. Since that time they have concentrated their efforts on matters other than metropolitan governmental reorganization.

Milwaukee Development Group

In August, 1959, a new organization known as the Milwaukee Development Group (MDG) was formed for the announced purpose of "stimulating private and public renewal of the City's downtown area." The group consisted of twenty-two top executives from the largest business and industrial firms in the community. Its membership included the presidents or board chairmen of Milwaukee's three largest banks, the heads of the electric, gas, and telephone utilities, the publisher of the two metropolitan dailies, and the presidents of such major corporations as Schlitz Brewing Company, A. O. Smith, Allis Chalmers, and Northwestern Mutual Life Insurance Company.

The MDG was largely an outgrowth of a controversy over downtown redevelopment that threatened to split the ranks of the economic notables. Late in 1958 the Marine National Exchange Bank, one of the major financial institutions in Milwaukee, announced plans to construct a twenty-eight-story office building in the heart of the central business district. Marine officials indicated that the project was contingent upon the granting of an assessment freeze by the common council. The attempt to secure this concession drew the vigorous opposition of Milwaukee's largest bank, the First Wisconsin, controlled by the Uihlein family, owners of Schlitz Brewery and of extensive downtown property. After considerable and at times bitter controversy between the banks, Marine obtained a seven-year assessment freeze (the law allows up to thirty years) and the office building is now a reality. The infighting in their own ranks disturbed business leaders and convinced them of the need for studying and coordinating downtown redevelopment plans. Formation of the small and highly selective MDG followed.

After its inception, the new committee unobtrusively encouraged a number of downtown developments, including the acquisition by the county of the Chicago and Northwestern Railroad property on the lakefront for future parkland use. The group, however, took no stand on metropolitan problems and did not concern itself with governmental reorganization. In late 1964 it disbanded as a separate entity and merged with the Greater Milwaukee Committee, "where it will continue to carry out its programs within the framework of that organization."

Milwaukee Association of Commerce

The Milwaukee Association of Commerce has a membership of 3,400 business firms located throughout the metropolitan area. Policy is made by a board of directors elected annually by the membership. The Association's activities, carried on through standing committees with staff assistance, are those traditionally performed by chambers of commerce: attracting new industry, promoting better air line service, lobbying for or against bills affecting business, and the like. Along with the GMC, the organization has played a part in pushing various capital improvement programs for the area, such as a stadium and an expressway system. It supported both the creation and extension of the Study Commission and, together with the City Club, took the lead in forming the Civic Federation for Community Cooperation. However, its status as the civic spokesman for the business community has been overshadowed by that of the more prestigious GMC.

League of Suburban Municipalities

Established in the late 1920's to combat the "imperialism" of the central city, the League of Suburban Municipalities has long been looked upon as the "voice of the suburban governments" and "the spokesman of the iron ring." With a membership consisting of all Milwaukee County suburbs and several from the adjacent counties, the League describes itself as "a voluntary organization of suburban officials that operates in exchanging and interchanging ideas." However, as one veteran participant bluntly described it, "The League was organized to fight the central city and it will continue to do this. Some persons ask the stupid question as to why Milwaukee isn't a member. We wouldn't have it; we are fighting the City."* Not all members feel so strongly and some privately resent the negative image that the organization has created and the great influence that it wields in setting suburban policy in external affairs. The League employs a lobbyist at the state capitol and has time and again proved its effectiveness in defeating legislation that it considers detrimental to suburbia. Few constructive measures have emanated from its tightly knit oligarchy.

The League started out as an association of suburban municipal attorneys, and it was not until 1952 that the chief executives of the local units were asked to participate. Several mayors now take part in its deliberations but the group still remains, as one of its officers recently called it, "a municipal attorneys' organization." The League operates under an unwritten rule that it will take no stand on an issue if a small minority of the member units dissent. It has been able to maintain a strong degree of cohesiveness over the years—with opposition to the central city supplying the common rallying ground—even though its positions have occasionally been contrary to the self-interest of some of its members.

Political Parties

Neither the Democratic nor the Republican party in Milwaukee County has demonstrated much interest in metropolitan reform or

* From an interview. Hereafter, direct quotations from personal interviews will be given without footnote reference.

in local governmental issues. The insignificant amount of patronage at the local level and the banning of partisan labels in elections for municipal and most county offices have not been conducive to partisan involvement in local governmental affairs. Party activity has occasionally been manifest in behalf of candidates for city and county offices but has been totally lacking in any of the reorganization movements.

The Democratic party in 1959 did adopt a county platform which contained, among other items, a local reorganization plank calling for "the ultimate organization of a multi-purpose metropolitan government with a popularly elected council chosen on a population basis." Recognizing the principle of municipal autonomy, the platform specified that "such a government should have sole charge of those functions deemed metropolitan in nature, while assuring existing municipal governments their territorial integrity and responsibility for all services deemed municipal in character."[4] The insertion of this provision, however, was largely the result of efforts by several University of Wisconsin–Milwaukee faculty members who served on the platform committee; it did not represent any widespread feeling of interest on the part of the membership. Nothing has been heard of the plank or, for that matter, of the platform itself since its adoption.

Labor

Labor, through the Milwaukee County Labor Council AFL-CIO, has cooperated actively with business and other groups in the private welfare activities of the community. It has also supported many civic projects including the expressway system, school building programs, and the construction of a war memorial and a county stadium. Aside from these physical improvements, labor's concern with local government has been confined largely to matters of direct relevancy to the economic interests of its members, such as urban renewal, building code changes, and public employee benefits. Some time ago, for example, when the Milwaukee mayor attempted to include the Building Inspector's office in a new department of city development, labor, especially the Building Trades Union, blocked the change through vigorous lobbying.

Labor has access to various members of the Milwaukee common council and the county board because of the electoral support that it can bestow or withhold; but it has shown little inclination or desire to exert its influence in matters of metropolitan reorganization. On occasions the joint council or individual unions have given some expression of interest in area-wide governmental affairs, but this concern has been mostly of a token nature. Many segments of organized labor looked upon the creation of the Metropolitan Study Commission with skepticism, and efforts to extend the agency's life received virtually no union support.

Other Organizations

Various other associations in the Milwaukee area occasionally take part in metropolitan affairs. Such groups normally become involved only in civic matters that touch upon their professional or occupational fields. Thus the local chapter of the American Institute of Planners actively promoted the creation of a regional planning commission and the medical society supported attempts to secure a county-wide health department. Two of the more active of these peripherally concerned groups have been the Milwaukee Board of Realtors and the Metropolitan Builders Association of Greater Milwaukee. The first contributed $1,000 to help finance the work of the Study Commission and supported the establishment of a regional planning body. The latter has sponsored several "growth conferences" to discuss governmental problems related to urban expansion and has been active in efforts to secure more centralized zoning administration and a uniform building code for the metropolitan area. Again, however, these are matters that relate closely to the groups' primary interests as organizations of realtors and builders. None of these associations has demonstrated any sustained or large-scale involvement in area-wide or general civic affairs.

The Press

Although newspapers are not in the same category as voluntary associations or interest groups, they are sources of pressure and influence in community affairs, and in this sense participants and activists. As communicators of information and advice to the citizen body, they are in a strategic position to win support for or arouse opposition against public issues. Their effectiveness in any given case depends, of course, on many factors: the prestige of the paper, the nature of the issue, the interest or concern of the readers in the matter at hand, and the conditioning circumstances. To assume that even the most highly respected newspaper can mobilize public action for any civic cause at any time would be patently erroneous.

Milwaukee County has two metropolitan dailies, the evening *Journal* and the morning *Sentinel*, and sixteen weeklies, seven of them in the central city and nine in suburbia.* The employee-owned *Journal*, with a daily circulation of approximately 365,000, is the area's leading paper. The *Sentinel*, long a member of the Hearst chain, was purchased by the *Journal* in July, 1962, and continued in operation with a separate editorial and reporting staff. Its circulation is slightly under 165,000.

Two of the weeklies within the city of Milwaukee are foreign language papers with a combined circulation of about 40,000. The others include the AFL-CIO labor press (circulation 105,000), the Milwaukee *Star*, a Negro weekly (circulation around 15,000), and several small neighborhood papers whose pages are devoted largely to advertising and local social events. In the suburbs, the

* This number does not include religious, fraternal, shopping, and trade type publications.

combined circulation of the nine weeklies is somewhat over 30,000. Important suburban weeklies include the *Reminder Enterprise Press* in Cudahy, the *Star* in West Allis, and the *Voice Journal* in South Milwaukee, each with a circulation well under 10,000.

Both major dailies give broad coverage to metropolitan civic affairs and both have consistently supported governmental reorganization efforts. Neither, however, has called for political amalgamation in recent decades, although suburban officials and the suburban press have occasionally accused the *Journal* of "pro-consolidation" leanings. In contrast to the dailies, the City weeklies give little space to area-wide affairs, while those in the suburbs devote their news columns primarily to matters of purely local interest. However, when the occasion seems to demand it or the Muse prompts them, the suburban papers gallantly rise to the defense of their communities against the "sinister designs" of the central city.

ORGANIZATIONAL LINKAGES

Examination of the list of community groups that have been active or interested in civic affairs reveals no organization with ability, motivation, or resources to mount a major offensive for metropolitan innovation. To the overwhelming majority of voluntary associations, area-wide governmental reorganization is at most a matter of incidental concern. Their primary objectives—whether economic, professional, or social—consume most of their available resources and leave little margin for significant participation in a metropolitan crusade. The burden of providing sustained citizen leadership in this field has fallen to a small number of organizations whose purposes are almost wholly of a civic nature: Greater Milwaukee Committee, City Club, Citizens' Governmental Research Bureau, and League of Women Voters. One special interest group, the Association of Commerce, should also be added to this list, although its many other concerns and its business orientation circumscribe the part that it can play in metropolitan reform.

Because of the limited base of support of individual organizations, the potential for meaningful action in metropolitan affairs must rest (as it does in most matters) in a coalition of many groups, but meaningful alliances among diverse organizations with specialized aims are difficult to form. The degree of interaction and communication among most groups on the local scene is not great. Each goes about its own business, concentrating attention on its own needs and problems. Motivation to join forces usually arises among such organizations only in matters that directly affect their primary interests. Socially recognized and non-controversial projects, such as a community chest drive, can also produce temporary working alliances, but issues of metropolitan reorganization seldom generate anything beyond mild interest or minimum involvement on the part of most groups. Any coalition formed under the latter circumstances is likely to be spurious and wholly ineffective.

It might be assumed that the more extensive the overlapping of membership among organizations, the greater is the possibility of forming significant and closely knit alliances. Although data are available for few communities, it is well known that considerable overlapping exists among local voluntary associations. There are, for example, close linkages among three of the top civic and business organizations in Milwaukee County. Greater Milwaukee Committee members comprise twenty-four of the forty-three members of the board of trustees of the Citizens' Governmental Research Bureau, and hold sixteen of the twenty-seven seats on the board of the Association of Commerce. Close business associates of GMC members make up most of the remaining membership on the Citizens' Governmental Research Bureau board, and the firms of virtually all GMC members belong to the Association of Commerce.

One might conclude from this close interrelationship that the civic activity of these three groups is well coordinated, but this is not always the case. The GMC and the Association of Commerce, for example, occasionally vie for the leadership of various civic projects. A recent instance of this competition occurred in the formation of the Civic Federation for Community Cooperation, an alliance spearheaded by the Association of Commerce and the City Club. The GMC had intended to establish a similar coalition under its own leadership and within its own organizational framework, but the action of the other two groups upset this plan.

This example, not an isolated one, points up the difficulty of coordinating civic activity even among relatively homogeneous groups with similar objectives. Each has its own projects and its own professional staff, and each tends to guard jealously its corporate personality and leadership role. An Association of Commerce committee hinted at this situation when it stated: "It should be pointed out that the need for reasonable cooperation between all individuals and groups working for civic improvement is desirable. It may well be that informal meetings of the professional executive or administrative heads of various civic groups would be helpful to analyze areas where cooperation between the various groups is desirable."[5] This diffusion of civic energies was also noted in several interviews with community leaders. As one respondent remarked, "Milwaukee's leadership is being directed into too many channels and too many groups"; or as another bluntly put it, "This community is too damned overorganized."

METROPOLITAN ORGANIZATION

The present state of knowledge about metropolitan influentials and area-wide decision-making is meager. Recent studies of power in various cities and towns have endeavored to identify the important policy formulators and describe the group relationships through which they wield their influence.[6] The majority of these efforts have been confined to small or medium-sized communities; and while such studies have made important empirical and theoretical contributions, their relevancy to decision-making in a politically fragmented metropolis is extremely limited. The Syracuse study by Martin and Munger was one of the first attempts to examine the capabilities of the local power structure to induce common action among several autonomous governments.[7] The study touched upon the nub of the problem; for the metropolitan activist is dealing not with a single political entity but with a cluster of local units, each with its own bureaucracy and presumably with its own network of power relationships. This fact adds a new dimension or variable to the investigation of power in a metropolitan context.

It would be misleading to assume the existence of an elaborate pattern of organizational participation in metropolitan affairs. The voluntary associations in the community are not arranged in any cohesive structural pattern, nor do they form a closely linked network that is capable of ordering the sprawling metropolis into an integrated unit. Even those groups that have evidenced most concern in this sector have other civic interests of a non-metropolitan nature which occupy their attention and consume their resources. It is extremely doubtful, moreover, that the true power complex of a community is operative in metropolitan reorganization movements. Portions of it are obviously called into play, but the issue has not been one to seriously activate the major constellations of influence.

The sophisticated student of the metropolitan scene may be able to delineate with reasonable accuracy the pattern of exercised power in any given situation. What he cannot do, except conjecturally, is ascertain the potential influence of the actors who might be brought into the play. Rarely does any group, whatever the nature of its program and objectives, attempt to utilize the sum total of its power potential in a specific project or cause. Such action would involve too great a risk to the organization and might denude it of its resources and weaken its capacity for future accomplishments. Voluntary associations, like individuals, weigh the costs and benefits of proposed courses of action. The more important a desired end is to the participants, the more heavily will they commit their stockpile of influence. The membership of the Greater Milwaukee Committee, for example, represents a strong reservoir of power. If this aggregation of influence were fully utilized to further a civic objective of a controversial nature, members of the group would necessarily incur corresponding obligations—to politicians, and to other associations, perhaps even to labor—that might diminish their power potential in matters relating to their private and business interests.

Philanthropic deeds aside, the notables can afford to commit only limited resources to a civic cause of no direct benefit to their economic enterprises. The tradition of community activity by the elite, their sense of noblesse oblige, the role expectations held by their peers and the general public, plus newspaper prodding, necessitate some involvement. Beyond this indistinct and fluid point, however, the exertion of additional power potential by the economic dominants rests upon the importance of the project to their personal and business interests. A metropolitan reorganization movement could conceivably induce a high output of power from an organization such as the GMC if its members became convinced that they had a vital personal stake in the outcome. Up to the present time, such conviction has been lacking among the important voluntary associations in Milwaukee, as in most urban areas.

3
Reorganization Efforts in Milwaukee: An Historical Perspective

Milwaukee's long history of central city-suburban hostility has been at least as intense and bitter as the usual pattern of core-ring animosity. For more than half a century, central city partisans have been condemning the suburbs as parasites while spokesmen of the ring have been extolling the virtues of small government and the sanctity of home rule. During this period of time, movements aimed at redesigning the metropolitan polity or effecting changes in its organizational structure have been commonplace. The circumstances surrounding these efforts have changed over the years, but the arguments of supporters and opponents alike have resisted the influence of time—they have merely worn thin from constant usage. The record of reform in this milieu has been one of perennial stalemate tempered by occasional gusts of accomplishment.

Appointment of the Metropolitan Study Commission in the summer of 1957 offered a fresh and seemingly promising approach to the governmental ills of the area. At the behest of Milwaukee civic leaders, the Governor and legislature intervened to establish a prestigious agency with power to investigate the local situation and make recommendations for possible state action. From the beginning, however, the Commission's actions and prospects were conditioned by the environment within which it functioned. Tradition, the record of the past, the circumstances that gave rise to its creation, the lack of public interest and understanding, the absence of crisis, and the endemic resistance of the system to change militated against the prospects of significant accomplishment.

Prior reorganization activities in Milwaukee County had ranged from annexation and political integration efforts to lesser remedies of functional consolidation and voluntary cooperation among local units. Each of these left its mark, sometimes deeply etched but mostly surface scratches, on the governmental structure. Through annexation the central city managed to extend its jurisdictional sway despite the failure of unification movements. Through consolidation of certain functions or services, the most visible and urgent area-wide problems were resolved. Through intergovernmental cooperation and ad hoc arrangements, lesser difficulties and inconveniences in the day-to-day functioning of the public machinery were corrected or mitigated.

The results of these efforts were not always adequate but the piecemeal accommodations to public needs and demands proved sufficient to keep the system functional. Time and again local officials demonstrated that they could act—on a minimal basis to be sure—when crisis threatened or when it was in their immediate interest to do so. What they consistently failed to demonstrate was a capacity or willingness to alter the present structure in anticipation of tomorrow's problems. Little public pressure existed for them to do so, since the average citizen exhibited faint interest in the logic or rhetoric of metropolitan reorganization. When his water supply was short or inadequate sewage disposal threatened his health, he was quick to make his voice heard in the political arena. But he, like the local official, was concerned with the present, not the future. So long as his immediate service problems were resolved, discussions about the rationality and effectiveness of the metropolitan political system had little meaning for him. Only the big city papers, the good government groups, and an occasional political maverick kept pressing the issue. This lack of general citizen interest in reorganization has proved a major handicap to those advocating major surgery on the political structure of the metropolis. But as one veteran of the local civic battles observed, "You can't expect citizens to be interested in the abstract."

The more significant of the earlier reform efforts in the Milwaukee area are reviewed here as a prelude to the latest reorganization movement. These are treated under three headings: political integration, functional consolidation, and intergovernmental cooperation. The first includes both merger of local units and annexation by the central city; the second relates to the creation of special districts and the transfer of functions to the county government; the third consists of voluntary arrangements, either contractual or informal, among local units.

POLITICAL INTEGRATION

Consolidation movements were started in Milwaukee County as early as 1870, when a bill was introduced in the state legislature to merge the City and county governments.[1] The Milwaukee common council opposed the measure, apparently feeling that it would increase the City's fiscal burdens. A short time later, legislation was passed calling for a referendum on the question of detaching the seven outlying towns (unincorporated) from Milwaukee County and annexing them to Waukesha County. The referendum failed of passage when City residents rejected the proposal although the majority vote in the towns favored detachment. Had the vote been favorable, Milwaukee County would have been reduced to fifteen square miles.

The push for consolidation was resumed in the early years of the present century, when citizen groups organized to battle municipal corruption. One by-product of the movement was an awakened interest in improving the efficiency and economy of local administration by joining together the City and county governments. World War I brought a temporary end to these activities, but the period following the cessation of hostilities witnessed renewed efforts to bring about political amalgamation of the City and suburbs. From 1919 to 1935 no less than fifteen bills were introduced in the legislature seeking constitutional changes to provide for or permit city-county consolidation. Most of the impetus came from central city officials and civic groups with strong support from the Socialist Party.

The depression years of the 1930's increased the tempo of merger efforts and led to the first comprehensive metropolitan study in Milwaukee County. Under prodding from civic groups, the Milwaukee common council in 1934 authorized its president to appoint a committee of fifteen citizens to study "the manner and method of procedure regarding the consolidation of city and county governments." Shortly thereafter a similar committee of fifteen was appointed by the chairman of the county board. The two groups then agreed to combine forces and organize as a joint committee. Extensive research was done for the committee by WPA employees under the direction of Mrs. Paula Lynagh, a staff member of the Citizens' Governmental Research Bureau. The findings were presented in a series of twenty-seven reports, each dealing with a specific service of local government including public health, parks, sewerage, fire protection, tax collection, and elections administration. All the reports stressed the need for more efficient management practices and emphasized the economies that would result from reorganization.[2]

While the study was under way, the joint committee requested the county board to hold an advisory referendum on consolidating municipal services and governments in Milwaukee County. The committee took this calculated risk in an effort to focus public attention on metropolitan reorganization. It reasoned that a favorable or even close vote would strengthen its hand considerably when the time came for implementing recommendations. Acceding to the request, the county board authorized a referendum on the question: "Do you favor effecting, by such county board or legislative action or amendment to the state constitution as may be necessary, consolidation of municipal services and governments in Milwaukee County?"

Before the vote, the joint committee began releasing its reports in rapid order with claims that large savings would result from consolidation. Suburban officials countered that there was no proof for such assertions. Identifying the committee with the central city, they bitterly attacked its motives and warned their constituents that merger would bring higher taxes and destroy popular control over local government. The results of the referendum were gratifying to the reformers, since the question carried by an overall county vote of 104,195 to 40,832. However, all suburban units with the exception of West Allis and Cudahy voted overwhelmingly against the proposal. The two defections caused considerable consternation among suburban officials and handicapped their lobbyists at the state capitol, who were working against pending consolidation bills.

Before the election, suburban officials and newspapers had contended that the question as presented on the ballot was vague and confusing. After the vote, this argument was renewed with greater intensity to explain away the Cudahy and West Allis breaches in the suburban wall. The contention was not without merit, since spokesmen for the joint committee had been ambiguous during the campaign as to the exact meaning of the proposition. When they addressed gatherings in the central city, they gave the impression that the committee was calling for a vote on complete political integration; when they spoke to suburban audiences, they talked in terms of functional consolidation.

Admittedly embarrassed by the pro-consolidationist vote, whatever the reason for it, West Allis officials decided to resubmit the issue to their residents. This time they made certain that the cards were stacked in their favor. Two questions were placed on the ballot:

1. Do you believe that the City of West Allis should by consolidation (annexation) join the City of Milwaukee and thus become a Ward or part of a Ward of the City of Milwaukee?

2. Do you believe that any municipal services now performed by the City of West Allis should by law be placed under the control of a County Board of twenty members, sixteen of whom would also be Aldermen of the City of Milwaukee?*

While the metropolitan press and pro-consolidationists complained bitterly of the "loaded" wording of the referendum questions, West Allis officials and the local paper conducted a vigorous campaign for a "no" vote. Directing their broadsides against the "giant octopus that is trying to devour everything within its reach," they called upon the sturdy citizenry of West Allis to reaffirm their municipal integrity. The response delighted the officialdom of suburbia. In the earlier county-wide referendum, 63 per cent of West Allis voters had supported consolidation. In the new election held just five months later the count was reversed, with only 27 per cent of the voters responding favorably to each of the two questions. The vote, together with the defeat of two consolidation bills in the 1935 legislative session, ended the last serious merger threat in the Milwaukee metropolis.[3]

Running parallel with the consolidation movements were efforts of the central city to extend its boundaries through annexation.

* This question referred to a proposed merger of the offices of alderman and county supervisor in Milwaukee city, a proposal that had received endorsement along with the consolidation question in the advisory referendum.

Although handicapped by the early incorporations, which blocked expansion at several key points around its periphery, Milwaukee city has been able to use its annexation powers with considerable effectiveness, growing from less than ten square miles at the time of its founding to its present size of almost 100 square miles.

The first major efforts at annexation began during the 1920's after the decennial census revealed a density of 17,000 people per square mile, an increase of 3,000 since the turn of the century. Convinced of the need to alleviate "urban congestion" by obtaining more *lebensraum,* the City created a department of annexation for the avowed purpose of promoting expansionist efforts.[4] The department circulated annexation petitions, formed booster clubs in fringe areas, advertised the advantages of joining the mother city, and otherwise aided residents and developers who were interested in bringing outlying land under City jurisdiction. These efforts increased the size of the central city from twenty-six to forty-four square miles in less than a decade. On the negative side they drew the suburbs closer together and strengthened their anti-City bias.

The second concerted expansionist drive came after World War II, when Milwaukee again embarked on an aggressive annexation-at-any-cost policy that doubled its territorial size by 1957. As a result of taking any parcel of land that could be obtained, no matter how small or where located, the City's boundaries came to present an irregularly shaped and jagged pattern of unusual design, with fingers or pockets protruding far out into the suburban fringe. Two factors were influential in prompting this policy: the necessity of securing additional land for industrial expansion in order to maintain a sound tax base; and high suburban zoning requirements that restricted the expansion of residential development for the small wage earner. Frank Zeidler, who served as mayor from 1948 to 1960 during the period of the City's greatest annexation activity, was particularly sensitive to this latter factor. He felt that unless Milwaukee expanded, low income workers would be barred from living in the outlying areas and crowded further into an already congested central city.[5]

The post bellum annexation efforts rekindled the "stop Milwaukee" movement and stirred up further suburban animosity. They also gave impetus to a wave of incorporations, not only in Milwaukee County, but also in adjacent Waukesha and Ozaukee counties. A law (the "Oak Creek" law), since repealed, lowering incorporation requirements was steered through the legislature by a suburban attorney. Its passage enabled two large and undeveloped townships in Milwaukee County to become "paper" cities and thereby immunize themselves against annexation. Thus by the end of the 1950's annexation had become a matter of past history, and the central city was hemmed in on all sides by an unbroken ring of incorporated municipalities.[6]

GRADUALISM

While the various attempts to steer political integration in Milwaukee County foundered on the sharp rocks of reality, other less radical approaches to the metropolitan "problem" showed a better record. Functional consolidation or unification of individual services was achieved in the fields of sewage disposal, parks, air pollution, and expressways but failed in public health, libraries, and transfer of the public museum from City to county control. The circumstances surrounding these successes and failures in partial consolidation provide some insight into the conditions favorable to metropolitan reorganization.

Sewage Disposal

Shortly after the turn of the century, pollution of the waters in the Milwaukee area from raw sewage discharge became a growing menace to public health. The City at that time discharged sewage untreated into the three rivers which flow through its confines on their way to Lake Michigan. Seven suburban communities also operated disposal facilities in the upstream area, dumping their raw sewage or inadequately treated effluent into the rivers. In 1913 the legislature, at the request of City officials and civic leaders, created the Milwaukee sewerage commission. The function of the new agency was to construct a city-wide network of sewers and a disposal plant and then turn the system over to a City department for operation. As work on the project progressed, it became apparent that Milwaukee had undertaken more than its financial resources would bear. In fact, the City was rapidly reaching the statutory ceiling on its bonded indebtedness and could complete the sewer system only by neglecting other badly needed capital improvements.

At this point, a movement for an enlarged sewer district to include the outlying communities began to take shape. The initiative for creating such a district came from the suburbs. Like the central city, most fringe area communities were faced with large expenditures for sewerage facilities that in many cases exceeded their debt limits. They were also concerned with the pollution of Lake Michigan in the vicinity of Milwaukee's water intake tank since a number of them purchased their water supply from the City. The time was thus opportune for action.

A bill to establish a metropolitan sewer district covering most of the then urbanized sections of Milwaukee County was introduced in the 1921 legislature by a suburban assemblyman. Backed by suburban officials and agreed to by the City because of its financial problems, the bill had little difficulty in passing the legislature. It provided that the city of Milwaukee would be reimbursed over a period of years for the suburban area's proportionate share of the costs of constructing the sewage disposal plant and the intercepting system. The City sewerage commission was to remain in existence and its staff and work force become the operating agent for the metropolitan district. This dual arrangement has prevailed up to the present day despite numerous attempts to consolidate the two agencies or transfer the sewerage function to the county government.

Parks

Unification of the park systems in Milwaukee County was a by-product of the merger attempts of the 1930's. Four factors gave impetus to the movement: existence of an active and capable county park commission; authority to effect the change under existing laws; a severe economic depression; and the decision of the joint consolidation committee to push for piecemeal or partial integration.

When the county park commission was created in 1907, the city of Milwaukee was the only municipality with a park system. Subsequently, several suburban communities also established parks within their corporate limits. From time to time suggestions were made by civic groups, particularly the City Club and the Citizens' Governmental Research Bureau, to consolidate these various systems under the county government. Little progress was made in this direction until the lean years of the early 1930's. The first move came when South Milwaukee and Cudahy officials, hard pressed for operating funds, offered to turn over their parklands to the county. In accepting the offers, the county government opened the way for total park consolidation.

The joint committee and various civic groups saw in the park issue an opportunity to win a major battle for functional consolidation. By capitalizing on the depression-generated interest in governmental economy and the suburban example of shifting their park costs to the county, these groups were able to muster considerable local support for the transfer of Milwaukee city parks to county jurisdiction. Some City officials resisted the move but after more than a year of constant effort and negotiation, including a favorable referendum by City voters, agreement on the divestiture was reached in December, 1936. Suburban leaders belatedly awakened to the tax implications of the transfer, but their protests came after the county board had committed itself to accept the City parks. Since statutory changes were not involved, the suburban leaders had no opportunity to kill the transfer at the state legislative level, where they usually enjoy a preferential position in matters of City-suburban controversy.

Air Pollution

Another functional consolidation of significance occurred ten years after the park transfer, when the county government assumed responsibility for air pollution control. Milwaukee, like other heavily industrialized areas, early became plagued by smoke problems. In 1914, the City adopted a smoke regulation code and established an enforcement division in the building department. Chronic complaints about soot and fly-ash increased with the passage of time in both the central city and the adjacent industrial suburbs, but it was not until 1945 that a serious movement for area-wide control was launched. Widespread publicity given by the press to successful accomplishments elsewhere in smoke abatement helped to stir up interest among Milwaukee-area residents and brought pressure on local officials for action.

Milwaukee city in 1945 began to draft a more comprehensive smoke inspection and abatement ordinance. At the same time a number of outlying communities, particularly those with large industrial concentrations, indicated an interest in air pollution control on a county-wide basis. Although several of them had smoke ordinances, none had either the staff or specialized equipment to enforce such laws. With prompting from civic groups and pushing by several supervisors from industrial suburbia, the county board agreed to consider the possibility of assuming the smoke control function by way of contract with the municipalities. When this approach became mired in a bog of prolonged discussion, supporters of area-wide control turned to the legislature.

Early in 1947 a state senator from the manufacturing-dominated suburb of West Milwaukee introduced a bill authorizing the county board to enact an area-wide smoke control ordinance. Spokesmen for a number of suburbs favored the measure. Many women's organizations in the area rallied to its support, and a petition signed by 4,500 housewives was presented to the legislature by the League of Women Voters. City of Milwaukee officials at first withheld their blessings but finally gave in when they saw the degree of favorable public sentiment. The outlying unincorporated towns generally opposed the bill on the grounds that they had no smoke problems and should not be asked "to pay for smoke control in Milwaukee."

The initial impetus for area-wide smoke control by civic groups had been sympathetically received by officials of the highly industrialized suburbs. Many of them had found themselves on the horns of a dilemma. On the one side they were receiving numerous complaints about soot and dirt from their householders; on the other side they were hesitant to antagonize local industries by enacting and enforcing a strict smoke abatement law. The proposal for area-wide control offered them a convenient way out. Milwaukee officials were in a somewhat similar position. They also were worried that a strong air pollution code enforced only in the central city might drive industry into the more lenient suburbs. County control seemed to offer a ready solution although it violated the City's long-standing policy of opposition to piecemeal consolidation.

The movement received a fortuitous boost when 7,000 tons of coal on the premises of a local industry ignited and burned for nearly a month. No better publicity could have been given to the consolidationist cause as smoke, gas fumes, and soot from the fire were carried over city and suburb alike by the variable winds. When some time later a mysterious blight that was killing grass in one of the outlying communities was traced to smoke from the electric utility plant, victory for the pro-consolidation forces was assured. The enabling act easily passed the legislature, and soon thereafter the county board enacted the necessary ordinances and assumed responsibility for the purity of the county's air.

Expressways

The latest instance of functional consolidation or transfer occurred in 1954, when responsibility for the construction and maintenance of an expressway system was vested in the county government. Expressways had been a topic of discussion for more than ten years when Milwaukee city inaugurated its program in 1952. Only a short time after actual construction started, the City found itself faced with two serious difficulties, one financial, the other a matter of suburban relations. In the first instance, the City had anticipated at least $17 million in state aids for the biennium but was informed that it would receive only $5 million. In the second, the expressway system proposed by consultants had to cross or touch several bordering communities. The need for suburban participation in the program was dramatized almost immediately after the start of construction in a dispute over location with West Milwaukee.

As the difficulties of financing and coordinating the system became more apparent, support for a county-wide expressway program grew. Sponsors of the original movement, such as the Greater Milwaukee Committee and the metropolitan newspapers, became alarmed that the program would break down if it remained solely a City undertaking. Suburban officials were also becoming cognizant of the stake that their communities had in the program. Not only were their own traffic problems and road-building needs increasing in magnitude but they could also visualize the day in the not too distant future when City-built expressways would be dumping thousands of cars on their doorsteps. Suburban residents, moreover, who commuted daily to the central city or to the industrial satellites were becoming increasingly expressway-conscious and their demands could not long be overlooked.

Early in 1953 a committee of twenty-one officials—seven each from the City, county board, and suburban communities—was organized to study the expressway problem. The group quickly agreed on the desirability of a county-wide program and decided to push for necessary legislation to accomplish this objective. With the committee's blessing a bill was introduced in the legislature providing for the creation of an expressway commission to be appointed by the governor. Fiscal control and final-approval authority over expressway plans were to be placed in the county board. Details of the bill provoked considerable controversy among public officials. Several from the central city, including the mayor, maintained that power to appoint the board should remain in local hands, while some county board members insisted that the program should be administered by a county department rather than a commission. Agreement to accept the original bill was finally reached when it became apparent that no expressway legislation would be enacted without such consensus. Once the issue was resolved locally, the bill quickly passed both houses without a dissenting vote. The Greater Milwaukee Committee with the assistance of the Citizens' Governmental Research Bureau played an important role in the negotiations by acting as arbitrator among the local units.

Gradualist Failures

In addition to those cases in which functional consolidation was achieved, there were several abortive attempts to bring about unification of other services. Efforts which attracted most attention involved creation of a county health department, establishment of a county-wide library system, and transfer of the Milwaukee public museum to the county.[7]

After several earlier efforts to secure a unified health department, the issue was again raised in 1949 when a privately financed survey of welfare and health services in Milwaukee County pointed to the desirability of a single agency. Soon thereafter an ordinance was introduced in the county board to create a county-wide health department. After considerable discussion and delay the board decided to appoint a high-level citizens' committee to make another study of the question. Suburban part-time health officers vigorously opposed even the making of such a study. They contended that excellent health services were being rendered by the individual municipalities and that the proposed survey would simply be a waste of time and money. Arrayed against them were the metropolitan press, League of Women Voters, Community Welfare Council, City Club, Medical Society, Citizens' Governmental Research Bureau, and a number of other civic groups. Milwaukee city officials were known to be hostile to the creation of a county system, although they took no public position on the proposed study.

The Citizens' Committee of five members, headed by the dean of the Marquette University Medical School, shied away from a single health department, convinced that this objective could not be attained. Instead the committee recommended that a county bureau of health services be established to supplement and coordinate the services of the part-time health departments. However, even this relatively mild proposal failed to win the concurrence of a physician member of the committee who was employed as a part-time health officer in one of the north shore communities. He and others who served in similar positions looked upon the creation of such a bureau as an opening wedge to county control of health needs. Their strong opposition at a public hearing before county officials led to the tabling of the proposal. Since that time little further agitation for health department reorganization has been evident, although the question is intermittently raised in the county board.

The movements for integrating the library systems in the area and transferring the Milwaukee public museum to county jurisdiction were closely linked together. Since 1915 Milwaukee city has furnished books and library services to suburban municipalities on a contract basis. The public museum has no similar relations with the outlying communities although suburban residents benefit from many of its facilities. Interest in county-wide administration of these services arose shortly after World War II, when both the library and the museum were vying for capital improvement funds —the former to build a $2.5 million addition to its central library; the latter to construct a new $6 million building.

Sentiment that suburbanites should bear a share of these costs began to be expressed by City aldermen. The time seemed opportune for action since several suburbs were also faced with the need to build new library structures to serve their expanding populations. In 1948 the common council and county board appointed a committee to study the feasibility of turning the two facilities over to the county. Opposition to library consolidation arose immediately, particularly among local library boards and officials in the six suburbs that operated their own systems. Because of the intensity of this opposition, the committee dropped the library question and turned its attention to the presumably less controversial museum transfer.

Five months after its appointment the study committee recommended the transfer of the museum to the county government and urged the common council and county board to seek the necessary enabling legislation. City officials, including Mayor Zeidler, favored the transfer. The common council unanimously adopted a resolution agreeing to convey the museum as soon as the county board secured the necessary enabling legislation. Little difficulty was anticipated in this regard until suburban opposition unexpectedly emerged. At legislative committee hearings on the bill, a large contingent of city attorneys and other local officials from suburban units appeared in opposition, contending that the museum was a useless expense and that Milwaukee city was forcing it on the outlying municipalities. Many educators in the same suburbs, however, supported the transfer on the ground that it would benefit their schools. It was apparent that suburban municipal officials were not concerned with the museum transfer as such but with the precedent it might establish for turning over other services to the county. Their opposition to the bill was sufficient to kill it.[8]

METROPOLITAN "TEAMWORK"

Localists and advocates of the status quo have consistently preached, if seldom practiced, the doctrine of voluntary cooperation among local units as the answer to the metropolitan problem. In recent years this approach has met with increasing, although reluctant, acceptance among reformers and students in the urban field, many of whom have become disheartened by the repeated rejections of metropolitan reorganization plans. Some of them reason that if major changes in the governmental structure of metropolitan areas are unlikely in the near future, the urban specialist should turn his attention and capacity for political inventiveness to the task of devising more effective ways of operating within the existing framework. This tendency has not been alien to the Milwaukee scene and, as we shall see later, it became an important factor in the Study Commission's thinking.

Wisconsin statutes give wide opportunity for the practice of intergovernmental cooperation. A 1927 law authorizes counties of 250,000 or more to render municipal services to cities and villages under contractual arrangements.[9] A later law gives local units broad authorization to contract with each other for services or for the joint exercise of any of their powers.[10] Little use of these enabling provisions has been made in Milwaukee County. The first has been almost totally neglected during the thirty-five years that it has been on the statute books even though the county government has shown its capacity for effective administration of urban type functions and its willingness to assume them. Suburban officials obviously look with no greater favor on an enlargement of county government influence in local affairs than they do on central city expansion.

Even the statute for intermunicipal cooperation has seen little use. In a comprehensive survey of intergovernmental cooperation made in 1960, the Citizens' Governmental Research Bureau found 124 cases of such cooperation in the county.[11] The majority of these were minor in nature and involved such arrangements as sharing the services of a vocational teacher by several school districts and the establishment of uniform traffic control regulations along a street that divides two municipalities. Almost half the cases consisted of informal agreements among administrative officials on such matters as mutual police assistance, lending of equipment, and exchange of purchasing information. The only significant instances of local intergovernmental cooperation were represented by the library and water contracts between the City and outlying municipalities, the typical mutual aid fire agreements among suburban departments, and most recently, the creation of a water utility by three north shore suburbs. The existence of so few contracts in a highly urbanized and governmentally fragmented area gives some indication of the extent to which each local unit has gone in developing its own services.

PHYSIOLOGY OF REORGANIZATION

Governmental reorganization in Milwaukee County has followed no single course. Most of the commonly advanced nostrums for metropolitan ills have been considered or tried at one time or another. Some have been successful, most have failed. Although the record is by no means clear or the data complete, a review of past reform movements in the Milwaukee area gives rise to certain conclusions and assumptions about metropolitan reorganization efforts.[12] None of them is particularly novel or unusual, but taken together they form an historical backdrop for the reorganization drama that featured the Study Commission—a backdrop that strongly suggested the outcome of the plot before the play began.

Two observations or conclusions will be disposed of quickly, one pertaining to political unification, the other to voluntary cooperation among local governments. Attention will then be concentrated on functional consolidation since the relatively extensive use of this approach in metropolitan Milwaukee and the varied experiences under it permit some generalization.

1. Few influentials, other than central city officials, have taken political amalgamation seriously in recent Milwaukee history. As early as 1927 a legislative interim committee was calling the consolidation of local governments unrealistic. Similarly, few members of the joint committee of the 1930's felt that complete integration was attainable even though they temporized on this issue in an attempt to resolve conflicting pressures. Their apparent indecisiveness is easy to understand since they were faced on the one hand with the demands of central city officials who told them to "go for total consolidation if you want us to play ball with you," and on the other hand, with suburban officials who were fighting for the retention of the status quo. The die was cast by the reformers in favor of partial consolidation when they openly rejected political integration in the mid-1930's and concentrated their efforts on park unification. Since that time the dilemma posed by the central city-suburban dichotomy has continued to plague reorganization efforts. Reformers have found themselves occupying a middle position between two adamant extremes that have seldom been willing to compromise. In this milieu, moderate proposals have often been subjected to attack from both sides although for diametrically opposite reasons.[13]

2. Local officials in Milwaukee County have shown little disposition to take the initiative in promoting intergovernmental agreements. The central city has been reluctant to contract with its neighbors since it feels that the latter have nothing to offer in return and that such cooperative arrangements serve only to subsidize and strengthen the suburban position. Officials in the ring communities, for their part, have refrained from exhibiting any more dependency on their traditional "enemy," whether by way of contract or otherwise, than absolutely necessary. Even among them-

selves, they have been willing to act jointly only when a compelling community need arises which they cannot meet individually without undue strain on local facilities and resources. The possible efficiency or economy which might result from joint performance of services is seldom sufficient to generate more than minor action.

3. As the historical record shows, seven major attempts at functional consolidation have been made in Milwaukee County since World War I. These involved sewage disposal, parks, air pollution, expressways, public health, libraries, and public museum. The first four were successfully accomplished; the last three failed. When these attempts are examined for factors determining success or failure, five significant variables emerge: (1) economic pressure, (2) service need, (3) citizen interest, (4) attitude of public officials, and (5) civic group activity. Although historical data do not permit precise evaluation of these variables, it is possible to (a) make rough approximations of the extent to which they were present in each case; (b) suggest certain interrelationships among them; and (c) offer several assumptions as to their relative influence on the outcome of reorganization efforts.

Table 6 represents an attempt to measure the intensity of the five variables as they appeared in each of the functional consolidation cases. A simple scale of three positions was employed for this purpose: (+) indicating presence of the variable in high degree; (o) present but not intense; and (−) not in evidence. Thus if strong economic pressure existed for consolidating a service because of needed capital outlays or other fiscal reasons, as in the case of expressway construction, a (+) rating was assigned to the economic variable. If economic factors were relevant but of lesser intensity, as in air pollution control, a score of (o) was given, and if they were negligible, as in the movement to secure a unified health department, the ranking was (−). The variable, attitude of public officials, was scored plus if officials generally favored the change, zero if they were divided in their position, and negative if a majority were against.

As Table 6 indicates, all five variables rank high in two of the

TABLE 6

Selected Variables in Metropolitan Reorganization as Related to
Seven Functional Consolidation Attempts in Milwaukee County

	Variables				
Subject of Consolidation	Economic Pressure	Service Need	Citizen Interest	Attitude of Public Officials	Civic Organization Activity
Sewers*	+	+	+	+	+
Parks*	+	o	+	o	+
Air pollution*	o	+	+	+	+
Expressways*	+	+	+	+	+
Public health	—	o	—	—	+
Museum	+	—	—	o	+
Library	+	o	—	o	+

(+) Present in high degree, or "for" in case of public officials.
(o) Present but not intense, or "divided" in case of public officials.
(—) Not present, or "against" in case of public officials.

* Consolidation achieved.

consolidation efforts (sewers and expressways), four in the case
of air pollution, and three in parks. No attempt that failed showed
more than two (+) variables. All the successful movements except park consolidation were marked by serious or urgent need,
demonstrated citizen interest, and had the strong support of public
officials. Conversely, the unsuccessful attempts were characterized
by lack of low perception of need, absence of citizen interest, and
opposition from a substantial segment of local officialdom. The
case of parks is the only significant deviation from the pattern of
successes. No major need for transfer of City parks to the county
existed at the time and the attitude of City officials was lukewarm
to such action. Civic organization activity was unusually high,
aided by the determined reform efforts of the joint committee, and
citizen interest was manifested in the favorable advisory referendum on park unification. Most important to the outcome, however,
was the economic depression of the period. In such a context, the
stock argument of reducing operational costs by consolidating gov-

ernmental agencies had more appeal than it would have in normal or affluent times.

Turning again to Table 6, the attitude of public officials can be viewed as the dependent variable and the remaining four factors as independent variables. Local public officials occupy the positions of formal authority in the governmental structure. No change that is dependent on official legitimation can, of course, be consummated without formal action on their part. More significantly, the Milwaukee experience—paralleled by that in other metropolitan areas—demonstrates that where legislative authorization for the change is necessary at the state or even county board level, such authorization will seldom be forthcoming over the opposition of local officialdom.

The crucial question, therefore, is what factors influence the position of local officials in reorganization issues. We have suggested four such factors or independent variables that appear applicable to the Milwaukee experience: economic pressure, service needs that cannot be met by unilateral local action, citizen interest, and civic organizational activity. The relative weight of each cannot be readily ascertained, nor is it certain that they exhaust the list of influential variables. Yet the evidence is persuasive that, taken together, they exert an important bearing on the outcome of metropolitan reform movements. The general hypothesis can be couched in this manner: the higher the intensity of these independent variables in a given case, the greater the possibility of mobilizing official support for reorganization.

Several further hypotheses can also be drawn from the findings.

(1) *The same factors that induce citizen interest in reorganization proposals also affect the attitude of public officials.* Economic pressures, a serious service need, and a high degree of civic organization activity tend to generate interest in both the citizen body and among local officials. Each variable, however, does not necessarily affect both groups in the same way nor is each of equal importance. In most of the cases discussed, citizens were less impressed than public officials by the economic factor. Milwaukee city officials, for example, supported museum and library consolidation less because of service needs than because of the necessity for large capital outlays.

(2) *The influence of civic organizations on the attitude of public officials toward reform will be minimal if other variables show a low degree of intensity.* The effort of civic groups to secure a unified health department of Milwaukee County is an instance in point. Despite considerable activity on their part, they were able to win virtually no backing from public officials. Both economic pressure and general citizen concern were lacking, and whatever need existed could not be readily demonstrated. When, however, a major service breakdown occurs or is imminent, as in the case of air pollution control, civic groups (including newspapers) play a useful function in articulating the problem for the citizenry and indicating ways of solving it. Once, also, public officials become convinced of a serious need or sense that it may be good politics to support a particular modification of the existing system, the role of civic groups is further enhanced. In such instances political leaders seek first the legitimation that prestigious organizations can bring to a cause, and secondly, the expertise and staff assistance which they can make available. Because of their community position and qualifications, Milwaukee civic groups have on more than one occasion been able to act as arbitrators or brokers between the governmental parties in negotiations leading to settlement. Thus in the park transfer and expressway consolidation cases, it was the participation and prodding of influential members of the major civic organizations that helped bring the negotiations to a successful conclusion.

(3) *Public interest in metropolitan reform is stimulated by specific service needs or crises, not by the logic or rhetoric of reorganization.* Where interest, other than that of civic groups and newspapers, has been evident, it has occurred in specific problem situations and has been focused on arrangements designed to handle the immediate issue. Even the "all-out" reorganization campaign of the early 1930's proved fruitless until reformers con-

centrated their efforts on the park issue and its economic implications. When no pressing deficiency existed that could be popularly dramatized, as in the case of public health, the possibility of arousing public concern has been slight. Such abstract generalizations as "disease recognizes no municipal boundaries," or "overlapping of governmental units is inefficient," seldom strike a responsive chord in the public arena.

(4) *Both central city and suburban officials must agree on area-wide reform measures before action is possible.* The initiation for change may originate with civic groups or with public officials themselves but unless the effective wielders of local governmental power in both jurisdictions can be co-opted into the cause, the chances of success are meager. In the instances of sewage disposal, air pollution, and expressways, agreements to support consolidation were ultimately reached between influential officials in both City and suburbs. In the unsuccessful museum and library efforts, central city officials strongly favored transfer of the functions to the county government but suburban officials effectively vetoed the moves. The one possible exception to this rule occurred in the park transfer, where Milwaukee city officials reluctantly agreed to the change while those in the suburbs took no position until it was too late.

AN OVERVIEW

The attitude of both central city and suburban officials toward metropolitan reform has changed little over time. The City's historic position has been one of opposition to piecemeal transfer of functions, although circumstances have forced it to yield on occasion. It has steadfastly adhered to the "single government" dogma, insisting that partial consolidation of services will hinder rather than expedite the achievement of this objective, strengthen the suburbs at the expense of the central city, and diminish the latter's prestige by divesting it of significant functions. This policy of "total surrender" has consistently impeded efforts to negotiate meaningful settlement of metropolitan issues. Fiscal pressures on the central city, however, have tended to soften this attitude in recent years.

Suburban officials, on the other hand, have long nurtured a tradition of localism that at times has been carried to the point of municipal chauvinism. Like their City counterparts, they also have opposed functional consolidation although they have always talked of their willingness to have "true" metropolitan services unified. However, a "true" metropolitan function, as they define it, is one over which they have no control and which they badly need, such as expressways or sewers, but cannot supply for themselves. Water supply was also such a function for the north shore suburbs until they decided to build their own plant. Now they argue that it is a local matter. The president of the League of Suburban Municipalities summed up the suburban attitude on partial consolidation when he said, "We are not prepared to yield any functions. We in the suburbs have always felt that the consolidation of functions of government would merely be putting the foot in the door toward the end of the suburbs. We believe we are sufficient unto ourselves."

County government officials have generally remained neutral in the city-suburban struggle. Although they have been receptive to the idea of functional consolidation under county jurisdiction, they have been reluctant to take the initiative or assume leadership in such movements. For the most part, they have followed a "wait and see" policy. Only when municipal officials in both central city and suburbs express interest in consolidating a particular function will the county board consider action.

This then is the background from which the Study Commission emerged and the political setting in which it functioned. That its actions were circumscribed and influenced by the tradition of governmental reorganization in the Milwaukee metropolis cannot be gainsaid. That it tried to rise above the limitations of the past is, as we shall see, equally true.

4
Creation of the Commission

As the decade of the 1950's advanced, metropolitan reform in the Milwaukee area again became an issue on the civic agenda. The City's annexation program, the resulting rash of suburban incorporations, and the problem of water supply focused renewed attention on the governmental structure of the metropolis. Water in particular served to trigger off the new interest. Hot, dry summers in 1953 and 1955 graphically demonstrated the incapacity of Milwaukee city's water system to serve the growing needs of the area, while the resulting restrictions on water use greatly irritated suburban customers as they surveyed their parched lawns and burnt-out shrubbery. Other problems such as sewage disposal in the outlying areas and the unsatisfactory state of City-suburban governmental relations contributed to the new interest. When local public officials failed to reach consensus on these issues through a self-constituted intergovernmental forum, civic leaders turned to the state for assistance. Their efforts resulted in the appointment of a citizens' committee on water and, shortly thereafter, a study commission of broader scope.

73

FORERUNNERS OF THE STUDY COMMISSION

The failure of local governments to act in concert in meeting area-wide problems was the target of much criticism by civic leaders and the metropolitan dailies in the early 1950's. Local officials generally discounted the significance of this agitation, convinced that metropolitan reform was a matter of little concern to most individuals. The more perceptive of them, however, feared that continued publicity of this kind could be politically damaging, particularly if linked to specific problems that were potential sources of citizen irritation. Suburban officials, moreover, saw themselves confronted with the task of meeting the growing water needs of their communities, while Mayor Zeidler and other Milwaukee policy makers looked upon the tightening ring of satellite municipalities as a threat to the City's well-being and future development. Both sides began to feel that a "proper" study would aid their cause. The important question was who would make it.

City officials saw little use in attempting to arbitrate locally what they considered the most important and vital issues of metropolitan concern—tax distribution and room for central city expansion. They were convinced that suburban negotiators would come to the local bargaining table with outstretched but empty hands. As Zeidler later expressed it, "The suburbs were willing to sit down with the City of Milwaukee to see how the city could furnish them with water, sewers, and incinerators, but they would not talk about unequal tax burdens, slum clearance, or problems that the city had."[1] Instead of a local study, Zeidler and members of the common council urged that a state-wide investigation be conducted by the Wisconsin legislature. They took this position even though they regarded the state's lawmaking body as politically unsympathetic to Milwaukee. In Zeidler's words, they were willing to take their chances with the legislature, "where we have been stung before, but we feel we can't find a solution to our problem elsewhere."[2] It was their hope that such a study would stimulate support for remedial legislation from other Wisconsin municipalities with fringe area problems, such as Madison, Green Bay, Racine, and Kenosha.

Suburban officials countered the move for a state-wide study by proposing the establishment of a conference of local governments to inquire into the area's problems. The purported rationale for this approach had been advanced by West Allis officials on an earlier occasion when the question of a state-wide study had arisen.

The suburbs feel that a great stride forward could be made in Milwaukee County by the establishment of a municipalities council, composed of representatives from the towns, cities, and villages to explore and define areas of cooperation, to decide upon projects of community-wide concern and to devise and set up methods of cooperation and cost sharing. We believe that the Milwaukee community has never had fair opportunity to solve its own problems and that Milwaukee should agree to participate in such an effort.[3]

In addition to the City and suburban proposals, a third approach—a metropolitan survey by a citizen commission—was suggested by civic groups. Irritated at the perpetual bickering between the central city and suburban governments, leaders of the Greater Milwaukee Committee and other civic organizations had become convinced that the most promising path to the solution of area-wide problems lay in citizen initiation and action. The prevailing fashion of metropolitan studies by high level citizen commissions helped to channel their thinking in this direction. Briefings by their civic secretaries had kept them abreast of developments in other large urban areas, and the examples of broad-scale studies in Pittsburgh, Atlanta, and elsewhere had greatly impressed them.[4] In their eyes metropolitan Milwaukee seemed a likely candidate for such an experiment.

Committee of 21

While discussion was going on over these various approaches, the county board of supervisors interjected itself into the picture.

In September, 1954, it voted to create a permanent Committee of 21—seven Milwaukee aldermen, seven county supervisors, and seven representatives of suburban municipalities—to consider matters of mutual interest to the local governments. The new instrument for generating metropolitan consensus was patterned after the temporary committee that had successfully engineered transfer of the expressway system from the City to the county government. Impetus for the establishment of the committee came from Bert Busby, a county supervisor from West Allis, who previously had been one of the leaders in the transfer of air pollution control to county jurisdiction. Although a staunch upholder of suburban prerogatives, Busby had proved more receptive to limited area-wide accommodations than most local defenders of the "republic in miniature." In the present controversy, like those over air pollution and expressways, he saw the need to seek out some means of resolving or mitigating the issues before they got out of hand.

The county board's move was acceptable to suburban officials, since it left control over any investigation of the area's problems at the local level where they wanted it. City officials were not happy but since their efforts to secure a state legislative study had met with no success, they reluctantly acquiesced in the proposal. At least they would sit down at the bargaining table with representation equal in number to that of the suburban units; and since the organization was purely a voluntary one, they could withdraw at any time they saw fit. Some of them also reasoned that the likely ineffectiveness of such an ad hoc committee would strengthen the City's case for a legislative inquiry.

The Committee of 21 held its first meeting in December, 1954, and elected Busby chairman. It then proceeded to adopt an innocuous declaration of policy that foreshadowed the future course of deliberations. The statement specified that "the committee is a voluntary organization without legal status or power, created in good faith by the municipal governments of Milwaukee County for the purpose of solving joint and mutual problems," and as such it will "carry out its task with patience and thoroughness and with

The *Milwaukee Journal*

The Way to Civilization

full respect for each government's right to self-determination."[5]

For the next year the group did little but argue over procedures, the kind of study the community needed, and the problems that should be investigated. In an effort to start some activity, a subcommittee on agenda finally recommended a long list of study areas and suggested that the group "first approach those problems which are relatively non-controversial" and turn to the more complex issues only after it had demonstrated its ability to be "an effective instrument for improved intermunicipal cooperation."[6] Logical as this approach may have appeared, a City representative showed its futility when he pointed out that most, if not all, the items on the proposed list were controversial. The seemingly irreconcilable positions of City and suburban officials ruled out the possibility of arriving at agreement even on the subject matter areas to be pursued. The former continued to insist that the committee examine the question of political consolidation while the latter persisted in demanding that the water problem be placed first on the agenda. At one point, a suburban representative bitterly complained, "I have the impression that Milwaukee will not vote for anything short of complete consolidation"; to which a City alderman retorted, "You're not too far off."[7]

The committee went through the motions of appointing subcommittees on various problems but by the end of 1955 chairman Busby was complaining of their inactivity and warning that "if something isn't done very soon, then truthfully there's not much point in meeting any more."[8] Following the chairman's admonition, a subcommittee of three was appointed to examine the feasibility of employing consultants to make a survey of the problems. Bids were solicited, and in June 1956 the subcommittee recommended that such a study be undertaken and that the county board be asked to appropriate the necessary funds. But again action was forestalled. Suburban and county board representatives generally favored the study while those from the City stated that they could not vote on it without approval of the common council. Such approval, however, was not forthcoming. The council temporized and came to no decision, a number of aldermen demanding that the scope of the survey be spelled out in detail before action was taken. "Let's be very honest," one of them remarked, "the study will undoubtedly include the water problem and we don't want it."[9] Matters remained at this stage until early in 1957, when it became apparent that a metropolitan commission would be created by the legislature. The committee then adjourned indefinitely.

Leadership Reaction to Committee

Civic leaders from the outset had doubted the wisdom of establishing a study group composed solely of local public officials.

They considered it improbable in the light of past experience that a politically motivated body of City consolidationists and suburban autonomists could make objective studies or reach decisions on solutions. Their reading of history was, of course, correct. If the objective was, as some civic leaders had in mind at the time, a restructuring of the metropolitan governmental system, a council of central city and suburban officials was not the instrumentality to accomplish it. To expect consensus on significant change to emerge from such a group is to disregard political reality. Without a strong third force, such as the state, that possesses the means to induce agreement, by either rewards or sanctions, neither central city nor suburban officials are likely to negotiate away any of their major prerogatives.

Unwilling to let the case for metropolitan reorganization rest solely on the findings of local officials, the major civic organizations in Milwaukee sought to have the investigation of the area's problems transferred to a committee of private citizens. At the very first meeting of the new Committee of 21, the Greater Milwaukee Committee, City Club, Civic Alliance, and League of Women Voters jointly petitioned the officials to sponsor a bill in the state legislature setting up a citizens' study commission. Such a body, the petitioners asserted, could carry out the necessary inquiries and make recommendations to the Committee of 21 and the local governmental units for their consideration. The suggestion elicited little support from the committee, but the request from such an array of prominent groups could not be wholly disregarded. The answer came easily to the political pros like Busby: offer an alternative that would give the petitioners their study committee and yet place control over it in the hands of the local officials.

In line with this strategy, the Committee of 21, over the protest of City representatives, voted to seek legal status for itself. A bill to make the committee permanent and give it authority to appoint an eleven-member subcommittee of citizens to study metropolitan problems was introduced in the legislature by Busby's brother, a state senator from suburban West Milwaukee. Supported by the League of Suburban Municipalities but opposed by spokesmen for the City government, the measure was defeated in the Senate by a narrow margin. City officials feared that if the committee were given statutory recognition all hope for a legislative study of the area's problems would be destroyed and "existing inequities permanently saddled on the people of Milwaukee."[10] Civic groups, although not enthusiastic, supported the bill on the theory that a slice of the loaf is better than nothing at all.

"Dineen" Committee

In May, 1956, while the Committee of 21 was still marking time, one of its members met with representatives of the Greater Milwaukee Committee to ascertain whether the group would be willing to finance the retention of an outside research firm. GMC officials, however, saw little purpose in allocating any of the organization's resources to a committee that had demonstrated capacity for little else than inactivity. They indicated that they would consider financing a study only if they were permitted to exercise control over its direction and extent, a proposal which they correctly anticipated would be unacceptable.

When the stalemate in the committee continued to prevail, the GMC leadership decided to take matters into its own hands. A delegation of four of the organization's most prominent members went directly to Governor Walter J. Kohler, a Republican, and urged him to appoint a citizens' study commission for the Milwaukee area. The group stressed the need for examining the water problem, a subject that GMC leaders regarded with particular interest at the time. Many of them lived in north shore communities which were dependent on the City for their water supply. The acuteness of the problem had been brought forcibly to their attention by personal experiences with chronic water deficiencies. The anomaly of such shortages in a modern urban area situated on the shores of a great fresh water lake struck them as ridiculous and convinced them of the need for some changes in the existing governmental system. When a solution did not appear to be forthcoming through local political channels, they turned to other means. This incident represents one of the few instances in recent Milwaukee history where the community's top influentials personally involved themselves and actively intervened in a metropolitan governmental issue. Their participation in such matters has commonly been limited to general endorsement of reform proposals or objectives, while the task of promotion and follow-up has been left entirely in the hands of the civic secretaries or lesser influentials in the organizational structure. The immediacy of the water problem and the personal experiences of the notables with it obviously proved a better stimulator to action than the more abstract question of metropolitan reform.

Governor Kohler, a former industrialist, acceded to the request of the delegation and appointed a seven-member committee of prominent business and professional leaders headed by Robert E. Dineen, vice-president of the Northwestern Mutual Life Insurance Company and an active GMC member. Dineen and his six colleagues were chosen from a list of fourteen names submitted by the GMC.[11] In naming the group, the governor pointed to the ineffectiveness of the Committee of 21 and its abortive efforts to reach a solution on the water problem. He stated that the circumstances which led him to act called for coordinated planning "to the end that the supply of water and disposal of storm water for the rapidly expanding population of Milwaukee shall be not only adequate but also economical." He instructed the committee to produce "some general conclusions and constructive suggestions" on these and "the many other municipal service problems which affect all people in the Milwaukee metropolitan area." Since Kohler's term as governor terminated at the end of the year, the committee was given only three months to perform its work. Those who sponsored the committee's appointment hoped that it could make enough progress in this short period of time to demonstrate what could be achieved by the establishment of a long-range citizens' commission under state auspices.

Appointment of the committee came as a complete surprise to most public officials. Those in the suburbs did not object since the group was charged with studying the two functions in which they were primarily interested, water supply and sewer expansion. City officials, on the other hand, made no effort to conceal their disappointment, charging that the governor had been "importuned by suburban leaders to follow a course of action which conceivably could lead to the suburbs taking over Milwaukee's water system without sharing total community costs."[12] Zeidler said he was concerned that "this stacked committee would obviously produce a report to give away the waterworks without giving the city tax equality," and that he "did not want the foes of the city to cite any report of such a committee as 'authority' for proposing legislation to take away the waterworks."[13]

The lack of rapport between the City administration and the business community is again evident here. The mayor and many Milwaukee officials were thoroughly convinced that the economic notables, most of whom lived in the suburbs, would throw their weight on the side of the little governments in any central city-ring dispute. As a matter of fact, most suburban officials were equally, although less overtly, suspicious of the elite and regarded them as "metropolitan government prone." They supported the creation of the Dineen committee and later the Metropolitan Study Commission only because they felt that the primary objective of the civic influentials at the time was solution of the water problem. Since they had no control over this function, one which was of real concern to them, they stood only to gain from such a study.

City officials, resigned to an unfavorable report, sought to broaden the inquiry of the Dineen committee by urging it to investigate the whole complex of area problems. Several civic organizations also asked the group to consider water as only one of

The *Milwaukee Journal*

Don't Snipe at the Piano Player,
He's Doing the Best He Can

several problems that must be solved "in one package." They saw little hope of settling the water issue without some *quid pro quo* arrangement that would offer the City certain advantages in return. The committee, pointing to the limitations of time, stated that it intended to devote its attenion primarily to the water problem. Most of its members felt that a strong case could be made for action in this field but that little would be accomplished if the group "spread itself thin" by becoming involved with other issues.

The committee held most of its meetings and conducted its deliberations in private. In December, 1956, it issued a 126-page report containing four major recommendations:

(1) Milwaukee's water department should be expanded to meet area needs, and a metropolitan water district considered only if the City remained unwilling to become the area supplier and to discard its fifty-year-old policy of using water as a lever to force suburbs into union with it;

(2) the territorial jurisdiction of the metropolitan sewerage commission should be expanded;

(3) a state-wide commission should be created by the legislature to study and re-evaluate the distribution formula under which state income and utility tax shares are returned to the municipalities;

(4) the legislature should create a permanent citizens' study commission of Milwaukee area residents to examine and make recommendations on governmental problems in the metropolitan community.[14]

Committee members had been impressed during their short tenure with the complexity of the issues and converted to the idea that the water problem could not be solved in isolation from other major issues. This awareness led them to call not only for a citizens' committee to examine service and other area-wide problems but also—in acknowledgment of the City's position—for a state study of the tax distribution formula.

Suburban governments indicated that the report "was in the right direction," particularly that portion dealing with the water question. City officials again criticized the committee for limiting "its efforts to the narrow scope of the water problem without considering the entire metropolitan problem." At the same time they were surprised that the report did not call for outright transfer of Milwaukee's waterworks to a metropolitan agency or the county government—a proposal they thought certain. Mayor Zeidler, who had viewed the establishment of the committee as an attempt "to steal the city's waterworks," commented that the report was "not as sharp as it started out to be," and that "it gave a more favorable aspect to the City's position than had the views voiced originally by some members of the committee."[15] The inclusion of the recommendation for a study of the distribution formula also came as a surprise to City officials. Zeidler called it a "sound conclusion," and a leading alderman commented that "if the tax laws were rectified, that would end debate over water and sewers."[16] The latter point was important, since it constituted the minimal basis on which the City would bargain. As a policy statement prepared by a committee of Milwaukee officials in the wake of the Dineen report emphasized, the City had no intention of changing its traditional water policy "unless a state-wide study of urban organization and tax structure first establishes an equitable distribution of tax resources within the metropolitan area."[17] But tax distribution was not a negotiable item in the eyes of suburban governments.

CREATION OF THE METROPOLITAN STUDY COMMISSION

In making its recommendations for a local study commission of private citizens, the Dineen report emphasized that the hostility between the central city and suburbs militated against the feasibility of any metropolitan study conducted by local public officials. It pointed to the Committee of 21 as an example, noting that it had proved incapable of providing even the facts, much less solutions, because of the veto power held by individual communities. Armed with this recommendation, the Greater Milwaukee Committee again went into action. Working through three Republican senators from the Milwaukee area—two from the suburbs and one from the central city—the Committee secured the introduction of a bill in the state legislature to implement the Dineen proposal for a study commission. Officials from suburban municipalities indicated their support of the bill, convinced that water was the major issue and that they would receive sympathetic treatment from a commission fathered by suburban representatives at the behest of leading suburban residents. Conversely, Mayor Zeidler and members of the common council announced their opposition to the bill and continued to insist that any metropolitan study should be conducted on a state-wide basis by a legislative committee. Civic groups and the two metropolitan dailies enthusiastically endorsed the measure.

With the support of prominent Republican legislators and with active lobbying on the part of the GMC, the bill passed the senate by a vote of thirty to two and the assembly by a margin of sixty-three to twenty-two. It was signed by Governor Kohler's successor, Vernon Thomson, also a Republican, in July, 1957. The bill provided for a commission of fifteen members to be appointed by the governor. Twelve of this number were to be residents of the county not holding an elective or appointive public office and the remaining three public officials: one from the city of Milwaukee and one each from a city and a village in the suburbs. The life of the commission was to extend to July 1, 1961, a period of four years. An initial appropriation of $30,000 was made to finance its activities. The statute directed the group to:

(1) investigate the adequacy, cost, and efficiency of the principal services provided by the various governmental units of Milwaukee County;

(2) examine the extent to which cooperative agreements or procedures had been established among these units;

(3) determine which services could be rendered most adequately on a local and which on a county-wide basis; and

(4) submit written reports to the Governor and legislature with findings, conclusions, and recommendations.[18]

With passage of the bill, the way was opened for the first comprehensive study of governmental problems in the Milwaukee area since the survey by the joint City-county consolidation committee of the early 1930's. Established to stimulate governmental adaptation to area-wide problems through investigation and recommendation, the Metropolitan Study Commission came to occupy the center of the stage in the mid-century movement for urban reform in metropolitan Milwaukee. Around it revolved the other dramatis personae: civic leaders, economic elites, public officials, news-papers, community organizations, and the general public.

THE ATTITUDINAL ENVIRONMENT

Before turning to an examination of the MSC and its work, some further observations about the setting in which it functioned are necessary. We have already described the political and organizational background of the Milwaukee community. In doing so we touched upon the factors and attitudes which historically have conditioned and influenced governmental reform efforts. That

The *Milwaukee Journal*

Gentlemen of the Jury

these forces continued to operate during the course of the Commission's tenure is a likely assumption. It would obviously be well, however, to have a more specific and precise picture of the general attitude toward metropolitan reform that existed at the time of the MSC's creation. Sources such as newspaper accounts and public statements by political and civic leaders are helpful but far too restricted and meager for purposes of reconstructing this climate. Another source, the leadership and citizen interviews which were undertaken as part of the present investigation, is more enlightening in this regard. Although not conducted until well after the MSC study was under way (during the fall of 1959), these interviews provide the best available data for assessing the attitudinal environment in which basic metropolitan problems and possible governmental changes were considered in the late 1950's.

Problems

An individual's role in society and his immediate interests strongly influence his perception of community problems. This obvious but frequently overlooked fact in metropolitan reform was graphically illustrated when a sample of eighty community influentials in both public and private positions was asked about the public problems and issues facing the Milwaukee area.* Typical of the responses was that of a public official who cited the need for additional revenue as the most important problem; a businessman who saw it as taxes; a welfare agency head who viewed it as social disorganization; a Negro leader who pointed to discrimination in housing and employment opportunities; a developer who complained of lack of uniformity in building codes; a socialite who mentioned poor cultural facilities; an improvement association official who stressed neighborhood rehabilitation; and a downtown merchant who considered parking the crucial problem.

* The nature of these interviews, the sample characteristics, and other details are described in Appendix B.

Most respondents found it difficult to list the problems in any order of importance; many said that it would be meaningless for them to make the attempt. A better indication of their relative importance as perceived by community leaders can be obtained from the frequency with which they were mentioned by the interviewees. As Table 7 indicates, problems associated with govern-

TABLE 7

Metropolitan Problems Most Frequently Mentioned in Interviews of Influentials, General Public, and Students

Problem	% of Influentials	% of Public	% of Students
Governmental finance (taxes, revenue needs, etc.)	61	35	34
Urban redevelopment	39	9	29
Governmental coordination	28	6	29
Water and sewerage	20	18	18
Traffic and transportation (including parking)	18	12	88
Land use and planning	13	1	4
Social and racial issues	11	1	7
Schools	2	10	2
	(N = 80)	(N = 307)	(N = 495)

mental financing—taxes, revenue needs, distribution of state aids and shared taxes—were listed by more respondents than any other issue. (By the time of the interviews the water problem was well on the way toward solution.) All but four of the twenty-four public officials interviewed mentioned the growing revenue needs of local government and the rising property tax rates. Many of them, particularly those in the central city, complained about the inequities in the method of distributing state aids and shared taxes. Business and industrial leaders, while generally recognizing the need for increased local expenditures in order to maintain a high level of public services, took issue with the personal property tax on business and pointed to the need for revision of the tax structure. The issue of tax reform has been predominant in Wisconsin politics in recent years and this fact no doubt contributed to the high degree of interest in the problem.

Next to the question of taxes the need for urban redevelopment was mentioned most often. Here again this result reflected the current interest in Milwaukee city's renewal program by the political and economic leaders. Blight and deterioration are no worse in Milwaukee than in other large metropolitan centers—if anything, conditions are better—but the local program had long been stymied by legal barriers and public indifference. Removal of the major legal obstacle by a recent constitutional amendment had opened the way for action and focused attention on the problem.

Less than one-third of the respondents mentioned items directly related to governmental reorganization. Labor leaders and businessmen active in civic organizations most frequently referred to such matters as governmental proliferation and lack of significant intermunicipal coordination. Only a minority of public officials, on the other hand, included such items in their list of major problems. Almost all of those who did so were from the central city.

Outside of the three categories of finance, redevelopment, and reorganization, no other problem was mentioned by more than 20 per cent of the respondents. Most of the social problems listed were cited by those in the welfare and educational fields. They centered largely around the Negro and included such issues as open occupancy, inadequate housing, and job discrimination. Few businessmen or public officials referred to these issues, although several indicated that the continued growth of the Negro population in Milwaukee city would generate difficulties. Only three of the eighty respondents mentioned schools as a problem, a reflection of the general satisfaction that Milwaukeeans have with their educational facilities.*

Few of those interviewed saw any significant changes in the kinds or seriousness of metropolitan problems in recent years. Running throughout their comments was the underlying theme that the situation in Milwaukee is "tolerable" and that the area is better off than most places. Only a small minority expressed any sense of urgency about changing the existing machinery to meet the community's problems. As one respondent observed, "Conditions around here have not become bad enough for anyone to get excited about metropolitan reorganization." Another noted that "if anything, Milwaukee's metropolitan problems are mild and call for small solutions." Public officials, both elective and administrative, did not feel that they were faced with any insurmountable service problems or widespread public dissatisfaction. Nor did businessmen as a group see any of the problems, except possibly taxation, as a threat to their economic interests—and the tax structure is a matter for state-wide reformation. Labor respondents similarly expressed no strong feelings that metropolitan problems were impinging on their interests.

Governmental Pattern

When respondents were asked directly how they felt about the local governmental pattern in Milwaukee County, their answers varied, depending largely on their position and place of residence. Milwaukee city officials were highly critical of the existing pattern. They considered it costly and wasteful, unfair to central city residents, and a major impediment to the proper development of the

* The interviews were conducted before the current civil rights movement with its repercussions in northern cities. More recently, the Milwaukee city school system has come under criticism from civil rights groups for its alleged failure to cope with de facto segregation.

area. Conforming to the historical stand of the central city, they viewed complete consolidation as the only solution, although they did not anticipate such action occurring in the foreseeable future. A few central city officials, however, evidenced some receptivity to functional consolidation. One of them noted, for example, that the transfer of certain costly functions to the county government would be one means of alleviating the City's fiscal burden. Another, serving in an administrative capacity, saw this approach as a means of raising the level of certain services. These expressions reflect some weakening in the City's traditional opposition to piecemeal consolidation.

Unlike their central city counterparts, suburban officials saw little wrong with existing arrangements other than the City's control of the water supply system. As one suburban officeholder remarked, "If the governmental pattern stays just as it is, it won't make a great deal of difference." Another stated that "We aren't aware of any problems that cannot be handled under the present system." Although several talked of their willingness to have "true" metropolitan functions consolidated, they actually meant those over which they had no control, such as sewage disposal and water supply. The attitude of suburban officialdom is summed up fairly accurately in the response of one of its leading spokesmen: "While admittedly there are problems, the Milwaukee area is pretty well off insofar as local government is concerned. We have high service levels and services are improving throughout the county. I don't see much need for reform. We need evolution, not revolution."

The attitude of county officials who were interviewed stands midway between those of their city and suburban colleagues. Looking upon the county government as the logical vehicle for handling metropolitan functions, they expressed strong opposition to the creation of any "new level of government." They noted, however, that while the county board has generally been receptive to taking on new activities, few of its members had any real consciousness of the need for metropolitan government and few of them would support any proposed transfer of functions in the face of opposition from local units.

Respondents other than public officials generally expressed the belief that the local governmental pattern was unsatisfactory. They complained mainly of its inefficiency, lack of coordination, and inability to handle service functions of an area-wide nature. Those who resided in the central city tended to look upon political consolidation as the ideal solution although they saw little hope for it and were receptive to other forms of accommodation. On the other hand, only one suburban respondent, a utility company executive, wholeheartedly endorsed such a remedy. He emphasized his view by citing the contrasting experience in extending water services in the Milwaukee area with that of expanding the privately owned utilities: gas, electric, and telephone. The others saw various justifications for suburban governments although they felt that there was need for area-wide handling of more services.

While place of residence seems to be most closely related to attitudes toward governmental patterns, occupation also appears important. Labor representatives, welfare administrators, and civic secretaries, regardless of residence, were more pronounced in their criticism of the existing structure than those in the business and professional sectors. This difference is not surprising since labor has traditionally favored local governmental amalgamation, private welfare agencies have long been engaged in consolidating their organizations on a county-wide or metropolitan basis, and civic secretaries are more conscious of the problems because of the nature of their work.

Attitude of General Public

The above findings involve the attitudes of those who may be referred to as community leaders or influentials. However, since many of the respondents were officials or active members of various groups and mass-based organizations their replies probably reflected the feelings of a far broader segment of the total community. Support for this assumption, at least with respect to problem perceptions, was provided by a random sampling of 307 area residents in the fall of 1960. Although the sample was not wholly representative of the Milwaukee universe, the interviews furnish further evidence of the popular climate at the time the MSC was carrying on its work. When respondents were asked what public issues or problems in the Milwaukee area were of greatest concern to them, the replies paralleled those of the influentials. The greatest number (35 per cent) singled out local governmental finance, particularly the high property tax levy, as the most serious problem. Of the other issues, only traffic-transportation and water-sewerage were cited by more than 10 per cent of the respondents. About one-fourth could mention no public problem that was of particular concern to them. (See Table 7.) Taken as a whole, the replies evidenced no great wave of popular dissatisfaction with the status of public affairs at the time nor any sense of urgency about metropolitan problems.

Similar results were obtained by an exploratory investigation into the attitudes of college students toward metropolitan problems and city-suburban relations. Short questionnaires were administered in December, 1960, to 495 students attending political science classes at the University of Wisconsin–Milwaukee. The respondents, with few exceptions, were in their freshman or sophomore years and taking their first political science course. All but 8 per cent of them resided in the Milwaukee area and over 75 per cent had lived for five or more years in their present municipality.

Among the items of inquiry, the students were asked to list the public problems in the Milwaukee area that were of greatest concern to them. Parking headed the list by a wide margin—a reflection of an extremely troublesome problem then existing around the University. Aside from this complaint, taxes, urban redevelopment, local governmental coordination, and water and sewerage were mentioned most frequently, while social and racial issues elicited little response. (See Table 7.)

In answer to a further question, "Which of the following solutions [those listed in Table 8] would best solve the problems of

TABLE 8

Preference for Solutions to Metropolitan Problems
(Student Interviews)

Solution	% of City Residents	% of Suburban Residents	% of Outside Milwaukee County	% of Total
Consolidate all local units into single government	20	13	15	17
Transfer more functions to county government	11	5	7	9
Transfer more functions to state government	5	4	3	4
Greater cooperation among municipalities	45	55	44	48
Just leave things alone	2	4	1	2
Other	5	5	1	5
Don't know	12	14	29	15
	(N = 274)	(N = 165)	(N = 56)	(N = 495)

the Milwaukee area?" almost one-half the students pointed to greater cooperation among local municipalities. Less than one out of five favored political consolidation, while the transfer of functions to the county or state governments attracted relatively little support. Suburban students showed a greater preference for municipal cooperation and less for political consolidation or stronger county government than those residing in the central city. Differences among them on the other solutions were insignificant. The responses of the students reflect parental attitudes as much as anything else. Students, however, to mention the obvious, are future citizen-voters and in a few cases, future community influentials; therefore, their attitudes have some relevance to the future of metropolitan reform.

Conditioning Factors

Two sets of factors, as seen by community influentials, newspapers, and other observers, summarize the general milieu in which the MSC functioned. The first includes those which serve to impede greater intergovernmental coordination; the second, those which tend to induce or encourage such coordination. As the listings indicate, the scales were weighted heavily on the side of the former:

Impeding factors:

(1) general public apathy—the average citizen sees nothing drastically wrong with the existing system;
(2) lack of "metropolitan consciousness" on the part of the citizenry;
(3) lack of a sense of area-wide responsibility on the part of most officials;
(4) lack of civic and political leadership at the metropolitan level;
(5) the long history of central city-suburban conflict and the suspicions it has engendered;
(6) vested interests of suburban officeholders and employees and the increasing bureaucratization of suburban governments;
(7) the central city's "all or nothing attitude" toward governmental coordination and the verbal attacks against the suburbs by city officials;
(8) the influence of suburban city attorneys over local governing bodies and their encouragement of an anti-central city attitude;
(9) the method of distributing state-shared taxes;
(10) the fetish of local autonomy; and
(11) the increase of racial minorities in the central city.

Integrative factors:

(1) rising costs of government, increasing taxes, and mounting fiscal pressure on local units;

(2) the county government's growing consciousness of its potential metropolitan role;

(3) increasing inconveniences experienced by residents in such matters as traffic and transportation;

(4) belief among some community leaders that the present governmental pattern is restricting growth and causing the community to fall behind other areas;

(5) increasing interdependency of the area in economic matters as specialization and industrial decentralization continue;

(6) willingness of the state to enact legislation authorizing governmental changes in Milwaukee County when sufficient consensus is arrived at locally, as in the case of creating the office of county executive; and

(7) continual pressure of population growth and expansion.

To what extent Commission members were aware of these various factors or how importantly they viewed them when they began their work is difficult to say. Some they were clearly conscious of, such as the hostility between central city and suburban officials and the problem of tax distribution. Others they misjudged, such as the attitude of the citizen body toward change; and still others, such as the influence of suburban city attorneys, they simply discounted or ignored. But whatever the impact of the environmental factors, the goals and perspectives of the MSC underwent radical revision during the agency's tenure. So did the roles and expectations of its members.

5
Personnel and Organization

On October 12, 1957, three months after the bill creating the MSC was signed into law, Governor Thomson announced his selection of the fifteen members who were to assume the role of metropolitan grand jurors. Two days later the appointees met to organize and consider plans for their work. Thus began an enterprise under official state auspices to examine governmental problems in the nation's seventeenth largest metropolitan area, an examination that was to extent over the next four years (until July, 1961).

Like any new and ad hoc agency, the Commission was faced immediately with problems of organization and with the necessity of appointing committees, working out procedures, recruiting staff, reaching consensus on an overall program, setting research goals and priorities, and establishing channels of communication with key groups and individuals. These are elementary tasks, yet the manner in which they are accomplished can be important to the success of an agency's mission. So also the personalities of the members, their drives and ambitions, their community linkages, and the individual biases they bring to the assignment are factors relevant to the outcome. Metropolitan reform is difficult—some would say highly improbable—under the best of conditions. Without a high degree of commitment, talent, influence, and organization on the part of those chosen to stimulate change, the battle is lost before the skirmishing even begins.

AN OVERVIEW

During the Commission's existence, a total of twenty-two individuals served as members. One death and five resignations occurred among the original appointees, and one death and two resignations among their successors. Nine of the original appointees remained on the MSC at the time of its demise. Two vacancies which occurred late in the group's life (by the resignations of Lobb and Foote) remained unfilled. Three different chairmen headed the Commission and three different research directors were employed by it during its life span of almost four years.

The Commission was assisted by a small professional staff and by outside consultants who were retained for a limited number of projects. It also had the help of some sixty-two non-commissioners who served as citizen or adjunct members of various committees. A substantial portion of the work, however, including both research and report writing, was performed by the members themselves. Financed by public funds and an insignificant amount of private contributions, the MSC spent a total of $125,000 during its lifetime.

The Commission worked hard and conscientiously to carry out its assigned task. It held monthly meetings throughout the four-year period, while its standing committees met with greater frequency. Public hearings were conducted on all important recommendations and efforts were made to keep the general public informed through speeches, newspaper releases, and monthly newsletters. Periodic reports reviewing the group's activities, findings, and recommendations were submitted to the governor, legis-

lature, and local units in Milwaukee County. The Commission in its work role placed primary emphasis on study, recommendation, and public enlightenment. Only in two or three instances did it take steps to promote adoption of any of its proposals by the state or local lawmaking bodies; and in each case its efforts were largely perfunctory and of brief duration.

MSC studies covered a variety of problems, from water supply and sewage disposal to land use control and municipal boundary adjustments. Some forty reports were issued, many of them including recommendations addressed to local governments and the state legislature. These reports concentrated primarily on specific issues and ways of solving them on an individual basis. Although the question of a metropolitan governmental agency was seriously considered during the early stages, in the end the Commission lowered its sights to less radical approaches: intergovernmental cooperation and increased use of the county government.

PERSONNEL

In announcing his selections, Governor Thomson remarked that he had received more suggestions for membership on the MSC than on any other commission he had been responsible for appointing. While not revealing the sources of the suggestions, he indicated that the Greater Milwaukee Committee was among the groups that had submitted names to him. Since six of the fifteen appointees were active GMC stalwarts and several others close business associates of members of the organization, its influence in the selection process was no mystery. A GMC official later stated that all but one of the appointees were on the list which his organization had submitted to the governor.

The high amount of organizational interest in the nomination of candidates was prompted by various motives. Some groups, particularly City and suburban officials, were anxious to obtain members who would be sympathetic to their interests; others, including the civic associations, wanted to assure a prominent and capable commission; and still others sought appointments for their members because of the prestige that presumably would be involved. In the end, the wishes of the GMC for an apolitical, business-dominated commission prevailed.

The appointees included nine businessmen, two attorneys (both closely associated with business interests), one labor union official, a housewife, an educator, and a suburban public official.* Nine of the members were suburbanites; the remainder resided in the city of Milwaukee. All but four, however, had their places of business or offices within the boundaries of the central city. The median age of the group was forty-eight, with the youngest thirty-seven and the oldest sixty-two. Seven were in their forties, four in their fifties, and three were sixty or over.

The composition of the membership was highly impressive though not widely representative. It was predominantly a commission of economic notables and middle-range businessmen, well educated, prominent, and respectable. Five of the appointees were members of the exclusive Milwaukee Club, the long-established symbol of upper class status in the community. Fourteen of the group were Republicans, although only a few were active partisans. All had extensive business or professional interests and all were active in various civic organizations and causes, serving on hospital and welfare boards, university councils, and governmental committees. The appointees were, in other words, extremely busy and active individuals, some of them at key points in their careers.

As Commission chairman, Thomson named John Lobb, a well-known businessman who had served on the staff of two former Republican governors. To fulfill the statutory requirement for representation from the three categories of local municipalities, the governor designated George Parkinson as official representative for the city of Milwaukee, Irvin Knoebel for the suburban

* A complete list of MSC members is given in Appendix C.

cities, and Richard Cutler for the villages. Parkinson, then vice-provost of the University of Wisconsin–Milwaukee, was technically eligible to serve in this capacity by virtue of his unpaid position as Milwaukee's deputy director of civil defense; Knoebel was West Allis comptroller; and Cutler, a lawyer, was a member of the planning commission of the village of Fox Point.

REACTIONS TO APPOINTMENTS

Initial reactions to the appointments were, with several significant exceptions, highly favorable. The *Journal* commented that the governor had chosen well, and the *Sentinel* editorialized that the high caliber of the Commission fully vindicated the judgment of those who sponsored its creation.[1] Business leaders called the appointments "superior." Labor was less enthusiastic, the *CIO News* referring to the appointment of Harold Beck, the one union official, as "window dressing."[2] Suburban officials expressed approval, with the president of the League of Suburban Municipalities referring to the selections as "splendid" and expressing confidence that "the appointees will approach the situation with a very thorough study of constructive ideas that will be beneficial to all inhabitants of the area, not just one segment."[3]

The comments of county government officials were generally favorable although several of them were critical that no one closely connected with the county board was selected. The total absence of top representatives from the ranks of local government was, in fact, the chief target of criticism by public officials. Sponsors of the Commission had wanted its membership restricted to private citizens and the requirement for limited political representation had been inserted in the MSC bill only to make it more palatable to the legislature. The gubernatorial appointments neutralized this requirement since two of the commissioners designated as official representatives of the governments—Parkinson and Cutler—had only peripheral connections with their local units while the third—Knoebel—was a career civil servant. None of the three could in any sense of the term be regarded as a major public official or acknowledged spokesman of the governmental units he was to represent. Of the three, Knoebel came closest to fitting this description, yet his personal association and ties with many members of the business community and his reputation as a civic leader made him a "safe" choice.

Unlike most who commented on the appointments, City officials were outspokenly critical. Mayor Zeidler left little doubt that he regarded the group as "suburban dominated" and unrepresentative of the central city. "As to the composition of this commission, and its limited objectives," he stated, "the city of Milwaukee and myself are opposed to it. We desire to be part of a state-wide study of the problems of the metropolitan areas. Milwaukee suburbs and certain powerful economic interests in the City did not want Milwaukee to be able to join with Madison and Green Bay and other central cities, and instead proposed this commission which was limited to Milwaukee County and which by nature would be weighted in favor of the suburbs."[4] The *Sentinel* undertook to answer this criticism editorially: "While it is true that more of its [MSC] members live in the suburbs than in the central city, it is also true that the chief interests of most of them—business, civic, and cultural—lie in the city. None is the type of citizen given to narrow sectional bias. It is unfortunate that Mayor Zeidler and a few other city officials already have sought to undermine public confidence in the commission by expressing doubts as to its impartiality."[5]

Milwaukee aldermen, particularly those with constituencies in the lower socio-economic categories, felt no restraints in attacking the Commission. Typical of their comments were such statements as "The Commission looks like a handpicked campaign committee for Governor Thomson in Milwaukee County"; "The almighty dollar is behind this study committee"; "We need no group of amateurs to tell the council what to do—yet here on this commission we have men completely unskilled in the science of government with the power of subpoena* . . . telling us how to run our government."[6] Even the few aldermen who counseled a wait-and-see attitude before condemning the MSC expressed disappointment that no representative of the common council or other elected city official was included among the selections.

ORGANIZATION

The Commission wasted little time in getting under way. At its initial meeting, it received the governor's personal blessing and heard him express "high hopes" that its work would be of great value not only to the Milwaukee area but to the entire state. This customary ritual out of the way, the group turned to matters of organizational structure and program. Three officers to fill the Commission's complement were selected in quick order: Parkinson, the City representative, as vice-chairman, Mrs. Sam Cook, a suburban village resident, as secretary, and Knoebel, the official suburban city representative, as treasurer. The rationale for the choices was fairly obvious: to give at least the appearance of balanced representation among the officers by political jurisdiction.

In his keynote remarks, Chairman Lobb stated that the MSC should seek as its overall objective the development of recommendations "leading to legislation that would enable the citizens' tax dollar to bring more and better services." Alluding to criticism that the Commission was suburban dominated, he denied that the members were biased against the central city. On the contrary, he said, they were well aware that "the presence of a strong, economically healthy city of Milwaukee is essential to the well being of the suburbs and the entire state of Wisconsin."[7] This profession

---

* The statute creating the MSC provided that the "Commission or any committee thereof may hold public hearings and shall have power to subpoena witnesses and require the production of documents, books, and records relevant to the subject of its inquiry." The power was never exercised by the Commission or its use even contemplated or discussed.

of benevolent concern had a hollow ring to City officials as they viewed Lobb's initial substantive move. Although in one breath he appointed a steering committee to recommend areas of study, in the next he told the commissioners to consider three major problems: water, taxation, and traffic and transportation. In fact, he stated, the first was so pressing that he was immediately appointing Willis Scholl, Allis Chalmers' top executive and a suburbanite, as chairman of a water committee. This precipitous action served to confirm the suspicions of City officials that the Commission's chief *raison d'être* was to help the suburbs gain control of the Milwaukee water works. As one alderman commented the next day during a verbal barrage against the MSC in the common council: "I am deeply disturbed that the only permanent committee established at the commission's first meeting was assigned the water problem."[8]

Standing Committees

Three standing committees grew out of the recommendations of the temporary committee on areas of study: metropolitan functions, land use and zoning, and revenue sources and distribution. There was general agreement that the first group would take over the water problem and that the committee established for this purpose at the earlier meeting would be dissolved. Scholl, who had previously been appointed chairman of the quickly disbanded water committee, was named to head the new functions committee. The City's criticism of the original action on water had struck a sensitive spot in the MSC armor. In an effort to dispel any public impression that the Commission was interested only in the water issue, the members decided to group this function with other metropolitan services under a broadly oriented committee instead of singling out the problem for specialized treatment.

Two of the initial three standing committees, land use and zoning and revenue sources and distribution, remained in existence throughout the four-year period, while that on metropolitan functions was succeeded in August, 1959, by separate committees on garbage and refuse disposal and on police services. In late 1959 a new standing committee of major significance was created to inquire into the question of intergovernmental cooperation. Each committee followed the practice of adding non-commissioners, normally four or five, to its contingent. These citizen-member appointments were made with two purposes in mind: to secure technical assistance and give broader representation to the various interests involved in the particular problem area. However, in most instances, the non-commission members participated only nominally in the work of the committees.

In addition to the substantive committees, the MSC also established a research advisory committee, later reconstituted as the research coordinating committee. Eight non-commission members together with Parkinson were named to the group, with the latter serving as chairman. Here the primary objective was to recruit research talent and experience. But again little use was actually made of the services of the non-commissioners. In the fall of 1959 the committee (which had met only on two other occasions since its inception) was reorganized as the research coordinating committee with a membership of two commissioners and two outside members. This committee, headed by Robert Foote, Red Star Yeast Company executive, was considerably more active than its predecessor, since it came into existence at a time when the MSC was without a research director and in the process of reorganizing under a new chairman. It served mainly as an advisor to the chairman and executive committee on matters of staff recruitment, retention of outside consultants, and research programming.

The original arrangements on structure and organization made no provision for an executive committee. As the need for policy considerations and decisions increased during the early months of the Commission, the chairman, vice-chairman, and heads of the three standing committees began to meet informally. The first sign of institutionalizing the committee came in June, 1958, when the group spelled out its powers in the initial minutes of its proceedings. These included authority to (1) approve order of priority of studies decided on by each committee; (2) act on behalf of the Commission between meetings; and (3) monitor the relationship between commissioners and the technical staff. Although the committee functioned with the knowledge and consent of the other members, its organization and powers were not officially ratified by the full Commission until more than eighteen months after it began to function. When University of Wisconsin–Milwaukee Provost Klotsche assumed the MSC chairmanship in the late summer of 1959 and began to reorganize the Commission, he found that "although the establishment of the executive committee had been taken for granted, a search of the records indicated the need for clarifying its functions."[9] A resolution formalizing its duties and setting its membership at six followed. Previously the number of members had fluctuated from five to nine with no fixed policy as to who should serve on it.

Committee Procedures

The rules of procedure gave the standing committees considerable latitude in defining the scope of their studies and the manner of conducting them. They provided that each committee prepare "a statement in writing setting forth its jurisdiction in sufficient detail to apprise the members of such committee and all other committees and the general public of the area which it will be permitted and directed to cover in its studies." This requirement proved of little value and compliance with it was no more than a gesture. The statements drafted by the standing committees were so broad and general that they communicated little as to the nature or scope of the proposed studies. The metropolitan functions committee, for example, noted only that it would "examine and study such of the services presently being rendered by various units of government in Milwaukee County as it shall determine," and that if it finds that any service "can be provided most equitably, effectively and efficiently, and at the least cost on a metropolitan basis, it shall then study and examine the methods by which the appropriate function of government can be performed and the service provided on a metropolitan basis. . . ."[10]

Vague as these statements were, they constituted the only formalized expressions of the Commission's research objectives. No overall study design was prepared, no long-range plans as to strategies and techniques formulated, and no operational goals defined. The Commission played largely by ear, improvising and working out its plans as it went along. Only during the latter part of its term were attempts made to develop a coherent framework for the studies, but by this time it was too late to change the pattern.

The rules permitted standing committees to issue progress reports at any time without formal Commission approval. Final reports, defined as those which include recommendations, were required to be presented at regular monthly meetings of the entire body. Action on the proposals could then be taken after a waiting period of at least thirty days. This intervening time was provided to give members and interested parties opportunity to submit comments and criticisms. The decision as to whether public hearings would be held before presentation of the reports was left to committee discretion. Seven such hearings were held, the majority of them occurring during the first two years of the Commission's tenure.

Research was conducted by the members themselves, by the staff, and by outside consultants. The procedure in each instance was determined largely by the desires of the individual committee chairmen and the resources available to them at the time. In the cases of the land use and zoning, revenue sources and distribution, and police services committees, much of the actual research and report writing was done personally by the chairmen. The metropolitan functions and the garbage and refuse disposal committees entrusted these functions to the staff, while the intergovernmental relations committee relied almost exclusively on the services of an outside research organization.

The limited funds available to the MSC did not permit the retention of a large staff. During much of its existence, it operated with only a research director and an office force of two or three persons. The staff reached its maximum size in the summer of 1958 when three advanced graduate students were employed to assist in various studies. For almost six months during the latter half of 1959 the Commission functioned with no professional staff members, and thereafter with only the research director.* Lack of staff was felt keenly; it was one of the most common complaints voiced when members were later asked to evaluate the Commission's operations.

Procedures on Recommendations

MSC policy on procedures beyond approval of the recommendations was never clearly resolved. At least three different viewpoints prevailed among the members at one time or another. The first, represented by Lobb, Parkinson, and Cutler, held that the Commission should see that bills were introduced in the legislature to carry out recommendations and even lobby for them if necessary. This view predominated during the initial phase of the work, largely because of Lobb's influence and his control over MSC policy. On several occasions the Commission requested the State Legislative Reference Library to draft bills covering its proposals, but no attempt was made to have the measures introduced. However, in one instance—amendment of the regional planning law—

---

* The first of the three research directors, Charles Ball, who served the Commission during its tenure, resigned in early 1959 when the position was placed under civil service. His successor, Charles Goff, resigned in the summer of 1959 over differences with Commission officers. It was not until the following February that the third director, David Mars, took over the post. (See below, Chapter Six.)

the Commission cosponsored and supported legislation; and in another—extension of the metropolitan sewer district boundaries—it endorsed the measure and had its research director appear at a legislative hearing in its support. This action was taken by the Commission leadership during the early period without any formal expression of policy by the full body.*

The second position, one which became more popular as the work proceeded, regarded research and recommendation as the basic responsibilities of the agency with implementation a matter for other hands—"for some champion," as one member expressed it, "who would come along and follow through on the proposals." Those who took this position, such as Foote and Robert Jensen, chairman of the revenue resources and distribution committee, felt that the Commission had neither the time nor the staff resources to serve in both research and activist roles. Several adherents of this viewpoint were also concerned that the sponsorship of legislation and related activities would involve the MSC in political controversy and thereby compromise its primary mission as a study group. So long as Lobb was chairman the issue remained moot. Shortly after his retirement, however, the question was formally raised in the Commission. In the ensuing discussion, the non-activist view prevailed although Cutler succeeded in keeping the door from being completely closed to the possibility of future action. The statement adopted by the Commission in June, 1959, constituted its first formal expression of policy on post-recommendation activities:

> In order to devote as much as possible of the Commission's time to ascertainment of relevant facts and the consideration of the causes and remedies of the problems under study, the Commission will engage in drafting legislation which would

* Toward the end of the Commission's life, the recommendations of the revenue sources and distribution committee were embodied in the form of a bill and introduced in the legislature at the "request" of two Commission members, acting as individuals and not as MSC representatives. (See below, Chapter Eight.)

implement its recommendations only in those instances where the drafting of precise legislation may be essential to either a better understanding of the problem and solution by the Commission or a more accurate public understanding of the Commission's recommendation.[11]

A third or middle position developed later in the Commission's life. After formal adoption of the non-activist policy, no further attempts were made to draft bills or press for implementation of recommendations. Proposals were simply adopted by the full Commission and the reports sent as a matter of routine to the governmental units and civic organizations of the area. A few members were critical of this policy and no one was altogether pleased with it since the recommendations had generated little activity. At the December, 1959, meeting the issue was again raised when Knoebel, the suburban city representative, inquired about the fate of the various MSC proposals. Stating that while he agreed with the policy of avoiding bill drafting or lobbying, he nevertheless felt compelled to ask, "But if the Commission has no way of assuring that anything will be done with recommendations contained in its study reports on metropolitan problems, can it accomplish anything?"[12] Although it is not clear as to what particular proposals Knoebel was referring to, most members felt that he was alluding to the water recommendations, in which West Allis was interested. The matter was referred to the executive committee, where the old arguments were rehashed. By this time the members had lost much of their initial fervor for metropolitan reform, and few were willing to commit the MSC to an activist role that would make further demands on their time and energies. They were unhappy, of course, that the recommendations were gathering dust, and they had an uncomfortable feeling that perhaps they should be doing something to stimulate activity, but no one had any concrete suggestions as to how this might be accomplished with the limited resources of the Commission.

The executive committee's report reflected the dilemma of the members. Emphasizing the research functions of the MSC, it noted that "it is quite apparent from reading the Statute that the Legislature intended the Metropolitan Study Commission to be primarily a study group instead of an action group. However, it seems clear that the Commission has the responsibility not only to make recommendations but also to outline steps or action necessary to put them into effect." To fulfill this latter duty at least in nominal fashion, the executive committee proposed that "all final committee reports on studies of individual functions and services shall henceforth contain, in addition to findings and recommendations, a further section specifically pointing out the steps that should be taken to accomplish the recommendations."[13] It also added the qualifying clause that "although the Commission should not be a propaganda agency or political action group, it should be available at all times to explain its recommendations to the legislature, to governmental units, and to citizen groups." The policy suggested by the Committee was followed for the remainder of the Commission's life. The "availability" section, however, saw virtually no use.

FINANCING THE COMMISSION

Of the $125,000 expended by the MSC during its lifetime, the state appropriated approximately $90,000 and the remainder came from Milwaukee County municipalities and private sources. Sixty-one per cent of the funds were used for staff salaries, 18 per cent for publication costs (reports, land use atlas, and monthly newsletters), 12 per cent for consulting services, and the balance for supplies and miscellaneous expenses. Not reflected in the total expenditures were office furniture and equipment loaned or given by local business corporations and labor services donated by Jensen's firm for reproducing reports. In addition, the Citizens' Governmental Research Bureau contributed services far beyond those for which it was compensated as a consultant. Spread out over four years, the funds available to the Commission were surprisingly small compared to the magnitude of its undertaking.

It became evident at an early stage that the initial appropriation of $30,000 from the state would be insufficient to finance the work program for the first two-year period at the level which Lobb and research director Ball desired. In May, 1958, the Commission authorized the chairman to appoint a committee to study the short- and long-range financial requirements of the agency. There is no record that such a committee was appointed. However, Lobb, in characteristic fashion and without consulting the other members, took it upon himself to secure additional funds. He appealed directly to the Association of Commerce and the local governments to supply the Commission's additional budget needs, which he estimated at about $40,000.

The Association of Commerce responded to Lobb's plea by asking its members to make donations but the results were minimal with less than $3,000 raised in this fashion. Lobb's failure to approach the Greater Milwaukee Committee first was a tactical blunder. The GMC had something of a fatherly interest in the Commission that it had fostered and it irked the group to be bypassed by its "protégé." Hence the poor response by top business leaders to the fund request.

The appeal to local officialdom proved more productive, but only after considerable byplay. The Milwaukee common council received the request coolly and delayed acting on it as several aldermen attacked the fund raising efforts of the Association of Commerce. "The study is a government function and government should pay for it," they asserted. "Financing by a special class would interfere with its obectives."[14] Kirby Hendee, one of the state senators from Milwaukee County who had sponsored the MSC bill, replied to this contention by pointing out that the law specifically permitted private contributions. "The reason we included this provision," he noted, "was that the state appropriated only $30,000 for the study. We knew that this would not be nearly enough for the job that was called for, but it was all the state could afford at the time. We felt that it was reasonable to expect groups in the Milwaukee area to contribute to the study, since it was intended to improve Milwaukee." Recalling that the aldermen opposed the creation of the Commission from the outset, he charged that they "are still trying to kill the whole study by cutting off its only available source of funds."[15] The Milwaukee *Journal* also chided the aldermen, commenting, "Quite without warrant, Aldermen Meyers and Mortier frown on the welcome effort of the Milwaukee Association of Commerce to find donors among its members. They say, 'government should pay for it.' Fine, if government will, but do you notice Meyers and Mortier putting in a resolution? We don't."[16]

Needled by the remarks of the press and civic leaders, the common council finally indicated its willingness to participate with other local governments in meeting the Commission's anticipated budget deficit. The League of Suburban Municipalities followed suit by recommending that its members contribute proportionately with the City on the basis of assessed property valuation in each community. Under this arrangement the central city donated approximately $22,000 and the suburban units (with all but two participating) $8,300. No further solicitation of funds was made by the MSC during the remainder of its tenure from any source outside the legislature.

The reluctance of the Commission to seek additional funds from non-public sources is difficult to understand in view of the common complaint about inadequate resources voiced by the members. One commissioner explained this unwillingness in the following way: "During the early period of the group's existence, some of the members felt that the Commission should set an example for other governmental agencies by demonstrating that it could operate on a Spartan budget. These members were very unhappy with Lobb's action in seeking additional funds. Later, after the blowup on the Commission in the summer of 1959,* the members were too embarrassed to ask for more funds from the community until the group could once again demonstrate its usefulness."

* See below, Chapter Six.

The decision by the Commission to restrict the scope of its research program during the last eighteen months of its existence also meant that fewer funds were needed. It could be implied, of course, that this decision was prompted by lack of fiscal resources, yet there appeared to be strong reluctance on the part of many members to start any new projects after 1959, a position they could rationalize on the basis of lack of funds. It is difficult to conceive that the Commission with its entree to the business community could not have obtained additional financing had it felt a strong urgency to broaden its research program.

PUBLIC INFORMATION AND EDUCATION

From its inception, the Commission toyed with the problem of public communication. How much of its time and resources should it allocate to an information and education program? Interest in this question waxed and waned during the four-year period but at no time became predominant. Most commissioners were too involved in committee work on the substantive issues and in their own personal and business affairs to devote much attention to the task of stimulating public interest. They were conscious of the need and made frequent gestures in this direction, but at no time were they willing to commit themselves or the Commission's scarce resources to a serious and sustained program of public education.

At an early stage in the proceedings, the suggestion was made that a public relations consultant be retained. No action was taken at the time since most members saw little need for such services until the Commission approached the point where it had a "a specific recommendation to sell." At the April, 1958, meeting, Mrs. Cook, the Commission secretary, proposed the appointment of a public information and education committee to keep the community apprised of the group's activities. The proposal was adopted and a committee appointed consisting of Mrs. Cook as chairman, three other commissioners, and seven outside members, including two newspapermen and three public relations directors of industrial firms. As its first project the committee prepared a ten-page popularly written pamphlet entitled "What the Metropolitan Study Commission Means to You." Twenty thousand copies were printed and distributed through local organizations and libraries.

After publication of the pamphlet, the committee showed no further signs of life, and public relations for the next eighteen months consisted mainly of occasional speeches by MSC members, press releases by the Commission chairman and research director, and distribution of reports. The chairmanship of the committee became vacant when Mrs. Cook resigned in June, 1959, and remained unfilled until Mrs. Norvan Gordon was appointed to the post six months later. Shortly thereafter the Commission began publication of an attractive monthly newsletter, "You and Your Metropolis," which ran throughout the remainder of the agency's existence. Working relations were also established at this time with the Junior Chamber of Commerce and the Junior Bar Association. The first conducted a mail survey of voluntary organizations in Milwaukee to determine which were interested or engaged in the study of metropolitan problems. Dovetailing with this project, the Junior Bar Association established a speakers' bureau to address interested groups on metropolitan problems and the work of the MSC. The number of requests for speakers, however, was disappointingly small; far less, in fact, than the number of young lawyers (twenty-seven) who offered their services.

THE SURVEY PATTERN

The MSC study differed little in organization, framework, and general orientation from the pattern of metropolitan surveys conducted in other American urban areas. A basis for ready comparison in this regard is provided by Daniel R. Grant's analysis of the many such studies, more than 100 in fact, that have taken place in recent decades.[17] Grant found that approximately two-thirds of the total were carried out under the supervision and responsibility of specially created commissions which, in the majority of cases, (1) were established by law or the official act of public agencies; (2) were appointed by a public authority—governor, state legislature, mayor, city council, county board, or a combination of these; (3) had fewer than twenty members; (4) consisted of more suburban than central city representatives; (5) had a small research staff of no more than two or three individuals, with occasional assistance from graduate students; (6) employed a function-by-function approach in its studies; and (7) received more financial support from private funds than from tax sources, with the amount inadequate in most cases.* Only as to the last characteristic did the MSC survey differ from the common pattern, since most of its funds came from public sources.

Grant's rundown further shows that the purpose of metropolitan surveys has varied from narrowly limited inquiries into particular problems to more comprehensive analyses of the relations among local governments. The emphasis, with few exceptions, has been on administrative or structural reforms designed to increase efficiency, eliminate duplication, provide better services on a more equitable basis, and reduce costs. Only in recent years has there been a noticeable trend toward investigating the broader political, social, and economic questions that underlie metropolitan intergovernmental relationships.

The Milwaukee Commission made no effort to pioneer into new paths. It proceeded along traditional lines with its focus on administrative and structural defects in the existing governmental system and on service deficiencies. Handicapped by lack of adequate professional staff and plagued by uncertainty over its proper role, the Commission experienced operational difficulties that similar groups in other areas have generally managed to avoid. In contrast

---

* The remaining one-third of the studies were conducted by existing organizations such as universities, community research agencies, chambers of commerce, and civic groups.

also to such metropolitan surveys as the Cleveland project in the late 1950's, involvement of influential community leaders and organizations in the Milwaukee Commission's work was minimal and insignificant. Yet despite these and other drawbacks, the MSC managed to turn out a prodigious amount of work, some of it of substantial quality. A few of its studies, moreover, particularly those on land use and governmental financing, indicated an awareness that there were more fundamental issues than administrative tidiness confronting metropolitan communities. This awareness, however, was never clearly articulated and the emphasis throughout the Commission's life remained on structural reform.

6
The Commission's
Life Cycle

The members of the Milwaukee Study Commission approached their task with a sense of mission. Imbued with the folklore of metropolitan reform, they believed that once the facts were ferreted out, the solutions would be so clear and persuasive that only the most adamant opponents of change would dispute them. Some members, of course, had strong notions as to the proper remedies and were certain that "objective" studies would substantiate their preconceptions. But others, and perhaps the majority, felt less confident that they understood the problems, let alone the solutions. Together with their colleagues, however, they anticipated that the magic of the study process would clear a well-marked path through the complex maze of metropolitan dysfunction. The task, as they saw it, was to seek out the facts and then formulate recommendations in the light of criteria familiar to every successful businessman: efficiency, economy, sound organization, and effective management. Aware that the realities of politics could not be overlooked, they nonetheless believed that where the case for reorganization was clear and convincing and where it was well supported by factual studies, the political obstacles would give way to rational action.

It was thus with considerable hope that the MSC began its work. Most members felt that the time was opportune for improving the metropolitan governmental system, although, as just indicated, few had any definite notions as to what form such improvement should take or how it could be accomplished. A majority of the group was also confident that the general public was ready for change even though they could point to few concrete indications to warrant such belief. The favorable reception they had received from the press and civic leadership together with the polite expressions of cooperation from public officials had helped to stimulate this spirit of optimism.

The present chapter shows in what manner and from what perspective the MSC carried on its work, and how both manner and perspective were modified over time. The environmental factors that impinged upon the group and influenced its operations become evident here. No metropolitan study commission, even the most purist dominated, has been successful in immunizing itself against political realities. Many have tried but like the successors of Frederick W. Taylor, the father of scientific management, they soon discovered that what may be perfectly rational from an engineering point of view may be wholly unworkable in the realm of human behavior. The experiences of the Milwaukee Commission graphically underscore this truism.

THE HONEYMOON PHASE

The life span of the Study Commission falls into three distinct time phases. The first extends from the agency's birth in October, 1957, to early 1959, when John Lobb resigned as chairman; the second from the time Lobb vacated the post to the appointment of J. Martin Klotsche as chairman seven months later; and the third during the remainder of the group's life. Each of these periods is characterized by a different emphasis and outlook, a different philosophy and approach, and a different mode of procedure. The initial period was one of considerable if not well-organized activity. Investigation into a wide variety of problems was instituted as each of the standing committees proceeded to map out its area of concern. Although the Commission's goals remained unexpressed, the question of some form of metropolitan government came to occupy a prominent plan on its agenda. By the end of the period, however, the earlier optimism had given way to disillusionment as outside reaction to the group's work began to manifest itself.

Lobb proved to be chairman of tremendous drive and vigor. Although a relative newcomer to Milwaukee, he had already acquired a reputation as a forceful and candid spokesman of the business community. Lobb saw the area's needs as twofold: establishment of a governmental agency with capacity to handle extra-municipal functions such as water supply; and creation of a tax climate that would stimulate industrial growth. Anxious to move the work along at a swift pace, he was impatient with and even neglectful of organizational arrangements and details. To him the goals were self-evident; research was needed only to convince the public and governmental officials. As one member described the situation: "The Commission was poorly organized during its early stage. It had no overall plan of approach, relations between the staff and committees were not worked out, operating procedures were not formalized, and clear lines of responsibility were not established. This was the way Lobb worked. He was poor on organization and didn't give a hoot whether minutes were kept or not. He believed in playing by ear and pushing ahead with studies and programs without clearly-drawn plans of execution."

Many of Lobb's characteristics were paralleled in the MSC's first research director, Charles Ball. A young man of only twenty-four, Ball was serving as capital budgeting officer of the city of Madison at the time of his employment by the Commission. Harvard educated and the holder of a master's degree in political science from the University of Wisconsin, he brought to his task an insatiable capacity for work together with youthful enthusiasm and ambition. In a short time he was playing a major role in helping the Commission formulate and carry out a research program. Never a closely knit team—each was too much of an individualist and the two were often at odds with each other—Lobb and Ball set the tempo and provided the initiative and direction for the group's work. With the former quarterbacking and the latter and his small research staff suggesting new plays and turning out work at an almost frantic pace, the majority of the commissioners found themselves in the position of bench-warmers rather than active players. In the words of one, "The Commission as a body sat on the sidelines during this early stage while the field was monopolized by a few prima donnas." Only the more aggressive members such as Cutler, who headed the land use and zoning committee, and Parkinson, the commission's vice chairman, helped in calling the signals.

This initial period might also be characterized as one of "metropolitan government consciousness." Most of the members soon came to anticipate the creation of some type of metropolitan agency, a "vehicle" as they called it, which could handle area-wide functions. Although differences of opinion existed as to the form of such an agency and the scope of its powers, the majority was definitely headed toward a metropolitan government recommendation of some kind by late 1958. According to Ball, the prevailing sentiment on the Commission at the time was to bypass the county as the metropolitan instrumentality because of its "organizational inadequacy and the fact that some problems transcended county lines." There was also some feeling, he stated, that "the initial proposals should be hard hitting and an attempt made to get something through the legislature before opposition had time to solidify."

One of the first indications of the Commission's thinking along these lines appeared in September, 1958, when Parkinson publicly stated that the MSC "is quite definitely moving toward a form of metropolitan government that will have jurisdiction over a large area—larger than the county," and "it also looks as though this metropolitan agency should have responsibility for a number of key metropolitan functions."[1] The Commission's first report to the governor, released shortly thereafter, contained further signs of this trend. Referring to future research plans, the report noted that one of the questions to be answered was: "What kind of metropolitan organization can most effectively handle metropolitan functions and at the same time guarantee government that is responsible to the people?"[2] Lobb at this time revealed his own sympathy for the "grand" approach when he told a Marquette University seminar that "formation of the commission was just another step toward some form of metropolitan government for the Milwaukee area, an idea which has been around for about 30 years."[3]

These public statements followed a series of executive committee meetings at which optional forms for a metropolitan government were discussed. The committee concluded that the way must first be paved for public acceptance of broad-scaled reorganization by presenting "factual studies on several different problems considerably prior to the time of making a recommendation on the form of government best designed to solve these problems." Several members felt that the facts on sewers, water, and other functions "would tend inevitably to imply to the public what the form of government ought to be, so that when it was suggested the public might consider the inevitable solution."[4] Or as one commissioner waggishly put it, the process was similar to the definition of seduction: "By the time the question is put, the decision has already been made."

Late in September the executive committee sent a confidential memorandum to all MSC members outlining five alternatives which it had considered for the metropolitan vehicle: consolidation of all local units, transfer of area-wide functions to the county government, a series of independent service districts, a multi-purpose metropolitan district, and federation. Indicating that it regarded the first as politically impossible and probably undesirable, the second as deficient since the county does not cover the "true" metropolitan area, and the third unwise since single purpose districts would further fragment the governmental pattern, it recommended that the last two—multi-purpose district and federation—form the basis for the group's consideration. When it became apparent from the response that some members were not yet ready to commit themselves to a specific metropolitan government recommendation, the executive committee suggested a procedure under which the Commission would: (1) define the standards or yardsticks for distinguishing area-wide from local functions; (2) consider each function in the light of these criteria, seeking the views of local officials in the process; and (3) invite all local governments to submit their views on the most desirable form of government for handling those functions identified as metropolitan. Cutler, in particular, was insistent on the involvement of local officials. Although he favored an activist role for the Commission, he did not feel, as Lobb initially had felt, that the necessary legislation for change could be secured without first winning local political support.

At a meeting in December, 1958, the executive committee, with Lobb and Parkinson absent, agreed to submit a report to the full Commission "Concerning the Determination of the Type of Government Best Suited to Discharge Metropolitan Functions." The report, like the confidential memorandum sent earlier to the commissioners, reviewed the five alternatives but this time excluded only two of them—political consolidation and creation of single-function districts—as unrealistic or inadequate. Without committing itself to any of the remaining alternatives, the report flatly stated that "there is a need to concentrate present metro-wide functions in one central metropolitan agency and to make sure that, in the absence of clear and compelling special circumstances, any future transfers of power from local governments will be assigned to that particular agency." It concluded with the recommendation that the MSC sponsor a bill in the forthcoming session of the legislature to create some type of metropolitan agency.[5]

When Lobb saw the proposed report, he immediately called another meeting of the executive committee and insisted that the type of metropolitan agency and the functions to be assumed by it were matters that should be left to a local charter commission. He stated that the experiences in other metropolitan areas such as Miami and Cleveland had convinced him of the desirability of this method. Cutler, who had been instrumental in getting the report through the committee, demurred at the creation of what he called "another study commission." After considerable discussion, Lobb accepted an amendment to the report which left the question open: "The Commission will either recommend legislation for the creation of a metropolitan agency and/or recommend the creation of a charter commission to draft a plan if constitutional or other considerations make such a course seem advisable." Lobb's unfavorable reaction to the report and his proposal for a charter commission came as a surprise to the other members since he had given no previous indication of favoring this approach. In fact, he conceded that up to this time he had "tended to think about the creation of an 'authority' of some kind."[6]

Apparently Lobb had become less optimistic in recent weeks at the prospect of securing metropolitan reorganization by legislative fiat and now felt that the best strategy was to move the issue from the state capitol to the local arena. In offering his new proposal, he stated: "I feel that we should make every effort to get the county, the city of Milwaukee, and the suburbs to go with us to Madison and ask for creation of a Charter Commission to set up a home rule county-wide form of government specifically protecting all the localities in the administration of local affairs."[7] The capture of the governorship and the lower house of the legislature by the Democrats in the preceding month's election was no doubt the primary factor that led to Lobb's almost complete reversal of attitude. As he later remarked, "With the state in the hands of a Republican Governor who would push a Republican legislature, I think we could have gotten some major reform enacted by the state. When there was a political change, I couldn't see much chance of getting this accomplished."

When the amended report of the executive committee was presented to the Commission at its monthly meeting late in December, Clifford Randall took exception to it on several counts. He questioned the advisability of eliminating two of the alternative forms, enlarging the territorial jurisdiction of the MSC, and asking the legislature to create a metropolitan agency or charter commission. At his insistence the report was toned down by substituting "may recommend" instead of "recommend" jurisdictional enlargement, and "believe" instead of "found" that two alternatives were inappropriate. The members also agreed that the views of the local governments be solicited and that a public hearing be held on the question of a metropolitan agency. Randall's position was revealing since he, of all members, was most intimately involved in the Greater Milwaukee Committee. His attack on the report, in the view of some observers, reflected the feeling of GMC leadership that the Commission was proceeding too fast and too far and that the proposal for enlarging its territorial jurisdiction was ill-considered and would do nothing more than arouse additional political opposition.

While these events were taking place within the MSC, interesting developments were occurring outside. Apparently both City and suburban officials at first interpreted the Commission's activities as favorable to their respective causes. Those in the central city purported to see a "leaning" toward a strong metropolitan government on the part of the group while suburbanites felt that a recommendation for a limited area-wide agency with jurisdiction over water and sewers was in the making. In September, 1958, Zeidler, who had been the Commission's most outspoken critic, told a meeting of the Milwaukee Advertising Club that the Study Commission had reached some "interesting conclusions" and that "nothing but good can come from its work."[8] Two months later, George Schmus, West Allis city attorney and a leading suburban spokesman of the "iron ring," similarly lauded the MSC in a speech before the Milwaukee Press Club as "a group of high-minded men who are trying to improve intergovernmental relations and the performance of governmental services without doing violence to existing institutions."[9]

The county board also injected itself into the act at this time with several of its members proposing that the county seek home rule powers in order to establish a metropolitan government patterned after the Dade County, Florida, system. Although the proposal was rejected, the board established a standing committee on metropolitan problems to study recommendations submitted to it by the MSC. In making the latter suggestion, John Doyne, who later (in 1960) became Milwaukee county's first elected executive, declared that "the county should take the lead in problems of metropolitan government. . . . Somebody has to take the lead and I think county government is the vehicle."[10] This flurry of activity prompted the Milwaukee *Journal* to editorialize: "When it comes to metropolitan government, few officials are saying 'let George do it.' They're saying 'let me do it.' If this indicated a general interest in finding the best solutions to metropolitan problems it would be fine. But, unfortunately, it doesn't. It indicates instead a reluctance by most officials to give up powers and a great eagerness to assume more."[11]

Following the Commission's action at the December meeting, questionnaires were sent to all Milwaukee County municipalities and the adjoining cities and villages in Waukesha and Ozaukee counties. Two questions were asked: what specific functions of local government should, in the public interest, be handled by a metropolitan type government; and what kind of metropolitan vehicle, if any, should be established to handle these services? The questionnaire suggested that at least four alternative answers to the latter query were possible: (1) modernization of the county government; (2) creation of a multi-purpose metropolitan district; (3) establishment of a federation of local units; and (4) retention of the status quo. Every municipality in Milwaukee County and five from the adjacent areas replied. They later reiterated their views at a public hearing that was well attended by local official-dom.

Use of the questionnaire with its "metropolitan government" overtones proved to be a major blunder. By putting the issue in this way to local officials before it had carefully prepared its case and formulated its strategy, the Commission exposed itself to broadside attack. The opposition was quick to take advantage of the opening. Typical of the suburban governments' reaction was the reply of the mayor of South Milwaukee. "The entire tone of your letter," he informed the MSC, "presupposes that there must be some form of metropolitan government. We again point out that South Milwaukee needs no Metro to handle any problem facing us. We believe that the present status of government is the best for our people, but will concede the need of central programming in sewerage and water for some of our neighbors. South Milwaukee takes the stand that metropolitan government is not needed, would be an overlapping of present government, and would merely add tax costs to an already saturated tax base." No substitute, the mayor warned, "has ever been found for local control of local affairs to sustain a sound democratic government."[12]

The other suburban communities followed closely the South Milwaukee line. While a majority answered that water supply and sewage disposal were functions that could best be handled on an area-wide basis, few listed other problems as metropolitan in character. In fact, the general tenor of suburban replies and of statements made by their spokesmen at the public hearing indicated strong hostility to any change in either the existing governmental structure or the allocation of responsibility among existing units for performing public services. Village of Fox Point officials, for example, stressed that "there should be very little change in transferring other functions from a local to an area control. The general structure of local government should not be changed. Various local governments, particularly suburbs, are closer to the people and the particular needs and wishes of the people within their boundaries, and are therefore able to take care of such needs and wishes with greater dispatch and at a lower cost." Wauwatosa officials, while favoring creation of a metropolitan water authority, reminded the Commission that "good government lives close to its people; super government is remote, cold, and unresponsive; the bigger the unit of government the smaller the man." West Allis declared that it would "resist any program of step-by-step functional consolidation which will eventually emasculate existing cities and villages, and leave them hollow government shells. West Allis is alert to the danger of consolidation being accomplished one small bite at a time, instead of in one gulp. The end result would be the same, the death of the smaller units of government. West Allis will not yield an inch to such a program."[13]

At the other extreme, the city of Milwaukee called for outright political amalgamation. Its official answer, in the form of a resolution adopted by the common council, reaffirmed the City's long-standing policy of opposition to lesser remedies, and stated that "if any change is made, the entire contiguous area of the Milwaukee region should be under one single unit of government, a municipality." It went on to point out "that important major functions which could logically be consolidated in a metropolitan government are so numerous and of such significance that the remaining functions left to any independent local units of government would be insufficient to justify their existence. . . . Other forms of metropolitan government become tortuous and too complicated for the citizens to understand. The City of Milwaukee with its system of wards with local representatives from each ward and a city wide, elected executive furnishes a tried and proven method of municipal administration which can meet the problems of this central area."[14]

The county government once again expressed willingness to

become the metropolitan vehicle, but few municipalities showed support for this approach. Nor did they express much sympathy for the extension of service districts beyond the Milwaukee County limits except on a voluntary and contractual basis. Only the central city's proposal for a metropolitan municipality envisaged a territorial unit larger than Milwaukee County. Communities in adjacent Waukesha and Ozaukee counties expressed interest in a metropolitan water and sewerage utility, but they also made it clear that they wanted no part of any political arrangement such as federation.

The responses revealed that the Commission's honeymoon period with the local units had been unhappily terminated by this ill-prepared and even naive plunge into the question of governmental organization and structure. The questionnaire had alarmed suburban officials, who construed it as a brief for some form of metropolitan government and an effort to put them on record in support of the concept. It also confirmed their growing suspicion that the MSC was thinking in far broader terms than they had originally anticipated; hence the overly negative nature of their replies with the strong polemics on local autonomy and the strictures against change. Only Mayor Zeidler and other City officials continued to speak well of the Commission as they waited to see what proposals would be forthcoming. Few of them expected the MSC to recommend political consolidation, yet they were amused at the discomfort of suburban officials over the actions of the "prestigious" Commission. City officials had long been the prime target of the daily press as obstructionists in metropolitan matters; now perhaps it would be their suburban colleagues' turn.

To most neutral observers the replies to the questionnaire dispelled any doubts they may have had about the prospect of significant reorganization in the Milwaukee metropolis. As a *Sentinel* reporter who had covered the Commission from its inception wrote: "The replies clearly indicate that the MSC is bucking a stone wall in attempting to legislate for any type of metropolitan government—either a new supergovernment, a federation of present governments, or a strengthened county government .... Metropolitan government? Where lies such hope in the bitterness reflected even in the answers to the commission's questionnaire?"[15]

MSC members had become more conscious in recent months of the formidable obstacles to metropolitan reform but they were taken aback by the completely negative character of the responses to their queries. They had hoped, as one of them remarked, "that somehow the replies would reveal common grounds for consensus and mark out the path to a feasible reorganization proposal." Instead they found themselves confronted with the same diametrically opposed and rigid positions that had stymied the Committee of 21. Even the civic groups, including the GMC, offered no expression of strong support during this flareup but remained strangely silent.

On March 1, 1959, less than a week after the public hearing on the metropolitan vehicle, Lobb unexpectedly announced his resignation as chairman. Citing the "press of personal business," he referred to the chairmanship as a "full time job" that should go to an individual who could devote considerable time to the task. That this reason constituted the impelling motive for his resignation is doubtful. There is little question that the chairmanship had proved a considerable drain on his time but, as other commissioners pointed out, he could readily have eased this burden by better organization and a wider delegation of responsibility. A few felt that he was irked by the group's refusal to support him in the matter of the charter commission and by the reluctance of many members to have the MSC assume an activist role. Others were of the opinion that he had initially viewed the Commission as a stepping-stone to the governorship and that he lost interest when it became apparent that no significant accomplishments would emerge from its work. After stepping down from the chairmanship, Lobb remained as a member of the Commission until August, 1960, but his participation was minimal.

Lobb's resignation as chairman had been preceded by that of Charles Ball, who had quit as research director a few months earlier purportedly because the state civil service commission had placed his position on the classified list and downgraded the pay. Only a month prior to Ball's action the chairman of the important metropolitan functions committee, Willis Scholl, had resigned from the Commission because of "pressure of business." Thus within a relatively short span of time the group lost its forceful chairman, its energetic research director, and its top industrialist. Matters stood at this crucial point as the curtain fell on the first act of the MSC drama.

THE INTERREGNUM

The second period in the Commission's life was marked by internal difficulties, lack of direction, disillusionment, and lessened research activities. Lobb's abdication came at a time when strong leadership was necessary to rally the group from its first serious setback, reassess its position, and map out future strategy. It left a power vacuum that, together with the other developments at the time, almost caused the collapse of the Commission. The resignation, moreover, had taken the other members by surprise. As one of them complained, "Lobb didn't tell us a thing about his intentions to resign. We first learned about it from the newspapers. If he was going to quit, he should have had his successor groomed and waiting in the wings, or at least have had some prior understanding with the governor. Instead he left us foundering while maneuvering for the post went on. The GMC and some members wanted Randall, some wanted Parkinson, some Cutler, and some just didn't give a damn."

With matters at this stage, Parkinson boldly introduced a proposal for a multi-function government at a meeting of the full Commission. His plan called for the establishment of a new metropolitan district authority to take over nine functions: sewage, expressways, parks, advisory planning and zoning, public library and museum, garbage and refuse disposal, assessment and tax collection, transportation planning, and public health administration. The proposal contained no suggestions on organization, structure, representation, or management, but merely indicated that the agency would have jurisdiction over the entire urbanized area regardless of county lines. In offering the plan, Parkinson stated that he favored a single government for the area but was aware that such a solution would be politically difficult if not impossible to attain. A multi-function agency, he said, appeared to be "the only acceptable compromise" between the consolidationists and local autonomists.[16]

Parkinson's long and active participation in local civic and educational organizations had given him considerable insight into metropolitan affairs. A forceful individual and one prone to act on his own initiative, he had introduced the district plan without consulting other members of the executive committee although the subject of a metropolitan agency was then under consideration by that group. Moreover, a majority of the functions included in the proposal had not as yet been studied by the Commission. Parkinson later stated that he took the step to stimulate action and restore the sagging fortunes of the MSC. "A majority of the members were in favor of some form of metropolitan government. I felt that we had reached the point where we had to act vigorously or lose public confidence."

The Parkinson plan was quickly endorsed at an executive committee meeting with only its author and Jensen, Beck, and Luetzow, all City residents, present. The other three members—Cutler, Knoebel, and the retiring chairman of the Commission, all suburbanites—were absent. Parkinson indicated that water supply was not included in the list because the Commission had already made recommendations covering this matter.* He might also have added that this was the one function which the City was most determined

* See below, Chapter Seven.

to retain. In presenting the proposal, Parkinson expressed hope that the MSC could have a bill drafted in time for the expected special session of the legislature in the coming fall.

The Parkinson proposal had the blessing of Milwaukee officials although it is doubtful that plans to implement it could have won serious support from a majority of the common council. Following his appointment to the MSC, Parkinson had won the confidence of Zeidler and other key officials and in a real sense had become the City's representative and spokesman on the Commission. As Zeidler later commented, "While no doubt the governor in his appointment of Dr. Parkinson intended to deliberately slight the City, he put on the commission the one man who was later to make the only positive step for a metropolitan government."[17]

The Parkinson coup, on the other hand, brought suburban officials and the small town papers screaming to their feet. The former demanded that Parkinson resign from the Commission, while the West Allis *Star* asked its readers if they wanted their public library and health department taken away from them and turned over to "metro" or if they wanted their city treasurer and assessor fired. "If you are awake to the dangers of metro super-government," the *Star* counseled, "if you are aware that metro government would cost you higher taxes and give you poorer service, you will speak up with the loudest 'No' you have uttered in your life. . . . And if you are awake, you will condemn Vice Chairman George Parkinson . . . who is hard at work on the study commission as the spokesman for Mayor Zeidler doing his best to consolidate the suburbs with Milwaukee. Come on, West Allis, let's fight this thing! Get your letters and phone calls in to the *Star*, the daily press, your county officials, your state officials, your city officials, STOP METRO MONSTER!"[18] Other suburban weeklies echoed the war cry. "Come hell and high water," the Whitefish Bay *Herald* cried out, "the people are determined to keep their way of life. They don't like the threat of an oligarchy."[19]

When Cutler, who had been out of town, learned of the executive committee's action, he immediately addressed letters marked "Confidential" to all members of the Commission expressing serious concern at the course of events. Cutler stated that suburban leaders who had been MSC supporters from the beginning (presumably as long as water was the issue) viewed the nine-function metropolitan proposal as an indirect effort to accomplish outright consolidation with the city of Milwaukee. "Premature suggestions of this kind," he complained, "which are judged by suburban leaders to be both an attack on the home rule of their municipalities, as well as being impossible of passage in the Legislature do very considerable harm to the standing of the Commission." Referring to further discussion of the proposal as "political suicide for the Commission," he stated that he would urge the executive committee to table it "until such a time, if ever, as studies of specific functions warrant entertaining such a proposal."[20] This was not the first occasion on which Cutler and Parkinson had clashed. Strong personality differences had developed between them during the prior year, and with Lobb's resignation these were accentuated as each sought to steer the Commission in the direction he considered to be in its best interest.

As these developments were occurring, Gaylord Nelson, a Democrat who had succeeded Republican Vernon Thomson as governor, named Albert F. Houghton to the chairmanship vacated by Lobb. Houghton, a well-known Milwaukee lawyer and a close personal friend of the governor, had been active in Democratic politics and had served in various civic capacities including the presidency of the Milwaukee Urban League. It was Nelson's intention that the new appointee become the official City representative on the Commission and that Parkinson remain to fill the vacancy caused by the death of one member, Earl R. Butter, in February, 1959. Houghton was technically eligible to serve in this capacity by virtue of his membership on the Milwaukee Harbor Commission. Since the statute barred more than one City official on the MSC, the Governor had proceeded with the Houghton appointment assuming that Parkinson would res¹gn his unpaid civil defense post and thus eliminate the technical difficulty. Parkinson, however, angered at what he regarded as a political maneuver to displace him, refused to withdraw from his City position but instead resigned from the Commission.

In face of the suburban outcry over the Parkinson plan, the movement on the Commission for metropolitan government collapsed. Houghton, at his first executive committee meeting in April, 1959, requested that the proposal be deferred until he had opportunity to study the question more thoroughly. His request was granted and nothing further was heard of the plan during the remainder of the MSC's tenure. Houghton became incapacitated by illness shortly after this meeting. Four months later he resigned as chairman but he remained on as a member until his death early in 1960. Direction of the Commission during this period fell to Cutler, who was elected vice-chairman when Parkinson resigned.

Cutler, at the age of forty-two, was regarded as one of the top municipal lawyers of the area. A brilliant and indefatigable worker, he at times antagonized others with his drive and initiative and his impatience with mediocrity. Cutler, to City officials, had become the symbol of the suburban "iron ring," which was wholly unwarranted, since his outlook on metropolitan affairs was far broader than the provincialism represented by the League of Suburban Municipalities, an organization that at no time looked to him as its spokesman. His municipal law practice, however, had occasionally placed him in opposition to the City in annexation and incorporation proceedings, and his aggressiveness in handling these matters had given rise to the "Cutler myth." At the time of the MSC appointment, for example, Zeidler had singled out Cutler "as one of the leading opponents of the city of Milwaukee."²¹

Cutler was probably too controversial a figure to head the MSC at this low point in its existence when it was under attack on several fronts. His position, moreover, was weakened by the fact that the incapacitated Houghton was still officially chairman. In addition, the chain of events which had brought disenchantment to the Commission and checked its momentum continued with two further resignations during this interim period. F. S. Cornell, executive vice president of A. O. Smith, who had succeeded Scholl in November, 1958, stepped down after serving less than eight months, citing the "pressure of business" as the reason; and Mrs. Cook was compelled to relinquish her post because her family was moving out of the state. When Cutler learned of Cornell's pending resignation, he wrote to the governor that "the already sagging prestige of the Study Commission would be further damaged if the story of the resignation appears prior to the time when you are able to announce the appointment of some person of stature to fill the position."[22] Aware of the various factors, including his own ambiguous position, Cutler worked closely with Foote, Jensen, and Beck, the three most active members at that time, in an attempt to reorganize the group and restore its working effectiveness.

The difficulties did not end at this point. Differences over staff procedures and work programs soon arose between some of the more active commissioners, including Cutler, and the new research director, Charles Goff, a University of Wisconsin–Milwaukee political science professor who had been selected under civil service procedures to succeed Ball. Goff had served under Parkinson at the University of Wisconsin extension center. A diligent and conscientious researcher, he had none of Ball's color or frenzied drive. He took over his duties at a time when the entire research program was in a transitional state and the Commission itself at a low ebb. Given little voice in policy-making after Parkinson's resignation, Goff devoted his time to research on several projects that had been initiated by the metropolitan functions committee. Less than six months after his appointment he resigned, contending that his job had been downgraded to routine work and that the acting chairman had consistently refused to consult with him on Commission matters. A public exchange of hostile letters between Goff and Cutler did little to help the "image" of the MSC in the community as the news media played up the controversy.

Mayor Zeidler had become decidedly cool toward the MSC after Parkinson had resigned; now Goff's departure further alienated him. He attributed both resignations to pressure by those unfriendly to the City's cause, a view that had no basis in fact. If anything, Parkinson's resignation resulted from a struggle within the Commission for the chairmanship while Goff's differences with Cutler and others were largely personal. Neither resignation was in any way associated with the individual's attitude toward the City. Zeidler, however, roundly criticized the Commission's treatment of Goff and proposed that the City hire the ex-director as a part time consultant on metropolitan affairs, stating that his purpose was to "protect the City from some very serious developments within the commission." Apparently alluding to indications that the water study might be reopened* and to the selection of Cutler as vice chairman, Zeidler charged that "recent changes on the commission indicate that it has decided to undo anything that was done under the administration of John C. Lobb and Dr. George Parkinson."[23]

Simultaneously with the mayor's statement, a strongly worded resolution sponsored by twelve of the twenty aldermen was introduced in the common council asking the governor and legislature to abolish the MSC. The resolution charged that a majority of Commission members had "a one-sided anti-city-of-Milwaukee viewpoint," and that continued studies would lead only to a "morass of misunderstanding."[24] One alderman stated that the MSC had demonstrated by "firing Goff" that "it doesn't want an objective study." Calling for immediate action on the resolution, he declared, "We should act quickly so those people will know they can't shove us around."[25] Other aldermen, uncertain of the political repercussions of such a direct attack on the Commission, were in favor of proceeding slowly. As one of them stated, "Let's send this

* See below, pp. 163–67.

to committee and invite Cutler over rather than antagonize the commission and the legislature."[26] This procedure was followed, and subsequent peace meetings between MSC leaders and City officials helped to calm the waters. With the future turn of events on the Commission, the matter was not revived.

THE FINALE

The third period of the Commission's history began with the naming of J. Martin Klotsche as chairman in August, 1959. This phase was marked by stability and harmony within the group and by less open bickering among City and suburban officials without. However, the dynamism and momentum of the earlier stages had disappeared to be replaced by a more cautious, conciliatory, and conservative approach on the part of the Commission. Klotsche described the difference between the first and final periods in these words: "During the Lobb regime there was a strongly activist philosophy pushed by the chairman with minimum participation by most members; while during the latter two years much time was devoted to mending fences, repairing the Commission's public image, and winding up our work in the face of the uncertainty of the future."

In announcing Klotsche's selection Governor Nelson stated that he was greatly concerned by reports of disagreements and personality clashes on the Commission, and he hoped that appointment of the University of Wisconsin–Milwaukee provost as chairman would lead "to overcoming these obstacles to progress."[27] The new appointee was a highly respected community leader who enjoyed the confidence of many groups in both the City and suburbs. His position as a public educator, moreover, placed him above charges of partiality and of political or business self-interest. In commenting on the selection, the *Journal* noted that Klotsche's past experience and his knowledge of the Commission's needs and problems recommended him highly. "Perhaps best of all, he is a moderator" with the capability "to pull the commission effort together, smooth frictions, and keep it on the track."[28] It is no secret that Nelson turned to the university provost to rescue a badly demoralized Commission. More resignations were in the offing at the time and the Greater Milwaukee Committee was conveying to the governor its concern about the agency's "disintegration."

The new chairman moved swiftly to reorganize the Commission and reassess its research program. He appointed two vice-chairmen, one responsible for liaison with public and private groups, the other to see that internal operations of the Commission were carried forward "particularly as they relate to program and studies." Clifford Randall was named to serve in the first capacity and Harold Beck was chosen to supervise internal operations. The executive committee was formalized and its membership reduced to six. The research coordinating committee was asked to examine the entire research program and status of current projects and to recommend a general work plan for the remainder of the Commission's tenure. Efforts to obtain a new research director to fill Goff's post were stepped up. Statutory changes initiated by the MSC after Ball's resignation had removed the position from civil service status and thereby broadened recruitment possibilities.

Two months after Klotsche assumed the chairmanship, the Commission announced the appointment of David Mars as research director. Mars, a member of the political science department at the University of Connecticut, accepted the position with the understanding that he would not report until the end of the current school semester in January, 1960. When he joined the MSC, plans for the final months had been formulated and the studies assigned to outside consultants or undertaken by the members themselves. He therefore had little opportunity to participate in shaping the research program or the direction it followed. Most of his time was occupied in coordinating committee activities, handling the administrative affairs of the Commission, and preparing reports. The quiet and effective manner in which he carried out these duties won the respect and confidence of the members, and the final report of the group reflects his influence.

After Klotsche's initial survey of the Commission and the status of its work, he concluded that two areas of concern should be particularly emphasized: communication with the public and intergovernmental cooperation. To push the first, he reconstituted the membership of the committee on public education and information and appointed Mrs. Gordon chairman. "I had a feeling from the beginning," he stated, "that this was an area that desperately needed attention. Few people knew of the Commission's research and findings. I was convinced that we had to reach and interest a wider audience if we hoped to build up support for our recommendations, and I wanted to make the work of the committee on public education and information a major effort." Unfortunately, inadequate resources as well as the magnitude of the task prevented more than minor attempts to publicize the Commission's work. "The fact that the results did not loom large," Klotsche later observed, "does not detract from the importance which some of us attached to this aspect of our work."

The second area of concern of the new chairman—intergovernmental cooperation—reflected at least partially his feeling and that of some civic leaders in the GMC that the Commission had badly mishandled the question of metropolitan government and had unduly alarmed suburban officials in the process. He felt that now the only hope for progress in reorganization lay in agreement among the local units. He was also aware from his examination of the MSC statute that one of the Commission's duties was to study the question of intergovernmental cooperation in the county and that no steps had been taken to perform this task. These factors prompted him to establish an intergovernmental cooperation committee to examine the past and current use of cooperative devices in the area and the prospects for their expansion.

Few new studies were inaugurated during this period as efforts were directed toward the completion of projects already under way, such as revenue sources and distribution, land use and zoning, and police services. There was little talk of metropolitan government, either within or outside the Commission, or of major changes in the existing structure. As one member described the situation: "The MSC stopped thinking in terms of a metropolitan government although some members hoped that it could reach agreement on a statement as to the future course of governmental reorganization in the area before disbanding." Such a statement emerged in the Commission's final report.

Toward the end of the Commission's life, Klotsche came to view the urban county approach as the long-range answer to Milwaukee's metropolitan problems. Reflecting on the work of the MSC during the time that he was chairman, he concluded that "development of the urban county concept was probably its most important single contribution, with public education and information and intergovernmental cooperation (having been the two major points that I was interested in when I took over as chairman) assuming lesser significance."

THE COMMISSION'S DEMISE

By the summer of 1960 MSC members were beginning to take note that only a year of the agency's tenure remained. Some of them expressed concern that many important areas of study would be left unfinished or untouched when the deadline arrived, but feelings were mixed as to whether an extension of the Commission's life should be sought. The subject was discussed by the executive committee at its August, 1960, meeting. When no clearcut consensus emerged, the group decided that a committee should be appointed to consider the question and that the major civic groups in the community should be represented on it. Nothing was said about involving local public officials in the decision.

The special committee named by Klotsche for this purpose consisted of three commissioners (Beck, as chairman, William Rasche, a recent appointee to the MSC, and John Kopmeier, president of Wisconsin Ice & Coal Company), and four non-commissioners: Edmund B. Shea, a prominent attorney and chairman of the GMC committee on metropolitan problems; Norman Klug, president of Miller Brewery Company and chairman of the civic affairs committee of the Association of Commerce; Karl Maier, a Northwestern Mutual Life Insurance Company executive and president of the Citizens' Governmental Research Bureau; and Gerald Rice, a Milwaukee attorney and president of the City Club. In addition to Shea, both Klug and Maier were active GMC members. The committee was asked to determine whether a need existed in the Milwaukee area for a group to do research in metropolitan problems after July 1, 1961, and if so, the specific form that such an organization should take. By establishing such a committee, the Commission sought to put the question of continuing its activities directly up to the civic leaders. If they answered in the affirmative, they would then be committed to provide the necessary support.

The special committee held three meetings. It quickly reached agreement on the need for further research and on the continuance of the MSC as the logical agency to perform this function. The group's swift action was due largely to Shea. A top community influential and a member of the governing council of the National Municipal League, he had been one of the original sponsors of the MSC and a staunch supporter of its work. Shea told committee members that he saw "no escape from the conclusion that the life of the Commission should be extended." Although he felt that the agency should be retained in essentially its present from, he was sympathetic to certain changes, including enlargement of its jurisdiction beyond the Milwaukee County lines and permanent status with fixed terms of office for the membership. The group considered these and other changes but rejected them when the executive secretary of the GMC and others cautioned that any modifications of the present law would complicate the problem of obtaining legislative approval for the extension.

In its report to the Commission the committee stated that it found "definite need for an agency to carry on research work into the problems of the metropolitan Milwaukee area after July 1, 1961"; and that the MSC "as presently constituted is the agency which should be given the responsibility for this work." It pointed out that many studies remained to be undertaken, such as civil defense, industrial development, public education, recreational needs, and water pollution; and that other projects instituted by the MSC had not been fully examined. The committee recommended that legislative extension of the Commission's tenure for two years be sought.[29] MSC members concurred in the recommendation, although several of them complained of the futility of prolonging the agency's life unless the legislature provided more operating funds than it had in the past.

Following the decision to seek an extension, the Commission submitted a budget of approximately $100,000 to Governor Nelson to cover the 1961-63 biennium. The governor reduced this amount by approximately one-half and included it in his executive budget to the legislature. Responsibility for securing legislative approval was taken over by the civic organizations, particularly the GMC, since Klotsche and other members felt that it would be improper for the Commission to promote its own existence. The governor was sympathetic but he was too deeply involved in the struggle over tax reform to give the MSC more than an approving nod. The strategy employed was to seek extension by means of an appropriation rather than through the introduction of a separate bill. This move failed, however, when the joint finance committee of the legislature eliminated the MSC item from the budget by a vote of twelve to one. The action was taken despite pleas from Milwaukee civic organizations and the lobbyist for Milwaukee County. Several committee members questioned the wisdom of spending state money to study local problems, and others remarked that the Commission had done nothing since its creation "except grind out a lot of reports" and "print elegant brochures."[30]

The action of the joint finance committee came as a surprise to MSC supporters. Although the committee was dominated by rural legislators, prior contacts with its members had indicated no great opposition. After this setback, Commission backers turned to the regular legislative channels and secured the introduction of a bill in the state Senate. At the hearing on the measure, an impressive array of representatives of Milwaukee business, labor, and civic groups appeared in its behalf, with the lobbyist for the county board again indicating support. No one spoke in opposition, but the lobbyist for the city of Milwaukee registered against the bill. The lobbyist for the League of Suburban Municipalities did not appear although he had previously opposed the appropriation before the joint finance committee. At that time he had apparently acted without instructions, taking it for granted that his clients were unfavorably disposed to the Commission's extension. His action undoubtedly reflected the feelings of most league members but since several of the north shore suburbs where GMC influence was strongest did not want to go on record against continuance, the organization took no official stand on the bill.

The measure was successfully steered through the upper house by Senator Jerris Leonard, a north shore Republican, who had succeeded to the seat vacated by Kirby Hendee, one of the sponsors of the original bill involving the Commission. The vote was nineteen to eight with all of the opposition coming from Republicans outside Milwaukee County. When the bill reached the Assembly, it met a different fate. Efforts to get it out of committee were defeated by a top-heavy vote of fifty-nine to thirty-four. Civic supporters of the MSC, with the executive secretary of the Greater Milwaukee Committee doing the lobbying, had been unable to find an influential assemblyman to play the role that Leonard did in the Senate. In a session dominated by such issues as tax reform and reapportionment, few lawmakers were willing to incur legislative obligations on a minor bill that, for no apparent reason, had become controversial. Rural Republicans registered heavily against the measure, but it was the negative votes of twelve of the twenty-four Milwaukee County representatives (eleven Democrats and one Republican) that helped to provide the margin of defeat. Thus, ironically, the coup de grace was administered to a metropolitan commission by a coalition of agrarian Republicans and urban area Democrats.

In opposing the Commission's continuance, the Milwaukee County assemblymen—the majority of whom had no strong personal feelings in the matter—were reflecting largely the attitude of municipal officials in their districts. As one of them stated in an interview, "I really can't say what the major problems of local governments are. I have to listen to people who are involved in these matters and in a position to know, such as a mayor or councilman. In this job you have to rely on such people for your opinions on something like this Study Commission." Another legislator who voted for the Commission's continuance explained, "As a legislator I can't possibly know all of the things that we have to work on and consider. On a matter such as the Commission I have to take the word of people like Klotsche, Schoenecker [executive secretary of GMC] and Rasche [MSC member]." It is interesting to note in this connection that five of the six representatives from suburban districts voted against continuance while a majority of the City assemblymen on the negative side were from wards of strong aldermanic critics of the MSC.

The legislature's refusal to extend the Commission's life brought to a close the mid-century crusade for metropolitan governmental reform in the Milwaukee area. Formally inaugurated with the Committee of 21, a product of local officialdom, the movement had proceeded through the Dineen committee, a creature of gubernatorial fiat, to the Metropolitan Study Commission, a locally based but state-established agency. The first ended in complete frustration; the second served a useful function by paving the way for the larger effort; the third concluded its activities with a record of slight tangible success on the one hand and major failures on the other. It is to this record that we now turn.

7

The Metropolitan
Functions Committee
and Its Successors

Public agencies of virtually all types are major targets of interest group activity and pressure. At the local, state, and national levels, special pleaders are engaged in lobbying at every stage of the policy-making process. Because of the pervasiveness of this trait in American political life, those interested in the subject of local governmental reform might assume that officially created metropolitan survey groups would be subjected to much the same kind of activity. Such an assumption, however, has little factual basis, as the experience of the Milwaukee Commission illustrates. At no time during the MSC's life did any outside organization make concerted efforts to exert "behind-the-scenes" pressure on its individual members or standing committees. The groups primarily interested, such as local officials and civic associations, made their views known through statements to the press, at public hearings and various gatherings, through written replies to MSC inquiries, and, at times, through individual Commission members. These efforts were, of course, a form of pressure, but they were disorganized and sporadic and could hardly be likened to interest group activity as we commonly understand the term.

The absence of direct pressures on metropolitan survey groups such as the MSC is not difficult to understand. In the first place, the non-political character of the body makes such attempts less meaningful. A study commission is intended to be a vector of influence which bears upon those who make policy decisions—the public officials or, in the case of referenda, the voters—but it is not a policy-making agency. It can propose and recommend, and in this capacity the commission itself resembles a pressure group. Second, those who might have a stake in the subject matter of the recommendations know that the road from proposal to accomplishment is long and arduous and that there are many points along the way—in the local assemblies, in the legislature, at the ballot box—where they can intervene if necessary. Third, few groups regard metropolitan study commissions as effective allies or formidable threats—in other words, as agencies that can exercise significant influence on public policy or governmental reorganization decisions. Hence they are unwilling to invest anything more than minimal amounts of time and energy in cultivating their support or neutralizing their opposition. Only the civic organizations which back such committees look upon them as meaningful instruments of reform. Finally, interest groups, such as political parties and labor, even if they had a direct stake in the outcome of a proposal, would be ill at ease in lobbying before a body of community notables endowed with the symbols of objectivity and civic virtue. This is not the kind of environment in which they are accustomed to operate. They prefer, if the matter goes that far, to make their influence felt when the issue moves into the political arena.

The subject of interest group activity is pertinent at this point since we are about to examine the role and operations of the MSC's standing committees. Given the large part that the committees played in initiating studies and formulating recommendations— their proposals were adopted by the full Commission in all but a few instances—the impact of external pressures can best be ascertained in the work of these units. The fact that virtually no lobbying type activity was evident in relation to their operations enables us to concentrate on other environmental factors that helped to shape Commission attitudes and policies.

THE WATER DILEMMA

As noted earlier, the metropolitan functions committee was one of three standing committees originally established by the MSC. Its creation grew out of the conviction of some members that all service problems should be assigned to a single unit for study. Such a step, it was hoped, would mute criticism that the Commission was singling out certain problems, particularly water, for specialized treatment. At this early stage in the proceedings, also, most members were uncertain as to what functions should be studied other than perhaps water supply and sewage disposal. As one commissioner stated, "Most of us came into this thing cold. We had a general idea that improvements were called for in the present way of handling services. We were convinced that there was a lot of duplication and waste going; but we didn't have any clear notions as to where or how to go about our job." Because of these factors, the Commission quickly shifted determination of the service-problem agenda to the committee that would be responsible for its execution. This action relieved the full body of a task for which it was unprepared and left the decision in the hands of a small group, where it could be handled with greater dispatch and less fanfare. Such action also assured better and more coordinated control over the range of services to be investigated and the priorities to be assigned them.

The chairman of the functions committee, Willis G. Scholl, was a high ranking executive at Allis Chalmers, the largest industrial employer in the area. A member of the GMC and a recognized economic notable, he had already served an apprenticeship in metropolitan problems and politics as a member of the Dineen committee. In the latter capacity he had the opportunity to observe at close hand the wide gulf between City and suburban officials over such issues as water and tax distribution. When his committee began work early in 1958, few observers doubted that the problem of water supply would be the top item on its agenda. Most commissioners thought similarly; and while none of them had any illusions that an easy solution could be found, they were hopeful of resolving the issue to the satisfaction of both the city of Milwaukee and the suburbs.

Scholl, however, felt that the time was inopportune for the committee to tackle what he considered an extremely delicate issue. He knew that the water problem would confront his group with two diametrically opposed positions, both charged with emotion. On the one hand, Milwaukee officials had made it crystal-clear that they would fight any attempt to remove the waterworks from their control or force the City to serve new municipal customers against its wishes. On the other side, suburban officialdom was equally insistent that the area's water supply system be administered by a non-political authority free from central city domination.* The strong reaction of Milwaukee officials to the Commission's initial emphasis on water had further convinced Scholl that it would be advisable to defer the matter for the time being. Moreover, two important cases relevant to the water issue were pending before the state Public Service Commission: the petition of suburban Wauwatosa for water service from the Milwaukee system and the petition of three north shore municipalities—Whitefish Bay, Fox Point, and Glendale—for authority to construct their own water utility.

In light of these developments, Scholl suggested that the water problem be set aside temporarily and attention turned to other

* The city of Milwaukee at this time furnished water to six suburban municipalities. South Milwaukee and Cudahy operated their own water utilities and several other cities and villages had partial systems that relied on community wells. The remainder of the county was served by individual wells.

functions such as sewage disposal and parks. Reminiscent of the philosophy of the disbanded Committee of 21, he argued that it would be better strategy for the committee to avoid the controversial subjects until it had an opportunity to get its teeth cut on the less difficult questions. This approach was accepted by the members but not without demurral. Foote in particular felt that water was the most important problem facing the Commission and that work on it should not be delayed. Parkinson, however, reflecting the City's position that water should be considered only as part of an overall metropolitan solution, strongly backed Scholl's strategy.

Assured of sufficient support among the committee members, the chairman publicly announced that the water study would be deferred until decisions were made on the Wauwatosa and north shore petitions. That the pending cases did not constitute the underlying reasons for the delay is made clear in a memorandum written at the time by research director Ball in which he summarized the committee's action. Listing the areas chosen for initial investigation—sewers, parks, and protective services—he noted that these functions "are not characterized by the political controversy which is associated with some other services." The committee felt, he stated, that it "would do well to demonstrate its objectivity and study capabilities on these essentially non-controversial services first before beginning work on others."[1]

SEWAGE DISPOSAL

With the water issue temporarily sidetracked the functions committee turned to the matter of sewerage, a problem less fraught with emotional overtones. Sewage disposal was already well established as a metropolitan function in the Milwaukee area. For almost forty years, the interception and treatment of sewage in the City and the older suburban municipalities (except South Milwaukee and Cudahy, which operated their own systems) had been handled by an independent district. In recent years support for enlarging the district to include the entire county had been expressed by many of the local governments; and at the time the Scholl committee began its deliberations, the metropolitan sewerage commission was considering legislation to expand its territorial boundaries.

The committee inaugurated its work by soliciting the views of local governments and other interested parties. Letters were addressed to municipal and county officials, the state health department, the metropolitan sewerage commission, and civic groups, asking for their opinions on extension of the sewer district boundaries and administrative reorganization of the agency. Should the territorial limits of the district include the whole county or should they take in an area beyond? Should the agency be converted into a department of the county government or of a new multi-purpose metropolitan government in the event one came into being? The latter question was prompted by the several attempts made by the county government to secure administrative jurisdiction over the agency. Many county board members resented the fact that they had no control over the district's budget but were obliged to appropriate whatever funds were requested.

The views expressed in the written replies and later reiterated at a public hearing showed that most local units and agencies favored extension of the district boundaries to the county line with service by contract to the adjacent areas. South Milwaukee alone registered strong protest, stating that it would oppose compulsory inclusion in the district. Only a few officials had any comments on the reorganization question. John Doyne, then acting chairman of the county board, stated that in his opinion the sewerage commission should be made a county department, although he saw constitutional impediments to such action. The city of Milwaukee's statement (signed by the mayor, president of the common council, and chairman of the streets and zoning committee) referred to the district as "an example of piecemeal functional consolidation, the fragmentation of government, and the dispersion of governmental functions." Agreeing that the sewer district should be expanded as a matter of public health protection for the area, it asked why the function should "not be assigned to a department of a properly organized single unit of government serving the entire area."[2] Mayor Zeidler later explained that the City decided to reverse its previous stand of opposition "because of the gravity of the sewage problems outside the City."[3]

While these opinions were being collected, the staff proceeded to document the sewerage problems of the area. It was assisted in this task by a sanitary engineer who was temporarily assigned to the Commission by the state health department. On the basis of this study and the views obtained in the poll, the committee formulated and released its findings and recommendations in July 1958. The report followed the usual pattern of survey literature. After outlining the history of the sewerage problem, it presented a dramatic picture of overflowing septic tanks and polluted roadside ditches, water courses, and private wells in the outlying areas of the county. Noting that "a grave threat to public health" existed, it warned that this threat would be magnified in the future as population and industrial growth changed the character of the rural-urban fringe.

Buttressed with these findings, the report recommended extension of the metropolitan district to embrace all of Milwaukee County and the bordering areas in adjacent counties. As to reorganization, it indicated that if and when jurisdiction over other municipal functions in the Milwaukee area was transferred to some form of metropolitan government, the sewerage district should then be integrated with such an agency.

The committee's recommendations were favorably received. Only South Milwaukee demurred to the proposals, reaffirming its intention to fight any attempt to include it in the district. Anxious to win unanimous support from the local governments for its first recommendations, the committee sought to convince South Milwaukee officials that it was to their advantage to join the district. A financial analysis was prepared by the Commission staff which purported to show that substantial savings would accrue to the community if it became part of a metropolitan system. The committee also endeavored to make the recommendations more palatable by specifying that the district would assume the outstanding debts on any municipal system that it took over. (South Milwaukee had a bonded debt of slightly over one million dollars on its sewage treatment facilities at this time.) When South Milwaukee continued to persist in its stand, the committee further amended its recommendations to provide that if a city were not included in the district, it should be required to install secondary treatment facilities within four years. This modification served only to provoke further attacks on the recommendations by South Milwaukee's officialdom and local press. Once again the committee retreated, finally proposing that the state board of health be empowered to set minimum effluent purity standards for municipal sewerage systems that remained out of the metropolitan district—a power that, as the South Milwaukee *Voice Journal* noted, the state board had already possessed for many years.[4]

The hassle had been one that the Commission could easily have avoided. Exclusion of South Milwaukee from the district would have interfered in no way with the extension of sewerage facilities to the remainder of the county; it would merely have violated the concept of a neat, aesthetic organizational arrangement in the form of a single district. South Milwaukee had made its position clear early in the proceedings when its long-time mayor, William P. Atkinson, flatly declared, "A metropolitan district cannot do anything for us that we cannot do better and cheaper."[5] The committee, however, failed to realize the depth of Atkinson's resistance and the fact that no approval would be forthcoming from the community over his objections. Taking its case directly to the people of South Milwaukee by talks before local service and business clubs, the committee sought to convince the public of the advantages to be gained by joining the district. These efforts to go over the heads of local officials and beard the lion in its own den proved completely abortive. The *Voice Journal* continued to attack the recommendations, and the South Milwaukee Junior Chamber of Commerce adopted a resolution supporting the position of the city fathers.[6] Had they been more experienced, the committee members would have realized the close relationship that usually exists in suburban communities between local officialdom and such local institutions as the newspapers and business-oriented groups.

When the prolonged skirmish was finally over, the committee's diluted recommendations were adopted by the full Commission. Shortly thereafter, a bill relating to expansion of the sewerage district was introduced in the legislature. Sponsored by the metropolitan sewerage commission, it provided for enlarging the district boundaries to the county line but giving municipalities the choice of inclusion or exclusion. The MSC, which had been considering the introduction of a similar bill, decided to support the agency measure rather than press for its own recommendations to enlarge the district beyond Milwaukee County. The local units also gave their blessing and the bill was enacted into law after certain minor differences had been compromised. As the chairman of the metropolitan functions committee reported to the Commission, "The legislature and public were presented with the somewhat unusual picture of all governmental bodies in Milwaukee County fighting on the same side for the passage of an important bill."[7] Actually, no fight took place; once consensus was reached locally, passage of the bill in the legislature was a mere formality. Subsequently, all Milwaukee County municipalities except South Milwaukee elected to join the district.

Members of the metropolitan functions committee, as one of them later recalled, "had remained confident, even after the first negative reactions from South Milwaukee officials, that a careful presentation of the facts would win community support for the original proposals." When these expectations did not materialize, the committee began to give ground, feeling that it could still salvage a workable plan to include the reluctant suburb. This strategy, however, was poorly conceived. It should have been evident to committee members by this time that South Milwaukee's support for any sewer recommendations could be obtained only at the price of total surrender on the part of the Commission, and this is ultimately what happened. Once Atkinson and his colleagues had taken the adamant position they did, further argument with them was useless. By sparring publicly with them, the Commission lost all advantage that it may initially have had. Not only did it demonstrate its vulnerability to suburban counterattack, but it also showed that it had few effective weapons for waging the battle.

WATER

While the metropolitan functions committee was engaged in the sewerage study, the Public Service Commission announced its decision in the Wauwatosa water case. Ruling that the City was a public water utility, the Commission held that it was obligated to serve its suburban neighbors. When Milwaukee officials indicated they would not appeal the decision,[8] Scholl announced that he and his colleagues were ready to begin study of the water problem. The committee's first step, at Ball's suggestion, was to authorize a comprehensive historical survey of water supply in the Milwaukee area. A number of members complained that the Commission's function was not to write histories but to examine existing conditions and prescribe ways of correcting them. Ball later said that he proposed the historical study in order to build up a case for removing control of the water system from the jurisdiction of the Milwaukee common council. He was certain, he stated, that such a survey would completely discredit the council's handling of the water problem in the Milwaukee area.

The study was assigned to Charles Beveridge, a young graduate student in history, who was temporarily serving on the MSC staff. The well-written and carefully documented report which he prepared traces in considerable depth the history of the Milwaukee water system from its inception in 1871 to the ruling in the Wauwatosa case in 1958.[9] It shows clearly that the extension of water services to the suburbs was inextricably bound up with the larger problem of metropolitan politics, with the City regarding water as an important weapon for carrying out its annexation policies and deterring industry from settling outside its corporate boundaries. From 1928 until the Wauwatosa order, the City had accepted only one new municipal customer, St. Francis, an action that had been ordered by the Public Service Commission when the City took over territory containing that municipality's source of water supply. The history also demonstrates that conflicts within the waterworks administration and the common council's unwillingness to authorize rate increases and major construction projects widened the gap between supply and the growing demands of the metropolis in the post-World-War-II period. Only after the disastrous summer of 1955 did the City authorize an extensive enlargement of its water system. This expansion has now given it adequate capacity to meet metropolitan needs.[10]

The functions committee stated that the purpose of the Beveridge study was to provide information about the capacity of existing municipal organizations to satisfy the water needs of the metropolitan community. "If, upon reading this history," the committee wrote in a preface to the volume, "the policy maker decides that present institutions and policies have been unable to guarantee the metropolitan community ample supplies of potable water, then he can legitimately ask whether new arrangements might be devised." The history substantiated Ball's prediction that it would place the common council's handling of the water problem in a poor light. Even City officials were compelled to admit that the study "for purposes of information" was "interesting." But, they said, the report is inapplicable since it deals "with the past and not with the present through a failure to recognize the full impact of the progressive changes which have been effected and are being effected."[11] Some of the criticism of the Milwaukee water system in the past was justified, Alderman Matt Schimenz, the City's spokesman at the MSC hearing on the water problem conceded, "but the sins of the fathers are not inherited by the sons. You ought to give us the courtesy of letting us act like a public utility."[12] Only two years before Schimenz had declared that the City's water would go to Wauwatosa over his dead body unless political consolidation of the municipalities took place.[13]

At the December, 1958, meeting of the MSC, the functions committee presented a concise and well-balanced set of conclusions based on the water history. In brief, these were:

(1) the city of Milwaukee has sought to use extension of water service as a weapon to promote political ends and this policy has contributed to city-suburban antagonisms;

(2) suburban municipalities unserved by Milwaukee have been unable to agree among themselves to create an independent metropolitan water system but have continued to wait, with a minimum of addition to their existing supply systems, in the expectation that the City would sooner or later be compelled by the Public Service Commission to serve them;

(3) the City did not cease almost constant challenging of the Public Service Commission's authority to order service extensions to the suburbs until the recent Wauwatosa decision;

(4) more realistic rate schedules are necessary if the City is to extend service on a metropolitan-wide basis without unduly burdening present customers within the City.[14]

Drafting of Recommendations

The committee next addressed inquiries to the various local governments and interested organizations asking them whether (1) a single metropolitan water agency should be established for the area; (2) the city of Milwaukee or a new metropolitan authority should be the agency to handle these functions; and (3) a metropolitan water system should charge differential rates so that distance and transmission costs could be built into the rate structure. Fifteen municipalities, including one in Waukesha County, and several civic organizations responded to the questionnaire. The replies showed little agreement; even the suburbs were unable to present a united front except in their opposition to Milwaukee as the metropolitan supplier.

The City, in a statement prepared by a special committee appointed by the common council, maintained that: (1) it was already supplying water to 83 per cent of the people in Milwaukee County; (2) it had now expressed its willingness to extend services to the remainder of the area; and (3) no need or justification existed for the creation of a new utility.[15] Suburban officials attacked the City's position, charging that "Milwaukee is incapable of nonpolitical management of a utility," but "uses water as an instrument of political blackmail."[16] South Milwaukee, this time joined by Cudahy, declared that it had no intention of giving up its own system although it would have no objection to a metropolitan agency if participation were voluntary. The north shore communities of Glendale, Fox Point, and Whitefish Bay indicated that they would be interested in a metropolitan authority only if their pending application for permission to construct a water utility was denied by the Public Service Commission.

Confronted with these conflicting viewpoints, the functions committee began to struggle with the formulation of recommendations. Some of the members, probably a majority, favored a proposal for an independent metropolitan water district. Parkinson, however, was strongly opposed to any recommendation that would divest the City of its water system without also settling the other major issues such as tax distribution. While these deliberations were taking place, the Public Service Commission ruled that the north shore suburbs were free to establish their own utility. The decision further complicated the task of the committee. If it recommended a single water authority for the area, both central city and suburban opposition—at least that of South Milwaukee, Cudahy, and the three north shore communities—would be aroused. Conversely, a proposal for a metropolitan district that would allow municipalities to exclude themselves would be of doubtful efficacy in view of the number that now would take advantage of this privilege. Hence when the City announced that it would appeal the north shore ruling to the courts, the committee reverted to a tactic that it had used earlier and agreed to table the matter until a judicial determination was made in the case. Scholl by this time had retired from the Commission and the vice-chairman of the committee, Ebner Luetzow, president of a local laundry chain, had stepped up to the chairmanship. Although the delay was attributed to the pending appeal, Luetzow had been convinced by Parkinson that action on the water issue should be forestalled until the Commission had resolved the question of metropolitan government.

When the functions committee reported its decision to the full Commission at the February, 1959, meeting, Lobb vigorously objected to the delay and accused the committee of "ducking the issue." It is "clear to me," he asserted, "that one of the main reasons for creating the Study Commission was to settle the water question. . . . Instead of delaying any recommendation now, it is time for the Commission to take more aggressive action and let the legislature know how we feel about this matter."[17] The executive committee itself had engaged in a game of musical chairs over this question. At its January 28 meeting, with Parkinson absent, it had agreed to support a combined water and sewerage agency. At another meeting two weeks later, with Parkinson present but Lobb absent, it had reversed its stand.

In arguing for temporary deferment of the issue, Parkinson declared that he was against any recommendation that would result in "interim management of Milwaukee's water utility." He maintained further that no permanent proposal could be made until the Public Service Commission determined whether "communities can or cannot pull out at will from the water district." Lobb retorted, "We have been studying the water problem for over a year and people are expecting us to make a recommendation."[18] Lobb was apparently anxious to push the water recommendations at this time in an effort to placate suburban officials who had been aroused by the recently issued metropolitan government questionnaire. According to Ball, the Commission chairman had met with leaders of the League of Suburban Municipalities and had assured them that the MSC would take early action on a metropolitan water district proposal. Lobb foresaw that tying the water issue to the question of metropolitan government would bring the incipient hostility of the now suspicious suburban officials to a head.

Previously the City Club had proposed to the Commission that Milwaukee city retain ownership of its water system and serve as the metropolitan agency, but that management of the utility be removed from control of the common council and vested in a commission. The joint committee now turned to this suggestion, hoping in this way to satisfy the City by making it the metropolitan supplier and to satisfy the suburbs by taking control over water out of the hands of the Milwaukee common council. Only one meeting was necessary to reach agreement on recommendations that (1) the city of Milwaukee be granted a monopoly to provide wholesale water service to the entire county outside those areas not currently served by the utilities of Cudahy and South Milwaukee; and (2) management of the utility be exercised by a board of seven commissioners, five appointed by the Milwaukee mayor with approval of the common council and two by the governor.

Reaction to Proposals

The proposals were formally adopted by the Commission at its March, 1959, meeting and the executive committee was directed to work with the State Legislative Reference Library in drafting the necessary legislation. The only dissent came from Knoebel, the suburban representative, who assailed the recommendations as "a short term political expedient based largely on the shaky and dubious foundation of being least objectionable to the city of Milwaukee." He also declared that it was unfair for the Commission "to interject itself in the dispute between the north shore suburbs and the city of Milwaukee by advocating a water monopoly which would negate the Public Service Commission order."[19]

Mixed reactions greeted the proposals. Only South Milwaukee and Cudahy, the communities explicitly exempted from the recommendations, were completely happy. City of Milwaukee officials received the proposals with reservations but with good grace. They were pleasantly surprised that the Commission favored a monopoly for the City—a position that buttressed their opposition to the creation of a north shore utility—although they did not like the proposal for divesting the common council of control. Glendale, Fox Point, and Whitefish Bay registered strong objections, asserting that they had no intention of abandoning their plans to construct a separate utility. Several municipalities maintained that the plan, although an improvement over existing arrangements, would leave the door open to continued political control by the City. The majority of suburban officials were outspokenly critical, condemning the Commission's proposals as "falling far short of an intelligent, realistic solution of the water problem."[20]

The water issue provided one of the few instances in which suburban governments were unable to present a united front on matters before the MSC. Municipalities such as West Allis and Wauwatosa wanted a metropolitan water authority so that they would be free from dependency on the City for their supply. Although their spokesmen publicly supported the right of the three north shore communities to construct a new utility, they realized that such action weakened the case for an area-wide water agency. Officials in the north shore municipalities, on the other hand, viewed the suggested metropolitan water system as a possible impediment to their plans. In a unique maneuver, attorneys for these suburbs had approached city of Milwaukee officials and informally suggested that their governments would oppose creation of a metropolitan water authority (which the City did not want) if the City would withdraw its opposition in the courts to the new utility. The proposed and somewhat bizarre entente was quickly dropped when Mayor Zeidler and other City officials said they would "have no part" of it.[21]

Reopening the Water Question

The Commission's involvement in the water question did not end with adoption of its recommendations. Several members, particularly Foote, who had actively participated in formulating the proposals, were disturbed over the cool reception given them and convinced that further efforts should be made to generate wider consensus. Foote believed that a stronger case might be established to show that adoption of the recommendations would be mutually advantageous to all parties concerned. The criticisms which he received from some influential north shore residents (who wanted no impediments placed in the way of the proposed utility for that area) alerted him to the fact that there were several unanswered questions about the efficiency of a single operation and the ability of the City's existing and planned facilities to furnish adequate water service within the near future. A north shore spokesman, for example, charged that the MSC had no data to substantiate its contention that metropolitan water service would be cheaper to consumers. Actually, he was correct in his charge since the Commission would have been hard put to produce such data from its files. It had simply proceeded on the assumption that a large utility could provide water more economically than many small utilities. Its research had been limited largely to the water history with only cursory attention to the details of costs and rates.

Foote convinced Cutler, who was then acting as Commission chairman during Houghton's illness, that the water question should be reopened and a new committee formed, bolstered by outside members with technical competency, to re-examine the issue. Prospective non-commission members for such a committee were discussed, and Foote then wrote to them setting out the questions that, in his opinion, required further consideration. He asked those who received the letter to treat it as confidential until formation of the committee was announced. When Mayor Zeidler learned of the letter from one of the recipients, he issued a public statement charging that a committee of the MSC was secretly trying to change the Commission's recommendation for a single water utility operated by the City. Zeidler said that he interpreted the move as an effort to justify the north shore utility and at the same time divest the City of its water system.[22] The plan to appoint a new water committee came at a time when the Commission's relations with the City were at a low ebb. Only a few months earlier the MSC had rejected the Parkinson proposal for a metropolitan government and shortly thereafter its author had resigned from the Commission under circumstances which some City officials construed as evidence that he had been "forced out."* This atmosphere was largely responsible for Zeidler's strong reaction to Foote's letter.

A New Look at the Recommendations

Plans to revive the water committee were quietly dropped after this incident. However, the subsequent court decision in the north shore water utility case again raised the issue in the Commission. In June, 1960, the state supreme court dismissed the City's petition for a review of the Public Service Commission ruling, thereby removing the last legal obstacle in the path of establishing the new utility. With construction of the north shore system now a certainty, sentiment arose among MSC members of taking a new look at the water situation. No action had been taken to implement the

* See above, Chapter Six.

original proposals since their adoption in March of the previous year. The legislative reference library had prepared a bill at the request of the MSC but the matter had been sidetracked by the internal difficulties which struck the Commission. Subsequently, the group discarded its activist role and gave no further consideration to sponsoring legislation.

Part of the impetus for re-examining the water question came from the Greater Milwaukee Committee, which previously had expressed reservations about several aspects of the recommendations. The group's position was set out in a letter to the Commission in November, 1960.[23] It suggested that the MSC proposals be qualified in two respects: (1) that Fox Point, Whitefish Bay, and Glendale be added to South Milwaukee and Cudahy as exceptions to the areas to be served by the Milwaukee water utility; and (2) that instead of a monopoly in the remainder of the county, the City merely be given the right to intervene in future applications filed by other parties to serve municipalities in the area. This latter provision would presumably permit existing suburban utilities, including the new north shore system, to extend their services to additional municipalities with Public Service Commission approval.

The GMC, through its metropolitan problems committee, headed by Edmund Shea, was particularly interested in the water recommendations since it was this problem that had first triggered off the group's efforts to secure a gubernatorially appointed study commission. It therefore wanted to see the MSC adopt a recommendation that it could endorse and promote. Shea saw the north shore utility as a reality; he himself had personally favored it because of his dissatisfaction with City service in that area. Several members of his committee were also known to oppose a monopoly for Milwaukee over the remainder of the county since expansion of the north shore utility into neighboring communities was a future possibility.

Following the north shore ruling, the executive committee concluded that further action on the Commission's part was now in order. As the first step, it decided to hold a series of informal meetings with municipal representatives to discuss the water question in the light of the new developments. This plan, however, never materialized. Efforts to arrange such meetings were delayed for various reasons, and in March, 1961, the committee concluded that it was too late to proceed in this way because of the "likely expiration of the Commission." It agreed instead to hold a public hearing in April on the original recommendations and any suggested alternatives. Letters of invitation were sent to all municipalities in Milwaukee County and the adjacent areas. Of the twenty-three communities invited, only Milwaukee and Wauwatosa sent representatives. The meeting was an obvious disappointment. The almost total lack of interest on the part of municipal officials dispelled any illusions which the Commission may have had—and admittedly by this time it had few—about the possibility of negotiating a satisfactory water settlement.

After the public hearing the executive committee again reviewed the recommendations but could not reach agreement. Three alternative proposals were then submitted to the full Commission: (1) the original recommendation modified by excluding the three north shore communities from the metropolitan service area; (2) a more carefully spelled out expression of the original monopoly proposal; and (3) an anti-monopoly approach similar to that suggested by the GMC, which would permit each of the four existing utilities—Milwaukee, North Shore, Cudahy, and South Milwaukee—to accept municipal customers subject to Public Service Commission rulings. At a meeting attended by only eight members, the Commission unanimously agreed to exclude the north shore communities from the service area. Several members stated that although they disapproved of the establishment of the new utility, "we have to recognize an historical fact." By a vote of five to three the members then accepted the second alternative—a monopoly for the City—with the exclusion clause added. Thus ended the MSC's long and unsuccessful involvement in the water problem.

Events that had occurred since the committee took up the water issue had removed much of the problem's urgency. The decision of Milwaukee officials to abide by the Wauwatosa ruling had given the suburbs access to a metropolitan water supply, while the large expansion program inaugurated by the City guaranteed sufficient water for all in the reasonably near future. In addition, the City's most dissatisfied customers—the north shore suburbs—had begun construction of their own utility and were no longer interested in a metropolitan system. On top of all this, recent summers had been reasonably moderate with ample rainfall, so that only minimal restrictions on water use had been necessary. Thus a problem which excited people four years earlier no longer appeared of any great urgency. The Commission had, in effect, lost a cause.

POLICE SERVICES

With the sewerage study completed in late 1958 and the investigation of the water supply problem well along, the metropolitan functions committee began to consider other items for its future work program. Two areas of inquiry were chosen for investigation: police protection and refuse disposal.[24] Consideration of the first was prompted not by any known public dissatisfaction with the existing system but by the members' feelings that police protection was an important function which ought to be examined. The fact, moreover, that there were fifteen municipal police departments, as well as the sheriff's force in Milwaukee County, was *prima facie* evidence to the committee of inefficiency and duplication. The second topic of study, refuse disposal, had been brought to the committee's attention by the concern which some public officials and civic groups were expressing over disposal practices and the scarcity of sanitary landfills in the county.

The police study got under way in the late spring of 1959 when the Commission retained Robert B. Notestein, a sociology professor at the University of Wisconsin–Milwaukee, to undertake the assignment. Because of the internal difficulties which the MSC was experiencing during this period, operations of the metropolitan functions committee had come to a virtual standstill. Not only had the committee lost the services of its two strongest members, Scholl and Parkinson, but the Commission itself was without a chairman and its research director was embroiled in difficulties with the ruling oligarchy. Because of these developments, Notestein was compelled to conduct his work without benefit of policy direction and with little indication of the kind of study that was wanted.

When the MSC was finally reorganized after its traumatic experiences during the spring and summer of 1959, the metropolitan functions committee was discontinued and two new committees were appointed to take over its work, one on police protection and the other on garbage and refuse disposal. Luetzow, who had been serving as head of the disbanded committee, continued on as chairman of the latter group. A recent appointee to the Commission, Dr. William F. Rasche, was named chairman of the police committee.

The Notestein Report

Notestein's report was not to the liking of the new police committee. What they wanted was simply a study which would survey the facilities, personnel, and operations of each police department in Milwaukee County. They believed that such a tabulation standing alone, without critical interpretation or comment, would make reasonably clear the deficiencies that existed and demonstrate the need for constructive change. Notestein, on the other hand, had approached his task on a much broader basis and had attempted to deal with police administration and law enforcement as a total county problem. This approach required an evaluation of existing police facilities and practices and a determination of their general adequacy. In his report, Notestein pointed out the deficiencies in such areas as recruitment, training, communications, record keeping, and general police coverage. He also noted the individual police departments that deviated from the norm, an inclusion that disturbed the committee members.

Although the report was temperate and fair, the committee felt that the critical evaluations would serve only to arouse the hostility of the suburban police chiefs and destroy any possibility of reform. As one member recalled in a later interview: "When I was appointed to the committee we had an excellent police study [the Notestein report] in the files. It is something I could willingly support on a theoretical basis, but I felt that this is not the way to proceed in Milwaukee. If we had published that report, all the police chiefs in the county and the sheriff would be shooting at us. In Milwaukee you have to work with these people, see their problems, and try to get them to work together. You have to see it from their side."

The Rasche Report

When it became clear that Notestein's report could not be reshaped to suit the desires of the committee, it was discarded and a new study instituted. This time the group's chairman, William F. Rasche, personally undertook the task. Rasche, an energetic and determined man of seventy-one who had retired after a long career of public service, visited every police department in the county (many of them on two or three occasions) and interviewed every police chief. In the process he collected and assembled a vast amount of comparable material on each department including personnel, salaries, facilities and equipment, expenditures, reporting, crime statistics, and number of traffic accidents. The committee's report, or more properly, Rasche's report, released in February, 1961, presented these data in the form of profiles of each department.[25] No attempt was made to evaluate the findings or make comparisons between communities; this task was left to the reader. As the report stated, "Sufficient information is given in each profile to enable the reader to make comparative studies and to place any one of the police departments in its true position in the total group of departments which protect life and property in Wisconsin's most densely populated county." The report indicated that the tabulations were "also prepared to serve as a basis for discussions with police chiefs, fire and police commissions, and other officials in studying the committee's suggestions and recommendations."

In addition to the profiles, the report contained two proposals, both of a relatively minor nature: inauguration of a central uniform reporting service to collect and distribute statistical information on the incidence of crime and accidents occurring in the county; and establishment of a central police records depository. In commenting on the recommendations, the *Journal* referred to them as essential but "too timid." Rasche would have been the first to admit that they were minor, but his contacts with suburban police chiefs had made him acutely aware of their deep resistance to any encroachment on the autonomy of local departments. He was convinced that progress in establishing a better system of law enforcement in Milwaukee County could be accomplished only with the cooperation of police officials in both city and suburbs. As the committee's letter transmitting the report to the full Commission states:

> The committee feels the challenge presented by the rising crime and traffic accident rates can be best met through the coordinated and united efforts of all the police departments, the local governments, and the people of Milwaukee County. It has proposed that this be achieved by voluntary cooperation of the 19 municipalities and that a series of cooperative studies be made by the committee and representatives of the municipalities to develop proposals for strengthening certain "common denominator" services listed in the report. The committee believes these objectives are attainable without sacrifice of the autonomy presently enjoyed by the municipalities and without need of additional legislation.[26]

Rasche was in effect a one-man committee although his group included Mrs. Gordon, Knoebel, and two citizen members. He was greatly disappointed when the legislature refused to prolong the MSC's life. He had extensive plans to study other aspects of the police problem—coordination of communication services was the next project on his agenda—and he felt confident that concrete results could be obtained by working closely with police administrators and encouraging them to support desirables improvements. Rasche was prepared to devote much time and energy to this cause, but he felt that the backing of a quasi-governmental body such as the MSC was needed to give official status to the work and take it out of the realm of private meddling. The demise of the Commission was a blow to him, but it did not deter him from continuing his efforts to secure adoption of the initial proposals made by his committee.

It is difficult to share Rasche's confidence that change could have been effected through the actions of the police chiefs. As heads of individual bureaucracies, small as these may be, each had a vested interest in maintenance of the status quo. The suburban chiefs, while personally friendly to Rasche, gave no indication that they were willing to discuss change seriously. The majority of them took the position that their departments were operating at a high level of efficiency, that cooperation among the various law enforcement agencies in the county already existed, and that placing certain police functions in a central agency, such as the sheriff's office, would be a "foot-in-the-door" to establishment of a single department for the area. Some of them privately admitted that certain changes would be desirable and beneficial, but none of them was willing to take a public stand for fear of antagonizing local political officials. Action by them, even with the gentle prodding of a Rasche, was at most a remote possibility.

Garbage and Refuse Disposal

The waste disposal study was inaugurated shortly after Dr. Goff joined the MSC as research director early in 1959. He defined the objective of the inquiry in these terms: "To examine refuse disposal practices in this metropolitan community and the degree of community satisfaction with the performance of such services, and to probe the practical possibilities of any kind of metropolitan-wide performance of such services." Inquiry was limited to disposal of refuse on the assumption that collection was a local or municipal function.* The research and report writing was done personally by Goff. He received help in data collection and analysis from the City Club's county affairs committee, which had been examining the problem of refuse disposal as one of the items on its current civic agenda. The chairman, Adolph Mandelker, a Milwaukee attorney, and several members of that committee had been appointed to the MCS's garbage and refuse disposal committee as citizen members.

When the first draft of the report was completed, it ran into much the same difficulty that Notestein's police study had experienced. Disagreements between Goff and some commissioners over various aspects of the draft delayed its publication for more than three months. Several members objected to the length of the document (ninety pages), while others felt that it did not contain sufficient evidence on comparative costs of disposal practices in the various communities and in cities outside the area.[27] Goff disagreed with these contentions and took the position that the garbage and refuse disposal committee should accept and release his report as a staff document. The committee would then be free, he said, to make whatever changes it desired before the report became the official statement of the group. This practice, however, had not been followed in the past, and no report, whether staff or other, had been released until the working committee, and in most

---

*Collection practices vary throughout the county with the city of Milwaukee and about one-half the suburban municipalities providing this service while the remainder rely on private collectors. The city of Milwaukee and six suburban communities dispose of garbage by municipally owned incinerators. The others use sanitary landfills, including a county-operated dump, for this purpose. All employ the landfill method for disposal of non-combustible refuse.

cases the executive committee, had tentatively approved its contents.

The argument between the research director and the committee was strictly over procedure and details. The draft contained no recommendations or criticisms of individual governments, and no substantive issues were involved. In fact, the report showed no serious deficiencies in present collection and disposal practices, but emphasized largely future difficulties that would arise from the scarcity of landfill sites. The incident is a minor one but illustrates the internal difficulties that plagued the MSC during the interregnum period. Resolution of the dispute was finally accomplished when Goff agreed to write an abbreviated report highlighting the findings of the study.

In March, 1960, the refuse committee submitted its recommendations to the full Commission. These called for the county government to construct and operate a series of incinerator plants in various parts of the county and to acquire and operate all existing landfill sites in the area. No mention was made of the acquisition of existing incinerators maintained by the City and several suburban municipalities. The committee avoided this question, having no desire to stir up potential opposition by proposing that the county take over existing facilities. Instead, the suggestion was made that as present facilities wear out, the operating municipalities would probably find it more economical to use the county incinerators than to replace their own equipment. As in the case of the police study, the committee's philosophy was to avoid proposals that would be distasteful to local officials, the assumption again being that no change would be accomplished without their cooperation and support.

The garbage and refuse report, like those of the other committees, contained considerable factual information of a general nature together with recommendations based on those data. What none of the reports did—and perhaps this is not the function and certainly not within the resources of the average study commission

—was to develop specific blueprints as to how the proposals could be carried out, including alternative methods and costs. The lack of such blueprints left a broad factual gap between recommendations and their execution by the relevant governmental units. Further studies, some of them costly, would be required before public agencies had anything concrete before them. There is no mechanism in existence, in other words, to perform this intermediate task other than the governmental units themselves. What usually happens in such cases is that the proposals gather dust even though some local officials might be interested in them if more specific information were available.

8
Land Use, Finance, and Cooperation

Among the most pressing problems of the metropolis are those relating to expansion and governmental financing. As urban areas grow in population and territorial size, the need for land use controls to assure orderly development becomes ever more important. At the same time, the mounting service and capital improvement requirements of the total community make increasing demands on the local public agencies that serve the area. Reform advocates have traditionally maintained that only governmental restructuring will bring solutions to these difficulties. Neither orderly land development, they say, nor the mobilization and equitable distribution of local public revenues can be achieved under the existing system of fragmented jurisdiction.

Individual members of the MSC, by virtue of their backgrounds, were cognizant of the importance of these two broad fields of concern. Cutler's legal experience in municipal work, for example, had forcefully brought to this attention the basic importance of coordinated planning and zoning to the development of a metropolitan area. Similarly, Lobb and the businessmen on the Commission were

175

convinced that fiscal problems constituted a key element in the urban picture. It was largely from these individual interests that two of the three original standing committees of the MSC emerged: land use and zoning, and revenue sources and distribution. The later establishment of a committee on intergovernmental relations was an outgrowth of the Commission's disillusionment with the possibility of significant structural reform and the belief that no change, however small, could be accomplished over the objections of local officials.

LAND USE AND ZONING COMMITTEE

The committee on land use and zoning proved to be one of the most active of the MSC sub-groups. Its chairman and principal sponsor, Richard Cutler, was a specialist in municipal law with broad experience in handling zoning and planning matters. As noted earlier, he was an individual of considerable drive and initiative who devoted many hours of his time to Commission work. He personally did much of the research for his committee, drafted most of its many reports and recommendations, and determined its agenda. The statement of jurisdiction which his committee adopted at the inception of its work was ambitious in scope: "To study, in whichever order seems desirable to it, all laws, rules, and governmental and private practices which affect the present and future use of land in Milwaukee County, including but not limited to zoning and related ordinances, transportation, state and local policies, and the extent to which benefited properties pay the full cost of public services and improvements."[1] The matter of implementing this statement was left almost wholly to Cutler's judgment.

Zoning Reform

Although the Cutler committee dealt peripherally with urban renewal legislation for Milwaukee city and also studied the question of municipal boundaries, its main efforts were directed toward planning and zoning administration and the establishment of a regional planning commission. Immediately after its organization, the group began to assemble data on land use and zoning in Milwaukee County. Local governments were tapped for information; private hearings were held with land developers, real estate brokers, planners, builders, and public officials; and the experiences of other metropolitan areas were examined in considerable detail. Dissatisfied with the amount of data available to describe the local situation and with the varying opinions received on the adequacy of the existing system, the committee authorized preparation of a land use and zoning atlas covering Milwaukee County. The intended purpose of the compilation was to provide a clearer picture of the land use pattern in the area and existing deficiencies in it.

Work on the atlas was done under Ball's supervision with additional staff assistance hired for the project. When completed, the colorful and impressive document depicted not only the actual use of land in every block throughout the 239 square miles of Milwaukee County but also the uses permitted under local zoning ordinances. The committee next retained planning consultants to prepare an analysis of the atlas showing the extent to which desirable zoning objectives were or were not being realized in the area.[2]

On the basis of the analysis and information gathered from other sources, the committee concluded that the existing system of zoning administration was not in the best interests of the county. It pointed to what it called substantial evidence of incompatible zoning along municipal boundaries, shortage of suitable land zoned for industry, failure to provide sufficient zoning for low-cost homes, and lack of coordination and even consultation among the nineteen separate zoning authorities in the county. This litany of common zoning offenses was set out in a statement of findings and conclusions adopted by the Commission at its July, 1959, meeting.[3]

Before the July meeting, the land use and zoning committee had presented the atlas and written analysis to a gathering of municipal officials, civic organization representatives, and builders. As it turned out, local officials attending the hearing were less interested in the committee's findings than in attacking a pending bill in the legislature sponsored by the Metropolitan Builders' Association of Greater Milwaukee to transfer zoning and subdivision control to the county government. To most of them the atlas was attractive and useful as any land use map would be, but neither it nor the analysis—which they largely ignored—struck them as particularly significant. The builders' association bill, on the other hand, had real meaning and concern for them. Here was a concrete and specific measure that if enacted into law would divest them of an important power which local governments have jealously guarded. Municipal spokesmen utilized the opportunity to condemn the bill in no uncertain terms and to make known their strong opposition to a county agency with mandatory zoning powers. In doing so they emphasized that no area-wide planning body with other than strictly advisory powers would be acceptable to them under any circumstances. The hearing began and ended on this negative note. (The bill was subsequently killed by the legislature.)

In October, 1959, after further soliciting the opinions of municipal officials on improving zoning administration but receiving few suggestions, the committee issued a carefully drafted report (by Cutler) tentatively recommending the establishment of a metropolitan plan commission.[4] This body would have the responsibility of preparing an "advisory" master plan for the physical development of the county. Municipalities would be required to submit all zoning changes to it for advice. If the local unit refused to follow the advice given, the metropolitan commission could appeal to the county board, where the questioned zoning change could be overruled by a two-thirds vote of the supervisors. In formulating the recommendation, Cutler and the other committee members conceded that any form of centralized zoning control for the county was unattainable. They hoped by their proposal, however, to strike an acceptable compromise between the opposition of local units to loss of their zoning autonomy and the need—which the committee strongly felt—for area-wide land use planning with some teeth in it.

Copies of the report were sent to all local governments and interested agencies in the county, and a public hearing was scheduled on the recommendations. The response was overwhelmingly negative. All nineteen county municipalities were represented at the hearing and all expressed vigorous opposition to the proposals. This display of unanimity found the central city and suburbs on the same side of the issue, although for different reasons. The City contended that centralization of planning should be considered only as part of a consolidation of the whole spectrum of governmental functions, while the suburbs branded the proposed veto power for the county board as a dangerous encroachment on home rule. Spokesmen for the latter declared that they would strongly oppose any plan to take away from local governing bodies full and final control over zoning. At the conclusion of the hearing Cutler commented pointedly that it would have been helpful if more communities had made their views known before the meeting. He noted that his group had solicited their opinions on several occasions, but only a few had bothered to reply. The previous hearing on the land use atlas, however, should have been sufficient to impress the committee with the unyielding attitude of local officials in the matter of zoning powers.

Disappointed by the reception accorded the report, Cutler and his group decided to make a further effort to elicit suggestions on zoning reforms from local officials. Another communication was accordingly addressed to the governmental units asking them to give their *constructive* views on needed changes. This request, like the earlier ones, was largely ignored. Finally, after struggling with alternative proposals and preparing three drafts of a new report, the committee in May, 1960, recommended establishment of a planning department in the county government.* Such a department would have authority to prepare a comprehensive advisory plan for the area but only with respect to county functions such

---

* One of the questions that troubled the members was whether the pending creation of a regional planning commission (see below, p. 180) obviated the need for a planning agency at the county level.

as sewers, parks, and expressways. It would also advise municipalities on land use and zoning problems affecting two or more communities. Eliminated from the recommendations were the mandatory referral and veto provisions of the earlier report.[5]

This watered-down version of the original proposals received general endorsement at a public hearing the following month, with only a handful of municipal representatives in attendance. But even in this modified form, the recommendations were not entirely satisfactory to the cautious-minded attorneys in the League of Suburban Municipalities. In a letter to the committee, the league stated that it approved the recommendations on three conditions: (1) the advice of the county planning department should not be binding on the municipalities; (2) no advice of the county planning department should be admitted as evidence in any court; and (3) no member or employee of the proposed department should be permitted to testify in any legal proceedings regarding the exercise of land use powers, such as zoning, which are delegated by law to municipalities. This nit-picking irked Cutler and his colleagues, who felt that they had already yielded too much ground in their efforts to satisfy local opposition. As they pointed out, the first qualification was already set out in explicit terms in the recommendation, and the other two were improper if not unconstitutional restrictions on the judicial process. The full Commission agreed with this position and adopted the committee's proposals by unanimous vote.

Regional Planning

Efforts of the Cutler committee in behalf of regional planning met a kinder fate. A movement had been afoot for several years to create a planning commission encompassing the seven counties in the southeastern corner of the state. Under a statute enacted in 1955, the governor was empowered to appoint such an agency when petitioned by two or more counties.[6] The City Club of Milwaukee and other supporters who were spearheading the movement had been endeavoring for some time to sell the idea of regional planning to the county boards of supervisors in the area. Several had indicated their receptivity, while others were hostile or reluctant, fearing that such an agency would be dominated by Milwaukee County. Several also objected to certain features of the law, particularly the method of representation, which would result in a commission of approximately 150 members.

At an early meeting of the land use and zoning committee, the members endorsed in principle the creation of a regional planning commission. They were undecided, however, whether corrective legislation should precede or follow its creation and whether its formation should be made mandatory by law. The committee established liaison with the urban problems committee of the Wisconsin Joint Legislative Council,* which was likewise studying possible revision of the regional planning act. It also consulted extensively with local supporters of the movement and representatives of the counties in the area. The City Club warned that any attempt to change the law at this point would only delay if not indefinitely prevent formation of such a commission. For the same reason it opposed any efforts to establish the agency by compulsion. Despite these warnings, Cutler's committee tentatively agreed in July, 1958, to recommend certain changes in the law including provisions that would substantially reduce the number of members and make it mandatory for Milwaukee and the three immediately adjacent counties—Racine, Waukesha, and Ozaukee—to form a regional planning agency.

Before the committee's recommendations were formally presented for Commission action, Governor Thomson informed the MSC that he considered it inadvisable to create a planning body for the southeastern area "until stronger support for such an agency

---

* The council consists of fifteen senators and assemblymen appointed by the legislature to study various governmental problems. The council in turn appoints subcommittees composed of both legislative and public members.

had been manifested."[7] Committee members by this time had also reached the conclusion that compulsory creation would be unwise and that the recommendations should be redrafted to eliminate this feature.[8] In view of the fact that the governor was not ready to act on the establishment of such an agency, the committee with formal Commission approval had the proposed changes to the planning law drafted in bill form. Working with the urban problems committee of the state legislative council, the two groups jointly sponsored a bill in the 1959 session of the legislature. Despite a number of weakening amendments, the measure passed with its main corrective feature—reduction in the size of the planning commission membership from 150 to twenty-one intact. Cutler worked vigorously for the bill, appearing several times before legislative committees.

Shortly after passage of the measure, Democrat Gaylord Nelson succeeded Republican Vernon Thomson as governor. Deeply interested in both state and regional planning, he and his director of resource development, David Carley, personally intervened in the southeastern area. With their active backing, the local supporters of area planning succeeded in persuading the boards of the seven counties to petition for the creation of a regional agency; and in August, 1960, the governor announced the establishment of the Southeastern Wisconsin Regional Planning Commission.

Municipal Boundaries

The third problem area considered by the land use and zoning committee was that of municipal boundaries. At a meeting of the committee in September, 1958, Cutler suggested that it investigate "whether the present boundaries of the nineteen municipal units within the county have any substantial beneficial or adverse effect upon local government."[9] The committee directed Ball to proceed with such a study. Six months later a report prepared by him and Cutler was presented to the group. It contained a strong indictment of the existing boundaries and their irrationality and called attention to some of the service problems which they created. It also pointed out that boundary alterations were virtually impossible to achieve under the cumbersome procedures provided by existing law.

The report was a well-written and interesting document and was intended as the basis for future recommendations. The matter, however, was dropped at this stage as the committee concentrated its attention on land use and zoning and regional planning. After the committee's recommendations for creation of a county planning department were adopted by the Commission in June, 1960, Cutler and his group again took up the question of municipal boundaries. The usual procedure of mailing questionnaires to the local governments was resorted to, and in February, 1961, the committee filed its final report and recommendations.[10] Reiterating the original findings as to the highly irregular character of the boundaries and the cumbersome legal requirements for altering them, it proposed statutory modifications to simplify boundary changes and suggested that county planning departments be authorized to study municipal boundaries and give advice to the local governments on desirable changes. These recommendations, largely of a technical and procedural nature, attracted little notice and aroused no comment. With the adoption of these proposals by the MSC the committee's work came to an end.

During its long tenure, the land use and zoning committee had scrupulously adhered to operating procedures that gave local officials and interested groups full opportunity to express their views before as well as after recommendations were formulated. It had also sought to maintain close contact and work cooperatively with other organizations and agencies in the field, such as the urban problems committee of the state legislative council. Like the other MSC standing committees, it had found local officials strong on resistance but weak on constructive suggestions. The reply that offered a positive contribution to a request for opinions and advice was the rare exception. The common practice of most municipalities after the earlier solicitations was to ignore the Commission's communications; and in instances where they took action, it was usually to express opposition to some indicated proposal.

The land use and zoning committee was by far the most active of the MSC subgroups in seeking implementation of its recommendations. This activity was due to and carried out almost wholly by its chairman. Until the Commission's policy on implementation was changed, Cutler had endeavored on several occasions to transfer his group's proposals from the drawing board to the policy-making arena. This was a time-consuming, frequently misunderstood, and discouraging role, as Cutler well knew, but one which he believed essential to the Commission's success.

REVENUE SOURCES AND DISTRIBUTION COMMITTEE

The committee on revenue sources and distribution operated steadily and consistently throughout the Commission's life. Although staff assistance and outside consultants were utilized, the bulk of the committee's work was performed by its chairman, Robert Jensen. A soft-spoken, reserved, scholarly (Phi Beta Kappa) business executive for a large appraisal firm, Jensen had extensive experience in the field of corporate finance. The substantial volume of work turned out by his committee, including seven major reports, attests to his considerable industry and the many hours he devoted to his assigned task. Unlike Cutler, Jensen had no liking for the role of lobbyist or publicist. He early informed Lobb that he was suited neither by temperament nor desire to play "Barnum," and that if selling the recommendations to the public and policy-making bodies was part of his responsibility as committee chairman, he would prefer that the post be assigned to someone else. These characteristics also caused him to remain aloof from the "politics" and personality difficulties of the Commission and to concentrate his efforts and attention on the work of his committee.

Lobb placed great stock in the revenue sources and distribution committee, so much so that he served as an active member of the group during the early period. His penchant for tax reform, which colored much of his work on the Commission, was reflected in his committee participation. When the question arose at the beginning whether the revenue or distribution side of the coin should be studied first, Lobb urged that the former be given priority. As he remarked in characteristically blunt fashion, "You have to get revenue first before you can distribute it." The question was a delicate one because of the City's insistence that inequalities in revenue distribution lay at the core of the metropolitan problem.

Lobb's view prevailed, and the committee authorized as its first major project a study to show the revenue needs of the area for the next ten years. Since this was a chore that would require substantial time for completion, the committee turned its immediate attention to two lesser revenue studies: property taxation and motor vehicle fees. Jensen and the other members reasoned that these latter projects could be accomplished relatively fast, thereby permitting the group to get some proposals before the policymakers and public while the broader and more time-consuming survey was proceeding. In Jensen's words, they felt that "if they could get one or two minor measures accepted by the governmental units, the status of the group would be enhanced and the way paved for more fundamental changes." Like most study committees, they also felt compelled to generate news as they went along, both to satisfy the newspapers and to arouse public interest.

The committee's first report, "Property Taxation in Milwaukee County," could more properly have been called "property assessment." All of its research findings dealt with the problem of assessment inequities and with weaknesses in the method of selecting assessors. The report and recommendations which emerged from the study were a curious mixture of findings on assessment practices and of value judgments on the existing tax structure. Although no research had been done on real property taxation as such, the committee under Lobb's influence could not refrain from expressing its strong feelings for tax reform. Calling for assessment at uniform and full value, it stated that "major new revenue sources" should accompany any attempt to achieve this desideratum. It noted further that with the imposition of additional revenue measures, "the property tax should be lowered simultaneously to reduce the burden on the home owner and on industry alike."[11] However, no recommendations were made as to new sources of revenue. In explanation, Lobb stated that studies of the revenue structure were currently under way, "which may make it desirable to prepare a package presentation of all the revenue sources and their distribution at one time."

The same situation prevailed in the motor vehicle taxation study, which was released at about the same time. Concluding that automobiles in Milwaukee County required far more in public expenditures than they generated in revenue, the committee predicted that additional taxes on real estate would be required unless new motor vehicle taxes were levied. It recommended an increase in automobile registration fees and enabling legislation to permit counties to levy gasoline taxes. In presenting the report to the Commission, Jensen requested that action on the proposals be deferred "until additional research material is incorporated to permit a more comprehensive report." Nothing further was heard of the recommendations until the increase in auto license fees was again raised in the committee's final report as part of a proposed overall revision of the state and local revenue system.

Committee members had become increasingly aware as their work proceeded that metropolitan fiscal problems are too closely interrelated for piecemeal recommendations. They had also become convinced that the pitfalls of partial recommendations outweighed the publicity advantages which such proposals generated. There was danger, as they sensed, not only that premature proposals might be at variance with the overall solution or package later formulated, but also that such recommendations might arouse needless controversy during the interim period. This latter possibility was brought to their attention when the tentative proposal for a motor vehicle tax became, as Lobb put it, "a political argument by both candidates for governor with neither knowing the facts."[12] After the motor vehicle report in July, 1958, the committee refrained from making any recommendations until the culmination of its work three years later. Although it issued a number of reports during this time, all were limited to findings of fact and general observations.

The "Gap" Study

The Jensen committee had started out with the basic assumption that a critical need for additional local government revenue would arise during the foreseeable future over and above that which existing tax sources would produce. To substantiate this assumption it retained the Bureau of Business and Economic Research at Marquette University to project anticipated expenditures and revenues of local units for the next decade. The Bureau's report, which became known as the "gap" study, was completed in September, 1959. According to its findings, local government expenditures in the area, on the basis of the present pattern, would exceed revenues by at least $84 million by 1970. The report suggested three alternative means of meeting this problem: curtailing expenditures; raising taxes or finding new sources of revenue; and widening the economic base of the area. It concluded with a hortatory statement—of a type seen often in survey reports—that metropolitan Milwaukee "is slipping behind the pace of development of the nation, and unless that trend is reversed by vigorous methods, the financial problems of local government may prove well-nigh insoluble."[13]

The report and its findings drew surprisingly little comment from local officials or the public generally even though they received wide coverage in the metropolitan press. Few seemed excited or perturbed over the prediction of future deficits and increased local taxes—the cry was by now a familiar one—or over the warning of economic stagnation, a warning that the average Milwaukeean found of little import to his relatively comfortable position. Considerably more interest was created some time later when local fiscal experts discovered that in projecting anticipated revenues the authors of the report had overlooked certain items of non-tax income, such as building permit fees, traffic fines, and water department earnings. Inclusion of these items would have narrowed the gap but would not have destroyed the point that the committee was trying to demonstrate, namely, that the present revenue structure would be unable to meet future governmental demands without substantial revision. The inaccuracy, however, received wide publicity and once again placed the Commission in an unfavorable light. One critic, for example, charged that the report grossly misrepresented the local situation, saying, "The notion that the county is slipping behind the pace of national development is sheer tommyrot—the unintended pure semantics of propaganda for tax favors."[14]

When the committee began to investigate the question of new taxing powers to fill the "gap," it found itself confronted with the close interrelationship that exists in Wisconsin between the local and state tax structures.* The importance which shared taxes and state aids play in the revenue pattern of local units made it wholly impractical to study Milwaukee area's fiscal problems without becoming immersed in the state revenue structure as well. This meant that the committee's recommendations would necessarily involve action at the state level—whether it be the raising of new revenue or changes in the distribution formula—that presumably would affect local governments throughout Wisconsin.

To provide a better factual picture of the distribution pattern the committee again retained the Marquette University Bureau to do a study of shared taxes and state aids. The report, completed

* See above, Chapter One.

early in 1960, comprehensively reviewed the entire subject and concluded that "it would be neither just nor practical to scrap completely the present system of state payments in place of a new one." If any major modifications are deemed necessary, the report stated, they "should be effected over a long period of time."[15] This conclusion coincided with the views of most committee members, who considered any major changes in the revenue distribution pattern politically impossible because of strong suburban and outstate opposition. It ran counter, however, to the views of Milwaukee city officials, who regarded such changes as of vital importance.

Formulating the Recommendations

With the preliminary studies out of the way, Jensen and his colleagues turned to the task of preparing a set of recommendations to cover the complex problem of fiscal reform. Most committee members were in substantial agreement that additional revenue would be needed to operate local governments in the coming decade; that the real property tax had reached the point of oppression; that the already high state income tax could bear little increase; and that the personal property tax on business and industry was impeding economic growth. Whether empirically established or not, these premises were taken for granted by most businessmen in the community. Reference to them can be found in numerous speeches and statements made by the area's economic leaders. It is hardly surprising that the revenue sources and distribution committee, composed almost wholly of businessmen, reflected these opinions.

Formulation of the recommendations and writing of the final document were almost wholly the work of Jensen. On the basis of the consensus which existed among most committee members, he drafted a report which proposed a general sales tax of 3 per cent, abolition of personal property taxes on business inventories, increased automobile license fees, and a modified distribution formula for the new revenue to permit reduction in local property taxes. The most controversial item was the first. Businessmen, the Association of Commerce, and leading Republicans had been advocating such a tax for several years, while the Democratic party, labor, and remnants of the old Progressive party stood in opposition.

Only one committee member, Shepard Magidson, the Milwaukee mayor's executive secretary, who had replaced Houghton as the official City representative on the MSC, demurred to the report. While agreeing with the analysis and indictment of existing fiscal arrangements within Milwaukee County, he questioned the remedies proposed. He particularly objected to the sales tax, abolition of the personal property levy on business, and the failure to recommend basic changes in the method of distributing shared taxes. When the report was presented to the full Commission for action, Magidson and Beck, the union representative, offered a series of six amendments to eliminate the "objectionable" features. All of the amendments were defeated by identical votes of nine to three, with Magidson, Beck, and Mrs. Gordon, all Democrats, dissenting. Jensen continued to insist, as he had in the committee, that the recommendations constituted a "package," and that any material change would make the proposals unworkable. Beck and Magidson, in arguing for the amendments, contended that a sales tax and abolition of the personal property tax would be unnecessary if distribution of present funds were handled more equitably. They also maintained that the Commission should make recommendations only for the local area and leave state problems to statewide committees and agencies. (This was a reference to the Continuing Revenue Survey Commission—commonly referred to as the governor's Blue Ribbon tax study committee—which was then in operation.)

Both Beck and Magidson in their opposition to the sales tax reflected the position of the City administration as well as labor and the Democratic party generally. They could muster little support, however, on a commission heavily weighted with businessmen, who, in turn, reflected the support of the business community for such a tax. The outcome was a foregone conclusion. After disposing of the amendments, the MSC adopted the recommendations of the Jensen committee in toto by the same margin of nine to three. This was one of only two instances during the MSC's life in which a committee recommendation failed to receive the unanimous approval of the full Commission; the other was the first water proposal, in which one member dissented.*

In taking on the problem of major tax reform, the Commission had ventured into an area with ideological and political implications, an area quite different from the efficient management, good government preserve of most metropolitan study groups. Consensus is far more difficult to obtain in matters of this nature than in functional and organizational questions, even among dedicated and reasonable members of such commissions. Until Magidson was appointed to the revenue sources and distribution committee in May, 1960, the group consisted of all businessmen and the West Allis comptroller, Irvin Knoebel. Homogeneous in composition and outlook, it was able to avoid the issues that might have provoked controversy in a more diversified group. This homogeneity enabled it to reach agreement quickly and make decisions with dispatch. The final product reflected the businessman's perspective and biases, but it was a product arrived at honestly and conscientiously.

"Blue Ribbon" Tax Committee

Unfortunately for the Commission's stature, much public attention which might otherwise have been focused on the recommendations of the revenue sources and distribution committee had

---

* There were, in fact, only three other occasions on which split voting occurred: a resolution favoring removal of impediments to urban renewal (one commissioner dissenting); a motion for the MSC to go on record in favor of a proposed constitutional amendment to permit taxation of personal property at different rates from real estate (three members opposed); and the three alternative water proposals considered by the Commission in April (three voting negatively).

been diverted to another tax study. Several months after Governor Nelson took office in 1959 he appointed a committee of prominent Wisconsinites to study and recommend changes in the state tax system. Known as the Blue Ribbon tax committee, the group was composed of legislators, businessmen, labor leaders, academicians, and political party officials. Lobb was named a vice chairman of the new committee and thereafter participated only nominally in the work of the MSC.

In December, 1960, the Blue Ribbon committee issued its final report recommending broad revision of the state's revenue and distribution system.[16] Almost simultaneously, the Jensen committee also released its recommendations. The proposals of both committees were strikingly similar in major respects: sales tax levy, elimination of personal property taxes on business inventories, and distribution of a portion of the additional revenue to reduce local real estate taxes. Jensen had kept in touch with the work of the Blue Ribbon committee and was familiar with the direction that its deliberations were taking. It was not so much this fact, however, that produced the similarity in reports as it was the consensus among business interests generally that a sales tax was the key to the state's fiscal problems. Like the MSC, the Blue Ribbon committee, although appointed by a Democratic governor, was weighted with members who were favorably disposed to a sales tax. As events later showed, neither Governor Nelson nor his top advisers were as strongly anti-sales tax as doctrinaire Democrats in the state. They were well aware, of course, that major tax revision without a sales tax was clearly impossible under a Republican dominated legislature—and such revision was a key item in Nelson's program.

Involvement of the MSC with revision of the state tax structure had obviously become less meaningful when the governor established a special committee for this purpose. Since the MSC and the Blue Ribbon committee were both state-appointed bodies, the incongruity of each pursuing the same task was apparent. The new committee, moreover, composed as it was of high-ranking business and professional members together with influential legislators and party leaders who could be directly instrumental in translating proposals into action, naturally overshadowed the local group in public interest and potential impact. The inevitable result was that public attention on fiscal reforms shifted from the local to the state scene. Jensen, however, felt that since his committee was already deeply immersed in the fiscal study, it had no alternative but to proceed.

Legislative Action

Since the question of tax reform was prominently before the legislature at the time the MSC recommendations were made, Jensen felt that the work of his committee should be made available to the lawmakers. At his request the Commission's research director, David Mars, prepared bills embodying the proposals and sought to have them introduced by a suburban Milwaukee assemblyman, Glen Pommerening, a Republican who had been an active member of the governor's Blue Ribbon committee. Pommerening refused to sponsor the bills since he had his own proposals, but he indicated a willingness to introduce them "on request." Jensen, consistent with his negative attitude toward an activist role for the Commission, decided that neither the MSC nor his committee should sponsor the bills. It was finally decided that Pommerening would introduce the measure "at the request" of Knoebel and Alfred Kliebhan, a savings and loan executive, who were members of the revenue sources and distribution committee but who in this instance would be acting as private individuals and not as official MSC representatives. Jensen's concern was merely to get the proposals in the legislative hopper, where, hopefully, some of their features would attract the support of those working on the tax problem.

Major tax reform ultimately came to Wisconsin in the closing days of 1961, but in the long legislative-executive struggle the earlier revision packages, including proposals by Governor Nelson, the Blue Ribbon committee, and the MSC, were virtually forgotten. Some features of the various plans were incorporated in greatly modified form in the bill finally passed.* How much, if anything, each of the plans contributed to the new tax structure of Wisconsin would be difficult to assess. That the "sponsorless" MSC recommendations received less attention than the others is generally acknowledged. All the proposals helped in one fashion or another to generate public interest in the tax problem, but basically it was the political situation that determined the final product.

COMMITTEE ON INTERGOVERNMENTAL COOPERATION

The committee on intergovernmental cooperation was a latecomer to the MSC scene, and in many ways it was a reflection of the changed attitude on the part of Commission members. By the time of its establishment in December, 1959, most reorganization proposals offered by the group had met discouraging rebuffs. Only one approach to the area's problems—that of voluntary cooperation among local units—remained unexplored. At the beginning, most Commission members would have placed little stock in this device as an effective instrument of metropolitan reform. Now, as the last resort, they turned to it in hopes of stimulating some activity on the local scene, even if minor in nature and scope.

Klotsche's preliminary review of the program and accomplishments of the Commission at the time he assumed the chairmanship convinced him of the need to examine the whole area of

* The tax bill enacted by the 1961 Republican controlled legislature and signed by a Democratic governor provided for a selective sales tax of 3 per cent on a limited number of items; a 50 per cent reduction in the personal property tax on merchants', manufacturers', and farmers' inventories; a small increase in income tax rates; and a return of a portion of the sales tax to local units for general property tax relief. An income tax withholding provision was also adopted as part of the "package deal."

voluntary cooperation. Calling attention to that portion of the statute which directed the MSC "to investigate the extent to which cooperative agreements or procedures have been established among units of government," he suggested that the Commission place major emphasis on this task during the remainder of its term, a suggestion readily concurred in by the membership. In December, 1959, Klotsche announced the appointment of a committee on intergovernmental cooperation to study the utilization of co-operative agreements by governments in Milwaukee County and to recommend ways and means of encouraging further inter-local cooperation.

The Committee's Approach

To head the committee Klotsche turned to Clifford Randall, a prominent Milwaukee attorney and a past president of the Greater Milwaukee Committee. Randall was an ideal choice for the task. A conciliator by nature, he had insisted from the beginning that the Commission proceed cautiously with its recommendations and consult fully with public officials and interested parties. Shortly after his appointment to the MSC in 1957 he had been elected president of Rotary International; and his duties in this capacity had taken him away from Milwaukee during most of the Commission's initial and interregnum periods. His participation and influence had consequently been minimal up to the fall of 1959. Had he been active from the beginning, he undoubtedly would have played an important role along with Lobb, Cutler, and Parkinson during the formative and transitional stages.

The committee, which consisted of two other commissioners and five non-commission members, operated in methodical fashion. It conducted a series of conferences with local officials and administrators, seeking not only to elicit their views but also to involve them in the formulation of recommendations. It engaged the Citizens' Governmental Research Bureau to undertake its fact-finding, including a detailed compilation of all voluntary agreements and procedures then in effect among the local units. Summaries of this list were then sent to public officials in advance of the meetings with them. The committee operated on the assumption that by stressing the positive accomplishments of intergovernmental cooperation in Milwaukee County rather than its failures a more favorable climate might be created among the local units for further action. Although hard pressed to find more than a few examples of significant agreements in operation,* the committee in its inventory of existing arrangements and its statements about the receptivity of public officials to cooperative devices painted a far more optimistic picture than the facts actually warranted.

During the course of its operations, the Randall committee met with library trustees, municipal attorneys, fire chiefs, and health officers. Local officials and administrators took part willingly in these conferences but gave no indication that they were ready to embark on any meaningful program of cooperation. In fact, the majority of them placed far more emphasis on how well problems were currently being handled than on the need for further cooperative arrangements.

As the committee proceeded with the study, it came to view its role as that of a catalytic agent to promote or accelerate action among those responsible for the administration of local public services. Randall struck this note when he said: "The natural desire for cooperation which the Commission found in all of the public officials in the Metropolitan Milwaukee area is stimulated and becomes a force rather than a state of mind when there is some outside catalytic agent at work."[17] By way of example he pointed to the formation of the library trustees' council of Milwaukee, a voluntary organization composed of representatives of the various library boards, which was suggested by and came into being as a result of the committee's efforts. Randall noted that his committee had actually convened the first meeting of the group and had

* See above, Chapter Three.

assisted in preparing an agenda and a tentative plan for a permanent organization. He also cited the recent agreement of the Milwaukee fire department to open its training facilities to suburban departments on a cost basis as another instance of cooperation that had resulted from discussions between the committee and the fire chiefs of the county.

The committee considered studying cooperative possibilities in a broad range of functional areas, such as purchasing, civil defense, the non-academic aspects of school administration, and public health; but lack of time and resources forced them to restrict their agenda. In the end they concentrated on the legal impediments to intergovernmental cooperation and on library and fire protection arrangements. Serving as a "catalytic agent," they found, was a time-consuming task with heavy demands. They soon decided that the most the committee could hope to accomplish was to experiment with the technique in a few functional areas and make suggestions for future action.

Findings and Recommendations

Randall and his group concluded that there were six major obstacles which discouraged or prevented greater use of cooperative devices in Milwaukee County: (1) legal uncertainty resulting from inadequate laws; (2) lack of communication between governments; (3) historic antagonisms between City and suburbs; (4) lack of public understanding and enthusiasm for joint municipal action except in emergency situations; (5) lack of initiative on the part of public officials; and (6) increasing competition for industrial development among local units. Although the committee stressed the first of these, it is quite evident that the other five obstacles are of far greater significance in explaining the relative lack of intergovernmental cooperation. Unwillingness or lack of interest, not legal impediments, is responsible for the low usage level of cooperative devices in metropolitan Milwaukee. If the local units were seriously interested in joint undertakings, they would have little difficulty in finding statutory authorization; for, as the committee noted, there are some sixty sections in the Wisconsin statutes dealing with this subject.

The Randall committee's foray into the field of intergovernmental relations convinced them of the potential value of further studies involving possible areas of cooperation—studies that would not merely suggest joint administration of a service or function but would also work out the details and mechanics of handling it. More importantly, the experience also convinced them that research of this "catalytic" type should be conducted under the aegis of the local governments themselves through survey committees appointed jointly by two or more units or by an intergovernmental council of local public officials. In this way, those responsible for putting the recommendations into effect would have a hand in their development.

The committee's final report made no effort to propose specific functions that might be undertaken jointly by the local units other than to review previous MSC proposals involving this question. It outlined the obstacles to progress in achieving greater cooperation, pointed up the need for better communication among high-ranking local officials, and concluded with five recommendations:

(1) statutory changes to clarify the authority of local units and the county government to enter cooperative agreements for services;

(2) a constitutional amendment establishing home rule powers for Milwaukee County to eliminate all doubt about the county's power to participate fully in cooperative arrangements;

(3) statutory authorization for counties and groups of local units to create joint survey and study committees;

(4) holding of regular meetings of existing intergovernmental organizations of public officials;

(5) formation of a permanent intergovernmental cooperation

advisory council consisting of the county executive, the heads of each city and village in the county, and the chairmen of standing committees on intergovernmental cooperation appointed by the governing council of each local unit.

These proposals were adopted by the full Commission without dissent. They received the usual broad coverage in the metropolitan dailies, but were ignored by the suburban papers. Public officials in both City and suburbs viewed them with little comment. Steps toward creating the mechanism which the committee hoped would serve as a continuing catalytic agent—an intergovernmental cooperation council—had already been taken before the MSC recommendations were made. For the most part, the efforts of Randall and his colleagues to "educate" and "stimulate" the local officials had produced few tangible results.

THE COMMISSION'S LEGACY

The philosophy and general approach of the Randall committee provided the basis for the MSC's final report. Early in 1961 Commission members revived the question of an overall recommendation on governmental structure. Many of them were of the opinion that the group had an obligation to make some sort of statement or proposal in this regard before disbanding. Since extension of the MSC's life appeared in doubt, they considered it advisable to prepare a report for release in June, 1961. Such a document, they felt, should outline the Commission's views on the future path to be followed by the community in its quest for an adequate metropolitan political system. If the MSC's life were terminated, the report could stand as the group's final legacy; and if the continuance were granted the statement could provide the framework and philosophy for a future work program.

There was general accord on the issuance of such a report but some disagreement as to its nature. Several commissioners argued that the group should "stop worrying about public sentiment and feasibility" at this late point and base its final recommendations on what "it considered to be the future public interest of the area." Those who took this position were not sanguine about the prospects of accomplishing any major changes but were disgusted with the attitude of local public officials and the apathy of the general citizen body. They felt that a strong statement might possibly awaken the public out of its lethargy. Others maintained that the Commission had to face the realities of the situation and make recommendations that ultimately would have some chance of acceptance. They pointed out that if its tenure were extended, it might find itself embarrassed in its future work by a strongly worded and far-reaching statement. The issue was resolved after Klotsche suggested that the proposed report, whether it be the MSC's final act or not, be built around the intergovernmental co-operation committee's anticipated recommendation calling for a larger role by the county government.

For some time before this discussion, the Commission had given indications of its receptivity to the county government as the area-wide agency. As research director Mars noted in the summer of 1960, when asked to give his views on the general approach to governmental change in the Milwaukee area: "I think an outsider reviewing our studies would be entitled to draw the conclusion that the Commission has already adopted the urban county approach. This appears very definitely in our recommendations on land use planning, refuse disposal and sewerage, and a little less definitely in our recommendations on water supply."[18] Since Klotsche's suggestion gave direction to what was evolving in the minds of most commissioners, it was readily accepted. By this time the members were only too glad to get the formality concluded.

The final report, drafted by Mars to embody this approach, contains an excellent statement of the Commission's final views. It begins by analyzing "the basic causes" of the difficulties faced by local governments in metropolitan Milwaukee: population growth, increasing automobile ownership, rise in governmental expenditures at a faster rate than disposable income, fragmentation of political power despite growing interdependence of the metropolitan community, and public apathy. It briefly summarizes the history of functional consolidation in the local area, noting that the transfer of services to the county government "is hardly a new or an untried technique," as exemplified by smoke control and the expressway system.[19] Apropos to this observation, it points out that "in most instances where a particular governmental function has reached the stage where it can no longer be handled adequately or effectively by small local units, that function has been transferred to the county government." It further notes that these transfers reflect a national trend which has witnessed the emergence of an entity known variously as the "urban county" or "metropolitan county."

The Commission's report defines the urban county approach to metropolitan problems as "the gradual or the rapid acquisition by the county of municipal-type functions." Acknowledging that the general ineffectiveness of American counties as administrative units has impeded their use as metropolitan vehicles, it cites the modernization of the Milwaukee County government in recent years and concludes:

Since the administrative structure of Milwaukee County is one which can accommodate the transfer to it of new functions of government, and since there is presently some parallel between the area of Milwaukee County and the logical area for furnishing certain governmental services, and since the people of the metropolitan Milwaukee area do not seem to be ready for any type of drastic structural reforms in government, the Metropolitan Study Commission recommends the urban county approach for Milwaukee County and further recommends that in all cases where a local governmental function in Milwaukee County is transferred in the foreseeable future, that such function be transferred to the government of Milwaukee County, unless it is transferred to the government of the State of Wisconsin.[20]

After thus committing itself to the urban county approach, the MSC left unanswered the question of what specific responsibilities should be handled on an area-wide basis. Instead it merely recommended that the legislature establish a procedure for the initiation and transfer of functions to the county government. In this way it hoped to establish the principle without subjecting it to the conflict that specific proposals would generate.

This last testament of the study group is conciliatory and moderate in tone. It makes no attempt to castigate local officials for their opposition to metropolitan reform, although it calls on them "to adopt a more positive approach to area-wide problems and to move forward cooperatively to try to solve them." The theme—intergovernmental cooperation—whether by contract or the transfer of functions to the county, predominates throughout the report. Commission members had obviously become convinced that if reform were to occur in the foreseeable future, it would have to take place within the existing framework of local government and with the assistance of public officials—an assistance unlikely to be forthcoming except in crisis situations, if past experience is any indication. On this note, another chapter in Milwaukee's long quest for metropolitan reorganization came to an end.

9
Images of the Commission

The term "image" has become common in American usage, thanks largely to Vance Packard, Madison Avenue, and a public-relations conscious elite. From the giant corporation to the ward politician, all who deal with the public in one capacity or another are concerned about the image they project. How do they appear to the public? What kind of impact are they making? What can they do to create a better picture of themselves in the popular eye? Regardless of their goal, whether the making of profits or election to public office, they are convinced—and not without reason—that a favorable image contributes to their success while an unfavorable one impedes it.

Metropolitan survey commissions, like other public and private agencies, are image creators. As actors in the public arena, they wittingly or unwittingly create impressions of themselves among the citizen body. These impressions may differ widely among their audiences and they may also change over time. To some, a study commission may appear as the tool of big business, to others as the handmaiden of politicians, and to still others as a dedicated body of able men seeking to rout out waste and inefficiency in government. Some will regard it with respect; others with hostility or amusement; while most will simply ignore it.

We have already observed how a sample of community leaders and other citizens in Milwaukee County regard metropolitan problems and the factors impeding or promoting greater area-wide integration.* Here we are principally interested in the attitudes of the same individuals toward the Metropolitan Study Commission, its work, its final recommendations, and its proposed continuance. We are also interested in the possible impact that the Commission had on the thinking of community leadership with respect to metropolitan government.

ATTITUDES TOWARD MSC

As explained in Appendix B, extensive interviews were conducted in the fall of 1959 with a sample of eighty community influentials, including public officials, business and labor leaders, and organizational representatives. Fifty of these respondents were subsequently reinterviewed during the summer of 1961. In both instances the interviewees were asked a series of questions relating to their impressions of the Commission and the functions it was performing. On the basis of the responses, "images" of the MSC can be grouped into four broad categories: very favorable, favorable, neutral, and unfavorable. As defined here, a respondent's impression is very favorable if he views the Commission as a highly prestigious and necessary agency that has performed its task well and served an important function. It is favorable if he recognizes its high character, usefulness, and good work but is critical of certain aspects of its performance. It is neutral if he has little interest in the Commission or no definite opinion about its usefulness. It is unfavorable if he regards it as biased, unnecessary, or lacking in competency.

* See above, Chapter Four.

As indicated in Table 9, 70 per cent of the respondents in the first round of interviews viewed the Study Commission either very favorably or favorably and only 9 per cent, mostly public officials,

TABLE 9

Attitudes Toward Study Commission (First Interview)

Occupational Category	% Very Favorable	% Favorable	% Neutral	% Unfavorable
Businessmen	61	26	9	4
Professional	40	40	20	—
Elected public officials	—	38	19	43
Appointed public officials	—	70	30	—
Social welfare administrators	12	25	63	—
Organizational secretaries	57	43	—	—
Labor leaders	60	—	40	—
Educators	67	33	—	—
Total (N = 80)	35	35	21	9

unfavorably. By the time of the second interview, the proportion regarding it with favor had dropped to 64 per cent while the percentages with unfavorable impressions had increased to 16. (See Table 10.) In both instances, one out of five expressed little

TABLE 10

Attitudes Toward Study Commission (Second Interview)

Occupational Category	% Very Favorable	% Favorable	% Neutral	% Unfavorable
Businessmen	44	44	12	—
Professional	20	60	20	—
Elected public officials	9	18	9	64
Appointed public officials	—	50	25	25
Social welfare administrators	—	25	75	—
Organizational secretaries	60	20	20	—
Labor leaders	50	—	50	—
Educators	67	33	—	—
Total (N = 50)	30	34	20	16

interest in the Commission or had no opinion of its usefulness.* Of those who were reinterviewed, 28 per cent showed some modification in their attitude, all toward a less favorable view. Most of these were business and professional leaders who had expected more activity to result from the Commission's work. Their disappointment was reflected in a change from "very favorable" to "favorable." The remainder were elected and appointed public officials who by this time were convinced that they had little to fear or to expect from the MSC, and who therefore felt free to express their outright disapproval.

Private Community Leaders

Some of the attitudinal shift of private community leaders is attributable to changes in their views about the role of a citizen commission. In the first round of interviews a substantial minority stated that the MSC should concentrate its efforts on research and recommendation and that the action phase should be left to other civic groups. Those who took this position maintained that the Commission would dissipate its energies if it assumed an activist role; and more importantly, that it would become involved in political maneuvering and thereby alienate itself from local public officials. In the second interview, a number of those who originally held non-activist views now expressed the feeling that the group "should have 'worn two hats': research and salesmanship," with accent on the latter. The fact that civic organizations displayed little, if any, initiative in taking up and promoting the recommendations while public officials evidenced no sign of even considering them contributed to this modification of opinion.

Business and professional men in general looked upon the MSC

---

* Greater differences would undoubtedly have been found if the first round of interviews had been conducted shortly after the MSC came into existence. As stated previously, the present study was not initiated until after the Commission had been in operation for almost two years and the most dramatic and active phase of its tenure had passed.

as a potentially significant instrumentality for stimulating governmental changes, particularly those which would lead to efficient and economical operation. They had no complaint about the Commission's research program or objectives; they were simply disappointed in its failure to achieve more tangible results. Respondents in the social welfare field, while not unfavorably disposed toward the MSC, believed from the beginning that it could accomplish little. They also felt that it had avoided some of the major issues facing the community, such as housing for lower income groups, racial discrimination, and acculturation of inmigrants. Organizational secretaries and educators were more sanguine about the Commission's work, pointing out that it had served a useful function by focusing attention on the problems of the area and providing factual data on which other groups could act. Labor leaders viewed it with considerable skepticism, although several of them spoke favorably of the Commission despite what they called its "blue ribbon aspects." The attitude of respondents other than those in the business and professional categories remained virtually unchanged during the period between the two sets of interviews.

Public Officials

The attitude of public officeholders toward the MSC underwent several modifications during the course of the agency's life. Originally, when the Commission was created, those from the city of Milwaukee viewed it with considerable hostility while suburban officialdom, although somewhat suspicious, considered it a potential ally in their battle for City water. When it became evident in late 1958 that the MSC had far broader objectives than the establishment of a metropolitan water agency, the uneasy friendliness of suburban officials changed to direct opposition. At the same time, central city officials began to regard the group more favorably. Recalling these impressions, a Milwaukee official stated, "At first I was strongly opposed to the Commission, looking upon it as part of a scheme to take control of the water system from the City, but my opinion later changed when it appeared that a metropolitan government plan was receiving serious consideration."

By the time of the first interviews in the fall of 1959, both City and suburban officeholders had come to regard the Commission with disfavor, although for opposite reasons. The former had reverted to their original position of hostility after Parkinson's resignation, again charging that the MSC over-represented the outlying areas and was suburban-oriented in its thinking. The latter continued to insist that the group was a threat to municipal autonomy. Typical of the remarks in the first interviews were: "We don't need it"; "It serves no useful purpose"; "These businessmen don't have the background to deal with these matters"; and "I wouldn't be disturbed if they abolished it tomorrow." An even more critical tone prevailed in the second round of interviews: "It was a waste of money"; "Municipal officials haven't the time to bother with all these people and their reports"; "I'm glad it's dead"; and "I can't see the value of spending money to come up with what we already know." One suburban official who had attended a Commission meeting described what he heard as "a lot of theoretical junk." Even those who had originally adopted a "wait and see what it does" attitude expressed dissatisfaction in the second interview. Most in the latter category had been basically suspicious of the Commission in the first place, and when they talked about waiting they meant waiting to see whether the MSC would place its stamp of approval on their own positions.

A small minority of elective municipal officials—mostly in the wealthy north shore suburbs—although not enthusiastic about the Commission, felt that it had served a useful purpose in drawing attention to area problems and relieving City-suburban tensions. Those who took this position in the second interview had expressed similar sentiments in the first. Few professional administrators in top-level appointive positions, such as city managers, showed any hostility to the MSC and its work, but most of them were skeptical that it could accomplish anything. As one of them remarked, "I felt from the start that it would be ineffective because of widespread opposition to change among local political leaders."

Only in the case of county government officials was the MSC successful in converting an unfavorable or neutral attitude to one of favor. The reason for this change is not difficult to understand since the county was the chief beneficiary of the group's recommendations. Although not overtly hostile to the Commission at the beginning, county officials were unfavorably disposed toward it. At the time of the first interview they were still expressing skepticism about its operations and intentions. Their doubts were dispelled, however, during the succeeding period as the MSC's sympathy for the urban county approach became more evident. As one county official observed in the second interview, "During the four years of its existence the commission changed from an obvious dedication to the establishment of a new level of government to emphasis on voluntary cooperation and use of the county government as the metropolitan vehicle." Another felt that its "work and recommendations would provide something of a blueprint for future action in enlarging the county government's metropolitan role."

The interviews indicate generally that public officials became less concerned with the MSC and its work as time passed. At first they were uncertain as to what effect such a prominent group might have on public opinion or, for that matter, on the governor and state legislature. Later, when it became apparent that it was having little impact on either grass roots thinking or the legislature, local officials tended to pay less attention to its work and even to ignore it. Several remarked that the suburbs lost interest in the Commission when the water issue was settled, while City officials saw little utility in it after the metropolitan government plan was dropped. Most officials felt that the Commission had lost its potential effectiveness by the end of the first two-year period. In the words of one, "We weren't sure in the beginning as to what a group of this kind might do to us. This was the first time something like this was thrown at us. We didn't think they had much pull, but you can never be too certain about things like this. Suppose they did stir up the public about waste and duplication and all this other stuff you hear from the good government boys. Or suppose they did get to the legislature. When we saw how they operated, however, and how politically naive they were, we knew we didn't have much to worry about."

Summary of Attitudes

In evaluating the MSC, respondents commented with favor most frequently on (1) the high quality of the research; (2) the dedication and fairness of its members; (3) its usefulness in pointing up metropolitan problems; (4) its value as an unbiased forum for articulating the needs of the area; and (5) its role in easing City-suburban tensions by elevating discussion of the issues from the level of political acrimony to that of rational consideration. Despite these favorable impressions only a small minority viewed the Commission at the end as a significant instrument of metropolitan reform.

The most common criticism of the study group, one voiced by almost 50 per cent of the respondents, was directed at its failure to play a more active role in selling the recommendations to the citizenry and public officials. Yet many of those who made this complaint admitted that the Commission was underfinanced and understaffed and therefore badly handicapped in what it could do. A second criticism, expressed by approximately one out of four interviewees, alleged that the MSC had "spread itself thin" by undertaking too broad a range of studies. Those who held this opinion felt that more in the way of action might have been stimulated had the group concentrated its attention and resources on fewer problems. Several who took this position complained of the Commission's failure to give reformist groups a "saleable" product. They suggested that it should have provided a "package deal" or *quid pro quo* arrangement whereby the gains or losses of both central city and suburbs would be balanced. A third negative impression, found principally among businessmen and civic organizational leaders, was that the MSC had been "too easily swayed" by the objections of public officials and had as a result "watered down" its recommendations to the point where they were innocuous and incapable of arousing any enthusiasm. While these and other criticisms occurred throughout the interviews, the feeling prevailed that the Commission had done "about as much as could be expected under the circumstances."

The interview findings substantiate at least one assumption commonly held about the efficacy of metropolitan survey groups: their almost total lack of impact on local officeholders. Attitudes of public officials toward the MSC did change during the course of its existence. These changes, however, are based almost wholly on respondents' expectations as to what the Commission might do; they do not reveal the agency as an educative force. In fact, the 1959 and 1961 interview comparisons are most significant as a measure of the Commission's inability to "educate" local officials or alter their perceptions of metropolitan affairs and issues. Thus, for example, the attitude of City officials changed from hostility to friendliness when the MSC headed toward a metropolitan government recommendation to which they were favorable; it reverted to hostility when this approach was dropped. No one was converted in the process by the findings and logic of the Commission.

ATTITUDES TOWARD RECOMMENDATIONS

When respondents were asked to give their reactions to the recommendations contained in the Study Commission's final report, the replies were generally favorable. Few took issue with the proposal for greater voluntary cooperation among the local governments, but one remarked, "Everyone favors cooperation—it is sort of like being for God and motherhood." Most respondents, while endorsing intergovernmental cooperation in principle, saw little prospect of any significant development along these lines.

"How are you going to get these officials to agree on anything?" was a common observation. The abortive experience of the Committee of 21 was referred to on several occasions to emphasize this point. One interviewee remarked that the cooperation proposal was meaningless since "suburban officials, particularly the lawyers, have built their political fortunes on central city-suburban conflict." A few administrative officials saw the possibility of increased cooperation among small groups of municipalities in such matters as purchasing, use of equipment, recreational programs, and refuse disposal. Most suburban elective officials admitted the desirability of more cooperation among local units but stated that this would be forthcoming "whenever a real need arises."

The urban county approach suggested by the MSC appeared to the respondents more realistic than voluntary cooperation. Only the elective officials in the central city and suburban municipalities demurred—the former because the proposal did not encompass complete consolidation; the latter because they saw an implied threat to local autonomy in an aggrandizement of the county government's role.[1] Those who favored the urban county recommendation observed that the county is the logical base on which to build a metropolitan government, particularly since such an approach eliminates the need for a new layer of government. Some central city respondents (private community leaders) stated that while they preferred a more drastic solution, functional consolidation of area-wide services at the county level was the most that could be expected. Suburban respondents, other than public officials, viewed the recommendation as sound and acceptable. Consolidating certain functions at the county level in the interest of better and more efficient administration made good sense to them as businessmen or professionals closely related to business.

Attitude Change

The views relating to recommendations provide an interesting case of attitude formation or change on the part of respondents.

In the initial interviews less than 10 per cent of the non-public officials had any definite notions as to the form that reorganization should take. The usual response was: "We need some type of metropolitan government"; or "Some consolidation of services would be desirable." Even central city residents who favored political integration as the ideal solution but acknowledged its unfeasibility had no specific alternative in mind. In the second round of interviews, the responses (again excepting those of public officials) followed an entirely different pattern with a high degree of unanimity on type of approach replacing uncertain and scattered views. The urban county recommendation had obviously helped to crystallize the thinking of many respondents and channel their attention to a common, if broadly defined, goal. The way had also been eased for general acceptance of the proposal by the favorable impression that the new county executive, John Doyne, had made since his election in April, 1960.

If nothing else, the interviews reveal that respect for county government in Milwaukee is on the increase among business and civic leaders, and presumably the general public. They also indicate that suburban officeholders are viewing this development with some uneasiness. With the central city effectively neutralized by loss of its annexation and water weapons, suburban officials may well transfer their hostility to the new "enemy." Some of them, in fact, are already beginning to look upon the county rather than the City government as the real threat to local autonomy or, more properly, to the vested interests of suburban officialdom. Growing resistance to enlargement of county powers is a likely consequence.*

The urban county approach offered nothing that was new or unknown to the Milwaukee area; in fact, it had been widely dis-

* Indications of increasing suburban hostility to the county government have already appeared. For example, in early 1963 the Wauwatosa common council adopted a report which charged that the county was attempting "to cripple local government."

cussed and to some extent followed in recent decades. But other solutions had also been mulled over and considered by reformist groups without any agreement on a common approach. At least for the civic elite, the recommendations now appear to have ended debate and uncertainty over possible remedies and determined the general direction that ideally should be followed. With what vigor, if any, this approach will be pursued is quite another matter. Certainly the interviews (and events since then) give no indication that community influentials are growing anxious or ready to take up the battle for metropolitan governmental reform with any degree of urgency or seriousness. If anything, they disclose a lessening of interest and concern.

Impact of Proposals

When queried about the impact of the recommendations on the citizen body, few respondents expressed any optimism. Most of them felt that the proposals had passed unnoticed by the general public ("The people don't give a hoot in hell about them") despite the widespread coverage given by the metropolitan press. In the earlier interviews, they had expressed some hope that the Commission's findings might awaken the community to the need for governmental change. By the time of the second interview, the majority of them were convinced that nothing short of catastrophe would accomplish this result. In the words of one respondent, "Trying to arouse the electorate over something like this is impossible. Unless we can get public officials to act, we may as well write off the possibility of reorganization."

That local officeholders would do little beyond ignoring the proposals was the general consensus among the respondents. The accuracy of this impression was clearly verified by the public officials who were interviewed. Both City and suburban representatives frankly admitted that they were paying little attention to the recommendations and expected little to result from them.

One official remarked that "the Commission's proposals aren't going to mean much," while another flatly stated that he and his colleagues "did not intend to do anything about them." Several criticized the recommendations as "generalized and vague statements that said nothing." As one put it, "If this is the best they can come up with after four years, it shows that there's damned little wrong with the present system."

Among public officials, only those at the county level expressed sympathy for the final report, a not unexpected finding in view of the nature of the recommendations. As one of them stated, "I am 100 per cent behind the Commission's proposal that the county assume more activities. It is a most practical alternative and much easier than trying to establish a new layer of government." However, when asked what he and his colleagues intended to do about the recommendations, he indicated that they would probably do little. "We have to proceed slowly in something like this or the mayors and municipal attorneys will start yelling that we are trying to grab more power."

ATTITUDES TOWARD CONTINUANCE OF MSC

The interviews revealed a sharp division of opinion about extending the life of the Study Commission for an additional two years as proposed. Most public officials reacted negatively; only those from the county government and several appointed City officials favored continuance. (See Table 11.) Educators and organizational secretaries strongly supported the Commission's extension, while businessmen and respondents in the other categories were almost evenly divided on the question. Those who favored continuance stressed the need for constantly focusing public attention on the problems of the metropolis and for alerting the citizenry to their importance. As one interviewee noted, "The Commission could keep the issues before the people and gradually things would begin to sink in." A few mentioned the need for further

TABLE 11

Opinions on Continuance of Study Commission

Occupational Category	% Favoring	% No Opinion	% Not Favoring
Businessmen	62	—	38
Professional	60	—	40
Elected public officials	18	18	64
Appointed public officials	75	25	—
Social welfare administrators	50	—	50
Organizational secretaries	80	—	20
Labor leaders	50	—	50
Educators	100	—	—
Total (N = 50)	60	6	34

research, but most felt that, if continued, the Commission should place more emphasis on education and action. A majority of the private community leaders who did not favor extension felt that the MSC had outlived its usefulness. Their views are summed up in the remark of one respondent, "We've had enough studying for a while. Now is the time to act and push for some of the reforms." However, no one who took this position gave any indication that he was willing and ready to take an active part in promoting the changes.

Although the interviewees were divided on the question of continuing the Commission, most of them evidenced a general feeling of need for some type of metropolitan study and action vehicle. Even those who were opposed or lukewarm toward an extension of the MSC's life acknowledged this necessity. Yet few respondents had any definite notions as to how such a successor committee or organization should be constituted. Their answers ranged from state-sponsored agencies of various types to foundation-supported study groups. Many felt that anything but a governmentally appointed commission would be ineffective. Those who expressed this view were skeptical that a private citizens' group could accomplish much since it would "be lacking in the prestige, sanction, and mandate that comes from public appointment." Several suggested that a representative committee of citizens might be appointed within the framework of the county government so that it would be attached, and have direct access, to a politically responsible body. Others agreed but felt that such a committee should also contain public officials to avoid what some referred to as "the political naivete of the study commission." Still others said that such an approach would be futile and that the only hope lay in a private citizens' group of top level business and civic leaders who would be sufficiently motivated and determined to push for action. No one felt sanguine about the prospects of organizing such a committee.

A Milwaukee alderman reiterated the City's original position that a state legislative committee is the proper vehicle for studying metropolitan problems. "One of our big difficulties," he stated, "is getting the legislators to understand the problems of the urban areas. Seeing some of these things first hand would be an education to them." Several suburban office-holders, on the other hand, indicated that a local group of public officials such as the proposed inter-municipal council of mayors could adequately serve the purposes of a study commission.

In the original round of interviews most respondents viewed establishment of the MSC by the state as the most desirable method. They said that it would be extremely difficult to mark out a significant role for such an agency or reach consensus on its membership through local channels. They also noted that as a gubernatorially appointed body, the Commission enjoyed high prestige and was elevated above local partisanship. About one-fourth of the respondents voiced the opinion that metropolitan reform on any meaningful scale would be accomplished only through state action. Another one-third indicated that the state should give the Milwaukee area more authority to solve its own problems. The remainder either opposed or were indifferent to state intervention of any kind. Several insisted that the Milwaukee area already had sufficient legal tools to attack its problems and that state action would only result in further inroads on the principle of home rule. By the time of the second interviews, some of the enthusiasm for a state-appointed citizens' commission had waned while the belief that the state should play a more direct role in solving metropolitan problems showed some gain.

COMMUNITY INFLUENTIALS AND METROPOLITAN REORGANIZATION

No startling or dramatic findings emerge from the interviews. For the most part they serve to confirm the common impressions held by many students of the metropolitan scene. They reveal, for example, no ground swell of dissatisfaction with the existing system of local government in the Milwaukee area. Most of the business influentials look upon the system as inefficient, but few regard it as detrimental to their economic interests. Although sympathetic to the reformist philosophy with its emphasis on local government as a business, they do not view the metropolitan pattern in the same light as their own private enterprises, where competition frequently dictates changes in corporate structure and management practices. Apparently they have become reconciled to the fact that some inefficiency is endemic to local government and is a price which must be paid for certain privileges, such as the maintenance of suburban enclaves. They recognize that urban growth generates problems, some of which could have serious consequences, but they are indefinite as to what these problems are or how they should be met. Their time, moreover, is so committed that they have little left to devote to the pursuit of area-wide governmental reform. At the same time, they feel that their position in the business and social community calls at least for a show of interest in metropolitan reorganization efforts. For these reasons, they are happy to see a high-level citizens' committee, such as the MSC, in being, whether its impact is great or not.

Leaders at the intermediate and lower levels in the "pecking order" of prestige and influence are generally more skeptical of "blue ribbon" study commissions and their usefulness. Like the notables, however, their notions about urban governmental ills and what might be done to alleviate them are vague and inconclusive. Their attention is focused mainly on issues of special concern to them, while their interest in the overall problems of the metropolis is extremely peripheral. Actually, one of the most revealing aspects of the interviews was the lack of understanding displayed by many leaders at all levels of either metropolitan governmental affairs or the work of the MSC. It became evident early in the interviews that reformist activities in the Milwaukee area had not resulted in a meaningful identification of basic community-wide problems and goals or imbued the leadership structure with any sense of urgency over them.

Local public officials gave no sign that they would act otherwise than in the apparent self-interest of the established governmental order. Those in the suburbs are well satisfied with the status quo and have few qualms about the ability of the existing system to sustain itself. Those in the central city are likewise confident about the self-sustaining powers of their own government and are far less militant than in the past about political consolidation. Obviously resigned to a fragmented local structure, they see little use in wasting their efforts on attempts to integrate the local governmental pattern. At the same time they are determined to resist a diminution of the City's powers by functional transfer or otherwise. They are extremely cool to an extension of cooperative arrangements with the suburbs, feeling that the City has everything to lose and nothing to gain by such devices. Like their suburban counterparts, they regard citizen study committees with suspicion and little enthusiasm. Few of them shed tears when the MSC was terminated.

The interviews reveal no indications that attitudes toward metropolitan reorganization are materially changing. Those who have supported reform efforts in the past continue to favor them today, although less hopefully and with less intensity. Those who have been opposed, lukewarm, or uninterested remain in the same frame of mind. Civic influentials are less optimistic at the prospect of reform after witnessing the reactions to the Commission's work and are convinced that no major alteration of the present governmental pattern is likely in the near future. The general citizen body remains indifferent largely because it does not perceive a need for change. Local public officials show no greater receptivity to governmental coordination than during the period of the Committee of 21. Only county officials have assumed a more positive attitude toward the role of the county government as an urban instrumentality, but they are not prepared or willing to push this concept in the face of municipal opposition. In brief, the interviews—to the extent that they are representative—offer persuasive evidence that the attitudes of Milwaukee area citizens and officials toward the metropolitan governmental pattern are basically static and give little promise at present of changing.

PUBLIC IMAGES OF THE MSC

Our discussion thus far has dealt only with the attitudes of community leaders toward the Commission. In concentrating on this group, we have implicitly assumed that metropolitan reorganization prospects can better be gauged from the attitudes of those who hold positions of influence in the polity than from the general citizen body. Sample surveys of popular opinion conducted in recent years in St. Louis, Dayton, Cleveland, and Miami have adduced impressive evidence that most urban residents have little information, slight interest, and few clearly formed opinions about the issues of metropolitan reform.[2] The results suggest that the first indications of genuine receptivity to governmental change in urban areas will be reflected not in the general public but among the community leaders or opinion formulators. They also suggest that short of crisis situations, little pressure on public policy-makers for significant change in the existing system can be expected from the grass roots. Thus, if reform is to materialize, it will depend on the willingness and ability of the few to stimulate and mobilize the support of the many.

The limited amount of data that we collected on attitudes of Milwaukee area residents substantiate the general assumption of low interest and concern in metropolitan governmental reform. When a sample of city and suburban dwellers were asked whether they had heard of the Metropolitan Study Commission, 53 per cent said "No." (At the time of the interviews in the fall of 1960, the agency had been in existence for over three years and during this time had received wide coverage from the press and other news media.) Even this proportion must be taken with reservation because of the tendency of respondents to feign knowledge when asked a question of this type. Almost 60 per cent of those who answered in the affirmative, for example, knew little or nothing about the Commission's role or purpose, or what it was doing. This finding, coupled with the fact that the sample over-represented the higher socio-economic groups where greater knowledge might be assumed, illustrates the low level of awareness about the Commission and the lack of interest in its work.

As Tables 12 and 13 show, extent of formal education and occupational ranking are closely related to knowledge of the Commission. Only 22 per cent of those with elementary education and 32 per cent of the unskilled workers claimed to have heard of it, compared with 71 per cent of the college graduates and 65 per cent of those in the professional and managerial class. Length of residence showed a similar but less significant relationship, with one out of four who had lived in the area for less than five years answering affirmatively as against one-half of those who had been residents for a longer period. These findings are comparable to those of other studies and as logically expected.

When respondents who claimed knowledge of the Commission's

TABLE 12

Knowledge of MSC's Existence as Related to Educational Level of Respondents (Citizen Interviews)

Educational Level	% Knowing of MSC	% Not Knowing of MSC	No. of Respondents
Some grammar school	22	78	18
Completed grammar school	22	78	37
Some high school	40	60	48
Completed high school	50	50	113
Some college	57	43	56
Completed college	71	29	35
Total (N = 307)	47	53	307

TABLE 13

Knowledge of MSC's Existence as Related to Occupational Level of Respondents* (Citizen Interviews)

Occupational Level	% Knowing of MSC	% Not Knowing of MSC	No. of Respondents
Professional, managerial, proprietary	65	35	63
White collar	62	38	37
Sales workers	48	52	27
Skilled workers	40	60	93
Unskilled workers	32	68	38
Retired	48	52	25
Other (students, farmers, etc.)	29	71	24
Total (N = 307)	47	53	307

* Housewives are classified according to occupation of head of household.

existence were questioned about the desirability of extending its life, 59 per cent replied favorably, 9 per cent unfavorably, and an unusually large number (32 per cent) had no opinion. The responses to the follow-up question as to what would be accomplished by the extension further reveal the low degree of concern with the Commission's work and objectives. Three out of every five interviewees who knew about the study group had no opinion on this point. Of those who did, the largest proportion (27 per cent) felt that nothing would be achieved by a continuance. A slightly smaller percentage believed that an extension would result in "just more studies." Only about 20 per cent expressed any hope that some improvement in metropolitan problem solving and governmental structure might emerge. A number of the less optimistic but more sophisticated pointed out that whether the MSC was continued or not, its work would be ignored unless it received political support. Most of those who expressed this opinion were convinced that such support would not be forthcoming.

NEWSPAPER IMAGES

Newspapers, in their role as a community institution, are reporters and interpreters of local events. As observers, commentators, and critics with a wide and regular audience, they enjoy a unique position of power and influence. The citizen must look largely to them for news and information, even for evaluation of local public affairs and local institutions. Community agencies in turn must rely heavily on the mass media, particularly the press, to reach and communicate with the citizenry. Thus what a newspaper writes or reports about a governmental unit will have much to do with the agency's public "image." News of one kind competes, of course, with that of another for the attention of the reader. If news about a particular local institution ranks low in readership priority, the impact of the press in reporting about that institution will likely be low also.

The Study Commission provides an apt illustration of this latter observation. Despite the efforts of the Milwaukee dailies to stimulate interest in the group's work and recommendations, the level of public responses remained patently low. The case of the suburban weeklies may be different, although we have no evidence on which to base an opinion. However, news about metropolitan governmental affairs—when it does appear in their columns—has little competition for readership attention from other items. This fact may tend to make suburban papers more influential than the large city dailies in shaping the thinking of their subscribers about area-wide governmental matters.[3] Whatever the case may be, both the metropolitan and the suburban press wrote many thousands of lines about the Commission.

Metropolitan Dailies

From its inception, the MSC received strong support from the two metropolitan dailies, the *Journal* and *Sentinel*, despite their decidedly different editorial and political policies. Both lauded its creation and voiced warm approval of the appointees. Both also projected a picture of the Commission as a group of high-minded, able, and top-level civic leaders dedicated to the cause of their community. Critics of the Commission were editorially spanked on numerous occasions and public officials chided for not acting on the proposals. Even during the "dark" days of the study group, the two papers treated it gently and sympathetically.

The metropolitan press looked upon the MSC's role as one of fact finding, public education, and recommendation, with this work in turn hopefully leading to a broad citizen movement to bring about "sounder metropolitan arrangements." As the *Journal* noted, "Certainly the commission cannot think of using its paid staff and public funds to propagandize public opinion, to generate support for specific proposals, to lobby, in short. Such activity, while proper and needful to be done by somebody, is nevertheless clearly political. . . . When the time does come for implementing and getting action, hope must lie in a citizen movement. . . . This would be in the manner of the national and state committees of citizens for the Hoover Report."[4]

Neither paper called for broad changes in the governmental pattern; both were content to accept and favor the milder recommendations of the MSC. Initially, they had been optimistic—as the Commission itself had been—that the community was ready for significant reform and that the studies would touch off an action program. By early 1959 this note of optimism had been replaced by the theme that the road to metropolitan change will be long, difficult, and gradual. As the *Journal* observed in February, 1959, any effort to say "here's the plan" and to attempt "to shove through legislative authorization for it without first winning full community backing is bound to fail."[5] It predicted, moreover, that such backing would not be forthcoming until public apathy and lack of concern were replaced by public interest and determination. Only education and enlightenment, in its opinion, could bring about this change.

Suburban Press

In contrast to the consistent support of the metropolitan dailies, the attitudes of the suburban weeklies fluctuated during the course of the MSC's life. Never enthusiastic about its creation, they gave it only minimum coverage or ignored it completely. Faithfully echoing the views of suburban officialdom and equating the metropolitan good with suburban interests, they condemned Commission proposals that impinged on the powers of suburban municipalities but in almost the same breath criticized Milwaukee officials for objecting to recommendations that would curtail the powers of the central city. So long as the study group dealt with water supply and sewage disposal—functions over which most of the suburbs had no control—the responses of the weeklies were generally favorable. When, however, the Commission probed into such matters as assessment, zoning, and police protection—functions which came under the direct jurisdiction of suburban municipalities—the reaction was uniformly unfavorable.

The first annual report of the MSC recommending extension of the metropolitan sewer district boundaries and alluding to the need for a metropolitan water system drew favorable comment from the suburban papers. However, when the Commission later gave indications of favoring some form of area-wide government with substantial powers, their attitude changed sharply. "This commission," the West Allis *Star* observed editorially in March, 1959, "was not originally founded by the legislature to search for a method of creating a super government here at the expense of personal freedom. Because it was led down this path, its work thus far has been largely a failure."[6] The north shore press was even more critical, calling the Commission a tool of the central city: "Milwaukee, abetted by the metropolitan study commission, is seeking a stranglehold on the suburbs. Today it is water. Tomorrow it will be the police force and fire departments, next garbage and rubbish collections, then health and schools."[7] The Whitefish Bay *Herald,* exhorting the people to cling to the government that was close to them, advised the study group to bury its plans for a "superimposed metropolitan government" and "concentrate solely on metropolitan water, expressways, and sewerage."[8]

After the flurry of interest over the issue of metropolitan government died down in early 1959, suburban papers paid little further attention to the MSC either editorially or in their news columns. Only on rare occasions did they take notice, as the West Allis *Star* did at the time a resolution was introduced in the Milwaukee common council to abolish the agency. In this instance the *Star* rose to the Commission's defense, declaring that Milwaukee officials were fearful that the group's work would turn the spotlight on the "deficiencies" in the City. "The commission would do well to tell the Milwaukee aldermen to jump in the lake on which they claim jealous monopoly and to continue with its studies."[9] Less than six months later, however, the same paper was berating the MSC for refusing the request of suburban municipalities to conduct a mass transportation study.* Referring to the Commission's position that it lacked resources for such an undertaking as "baloney," the *Star* retorted that the study group apparently had the time and means to "flirt with fuzzy-headed theorists who seek their cherished one Metropolitan Government—with no suburbs," or "to endorse the continued existence of the mismanaged, mishandled, miserable Milwaukee water utility when every test of common sense calls for a new businesslike, soundly run Metropolitan Water Authority."[10]

Suburban papers ignored the MSC's final recommendations and only a few commented on extending its term. The West Allis *Star*, for example, stated early in 1960: "As we look back on its [Study Commission's] record, and as we look ahead to the future, we have this advice for the legislature—let it die. The problems of government ultimately must be solved by the men of government, not by part-time do-gooders in the field. Let's face it, their social and business commitments do not permit more than a lick and a promise at governmental problems; and they do not have the necessary experience in the field, either."[11]

IMPRESSIONS OF COMMISSION MEMBERS

Not only the outside viewer but the "image-maker" himself forms impressions of his position, his role, and his efficacy in relation to the public. These impressions may also change over time as experiences impinge upon them. We have already observed some of the views and attitudes of MSC members at various points in preceding chapters. We saw, in general, that their impressions

---

* The Commission decided not to undertake a transportation study because of limitations of time and money even though it acknowledged the need for such a survey. It indicated, however, that it would accept the responsibility of supervising the preparation of a research design for a transportation study provided the county would appropriate the money. The proposal did not materialize during the life of the MSC because of legal issues regarding the expenditures of county government funds for this purpose. Since that time the Southeastern Wisconsin Regional Planning Commission has undertaken a comprehensive transportation study of the entire area.

of metropolitan problems and of the Milwaukee community corresponded closely to those of other business and civic influentials. Their self-analysis, prompted by interviews which we conducted with all Commission members, furnishes additional insight into the local reorganization movement.

As a result of their experiences on the MSC, most commissioners came to regard two factors as the strongest impediments to metropolitan governmental reform: the intransigent attitude of local public officials, and citizen apathy. They were particularly disturbed by the first since their service on the Commission had convinced them that few officials were seriously interested in considering progressive changes in the existing system or willing to think in terms broader than their own city or village. Some members felt that opposition to the group's recommendations "did not reflect the attitude of the people but only of those who were seeking to protect their vested interests." Yet they were disappointed with the low degree of concern displayed by the general public and baffled as to how they might "break through the barrier of public officials and awaken interest in the citizen body."

Impact

The members had few illusions about the Commission's impact on either public officials or the citizen body. They believed that most officials were totally ignoring their proposals and that the general public was simply not being reached. The interviews clearly indicate that long before the MSC terminated, a majority of its members had lost hope that their work would have significant influence on community thinking. A minority seemed reconciled to a piecemeal, evolutionary approach via intergovernmental cooperation, but most were far from enthusiastic or even sanguine about the possibilities of this strategy. Several mentioned that political leadership, such as the county executive might exercise, was the only hope for change.

The majority of members were dissatisfied with the accomplishments of the Commission. They believed, however, that it had made the public more aware of the problems, engendered some interest among civic groups to carry on the work, contributed to several progressive measures (regional planning and extension of sewer district boundaries), and helped ease City-suburban tensions. They attributed their failure to accomplish more to the turnover of MSC personnel—members, chairmen, and research directors—to meager budgets and lack of staff, and to the fact that Milwaukee's metropolitan problems have not reached crisis proportions. As one commissioner remarked: "Intergovernmental coordination will come about only when communities reach the point where particular problems get out of their reach or taxes get so high that the people begin to demand consolidation of some kind."

Extension of Tenure

Although the Commission voted unanimously for extension of its life, no more than one-third of the membership felt strongly about its continuance, another one-third was lukewarm, and the remainder saw little purpose in prolonging its tenure. Several expressed the opinion that many members had lost interest in the work and were only "marking time until their terms expired." Others said that the MSC had already been in existence too long and had "run out of steam," as one put it, or "lost its original militancy," as another remarked. Several members suggested that if the Commission was continued, it should have new faces. One of those who made this suggestion observed that the most influential members had either resigned or become inactive. More than half the group stated that they definitely did not want to continue on as members if the Commission's life was extended.

When asked why the MSC supported the proposed two-year extension when many of its members were less than enthusiastic, the replies were uniformly similar. Virtually all commissioners remained convinced of the need for some continuing agency to study and keep public attention focused on the problems of the area.

However, they saw little prospect of an instrumentality of this kind coming into being as a substitute for the MSC, nor were they at all certain as to the form or character that such a new body should take. The simple solution, at least for the time being, seemed to rest in a prolongation of the MSC's life.

In Retrospect

The commissioners had few definite answers when asked what they would do differently were they to start over again. Some frankly admitted that they were at a complete loss to answer the question. They surmised that no matter what course they might have taken the results would have been about the same. Several said that they would define their objectives more clearly and try to reach firm consensus on the methods to be used in pursuing them; many indicated that they would insist on a larger staff and more operating funds; and others replied that they would narrow the work program down to a manageable number of items and then concentrate intensively on these. The members remained almost equally divided on the question of action versus research, although many of them felt that a greater effort should have been made to stimulate reformist activity by other civic groups.

One commissioner, expressing the general feelings of others in the group, summed up the total picture in these words: "I would concede that there was an immense amount of frustration and disappointment on the part of the Commission itself. While one cannot say that there was great enthusiasm among the members at all times, there was determination on the part of some to face up to the task which had been given to them." No one who observed the Commission over a period of time would deny this statement. But four years of frustration and disappointment are a lot to bear. That they took their toll on the members and their spirit and determination stands out in this attempt at metropolitan reform.

10
The MSC in Retrospect

The story of the MSC is another in the long and complex record of attempts to modify local governmental arrangements in the Milwaukee metropolitan area. As history, it affords opportunity to examine a metropolitan reform movement over time and to observe the major variables that condition its operation. As a case study of a single action campaign, it contributes to the growing stockpile of material available for comparative analysis of metropolitan reorganization movements. And as an example of reformist activity in a large urban center, it adds to our understanding of the efforts and failures to adjust governmental mechanisms to the massive forces at work in the nation's metropolitan areas.

Scott Greer, in a recent study, describes metropolitan action movements as "minor revolutions, bloodless to be sure, but far from pacific and rational." He characterizes them in this manner because, as he describes it, they intend "a radical change in the division of power, rewards, and esteem within the metropolis."[1] In the three cases that he examines—Cleveland, Dade County (Miami), and St. Louis—plans embodying major alterations of the governmental structure had been drafted and submitted to popular referenda. In each instance, the presentation of the charter to the electorate had been preceded by an "objective" study or survey conducted by non-governmental bodies: in Cleveland and Dade County under the auspices of citizen committees and in St. Louis by local universities. The Milwaukee movement, in contrast to these three cases, did not advance beyond the survey stage. It terminated with the demise of the MSC and with a report that outlined only in general terms the future path that reorganization should take. The Commission's recommendations, moreover, were in no sense of the word revolutionary. They contemplated no radical change in the division of power and rewards but only a continuation of an evolutionary trend that had long been noticeable although not clearly articulated. Yet the movement started out with Don Quixote mounted on his steed ready to charge the ramparts of the status quo. Somewhere along the way the horse became lame and the rider lost his armor. The era of the Milwaukee Study Commission is but another phase in the area's political history, yet it raises the question: Why the deceleration from crusade to tinkering?

In preceding chapters we sought to do four things: (1) provide historical background for the current metropolitan reform movement in Milwaukee; (2) present a picture of the institutional and environmental structure within which the MSC operated; (3) examine the work of the Commission and the forces that impinged upon it; and (4) describe the public images of the MSC and the responses that its work evoked. Here we endeavor to order the findings that emerge from these various facets into some sort of logical relationship so that their meaning and significance become clearer and the results of the reform movement more understandable.[2]

The analytical framework employed for this purpose can be described in the following way. Our subject of analysis is a metropolitan survey commission created to pursue certain goals and objectives, some of them specified, others implied. This agency operates in a social and political environment which it seeks to affect or change in accordance with its goals. The environment, in all probability more change-resistant than change-promotive, has certain built-in factors, some of which are sympathetic to the objectives of the actor, others neutral, and still others hostile. To achieve its goals, the Commission brings to or has available for the task certain resources—actual and potential—which it may fully or partially exploit or even ignore entirely. Operating in the given setting and conditioned by it in various ways, the Commission utilizes these resources to influence the environment in some measure, however large or small. In turn, the group is influenced and its behavior structured by the environmental responses that it precipitates. From this interplay of forces emerge certain results that measure the extent to which the goals of the Commission are realized or frustrated. These consequential products may range from basic governmental alteration to retention of the status quo and mobilization against change. The analysis, in other words, centers around five key variables: goals, environment, resources and the extent of their utilization, environmental feedback, and results.

GOALS

In the Milwaukee case, the official instrumentality of reform efforts—the MSC—grew out of some vaguely defined notions about metropolitan malfunctioning. The civic and good government groups that promoted the creation of the Commission assumed that the existing pattern of local government was pathological. How much of this concern was due to specific deficiencies which they were able to clearly identify, such as water supply, and how much to the current fad of metropolitan reformism is a matter of speculation. One fact, however, appears certain. At no time did they define their goals in other than the most general terms.[3] On those occasions when they did attempt to be specific, they found themselves forced to resort to the shopworn phrases of reformist literature: elimination of overlapping units and duplication of services, greater governmental coordination, more efficient and economical management. The statute creating the MSC illustrates this point. Drafted largely by civic representatives, it directed the Commission to study the character and cost of local public services and determine which can be rendered "most adequately and efficiently" on a local and which on a county-wide basis. But these were narrow goals that hardly encompassed the problems of the metropolis, as many who were involved in the movement well know. Yet the belief persisted that somehow poor governmental organization was the prime cause of most metropolitan difficulties and deficiencies.

The MSC was created by the efforts of civic notables; it was not the result of grass roots dissatisfaction or of demands by public officials. When it came into existence it fell heir to the uncertainties that characterized the metropolitan perspectives of its sponsors. It found also that it must act within an on-going community system that placed formidable restrictions upon its objectives and even its procedures. At first it largely ignored the question of goals and strategies and the environmental milieu in which it was operating. A few individual members such as Lobb had definite objectives in mind, but the Commission as a whole had no clear idea of its role or function. It made no effort to formulate goals in operational terms or to define procedures in any methodical fashion but plunged directly into the task of examining those problems that were suggested to it by its chairman and by one or two of its stronger members. This lack of goal definition and clearly established procedures was to haunt the Commission throughout its existence. As one commissioner commented, "We made a serious mistake when we did not sit down and devote about six months of our time to thinking and laying out plans. As it was we started our projects too quickly without a clear idea of our objectives and without any real sense of direction." Some members were still debating the Commission's proper role when it closed its doors. The evidence is strong that the failure to clarify goals caused a marked dissipation of the group's energies and impeded its output. Uncertainty generated doubts, and these in turn militated against vigorous and decisive action.

The general and formal goals of the MSC were prescribed by statute. As noted earlier, they were wholly within the tradition of the administrative reform movement. But as Commission members realized, the legislative specifications were more in the nature of loosely defined directives than of operational objectives. The ultimate goal was presumably a better and more effective system of local government for the Milwaukee metropolis; but how was this desired end to be achieved and what role was the Commission to play in the process? Was it to confine itself to study and recommendation? Was it to stimulate efforts by others to implement its proposals? Was it to initiate action and press for adoption of its prescriptions? Neither the MSC nor its civic supporters had ready answers to these questions.[4]

The conflicting opinions among MSC members over the manner of accomplishing reform further illustrate the difficulties that the group experienced in defining its goals. Three basic views in this regard can be distinguished. The positions which they encompass are not mutually exclusive or contradictory—some members would have supported all three; the question is essentially one of emphasis and priority. The first viewpoint, typified by Lobb, held that reform would be achieved only if it were superimposed from above by some outside agency such as the governor and state legislature. The second, represented mainly by Randall and Rasche, maintained that change would be brought about only if substantial agreement were generated among local public officials. The third, which found expression first in Mrs. Cook and later in Mrs. Gordon and Klotsche, believed that reform was possible only if the public became insistent on demanding it.

These views in turn called for three different strategies. Under the first formula, the MSC would translate its recommendations into bills and take them directly to the governor and legislature. Those who supported this position were aware of the influence of municipal officials and the force of public opinion, but they saw little payoff in expending scarce Commission resources on efforts to cultivate the good will of the local guard and to educate the citizenry. As Lobb insisted, the path for solving the metropolitan dilemma lay in political action at the state level. He saw hopes of accomplishing reform as long as there was a Republican commission, a Republican governor, and a Republican legislature. (He stated that he would have felt the same had these three agencies been under Democratic control.) This approach assumes that questions of metropolitan government can be decided at the state level through political party channels. It overlooks the fact that issues of this kind have seldom commanded party loyalties in Wisconsin, or for that matter elsewhere, where the rural-urban dichotomy remains strong.

The second approach, while not denying the need for state intervention, held that the legislature would not act over the opposition of local public officials. As envisioned by its proponents, the Commission's task was to work out some kind of consensus on proposed changes at the local level or at least enlist the support of a substantial number of municipal officials. This strategy places principal emphasis on persuading (or in Cutler's words "even teasing") the local units to sponsor changes or initiate the necessary enabling legislation.

The third, or public stimulation, approach assumed that neither state nor local officials would act except in response to public demand. Those who subscribed to this view were not oblivious to the relatively low saliency of metropolitan affairs in the life of the average citizen. They were convinced, however, that any talk of modifying the local bureaucratic structure was idle speculation until the public became interested and concerned. They felt, therefore, that the Commission should utilize a significant portion of its resources on a program of public information and education.

Klotsche struck this note in the 1959 report to the governor when he stated, "In the remaining 20 months of the Commission, more and more emphasis must be placed upon acquainting the public with the problems being studied by the Commission and with its findings and recommendations."[5] Later, in pleading for more public interest in MSC activities, he observed that "the role of the citizen is indeed a strategic one in the whole area of metropolitan affairs. The public should be aroused to an awareness of the seriousness of the metropolitan problem."[6]

To a large extent the loosely defined goals of the MSC were shaped by two factors: what the members thought the community needed, and what the members thought the community expected of them. A third factor, the influence of a professional staff in goal formulation, was less important in the Milwaukee situation than is normally true because of the high turnover and other staff troubles which the Commission experienced. The members who had definite notions as to what the group should do had little difficulty in getting their ideas accepted. Thus Lobb, who viewed tax reform as a crucial need, and Cutler, who regarded changes in land use and zoning as critical, were able to demarcate these areas as major MSC objectives. At the same time, other goals were dictated by public expectations—or more properly by what the members believed these expectations to be, as the much debated multi-function district illustrates.

When the Commission began operation, a majority, if not all, of the members felt at least in a vague way that it was incumbent upon the group to devise some form of metropolitan government. As civic-minded influentials, they were aware of the national movement for metropolitan reform and the customary recommendations of citizen committees with their emphasis on broad structural changes. Cutler alluded to this factor when he said that "none of us could escape noticing the frequency with which study commissions in other metropolitan centers have recommended the creation of some form of metropolitan government."[7] But more importantly, the Commission members were convinced that local civic organizations, the daily press, and Milwaukee County residents in general anticipated major recommendations for governmental reform. This feeling is well illustrated in the debates over a metropolitan vehicle. As the land use and zoning committee noted at one point, "The general public seems to be expecting and desiring the Metropolitan Study Commission to come up with some far-reaching proposal." The group concluded that if the Commission reached agreement on a multi-purpose service district, it would be well to attach more than two functions to the new agency, since "a two-function district might appear too timid an approach to the general problem when the public is expecting a substantial new approach toward the solution of long accumulating metropolitan problems."[8]

In addition to the difficulties of formulating specific or operational goals, Commission members were also plagued with the common dilemma that confronts action-oriented study groups. Should the group be concerned with the hard realities of politics—with what is politically feasible or acceptable—or should it recommend the theoretically "proper" solution?[9] The question is not one solely of the ideal versus the practical or of political transcendence versus political obeisance. It is also a question of where the inevitable compromises should take place: within the study group or in the political arena. Magidson raised this point in his dissent to the tax reform proposals when he stated: "It is true that some political compromise may be necessary. However, compromising is a problem which should be left to the legislature. It is the job of a citizens' committee, such as this one, to recommend what is right and proper so that the legislature has clear choices to make."[10] The case for this approach was tersely summed up by research director Mars: "The question is one of history versus immediacy, and the Commission should be on the side of history. It should recommend what is intellectually honest and let the compromises be hammered out by the policymakers."

Several other members made similar observations, complaining that after the initial setbacks the Commission sought to please everyone by "watering down" its proposals and becoming "timid in its approach." The obvious result, they stated, was to lessen the prestige of the MSC and leave nothing for negotiation and compromise at the political bargaining table. Those who held this viewpoint agreed with the observation made by one student of the metropolitan scene: "Everywhere the governmental reorganizers will face the same challenge. They must raise a standard to which the wise and honest can repair. They must remember, however, that the wise and honest will not rally around that standard if it is either mean and paltry, or the banner of a hopeless cause."[11]

On the other side of the coin, the conception of the Commission's role as a catalytic agent—a conception that became more prevalent with the passage of time—eschewed the ideal and concentrated on what seemed attainable. Here the emphasis was on stimulating local officials to action. This strategy forced the Commission to shape its proposals in such fashion that they were acceptable or at least not distasteful to those at whom the stimuli were directed. Diluted and mild recommendations and a lowering of the Commission's overall goals were unavoidable consequences, as the experiences of the Randall and Rasche committees demonstrate. The question here is not the value of the catalytic or broker's role but whether a study commission is the proper actor to play it. The fact that one of the goals of such an agency is the stimulation of citizen concern in metropolitan affairs raises the question of whether it can serve as both a catalyst for local officials and a goad to public action. If it calls for broad changes it alienates the former; and if it suggests only minor reform, it generates little interest among the citizenry.

Goal diffusion or uncertainty is seemingly endemic to metropolitan study commissions. In Milwaukee the situation was aggravated by still another factor. Most members initially contemplated recommendations that would embody an overall solution to the area's problems, as their early and oft-repeated references to a metropolitan agency or vehicle indicate. Yet at the same time each committee was busily engaged in formulating proposals of a partial nature that jeopardized an integrated approach. Ball called this fact to Lobb's attention as early as April 1958:

> You may or may not agree that full commission recommendations should be held off until the Commission is prepared to offer the legislature and the public a package program. The danger of piecemeal recommendations is that they will not fall into the pattern of metropolitan government which the Commission might finally propose. Equally important, the Commission may wish to conclude trades with various elements in the community through which the Commission would make certain recommendations in return for support for others.[12]

The matter of overall as against piecemeal recommendations was settled only by the collapse of the metropolitan government movement within the MSC. Thereafter the emphasis was on accomplishing partial goals, first through legislative action on individual measures and later through stimulation of local officials.

THE ENVIRONMENT

The environmental factors that have given rise to the mid-twentieth century spate of metropolitan surveys are not difficult to identify. In some instances they have been sewerage or similar problems; in others, an accumulation of service deficiencies; and in a few the feeling that the scale of local government is lagging behind that of urban growth and expansion. Although the proximate cause may differ in each situation, the common underlying theme has been the same: the need for more administrative efficiency and effectiveness in the existing governmental system. In each, the arguments for reorganization or change based on this theme have been forced to compete with counter arguments that favor administrative separatism and autonomy.

The Milwaukee experience follows the usual pattern. Here it

was largely the disputes over water supply and annexation that provided the immediate and most apparent impetus for a metropolitan survey. To the business influentials, the problem was basically one of organization. As several of them stated, they pushed for the creation of a study commission because of the constant frustrations which they experienced in promoting civic projects. They mentioned particularly the expressway system and the county stadium, noting that in each instance "innumerable questions kept arising over governmental jurisdiction. Who would put in the streets to the stadium? Who would be responsible for this function and that?" Few people, however, saw the problem in these concise terms.

The general environmental setting in which the MSC functioned was not especially propitious for the achievement of the Commission's statutory mandate. The long history of City-suburban conflict had provided fuel that could easily be sparked by the entrenched bureaucracies of both jurisdictions. City political leaders, invoking the principles of justice and efficiency, had demonstrated a willingness to accept governmental change only if it involved total surrender on the part of those beyond the walls of the citadel. Suburban officials, in the name of local autonomy and small town democracy, had indicated a receptivity only to such change as would fulfill their major service needs, particularly water. County government officials were playing the role of neutralists, although they were not averse to accepting the metropolitan crown if voluntarily tendered them. They were not prepared, however, to take any political risks to induce the offer. Officials at the state level, although they had created the MSC, displayed little readiness to intervene in the local situation.

The public climate for Commission activities was neither friendly nor hostile, it was simply apathetic or unknowing. Citizens generally, as well as the majority of voluntary organizations in the area, were little concerned about metropolitan reform or committed to MSC goals. Even in the case of the interested groups, their concern hardly involved a sense of primary dedication to the cause of area-wide reform. As we know, it is easier to be interested than to be active.

When the MSC came into existence, the metropolitan community was not faced with any critical breakdown of public functions or any imminent collapse of its local governmental system. In fact, the service level in the area was relatively high despite some deficiencies in sewage disposal, water supply, and the usual minor inconveniences in the outlying sectors. No local unit was in danger of bankruptcy and none was pleading for assistance. School district reorganization was making substantial headway and correcting many of the most patent inequities in the process. By this time, also, one of the most troublesome issues, annexation by the central city, had been eliminated from the arena of controversy with incorporation of the last remaining township land in the county in late 1956.

A second major issue, water supply, was also settled before the Commission could capitalize on it. The urgency of this problem was removed early in the MSC's life when the Public Service Commission's ruling in the Wauwatosa case gave the suburbs what they most wanted: access to the City's water system. The Wauwatosa decision did more than settle the water dispute; it took away from the MSC the one issue that was potentially capable of opening the door to a larger measure of metropolitan reform. Although some suburban agitation for an area-wide water authority continued after the ruling, the issue had lost its appeal. Mayor Zeidler's earlier prediction that suburban officials would lose all interest in the MSC once they obtained a source of water supply for their communities proved substantially correct.

The more perceptive supporters of metropolitan reform in Milwaukee—only a few to be sure—looked beyond the immediate housekeeping problems of waste disposal and traffic control to the future urban environment. They sensed that the existing governmental structure failed to provide adequate means of formulating overall policy for the orderly development of the area. They appeared aware of the potential dangers of uncoordinated land use planning and continued urban sprawl. But these were matters of tomorrow remote from popular understanding and concern. Not even the economic notables, much less the average citizen, saw any serious threat to their present or future interests in the existing metropolitan system. How was "revolution" to be generated in this environment? As Robert Wood has written, "Political change when public problems become pressing seems quite possible. But the anticipation of problems by the localities and the development of policies and structures to meet them is another matter."[13]

RESOURCES

The MSC functioned in an environment that was obviously more favorable to the defenders of the status quo than to the champions of reform. If it was to succeed in its objectives, the Commission had to survive the attack of that which existed. To change the system in any major respect would require Herculean effort and substantial resources. As one member later reflected: "I wonder whether we would ever have undertaken the job had we known what we were up against." Certainly the task of redesigning the local polity is difficult under the best of circumstances, and the Milwaukee environment was far from auspicious for this purpose. But possible or impossible as the assignment may have been, the MSC was the chosen instrumentality to formalize and activate the reform ethos. What resources did it have for achieving this objective? How and to what extent were they utilized?

The amount of resources available to individuals and organizations and the extent to which they are willing to use them are crucial variables in determining actual and potential influence. Means at the disposal of community actors for effecting public decisions, moreover, vary widely. Outside the ballot, great disparities exist in the knowledge, wealth, social position, and other means of power possessed by the participants in the political system.[14] Since metropolitan reform is by its very nature a matter of political decision making, the question of resources and their utilization in the public arena is of considerable relevancy to an analysis of survey commissions.

Character of Resources

The Commission brought to its task a stock of assets that to the casual observer might seem impressive. It enjoyed high social and economic standing, the prestige of gubernatorial appointment, a legislative mandate, full support of the metropolitan press, and the backing of civic organizations. Through several of its members, it had entree to the top influentials in the commercial and industrial sectors of the community. By means of these members it also had access to sources of financial support over and above legislative appropriations. Its roster contained several strong and highly motivated individuals who viewed service on the Commission as an opportunity for personal career development as well as a civic responsibility. Talented, able, educated, and highly respectable, its personnel was well representative of the community elite.

The very qualities which made the MSC an impressive body also militated against its effectiveness as an instrument of reform. Its prestigious composition caused it to be suspect in some circles and its apolitical character gave it little access to the centers of political power. Presumably, as a creature of the state it would have admittance to the decision-making machinery of state government, but its composition as a citizen commission denied it status among the lawmakers. It did enjoy the overt support of the governor, and because of its sponsorship it could expect sympathetic treatment from local Republican legislators. Theoretically it had open channels to the local governments through their officially designated representatives on the Commission. But as we have seen elsewhere, these appointees were only nominally connected with their municipal units and could in no sense be considered influential opinion-makers in local governmental circles. Parkinson and Knoebel, for example, did not enjoy the same status among central city and suburban officials as did Scholl and Carpenter among their social and economic peers.

Common to all citizen study groups, the MSC was also deficient in certain critical resources. First of all, it did not enjoy the advantages of numbers or a basis of mass support such as is available to labor unions and political parties. Second, it lacked access to means that are normally at the disposal of elected officials, such as the legal powers of public office with their rewards and sanctions. Finally, it did not have the resources for communicating with and motivating the wide strata of intermediate and lower opinion formulators, such as neighborhood influentials, ethnic leaders, and union stewards. As the interviews indicate, the Commission's influence seldom penetrated beyond the good government groups, and these were already in its camp.

Use of Resources

The potential influence of an individual or group is dependent not alone upon the possession of resources but also on the willingness to employ them for a given purpose and on the rate and efficiency with which they are used.[15] Politicians normally utilize their resources at a high rate with considerable efficiency for political ends; businessmen do the same for business objectives. The situation, however, is different in the case of metropolitan reform. Few politicians will risk their scarce means to support modifications of the local governmental pattern, but they will expend them in opposition if the proposed changes encroach upon their interests. To the businessman, metropolitan reform is merely a "sideshow in the great circus of life." Seldom does he utilize his assets to any significant degree in furtherance of the crusade. Even if he were willing to do so, the political structure in which he operates frequently circumscribes his activity. The economic notable whose plant is situated in a suburban community may expend substantial resources to influence local officials on matters that concern his business, such as a zoning change to permit expansion of his factory. It is highly improbable that he will use his means at this rate in supporting recommendations for metropolitan reform that have little direct reference to his economic interests. He will be particularly reluctant to do so if the proposed changes are anathema to local officials with whom he finds it advantageous to maintain good relations.

Even in those cases where the businessman is willing to expend a share of his resources on metropolitan reorganization, he frequently utilizes them inefficiently and unskillfully simply because he lacks the experience and desire to be a political entrepreneur. The Milwaukee experience demonstrates the relatively low level at which potential assets are commonly employed in metropolitan reform movements. Many sources of aid and influence both within and outside the MSC were either ignored entirely or utilized at only minimal rates. Internally, several members contributed generously of their time, but the talents and potentialities of the majority were scarcely tapped. Nor was the prestige and legitimacy which the agency enjoyed at its inception fully exploited. In fact, poor strategy, resignations, and lack of clearly articulated goals soon dissipated the advantages of high public status.

The exodus of the economic elites from the Commission was a particularly damaging blow to the group's prestige. The busy executives had early discovered that effective leadership of a metropolitan reform movement entails sacrifices—time, energy, involvement in controversy with public officials—which they were not prepared to make. Of the four members who could be ranked among the top business notables of the community—Carpenter, Cornell, Lobb, and Scholl—only Carpenter remained on the Commission at its demise; and he had long ceased to be active, attending but one meeting during the last eighteen months of the agency's life.

Financial resources allocated to the MSC were small ($125,000) considering the task imposed upon the group. Yet a large potential source of monetary support—the economic influentials—remained almost wholly untouched. Only on one occasion did the Commission endeavor to solicit aid from individuals or organizations. This effort yielded less than one-third of its total funds, most of it coming from local governments. Until the very end of the MSC's life, a common complaint of the members was lack of sufficient finances to conduct their operations properly. Yet the commissioners themselves were reluctant to pursue actively the financial potential that was theirs.

Research Resources

A more revealing picture of MSC resources can be obtained by examining them in relation to each of the group's expressed objectives: study and recommendation, public information, reform initiation, and action stimulation. The Commission had several categories of research means on which to draw: its staff, the members themselves, consultants, and technicians from local businesses, government, and the universities. During the initial period it employed a moderate-size staff, but after Ball's resignation it operated with only a research director.[16] The reluctance to seek additional outside funds ruled out the possibility of retaining an adequate staff and placed severe limits on the scope and depth of the research. It also deprived the various committees of professional assistance other than that provided by consultants and the director. Much of the research burden during the latter years of the group's life was carried by Commission members. The talents and time of several individuals, including Cutler, Jensen, and Rasche, were utilized in research and report writing to an extent seldom observed on metropolitan commissions.

The Commission employed consultants only on a minimal basis. On several occasions it discussed plans for making broader use of outside research agencies, but here again its small budget deterred action. Assistance from technicians in the community also remained largely untapped. Although the Commission early appointed a research advisory committee with the intention of enlisting professional research talent, the matter was not pursued. No efforts were made, for example, to have local firms assign technical personnel to the Commission for limited periods in the same way that they release their junior executives to participate in community chest and other civic drives. Possible assistance from governmental agencies likewise remained unexplored except in the one instance, where the state health department was persuaded to assign an engineer to the sewerage study.

The MSC's heavy reliance on the members themselves for its research needs had serious drawbacks. In the first place it compelled them to perform work for which they were not trained. Secondly, it diverted their time and energy from other goals of the group. Last and perhaps most important, it annoyed the business executives on the Commission. As one of them complained, "We handled and discussed too many matters that should have been left to the staff. Business leaders are accustomed to have the facts carefully assembled and brought before them by their staff. They are then in a position to make quick decisions."

Public Information Resources

MSC resources for its second goal, public education and information, consisted largely of the mass media, the communications network of civic organizations, and the facilities of the Commission itself. The metropolitan dailies and major radio and television stations of the area gave prime coverage to MSC activities, and both the *Sentinel* and *Journal* editorially supported its recommendations. The communications resources of the civic groups were less fully utilized. The League of Women Voters made consistent efforts to keep its membership informed and to generate interest in those proposals on which the various local leagues could reach consensus. A few other organizations, such as the Citizens' Governmental Research Bureau and the City Club, also covered the Commission's activities for their members, but their audiences were already among the "believers."

The MSC had hoped that with the aid of the Junior Chamber and Junior Bar a large number of voluntary organizations could be encouraged to establish metropolitan problems committees. As Klotsche and several others saw it, the Commission's public education program should be broader than selling its recommendations and "should be geared to the opinion molders rather than to individuals; the opinion molders being the members of the study committees on metropolitan problems in the various organizations."[17] This sophisticated approach to opinion formulation was not pushed with vigor and the program soon collapsed.

The MSC's own efforts to perform the role of preceptor to the metropolitan community were sporadic and limited largely to the distribution of brochures, newsletters and reports, and to speeches by the chairman and individual members. Although the need for informing the public was repeatedly discussed by the members, they were at no time willing to commit the MSC and its resources to a major educational effort. Throughout the Commission's life they continued to skirt the problem by making token gestures toward a public information program. Even Klotsche, who was firmly convinced of the need, felt that the agency's resources were not commensurate to the task. Actually, the whole matter of communications both within and outside the Commission was a frustrating one for the members. As Houghton told an audience of civic leaders and public officials, one of the MSC's "biggest problems is in the field of communications. We have very real problems in communicating internally with members of the Commission who after all are busy men and women . . . who have to make a living in addition to performing a civic duty by serving on the

250 THE MILWAUKEE METROPOLITAN STUDY COMMISSION

Study Commission. We also have had some difficulties in our communications with the governments in greater Milwaukee and in our communications with the general public."[18]

It is extremely doubtful that the MSC could have served as an effective agent of public education even if it had made maximum use of its resources. Most metropolitan reform issues, particularly those of governmental reorganization, lack direct relation to the on-going life of the average citizen and consequently have little capacity for attracting and holding his attention or shaking him from his civic complacency. Transmitting complex issues of this kind to the electorate is a well nigh impossible task that certainly cannot be accomplished by newspaper publicity or the pronouncements of ad hoc committees, highly endowed as they may be with the symbols of legitimacy. If public support is to be mobilized for metropolitan reform, the impetus must come from mass-based sources that can influence political behavior, such as labor unions and political parties. Citizen commissions such as the MSC usually have little access to resources of this nature.

Reform Initiation Resources

The MSC's third goal—initiation of reform—cast the group in an action-oriented role. Never fully accepted by the majority of members, the part was played only during the early phase of the Commission's life. After Lobb's resignation as chairman and the tabling of the metropolitan government proposal, the role was formally discarded although not forgotten. The talents and means available to the Commission for enacting this part were not impressive. Its own personnel had little political experience while its access to the resources of political leaders was minimal. It could secure the introduction of its bills as any organization can, but it lacked the means to mobilize support for their passage.

With the exception of Lobb, the high-ranking businessmen on the MSC did not favor an action role for the Commission; this task, they felt, should be left to other groups. Officials of the Greater Milwaukee Committee held similar views. In fact, a noticeable coolness developed between the GMC and the Commission during the early period when the latter was behaving as an activist. Cutler alluded to this situation when he wrote the governor in June, 1959:

> We believe that the Commission will fail unless there is a three-way understanding between you, the Commission, and business and civic leaders in Milwaukee County concerning the role of the Study Commission. We fear that through a series of failures of the Commission the three groups mentioned do not at this time have a mutual understanding of the role of the Study Commission.[19]

The position that research and recommendation should be separated from implementation may be logical but it leaves unanswered the question as to who will champion the proposals in the political arena. Civic groups standing alone do not possess sufficient resources for the task, while other large organizations and the overwhelming majority of political leaders have shown little interest in the cause. It was this factor that troubled even those Commission members who were convinced that their role should be limited to study and prescription.

Catalytic Resources

The fourth goal—stimulating reform activity among local officials —called for still another set of resources. For the MSC to serve as a catalytic agent, time, staff, and negotiating skill were required. All except the last were in scarce supply. The staff was far too small to conduct the fact-finding and assist in the continuing negotiations and follow-ups necessary for the Commission to function effectively in this capacity. The catalytic role, like that of research, is ill suited to a group of busy executives. They have neither the time nor patience for such a task. As one of them observed: "It's an extremely frustrating experience to try to get these officials to work together and do something. All these little mayors are jealous of their powers. They think only of their own little domain and can't see the good of the whole metropolitan community."

The experiences of the Randall and Rasche committees indicate that the catalytic role involves certain prerequisites and demands: (1) a continuing or long-term committee of citizens with sufficient time to devote to the task; (2) legitimization of the committee by public appointment; (3) a full-time professional staff; (4) consensus between the committee and local officials on the specific areas of cooperation to be explored; and (5) research in sufficient depth and detail to give local policy makers the kinds of data on which they can base decisions (e.g., costs of proposed changes, blueprints for carrying them out, estimated results). If a citizens' committee is appropriate to play the role of public catalyst, its responsibilities should be so understood and its membership selected specifically with this function in mind.

ENVIRONMENTAL FEEDBACK

The term "feedback" might be simply defined as the flow of information to the place where analysis is made of conditions in the environment. A furnace thermostat is a good example of feedback in operation. Temperature in the area served by the heating equipment is communicated to the thermostat—the point of analysis—which in turn causes adjustments to be made in the output of the furnace. Human organizations such as the study commission are subject to analogous feedbacks. Their outputs or activities cause reactions in the social and political environment. These reactions are relayed back to the organization, where they induce certain changes in the group's behavior. In the case of the MSC, the influence of the environmental feedback was unusually great. The members' conception of metropolitan reform and the character of Commission recommendations were substantially modified by the external responses to their work.

Attitude Changes

Early in the life of the Commission most members believed that significant metropolitan reorganization was possible and that widespread latent sympathy for action in this field existed. They had little evidence to warrant those beliefs but assumed, as one of them remarked, that "People must be sick and tired of all the quibbling between City and suburban officials and all the talk—with no action forthcoming—of doing something about metropolitan problems." Many of them felt also that the studies which the group was about to engage in would provide answers to the problems of the area and convincingly point out the way to needed governmental changes. Less than eighteen months later—after the tabling of the metropolitan district proposal—none of the commissioners were speaking in these terms. Their aspirations had tended to adjust to what they believed was attainable. By this time they had experienced the adamant and rigid opposition of public officials and had learned that their impression of latent popular support for reorganization was a grand illusion. By this time, too, they were beginning to realize that metropolitan research contains little magic and seldom provides cookbook recipes or such clear-cut answers that only the unintelligent can dispute them.

When the MSC started its operations most commissioners were convinced of the need for area-wide administration of certain functions. This conviction remained at the end but in altered form. Originally, many of the members were sympathetic to the creation of a new metropolitan agency with jurisdiction extending beyond the county lines and with control over a substantial number of services. At the time MSC terminated its activities, all these notions —new agency, extra-county jurisdiction, broad range of functions— had been discarded or modified. An existing governmental unit, the county, was proposed as the metropolitan vehicle; problems that transcended county lines were to be handled by inter-county agreements; and the question of what services might better be handled on an area-wide basis was left open.

Environmental Impact

The first serious shock to the MSC's expectations came in early 1959 with the replies of the suburban governments to the questionnaire on metropolitan reorganization. The inflexible attitude exhibited by local officials and the failure of the public generally to give any signs of support for area-wide reform convinced Commission members that it was futile to think in terms of a holistic or total approach to the problems of the metropolis. This recognition led them to abandon the large solution and turn to partial remedies relating to specific functions.

The second major setback to MSC aspirations occurred late in 1959 when the initial recommendations of the land use and zoning committee on establishment of a county planning commission met solid opposition from both central city and suburban governments. The reaction to this proposal to give the county government veto powers over local zoning caused Commission members to doubt the feasibility of even a piecemeal approach that involved any element of compulsion. Thereafter the MSC shifted its emphasis to voluntary cooperation, urging local units to reach agreement among themselves on joint activities and on turning over area-wide functions to the county government.

Commission Reaction

As early as February, 1959, the Milwaukee *Sentinel* was reporting that the MSC "has learned how it feels to burn its fingers. . . . It's no secret, that most members of the Metropolitan Study Commission have lost hope for any metropolitan government here in the foreseeable future. The citizen commissioners had such a vision when they started their study of metropolitan problems 16 months ago. But this vision went up in smoke in the cross fire of city-suburban rivalry."[20] As one commissioner stated, "When I was first appointed to the MSC I had high hopes that we could get something done for the community; but after a time I began to doubt that anything could come of our efforts." Another observed "The commission started out with bright hopes and the belief that it could accomplish something by pointing out the problems and showing the way to their solution. There was a lot of enthusiasm among the members for some form of metropolitan government. This ideal vanished in face of the opposition that we met."

The instrument ultimately recommended by the Commission for promoting cooperative activity was an intergovernmental council of elected local officials. Ironically, the MSC has been created largely because of the failure of a similarly constituted body of public officeholders—the Committee of 21—to act on metropolitan problems. During its tenure, the MSC had run the continuum from compulsory and large-scale reform to voluntary and minor change, although at the very end it suggested greater use of the county as the metropolitan vehicle. It had retreated from its original position in the cases of metropolitan government, sewage disposal, water supply, and land use and zoning. Only its recommendations on revenue sources and distribution had remained firm, but tax reform was an issue that was being contested at the state and not the local level.

During the initial phase of its operations, the MSC had evidenced little interest in the county government as the possible metropolitan instrumentality. At one point the executive committee had flatly stated that the county was not an appropriate agency to serve in this capacity since its territorial jurisdiction was too narrow. The first indication of receptivity to the urban county approach occurred late in 1959 in the tentative although soon abandoned proposal of the land use and zoning committee to establish a county planning commission. The first county-oriented recommendation actually adopted by the MSC was the proposal that the county government build and operate a series of incinerators. It was not, however, until the closing months of its tenure that the Commission unequivocally embraced the principle of the urban county.

Several factors contributed to the espousal of this approach. Experiences on the Commission had convinced the members that major reorganization of the governmental pattern in the foreseeable future was highly improbable. The only course that appeared open to them was to accept the present system in its entirety and encourage better utilization of its potential. The national trend away from the creation of "new levels of government" and the favorable attitude of their last research director, David Mars, toward the urban county concept were additional elements that impressed them. Perhaps the most important factor was the receptive attitude of several county government officials, particularly John Doyne, toward the MSC and its recommendations. After Doyne assumed the newly-created post of county executive in January, 1960, he indicated more affirmatively his support of the Commission but at the same time reiterated his strong opposition to the establishment of any new metropolitan agency or district. By this time MSC members were convinced of the necessity of political support and leadership if reform was to be accomplished. Only the county government seemed to offer any hope, tenuous as it was, for the future of metropolitan reorganization in Milwaukee.

The MSC's impact on the environment was far less than the effect of feedback on its own thinking and actions. Service on the Commission was in effect a learning process for most members. Not only did their work better acquaint them with the area's problems but more significantly it materially altered their views on metropolitan reform and the manner of accomplishing it. As one member described it, "When I first came on the Commission, I had little experience with politics. My first inclination was to roll up my sleeves and get the job over with. But I soon learned that this is not the way you operate if you hope to get anything done. This kind of job requires a lot of patience and the willingness to negotiate and compromise." Metropolitan reorganization, as the Commission belatedly discovered, is not above the hard realities of politics.

RESULTS

The MSC operated for almost four years. During this time it enlisted the time and energy of some of the community's ablest citizens. Countless hours and the combined talents of many individuals were devoted to its work. Thousands of words went into its numerous reports, and many more thousands appeared in the press or were uttered in public presentations of its findings and recommendations. What were the results of all these efforts? Previous pages do not portray an impressive list of accomplishments. They reveal no major victories for the cause of urban reform and no dramatic changes in the local governmental structure. Whatever results there were must be sought in less spectacular items: research products, articulation of problems, modification of statutes, stimulation of action, and crystallization of reformist thinking. Some of these results are not difficult to recognize and assess, but most are intangible and not easily identified or measured.

Research and Problem Identification

The research output of the MSC was substantial—far beyond what one might predict on the basis of its budget. Evaluated in terms of amount of research rather than reform action, the Commission would be rated highly successful. The legacy of reports and information that it bequeathed to the community continues to be referred to by the press and by civic groups such as the League of Women Voters. The research, like that conducted by most metropolitan survey groups, consisted mainly of fact gathering and data recording with some attempt at analysis. As inventories of existing conditions in the problem areas examined, the findings served a useful purpose. As contributions to a better understanding of the factors involved in the functioning and development of the metropolis, they offered little. The Commission's failure to prepare a study design based on some concept or rationale of the metropolitan community led to diffusion of research efforts and a lack of depth in many of the studies.

Reform Initiation

The MSC saw two of its recommendations translated into action: extension of the sewer district boundaries and creation of a regional planning agency. Both measures had already been proposed and initiated by other groups prior to appointment of the Commission. Both would eventually have been adopted whether a study group had been established or not although the Commission's work probably hastened their accomplishment. In each instance, the MSC played the role of activist. It endorsed and supported the sewer district bill in the legislature and jointly sponsored corrective amendments to the regional planning law and encouraged its utilization locally.

The two achievements, it is interesting to note, met the historical preconditions for local governmental reorganization.* Enlargement of the sewer district boundaries involved an increase in territorial jurisdiction for an already existing metropolitan agency and was of primary concern to the outlying suburbs. Among other factors, the measure (1) had the support of local officials in the affected area; (2) pertained to a service that could not be met by unilateral action on the part of the municipalities, and (3) grew out of citizen dissatisfaction with the lack or inadequate level of the service. Where these prerequisites did not exist, as in South Milwaukee with its locally operated sewer system, there was strong and successful opposition to inclusion.

Establishment of the regional planning commission was a somewhat different matter although the same factors were in evidence.

* See above, Chapter Three.

Regional planning was a new function of a purely advisory nature that posed no threat to the established bureaucracy. It had the active support of the planning administrators of the area and the blessings of many local officials. It also had the strong support of the governor, who had espoused state and regional planning as a major item in his political program and who personally intervened in the move to create the new agency.[21]

Action Stimulation

Some MSC supporters had hoped that the existence of such a body would stimulate public officials to put the metropolitan house in order. They reasoned that the group's prestige and its potentiality for affecting change would prompt local officialdom to act constructively in its own self-interest. Reaction took place, but it was the negative response of change-resistant interests, not the resolution of those in authority to improve the system. When the MSC continually retreated in face of this resistance, it "lost face" among supporters as well as the guardians of localism; for if the existing system was no worse than recommendations of the Commission indicated, there was little reason why either public officials or the citizen body should become concerned.

When the MSC first came into existence, its potential for stimulating action was an unknown quantity. Even the seasoned officials in both central city and suburbs were not sure just what kind of game they were about to engage in or what the public would demand. The City set up a special committee to analyze the group's reports and instructed Parkinson to get in touch with key officials if any unexpected questions affecting its interests arose in the Commission. The president of the common council stated that in such an event he would immediately summon the aldermen into special session to review the matter. Suburban governments similarly kept close watch over Commission activities through the League of Suburban Municipalities.

By the time the MSC closed its doors, the situation had completely reversed itself. Whatever advantages or initiative the Commission may have enjoyed at its inception had long since been lost. During the latter months of its life it was largely ignored by both City and suburban officialdom. The low state to which its standing had deteriorated is illustrated by the final public hearing on the water question. In contrast to the first hearing two years earlier, where all local governments were represented, only the City and one suburb bothered to send spokesmen to the second. As far as suburban officials were concerned, the problem had been solved; the Commission was no longer of any potential use to them. Interest in the recommendations on revenue sources and distribution was similarly low. Even the inclusion of a proposal to abolish local assessing departments and transfer the function to county government failed to evoke any protest or comment, even though it involved local autonomy, of traditional concern to local public officials. By this time the inability of the MSC to stimulate either public or political support for its recommendations had been well demonstrated. After the collapse of the metropolitan government movement and the subsequent dilution of Commission goals, local officials had become convinced that they had little to fear from the group's activities.

The efforts of the Commission to stimulate activity on a lesser level by serving as a catalytic agent produced few tangible results, possibly because this approach was undertaken after the MSC had already lost face among local officials. Randall, as chairman of the intergovernmental cooperation committee, made a determined bid to test the efficacy of this approach. He felt, as a result of his experiences, that a citizen committee could probably be effective in inducing modest cooperative activity. At the same time, he was convinced that long and sustained efforts in working closely with local public officials would be required if the task was to prove at all fruitful. Rasche was also certain that the "soft sell" approach could be productive. He felt that his work with the police chiefs was beginning to lay a foundation for cooperation and that some constructive results could have been achieved if the Commission's tenure had been extended. Few other members, however, were as sanguine. A majority felt that the results which could be expected from this approach would be far from commensurate with the amount of resources necessary to bring them about.

Effect on Reformist Thinking

The MSC's experiences convinced most civic leaders that only minimal accommodation of the governmental structure to the realities of metropolitan life can be expected in the foreseeable future. As a result of the group's work, and particularly its final report, most reform advocates appear willing to accept the present pattern of government as a given framework and work for improvement within it. The Commission's recommendations have also served to focus attention upon county government as the metropolitan vehicle and have crystallized reformist thinking around this approach. Thus for the first time in recent decades local civic organizations and interested citizens have an overall objective defined for them on which they can base their activities. Up to the present, however, they have taken no significant steps to further this goal. In fact, civic group activity in the field of metropolitan reform has come to an almost complete standstill.

THE PRESENT STATE OF REFORM

The MSC was largely an outgrowth of disillusionment with intergovernmental cooperation. At the time of the Commission's establishment, civic leaders anticipated that some measure of functional consolidation, if not a new metropolitan agency, would result from its activities. By 1961 these expectations and hopes had vanished. Little talk of metropolitan government or broad-scale reallocation of functions is now heard. The urban county concept has won approval in theory from civic activists, but only a small minority view this remedy as anything more than a long-range goal to be pursued slowly and by piecemeal arrangements. The short-term objective is to be intergovernmental cooperation, an approach discarded as inadequate only a few years back.

The return to the old approach is illustrated by the Civic Federation for Community Cooperation (CFCC), which was formed after the demise of the MSC. Sparked by the City Club and Milwaukee Association of Commerce, some twenty organizations joined in a loosely knit alliance for the announced purpose of seeking implementation of MSC recommendations. The CFCC intended to model its activities after those of the Randall committee and to serve as a stimulator or catalytic agent for action by local officials. Its theme—one that has returned to popularity among civic groups—is "intergovernment cooperation." As the Milwaukee *Journal* (in editorially commenting on the "hopeful new civic movement") noted at the time: "Basic to achieving specific ends will be nurture of a warmer climate for intergovernment cooperation as the vehicle." The same theme was highlighted at the Greater Milwaukee Committee's annual dinner for public officials in November, 1961. Little of substance, however, has emerged from the CFCC since its organization, and the GMC for all practical purposes has dropped metropolitan reorganization from its agenda.

Local officials, moreover, have given no indication of responding any more constructively to the plea for cooperation than they did in the days of the Committee of 21. In fact, history is repeating itself with the embryonic council of municipal heads. In January, 1961, the county executive brought the mayors and village presidents together at a meeting called by the GMC. The group tentatively agreed to form an intermunicipal council but to exclude controversial items from its agenda. Although a steering committee met on several occasions with inconclusive results, the council has not been organized up to the time of this writing more than four years later.

Does this state of affairs portend governmental or administrative chaos for the Milwaukee of the year 1975 or 2000? Probably not, although the failure of local units to act in concert may prevent the community from attaining much of the potential of its urban environment. Metropolitan Milwaukee, like similar areas throughout the nation, will likely continue to make piecemeal adjustments to its governmental system as new needs or crises arise. It will continue to "muddle through," as economist Lindblom so aptly described the process—or if not through, at least to muddle.

11

The Twilight of
Metropolitan Survey
Commissions

The Milwaukee Metropolitan Study Commission provides more than an isolated instance of efforts by an officially appointed group of local citizens to redesign the urban polity. Operating during a period when new winds were beginning to stir in the field of metropolitan reorganization, the Commission found itself caught in the cross currents of a minor revolution in urban research. A product of the old tradition, it came at a time when basic disagreements among the "experts" were rising to the surface; when long-standing assumptions about governmental reorganization were being questioned; when academic criticism of traditional local government studies had reached a high peak; when research in the urban field was taking on new orientations, new emphases, and new approaches; and when controversial social issues were demanding greater public attention. These emerging trends ran counter to the classical notion of the lay study commission and its philosophical predispositions. In a sense a victim of the new forces, the MSC represented what may well have been the twilight or demise of such commissions as we have known them.

Metropolitan surveys began to make their appearance during the 1920's. Most often, the initial impetus for such studies came from organizations that were heirs of the municipal reform spirit and ideology of the early century: citizens' leagues, good government councils, chambers of commerce, and leagues of women voters. These groups began to turn their attention to the larger community as central cities became better governed and the critical urban problems outgrew corporate boundaries. Well before World War II, metropolitan reorganization had come to occupy the place on the civic agenda that municipal reform had held earlier. The movement reached its heyday during the five-year period from 1953 to 1957, when approximately seventy such studies were instituted, the majority of them under the direction of specially created commissions or committees. Since that time the number has radically declined, until today less than a handful are in existence and few new ones are contemplated.

The history of study commissions is a history of the whole complex of folk-thought on metropolitan reorganization. It is a story of the timidity and hesitancy of the economic notables about involvement in public issues, of the tenuous relationship between business and political elites, of the moral and technical complexity of the problem, of the lack of citizen concern, and of the deep resistance of the ongoing system to change. Above all, it is a tale of often bootless enterprises that fell far short of the expectations of their sponsors. The curious question is where the civic reformers and their academic mentors ever got the notion that citizen study commissions could become effective instrumentalities of governmental restructuring in the modern-day metropolis.

ASSUMPTIONS

The rationale underlying the creation of citizen survey commissions merits exploration, since it focuses attention on the wisdom or feasibility of trying to achieve metropolitan reform through this type of instrumentality. Perhaps the best way to approach the question is to look at the basic assumptions that prompted the creation of these agencies. Many such assumptions could probably be identified, some peculiar to a single or limited number of study groups, others of more universal applicability. We suggest four which appear to be of major importance and wide relevancy: (1) power and influence of economic notables over the community agenda; (2) need for major change in the existing governmental system; (3) self-evident nature of the solutions; and (4) latent receptivity of the citizen body to reorganization.

Influence of Economic Notables

Advocates of metropolitan surveys have long insisted on study commissions of high-ranking citizens drawn largely from business and industrial circles. Conceiving the structure of community power as monolithic, they have assumed that key civic decisions are made by a select group of individuals of upper socio-economic status who stand at the top of a stable power hierarchy. With the blessings of this coterie, projects move ahead; without its express or tacit consent, little of significance can be accomplished. This group is presumed to exercise (or at least possess the latent power to exert) predominant influence over local public policy and to have control over or access to lower levels in the community structure where decisions are formally legitimated and executed. Moreover, because of its prestigious character, it is also presumed to have considerable influence over the formation of public opinion on matters of civic concern.

Were this an accurate picture of the pattern of community power in the metropolis, tangible results might be expected to flow from a survey commission selected from the ranks of the economic elites or their subalterns. But the mythology of civic power and the facts of the urban world do not coincide. Influence over the course of community affairs in metropolitan areas is possessed by many individuals and groups in a considerable variety of roles, each exercising power only within a fairly limited scope. As Dahl states it, "The economic notables, far from being a ruling group, are simply one of many groups out of which individuals sporadically emerge to influence the politics and acts of city officials."[1] Individuals in top economic positions may have more power than those in lower posts, but the value system of the economic elites closely circumscribes the exercise of this power outside the business sector. To the corporate executive, non-conflict and smooth-running efficiency are the desiderata. Involvement in the problems of the polity necessitates entry into the local political world, where conflict and a certain lack of efficiency are predominant characteristics of the system.[2] Consequently, the economic notables have only rarely been willing to face up to the necessity of realistic political action in the metropolitan sphere. Instead they have sought to fulfill their role obligation as civic influentials by sponsoring and supporting "non-partisan" studies.

When metropolitan reorganization is at issue, political forces representative of local officialdom are invariably called into play. These forces, as the record of reform accomplishment demonstrates, are not readily amenable to the purported influence of business leaders. Lay survey commissions seek access to public officials since their support is helpful, if not essential, for translating recommendations into action. Such efforts to woo or influence the reluctant bureaucracy have been notoriously unsuccessful. In fact, local officeholders generally regard citizen survey commissions as amateur intruders or civic nuisances that must be politely tolerated. Seldom are they interested in considering the proposals which emanate from such groups as the basis for serious discussion of governmental reorganization. To their way of thinking, major changes, if needed—an assumption which the overwhelming majority of them deny—should be instituted and negotiated through established political channels.

The Milwaukee experience offers further proof that the ties between top businessmen and the local bureaucracy are at best tenuous. Local political leadership can afford to bargain with the economic elites on many community matters, and such bargaining sporadically takes place. Reorganization, however, is seldom a negotiable item in the eyes of local officialdom, since this poses a threat to the established system. Even were the economic notables firmly committed to achieving metropolitan restructuring, they could not impose such a decision on the political leaders without their acquiescence. The latter, with their own independent bases of power, have the means to resist governmental modifications which they perceive as detrimental to their interests. When the occasion demands, they are able to draw on a cadre of political resources that can quickly be mobilized through the existing web of mutual ties. Suburban leaders can act in terms of a common threat to suburbia, and on the basis of their collective identity can effectively marshal support at both the state and local policymaking levels. Central city officials can act in a similar manner, through the political leaders and mass-based interest groups that are closely linked to the core municipality.

Need for Governmental Change

The second reformist assumption—the need for basic governmental restructuring if the metropolis is to survive—has been subjected to skeptical comment from urban scholars in recent years. Political scientist Charles R. Adrian, for example, has written that most of the needs and problems discussed in survey commission reports are not abnormal crisis situations but part of the ordinary problems of living in a wealthy, changing, complex nation. According to him, many of the leaders who guide the policies of our larger communities hold to beliefs that are based on unrealistic assumptions of how metropolitan areas should be governed. "Collectively, these assumptions represent the folklore that determines in large part the policy statements found in the reports of Chamber of Commerce committees, 'citizen committees' on metropolitan area problems, and local government research bureaus."[3] A similar theme is evident in a collection of articles entitled "Metropolis in Ferment," which appeared in the November, 1957, issue of the *Annals of the American Academy of Social and Political Science.* Running throughout much of the treatment is the implicit assumption that time would heal, and that the crazy quilt of metropolitan life would eventually right itself in the tugging, hauling, and compounding of a democracy.

Reaction against the stereotyped problem statements and prescriptions of the administrative management approach to metropolitan reorganization has brought about an almost complete reversal of the earlier emphasis on major structural change. In many academic circles it has now become fashionable to regard the present fragmented system of urban government as functional and adequate. Whatever adjustments are needed, so the rationale runs, will be accomplished in the normal push and tug of the political process. A natural consequence of this view is the tendency to dismiss governmental structure as a major variable in determining the course and operation of the metropolitan community. In one sense, this tendency has been healthy since it has diverted attention from the narrowly circumscribed framework of administrative reform to deeper analyses of metropolitan behavior. But in another sense, it had led to overly sanguine appraisals of the existing governmental system and a disregard of the possible effects of political structure and form on urban functioning.

The declining popularity of the "disaster" thesis has not been confined solely to the ranks of social scientists. Even the tune of reform activists has changed, less, however, for intellectual reasons than because of the repeated failures of metropolitan reorganization campaigns. When the civic knights first began their rational assault on the ills of the modern metropolis, they took for granted the indispensability of political unification. Later, they gave ground and turned to the advocacy of "local federalism" in its various forms. More recently, they have lowered their sights still further until today voluntary intergovernmental cooperation has become the widely acceptable answer to the governmental problems of metropolitan areas.[4]

Nature of Solution

The third assumption, the self-evident character of the remedies, has also undergone modification. Reformist dogma from the beginning had been based on a simplistic view of the metropolis and the maladies which afflict it. Critics of metropolitan political structure have in the past been virtually unanimous in their diagnosis: too many governments, overlapping jurisdictions, duplication of functions, lack of coordination. Few doubted that the system was pathological; the objective was to effect a cure before the patient succumbed. By the late 1950's, however, a new note was finding its way into the literature. Social scientists were beginning to ask whether fragmented local government was really the villain in the play and whether the proposed forms of area-wide government were the answer to the problems of the nation's burgeoning urban centers. Political scientist Edward Banfield gave voice to the growing doubts about structural reform when he speculated that one reason for the low batting average of study commissions might be the "spurious" nature of the metropolitan area problem.

That there are (for example) 1,071 independent local governments in the New York area may not be as bad as it is made to sound. Perhaps there should be even more. There are some real and important problems of metropolitan reorganization, of course, but the 'one local government for one local area' idea reflects a taste for symmetry, simplicity, and, in a special sense, logic.[5]

Banfield and others also cautioned against the failure to distinguish between problems which exist in metropolitan areas regardless of the form of government and those which exist by virtue of the inadequacies of administrative structure. The tendency of the reformers has been to equate the two and to hold that most of the phenomena troubling metropolitan communities could be controlled through governmental reorganization. Viewing decentralization of the local polity as the real enemy and the root of urban maladies, they insisted that creation of a central instrumentality for area-wide administration and decision-making would provide the means for effectively handling the social as well as service problems. When questions were asked about the political and social costs of a centralized system, the citadel of administrative orthodoxy bristled with indignation at such impudence. To the reformer, the logic of his position appeared irrefutable; only the procrastination and selfish resistance of politicians and public officeholders stood in the way of achieving the Heavenly City.

All this has now changed. The passage of time has brought with it increasing awareness of the complexity of the problems and a reaction to the old nostrums. What seemed self-evident only a decade or so before now appears highly problematical. Luther Gulick, long a keen observer of the metropolitan scene, described the changing perspective in the William W. Cook lectures at the University of Michigan in 1961:

> The answer is not as easy and simple as most American reformers thought as recently as five or ten years ago. When we first faced the problem of urban explosion it was natural to seek a solution of emerging governmental difficulties through the direct application of simple measures such as annexation of the suburbs, consolidation, public utility extensions, and the simple direct enlargement of the boundaries of the local general government. Where this approach encountered difficulties, we turned to 'authorities' and other special districts and created state commissions without much thought as to where this might lead us. Thus we met what we thought were simple problems with simple, direct answers.[6]

But when the simple answers proved unacceptable, urban specialists began to probe more deeply into the causes of metropolitan dysfunctioning. The results were disquieting to those who viewed the problem primarily in terms of governmental organization. To tackle the underlying causes would take the reformers outside the realm of administrative orthodoxy into the more complex and controversial field of social and political behavior. Neither the business leaders nor their dependent civic organizations were prepared to engage in such an undertaking.

Potential Citizen Interest

The last assumption, that of popular interest, has also been badly punctured by empirical research. We are commonly told that metropolitan study commissions serve a useful function by articulating the problem, pointing out the solutions, and generating public interest and discussion. These results in turn presumably lead to citizen pressure on public officials to institute desired changes. For, so the argument goes, once the public is made acquainted with the "convincing" facts of the case, the resistance of petty interests and small minds will be swept aside in an inexorable march toward civic redemption. Logical as this line of reasoning may appear, the postulated sequence of events rarely takes place in the real world of metropolitanism.

The lack of public response to the work and recommendations of metropolitan study commissions is too well known to require further documentation. One reason for this indifference is the relative satisfaction of most urban residents with their local governments. The myth of a highly discontented metropolitan constituency standing ready to storm the walls of the status quo has been thoroughly dispelled by sample surveys of citizen attitudes toward reorganization. In St. Louis, Dayton, and Cleveland, for example, interviews with a cross section of the population showed that residents in those areas had no strong criticism of their local units and relatively few service complaints.[7]

A second reason is found in the nature of the issues that constitute the stock in trade of the typical survey commission. As traditionally formulated by such groups, the metropolitan problem is simply one of relating sound engineering and administrative solutions to such matters as sewage disposal, traffic congestion, water supply, and land use. Even a cursory review of survey literature will impress one with the strong emphasis that the reform movement has placed on the technical nature of urban problems. The announced purpose of the comprehensive study by the Cleveland Metropolitan Services Commission in the late 1950's was "to study the administration of local governmental services, in particular those problems which necessarily transcend municipal boundaries. . . ."[8] Similarly, the legislative mandate to the Milwaukee Commission, as we saw earlier, called for an investigation of "the character, extent, adequacy, cost, and efficiency of the principal services provided by governmental units."[9] Considered in this light, the avowed objective of the metropolitan reform movement is reorganization of the local bureaucratic machinery so that it can furnish essential public services in an efficient, economical, and apolitical fashion. This seeming obsession with the structural features of the local polity has led most study commissions to ignore the metropolitan community as a social system and to regard it merely as an administrative mechanism for providing services.

Scott Greer's incisive study of reform campaigns in three major metropolitan areas clearly demonstrates that it is a thankless and nearly impossible task to transmit to the electorate the complex question of structural change in government.[10] By presenting the metropolitan problem primarily as one of organization and administration, study commissions have minimized their chances of attracting widespread public interest. Social science research offers persuasive evidence that the more a population perceives a problem as technical in nature, the less it is likely to be concerned or to participate in its solution. As sociologist Warner Bloomberg has observed: "If decisions are viewed as involving mainly judgments about right and wrong, good and evil, more people will believe themselves qualified to affect the outcome than when decisions are viewed as requiring some more esoteric technical knowledge."[11]

Citizen study commissions are confronted with a dilemma in this regard. They can undoubtedly raise the level of popular interest and participation by redefining metropolitan reorganization in non-technical or ideological terms. To do this, however, they must shift their case for change from the rationale of management efficiency to the larger and more controversial issues of the metropolis such as race relations and social disorganization. But the other horn of the dilemma is equally sharp since they cannot move in this direction without running into two possible dangers: alienating their sponsors and arousing more opposition than support among the populace. Business leaders, as we have seen, assiduously avoid involvement in community issues with ideological overtones. They have felt free to support metropolitan reorganization, since it has traditionally been defined in technical terms. This support would quickly have been withdrawn had the question of governmental change become linked to the ideologically controversial issues of the community. The attitude of the economic notables toward participation in these matters shows signs of changing under the pressure of current events, but the day has not yet arrived when involvement is the accepted rule.

The possibility of creating added opposition of major importance is even more serious. Presenting the case for metropolitan reform in ideological terms will in all probability engender more public interest and will win support from individuals and groups who have been uncommitted. At the same time it will arouse opposition from many who have been disinterested or quiescent spectators. In fact, the opponents of metropolitan reform have frequently and effectively capitalized on ideological arguments in referenda campaigns, depicting the movement as everything from

an attack on individual freedom to a battle between the forces of evil (central city) and the forces of good (suburbs). On which side the net gain will accrue if the reform cause should also shift its case to ideological grounds is uncertain.

These observations lead to the drawing of an interesting contrast. Lay survey commissions can effect change only when they are able either to influence directly the responsible public bodies or to move the citizenry to demand change. Official governing bodies, on the other hand, can effect structural reform (within, of course, statutory and constitutional limitations) even when the citizen body is totally uninterested or apathetic. In other words, an active and overt public concern is crucial to the success of citizen study commissions, given the fact that they have little direct impact on public officials, whereas local governing bodies can take action in circumstances where such interest is not manifest. So long as metropolitan reform is perceived as a technical problem, the general public is unlikely to become involved, in the absence of a crisis situation. Instead, most citizens will continue to leave the question in the hands of their governmental officials, where they presume the expertise lies. Hence until those who man the bureaucratic helm see need to act, little change is likely to be forthcoming. If by some chance, however, they should desire to effect organizational reform, it would be to their advantage to keep the problem defined in technical terms. By so doing they would meet fewer obstacles and arouse less opposition than if the issue became ideological.

CAUSES OF DECLINE

Today little enthusiasm remains for the use of lay study commissions as instruments of metropolitan reform. The situation is in decided contrast to that of only a few years ago, when scarcely a month passed without the creation of such an agency in one metropolitan area or another. What was then a high-ranking item on

the civic agenda and a favorite topic of community leaders has now become a casualty of the reform cause with little immediate prospect of revival. What has brought about this precipitous decline in popularity? A partial answer can be found in the already discussed assumptions on which such commissions were based. In addition, three other factors can be cited as major contributors to the diminishing fortunes of these agencies: their negative record of reform accomplishment; the new orientations of urban research; and the emergence of overriding social and racial problems.

Record of Accomplishment

We need not dwell long on this first factor although its psychological impact on the popularity of metropolitan surveys has been great. The unexciting story of meager results that have followed in the wake of such studies is too well known for reiteration. Of the more than 100 surveys undertaken during the past several decades, only a few—notably in Miami and more recently in Nashville—have led to any significant reorganization. Senator Joseph E. Clark of Pennsylvania expressed what was in the minds of many when he said: "Studies have been made of almost every major metropolitan area in the country, but they have produced little more than a library of frustration."[12] Some observers find consolation in the fact that small gains have been made and that studies which have gathered dust are occasionally resurrected as authority for later action. But these sparse and unspectacular accomplishments, meaningful as they may be in some cases, are hardly enough to generate continued enthusiasm among the ranks of top civic leaders, where the principal support for the movement has rested.

Since metropolitan study commissions were largely the product of the business community—in league, of course, with the good government groups—the attitude of the economic leaders was of critical importance to the existence and support of such bodies.

Top-level businessmen are accustomed to achieving results in their own establishments; heads are likely to roll and organizational changes are quickly made if satisfactory performance is not forthcoming. When commercial and industrial leaders became champions of metropolitan reorganization, they soon discovered that they could not act with dispatch as they do in the business world. They found instead that the process of governmental change is long, involved, and frustrating. Every attempt to translate into action what seemed to them perfectly rational recommendations met with countless political obstacles, long periods of negotiation, little public response, and negligible results. As survey after survey failed to receive political implementation, the enthusiasm of the post-World-War-II period for metropolitan commissions waned. Economic notables grew weary of sponsoring such abortive efforts and turned their attention to other aspects of the civic scene. Much the same thing happened in the case of foundation support. A number of major metropolitan surveys of the last decade were partially financed by foundation funds. But like the businessmen, the foundations were interested in seeing tangible results, not quixotic ventures; and when none were forthcoming, they too lost interest.

The "New" Urban Research

As late as 1957 political scientists were under attack for failure to study seriously the impact of urbanization on governmental institutions and political life.[13] One critic charged that "while the literature of municipal government continues to grow, fed by bureaus of government research and the teaching concerns of political scientists, there is little in this literature that is of substance sufficient to rise above the level of specialized reporting and into the general stream of political science."[14] These views echo the concerns of the new breed of urban political scientists who have emerged in recent years. Highly critical of the traditional preoccupation with government form and structure and with the historical-descriptive approach to the urban community, the "modernists" stand for empirical testing of long-held assumptions and the systematic study of political behavior.

In the eyes of the new generation of urban scholars, the classical metropolitan studies were based on nothing more than what Coleman Woodbury has referred to as "folk political science," plausible, often repeated, but without any firm empirical foundation. Much of the work undertaken by study commissions might, in fact, be described as highly stereotyped inventory research: gathering and recording of data, summarization of revenues and expenditures, tabulation of services, and description of governmental patterns. Existing arrangements are measured against either the criteria of professional associations in the various fields or some generalized notions as to how matters should be. Recommendations for change are then made based on a set of principles drawn largely from the standard texts on local government and public administration. This was the kind of research that the business-dominated sponsors of metropolitan surveys wanted and were willing to support. They had little doubt that governmental restructuring was necessary. Research was needed only to document the case and provide the reformers with ammunition to sell their product.

Starting in the late 1950's, metropolitan research took a new turn as foundation funds became available to those working in the urban field. With this assistance several metropolitan studies, including those in Cleveland, Dayton, St. Louis, and New York, attempted to break away from the common mold and employ more sophisticated social science approaches and techniques in the investigation of the metropolis. Economists and sociologists joined political scientists in these endeavors. Studies of urban governmental patterns and administrative efficiency became secondary to more basic inquiries into economic and social structures, citizen perceptions and behavior, and political processes.

The new studies were characterized by inquiries into the economic base of the metropolis, its power structure and decision-making patterns, its political and social interests, and the attitudes of its citizens. Social science research of this type is not only costly but it is also unappealing to lay commissions. Reform activists and sponsors of metropolitan surveys were dubious from the beginning about spending time and resources on projects which they little understood. They were willing to go along at first since this was the type of research that was attracting foundation funds. However, when this support dried up after the initial wave of interest, civic leaders lost whatever taste they may have had for involvement in the new research.

Recent years have found metropolitan commissions in an awkward position. On the one hand, the traditional studies which they have been accustomed to undertake have come under heavy fire from academic and professional circles and have consequently lost much of their aura of legitimacy. On the other hand, the more basic type of research that is being called for by urban specialists does not readily lend itself to study commission sponsorship. Such bodies are under constant pressure to provide solutions, not to conduct general inquiries into social and organizational behavior. This latter function can best be performed in an atmosphere free from the demands of time and the necessity of providing answers to immediate problems.

The changing orientation of urban research and the correlative trend away from the lay survey commission can also be observed in the types of metropolitan studies currently under way. The first annual digest of metropolitan surveys published in 1958 listed a total of fifty-one local and regional studies in progress.[15] Thirty-nine of this number dealt with governmental reorganization, twenty-seven of which were under the direction of citizen study commissions either appointed by public bodies or sponsored by private organizations. (See Table 14.) The 1964 tabulation, in contrast, showed 160 local and regional studies, only eight of

TABLE 14

Metropolitan Studies by Type, 1958 and 1964

Type of Study	Number (1958)	Number (1964)
Governmental reorganization	39	8
Official study commissions	12	1
Private organizations	15	5
Universities	3	1
Local governments	7	1
Charter commissions	2	—
Mass transportation	5	56
Social and economic	5	36
Planning and development	2	60
Total	51	160

Adapted from *Metropolitan Surveys, 1958* and *Metropolitan Surveys, 1964*, Graduate School of Public Affairs, State University of New York, Albany, New York.

which could be referred to as reorganization surveys and only six of which were under the auspices of citizen commissions. The most notable difference is the shift from administrative and structural investigations to broader social and economic, transportation, and planning and developmental inquiries. In 1958 only twelve of the listed studies fell into these latter categories; by 1964 this number had increased to 152. Virtually all of these, moreover, were under the direction of regular governmental agencies or departments and not of ad hoc survey commissions.

A distinct trend in the institutional division of metropolitan-related research now appears to be emerging. Studies referred to as "basic" (not aimed at the solution of immediate and specific problems) are confined largely to the universities and a few privately endowed organizations such as Resources for the Future and the Urban Land Institute. Studies that deal with the growth and developmental problems of individual urban areas are being carried on by the increasing number of metropolitan and regional planning agencies. Finally, research which involves metropolitan governmental organization and administration is falling more within the purview of (1) state legislative committees on urban problems; (2) state offices for local government, as in New York; (3) local intergovernmental councils, such as the Association of Bay Area Governments (ABAG) in San Francisco, the Intergovernmental Cooperation Council in the Willamette Valley in Oregon, and the Supervisors Inter-County Committee in the Detroit Area; (4) federal agencies and committees, such as the Advisory Commission on Intergovernmental Relations established by Congress in 1959.[16]

These last developments reflect the feelings of some urban specialists that studies of structural changes and reallocation of functions should be entrusted to committees or arms of governmental units which have authority to put recommendations into effect or at least influence their adoption. This method has considerable merit if one accepts the view currently popular among many academic observers that radical modification of the metropolitan governmental structure is not needed. If only lesser adjustments are required to keep the system reasonably functional, public officials at both the local and state levels are in the most advantageous position to negotiate and work out the necessary settlements. It is true that the Milwaukee Committee of 21 proved a total failure as an instrument of change, but it was assumed at the time that major restructuring was the intended goal. Under a different set of premises and with involvement by or pressure from higher levels of government, the outcome might have been different.

The Crucial Problems

The third factor contributing to the declining use of study commissions is found in the changing social climate of the nation. Americans today are witnessing an essentially peaceful but determined revolution in race relations. Although the problem is not peculiarly urban, the battle is being waged principally in the cities and metropolitan centers of both North and South. Sit-ins, school boycotts, and protest demonstrations have become familiar scenes in many communities during the last several years. These events are manifestations of a growing unwillingness among Negroes to adjust their hopes and behavior to a system in which they are relegated to second class citizenship. Community leadership has been taxed to the full in efforts to meet the problem either by resisting the demands or by seeking ways of increasing job opportunities for minority groups, providing greater freedom for them in the choice of housing, and integrating school systems.

Other related problems are also adding to the complexity of modern urban life. Two in particular have become of increasing concern: poverty and automation. Numerous books, articles, and public pronouncements, as well as President Johnson's "war on poverty," have dramatized the fact that a substantial segment of the American population is not sharing in the abundance of our affluent society. At the same time, numerous reports of unemployment and layoffs are calling attention to the large number of workers who are daily being displaced by technical advances in the means of production. This latter development, moreover, is occurring at a time when a record number of young men and women are entering the labor market. Although poverty and automation, like racial integration, are national problems that can be met only by national action, their greatest impact is being felt in the large population centers. They are problems that cannot be ignored by local leadership even though local communities are individually powerless to cope with them. As such, they, too, are absorbing an increasing amount of attention from both political and non-political leaders in our metropolitan areas.

In the face of these critical social and economic problems, it is somewhat incongruous for prominent citizen commissions to limit their involvement in metropolitan public affairs to campaigns against governmental fragmentation, overlapping political jurisdictions, and management inefficiency. The simple truth is that the urban world is not the same world which existed just a few years ago. Whether they view the prospect with enthusiasm or not, the attention of the community elites and their allied civic associations is likely to be increasingly diverted from the technical problems of the metropolis to the more crucial issues of race and social disorganization.

THE FUTURE

After the failure of the Wisconsin legislature to extend the life of the Milwaukee Study Commission, a civic activist asked, "Where do we go from here?" Where indeed does the movement for metropolitan governmental reform go when repeated rebuffs in community after community have dulled the enthusiasm of the crusaders and caused them to hang up their arms? If the study commission will not work, what, if anything, will? The history of efforts to reshape the urban polity provides few concrete clues to these queries. Nor do the amateurs and professionals working in the civic vineyard have any clear notion as to what should be done. Some argue that we should forget the whole thing since matters will somehow work themselves out in the course of events. Others continue to insist that metropolitan reform can be effected by the economic notables if only they become seriously committed to the cause. Still others see the prospect for change dependent almost entirely upon the initiative of responsible public officials and on pressures from higher levels of government.

One of the most important factors to be kept in mind in discussing the future course of metropolitan reform is the diminishing degree of control that local areas have over their own destiny. Large-scale society has become so structured in the modern world that many of the crucial decisions relating to the local community are made by agencies outside its borders: in the halls of Congress, in the Housing and Home Finance Agency, the Bureau of Public Roads, and the Department of Health, Education and Welfare, in the state legislature and the governor's office, in state administrative agencies, and in the plush corporate board rooms in the New York skyscrapers. As Scott Greer has noted, "The discrepancy in organizational scale between local government and the nature of large-scale society results in a movement of power upward, to organizational centers outside the control of the local polity. Such organizations wield power that is area-wide in scope and consequences."[17]

These are forces that are helping for better or worse to shape the metropolis of tomorrow. They are also forces that are gradually compelling local governments in urban areas to act in self-defense by fashioning devices of a potentially integrative nature, such as regional planning agencies, intermunicipal councils, and intercounty committees of officials. The national government is giving increasing encouragement to this trend through financial incentives. Both by law and regulations, an increasing number of federal programs relating to urban communities are providing as a condition of aid that local projects be consistent with comprehensive plans for the development of the entire area. The Advisory Commission on Intergovernmental Relations stressed this strategy in stating that the national government "must be prepared to accept, as a permanent and continuous responsibility, the stimulation and support of state and local efforts to achieve an effective and orderly pattern of metropolitan area development."[18] The commission's assistant director enlarged on this point when he pointed out:

> From their inception, federal (and state) grant programs have conferred benefits, primarily in the form of money, in exchange for acceptance by local governments of procedural requirements. The challenge now is to see how effectively this classic activity (grants-in-aid) of intergovernmental relations can be applied in strengthening governmental organization, structure, cooperation, and planning in metropolitan areas.[19]

The states, except in the case of school district consolidation, have been slow to follow the federal lead in using their financial and other powers to effect greater integration in their metropolitan centers. The (Kestnbaum) Commission on Intergovernmental Relations as early as 1955 reported to Congress that "it is clearly the responsibility of the States to assume leadership in seeking solutions for the problems of metropolitan government."[20] Shortly thereafter, a report prepared for the Council of State Governments by John C. Bollens emphasized that while national and local action was indispensable, the states held the key to the metropolitan solution.[21] Since that time, the states themselves have begun to move slowly in this direction by creating legislative interim committees on local government, and in a few cases, by establishing offices of local affairs.

The minor results which have thus far followed pleas for more state intervention in metropolitan governmental affairs have led many to dismiss this approach as unfeasible. Several emerging developments, however, warrant careful reappraisal of the state's potential role in this regard. One is awareness on the part of state officials that federal urban programs will increasingly bypass state governments unless the latter assume greater responsibility for their metropolitan areas. Another is the Supreme Court decisions on reapportionment, which hold out the prospect of making state legislatures more responsive to the needs of urban communities. A third is the growing political dependency of state governors on the large population centers and the consequent necessity for them to devote more attention to the problems of these areas.

Those skeptical of state action in the metropolitan field can point to the meager results of the Milwaukee Study Commission, since here was an agency embodying the principle of state intervention in modernizing the local political structure. The reference, however, is not entirely appropriate, for the MSC's ties to the organs of state government were negligible. The legislature in no way considered the group as an adjunct agency assisting it by fact-finding and recommendations relative to the governmental

286 THE MILWAUKEE METROPOLITAN STUDY COMMISSION

system in the Milwaukee area. It created the Commission to accommodate a few of its members, and that was about as far as it intended to go. If anything, the experience simply reiterates the fact that the approach to legislative intervention in the local sphere must be through normal political channels with political techniques and means. High-ranking citizen study commissions have generally been unwilling to play this game, preferring to remain, like Caesar's wife, above reproach.

The closest analogue to the MSC is the British royal commission, which has long been an instrument of investigation and reform in that country. In fact, at the time the Milwaukee agency was created, a royal commission was established by Parliament to examine the local governmental system of the Greater London area. In contrast to the Milwaukee experience, the recommendations of the British commission led to action by Parliament in 1963 radically reorganizing the governmental structure of metropolitan London.[22] The English tradition of appointing and then seriously considering the advice of prominent citizen commissions is unknown in the United States. Neither state legislatures nor Congress have looked with favor on such bodies; they have preferred to do their own investigation through committees of their own members and, in some instances, through mixed bodies of legislators and private citizens. The latter device was employed with considerable success by several state reorganization or "Little Hoover" commissions in the post-World-War-II period.[23] The approach has considerable merit, for the presence of prestigious citizens tends to act as a leavening force on the legislators. Consensus may be more difficult to reach in a heterogeneous group of this kind than in a committee of like-minded businessmen, yet the effort is more likely to pay off in action, particularly if the legislative appointees are influential members of their respective bodies.

Perhaps most important of all to the future course of metropolitan reorganization is the perspective of community leaders and civic activists. For the most part they have tended to dismiss or overlook the possibility of achieving change by relating external forces and agencies to the local political structure. Such an approach has little meaning or appeal if they are to be concerned only with items of administrative management. Once, however, they become willing to turn their attention to the question of policy formulation on the key developmental and social issues of the metropolis, the relevancy of external pressures becomes clear. It really matters little in the shaping of the urban environment whether we have one or fifteen fire departments, whether some duplication of functions exist, or whether sewers are administered by one district, water by another, and air pollution control by a third. Some inconvenience and inefficiency will undoubtedly be present under such arrangements, but it is unlikely that these drawbacks will render the system dysfunctional. What does matter is that there be some institutional means of bringing all affected public agencies and their resources in the area—local, state, and federal—to bear on the achievement of broad community goals.

If the premise is accepted that only pressure from higher levels of government will bring about significant change in the structure of metropolitan public decision-making, a new strategy is called for on the part of the civic notables. In view of the growing size and complexity of the modern urban community, they might give serious consideration to diverting the main thrust of their efforts from local persuasion to concerted activity at the state (and even national) level.[24] This approach would require the joining together of civic elites and their subsidiary organizations from the various metropolitan and urban centers of a state in some sort of formal association. A permanent office staffed with skilled lobbyists and research personnel could be established at the state capital to promote legislative and administrative policies designed to reduce governmental "separatism" at the local level and stimulate state activity in the solution of urban problems. Such a procedure would be a logical outgrowth of contemporary society. As the metropolis becomes more and more dependent upon higher echelons of government, civic leadership must also move upward in order to influence urban policy that emanates from these levels. For its sights to remain trained solely on local agencies and decision makers would be to disregard forces that are shaping the course and development of the nation's metropolitan areas.

In last analysis, the question of metropolitan governmental reform will not be determined by survey commissions, scientific studies, and rational discourse. No amount of wishful thinking can make the issue apolitical. It is a question that must be resolved in the political arena with political weapons and techniques. It is not, moreover, a contest between the enlightened and unselfish on the one side and the ignorant and self-seeking on the other. The tendency to view reorganization in these simple and moralistic terms has handicapped the movement for change by divorcing it from reality. Neither its supporters nor its opponents have a monopoly on virtue. Just as the most vigorous adversaries of reform are those who profit from retention of existing arrangements, so the most highly motivated proponents of reorganization are those who stand to gain by alterations to the system. Actually, the weakness of the reform movement is that too few in its ranks have seen any real personal benefit in the proposed changes.

The successful Nashville consolidation in 1962 points up these elementary facts. What in an abortive effort only four years earlier had been presented simply as a question of administrative reorganization fostered by the good government groups became a political issue in the later campaign when opponents of the central city mayor (who opposed consolidation) seized upon the proposal as a means of driving him from office.[25] The issue of reorganization in this case was brought down from the heights of abstract speculation to the political arena, where the stakes were real and understandable. Voters who identified themselves with one or the other faction now had an "authoritative" referent for reaching a decision even though they may have been completely ignorant of the proposal or its potential effects on their own interests.

The twentieth century finds itself in an ever-expanding web of activity and ever-widening radii of interdependence. To work out a satisfactory and acceptable system of government for this complex polity is a challenging task for urban man. Regardless of the fate of various reform efforts, the metropolitan governmental structure is certain to undergo modification with the passage of time. Only by so doing can it survive the great changes in the urban environment that the future will bring. This adjustment may be only a minimal accommodation to the emerging forces or it may involve a radical alteration of the system. Whatever the change, it will almost certainly take place through political channels, under the initiative of political actors, and through the process of political bargaining. Civic notables and good government groups will remain important, but less as carriers of the movement than as legitimating symbols.

APPENDIX

NOTES

INDEX

APPENDIX A
Metropolitan Study Commission Chronology

September 16, 1954 Milwaukee County Board of Supervisors authorizes establishment of the "Committee of 21."

September 9, 1956 "Dineen" committee is appointed by Governor Kohler to study water and sewerage problems in Milwaukee County.

July 20, 1957 Governor Thomson signs bill creating Metropolitan Study Commission.

October 12, 1957 Governor Thomson announces appointment of MSC members.

October 14, 1957 Metropolitan Study Commission holds first meeting.

October 14, 1957 Chairman Lobb appoints special committee on water.

November 11, 1957 MSC establishes three committees: Land Use and Zoning, Metropolitan Functions, and Revenue Sources and Distribution.

February 1, 1958 Charles Ball is appointed research director.

February 24, 1958 Commission appoints research advisory committee.

April 28, 1958 Commission establishes public information and education committee.

May 19, 1958 Public hearing on regional planning recommendations is held.

June 5, 1958 Public hearing on sewerage recommendations is held.

June 18, 1958 Public hearing on property assessment is held.

August 25, 1958 Commission approves recommendations on property tax assessment.

September 29, 1958 Commission approves recommendations extending boundaries of metropolitan sewerage district.

November 24, 1958 Commission votes amendment to sewerage recommendations, relative to South Milwaukee.

December 23, 1958 Ball announces his resignation as research director, effective February 1, 1959.

December 29, 1958 Commission approves recommendations to facilitate creation of regional planning agency.

December 29, 1958 Executive Committee presents "Report Concerning the Determination of the Type of Government Best Suited to Discharge Metropolitan Functions."

January 22, 1959 Public hearing on first water recommendations is held.

February 7, 1959 Charles Goff is appointed research director.

February 25, 1959 Public hearing on possible creation of metropolitan government in Milwaukee area is held.

March 1, 1959 John Lobb announces he will resign as chairman by April 1.

March 23, 1959 Commission adopts water recommendations to create a new water authority for Milwaukee County with the City retaining ownership of the facility.

March 23, 1959 Vice-chairman Parkinson presents proposal for creation of a multi-function metropolitan agency.

April 11, 1959 Parkinson resigns from Commission.

April 13, 1959 Albert Houghton is appointed to MSC as chairman.

June 22, 1959 MSC authorizes Bureau of Business and Economic Research at Marquette University to undertake study of revenue needs and trends in Milwaukee County.

June 22, 1959 New research coordinating committee is created.

July 22, 1959 Charles Goff resigns as research director.

July 27, 1959 Albert Houghton announces his resignation as Commission chairman.

August 19, 1959	J. Martin Klotsche is appointed MSC chairman.
August 24, 1959	Police Protection and Garbage and Refuse Disposal committees are established.
September 5, 1959	Metropolitan sewerage bill supported by MSC becomes law.
October 20, 1959	Public hearing on proposed metropolitan plan commission is held.
November 4, 1959	Regional planning bill amendments supported by MSC become law.
December 28, 1959	Intergovernmental cooperation committee is created.
December 28, 1959	MSC authorizes Marquette University Bureau of Business and Economic Research to conduct study of distribution of shared taxes and aids as related to governmental units of Milwaukee County.
February 1, 1960	David Mars assumes position as research director.
April 25, 1960	MSC approves recommendations transferring refuse and garbage disposal to county government.
June 14, 1960	Public hearing on revised proposals for land use and planning is held.
June 27, 1960	Commission approves recommendations calling for creation of county planning department and regional planning commission.
August 22, 1960	Commission reopens study of water question and recommendations of March, 1959.
August 22, 1960	MSC appoints special committee on determination of the need for research into governmental problems of the metropolitan Milwaukee area after July 1, 1961.
October 24, 1960	MSC approves recommendations on inter-library cooperation.
February 27, 1961	MSC approves recommendations on tax reform, including a 3 per cent sales tax.
February 27, 1961	MSC approves recommendations facilitating resolution of municipal boundary problems.
March 27, 1961	MSC approves recommendations calling for greater cooperation in keeping crime records in Milwaukee County.

March 27, 1961	MSC goes on record as favoring bill to establish single county department of assessment.
April 12, 1961	Public hearing on revised water recommendations is held.
April 24, 1961	Commission approves series of recommendations urging a stronger county government and an intergovernmental advisory council.
April 24, 1961	Commission approves revised water recommendations to exclude new north shore water utility from MSC recommendations of March, 1959.
May 12, 1961	Municipal boundary disputes bill supported by MSC becomes law.
June 19, 1961	MSC adopts final report.
June 26, 1961	Bill extending life of MSC for two years passes Wisconsin Senate.
July 13, 1961	Bill continuing MSC is defeated in Assembly.

APPENDIX B

Interview Sample

Extensive interviews were held with eighty community leaders during the fall of 1959. Fifty of these respondents were subsequently reinterviewed during the summer of 1961 after the final report of the MSC was issued. It was originally planned to select a smaller panel of respondents for three and possibly four rounds of interviews, timed to coincide with the issuance of important recommendations by the Commission or the occurrence of major events relevant to metropolitan reform. The absence, however, of significant reform activities during the study period made this procedure impractical. Issuance of the MSC's final report provided the first adequate opportunity to assess reaction to a major recommendation for governmental reorganization and to measure attitudinal changes.

The first round of interviews was designed primarily to:

(1) obtain background material about the Milwaukee area and its problems;

(2) ascertain how major issues facing the community were perceived or defined by representatives of various groups and organizations;

(3) secure information that would be helpful in formulating assumptions about forces and influences which bear on the shaping of local public policy;

(4) determine the attitude of community influentials and public officials toward metropolitan problems and the work of the MSC;

(5) learn something about the general power structure of the community, particularly as it relates to metropolitan decision-making.

The second or follow-up interview inquired into respondents' reactions to the Commission's final recommendations, their evaluation of its work, and their current views of metropolitan problems and solutions. Taken together, the two interviews sought to ascertain whether the attitudes of representative local influentials toward metropolitan reform in the Milwaukee area were relatively static or developing toward or away from the point where changes in the governmental pattern appear likely in the near future.

Each interview normally lasted from one to two hours. The schedules employed in the initial and later round of interviews were structured to assure uniformity in data collection and provide a basis for analysis. They were designed, however, to give respondents wide latitude in their answers and the investigator broad discretion in the interviewing.

Selection of Respondents

In selecting the individuals to be interviewed, attention was concentrated on finding those who met these criteria:

(1) active in local public affairs in Milwaukee County, either as public officials or as private leaders;

(2) reputation for knowledgeability about local issues;

(3) representative of various segments of the metropolitan community;

(4) in positions to influence or reflect community or group opinion.

Names were obtained from a variety of sources, including informants who were well acquainted with the area, newspaper files, and organizational rosters. This stockpile of potential respondents was carefully considered in light of the above criteria and tentative selections made. The list was then discussed with several responsible and perceptive individuals in various sectors of community life and modifications made. The list originally consisted of fifty names, but this number was expanded to eighty as additional individuals were nominated during the course of the interviews. Because of limitations of research resources, the number was cut back to fifty for the second round of interviews by random selection from each occupational category that was utilized for analytical purposes.

Characteristics of Respondents

The full panel of respondents consisted of 23 businessmen; 24 public officials (14 elective and 10 appointive); 10 prominent professional men (mostly lawyers); 8 administrators in social welfare agencies such as the community chest and urban league; 7 executive secretaries of civic, ethnic, and neighborhood organizations; 5 labor representatives; and 3 educators. The list was broadly representative of city and suburban public officials in both small and large units, including the county government. It contained councilmen, mayors, city managers, agency heads, and state legislators. Included also were several newspaper publishers, financiers, presidents of large and small corporations, political party leaders, officials of business and professional interest groups, service club chairmen, racial and ethnic spokesmen, and other leading civic activists. Forty-four respondents resided within Milwaukee city; the other 36 were suburbanites.

In age, the respondents ranged from 26 to 72, with fifty the average and with a majority falling within the 45 to 55 bracket. In education, they far outdistanced the general population: 68 of the 80 held college degrees, including 28 LL.B.'s, 12 M.A.'s and 3 doctorates (the latter all educators). The panel was heavily weighted on the side of the males, with only 6 women included. Economically, there was wide variation among the respondents although all but two of them exceeded the median income of the area's population and a number of them enjoyed top incomes. Over 90 per cent were home owners and 71 per cent natives of the area. Some of the interviewees were members of old-line and socially prominent Milwaukee families, while the majority fell within the middle and upper-middle social strata. With few exceptions, all were members of more than one voluntary organization; and over 50 per cent of the non-governmental respondents were serving or had served in some public capacity either as part-time officeholders or Commission members. (For the "typicality" of the sample see W. Bell, R. Hill, and C. Wright, *Public Leadership*, San Francisco: Chandler Publishing Co., 1961.)

Citizen Interviews

A class in public opinion research at the University of Wisconsin–Milwaukee afforded an opportunity to inquire into the attitudes of the general public toward the Metropolitan Study Commission and its activities. As a major part of their course responsibilities, the students participated in the preparation and execution of a sample survey of citizen attitudes and participation patterns. The occasion was used to include three questions pertaining to the Commission in the schedule:

(1) Have you heard of the Metropolitan Study Commission?
(2) There has been talk about extending the Commission's life for another two years. What do you think of the idea?

(3) What do you think will be accomplished by the two-year extension if it is granted?

The last two questions were asked only of those who answered the first affirmatively. At the time the interviews took place (fall 1960), the Commission had been in existence for over three years.

A total of 307 respondents (145 adult males and 162 adult females) were interviewed. The sample was drawn by the student interviewers from thirty Milwaukee County election precincts chosen by a process of random selection. Although the sample included neighborhoods of varying social and economic characteristics in both the central city and suburbs, it tended to be somewhat over-representative of the middle and upper socio-economic populations of the area.

APPENDIX C
Roster of Commissioners

Harold E. Beck

Business Representative, Office Employees Union No. 9, AFL–CIO. Native Milwaukeean; age 47. Residence and place of employment in Milwaukee city. Member of American Veterans Committee, Eagles, Masons, National Conference of Christians and Jews, and National Association of Housing and Redevelopment Officials. Served as chairman of Citizens Urban Renewal Committee and Mayor's Cost of Living Committee, and as member of Mayor's committee to study municipal needs and finances. Served full life of Commission.

Earl R. Butter

President, Butter Hardware Company. Native Milwaukeean; age 61. Place of residence and business in Milwaukee city. Member of Greater Milwaukee Committee, Milwaukee Association of Commerce, Better Business Bureau, Mitchell Street Advancement Association, and Mayor's Advisory Council. Served as chairman Milwaukee Parking Commission. Died February, 1959.

O. W. Carpenter

President, Chain Belt Company. Native of Ohio, moved to Milwaukee area in 1934. Age 53. Suburban resident (Fox Point). Place of business West Milwaukee. Graduate of Ohio Wesleyan University and Atlanta Law School. Member Greater Milwaukee Committee and Milwaukee

Club. Director Columbia Hospital, Pabst Theatre Foundation, Kearney Negro Welfare Foundation, Milwaukee Orchestral Association, Goodwill Industries, and Citizens' Governmental Research Bureau. Past president Community Welfare Council, United Independent School Foundation, and Milwaukee Boy's Club. Former trustee of Village of Fox Point. Served full life of Commission.

Mrs. Sam M. Cook

Housewife (husband an official of Graybar Electric Company). Native of Kansas City, Missouri; moved to Milwaukee in 1953. Age 37. Resident of suburban Bayside. Graduate of University of Kansas. Director of Milwaukee Junior League, Milwaukee Art Institute, and Planned Parenthood Association. Member American Field Service Committee and St. Lawrence Seaway celebration committee. Served on Fox Point citizens' committee on school budgets. Resigned from Commission in June, 1959.

Richard W. Cutler

Attorney, member of firm of Wood, Brady, Tyrrell and Bruce. Native of Connecticut, moved to Milwaukee area in 1949. Age 40. Resident of suburban Fox Point; law offices in Milwaukee city. Graduate of Yale University. Member Greater Milwaukee Committee, Milwaukee Club, World Affairs Council, Children's Service Society, and Junior Achievement. President, Milwaukee chapter of Foreign Policy Association. Served on Fox Point Planning Commission, Fox River Basin Planning Committee, and subcommittee on urban problems of Wisconsin Legislative Council. Served full life of Commission.

Robert T. Foote

Executive vice president, Red Star Yeast and Products Company. Native of Milwaukee area; age 40. Resident of suburban Shorewood. Place of business in Milwaukee city. Graduate of Cornell University. Member Milwaukee Club and Friends of the Museum. Director Country Day School, Milwaukee University School, and Milwaukee County Zoological Society. Resigned from Commission in August, 1960.

Robert E. Jensen

Executive vice president, American Appraisal Company. Native of Sheboygan, Wisconsin. Moved to Milwaukee in 1949. Age 45. Both residence and place of business in Milwaukee city. Graduate of University of Wisconsin. Member of City Club and Milwaukee Athletic Club. Trustee of Citizens' Governmental Research Bureau. Served full life of Commission.

Alfred S. Kliebhan

Secretary-treasurer, St. Francis Building and Loan Association. Native of Milwaukee area; age 62. Resident of Milwaukee city; place of business in suburban St. Francis. Graduate of Pio Nono College. Vice president of Trinity Memorial Hospital; past governor of National Savings and Loan League; member advisory committee of Cardinal Stritch College, and board of consultants of St. Francis of Assisi Convent. Served full life of Commission.

Irvin F. Knoebel

Comptroller, City of West Allis. Native of Milwaukee area; age 60. Resident of suburban West Allis. Director of West Allis Memorial Hospital and West Allis State Bank. Past state chairman of Municipal Finance Officers Association. Chairman, West Allis Housing Authority. Served as chairman of the suburban delegation on the Committee of 21. Served full life of Commission.

John H. Kopmeier

President, Wisconsin Ice and Coal Company. Native Milwaukeean; age 48. Resident of suburban Bayside; place of business in Milwaukee city. Graduate of Yale University. Director, Association of Commerce, Children's Service Society, and Marquette University Medical School. Member Kiwanis Club, Knights of Columbus, Milwaukee Athletic Club, and St. Michael Hospital Advisory Board. Served full life of Commission.

John C. Lobb

Executive vice president, Marine National Exchange Bank. Native of Minnesota. Moved to Milwaukee area in 1955. Age 43. Resident of suburban Shorewood; place of business in Milwaukee city. Graduate of University of Minnesota and University of Wisconsin Law School. Member, Milwaukee Club and University Club. Served as secretary to Wisconsin Investment Board and as chairman of the Governor's Advisory Committee on Industrial Development. Resigned from Commission in 1960.

Ebner F. Luetzow

President, South Side Laundry and Dry Cleaners. Native Milwau-keean; age 58. Both residence and place of business in Milwaukee city. Member of Greater Milwaukee Committee and Kiwanis Club. Chairman, Civic Affairs Committee of Association of Commerce. Director, St. Luke's Hospital, Kiwanis Foundation for Cerebral Palsy, Milwaukee Vocational School, and Better Business Bureau. Served full life of Commission.

George Parkinson

Vice provost, University of Wisconsin–Milwaukee. Native of Ohio; moved to Milwaukee area in 1927. Age 58. Resident of Milwaukee city. Graduate of Ohio State University (B.A. and M.A.) and University of Wisconsin (Ph.D.). Vice president, Milwaukee Council of the Navy League; president, Wisconsin Society of Sons of the American Revolution; director, Milwaukee YMCA. Served on the "Dineen" committee. Resigned from the Commission in April, 1959.

Clifford A. Randall

Attorney, with firm of Zimmers, Randall, and Zimmers. Native Milwaukeean; age 51. Resident of suburban Shorewood; offices in Milwaukee city. Graduate of Dartmouth College and Marquette University Law School. Director and general counsel for the Association of Commerce. Member Milwaukee Club and Greater Milwaukee Committee (past president). President, Rotary International. Former chairman, Milwaukee chapter of Red Cross. Director, Milwaukee County Zoological Society. Member of advisory board, Salvation Army, and Boy Scouts Council. Served full life of Commission.

Willis G. Scholl

Executive vice president, Allis-Chalmers Manufacturing Company. Native of Michigan; moved to Milwaukee area in 1947. Age 49. Resident of suburban Wauwatosa; place of business in West Allis. Member, Greater Milwaukee Committee, Marquette University Advisory Council, Business Advisory Board of University of Wisconsin–Milwaukee. Director, Milwaukee Hospital Auxiliary, Milwaukee Children's Hospital, and Association of Commerce. Served on the "Dineen" committee. Resigned from Commission in October, 1958.

Francis S. Cornell (replaced Scholl)

Executive vice president, A. O. Smith Corporation. Native of New Jersey; moved to Milwaukee area in 1945. Age 59. Resident of suburban Whitefish Bay; place of business in Milwaukee city. Graduate of Lehigh University. Member Greater Milwaukee Committee. Director, Neighborhood House, YMCA, and Marquette University Medical School. Served on Commission from November, 1958 until resignation in June, 1959.

Mrs. Norvan F. Gordon (replaced Mrs. Cook)

Housewife (husband a physician). Native Milwaukeean; age 39. Resident of Whitefish Bay. Graduate University of Wisconsin. Director, League of Women Voters and Girl Scouts. Member Corporation of Child Care Centers. Served on Commission from July, 1959 to its demise.

Albert F. Houghton (replaced Parkinson)

Lawyer, member of firm of Houghton, Bullinger, Nehs and Houghton. Native Milwaukeean; age 38. Residence and office in Milwaukee city. Graduate of Amherst College and the University of Wisconsin. President Urban League; member State Historical Society and World Affairs Council of Milwaukee. Former assistant district attorney in Milwaukee County, member Milwaukee Harbor Commission, and chairman United Nations Observance Commission. Served as chairman of MSC from April to August, 1959, and as a member until his death in February, 1960.

J. Martin Klotsche (replaced Cornell)

Provost, University of Wisconsin–Milwaukee. Native of Nebraska; moved to Milwaukee area in 1931. Age 51. Resident of Milwaukee city. Graduate of Midland College (A.B.) and University of Wisconsin (Ph.D.). Member Greater Milwaukee Committee and World Affairs Council of Milwaukee. Director, Milwaukee Art Institute and National Conference of Christians and Jews. Previously served on Milwaukee Housing Authority and Governor's Commission on Higher Education. Served as chairman of MSC from August, 1959, to its demise.

Shepard A. Magidson (replaced Houghton)

Executive secretary to mayor of Milwaukee. Native Milwaukeean; age 39. Resident of Milwaukee city. Graduate of University of Wisconsin (A.B.) and Syracuse University (M.A.). Member Milwaukee Government Service League, Municipal Finance Officers Association, and National Tax Association. Served on MSC as official representative of the city of Milwaukee from his appointment in April, 1960, to termination of Commission.

William F. Rasche (replaced Vonier)

Retired. Former head of Milwaukee Vocational School. Resided in Milwaukee area since 1940. Age 71. Resident of Milwaukee city. Board chairman, Milwaukee Cerebral Palsy Work Center, and chairman Metropolitan Youth Commission. Served on Commission from October, 1959, to its demise.

Sprague Vonier (replaced Butter)

Program director, WTMJ television station; lived in Milwaukee area since 1945. Age 42. Resident of Milwaukee city. Graduate of University of Hawaii. Served previously as assistant secretary to former Milwaukee mayor. Appointed to Commission in July, 1959, resigned September, 1959.

APPENDIX D

Major Reports and Recommendations of Metropolitan Study Commission

GENERAL

1958 Annual Report to the Governor of the State of Wisconsin. iv, 53 pages. October 13, 1958.

1959 Annual Report to the Governor of the State of Wisconsin. 3, vii, 38 pages. October 15, 1959.

1960 Annual Report to the Governor of the State of Wisconsin. ii, 67 pages. October 13, 1960.

Report to the 1961 Legislature of the State of Wisconsin. i, 39 pages. January 3, 1961.

Metropolitan Milwaukee, Problems-Solutions. 26 pages. June, 1961.

EXECUTIVE COMMITTEE

Report Concerning the Determination of the Type of Government Best Suited to Discharge Metropolitan Functions. 7 pages. December 29, 1958.

INTERGOVERNMENTAL COOPERATION COMMITTEE

Interlibrary Cooperation in Milwaukee County. Report by the Citizens' Governmental Research Bureau. 48 pages. July, 1960.

Fire Department Interlocal Cooperation in Milwaukee County. Report by the Citizens' Research Bureau. 32 pages. September, 1960.

Final Report on Intergovernmental Cooperation in Milwaukee County. iii, 44 pages, exhibits. April 24, 1961.

LAND USE AND ZONING COMMITTEE

Report on Regional Planning Legislation. ii, 34 pages, exhibits. May 26, 1958.

Regional Planning Legislation in Wisconsin: A Final Report with Recommendations. ii, 13 pages. July 28, 1958.

The Milwaukee Metropolis in Maps. 24 pages. September 29, 1958.

Report and Recommendations on Regional Planning. iii, 30 pages. December 8, 1958.

Report on Municipal Boundary Problems. 22 pages, exhibits. February 23, 1959.

Milwaukee County Land Use and Zoning Atlas. 32 pages. April, 1959.

Land Use and Zoning Analysis. By Nelson-Ball & Associates. v, 59 pages, exhibits. April, 1959.

Land Use Planning and Control in Milwaukee County. iii, 62 pages. October 2, 1959.

Land Use Planning in the Metropolitan Milwaukee Area. iv, 49 pages. May 23, 1960.

Findings and Recommendations on Municipal Boundary Problems. 5 pages. February 27, 1961.

METROPOLITAN FUNCTIONS COMMITTEE

Report on Sewage Disposal in the Milwaukee Metropolitan Area. iv, 101 pages. July 28, 1958.

Report of the Metropolitan Functions Committee Relating to Sewage Disposal in the Milwaukee Metropolitan Area (recommendations). 9 pages. August 25, 1958.

History of Water Supply in the Milwaukee Area. ii, 192 pages. November 24, 1958.

Conclusions Based on the History of Water Supply in the Milwaukee Area. 7 pages. December 29, 1958.

Statements on Water Supply Prepared for January 22 Hearing of the Metropolitan Functions Committee. 34 pages. January 26, 1959.

POLICE PROTECTION COMMITTEE

Technical Report on Police Protection in Milwaukee County. 149 pages, exhibits. February 27, 1961.

Recommendations on Uniform Accident and Crime Reporting and Es-

tablishment of a Central Police Records Depository for Milwaukee County. 5 pages. February 27, 1961.

REFUSE AND GARBAGE DISPOSAL COMMITTEE

Refuse and Garbage Disposal in Milwaukee County. 78 pages, exhibits. December 1, 1959.
Recommendations on Refuse and Garbage Disposal in Milwaukee County. 2 pages. March 28, 1960.

REVENUE SOURCES AND DISTRIBUTION COMMITTEE

Report on Property Taxation in Milwaukee County. iv, 40 pages, exhibits. April 28, 1958.
Property Assessment Recommendations. 4 pages. July 28, 1958.
Report on Motor Vehicle Taxation. ii, 18 pages. July 28, 1958.
Study of Revenue Needs and Trends in Milwaukee County. Report by the Bureau of Business and Economic Research of Marquette University. 105 pages. September 4, 1959.
Filling the Gap. Progress Report by the Revenue Sources and Distribution Committee. ix, 61 pages. November 23, 1959.
State-Local Financial Relationship: A Study of Shared Taxes and Aids in Wisconsin. Report by the Bureau of Business and Economic Research of Marquette University. iv, 71 pages. March, 1960.
Final Report and Recommendation on Taxation and Revenue Distribution in Milwaukee County. iii, 34 pages, tables. December 19, 1960.
Final Recommendations on Taxation and Revenue Distribution in Milwaukee County. 12 pages, exhibits. March 9, 1961.

Notes

1. The Setting

1. Quoted in *Milwaukee Journal,* January 31, 1961.
2. Richard S. Davis, "Milwaukee: Old Lady Thrift," in Robert Allen (ed.), *Our Fair City* (New York: Vanguard, 1947), p. 189.
3. George S. Perry, *Cities of America* (New York: McGraw-Hill, 1946), pp. 45–56.
4. See *Milwaukee's Community Renewal Program: Projects and Objectives* (Milwaukee: Department of City Development, May, 1964).
5. See Glenn Fuguitt, *Rural and Urban Population Changes in Wisconsin, 1950–1960* (Madison: Department of Rural Sociology, University of Wisconsin, 1961), p. 78.
6. Bayrd Still, *Milwaukee, The History of a City* (Madison: State Historical Society of Wisconsin, 1948), p. 70.
7. Quoted in *Milwaukee Sentinel,* June 25, 1893.
8. U.S. Bureau of the Census, *County and City Data Book,* 1962.
9. See John H. Kessel, "Governmental Structure and Political Environment: A Statistical Note about American Cities," *American Political Science Review,* LVI (September, 1962), pp. 615–620.
10. Economic data are derived from a number of sources, including: *Census of Manufactures, 1958; Census of Business, 1958; Report of the Commission on the Economic Study of Milwaukee, 1948* (Milwaukee: City of Milwaukee, 1948); *Annual Report, 1958,* Federal Reserve Bank of Chicago.
11. Still, p. 379.

12. "Growth of Governmental Activities in Milwaukee County," unpublished MS (Milwaukee: Citizens' Governmental Research Bureau, 1960). See also H. J. Schmandt and G. R. Stephens, "Measuring Municipal Output," *National Tax Journal*, XIII (December 1960), pp. 369–375.

2. The Community's Organizational Pattern

1. Robert A. Dahl, *Who Governs* (New Haven: Yale University Press, 1961); Linton C. Freeman, Warner Bloomberg, Jr., Stephen P. Koff, M. H. Sunshine, and T. J. Fararo, *Local Community Leadership* (Syracuse: University College of Syracuse University, 1960); Floyd Hunter, *Community Power Structure* (Chapel Hill: University of North Carolina Press, 1953).

2. Roscoe C. Martin, Frank J. Munger, and others, *Decisions in Syracuse* (Bloomington: Indiana University Press, 1961), p. 328.

3. *Directory, Milwaukee County Organizations, 1959–60* (Milwaukee: Milwaukee Public Library, 1960).

4. "A Platform for Better Government in Milwaukee County," adopted by the Delegate Council of the Democratic Party of Milwaukee County, November 18, 1959.

5. Milwaukee Association of Commerce, *Progress Report in the Development of a Civic Affairs Program*, October, 1960, p. 2.

6. See, for example, Robert Presthus, *Men at the Top* (New York: Oxford University Press, 1964).

7. *Decisions in Syracuse*.

3. Reorganization Efforts in Milwaukee: An Historical Perspective

1. A summary of bills pertaining to governmental consolidation in Milwaukee County is contained in a compilation by the Citizens' Governmental Research Bureau, dated October 6, 1947. For a detailed and well-documented account of governmental integration efforts in Milwaukee County, see Charles D. Goff, "The Politics of Governmental Integration in Metropolitan Milwaukee," Northwestern University, 1952 (unpublished Ph.D. dissertation).

2. Joint Committee on Consolidation in Milwaukee, *Metropolitan Milwaukee: One Trade Area Burdened with 93 Local Governments* (Milwaukee: Joint Committee on Consolidation, 1936). Also reports of the Committee, numbered 1 through 27, on various functions.

3. The suburban victory was memorialized by a mock funeral held at the annual dinner of the Milwaukee County League of Municipalities. At an auspicious moment in the festivities a black coffin marked "Mr. Consolidation" was wheeled down the center aisle of the dining hall followed by thirty mourners representing the joint committee. After an appropriate funeral eulogy delivered by the president of the league, the body of Mr. Consolidation was put to rest "forever."

4. Arthur M. Werba and John L. Greenwald, *Making Milwaukee Mightier* (Milwaukee: Board of Public Land Commissioners, 1929).

5. For a first-hand account of the philosophy underlying Milwaukee's annexation effort and the tactics employed see Frank Zeidler, "The Expansion of the City of Milwaukee from 1940 to 1960 and Some Related Matters," (unpublished MS in Milwaukee Public Library).

6. Since this time Milwaukee has annexed fifteen acres of land in the township of Germantown in Washington County, adjacent to the City's northwestern boundaries. Further expansion in this direction was promptly cut off by annexation of the remaining township area into the Village of Germantown.

7. The Milwaukee County government has long engaged in services of an urban character. Public welfare and public hospitals have been county responsibilities since the middle of the last century. The county government also operates the area's two public airports and the stadium, which serves as the Braves' ball park.

8. Mayor Henry Maier of Milwaukee revived the issue in his charter message of 1964 when he called for the transfer of the central library and museum to county control on the ground that all who receive the benefit of these facilities should share in their costs. The proposal was part of the Mayor's program to eliminate financial inequities suffered by the City because of suburban and state legislative policies.

9. Sec. 59.083 *Wisconsin Statutes.*

10. Sec. 66.30 *Wisconsin Statutes.*

11. Intergovernmental Cooperation Committee, *Final Report on Intergovernmental Cooperation in Milwaukee County* (Milwaukee: Metropolitan Study Commission, April 24, 1961).

12. Charles D. Goff in his study of governmental integration in Milwaukee County concluded that "proposals for functional consolidation have the best chance of success when (a) a governmental service is historically new, (b) only a minority of the metropolitan governments have begun to provide the service, (c) the number of public employees affected by the consolidation is small, (d) a majority of the

metropolitan governments are impressed with the desirability of the service, (e) the problem of government which the service was instituted to help solve, is a matter of concern to an existent or potential majority of the people. "The Politics of Governmental Integration in Metropolitan Milwaukee" Northwestern University, 1952 (unpublished Ph.D. dissertation), p. 750.

13. There are indications that even consolidation is no longer attractive to central city officials and residents. In 1962, for example, St. Louis city officials and voters opposed a constitutional amendment that would have merged the city and suburban governments. See Frank S. Sengstock and others, *Consolidation: Building a Bridge between City and Suburb* (Worcester, Mass.: Heffernan Press, 1964).

4. Creation of the Commission

1. Frank Zeidler, "The Expansion of the City of Milwaukee from 1940 to 1960 and Some Related Matters," unpublished MS in Milwaukee Public Library, p. 62.

2. Alderman Mortier struck at the heart of the problem when he said: "Because of the strong conflict of interest between Milwaukee and the suburbs, study at the local level is impossible. The suburbs can no more discuss ways and means of breaking up their tax free status than we can discuss waiving away City services without compensation." (Milwaukee *Journal*, October 31, 1956.)

3. Milwaukee *Journal*, February 5, 1953.

4. The influence of these studies on community leaders is indicated in a letter, dated December 1, 1954, addressed to the Committee of 21 and signed by representatives of nine Milwaukee civic groups. The letter notes that the organization had carried on intensive studies of efforts to solve metropolitan problems in other areas and found the use of citizen study commissions an effective device.

5. Minutes of the Committee of 21, December 22, 1954.

6. Ibid., July 14, 1955.

7. Milwaukee *Journal*, June 26, 1956.

8. Ibid., November 22, 1955.

9. Ibid., September 15, 1956.

10. Ibid., March 4, 1955.

11. Ibid., September 9, 1956.

12. Ibid.

13. Ibid., September 15, 1956.

14. Report of Governor's Metropolitan Study Committee (Milwaukee, December, 1956).

15. Milwaukee *Journal*, December 16, 1956.

16. Ibid.

17. Cited in summary of City position on metropolitan problems prepared by Gerald P. Caffrey, municipal reference librarian, City of Milwaukee, dated February 26, 1957.

18. Sec. 59.075, *Wisconsin Statutes*, 1959.

5. Personnel and Organization

1. Milwaukee *Journal*, October 14, 1957; Milwaukee *Sentinel*, October 17, 1957.

2. *CIO News*, October 18, 1957.

3. Milwaukee *Journal*, October 13, 1957.

4. Statement issued by Mayor Frank Zeidler, dated October 14, 1957.

5. Milwaukee *Sentinel*, October 17, 1957.

6. Ibid., October 16, 1957.

7. Ibid., October 15, 1957.

8. Milwaukee *Journal*, October 16, 1957.

9. *Minutes*, Metropolitan Study Commission, December 28, 1959.

10. Ibid., January 27, 1958.

11. Memorandum from executive committee of MSC to all Commission members, dated June 1, 1959.

12. *Minutes*, Metropolitan Study Commission, December 28, 1959.

13. Ibid., January 25, 1960.

14. Milwaukee *Journal*, August 5, 1958.

15. Ibid., August 11, 1958.

16. Ibid., August 6, 1958.

17. "General Metropolitan Surveys: A Summary," in Governmental Affairs Foundation, *Metropolitan Surveys: A Digest* (Chicago: Public Administration Service, 1958), pp. 3–24.

6. The Commission's Life Cycle

1. Address by Dr. G. A. Parkinson to Mayor's Advisory Committee, dated September 10, 1958, p. 9.

2. *1958 Annual Report to the Governor* (Milwaukee: Metropolitan Study Commission, October 13, 1958), p. 3.

3. Milwaukee *Journal,* November 9, 1958.

4. *Minutes of Executive Committee,* Metropolitan Study Commission, August 27, 1958.

5. Ibid., December 17, 1958.

6. Ibid., December 24, 1958.

7. Ibid.

8. Milwaukee *Journal,* September 26, 1958.

9. West Allis *Star,* November 26, 1958.

10. Milwaukee *Sentinel,* November 22, 1958.

11. Milwaukee *Journal,* December 3, 1958.

12. Letter from Mayor W. P. Atkinson to MSC, dated January 26, 1959. Reproduced in *Essentials of Replies by Municipalities to Questionnaire of December 31, 1958* (Milwaukee: Metropolitan Study Commission, February, 1959).

13. The reply of West Allis is reproduced in *Essentials of Replies by Municipalities.*

14. Resolution adopted by Common Council, City of Milwaukee, February 13, 1959. Reproduced in *Essentials of Replies by Municipalities.*

15. Milwaukee *Sentinel,* February 25, 1959.

16. Ibid., March 24, 1959.

17. Milwaukee *Journal,* July 23, 1959.

18. West Allis *Star,* April 9, 1959.

19. Whitefish Bay *Herald,* April 9, 1959.

20. Letter from Richard Cutler to all MSC members, dated April 9, 1959.

21. Milwaukee *Journal,* October 13, 1957.

22. Letter from Richard Cutler to Governor Gaylord Nelson, dated June 15, 1959.

23. Milwaukee *Journal,* July 23, 1959.

24. Milwaukee *Sentinel,* July 24, 1959.

25. Milwaukee *Journal,* July 24, 1959.

26. Milwaukee *Sentinel,* July 24, 1959.

27. Milwaukee *Journal,* August 19, 1959.

28. Ibid., August 22, 1959.

29. "Report to the Metropolitan Study Commission on the Determination of the Need for Research into Governmental Problems of the Metropolitan Milwaukee Area after July 1, 1961."

30. Milwaukee *Journal,* February 14, 1961.

7. The Metropolitan Functions Committee and Its Successors

1. Memorandum from Ball to Scholl, dated February 12, 1958.
2. Statement of city of Milwaukee, dated June 4, 1958. Reproduced in *Report on Sewage Disposal in the Milwaukee Metropolitan Area* (Milwaukee: Metropolitan Study Commission, July, 1958), p. 80.
3. Frank Zeidler, "The Expansion of the City of Milwaukee from 1940 to 1960 and Some Related Matters," unpublished MS in Milwaukee Public Library, p. 178.
4. South Milwaukee *Voice Journal*, December 4, 1958.
5. Ibid., November 6, 1958.
6. Ibid., October 9, 1958.
7. *Minutes*, Metropolitan Study Commission, May 25, 1959.
8. In vetoing a resolution of the common council to appeal the decision to the courts, Mayor Zeidler stated that Milwaukee must resign itself to the inevitable. Responsibility, he declared, now rested with the state government, which had taken away the City's means of survival by the water decision and by laws removing restrictions on the incorporation of suburban communities. Later Zeidler wrote that he had vetoed the resolution on the advice of an assistant city attorney who informed him that the City might possibly be sued for damages if it lost its challenge of the Public Service Commission order. Zeidler, p. 180. The story of the water fight with Wauwatosa is told by David G. Gladfelter, "Water for Wauwatosa," in *Cases in State and Local Government*, Richard T. Frost (ed.) (Englewood Cliffs, N.J.: Prentice-Hall, 1961), pp. 280–301.
9. *History of Water Supply in the Milwaukee Area* (Milwaukee: Metropolitan Study Commission, November, 1958).
10. Following a report in November, 1956, by an engineering firm retained by the City to study the water problem, a large-scale construction program at an estimated cost of over $54 million was authorized by the Common Council.
11. Statement of city of Milwaukee, filed with MSC on January 2, 1959. This and statements from other parties are contained in *Statements on Water Supply Prepared for January 22 Hearing of the Metropolitan Functions Committee* (Milwaukee: Metropolitan Study Commission, January 26 ,1959).
12. Milwaukee *Sentinel*, January 23, 1959.

13. The water went there without political consolidation and nearly over Schimenz's political corpse. Schimenz's appointment to the Wisconsin Public Service Commission some time after this hearing failed to receive legislative confirmation when Milwaukee suburban officials and representatives vigorously opposed it. They obviously wanted no ex-Milwaukee alderman passing on water matters. He was instead named by Governor Nelson to the State Industrial Commission.

14. "Conclusions of the Metropolitan Functions Committee, based on Review of History of Water Supply in the Milwaukee Area," December 29, 1958.

15. Statement of city of Milwaukee, January 2, 1959.

16. Milwaukee *Sentinel,* January 23, 1959.

17. Milwaukee *Journal,* January 24, 1959.

18. Milwaukee *Sentinel,* January 24, 1959.

19. Milwaukee *Journal,* March 24, 1959.

20. West Allis *Star,* March 26, 1959.

21. Milwaukee *Journal,* January 4, 1959.

22. Ibid., July 21, 1959.

23. Letter from Greater Milwaukee Committee to J. M. Klotsche, chairman, MSC, dated November 3, 1960.

24. Preliminary inquiries into police protection had already been instituted by research director Ball before his resignation.

25. *Technical Report on Police Protection in Milwaukee County* (Milwaukee: Metropolitan Study Commission, February 27, 1961).

26. Letter from William F. Rasche to J. Martin Klotsche, chairman, MSC, dated February 27, 1961. Reproduced in *Technical Report on Police Protection in Milwaukee County.*

27. Draft of report prepared by Charles D. Goff for Committee on Garbage and Refuse Disposal, dated August 1, 1959.

8. Land Use, Finance, and Cooperation

1. Statement of Jurisdiction of Land Use and Zoning Committee, *Minutes of Metropolitan Study Commission,* December 23, 1957.

2. Ball by this time had resigned as research director and together with a local planner, William Nelson, had formed a private firm of planning consultants. It was this firm which prepared the analysis.

3. "Findings and Conclusions Concerning Zoning in Milwaukee County," dated July 19, 1959. See *Minutes of Metropolitan Study Commission,* July 27, 1959.

4. "Land Use Planning and Control in Milwaukee County," dated October 2, 1959.

5. "Land Use Planning in the Metropolitan Milwaukee Area," dated May 23, 1960.

6. Section 66.945, *Wisconsin Statutes.*

7. Milwaukee *Sentinel,* October 14, 1958.

8. Report and Recommendations on Regional Planning, Land Use and Zoning Committee, dated December 8, 1958, p. 30.

9. *Minutes of Land Use and Zoning Committee,* September 15, 1958.

10. Report on Municipal Boundary Problems, Land Use and Zoning Committee, dated February 23, 1959.

11. Report of the Revenue Sources and Distribution Committee, dated April 28, 1958.

12. Milwaukee *Sentinel,* September 19, 1958.

13. *Study of Revenue Needs, Expenditures and Trends in Milwaukee County* (Milwaukee: Marquette University Bureau of Business and Economic Research, 1959), p. 87.

14. Milwaukee *Journal,* June 13, 1960.

15. *State-Local Financial Relationship* (Milwaukee: Marquette University Bureau of Business and Economic Research, March, 1960), p. 60.

16. Report of Continuing Revenue Survey Commission, State of Wisconsin, December, 1960.

17. Statement on Behalf of the Intergovernmental Relations Committee by Clifford A. Randall, chairman, dated January 19, 1961.

18. Letter from David Mars to Richard Cutler, dated July 26, 1960.

19. *Metropolitan Milwaukee: Problems—Solutions* (Milwaukee: Metropolitan Study Commission, June, 1961).

20. Ibid., p. 20.

9. Images of the Commission

1. Arguments against any appreciable enlargement of county powers ran two ways. Suburban officials contended that since eighteen of the twenty-four supervisors are Milwaukee residents, the City would in effect control the county board. City officials, on the other hand, maintained that the county board was actually more representative of the suburban viewpoint, anti-City, and a competitor for tax resources.

2. John C. Bollens (ed.), *Exploring the Metropolis* (Berkeley and

Los Angeles: University of California Press, 1961); *Metropolitan Challenge* (Dayton: Metropolitan Community Studies, November, 1959); James A. Norton, *The Metro Experience* (Cleveland: The Press of Western Reserve University, 1963); Edward Sofen, *The Miami Metropolitan Experiment* (Bloomington: Indiana University Press, 1963).

3. See Morris Janowitz, *The Community Press in an Urban Setting* (Glencoe, Illinois: The Free Press, 1952).

4. Milwaukee *Journal,* February 2 ,1960.

5. Ibid., February 4, 1954.

6. West Allis *Star,* March 5, 1959.

7. Shorewood *Herald,* April 16, 1959.

8. Whitefish Bay *Herald,* February 12, 1959.

9. West Allis *Star,* July 30, 1959.

10. Ibid., January 7, 1960.

11. Ibid.

10. The MSC in Retrospect

1. Scott Greer, *Metropolitics: A Study of Political Culture* (New York: Wiley & Sons, 1963), p. 1.

2. The framework of analysis borrows from Robert Dahl's studies of influence and power. See particularly his *Who Governs* (New Haven: Yale University Press, 1961), and his "The Analysis of Influence in Local Communities," in *Social Science and Community Action,* Charles Adrian (ed.) (East Lansing: Michigan State University, 1960), pp. 25–42.

3. At one point Parkinson and Foote prepared a list of broad principles to be used in evaluating proposals for changes in governmental structure, but little use was made of the document and it was soon forgotten. ("Principles," MSC, dated February 10, 1958.) Research director Mars later called the members' attention to the document when they were considering the final reports, but they showed no inclination to utilize it.

4. The League of Women Voters, for example, at one point noted that it was faced with a number of troublesome questions as it reviewed the work of the Commission. Once the recommendations are approved, what then? Is it the duty of the Commission to seek support for them? Where does study and recommendation stop and action begin? ("Progress Report on Metro Problems," League of Women Voters, Milwaukee Metropolitan Area, September, 1960.)

5. *1959 Annual Report to the Governor of the State of Wisconsin* (Milwaukee: Metropolitan Study Commission, October 15, 1959), p. v.

6. Milwaukee *Sentinel,* April 16, 1960.

7. Memo to MSC members from Richard Cutler, dated June 30, 1959.

8. *Minutes of Land Use and Zoning Committee,* October 6, 1958.

9. See in this connection an article later written by research director David Mars, "Work for the Future," *National Civic Review* LII (May, 1963), pp. 251–254.

10. Letter from Magidson to Klotsche, dated December 19, 1960.

11. Thomas H. Eliot, "Dilemmas in Metropolitan Research," II *Midwest Journal of Political Science* (February, 1958), p. 37.

12. Letter from Ball to Lobb, dated April 22, 1958.

13. *1400 Governments* (Cambridge: Harvard University Press, 1961), p. 197.

14. See Dahl, *Who Governs,* chapter 1.

15. Ibid., chapter 24.

16. One additional staff member, Professor Robert Notestein, was employed during the summer of 1959 to do the police study.

17. *Minutes of Executive Committee,* January 20, 1960.

18. Address before Metropolitan Milwaukee Citizens' Conference on Government, April 17, 1959.

19. Letter from Cutler to Governor Nelson, dated June 15, 1959.

20. Milwaukee *Sentinel,* February 25, 1959.

21. Concessions to local autonomy had to be made in both the sewer and the regional planning bill. The sewer bill as finally enacted into law gave municipalities the choice of joining the district or remaining outside its jurisdiction. The regional planning act permitted local units to withdraw from the jurisdiction of the regional commission at their discretion. This latter provision enabled some eight cities and towns to withdraw from the commission immediately after its creation and for a time to threaten its existence.

11. The Twilight of Metropolitan Study Commissions

1. Robert Dahl, *Who Governs* (New Haven: Yale University Press, 1961), p. 72.

2. See in this connection Herbert Gamberg, *The Escape from Politics: Power in Middle-Sized Cities* (Champaign, Illinois: Office of Community Development, 1964), chapter 6.

3. "Metropology: Folklore and Field Research," *Public Administration Review*, XXI (Summer, 1961), p. 149.

4. A Rockefeller report, *The Challenge to America: Its Economic and Social Aspects* (New York: Doubleday, 1958) typifies this trend in its treatment of urban problems, noting that "cooperation among existing governmental units, under existing authority, can often go far to meet these problems, and this, rather than the creation of new layers of government, may be the most effective means of coping with metropolitan growth." Report of Panel IV of the Special Studies Project.

5. "The Politics of Metropolitan Area Organizations," I *Midwest Journal of Political Science* (May, 1957), pp. 77–78.

6. *The Metropolitan Problem and American Ideas* (New York: Alfred A. Knopf, 1962), p. 119.

7. John C. Bollens (ed.), *Exploring the Metropolis* (Berkeley and Los Angeles: University of California Press, 1961); *Metropolitan Challenge* (Dayton: Metropolitan Community Studies, November, 1959); and James A. Norton, *The Metro Experience* (Cleveland: The Press of Western Reserve University, 1963). York Willbern touched upon a related aspect of this question in the Southern Regional Training Program lectures at the University of Alabama in 1961 when he said: "The facts seem to be that the great sprawling urban areas of this country fall short not so much in their achievement of the goals and ambitions of their residents, as in the degree to which they achieve or fail to achieve the speculative constructs of the intellectuals who concern themselves with the matter. The disparity is not between metropolis as it is and the metropolis as its residents wish it; the disparity is between the existing metropolis and the City of God of the planners and the dreamers." *The Withering Away of the City* (University, Ala.: University of Alabama Press, 1964), p. 47.

8. For a careful analysis of the Cleveland survey, see Norton, *The Metro Experience*.

9. Sec. 59.075 *Wisconsin Statutes*.

10. Scott Greer, *Metropolitics* (New York: Wiley & Sons, 1963).

11. Warner Bloomberg, Jr., "Notes for a Theory of Local Governance" (mimeo.), 1964.

12. Joseph E. Clark, "To Come to the Aid of Their Cities," *New York Times Magazine*, April 30, 1961, p. 90.

13. Robert J. Daland, "Political Science and the Study of Urbanism," *American Political Science Review*, LI (June, 1957), pp. 491–509.

14. Lawrence J. R. Herson, "The Lost World of Municipal Government," *American Political Science Review*, LI (June, 1957), p. 330.

15. The tabulation of on-going studies in *Metropolitan Surveys* is based on responses from correspondents in each state and hence is probably lacking in comprehensiveness. It is highly unlikely, however, that any major reorganization studies by metropolitan survey commissions have been omitted.

16. For a recent analysis of local government adaptation to change in various metropolitan areas see Roscoe C. Martin, *Metropolis in Transition* (Washington: Housing and Home Finance Agency, 1963).

17. Scott Greer, *The Emerging City* (New York: Free Press of Glencoe, 1962), p. 192.

18. *State Legislative Program of the Advisory Commission on Intergovernmental Relations* (Washington: Housing and Home Finance Agency, 1963), p. 6.

19. Norman Beckman, "Our Federal System and Urban Development," *Journal of the American Institute of Planners,* XXIX (August, 1963), p. 159. See also Webb S. Fiser, *Mastery of the Metropolis* (Englewood Cliffs, N.J.: Prentice-Hall, 1962), chapter VI.

20. Commission on Intergovernmental Relations, *A Report to the President for Transmission to Congress* (Washington: Government Printing Office, 1955), p. 52.

21. *The States and the Metropolitan Problem* (Chicago: Council of State Governments, 1956). See also Harold Herman, *New York State and the Metropolitan Problem* (Philadelphia: University of Pennsylvania Press, 1963).

22. See William A. Robson, "The Reform of London Government," *Public Administration,* 39 (Spring, 1961), pp. 58–71; and Frank Smallwood, *Greater London: The Politics of Metropolitan Reform* (Indianapolis: Bobbs-Merrill, 1965).

23. The State Reorganization Commission of Missouri, which functioned during 1954–55, is one example of a successful mixed body. Composed of both prominent citizens and influential members of both houses, it saw a substantial percentage of its proposals adopted in subsequent years.

24. Support would, of course, continue to be given to the local watchdog organizations such as citizens' governmental research bureaus, since the work of these groups has resulted in incremental improvements to the metropolitan system as well as to the administrative processes of individual local governments.

25. See David A. Booth, *Metropolitics: The Nashville Consolidation* (Lansing: Institute for Community Development and Services, Michigan State University, 1963).

Index